HERE'S WHAT READERS ARE TELLING US ABOUT THE FIRST BUG MAN NOVEL!

"I read this book on vacation this past weekend, and once I began, I couldn't put it down. The writing is clever, intelligent, humorous, and suspenseful. The words are so visual that the whole time I was reading, I was picturing the book as I would a movie. I'm already looking forward to the next Bug Man mystery."—MD

"I've read every Grisham novel and loved them all; however, not since *The Firm* have I enjoyed a book this much."—LA

"I loved Nick Polchak! He is quirky and fascinating. The humor is great and the story had a ton of fun twists and surprises."—DG

"Being a big fan of the TV show *CSI*, I looked forward to the release of this novel. But it blew my expectations away! If Bug Man is any indication of the types of novels Howard Publishing will publish, this new series will be a fantastic hit!"—SH

"I can honestly say that I was held by every page. The characters were so unique and believable. I learned a great deal about insects in a very pleasurable format."—LD

"I could hardly put it down—when I get one this good it always makes me mad at myself because I finish it too fast and it is over."—WH

"How wonderful to discover a hero who hasn't stepped out of the pages of *GQ*. His human frailties and quirky personality give hope to mere mortal men! My hat is off to Tim Downs. A masterful job!"—RF

"I loved the Bug Man. What a wonderfully funny and bright character—well done."—DC

"I LOVED THIS BOOK ⟨...⟩ to say that this is one of the best I ⟨...⟩ waiting for the sequel with great an⟨...⟩

"It was so well written ⟨...⟩ I could hardly put it down once I started reading it . . . and I hate bugs."—MD

"I was surprised that I liked it so much because I am not fond of bugs myself and secondly I don't really like mystery novels, but I could hardly put the book down!"—MT

"I seriously could not put it down. I loved Nick Polchak's character and was amazed at the level of detail regarding forensic entomology. It was fascinating. The mystery kept me turning the pages and I am eager to read the next installment."—BC

SHOO
FLY PIE
& CHOP
SHOP

A BUG MAN NOVEL

 **HOWARD BOOKS**
A DIVISION OF SIMON & SCHUSTER, INC.
New York • Nashville • London • Toronto • Sydney

TIM DOWNS

Our purpose at Howard Books is to:
- *Increase faith* in the hearts of growing Christians
- *Inspire holiness* in the lives of believers
- *Instill hope* in the hearts of struggling people everywhere

Because He's coming again!

 Published by Howard Books,
a division of Simon & Schuster, Inc.
1230 Avenue of the Americas, New York, NY 10020
www.howardpublishing.com

Shoofly Pie and Chop Shop © 2009 Tim Downs

Library of Congress Cataloging-in-Publication Data is available

ISBN 978-1-4391-3615-7
ISBN 978-1-4391-6691-8 (ebook)

10 9 8 7 6 5 4 3 2 1

HOWARD and colophon are registered trademarks
of Simon & Schuster, Inc.

For information regarding special discounts for bulk purchases,
please contact: Simon & Schuster Special Sales at 1-800-456-6798
or business@simonandschuster.com

Cover design by David Carlson Design
Interior design by Gabe Cardinale

SHOO FLY PIE

BUG MAN NOVEL 1

For my beautiful Joy,
whose constant love and encouragement
keep the bugs away.
Remember, I can do anything you think I can do.

ACKNOWLEDGMENTS

I would like to thank the following individuals and organizations for their generous contributions to this book: Dr. John Butts, chief medical examiner of North Carolina; Steve Bambara of North Carolina State University for his help with beekeeping; Major Dominic Caraccilo, commander of Headquarters Company, 2d Brigade, 82d Airborne, during Operation Desert Storm; Bill Poston of the North Carolina Department of Correction; Randy Young of Young Guns, Inc., in Apex, North Carolina; Chuck Henley at the Defense POW/Missing Personnel Office; the Department of Entomology, National Museum of Natural History, Smithsonian Institution; the U.S. General Accounting Office; Walter Reed Army Medical Center and Biosystematics Unit; Gulf War Health Center; U.S. Army's *Armor* magazine; U.S. Army Center of Military History; Brown-Wynne Funeral Homes of Cary, North Carolina; the American Beekeeping Federation; and scores of others who took the time to respond to my e-mails, letters, and phone calls.

I would especially like to thank the forensic entomologists who generously gave their time to help me understand their remarkable field: Dr. Boris Kondratieff of Colorado State University, for helping me with the basics of FE; Dr. Robert Hall of the University of Missouri, for introducing me to Chrysomya megacephala; and Dr. Neal Haskell, for allowing me to attend his fascinating Forensic Entomology Workshop (a.k.a. Maggot School) in Rensselaer, Indiana. Thanks for assisting me with the science behind what is, in the end, a work of fiction.

I also want to thank the individuals who made the publication of this book possible: literary agent Kathryn Helmers, who was as tenacious as a tick in shopping my manuscript; Jeff Tikson, my longtime advisor and friend; Ed Stackler, for his invaluable skills as an editor and story consultant; and the wonderful people at

Howard Publishing, for their creativity, vision, and passion for the written word.

Thanks, too, to the faithful friends whose opinions helped shape this book into its final form: Tim Muehlhoff, Kent Kramer, Joy Downs, Bill and Laura Burns, Jim and Renee Keller, and Dan and Julie Brenton.

And thank God for the Internet.

Holcum County, North Carolina, 1975

Zachary Sloan stepped out of the Rayford ABC Package Store and walked to the bed of his primer-gray Ford pickup. Two eager dogs greeted him. The first, Sloan's favorite, was an aging black Labrador, now walleyed and graying at the muzzle; the other was a spotted pup of questionable lineage but unlimited enthusiasm. The dogs nuzzled the paper package in the old man's right hand.

"Get back, mutt. That's for me." He slipped the bottle into the right pocket of his khaki hunting coat and took a crumpled sack from under his arm. "This is for you two no-goods." He tossed a fat pig's knuckle onto the rusty truck bed, then climbed into the cab. He revved the engine, coaxed the transmission into reverse, and backed out on to Highway 29. The dogs took two quick steps back as he accelerated east.

Fifty yards away to his right the tracks of the Norfolk and Southern ran parallel to the road, the side of the towering embankment silhouetted gray-blue by the afternoon sun. Sloan watched the telephone poles click by, each one clipping the hood of his truck with the tip of its shadow. Not far ahead, County Road 42 descended from the left through a vast, open expanse of fledgling corn and tobacco. It dipped down to cross Highway 29, then abruptly rose again to traverse the train tracks fifty yards away. There was no stoplight or sign at the intersection; none was necessary. Sloan could see vehicles approaching for miles in all directions—except from the right on County Road 42, where the Norfolk & Southern shielded the intersection like an ancient fortress wall.

Three miles away, a forty-foot flatbed trailer lumbered cautiously down a dirt road and passed beneath a brightly painted sign that hung across the exit to the Good 'N Plenty Orchards. Strapped to the bed of the open trailer was stack after stack of neat, white cabinets, each with a kind of oversize box top that overlapped at the edges. Each cabinet seemed to contain several drawers, expertly dovetailed at the edges. In the lowest drawer of each cabinet was a long horizontal slot stuffed tight with a rag and secured with twine. The drawers could not be opened, yet each cabinet was completely filled . . . with 40,000 honeybees.

The dirt road ended with a sudden rise to join the county highway just north of the town of Rayford. The teamster cautiously eased the left wheel up onto the roadway. With one great gun of the diesel engine, the right wheel followed. The flatbed behind him rocked right, then lurched left. The beehives flexed and shifted uneasily like tottering stacks of cups and saucers. An angry murmur rose from within the whitewashed columns, then quieted once again as the flatbed settled onto the level roadway of County Road 42. With each grinding shift of gears, the diesel sent a plume of blue smoke into the sky, slowly gathering speed as it headed south toward the tiny town of Rayford.

Sloan spotted the long flatbed with the alabaster cargo approaching from far away to his left. He eyed the intersection, then the flatbed, then the intersection again. Their two vehicles seemed to be approaching at equal speeds. Sloan pushed steadily on the accelerator, and the flatbed accelerated in kind.

"Grits-for-brains," the old man muttered. There was a common understanding in Rayford that commercial rigs should always yield to the locals—a common understanding, that is, among locals. Sloan took a different view entirely. His tariffs and duties had paid for these roads, thank you, and the meandering locals could get out of the way.

Now Sloan had the accelerator pushed flat against the floor. Behind him, the dogs stood straight and alert, sensing a force of wind and a whine from the engine that they had never felt before. The pup stepped nervously to his left, stopped, then started right again. He began to whimper and pushed his nose into the side of his more experienced companion. The aging Labrador slowly hung his head, circled once, and lay down.

High atop the railroad tracks fifty yards to Sloan's right, three bicycles raced side by side in a dead heat, clattering across the half-buried crossties of the old Norfolk and Southern railway.

Eight-year-old Andy Guilford suddenly veered to the right, forcing Pete St. Clair's bike up against the steel railhead.

"No fair!"

Pete jerked back on the handlebars and jumped the rail altogether. His back wheel spun wide and cut a deep arc in the loose gravel ballast.

"You can whine or you can win," Andy shouted back. He swerved left now and jammed his foot into the rear tire of Jimmy McAllister's rusting red beach cruiser. The bike lurched violently, almost throwing Jimmy onto his handlebars.

The three bicycles simultaneously crunched to a stop at the crossing of County Road 42. For a while the three boys said nothing; they stood straddling their bikes, panting and mopping their foreheads, staring up the road one way and then down the other.

"We did it!" Jimmy beamed. "We beat her!"

"And I beat the both of you," Andy chided.

"Like fun you did!"

Andy glanced to the left. He saw the great white flatbed barreling toward them, still a good mile away, and an old gray pickup streaking down from the left. Now he cupped his hand above his eyes and followed County Road 42 to the right. There was no sign of an automobile as far as the eye could see—no sign of her automobile. This is the way she would come—this is the way she came every Saturday afternoon when her father made his weekly drive into Rayford.

"We beat her, all right," Pete said. "But she's bound to be along any minute. Better get ready!"

The three boys tossed their bikes aside and scrambled for position. Jimmy hoisted himself up on top of the big metal signal box beside the tracks. He steadied himself, then slowly stood aright and spread his arms out wide.

"This is where I'm going to be," he said. "She'll see me before she sees either one of you!"

Andy stood eyeing the great gleaming crossing signal on the far side of the road.

"No way!" Jimmy shouted over to him.

"Just watch me," Andy called back. He shinnied up the silver post as far as the flashing red target lights, then pulled himself up and over. He climbed past the black-and-yellow Norfolk and Southern sign, up past the great white X formed by the RAILROAD CROSSING signs, until he straddled the post cap like a skull atop crossbones.

"Now who's she gonna see first?" he shouted down. "She'll spot me a mile away!"

Pete peered up at Andy, then at Jimmy, then Andy again.

"Hey, Pete!" Andy called down. "Maybe you could wave your hankie!"

"Or drop your drawers!" Jimmy joined in. "She's sure to see that!"

Pete stood gloomily for a full minute, saying nothing. Then he stepped across the railroad tracks onto the pavement.

He lay down in the center of the right lane—her lane.

"Are you nuts?" Andy called down. "Get out of the road!"

Pete lay motionless, staring at the sky.

"Pete!" Jimmy shouted. "She'll run right over you!"

"She won't neither. When the car hits the tracks, it leaves the ground. She'll fly right over me."

"What if the car slows down this time? What if you're too far from the tracks?"

Pete said nothing.

"She'll never even see you!" Andy was almost screaming now. "She'll run right over you and squash you like a bug, and she'll never even know it!"

"She'll know," Pete said under his breath. "She'll know I did it for her."

Andy looked up. Far down County Road 42 he saw a tiny blur coming over the horizon.

Inside that tiny blur, seven-year-old Kathryn lay on her back, sandwiched between the rear window and backseat of her father's crumbling green '57 Chevy Bel Air. Her left shoulder was wedged tight between the glass and vinyl, and her nose just cleared the window as it curved up toward the roof above her.

She closed her eyes and felt the warmth of the afternoon sun on her full body. The wind from the single open window swirled around her and carried the smell of tobacco from her father's cigarette. She rolled her head to the right and studied the back of her father's head: the sun-furrowed neck, the leathery ears that protruded proudly into space, and the thick shock of auburn hair that always lay carelessly to the left. Last of all, she saw her father's emerald green eyes in the rearview mirror. They were focused directly on her.

"Know what I think?" he said, grinning. "I think you wish you was a big ol' whitetail deer, so's you could ride strapped across the hood."

Her heart raced at the thought that somehow it might be possible—to feel the wind in her hair, to watch the road rushing to meet her instead of always disappearing into the past.

"Could I, Daddy?" she asked with childish hope.

He laughed. "Your momma would shoot me dead. Why, she'd tan my hide if she knew I let you ride without a seat belt."

He glanced again in the mirror at Kathryn's body stretched out atop the backseat beneath the rear window.

"You be careful back there, hear?"

He flicked his cigarette out the window and rolled it up, leaving just a hairline crack at the top.

"Are the tracks coming, Daddy? Are we there yet?"

"Almost! Get ready!"

With a squeal, Kathryn wedged herself even tighter against the glass. She was in her favorite place on the best of days, and now she was coming to the best moment of all—when they came to the sudden rise in the road where the Norfolk & Southern crossed County Road 42. When no train was in sight it was agreed—it was expected—that her father would accelerate up the rise just as fast as the aging Chevy could possibly go. As they crossed the tracks and the road dropped suddenly away beneath them, the hulking sedan would magically lift from the ground like the pirate ship rising from the Blue Lagoon. Then, for one eternal moment, Kathryn would float weightless above the seat, above the car, above even the gigantic town of Rayford itself. It was the longest two seconds in the universe, an entire world within a world, a glimpse of eternity— Kathryn was not about to let her father forget about it.

"Faster, Daddy! Faster!"

The signs flashed past like confetti now, and the code of dots and dashes on the pavement blurred together into yellow and white ribbons streaming out behind the car. She heard the growling complaint from the aging engine and the rising pitch of her father's voice.

"Here it comes, sweetheart! Get ready!"

Zachary Sloan glared at the center of the intersection and shot defiant glances at the great white blur closing fast from the left.

Two hundred yards . . .

One hundred yards . . .

Fifty yards from the intersection, Sloan slammed his hand down on the horn in a final act of anger and defiance and was instantly answered by the shattering bellow of the diesel's great air horn. Both vehicles went raging, shouting, screaming into the center of the intersection.

The Ford arrived a split second before the flatbed. The left headlight of the pickup smashed into the right fender of the diesel just behind the bumper. The hood sprung open and was instantly ripped away in the wind. The pickup spun right across the front of the flatbed, heaved onto its side, and continued through the intersection amid a shower of sparks and the deafening scream of metal on concrete.

The force of the impact spun the diesel cab fully to the left, jackknifed at a right angle to the flatbed behind it. The aging retreads of the diesel skidded, then stretched, then exploded into shards of smoking rubber. The bare metal wheel rims dug into the pavement, and the cab slammed onto its side with astounding force. The flatbed trailer, sheared from its shattered cab, lurched right, then left, then right once again—and then flipped side-over-side down the middle of County Road 42.

The hives that were not strapped down seemed to float in the air for an instant before crashing to the roadway below. Those that were bound to the bed of the trailer were whipped to the pavement as the flatbed began its roll. In both cases, the hives did not seem to simply break or crush or fall apart; they literally exploded. Eighty-five hives had lined that trailer, each weighing almost a hundred pounds. As each hive struck the roadway, the brittle drawer-like supers separated, then splintered into a thousand pieces, vomiting a tangle of wood, wire, wax, and honey. At first, the bees seemed to spill out from the wreckage like pouring gravel. Then, slowly, the million-or-so that survived the crash began to rise into the sky in a black, boiling, living cloud of venom.

Pete sat upright in the center of the road.

All three boys stared wild-eyed, gawking at the carnage spewed out on the road behind them and the slowly rising cloud above. Almost simultaneously they remembered—and they turned back again to see the flash of the green Bel Air less than a quarter of a mile away.

Andy and Jimmy dropped to the roadway and Pete scrambled to his feet. All three boys stood jumping, shrieking, and waving their arms in frantic, futile arcs.

"There they are!" Kathryn's father called to the backseat. "All three of them, waving their hellos!" He lay on the horn and shoved the accelerator to the floor.

The nose of the sedan tipped upward as they reached the rise. Kathryn heard the whine of the engine as the wheels spun free of the ground, and she felt the lug of the tires as they dropped away below the car. Then at last came the glorious moment when she floated free of the car—or was the car falling away from her? It didn't matter. To Kathryn, it was the sacred moment when she rose from the dead and ascended into heaven.

For an instant, only clouds and sky were visible through the windshield of the airborne sedan. But as the weight of the engine forced the nose of the car back to earth, a hellish landscape rose into view. In the left lane lay a broken and twisted flatbed; to the right, the crushed shell of a diesel cab and the smoldering undercarriage of a gray pickup; straight ahead, a graveyard of crumpled and shattered white bones. And above it all was a massive, swirling black cloud of . . .

"Holy . . . Hold on, Kath!"

Less than a second later the sedan smashed into the first of the hives. The tires lost all traction on the sea of honey and insect parts and spun helplessly to the right. The right fender struck the twisted chassis of the diesel, and the sedan lurched onto its left side. To Kathryn's astonishment she found herself standing perfectly erect, still pressed between the rear window and seat, as if she were suddenly back home standing in front of the storm door, watching the backyard rushing toward her. Just as suddenly, the car flipped onto its rounded top, and Kathryn was thrown face-forward against the window glass. Six inches below her nose she saw a yellow dash streak by, then a dot, then a much longer dash, and then at last the car came to rest.

For a few moments Kathryn lay perfectly still, unable to move but perfectly aware of everything around her. Above and to her right she heard the engine cough and sputter and die. She heard the wheels somewhere above her continue to spin a full minute longer. She detected the acrid stench of burnt rubber, the thick, sweet smell of diesel fuel, and—strangely, more than anything else—an odor like smashed bananas.

She lifted her head a few inches and saw a spatter of blood from her nose on the glass below her. She watched as tears began to fall straight away from her eyes, splash, and run down the window to her right. Out of habit, she rolled her body to the right—but this time she found herself lying on the crumpled ceiling of the car amid paper cups, floor mats, cigarette butts, and coins. She slowly turned to look at the back of her father's head, and through a wash of tears saw his body hanging behind the wheel, suspended by his seat belt. His shoulders sagged against the ceiling with one arm extending straight out, and his head was tucked under like the ducks she had seen on the pond behind her house.

But she had never seen her father's neck bent at an angle like that.

She reached out to touch her father's arm, but then she heard a shout from somewhere outside the passenger side of the car. She turned to the window—all of the glass was still intact. She looked out to see an old man in a khaki jacket standing not more than twenty yards away.

Far beyond him, still atop the rise of the railroad tracks, stood the figures of three helpless boys.

The left side of the man's face was covered with blood, and he stumbled toward a motionless black form on the ground ahead of him. He dropped to his knees and buried his face in the dark fur. Beside him, a mottled gray pup paced anxiously back and forth.

Suddenly the pup started, then spun to its left and snapped at the air. It jumped again and whirled back to the right. In another moment it was leaping, whirling, and kicking like the wild horse Kathryn once saw at the state fair in Raleigh.

The man staggered to his feet. He swung at the air around his face with one hand, then both. He began to duck and weave and flail at the air like a boxer facing some menacing shadow. Now he began to wave his arms frantically around him and pulled his jacket up over his head, running a few steps one way, then the other.

For the first time Kathryn looked up into the sky. She saw a great, swirling black cloud that seemed to be slowly descending around them like a plague, and a single word screamed out in her mind: FIRE! She saw no flames, but she remembered what the fireman once told her class: The hottest fire is the one you can't see. It was like watching hell itself. The man and his dog were being tortured by flames but were never consumed.

A wave of panic swept over Kathryn. "Daddy! Wake up! We have to get out of here!" She twisted around and put her feet against the window glass. She pulled back and with all of her might kicked out against the glass.

Nothing.

She kicked again and again as the cloud outside grew thicker and darker and closer. She began to weep hysterically, but stopped with a gasp. She saw the man, now barely visible through the whirling cloud, begin to stagger directly toward her. His face looked swollen and blue with patches of black and gray, and his hands clutched at his throat. He bent forward, then straightened and threw his shoulders back and his chest out, as though he were straining to draw each breath through a long tube. He stumbled forward two steps, then suddenly stopped and dropped his arms limp at his sides. For a moment he stood perfectly still, as if somehow at peace with this unexpected fate, and then fell headlong on the pavement not more than ten feet from Kathryn's window.

Kathryn screamed and scrambled back from the glass. There were no flames, yet the man's body grew steadily darker—and the black patches seemed to be moving.

Kathryn's eyes were fixed in horror on the blackened figure before her. She crawled back, back, until she was flattened against the opposite window glass, her arms frozen down and out to her sides. She felt a tiny tickle on her left wrist and frantically jerked it away. She turned.

Near the ground, her father's window was still open just a hairline crack. The crack was lined with the wriggling heads, legs, and wings of a thousand enraged bees struggling to squeeze through. Behind them, a thousand more pressed forward. Both windows were completely covered with a shifting, throbbing, crawling mass of black-and-yellow insects.

Seven-year-old Kathryn took a deep breath, closed her eyes, and screamed.

Cary, North Carolina, April 21, 1999

Nick Polchak rapped his knuckles on the frame of the open doorway. He glanced back at the Wake County Sheriff's Department police cruiser blocking the driveway, orange and blue lights silently rotating.

"Yo!" Nick called into the house. "Coming in!"

A fresh-faced sheriff's deputy in khaki short sleeves poked his head around the corner and beckoned him in. Nick wondered where they got these kids. He looked younger than some of his students.

Nick stepped into the entryway. Dining room on the right, living room on the left. It was a typical suburban Raleigh home, a colonial five-four-and-a-door with white siding and black shutters. A mahogany bureau stood just inside the door. At its base lay three pair of shoes, one a pair of black patent leathers. Nick shook his head.

He knew the layout by heart: stairway on the left, powder room on the right, down a short hallway was the kitchen, and the family room beyond that.

Nick paused in the second doorway and took a moment to study the young officer. He stood nervously, awkwardly, constantly checking his watch. His right hand held a handkerchief cupped over his nose and mouth, and he winced as he sucked in each short gulp of air. Nick followed the officer's frozen gaze to the right; the decomposing body of a middle-aged woman lay sprawled across the white Formica island in the center of the kitchen.

Nick knocked again.

"Officer . . . Donnelly, is it? I'm Dr. Nick Polchak. Are you the first one here?"

"I was just a few blocks away, so I took the call." He glanced again at his watch. "Our homicide people ought to be along within the hour."

Nick began to stretch on a pair of latex gloves and stepped around to the victim's head. "The name on the mailbox said 'Allen.'"

"Stephanie Allen. That's all I've been able to get so far." The deputy nodded silently toward the family room, where a solitary figure sat slumped forward in a red leather chair with his face buried in his hands. Nick raised his own left hand and wiggled his ring finger. The deputy nodded.

"I didn't get your name—did you say Kolchek?"

"Polchak. Nick Polchak."

"You don't sound like you're from around these parts."

"I'm from Pittsburgh," Nick said. "And I'd say you're not."

The deputy grinned. "How'd you know?"

"You left your shoes at the door."

"They don't do that in Pittsburgh? I guess they don't have the red clay."

"The police don't do that in Pittsburgh. They figure if you've got a dead body in the kitchen, you've got more to worry about than dirty carpets."

The body lay faceup, stretched out diagonally across the island under the bright kitchen fluorescents.

"Very handy," Nick said. "Too bad I don't find them all like this."

The head rested in one corner, with medium-length blond hair flowing out evenly on all sides. There were deep abrasions and contusions on the neck and lower jaw. The body was in putrefaction, the second major stage of decomposition. The skin was blistered and tight from expanding gases, and the stench was considerable. There were sizable maggot infestations in both eye sockets and in the gaping mouth cavity. She had been dead for several days—maybe a week or more.

"You got here fast, Doc. I thought the medical examiner's office was in Chapel Hill."

Nick shook his head. "I didn't come from Chapel Hill. I came from NC State. I picked up your call on my police scanner."

"From the university? What were you doing there?"

"That's where I work."

Nick removed a pair of slender forceps and a small magnifier from his coat pocket. He bent close to the victim's head and began to carefully sort through the wriggling mass of maggots in the left eye socket.

"Wait a minute. You're not from the medical examiner's office?"

"Never said I was."

"Then who in the—"

"I'm a member of the faculty at NC State. I'm a professor in the department of entomology."

"A professor of what?"

"I'm a forensic entomologist, Deputy. I study the way different necrophilous arthropods inhabit a body during the process of decomposition."

The deputy stood speechless.

Nick plucked a single plump, white larva from the wriggling mass and held it under the magnifier. "I'm the Bug Man."

The deputy began to blink rapidly. "Now just hold on . . . you're not supposed to . . . you're not a part of this . . ."

"Relax," Nick held the forceps aloft. "It's just one bug. There's plenty more where that came from."

"You need to leave, Dr. Polchak."

"Why?"

"Because—you're not a medical examiner, and you're not with the department. You shouldn't be here. It's not procedure."

"Not procedure. I have assisted the authorities on seventy-two cases in thirteen different countries. How many homicides did you have in Wake County last year? Five? Ten?"

The deputy shrugged.

"And how many of them did you work?"

"I never heard of any Bug Man," the deputy muttered.

Nick glanced down at the man's stocking feet. "Now there's a surprise."

Now Nick turned to the motionless figure in the red chair. "Mr. Allen," he called out. "I'm Dr. Nick Polchak. I'd like to ask you a few questions, if you don't mind."

"No," came a whisper from under the hands. "No questions."

"Mr. Allen," the officer broke in. "This man is not a part of the official police investigation. You don't have to answer his questions."

"He's right," Nick said. "But you can if you want to. And when the homicide people get here, Mr. Allen, they're going to ask questions—quite a lot of them. First the police will ask you when you first discovered your wife's body."

The man looked up for the first time. His face was ashen and drawn, and a deep purple crescent cradled each eye.

"It was less than an hour ago," the man said. "I called the police immediately."

"Immediately? Your wife has been dead for quite some time, Mr. Allen."

"I've been out of town. I just got back, just today. And then I found her, like . . . like this."

Nick nodded. "Next the police will ask you where you were during that time."

The man did a double take. "Me? Why me?"

"Because the one who discovers the body is always a suspect."

"Like I said, I was out of town. I was in Chicago, on business. For a whole week—they can check it out."

"I'm sure they will," Nick said, "and I'm sure they'll find you're telling the truth. Their next question will be: What day did you leave for Chicago?"

The man thought carefully. "Last Wednesday. The fourteenth."

"That would be . . . seven days ago exactly. And prior to that time, Mr. Allen, did you see your wife alive and well?"

"We said good-bye right here, on Wednesday morning. She was perfectly healthy."

"You're sure you left that day? On the fourteenth?"

"Of course I'm sure! You think I can't remember a week ago?"

Nick held the specimen up and studied it closely. Then he looked back at Mr. Allen.

"Care to try again?"

Nick dragged a chair from the breakfast nook into the family room and sat down opposite the man, with the tiny white specimen still writhing in the forceps in his right hand. He offered the magnifier to the man. "I want you to take a look at something."

"I can't look at that. Get that thing away from me!"

"Oh come now," Nick whispered. "You have a stronger stomach than that—don't you, Mr. Allen?"

The man looked startled; he hesitated, then reluctantly took the magnifier in his left hand.

"Pull up a chair," Nick called back to the deputy. "Learn something." Nick slowly extended the forceps. "Take a look at that end. Tell me what you see."

The magnifier trembled in the man's hand.

"Little lines," he mumbled. "Sort of like slits."

"How many little lines?"

"Three."

"Give the deputy a look, Mr. Allen. Those 'little lines' are called posterior spiracles—think of them as 'breathing holes.' The maggot you're holding is the larva of a common blow fly. That fly landed on your wife's body shortly after her death and began to lay eggs in the softest tissues—the eyes, the mouth, and so on. Those eggs hatched into larvae, and the larvae began to feed and grow.

"Now when a larva grows, it passes through three distinct stages of development. Are you following me, Mr. Allen? Because this is the important part: The larva doesn't develop those breathing holes until the third stage. And after many studies, we know exactly how long it takes for this species of fly to reach that third stage of development. Guess what, Mr. Allen? It takes more than a week."

The man began to visibly shake as Nick rocked back in his chair and folded his hands behind his head.

"Let's see what we've got so far. You've been out of town for a week—exactly a week. You say that you saw your wife alive one week ago, yet there are insects on her body that prove that she died more than a week ago."

"Well...uh...," the man stammered, "maybe I was gone...longer than I thought."

"The airline's records can clear up that little point. And I'm betting those same records will show that you made your reservations the same day that you traveled—sort of a last-minute business trip, you might say. I have just one more question for you, Mr. Allen. The police won't ask you this one, but it's something I've always wondered about . . ."

Nick leaned forward again.

"When you strangle someone, can you feel the hyoid bone break, or is it all just sort of soft and squishy?"

The man jumped frantically from his chair and lunged toward the door. He ran like a man in a funhouse, stumbling first one way and then the other, throwing himself from wall to wall, ricocheting wildly down the hall toward the open door.

The deputy sat frozen in astonishment, staring wide-eyed at the doorway.

"I think you're supposed to run after him," Nick said. "That's what they always do on TV."

The deputy thrust the magnifier and forceps into Nick's hands and raced barefooted down the hallway. Nick rose slowly from his chair, shook his head, and headed back toward the body. As he passed the hallway he caught a glimpse of the mahogany bureau just inside the front door.

The top drawer was open.

Nick ran to the door and leaped out onto the brick porch. There was no sign of the deputy or his quarry—they had already rounded the house, probably headed for the woods in back.

"He's armed!" Nick shouted. "Your man is armed!"

No response.

Nick looked both directions. He chose left and raced toward the corner of the house. "An amateur cop chasing an amateur murderer," he said aloud. "Someone could get killed this way."

He rounded the corner in a wide arc, expecting to lengthen his stride into a long run for the woods—but there, bracing himself against the far corner of the house, leaned the quivering figure of Mr. Allen. In his right hand a .357 magnum dangled toward the ground.

Nick skidded to a halt. The man saw him, straightened, and wobbled out away from the house. He turned to face Nick and slowly raised the weapon. He couldn't steady it; Nick felt the barrel sweep back and forth across his body again and again.

The man's arm shook so violently that he looked more like he was whitewashing a fence than aiming a firearm. Nick marked the distance between them—fifty feet at least. At this distance, it would take several tries for the man to hit him.

But it only takes one.

"Listen to me, Mr. Allen. You did something stupid. Don't make it worse. You cannot get away, and you know it. You're only running because you're scared."

The gun swept past twice more, marking Nick with a broad X.

"Think, Mr. Allen. Maybe you didn't mean to kill your wife—but if you shoot someone else, they'll hang you for sure. Put the gun down. Call a lawyer and see what you can work out."

The gun began to steady . . .

Over the man's shoulder Nick saw a khaki figure step out silently from behind the house. The deputy drew his own handgun, leveled it, then opened his mouth as if to shout. Nick held up both hands and shook his head violently.

You idiot! I'm in your line of fire!

Too late.

"FREEZE!"

The man spun around, firing wildly before he even faced his foe. The officer fired back; the first shot streaked over the man's left shoulder. Nick could feel it coming, he could sense the air compressing ahead of the bullet as it tore past his left ear.

Nick dove for the ground. The man continued to fire blindly—three shots into the ground, one into the air, two into the side of the house.

The officer fired twice more, shooting for the torso, not trusting his own aim. The first shot caught the man in the lower abdomen and the second hit square in the chest. Nick watched the man take both bullets. It was not at all like the movies—no violent recoil, no sense of impact at all. The man stood motionless for a moment, then his knees suddenly bent in opposite directions, and he sagged to the ground like a crumpling sack.

Nick crawled toward the broken body. He pulled the gun away and tossed it aside; the barrel burned his hand. He placed two fingers on the carotid artery and waited.

Nothing.

Nick looked up at the deputy and shook his head. The officer's knees buckled, and he dropped to the ground, vomiting.

Nick rolled onto his back and stared up into the April sky.

"Seventy-three cases," he said.

North Carolina State University, April 22, 1999

"Nicholas? A word, if you please."

Nick stepped into the office of Dr. Noah Ellison, chairman of the department of entomology and by far the most senior professor in any department at NC State. Dr. Ellison quietly closed the door behind them.

"Nicholas," he began, wagging a spindly finger, "it has been brought to my attention that you failed to appear for another of your classes yesterday."

"Sorry, Noah, I had to make a house call."

"It is my responsibility as chairman of this department to remind you that your contract involves a certain amount of teaching—and your colleagues have reminded me that it is my duty to discipline you appropriately."

Noah picked up Nick's right hand and slapped him on the wrist.

"Consider yourself disciplined. Please do not force me to resort to such extreme measures again."

The old man motioned for Nick to sit.

"I have good news and I have bad news, Nicholas. Which would you like first?"

"Give me both at the same time."

"Very well. The good news is the National Science Foundation has granted funding for your summer research proposal—continuing study in your beloved field of forensic entomology. The bad news is that the grant is woefully inadequate, hardly more than a one-way ticket out of town."

Noah slid a check across the desk. Nick glanced at it and rolled his eyes.

"Can't we do any better than this, Noah? Aren't there any departmental funds?"

He shook his head. "I control the purse strings, Nicholas, but not the size of the purse. I'm afraid that's it; take it, as they say, or leave it."

Nick studied the check again, hoping to discover a floating decimal point. "What am I supposed to accomplish with this?"

"You have the faculty committee's permission to spend the summer at our Extension Research Facility in Holcum County. And you may take your research assistant, Dr. Tedesco, along with you."

"Holcum County? Is that in North Carolina? Please, tell me it's not."

"Forgive me, Nicholas." Noah smiled. "Sometimes I feel like the poet Virgil, leading you to ever deeper levels of hell."

"Holcum County." Nick groaned. "Just the sound of it."

"Try not to think of it as a place, but as an opportunity—an opportunity to get away from the university, away from the classroom, away from students . . . and, I might add, away from the authorities."

"The authorities?"

"I received a rather belligerent phone call this morning from the Wake County Sheriff's Department regarding the way you—how shall I put it—expedited one of their investigations. I've spoken with the chancellor; he agrees that this would be a propitious time for you to take an extended leave. Purely in the name of science, of course. May I make a suggestion, Nicholas? As a friend? The next time you desire to assist the authorities, you might consider—just once—asking them first."

Nick grinned at the old man, slid the check from the desk, and headed for the door.

"One more thing, Nicholas. This is to be a summer of theoretical research, not applied science. Please . . . for the sake of the university, the department, and your weary old mentor—for the sake of your job—try to stay out of trouble."

"Noah," Nick said yawning, "what kind of trouble can you get into in Holcum County?"

Holcum County, North Carolina, June 1999

Sheriff Peter St. Clair stood in the center of the knee-high meadow, staring at the decomposing body of his oldest friend.

The cadaver lay on its back, fully stretched out, both arms extending down and to the sides. It was dressed in khaki pants and a mottled blue corduroy hunting shirt. The torso was bloated and distended, causing the seams of the shirt to split apart between buttons as if the shirt were three sizes too small. The skin was stretched and shiny, and the face was badly decomposed around the eyes and mouth. The only thing that looked at all natural about the corpse was the hair, which still lay neatly and almost comically combed to one side. The left hand was missing almost entirely, thanks to occasional visits by some forest scavenger; the right hand held a gleaming chrome handgun bearing the single engraved word, AIRBORNE, followed by the twin AAs of the All American Division.

The sheriff turned and stepped a few paces from what remained of his childhood friend and comrade at arms. He stood facing away, staring at the ground and grimly shaking his head.

"It's Jim, all right."

On the other side of the body three hunters stood watching. The first hunter, Ronny, nudged Wayne and nodded silently toward the sheriff; Wayne passed the observation on to Denny, who reached up and slid the bright orange cap from his head. They all stood silently until the sheriff turned back to face the decomposing carcass once again.

"Sorry to have to call you like this, Pete," Denny said. "What with Jim being an old friend of yours and all, we thought you'd want to know straightaway."

"You did the right thing." The sheriff paused. "You boys didn't touch anything, did you?"

"Hey, give us a little credit, Pete. We didn't even move the gun. See? It's still in his hand. He didn't even drop it after he . . ."

An awkward silence followed. No one wanted to finish the sentence.

"Let's get something straight." The sheriff glared at two of them. "I don't want to hear any more talk about 'suicide' until the coroner has a chance to look things over. All we know for sure is that Jim McAllister is dead."

"I s'pose we know what suicide looks like," Wayne grumbled.

"It's not a suicide until I say it's a suicide. That's the law." Sheriff St. Clair folded his arms and kicked at the ground. "As far as we know, it might have been an accident. Maybe even murder."

Ronny and Wayne stood with heads hung low and hands in pockets, looking suitably repentant. Denny, suffering from a life-long case of what his childhood friends referred to as "diarrhea of the mouth," was the only one foolish enough to respond.

"C'mon, Pete. I know you and Jim went way back and all, but . . . an accident? Shot in the side of the head? Nobody has an 'accident' like that—least of all an Airborne ex. And who would kill Jim? Nobody liked him—but at least he stayed to himself, stayed out of everybody's way. Besides, we just don't have many murders in these parts." Then he added for good measure, "Look who I'm telling."

It was true. The last murder in Holcum County was over a year ago, when old Mrs. Kreger decided to stop feeding her invalid husband. Her attorney got her off on the grounds that she just might have had a touch of Alzheimer's herself, but the people who knew Mrs. Kreger best weren't so sure. In any case, Denny was right; there weren't many murders in Holcum County, but the sheriff was not about to surrender the point. He took a step closer and spoke quietly, as though he might be overheard.

"Look. You boys know what it's like in a town like this when somebody does hisself in. Remember when they found Alvin

Rafferty in his garage a few years back? I don't think his family ever got over it—the way people look at you, the way they talk behind your back. Well, Jim's got a sister, remember? I don't want that to happen to her. Let's keep this quiet, okay? Can I count on you? Ronny? Denny? Wayne? For Jim's sake."

Each man nodded gravely. They were a part of the inner circle now, Keepers of the Secret—certainly one of the best secrets in Holcum County for quite some time.

They were interrupted by noise from the edge of the clearing—the heavy, clumsy, crashing footfalls of someone obviously not at home in the woods. From an opening in the small pines emerged the figure of a deputy, a young man of startling stature. He was a full head taller than the sheriff. His shoulders were heavy and rounded, and they hung down over a hulking torso. His arms were shapeless and pale but as thick as an average man's thigh. His blunt-fingered hands swelled into two great drumstick forearms that belied the overall softness of his appearance. His pale blue eyes were set narrow but were large as buckeyes, and he seemed to wear a constant grin. It was the body of a man—an enormous man—but it was the unmistakable face of a child.

He grinned at the sheriff as he approached, and each of the hunters greeted him in turn.

"Hey, Beanie."

"How's it going, Beanie?"

Now there was another sound from the edge of the clearing, and a short, stout, white figure stepped out, panting and mopping his forehead from the early morning humidity. He ran a finger around his collar, peeling it away from his glistening stump of a neck, and stepped toward the already assembled party.

"Mornin', Sheriff. Deputy. Boys. I came as soon as I got your call."

"Mr. Wilkins." The sheriff nodded and extended his hand. "Thanks for coming so quick. I think you know the boys here— Ronny, Denny, Wayne. Boys, you all know Mr. Wilkins, the county coroner."

They all knew Mr. Wilkins, of course, but not as county coroner. They knew him as Mr. Wilkins the drugstore owner or Mr. Wilkins the American Legion coach, but few people knew Mr. Wilkins in his official capacity. There was very little for a coroner to do in a county the size of Holcum.

"Where is the decedent?" Mr. Wilkins asked impatiently.

The four men turned and pointed to a spot at the crest of the meadow where a cloud of black flies hovered in tight circles just above the grass. The group approached cautiously, carefully seeking the upwind side, and formed a line to the left of the body—all except Mr. Wilkins, who, having caught the brunt of the stench, was still ten yards back, doubled over and retching into a stand of foxglove.

They waited awkwardly until Mr. Wilkins recovered and approached again with far more caution. The sheriff and the three seasoned hunters braced themselves against the odor and stood motionless. The deputy pinched his nose and winced in his childlike way, as all of them secretly wished to do, and Mr. Wilkins gagged and covered his mouth and nose with his dripping white handkerchief.

Denny broke the silence. "I'm the one who found him, Mr. Wilkins—that is, we all did. We come through this way a lot in the summer, getting ready for deer season."

"Deer season? That's not till September."

"Georgia Pacific leases out these woods to a group of us to hunt on. They timbered a couple hundred acres last month and they tore the place up real good—and right near where we got our deer stands too. So we were out planting clover and beans, laying out salt blocks, you know—trying to draw the deer back in."

The sheriff nodded.

"To get to our deer stands we got to cross this meadow. Right in the middle we spotted that big cloud of flies. Figured maybe it was a deer carcass, maybe somebody poaching on our lease. Thought we better check it out—and here was Jim McAllister stretched out on the ground. Shot hisself right through the head. At least"—he glanced quickly at the sheriff—"that's what it looks like. Appears he's been dead a long time."

"I'll decide how long he's been dead," Mr. Wilkins said in utter misery, still tugging at his collar. As coroner, Mr. Wilkins was not required to visit the death scene—but as it was only his second opportunity in his three-year term as coroner to exercise his official duties, he had gone the extra mile. The sheriff hadn't told him it would be more like a mile-and-a-half, through thick North Carolina woodland on a sweltering summer morning.

Sheriff St. Clair opened a chrome case and pulled out a 35-millimeter Nikon and two rolls of film. He handed a bright yellow roll of barrier tape to the deputy. "Benjamin—secure the perimeter of the death scene." The deputy looked bewildered; he started off one way and then the other and finally just stood staring at the roll of tape as if it might offer some explanation of its own.

"Find some branches," the sheriff said quietly. "Long, straight ones. Stick one there and there and there and over there. Then stretch this tape around 'em."

Beanie smiled gratefully and bounded off toward the woods.

"Take a look, Mr. Wilkins. What do you make of it?"

Mr. Wilkins slowly approached the body for the first time, his handkerchief still clutched tightly over his face. He turned his head away, sucked in a deep breath, then took a few quick steps toward the body. He poked and prodded and probed until his face began to grow red, then took several quick steps away to explode and pant and then once again fill his lungs with air. Wayne began to snicker, but the sheriff shot a burning look his way, and Wayne thought better of it and struck a more solemn pose. Mr. Wilkins repeated this process several times, until it became obvious that he was in danger of fainting dead away. Finally, still facing away from the body, he spoke.

"Suicide. Plain and simple."

"What makes you so sure?"

"Single gunshot wound to the side of the head—two wounds and you might have a murder. Entry wound is on the right—he was right-handed, wasn't he? Exit wound on the left. No chance of ever finding the slug out here, but the angle of entry and exit look about right." He spoke with more and more authority as he continued. "Classic suicide scenario. Most suicides are with handguns, you know, and almost always to the head. Never seen one otherwise." In point of fact he had never seen another suicide at all, and everyone knew it—but they all held their tongues. "The weapon is still present, no signs of struggle or conflict, no indication that the body was moved or disturbed in any way. Yessir, a classic suicide."

The sheriff put his hand on Mr. Wilkins's shoulder and turned him aside. They walked several steps away, much to Mr. Wilkins's relief, but they were still easily within earshot of the others.

"I hate to admit it, Will, but I think you're right," the sheriff said. "You know Jimmy McAllister and I go way back. We grew up together here in Rayford. We were both at Fort Bragg, and we served together in the Gulf. But the fact is"—he glanced over to be sure that no one overheard—"things didn't go so well for Jim after Desert Storm. A lot of chronic fatigue, long bouts of depression. He even made a few trips up to Walter Reed to be treated for Gulf War Syndrome. Nothin' helped for long. He started stickin' to himself more and more, went on hunting trips for weeks at a time. Some of us were beginning to wonder how long it would be before something like this happened."

"That settles it, then," Mr. Wilkins said. "A definite suicide. I'll notify the medical examiner's office in Chapel Hill that no autopsy is necessary."

"You're the expert. What else do you need to do here?"

"In most cases," he said, "we draw a blood sample for a standard toxicology screening. Drugs and alcohol, that sort of thing. But I doubt we could get a sample at this stage. So, I sign the death certificate, and then I call Schroeder's to pick up the body and hold it until we can notify the next of kin. Didn't he have a sister?"

"Amy. I'll make sure she knows."

Mr. Wilkins made a final inquiry of the hunters. "Any of you boys know a reason I shouldn't call this one a suicide?"

Each man solemnly shook his head.

"Then it's uncontested." He paused to look at his wristwatch. "I'm recording the legal time of death as 8:04 a.m. on June 14, 1999. And I'm getting out of this kill-dog humidity just as fast as I can." And wringing out his handkerchief as he went, the Holcum County coroner lumbered back toward the opening in the woods.

Sheriff St. Clair pulled out a cell phone and flipped it open.

"You callin' Amy?" Ronny asked.

"I got one other call to make first." The sheriff paused, waiting for an answer at the other end.

"Good morning, Central Carolina Bank."

"I want to talk to Kathryn Guilford," the sheriff said. "Just tell her it's Peter—and tell her it's important."

CHAPTER 3

Thirty-year-old Kathryn Guilford slowed her car as she approached the small gravel road that cut a hole deep into the woods just outside of Sandridge. Sandridge was the extreme western boundary of Holcum County, a remote area of old abandoned home fields that had been slowly but thoroughly reclaimed first by brush, then by pines, then by the overpowering hardwoods. She turned the nose of her '97 Acura onto the crunching gravel and peered as far as she could down the path. Thirty yards ahead of her, it curved slowly to the right and disappeared behind a gnarled red oak. To her left was a rectangular white sign, too small and with too many letters to be read from the main road. It didn't seem to advertise or welcome, Kathryn thought; it seemed to exist simply to mark a location, like a survey marker or a gravestone. In red gothic letters it stated plainly, NORTH CAROLINA STATE UNIVERSITY—DEPARTMENT OF ENTOMOLOGY—HOLCUM COUNTY RESEARCH STATION. In the center of the sign was the seal of the university, but freshly pasted across the seal was a blue and gold bumper sticker emblazoned, GO NITTANY LIONS.

Kathryn rolled down her window and listened. From the woods came the slow, heavy, rolling chant of the cicadas, already laboring in the rising morning steam. A thousand invisible wood crickets joined the lament, and blunt-bodied beetles, weighed down by the morning haze, buzzed slowly back and forth across the path.

The woods were thick and crowded with life, all groaning and complaining in the early summer heat.

Kathryn felt a shudder flutter down her spine. She fastened the top button of her white satin blouse and rolled the window up tight, instinctively glancing in the rearview mirror to make sure that each window had sealed completely. Then, flipping the air conditioning to high, she proceeded slowly down the gravel path.

Thirty yards past the red oak she came to a tall chain-link fence topped by a spiraling roll of razor wire. An unchained gate swung open away from her, and beside the gate was a bright yellow sign bearing a single word: BIOHAZARD. Below the sign was a piece of weathered poster board with a frowning face markered at the top. Below it in rough hand-lettering were the words Mr. Yucky says GO HOME.

"Strange sense of humor," Kathryn whispered, and proceeded through the gate.

The road straightened and widened now, and she relaxed a little and accelerated down the path. Her eyes began to pool with tears when she remembered Peter's phone call, less than three hours ago, with the gut-wrenching news that Jimmy McAllister was dead—and by his own hand. The coroner checked everything out. He was depressed, they had said. It was only a matter of time before something like this would happen. Everything fits; everything is in order; everyone is so sure.

Everyone but me.

Kathryn snapped back to attention at a buzzing sound from under the dashboard. To her utter horror, a single wriggling yellow jacket squeezed from the left floor vent and fanned its cellophane wings. Before she could even scream, the yellow jacket shot forward and landed on her left thigh just below the hemline, then crawled a few quick steps upward. Kathryn found her voice and let loose a scream, snapped both legs straight, and slapped violently at her leg. The car lurched abruptly left, and she jerked the wheel back toward the center of the road. The yellow jacket, now decidedly annoyed, shot upward and buzzed close across her face, then disappeared into the backseat behind her. She threw herself forward and flailed her right arm wildly over, around, behind her head. A venomous hiss sizzled past one ear, retreated, then streaked across the other.

With a shriek of terror and rage, Kathryn released the wheel with both hands and swung madly at the air.

In that instant Kathryn Guilford was no longer a thirty-year-old bank executive driving a shining silver Acura. Somehow, one tiny black-and-yellow insect had projected her back through time and space, back to that place that was so long ago and yet never far away . . . She was once again a seven-year-old girl in an upside-down '57 Chevy Bel Air.

The car weaved from side to side in a widening arc, then abruptly lunged from the road. With a crumple of metal and the dull whump of exploding air bags, it came to a final stop against a massive, smooth-faced silver beech.

She was stunned for only an instant—then she groped frantically for the chrome handle, flung open the door, and bolted out. She spun to face the car and her invisible assailant, her arms still beating at the air, backing away into the center of the road. Exhausted, she began to slow down and then stopped. She stood silently for a moment, panting, then lifted both arms and examined herself. Her navy blue A-line skirt was blotched with a musty white powder. Her blouse hung loose and her silver wire choker was nowhere in sight. She stared in dismay at her shoes, her legs, and her arms; she wiped her face with the back of her forearm and studied her hands.

Finally, she looked at her car.

The gleaming silver hood lay crumpled back, echoing the contour of the stately beech, and steam hissed up through the grill and from under both sides. The driver's door was still open, revealing two limp air bags sagging from the console, and the once-spotless black interior was now blasted with the same white powder that thoroughly covered her.

Kathryn took a deep breath and inched back toward the car, hesitating at the open door; there was her purse, still resting in the center of the passenger seat. She ducked her head, anxiously searching every inch of air space inside. Then, with a lunge, she snatched her purse and scrambled backward, taking one last swing at the air in front of her face.

She dusted her skirt, straightened her blouse and hair, and then stopped. She listened again to the chorus of cicadas, crickets, and beetles that now seemed to completely surround and press in on her. She stood for a moment weighing her options. She glanced back up the road toward the open gate now a quarter of a mile behind her. She could go back—but back to what? Back to ignorance and frustration and doubt? Back to where no one would listen or help? Back to a funeral where the truth would be buried forever along with the body? Along with Jimmy's body . . .

She peered down the road in the direction of the mysterious biohazard, still nowhere in sight. She refastened the top button of her blouse and then, turning toward the invisible research facility somewhere in the distance, Kathryn Guilford continued to do what she came to do.

Ten sweltering minutes later her blue sling-back sandals were coated with gravel dust. Sweat ran freely down her face and neck, and her satin blouse clung heavily to the center of her back. Rounding a bend, she came at last upon a building—a pale green Quonset hut attached to a rectangular outbuilding at the back, forming a large T. The curved, corrugated surface of the roof was broken by a series of large skylights, giving it more the appearance of a greenhouse than a building. The gravel road dead-ended into a small parking lot directly in front of the Quonset.

In the parking lot were two automobiles. On the right was a tidy, silver-blue Camry; on the left was a faded, rusting relic that during some geologic era had been a '64 Dodge Dart. The car slumped decidedly to the left; the original color was anyone's guess. The backseat was split open across the top with puffs of twisted oatmeal poking through. The seat itself was piled with stacks of black and blue vinyl binders and thick stapled papers, accented by a single Papa John's Pizza box on top. In the rear window black-and-gold Pittsburgh Pirates and Pittsburgh Steelers caps posed proudly side by side.

Kathryn stepped up onto the narrow landing, took one last accounting of herself, and knocked. There was no answer. After several moments she knocked again; still nothing. She turned and looked again at the two cars behind her. It occurred to her that the rusting relic on the right may not be in working order. Judging by its appearance, it may not have been driven since Watergate, but the Camry looked in perfect condition. Someone must be home.

Just then the screen door began to open, and Kathryn had to step back to make room for it. Behind the door stood a pleasant looking, round-faced little man no more than five feet in height. He was balding down the middle and long strands of chestnut hair were combed strategically from one side to the other. He wore small, round spectacles, which accented perfectly the roundness of his cherubic cheeks and nose. It was an altogether kind and friendly face.

"May I help you?" he asked, self-consciously raking his hand from left to right across the top of his head.

"I'm here to see Dr. Polchak."

"You are?" His eyebrows rose up behind the little spectacles. "Is he expecting you?"

"No . . . Actually, I was just driving by, and I thought I'd stop in."

He peered over Kathryn's shoulder into the driveway. There was a silver-blue Camry and a Dodge Dart—nothing else.

"I . . . had a little car trouble."

The little man seemed to come alive at this news. "Where are my manners? Please forgive me. Won't you come in? Please do."

Kathryn gladly stepped into the open doorway, anticipating the cool rush of air conditioning that is the salvation of every home and business in the South. Instead, to her dismay she found that it was just as hot inside the structure as it was outside—but without the breeze.

"Please forgive the appearance of the place—we're not accustomed to receiving visitors here, especially such lovely ones. I am Dr. Tedesco, a research associate of Dr. Polchak," he said, extending his hand. "You look dreadfully hot. Can I get you anything? Water? A cold drink?"

"No, thank you, I'm fine. If you could just tell Dr. Polchak I'm here?"

"Of course, of course." He glanced back into the laboratory doubtfully. "And whom shall I say is calling?"

Kathryn reached into her purse and handed him a card. In green thermographic letters it declared: Kathryn Guilford, Central Carolina Bank & Trust, Commercial Mortgage Capital.

"And please—tell him this is not about banking."

The little man held up one finger, winked, and scurried back into the lab.

The interior of the Quonset was a large, open rectangle. Light from the twin rows of skylights streamed down onto a long, double-sided worktable that occupied the center of the room. Worktables lined all four walls, in fact; stopping only for the doors at either end. The only open space in the room was a narrow aisleway that ran the perimeter of the room, separating the tables along the walls from the one in the center. On the far wall was a door, and the center of the wall was filled with one great, rectangular window looking out into the office beyond.

Kathryn watched the little man disappear through the door and approach a seated figure in the office beyond. The figure was facing away from Kathryn, bent over a desk, intently occupied by some task before him. The little man began to speak in his effervescent style, holding out the tiny business card and gesturing occasionally in Kathryn's direction. The figure never moved or looked up; he simply continued to focus on the task at hand.

Kathryn's eyes wandered back to the room immediately before her, stopping first on the far worktable just below the great window. It was lined with different sizes and shapes of glass terraria. Her eyes followed the path of the cases around the table to the right; it, too, was completely covered, as was the table on the left and the double-sided counter in the center. The entire room was one vast collection of display cases overhung by long banks of fluorescent lights. She could see that each terrarium contained some kind of plant or rock or limb. Some were lined with sand, others with yellow or gray or chocolate soil. Her eyes came to rest on the terrarium directly before her, not more than twelve inches away. It was covered with glistening sand, with a large flat slab of pink sandstone in the center. It was otherwise empty, except for a shallow dish of water in one corner. Kathryn bent closer to study this strange, lonely landscape. Instinctively, she reached out and tapped on the glass.

From under the stone a brown desert scorpion skittered out, menacing tail aloft, pincers ready.

Kathryn drew a sharp breath and leaped away from the glass. She stumbled backward against the screen door, punching her elbow through the stiff wire mesh as it crashed open. She staggered back to the gravel driveway and stood, trembling.

At the crash, the studious figure in the office at last turned to stare in Kathryn's direction—but the lab was now completely empty. He rose, taking the business card from the little man's hand, and stepped out into the lab.

A moment later Kathryn saw the screen door open. A tall silhouette in the doorway stood silently studying her, carefully rereading the business card in his right hand, then slowly looking her over once again.

From inside the lab the little man urgently pushed his way past and hurried to her side. "My dear, whatever happened? Are you quite all right? Please, come back inside, out of this dreadful sun."

"If it's all the same to you, could we speak outside?"

She turned to look at the figure still standing in the doorway. He was holding her business card at eye level now, still glancing from the card to Kathryn and back again, as if he had been handed the driver's license of a bald-headed man from New Jersey.

It was the little man who broke the silence. "Where are my manners? Ms. Guilford, may I present Dr. Nicholas Polchak. Dr. Polchak, allow me to introduce—"

"Kathryn Guilford," the tall figure interrupted, "Central Carolina Bank and Trust, Commercial . . . Mortgage . . . Capital." He said the last three words slowly, as if to emphasize the disparity between the dignified title and the disheveled woman who stood before him.

"As I told Dr. Tedesco, I'm not here about banking."

"What exactly are you here about?"

"I've come to talk to you about a matter of utmost importance," she said with all the solemnity she could muster, but the words sounded ridiculous even to her.

He glanced at the curling shards of screen wire. "Were you in too big a hurry to open the door?" He looked at the little man beside her. "Teddy, we need to fix this. We don't want any local dermestids paying us a visit."

At last the tall figure stepped from the doorway, and for the first time Kathryn could see him in detail. He was lean and angular, with very large hands and feet. He wore a white ribbed polyester shirt with a large open collar, which hung open over a blue and green Fubu T-shirt. Below, a pair of enormous olive green cargo shorts overshadowed two alabaster limbs that protruded into a pair of ancient leather thongs.

He looked about Kathryn's age. His head was rather large and shaped like an inverted triangle. It narrowed from a wide brow to a strong chin with a deep dimple pressed into the center. His skin was fair and smooth, the skin of a man who spent far too much time under fluorescent light. His hair was dark and straight and his hairline receded slightly on both sides, emphasizing the triangularity of his features. It was a handsome face for the most part, Kathryn thought. She glanced quickly over his features, taking an instant accounting of each, but came abruptly to a halt at his eyes.

He wore the largest, thickest eyeglasses Kathryn had ever seen, which so distorted his eyes that they seemed to float behind the lenses like two soft, colorless orbs. They reminded Kathryn of the pickled eggs that eternally floated in a jar beside the cash register at Wirth's Amoco. She almost laughed aloud at the mental image.

His eyes never seemed to rest and never focused long on a single object. It was impossible to tell exactly where he was looking at any moment. Kathryn watched the eyes moving over her. They darted to one side, then the other. They floated upward, then slowly sank again. They studied her, they analyzed her, they examined her; they saw everything but focused on nothing. Kathryn wished that his eyes would come to rest on hers; she wished that she could make contact with them—but the eyes always moved on.

"I came here to make a legitimate business proposition," she said. "If you're not interested, perhaps I should take my business elsewhere."

Nick smiled. "I suspect there is no elsewhere, or you wouldn't be here."

She softened her tone. "A friend of mine has died—a very old and dear friend. The police say it was suicide, but I think they're wrong. I'm sure they're wrong," she added, then paused for emphasis. "I think he might have been murdered."

"Mrs. Guilford," Nick cut in. "Dr. Tedesco and I are members of the faculty of North Carolina State University. We were sent here this summer to do research."

"You do research on dead people."

Nick's eyes darted rapidly over Kathryn once more, as if he might have missed some detail in his initial estimation. "I do research on arthropods—specific insects that inhabit dead people."

Kathryn opened her purse and removed a folded photocopy. "From the *Holcum County Courier*," she said, beginning to read. " 'Bug Man Comes to Holcum County.' "

"May I?" he said, taking the photocopy from her hand. " 'Dr. Nicholas Polchak'—that would be me—'Professor of Entomology at NC State University in Raleigh, will spend the summer at the extension research facility here in Holcum County to continue his studies in the emerging field of forensic entomology, the use of insects to solve crimes.' "

He quickly scanned the rest of the document. "Blah blah blah and so on, and—here's the good part—'Dr. Polchak, a tall, muscular man . . .' Now that's outstanding journalism. Yes indeed, very well put."

A faint groan came from Teddy, who stood quietly staring at the pavement, shaking his head slowly from side to side.

"Dr. Polchak, I need your help. And I need it right away."

He handed the photocopy back to her. "Mrs. Guilford, you need to go to the police. If the police won't help you, you need to call the medical examiner's office in Chapel Hill and talk to them. Or you can even hire a private investigator. I'd like to help you—really I would—but this summer I'm under strict orders to stick to research."

He turned back toward the Quonset. "Come on, Teddy," he said, disappearing through the doorway, "we've got some sarcophagids to pin. Let's not waste any more of the lady's time."

Kathryn watched the door swing shut behind him.

"I'm very sorry," Teddy said, looking truly regretful. "He meant what he said—he really would like to help you. But to tell you the truth, this summer he's been given strict orders to stay out of trouble."

"There won't be any trouble."

"Trust me. With Nicholas, there's always trouble." And with a heavy sigh he turned and followed his colleague back into the lab.

Kathryn turned slowly back toward the path to her crumpled car. She stood motionless for several seconds, staring directly ahead.

Suddenly she wheeled around, fists clenched, her face flushed with anger. She marched up to the broken screen door, flung it open hard, and charged through the open doorway—then just as quickly drew back again. There was the same glass case, now occupied by three brown scorpions. The terrarium at her left elbow contained a tree branch where black, metallic-shelled beetles swarmed up, then dropped off in clusters like thick blobs of oil. In the terrarium on her right, a gray-and-brown wolf spider held a struggling black cricket in its slender, tapering legs.

Kathryn stared desperately across the lab at the large window into the office beyond. Inside she could see the figure of Dr. Polchak already seated again at his work. Her eyes slowly traced the path of the aisleway to her left, pausing at each glass case to imagine the unspeakable horror it might contain. The aisle seemed so much narrower now than at first sight. She measured the distance from her present location to the doorway beside the large window. It couldn't have been more than fifty feet. Or was it seventy-five? Or a hundred?

It might as well be ten miles.

With her left hand she turned her collar up high and squeezed it tight, completely covering her neck. With her right hand she clutched the front of her blouse, wadding it into a ball. She hunched her shoulders forward and pinned her arms tight against her torso. Her breathing was shallow and rapid, and her legs felt thick and rubbery. She closed her eyes, took a deep breath, and stepped slowly forward like a tightrope walker on a windy day.

She forced herself to stare directly ahead, though the hideous temptation to turn and look directly into each terrarium was almost irresistible. From the corners of her eyes she watched each glass case pass slowly by—nothing more than blurs of brown and green and tan—but in her mind's eye she imagined swarms of wriggling insects sucking up to the glass, pressing up against the terrarium lids, their hairlike antennae protruding through the screened tops, probing the air, stretching toward her, reaching for her.

The office door was directly ahead of her now, no more than thirty feet away. She was halfway there, but the thought that kept forcing its way into her mind was that she was now directly in the center of this living nightmare. She felt herself begin to lose her balance, and a wave of panic and nausea almost overwhelmed her. She imagined falling suddenly to one side, drawn irresistibly by the darkness behind the glass, reaching out to stop herself. Then she imagined her hands crashing through the glass and reaching helplessly into the black abyss.

The panic swelled up within her like a tidal surge. She commanded her legs to run for the office door, but they seemed to move in slow motion. She felt the glass cases begin to slide toward her, and those behind her seemed to swirl in and pursue her like paper boxes whipped into the draft of a passing car. She looked like a toddler taking its last hurried steps before collapsing into the arms of a waiting parent—but to Kathryn, it felt as though she were running down an endless, windowed hallway for all eternity.

With a crash, the office door flew open and Kathryn burst into the room. Nick looked up from his microscope with a start and saw Kathryn, still tightly clutching her collar and blouse, trembling and panting like a spent mare. He rose from his stool and walked slowly toward her.

"Mrs. Guilford," he said, cocking his head to one side, "are you cold?"

"Dr. Polchak," she growled through clenched teeth, "I need your help—and I need it right now!"

For a moment he stood perfectly still, observing her. Then he slowly reached out and took hold of the hand still clutching at her collar. He pulled gently but said nothing. She resisted. He pulled again, steadily, until she understood and slowly loosened her grip. With his other hand he tugged at the clenched fist on her blouse. He softly lowered both hands to her sides and then began to straighten and smooth her collar and blouse. As he worked, his eyes began to float over her once again, watching, examining, studying.

"Have a seat," Nick said as he returned to his stool. Kathryn looked around the office for the first time. It was smaller than it looked from the outside, and impossibly crowded. The largest single item in the office was a tall stainless steel unit that looked like a double-wide refrigerator with glass doors. The back wall was covered with particle-board bookcases of various colors and sizes, and each shelf sagged under the weight of endless dull-colored volumes with tiny gold or silver titles. Some books were placed well back on the shelf, others stuck out half-returned, and between every few books a manila file or stack of loose photocopies projected. Under the great window was a long worktable, completely cluttered with binders, tweezers, magnifiers, plastic containers, and a hundred other mysterious tools of the forensic entomologist's dark trade. More than anything there was paper: stacks of articles atop the bookshelves, printouts on the tables, manuscripts on the floor. The only break in the endless clutter was two narrow doorways, one at each end of the room—the only means of escape.

Kathryn stood looking awkwardly about the room. There seemed to be no other place to sit. Nick leaned forward and slid a second stool out from under the worktable, topped with a cascading pile of technical journal articles. With a sweep of his hand he sent the mound of paper back under the table and gestured to the seat.

"Don't you ever put anything away?" Kathryn asked, sliding onto the stool.

"That is away. Away from me."

They sat in silence for a few moments as Kathryn gathered her thoughts. Nick spoke first.

"Only one of us knows why you're here. I'll bet it's you."

So much for formalities, Kathryn thought, and plunged ahead. "As I said outside, I have a very dear friend—"

"Had a dear friend," Nick interrupted. "When was the body discovered?"

"Early this morning—by some hunters in the woods not far from here."

"And what was the estimated time of death?"

"They said a week ago. Maybe longer."

"Now tell me about the disposition of the body."

She stared at him blankly.

"How it was situated," he explained, "how it was dressed, the position of the arms and legs, the contents of the hands . . ."

"I don't know a lot of . . . details," she stammered. "They said he was found lying on his back. He was still holding his pistol in his hand—the one he got in the army. He had . . . they say he . . ."

She grimaced, made a gun with her right hand and held it to her temple.

"A contact wound to the right temporal region—and no doubt an exit wound on the left. The standard service sidearm is a nine-millimeter, and as they say around these parts, you just can't keep that chicken in the henhouse."

She glared at him hard but said nothing.

"The sheriff's department was satisfied that this was a suicide?"

"Yes, but—"

"And the medical examiner's office—what did they say?"

She looked at the floor. "The coroner said nothing looked suspicious to him either."

"Maybe the autopsy will turn up something."

"There won't be an autopsy."

Nick raised one eyebrow. "No autopsy was ordered?"

"No."

"In cases of unattended death—as in the case of a suicide—an autopsy is usually ordered to verify cause of death. Things must have looked pretty straightforward."

Kathryn had nothing to say in response.

"This dear friend of yours—I assume we're talking about a male? He was about your age, thirty to thirty-five? Caucasian?"

"That's right. How did you—"

"Three-quarters of all suicides are by white males. Two-thirds of them are by gunshot, generally to the head. That fits too. He did it outside, probably standing up—men usually do. Women like the comforts of home and almost always lie down. He used his own gun, which was still in his hand. And there was no note, was there? Nothing to explain his motive or timing?"

She shook her head.

He let out a sigh. "You just can't get men to write, can you?" He paused a full measure for dramatic effect. "So, Mrs. Guilford. What can I do for you?"

Kathryn's face was red and hot. "I knew Jimmy since we were kids together here in Holcum County. We grew up together, like a brother and sister. I knew him better than his parents, better than his own sister—better than anyone. He would not, he could not have done this to himself. I don't care what the sheriff or the coroner says, they're wrong about this—and I have to know what happened."

Nick took a deep breath. "Let me see if I understand you. The sheriff's department, drawing on its considerable experience in homicide investigation, closed this investigation almost before it opened. And the county coroner, representing all of the forensic knowledge of the North Carolina State medical examiner's system, verified the cause of death without even a second look. But you're convinced they're both wrong—because you have this feeling."

It was fortunate at this moment that the door behind Kathryn opened and Dr. Tedesco stepped into the room, providing a momentary respite from the tension. He was startled to see Kathryn again but said nothing. He stepped quietly to the side, pretending to resume his duties, and waited for the conversation to resume.

"I have to know," Kathryn repeated, barely containing her anger. "The sheriff won't help me—he thinks I'm wasting my time. The coroner can't help me either. Since he already signed the death certificate, the body is no longer under his authority. I could hire a private investigator, but not in a town the size of Rayford—and even if I found one, I'm not sure he'd know what to look for. I'm out of options, Dr. Polchak—and I'm out of time. The body is being moved right now to a funeral home, and from there it will be turned over to the immediate family. Soon it will be too late to do anything."

Nick said nothing for a long time.

"You'd be helping the authorities," she added.

"I have a long history of helping the authorities," he said. "Trust me, it isn't always welcome."

"Then you'd be helping me."

"I just can't look into every mysterious death that comes along—and to be frank, Mrs. Guilford, this one hardly sounds mysterious."

Kathryn paused. "What about money? Are you motivated by money?"

"Money?"

She leaned forward and stared directly into his imposing spectacles. "I will pay you twenty thousand dollars to look into this for me."

There was an audible gasp from behind Kathryn. Dr. Tedesco did his very best to contain himself, but bits of words and phrases still tittered out: "Twenty thousand . . . oh my, I . . . twenty thousand?"

"This is why Teddy never plays poker," said Dr. Polchak.

"I know more about you than you think," Kathryn said. "I know that you're a forensic entomologist, and that there are very few of you around. I know that it's almost impossible to make a living at it. I know that most of you are employed by museums and universities, and that means you depend on departmental funding and research grants to survive. In other words," she said, adding her own pause for emphasis, "I know you need that money so bad you can taste it."

Nick slowly smiled. "And you said this visit wasn't about money."

"I said this visit wasn't about banking. What would this really require of you, Dr. Polchak? One look at a body? A trip to a funeral home? A little work right here in your own laboratory? Twenty thousand dollars buys a lot of bug food."

From behind them Teddy conducted an elaborate pantomime of hair-pulling, eye-rolling, and desperate pleading. Nick ignored him.

"I don't want to waste your money, Mrs. Guilford. Don't misunderstand me, I want your money—but I don't want to waste it. I feel I should tell you that there's a very good chance I'll come up with nothing at all."

"I'm willing to take that chance."

Nick sat silently for a full minute. "Plus expenses," he said at last.

"I beg your pardon?"

"Twenty thousand dollars plus expenses."

"What sort of expenses?"

"Travel, if necessary. Meals. Supplies. Valium for Teddy. I don't know what else . . . expenses."

"Done." She extended her hand, and as Nick cautiously reached for it she added, "There is one small condition, Dr. Polchak, and this is not negotiable. I want to work with you. I want to be there every step of the way."

Nick pulled back, and Teddy buried his face in his hands. "That's entirely out of the question."

"It's not negotiable," Kathryn repeated. "I'm not a fool, Dr. Polchak. Twenty thousand dollars is a great deal of money. What am I supposed to think if you report back in two weeks and say, 'Sorry, I found nothing'? I want to see what you do. I want to know that nothing was overlooked. I want to know that if we find nothing, it won't be because we didn't look hard enough. I want to know."

After another full minute, Nick spoke again. "The investigation will take a full week, perhaps two. And if what you say is true—if the body is already on its way to a funeral home—then we have to begin immediately. That means right now."

Kathryn extended her hand again. As Nick took it, he said, "I have one condition of my own, Mrs. Guilford. If you're going to work with me, it has to be—as you said—every step of the way."

"Agreed."

"Mrs. Guilford," he said, smiling, "you have no idea what you've gotten yourself into."

CHAPTER 4

The interior of Dr. Polchak's crumbling Dodge Dart was even worse than Kathryn had imagined. The brittle vinyl seats were split apart in sharp ridges, and the dashboard was a canyon of cracked ravines and gullies with rivers of dusty foam flowing beneath. Above her head the roof liner draped and sagged. Below, the floorboard was pockmarked with rust holes that allowed her a more than adequate view of the pavement streaking by beneath her feet. She sat rigidly, legs apart, straddling the cratered floorboard as if it were an open bomb-bay door.

"Watch your skirt," Nick said with a sideways glance. "I'd rather you didn't get that sodium azide powder all over my upholstery."

"What upholstery?"

"I like to take care of my car. For example, I try to keep beech trees out of my engine." He glanced at her again. "Care to tell me what happened back there?"

"No." She pointed up ahead. "Schroeder's is on the left at the next corner. If you don't mind, park on the street."

"There are hundreds of unexplained traffic fatalities every year," Nick said. "No heart attack, no stroke—for some reason the driver just swerved off the road. Some experts—like me—think the answer may be insects. A bug flies in the window, the driver panics, there's an accident." He looked at Kathryn. "Entomophobia is one of the more common irrational fears, Mrs. Guilford."

Kathryn glared straight ahead. "You're just a bushel full of interesting information, aren't you?"

Nick stopped the car and pulled up on the emergency brake, which moved without a sound. "I don't think it's actually attached to anything," he said. He turned to the backseat, grabbed a large canvas knapsack and then paused, eyeing the two black-and-gold hats resting side-by-side in the rear window.

"This one," he said, pulling it on tight. "I think this might be a job for a pirate."

Great, Kathryn thought. Just the final fashion touch he needed.

"No offense"—she looked him over quickly—"but I wish you had changed."

"I wish I had a dollar for every time a woman told me that."

Schroeder's Funeral Home was a landmark in the town of Rayford. For decades it had been known as the Lampiers' Home, the largest private residence in Holcum County. It was still remembered that way by most of the older residents of Rayford. With its white beveled siding, long black shutters, and green-and-white canvas awnings, it had the perfect image for its current function. Mr. Schroeder simply added the embellishments of his trade: the chapel, the garage, and the tonguelike porte-cochere that jutted out above the circular asphalt driveway.

Kathryn hesitated at the tall black door. "Do me a favor—let me do the talking."

Nick shrugged. "It's your money."

As Kathryn stepped through the doorway, a wave of frigid air engulfed her. As sweltering as her morning had been, the air felt much too cold. She shivered—not simply because of the abrupt change in temperature but because of the total change of environment. Everything around her was suddenly dark, cold, heavy, and silent. She had the eerie sensation that she had just stepped on an unmarked grave.

The ancient red oak flooring creaked and groaned as they stepped into the center of the high, arching atrium. The walls were lined with dark cherry paneling that disappeared into the darkness above. Directly ahead, a wide doorway opened into a small chapel lined with short pews. On the far wall a Gothic stained-glass window sent streams of multicolored light to meet them. To their left, a smaller doorway opened into an office.

"Remarkable." Nick's voice shattered the silence. "It's amazing the trappings that your species attaches to a simple biological function like death."

A moment later the figure of Mr. Schroeder appeared in the office doorway. His hands were folded in front of him as he walked, and the floor made no sound, as if he had somehow learned to become a part of the stillness around him. He wore a dark suit with a black-and-silver tie, and a white carnation glowed from his left lapel. His silver hair was combed neatly back, and his face seemed to be frozen in an expression of permanent compassion, deep sorrow, and profound concern.

"Kathryn, Kathryn, Kathryn!" he said in a half-whisper, taking both of her hands in his. "How good it is to see you again. I don't believe we've had a visit from you since . . . why, since we had the privilege of caring for your mother."

"I assume you mean since her mother died," Nick said, running his hand admiringly over the cherry paneling.

Mr. Schroeder cringed slightly at the sound of the forbidden word, taking note for the first time of the bizarrely clad stranger beside Kathryn. Whatever his thoughts, his expression never faltered; Mr. Schroeder had long ago learned that constant politeness, tolerance, and patience were vital assets in his profession. After all, in a town the size of Rayford, almost everyone was an eventual customer.

"And who might this be?" he smiled warmly to Kathryn.

"Mr. Schroeder, I'd very much like you to meet Dr. Nicholas Polchak."

Nick smiled broadly, folded his hands in front of him, and cocked his head slightly to one side. Mr. Schroeder didn't seem to notice, but the mimicry didn't escape Kathryn. She shot him an angry glare.

"It is an honor, Doctor," Mr. Schroeder said warmly and then turned to Kathryn again. "Tell me, does your visit today concern Andrew? Has there finally been some resolution to the situation? I do hope so, for your sake."

Kathryn winced slightly and looked at the floor. "No, Mr. Schroeder. Nothing has changed. His body has never been recovered. This is not about Andy."

"Ah," he said, sighing deeply, "perhaps one day." There was an appropriate moment of silence—Mr. Schroeder's stock-in-trade—and then he smiled at both of them again. "Well then, how can we be of service to you today?"

"Mr. Schroeder, I understand that you are receiving the body of Jimmy McAllister."

Mr. Schroeder looked suddenly overwhelmed with sorrow. "Oh yes, a very sad affair, very sad. We were happy to make our facility available to the sheriff's department until the immediate family can make their wishes known regarding the final disposition."

"Mr. Schroeder, please—may I see him?"

At this, Mr. Schroeder uttered a deep moan and closed his eyes tightly, shaking his head slowly from side to side. Kathryn thought he looked exactly like the ghost of Jacob Marley; she saw Nick turn away to disguise a smile.

"My dear Kathryn," he intoned, "you must understand the situation. I'm told that Mr. McAllister has been deceased for almost a week now. How can I put this delicately? He will be in no condition to receive visitors—as I'm sure the good doctor can testify."

"The body will be in a stage of decomposition known as putrefaction," Nick said abruptly, "perhaps even black putrefaction, considering the ambient temperature lately. The gut will be bloated by intestinal bacteria—so will the eyes and tongue, if there's anything left of them. The skin will be blistered and loose. There will be major larval infestations here, here, and here"—he pointed casually to Kathryn's temple, eyes, and mouth—"and brother, it will stink to high heaven."

Each additional description seemed to rocket off the walls and violate the solemn atmosphere like an obscenity shouted in a cathedral. Mr. Schroeder looked as though he might never recover.

"Nevertheless," she continued, "I still want to see him."

"Kathryn, please," Mr. Schroeder implored. "This is not how Mr. McAllister would want you to remember him. Don't do this to him. Don't do this to yourself."

"Please. It will only be for a few minutes."

"I'm very sorry," he said, sighing. "I'd like to accommodate you, but you must understand my situation. First of all, the deceased has not arrived yet. And even when he does, without direct permission from the next of kin I cannot allow a viewing. Have you such permission?"

"I know Jimmy's sister, but . . . well . . . it's kind of complicated . . ."

"There isn't time," Nick cut in. "When the body arrives, you won't bring it in the house—not in the shape it's in. You'll store it in the garage, and you'll dust it with Formalin powder as fast as you can to control the stench. That will kill every insect on the body."

Mr. Schroeder looked at him closely, as if for the first time.

"Look," Nick said, "we're not asking to do an autopsy here— we just want to collect a few bugs."

A look of astonished realization swept across Mr. Schroeder's face. "I'm sorry," he said firmly, "what you ask is out of the question. You're not requesting a viewing at all, you're intending to conduct some kind of examination. What you suggest is quite unethical and improper—and possibly illegal as well."

"Please," Kathryn pleaded now, "I have to see him. If only you knew how important this is to me . . ."

A prolonged and awkward silence followed—then Nick spoke up abruptly. "Mr. Schroeder, I understand your situation completely. As a fellow professional I can appreciate the awkward position that Mrs. Guilford has put you in. We'll contact the immediate family in the next few days to see what options might be available to us. Thank you for your time."

Kathryn watched open-mouthed as Nick wheeled around and walked quickly out the door. She turned, muttered something incoherent to Mr. Schroeder, and hurried after him. She caught up to him halfway to the car.

"What's the matter with you?" she shouted after him. "Are you out of your mind? What were you thinking back there?" Nick said nothing, but got into the car and started the engine. Kathryn hurried around and climbed in, slamming the door hard behind her.

"Easy on the door," he said, pulling away from the curb in a puff of blue smoke. "It's held together by Bondo."

"I thought you said we don't have a few days! What happens if he puts that powder on the body?"

"Then you've got no bugs. No bugs, no Bug Man."

"No Bug Man, no twenty thousand dollars!" she reminded him. "I don't understand why in the world you—"

"This should be far enough." Nick pulled over to the curb again a single block farther down the road, just out of sight of Schroeder's Funeral Home. "You coming?" he said as he climbed from the car. She stared for a moment in utter disbelief, then hurried after him.

"It was obvious we were getting nowhere with Mr. Schroeder," he called back over his shoulder. "But he still helped us out in his own small way, bless his icy little heart. He told us that the body hasn't arrived yet."

"So what?"

"Mr. Schroeder can't show us what Mr. Schroeder doesn't have, so why waste our time on him? Let's go around to the garage and wait for the delivery man."

"But won't the delivery man tell us the same thing?"

"Maybe, maybe not. Funeral directors often contract out to have somebody else do the dirty work of collecting bodies. If the collector is an employee of the funeral home, he'll probably tell us to get lost. But if he's just some local yokel, then what does he care?" Nick turned and winked. "He just might let us take a peek."

The garage was the business end of the stately funeral home, providing direct access to the chrome-and-porcelain preparation rooms inside. Schroeder's Funeral Home was first and foremost a place of comfort and condolence and dignity, so it was prudent to attempt to conceal the true nature of the business—the receiving and processing of dead bodies. The garage and driveway entrance were masked by a screen of tall redbuds.

Nick slung off his knapsack and dropped it on the driveway in front of the garage. He stretched out on the pavement and laid his head against the knapsack, folding his arms across his chest and tipping his Pirates cap down over his spectacled eyes.

"Wake me if you see a car." He yawned. "A big black one."

Kathryn was in no mood for sleep—or for humor. She paced nervously back and forth, looking first down the driveway, then around the side of the house, then at the reclining form of Nick—but mostly at Nick.

"Is this against the law?" she demanded.

"Maybe," he said without moving. "Does it matter? I thought you said you have to know."

"I just like to know what I'm getting myself into. I do have a position in this town, you know. I don't want the headline in tomorrow's Courier to read, 'Bank Officer Charged with Breaking and Entering.' "

"We're not breaking and entering," he assured her. "The headline will read more like, 'Woman Charged with Molesting Dead Man.' "

"That's not funny! What if Mr. Schroeder comes out?"

"It's still daylight. I'm sure Mr. Schroeder stays in his coffin until midnight."

Nick peeked out from under his cap and took note of the stone-cold expression on Kathryn's face. "Relax," he said, pulling his cap down once again. "The law is a little fuzzy about this kind of thing. When a body is first discovered it belongs to the local medical examiner until he signs off on the death certificate. Later on the funeral home releases the body to the immediate family, and then they own it. But in-between—whose body is it? It's not exactly clear. We're not hurting anyone, Mrs. Guilford—least of all your pal Jim."

"What happens if we get caught?"

Nick sighed heavily and sat up. "Mr. Schroeder will raise the roof, and he'll probably call the next of kin. If he's really mad, he'll call the police too. You'll get a nasty call from the sister, and the police will say, 'Don't make a hobby out of this.' Finito."

"What would happen to you?"

"Don't worry about me," Nick said under his breath. "They can't send me anyplace worse than this."

Behind them there was a loud click and the whir of an electric motor, and the garage door suddenly began to rise. Nick jumped to his feet and peered down the driveway. The long Cadillac hearse rolled slowly up the pavement and pulled into the garage. Behind the wheel was a young man of no more than eighteen, with an even younger boy beside him.

"This looks good, very good. Tell you what"—he smiled, glancing at Kathryn—"this time, why don't you let me do the talking?"

The boys stepped from the car and nodded to their unexpected visitors, then proceeded silently to the rear of the car. The older boy wore baggy denims that hung low on his hips and draped about his feet. He wore a green plaid button-up that hung open over a gray T-shirt beneath, and he sported a pair of silver rings in his left ear. His hair was shaved close on the sides, and his sideburns were thin and long. A tangled tuft of red hair lay atop his head. The younger boy was similarly clad. Both wore bright bandannas around their necks, one red and one blue.

"Can I give you fellas a hand?" Nick asked, taking a position opposite them as they rolled the long gurney from the hearse. "Ready? One, two, three." They lifted and pulled, and the stretcher's wheels dropped and locked in place. Atop the stretcher was a black vinyl bag, zippered down the center.

"I'm Dr. Nicholas Polchak." He smiled, extending his hand to each of them. "Call me Nick."

"I'm Casey," said the older boy, returning the handshake.

"Griff," said the second, his voice a full octave higher.

"I'm with the medical examiner's office in Chapel Hill," Nick lied.

Kathryn winced.

"It seems we missed a few things in the initial investigation, and they sent me down to take a final look. Why don't we set up over here?" He guided the gurney into the left side of the garage, out of sight of the driveway.

"You guys know Mrs. Guilford? It seems she knew the deceased here, so I said she could tag along." Both boys looked at Kathryn, but Casey looked a little longer. Kathryn smiled back nervously and waved, not trusting her voice.

"Can we watch?" Casey asked hopefully.

"I could use your help. Tell me what you've got here."

"We picked him up this morning, in the woods off Weyerhaeuser Road. Musta had to carry him a mile, maybe more. A big guy, weighed a ton. He's been dead a week—a real rotter. Another few days and we woulda had to use the straps to bag him."

"Well, let's take a look." As he reached for the zipper, each boy slid his bandanna up over his nose and mouth. Nick stopped, closed his eyes, and took a deep breath through his nose.

"You don't use anything?" Griff asked in astonishment.

"Whoa," Casey muttered through his bandanna, "you're the man."

As Nick slowly pulled the zipper, it suddenly dawned on Kathryn that she was about to view the remains of one of her oldest and dearest friends—and it wasn't going to be pretty. "Don't do this to him," Mr. Schroeder's words returned to her. "Don't do this to yourself."

A wave of doubt came over her. Did she really need to do this? Did she really want to? Is this the way she wanted to forever remember her friend—not as a handsome, always-smiling companion, but as a decomposing, insect-infested corpse? She had hired Dr. Polchak to do the examination. Why did she need to be here at all? She remembered Dr. Polchak's words: "You have no idea what you've gotten yourself into." Was he really warning her, or were his words just more of his arrogant posturing? She edged closer to the body, then stepped quickly back again. She wanted to know—but did she really need to see?

Nick spread open the body bag near the head and tucked the flaps under the shoulders. "Mrs. Guilford," he said without looking up, "you might want to watch out for—"

Too late. The stench hit Kathryn like a punch in the gut. It was more than a smell—the word was ridiculously inadequate to describe what Kathryn now experienced. Something had reached deep into the limbic region of her brain and triggered an ancient memory—a memory that every human being possesses yet no one needs to learn—the smell of death.

The three men watched as she lurched for the open doorway and dropped to her knees, convulsing. "Now that," Nick sneered, "is what I call gross."

Casey stooped over Kathryn and slid off his bandanna. "Try this. It's covered with Vicks."

"That's an old gravedigger's trick," Nick said. "They used to use camphor. You guys really know your business."

Both boys grinned from ear to ear.

"Casey, open that backpack. We've got to work fast—I mean, I'm on a tight schedule here. See those plastic containers? Pop off the lids and take out the labels. Griff, you hold the containers for me. Casey, you write what I tell you on the labels." He took out a penlight and a pair of long forceps.

Kathryn was already on her feet again, though both legs fluttered like sparrows. She felt a wretched emptiness inside as though her very soul had been sucked from her body. With her right hand she pressed the life-saving bandanna tight against her face; her left hand clutched her stomach, hoping to prevent it from once again hurtling into the abyss. She staggered around the gurney half-doubled over, slowly regaining her strength, taking in everything she could.

She watched Nick pluck several plump white maggots from the open wound in the right temple and drop them into one of Griff's containers.

"You can close that one," he said. "Put, 'right temporal region, entry wound.' " From the opposite side he selected several more. " 'Left temporal region, exit wound.' "

He collected specimens from each ocular region, then used his penlight to prop open the jaw and peered inside. "We've got a cave full of bats," he said, as he stepped aside to allow Casey and Griff to have a look, much to their delight. Kathryn felt her stomach convulse like kneading dough.

From deep within the nasal cavity, Nick slowly removed one fat, wriggling larva that was easily twice the size of any he had collected yet. "Jimmy's been a bad boy." He whistled and held the specimen aloft for all to see. "Would you look at the size of that bugger? Label this big boy 'nasal septum.' "

Casey pointed to a missing hand. Nick gathered a few specimens and scraped away several others to examine the exposed stump. "This is from predator activity. Looks like everybody liked Jimmy." He winked at the boys.

He worked quickly now. "The infestation is consistent with the estimated time of death," he noted to Kathryn, "and so is the general condition of the tissues." He pulled the tattered shirt sleeves up and observed the purplish black coloration on the dorsal surface of the arms where the skin lay against the gurney. He moved around to the legs and removed the shoes and socks. The left foot had the same burgundy discoloration along the heel and continuing up the leg—but the right foot was completely purple from heel to toe. He jerked up the right pant leg. The color ended abruptly just above the ankle. The leg above it had no stain at all.

"How did you find the body? How was it lying? Show me." He nodded toward the floor. Griff lay down and stretched out on his back, arms and legs straight out.

"You're sure? Exactly like that?" Both boys nodded confidently.

He moved around to the side of the body and began to search inside the bag itself. "Help me out here, all three of you," he said, pointing to the opposite side of the bag. "I'm looking for late-instar larvae—really big ones—and especially for little brown capsules about this big. Sort of like brown rice. Check the pockets and the folds in the clothing too—quick now."

The boys scrambled over one another to set to the task. Kathryn edged up to the bag herself and pretended to search, but her mind was desperately focused on something else, anything else that could block out the horror before her.

Nick came around once again to the head. "I guess this will have to do," he said, glancing back over his shoulder at the door. He reached for the zipper and began to slide it up, but as it approached the head, he abruptly stopped. "Well hello there," he said, peering closely at a small, sparsely infested wound in the center of the forehead. "You boys almost missed the party—and you just might be the guests of honor." He plucked a single specimen from the wound and held it up, examining it closely.

At that exact moment the door swung open and Mr. Schroeder stepped into the garage, and with a single sweep of his eyes comprehended the situation. His face began to grow red and to contort, as though he were rapidly trying on a variety of new facial expressions in sizes and styles unfamiliar to him.

"What," he blurted out, "is the meaning of this?"

"Oh no," Kathryn said aloud. It was her worst fear realized; in her mind's eye she could already see the morning headlines.

"Mrs. Guilford," Nick said quietly, still studying his specimen, "I could use a little help here." Kathryn rushed to intercept the furious Mr. Schroeder.

"I distinctly forbade you to conduct this kind of examination!"

"Mr. Schroeder, if you'll just listen to me for a moment, I—"

"You have gone behind my back to conduct this reprehensible procedure in my own facility!"

"If you'll just give me a minute to explain, I'm sure I can—"

Casey leaned over to Nick. "You're not really from the medical examiner's office, are you?"

"Nah." He shrugged. "But we're having a good time, aren't we?"

With each exchange Mr. Schroeder grew more and more livid, and soon he began to spit and splutter accusations and invectives so rapidly that it was impossible to understand him. For her part, Kathryn kept apologizing and explaining, calming and reassuring, all the time keeping herself strategically positioned between Mr. Schroeder and "the good doctor." But she was quickly coming to the end of her diplomatic abilities.

"Griff," Nick said urgently, "toss me another container— quick."

"We're out of containers," Griff said, holding open the knapsack. "See?"

"Hold this!" he commanded, shoving the forceps and its tiny captive into Casey's hand. "Very gently!" He hastily searched through the already-filled containers and chose the one marked "left ocular cavity." He popped off the lid and with a flip of his wrist flung its contents across the room. The larvae rebounded like tiny marshmallows off the side of the gleaming hearse. "Sorry, boys," he said, taking the forceps carefully from Casey, "somebody else needs this cab."

Mr. Schroeder was almost on top of him now, shouting and threatening and waving his arms around Kathryn. Nick tossed the last of the containers into the knapsack, cinched it shut, and stood up so abruptly that Mr. Schroeder stopped in midsentence.

"I believe we have everything we require here," Nick announced with great dignity. "Thank you, Mr. Schroeder, it was a lovely service." He rubbed Griff's head, gave Casey a quick thumbs-up, and proceeded out the garage door. Kathryn watched him wide-eyed, then turned back to Mr. Schroeder, as if there might be some appropriate parting words for such a situation. She stood silently with her mouth half open, her eyes darting desperately from side to side. At last she smiled weakly, shrugged, and hurried down the driveway.

They sat in the car a long time, silently staring out the windshield. Kathryn pulled at the sun visor; it came off in her hand. She studied herself in the mirror. She was white as paste, and there were red circles around her eyes that almost matched the red bandanna still stretched across her face. She was panting hard, and with each breath the bandanna fluttered out in front of her like a crimson pennant. She sat slumped in the seat, her arms limp at her sides, and both her legs were trembling uncontrollably.

"I don't know about you," Nick said, "but I'm starving."

CHAPTER 5

Kathryn sat slowly sipping black coffee in a remote corner of the Smithfield Chicken and Barbecue in Rayford. She insisted on a table as far as possible from the All-You-Can-Eat Pig Pickin' Buffet and positioned herself with her back to any possible view of food.

She stared blankly at the emergency exit door, not more than ten feet away, while she mentally reviewed the events of the day. She had wrecked her new car, ruined an entire outfit, promised her second mortgage to a man who just might be a raving lunatic— and to top it all off broke into a funeral home to pick bugs off a decomposing corpse. She looked again at the emergency exit. Does the alarm really go off if you open the door?

"You're not having anything?" Nick said, returning to the table with three loaded plates balanced on his arms. "How do women do it?" He stooped down and slid the dinner plate forward. It was heaped with pulled pork, potato salad, and a pool of beans with a pallid cube of pork fat bobbing in the center. His salad plate held only a few leaves of lettuce, smothered with a great mound of black olives and bacon bits. His dessert plate was piled high with a thick white ambrosia salad of marshmallows, mandarin oranges, coconut, and whipped cream.

"How in the world can you eat after . . . that?"

"You'll notice I passed on the macaroni and cheese," Nick said through a mouthful of potato salad. Kathryn shut her eyes hard. "Sorry. Inside joke."

"I never felt so useless in my entire life," she muttered.

"I thought you did very well back there."

"I spent half the time on my hands and knees vomiting!"

"Well . . . you were very good at vomiting."

Kathryn closed her eyes again and dropped her head to the table with a thud.

"Don't take it personally," Nick said. "A decomposing body emits two unique chemicals. One is known as putrescine and the other cadaverine—cute names, don't you think? When they team up, they can reach down your throat and jerk your insides out."

"They didn't seem to bother you."

He shrugged. "It's an acquired taste."

They sat in silence for several minutes. It was all Kathryn could bear to sit and listen to the sounds of her companion munching and crunching his way through plate after plate of vile obscenities. She wanted to ask him if he had been able to learn anything from his hurried investigation, but she knew she couldn't tolerate a detailed evaluation—not yet. She really didn't want to talk at all. More than anything she wanted to go home and take an endless, steaming shower—but anything was better than listening to that sound.

"Do you think Mr. Schroeder will call the police?" she asked.

"Probably. We dared to disturb Cerberus, guard dog of the dead," he said in an ominous tone, "though I suspect his bark is worse than his bite. I wouldn't worry about it."

She watched him wipe a bit of marshmallow from the corner of his mouth. "You don't strike me as the kind who worries about much of anything."

"I've found that worrying takes a lot of energy and produces few results."

"Must be nice," she said, picking at the plastic chrome peeling from the top of the salt shaker. "I just hope nobody finds out about all this."

Nick shook his head in disdain.

"You're not from a small town, are you, Dr. Polchak?"

"Not quite. I'm from Pittsburgh."

"In a small town, if one person knows, everybody knows. Then come the funny looks and the whispers behind your back when you pass. 'Did you hear what happened at Schroeder's Funeral Home? Did you hear what she did?' But to your face it's always, 'How do,' or, 'Nice day.' "

"And all your friends are thinking, 'Why can't she find herself a nice, living man?' "

"I'm serious!"

"Mrs. Guilford," he said, pushing aside the last of his empty plates, "there is a difference between small-town people and small-town minds. The first you can live with, the second you can live without. Just let it go."

"That's easy for you to say."

"Yes," he said, "it is."

The front door opened with a jingle, and Kathryn looked up to see Sheriff Peter St. Clair step inside. He was tall, wide-shouldered, and narrow at the waist, looking like an athlete just barely past his prime. His hair was sandy blond and stiff as wire, cut close, a throwback to his last tour of duty less than a decade ago. Kathryn smiled. Everything about Peter was still army; head to toe he was sharp, tight, lean, and hard.

The sheriff tucked his Ray-Bans into his front shirt pocket and refastened the button. The waitress smiled and greeted him from behind the counter. He nodded to her without a word, pointed to the percolating Bunn-O-Matic, and headed directly for Kathryn and Nick.

The sheriff stopped abruptly in front of the table and stood, hands on hips, staring silently at Nick. Then he bent over, kissed Kathryn on the cheek, and sat down.

"So much for your fears of police brutality," Nick said sotto voce.

"Okay, Kath," the sheriff said. "What's going on?"

"Hello, Peter," she said, squeezing his forearm.

"I just got a call from old man Schroeder. He said you came by this afternoon with some guy he'd never seen before—some kind of doctor." He glanced at Nick again. "He accused you two of everything from breaking and entering to burglary to desecrating a graveyard. It sounded like *Invasion of the Body Snatchers*!" He turned back to Kathryn and lowered his voice. "He claims you two did some kind of autopsy on Jimmy's body."

"We did not!" she shouted back just as the waitress arrived with the sheriff's coffee. There was a moment of frozen silence as the waitress clacked the cup and saucer onto the table, and Kathryn was greatly annoyed that she took an extra minute to tidy up the table and wipe the ring of water from under each glass.

As the waitress turned away, Kathryn leaned forward. "We didn't break into anything, we didn't desecrate anything, and we didn't take anything!"

"Well," Nick held up the canvas knapsack, "that's not exactly true." Before Kathryn could protest, he dumped the knapsack over and sent its contents clattering onto the table. She watched in horror as a single container rolled slowly toward the sheriff until it stopped against his cup. With each revolution the milkwhite passengers rode the plastic wall to the top, dropped off, then began the upward ride again. It was like watching the popcorn machine in the lobby down at the Imperial Theater.

The sheriff looked in astonishment at the assortment of plastic containers. He lifted the one before him and stared at a trio of writhing, white maggots on a folded piece of damp paper towel.

"Peter," Kathryn said quietly, "I want you to meet Dr. Nicholas Polchak of North Carolina State University. Dr. Polchak is a forensic entomologist. I hired him, Peter—to investigate Jimmy's death."

"How do, Sheriff." Nick extended his hand with a flourish.

The sheriff groaned and dropped his head into his hands. "Kath, what have you done? I told you not to do anything!"

"You told me there was nothing more you could do," she said defiantly. "So I decided to do something myself."

"You," he shook his head in bewilderment, "are the most muley, stiff-necked, bullheaded woman I ever met." He reached out and made a mock strangling gesture at her throat, then placed his hands on hers and squeezed hard. Kathryn smiled faintly in return.

The waitress slowly approached the table once again, uneasily eyeing the pile of transparent containers and their contents.

"You folks got anything you need me to . . . dispose of for you?"

Nick looked quizzically around the table. He handed her a single crumpled Sweet 'n Low packet.

"By the way, Darlene, do you have any liver back there?"

"Liver?" she said suspiciously. "We got the fried chicken livers over by the chickpeas."

"Yes, but can I have them prepared a different way?"

"How you want 'em?"

"Raw. About a half a pound will do." He held up the largest of the containers. "Your sign says, 'Kids Eat Free.' "

She turned away again, stopping every few paces to glance back at Dr. Polchak. "Her name is Beverly," Kathryn scolded.

"Really? I thought everybody down here was named 'Darlene.' "

Sheriff St. Clair set the container back on the table and slid it well away from him. "Down here? And where might up there be, Doc?"

"Pittsburgh."

Kathryn watched uneasily as the sheriff studied Nick. He glanced at the Pirates cap that still sat tight atop Nick's head and the tufts of dark hair that protruded from underneath on both sides. He stared a long time at Nick's colossal eyeglasses and the floating orbs behind them. He cocked his head from side to side, as if he were trying to guess the contents of the Mystery Jar in the sideshow at the Holcum County Fair.

Kathryn kicked him under the table.

"You must be just about blind." The sheriff nodded at Nick's glasses.

"Oh, I don't know. You'd be surprised what I can see."

The sheriff carefully considered each feature of Nick's face, then turned his attention to the bizarre polyester anachronism Nick wore as a shirt. His eyes moved slowly from button to button, and he smiled and shook his head slightly at the fresh barbecue stain on one side. When his eyes reached the table, he slowly pushed his chair back, bent over, and stared under the table for a good long time.

"I really should learn to cross my legs," Nick said to Kathryn.

The sheriff sat upright again and stared silently into the enormous eyes for a full minute.

"Hey Kath," he said, without removing his eyes from Nick, "I saw a bumper sticker the other day on Denny Brewster's truck. It said, 'I don't care how you do it up North.' "

"He's had that bumper sticker for ten years," she hissed.

"I know. It just came to mind."

"That's a good one," Nick said, "but my favorite is, 'Dixie: Where the family tree does not fork.' "

The sheriff squinted. "What's with all this Bug Man stuff?"

"True bugs belong to the order Heteroptera. I don't just study bugs; I study other orders of forensic value as well. Bug Man is a misnomer, really—sort of like the term Law Man."

"Stop it," Kathryn broke in. "You two hounds can sniff each other all day if you want to. But the fact still remains, Peter"— she leaned forward and looked directly at him—"Dr. Polchak is working for me."

The sheriff opened his mouth to speak twice, but each time seemed to think better of it. He slumped back in his chair and stared at her.

"As a private citizen, you have the right to investigate any-thing you want—within limits." He turned again to Nick as he said this. "If you were a private investigator, I'd say, 'You could lose your license doing what you did today.' But you don't have a license, do you? So consider your hand slapped—and consider yourself lucky." Now he turned back to Kathryn. "Investigate away. It's your money. But I'm telling you, you're wasting your time."

"You seem very certain of that," Nick said.

"You're a forensic what? Etymologist?"

"No. That would be the study of word origins—not much help in a case like this. I'm a forensic entomologist."

"Whatever. I suppose from the forensic part that you've investigated a few deaths before."

"Quite a number."

"Then you'll be able to appreciate that there was nothing unusual about this one."

"Convince me."

"Male caucasian, thirty. Military background, lots of firearm experience. Gulf veteran, posttraumatic-stress victim with long-term depressive tendencies. A hunter, a loner, disappeared for weeks at a time. Turns up in the woods flat on his back, shot once through the head. The handgun was still in his hand—his handgun. No note, but no indications of struggle or conflict—no indications of anything."

"Did you do a gunpowder residue test on the hand?"

The sheriff paused. "Yeah," he said. "It was negative."

Nick raised one eyebrow, and Kathryn looked quickly back at Peter. "When a handgun is fired," the sheriff explained, "it sometimes leaves a residue of gunpowder on the hand that fired it—sometimes. I tested Jim's right hand—no gunpowder."

Kathryn's eyes widened with excitement.

"But," the sheriff interrupted, "the better the weapon, the cleaner it fires. Jim had a Beretta nine-millimeter—a fairly clean gun. I didn't expect to find any gunpowder."

"So you ran a neutron activation analysis to make sure," Nick continued.

The sheriff rolled his eyes and sank back into his chair. "Look, I'm the sheriff of a little county with an even smaller budget, which has to cover everything from crime-scene investigation to printing posters that say, 'Clean up after your dog.' You got any idea what an NAA costs?"

This time Nick turned to Kathryn to explain. "No matter how clean the weapon, it may leave microscopic traces of barium and antimony on the hand—traces that can't be detected by traditional tests. What the sheriff is telling us is that he's very certain about the cause of death—as certain as his budget will allow."

"I would have run that test no matter what it cost," the sheriff protested, "if there had been any indication that something was out of line. The coroner checked everything—he says suicide. I talked to Jim's sister—she buys it too. I asked some questions around town—nobody is surprised, nobody has a doubt—except one person." He looked directly at Kathryn as he said it. "I'm telling you, there was nothing out of the ordinary, and there was no reason to do any more than I did."

There was a long silence that followed as the impact of the sheriff's words sunk in. It was Nick who broke the silence.

"How long had Jim McAllister been using cocaine?"

Kathryn's mouth dropped open, and she began to blurt out an angry and absolute denial—but she was instantly aware of the silence from the chair beside her. She turned to Peter, and one look at his face told her that the unthinkable was quite true. Even worse, it told her that Peter had probably known about it for quite some time—and for some reason had kept it from her.

Peter could not meet Kathryn's eyes. He turned to Nick instead. "How did you—"

"Bubba told me," Nick said, holding up a container with a single plump white maggot within—by far the largest of all the specimens. "Bubba is probably an ordinary blow fly or flesh fly larva, but he is not of ordinary size. An average larva at this stage of development should be about ten millimeters in length. Bubba is close to twenty. I removed him from the nasal septum. The only thing that can account for his accelerated growth is the presence of cocaine in the tissues where he was feeding. Your friend must have ingested within several hours of his death—and I think it's safe to assume that it probably wasn't the first time."

Kathryn continued to stare at Peter, searching his face for some excuse, some explanation.

"It . . . started in the Gulf," he stammered. "It wasn't just

Jimmy—it happened to a lot of boys going into combat for the first time. He thought it would stop after the war. It didn't . . ."

His voice trailed off. He looked up into Kathryn's eyes, but the intensity of her stare drove him away again. Even as a child her pale green eyes could burn like emerald fire when they were fueled by anger or injustice. In this case it was both.

Kathryn sat in stunned silence, feeling her face and neck grow redder by the minute. The entire reason for this investigation, which flew in the face of all the available evidence and expert opinion, was her unshakable conviction that Jimmy McAllister would never take his own life. But two minutes ago, it had also been her unshakable conviction that Jimmy would never have used cocaine. If she was so badly mistaken about one part of his character, could she be wrong about another? Her car, her clothes, her mortgage; the fear, the exhaustion, the utter humiliation—had it all been for nothing? Was she nothing more than a stupid schoolgirl acting on an emotional impulse, too simple and naive to accept how the world really works? The tears welling up within her made her feel all the more childish and silly, and she drove them back fiercely with anger and contempt.

"I need some time alone," she said quietly, rising from her chair. The sheriff rose with her and reached out to put his hand on her shoulder, but she pulled away.

Nick watched until the door closed with a jingle behind her. The sheriff slowly sat down again to face him.

The waitress returned with a brown paper bag rolled down tight and sealed with a clothespin. She opened her mouth to speak, but noting the look on the sheriff's face, she simply set the bag in the center of the table and backed away.

"That was cute, Doc. Real cute. You remind me of one of those psychic hotline people. You got nothing real to offer so you toss out a bone—that cocaine thing—just to keep her on the line, just to keep her believing—just to keep her paying."

"You should have told her."

"Why? What would it have proved? That Jimmy's depression might have been chemically induced? That his suicide might have been encouraged by the drugs? Let me tell you, his weirdness started a long time before the coke."

"You should have told her."

"What do you know about it? Look"—he lowered his voice, glancing around for listening ears—"we all grew up here together—Jimmy, me, and Kath. We were family—about the only family any of us had. She loved Jim like a brother. What good would it do to drag his memory through the dirt by bringing up a drug problem? But I guess you took care of that."

"So her 'brother' had a serious drug problem, and you kept it from her for almost a decade? That's some family you've got there."

The sheriff looked down at his coffee cup. "Jim made me swear. He would have died before he let her find out."

"Looks like he did."

"He thought he could beat it on his own—and he did, a couple of times. He went through rehab a couple of years after the Gulf. He was clean for a year, maybe two. Then he went on it again. He'd kick it for a while, then go back. After a while even I didn't know how he was doing."

"Now you know."

"The point is"—the sheriff leaned in for emphasis—"I knew Jim McAllister since he was a kid. I knew him. He came from one suck-egg family—if you don't believe me, go meet his twisted sister, Amy. Jim started showing signs of depression real early, and I'm telling you, his depression led to his drug problem and not the other way around. He was headed for a sudden stop anyway. Some of us saw it coming a long time ago."

"But not Mrs. Guilford."

"She only saw the good side. That's all she wanted to see. It's a bad habit of hers. I wanted to protect his memory for her, so . . . I kept the cocaine thing quiet."

"And as a result, she believed that little Jimmy could never have done anything as nasty as suicide. And she hired me to prove it."

"I guess I owe you an apology for that," the sheriff conceded. "But at least we know that all this is no longer necessary." He gestured to the pile of containers still scattered across the table.

"How so?"

The sheriff hesitated. "The cocaine. I told you that—"

"You told me that his depression led to his drug problem and not the other way around. That means that the cocaine had nothing to do with his death—so nothing new has been introduced into the equation. Mrs. Guilford will still want to know what happened to her friend."

The sheriff stared blankly at Nick for a long time.

"Don't take her money," he said at last.

"Excuse me?"

"I assume she's offered to pay you. How much? Five thousand? More?"

"That's between me and my client."

"Don't take her money," he said again. "No matter what you may think, Doc, she's not a rich woman. She works at a bank, for crying out loud. If she's offering you that kind of money, she's putting her house in hock, I can tell you that. Don't take it."

Nick leaned back and folded his arms across his chest. "Ten minutes ago she couldn't believe that Jimmy would kill himself, because she knew Jimmy. Now—thanks to you—she isn't sure what she knows. Unless I miss my guess, she'll still want to do everything in her power to find out anything she can."

Nick began to carefully place each container back into the knapsack, followed by the wrinkled paper bag.

"You know"—the sheriff nodded toward the knapsack—"I could confiscate all this and put an end to it right now."

"But you won't," Nick said, smiling, "because she might not forgive you for it. And I have a feeling that's a risk you're not willing to take."

"I won't let Kathryn be taken advantage of," the sheriff said without emotion. "I will do everything in my power to protect her."

"Are you sure it's Kathryn you're trying to protect?"

Nick slung the pack over one shoulder and stepped toward the door. He stopped and turned back to the sheriff.

"I intend to take her money," he said. "And I intend to earn it."

From each plastic container Nick selected two or three plump maggots, carefully avoiding both the largest and smallest specimens, and dropped them into a small vial of 70 percent isopropyl alcohol to preserve them. Each died almost instantly and floated softly to the bottom. He capped each vial tightly and labeled the victims exactly as he had designated their living counterparts: left ocular, right temporal, left temporal . . . He treated the hungry survivors in each plastic container to several strips of raw liver and transferred the lot to the wire shelves of the large chrome and glass unit in the corner of the room.

It was after midnight now, and Nick was still hard at work under the glaring blue fluorescent lights of his office lab. He sat down at the gray-and-white dissecting microscope and maneuvered a glass slide directly under the lens. No sooner had he reached for the focus knob than the exterior door to his left suddenly swung open. There in the darkness stood the exhausted figure of Kathryn Guilford.

"Close the door," Nick said without looking up.

"Are you worried that I might let out some of your precious bugs?"

"I'm worried about the bugs you might let in—especially the dermestids. They're dry-tissue eaters, and they'd love to make a snack out of my mounted specimens."

Kathryn stood motionless in the open doorway until he finally glanced up reluctantly from his microscope.

"Pretty please?"

Nick studied the standing form of Kathryn Guilford. She was tall, he observed, about 175 centimeters—maybe more. She was wide in the shoulders, with a very lean body mass—perhaps an athletic background. The thorax tapered tightly toward the abdomen, producing a full, rounded curve of the hips. The legs were long and tanned and very lean. The face was equally lean; the zygomatic arch was prominent, producing a high cheekbone, and the nose was long and straight, ending almost in a chisel point. The eyes were wide and very green. The hair was a deep auburn, and she seemed to make less fuss about it than women typically do. Right now she wore it down, but he could imagine it pulled back in a thick ponytail. Green eyes, auburn hair, and a spray of freckles across the nose. Overall it was a pleasing figure, one that Nick imagined some men would find quite beautiful.

Kathryn stepped inside and pulled the door shut behind her. She rolled out a chair from under the table to her right and sat down across from Dr. Polchak. "You're probably surprised to see me."

"I'm surprised to see anyone at this hour. Don't you ever sleep?"

"I have something for you." She reached into her purse and handed him a folded slip of paper. "It's a check."

"Yes, I've seen one before." He turned the check over and held it up to the light as if it might not be real. "One thousand dollars. That's slightly less than the amount we agreed upon."

"I think a thousand dollars is an adequate fee for a single day's work," she snapped. "I see no reason to continue this investigation after . . . after tonight."

Without a word Nick turned back to his microscope. He carefully removed the glass specimen slide and slid the edge of Kathryn's check under the chrome holding clips instead. He peered once again into the eyepiece. For several moments he studied it—focusing, shifting, then focusing again.

"For crying out loud," Kathryn said, "it's good."

"Not good enough." He looked at her again. "Give me one good reason why you should drop this investigation."

"One good reason! The only reason I started all this is because I believed that Jimmy could never have taken his own life—and then tonight I learn that he was a user! I never thought that could be true of him either. Maybe I was wrong about him . . . maybe I was wrong about everything."

"The sheriff believes that cocaine had nothing to do with your friend's death—that his drug use was a symptom of his struggle, and not the cause. Do you agree?"

She thought carefully. "Yes," she said slowly, and then with more confidence, "yes, I do."

"Then the cocaine tells us only two things: one, that your friend was indeed troubled—which we already knew—and two, that your friend the sheriff is willing to withhold information from you."

"He did it to protect me."

"So he said." Nick studied her eyes closely. "And you obviously believe him."

Kathryn ignored the remark. "So you think there's good reason to continue the investigation?"

"I don't think there was ever good reason to begin—but then, this is not about reason, is it? You came to me because you had a hunch. Your friend could not have died by suicide, you said, because he was incapable of taking his own life. Nothing has changed about that. I just hate to see you give up a good hunch for a bad reason."

Kathryn gazed at him in confusion, trying to make sense of this strange assortment of riddles. Suddenly it all became clear to her.

"This is all about money, isn't it? Give me back my check!"

Nick reached into his breast pocket with two fingers and removed the folded paper. Straightening his arm, he dropped the paper to the floor in front of him and slowly slid it forward with his left foot. Kathryn snatched up the check and spread it out on the worktable beside her, furiously crossing out numbers and figures and writing new ones in their place.

"There!" She tossed the check back on the floor in front of him. "Five thousand! Now is there a good reason to call it off?"

Nick sat motionless, continuing to study Kathryn's eyes.

"The body was moved," he said quietly.

Kathryn was stunned. Jimmy's body—moved? But who would move it? And why? Her mind raced with all the possible implications of this revelation—but all that came out of her mouth was an astonished, "What?"

"The blood that circulates in your body is red due to the presence of oxygen. When a body dies, the blood becomes purple—almost black—and it pools in the lowest parts of the body. The blood actually stains the surrounding tissues, and after six to eight hours the stain becomes permanent. This is a condition known as 'fixed lividity.' "

Nick laid his right arm out flat on the table beside him, palm up. "I die. My body falls to the ground—like this." He nodded to the arm. "The blood drains to the dorsal surface—down here—and eight hours later the bottom of my arm is permanently stained. Now if someone comes along after eight hours and flips me over, the blood will no longer pool to the bottom—the stain will stay on top. I died this way"—he flipped his arm over—"but my body was discovered this way. Guess what? I was moved."

Kathryn squinted hard.

"At the funeral home, our two young body baggers told us that they found the body like this." He leaned back in his chair and extended his arms and legs straight out. "Exactly like this. The sheriff seemed to concur. Flat on his back was the way he put it, I believe. But during our little examination I removed your friend's shoes. The left foot was stained along the heel, continuing up the back of the leg—exactly as it should be if the leg lay flat for the first few hours after death. But the right foot was completely purple, top and bottom, with the stain ending just above the ankle. That means, Mrs. Guilford, that he may have been found 'flat on his back'—but he didn't die that way."

Kathryn sat more and more erect as the full meaning of his words began to sink in.

"That means," she said excitedly, "that when Jimmy died his leg must have been in a position more like . . . like . . ." She dropped to the floor and stretched out, then drew her right foot up tight against her buttock with her knee pointing toward the ceiling. "Something like this."

"Very good, Mrs. Guilford."

"And then later—six to eight hours later—someone must have laid it flat. But if someone was there within hours of his death, then someone may have been involved in his death. That means Jimmy didn't kill himself!"

"No, it doesn't."

"But," she said, snapping upright, "somebody moved the body!"

"Not necessarily. All we know is that somebody—or something—moved the leg. Suppose your friend shot himself, as the sheriff is convinced, and when he fell the leg was somehow propped up."

"But what would keep the leg in that position?" She lay back again and experimented with her foot in different positions. Each time her leg swung outward and fell. "There's no way," she said. "It won't stay like that."

"Suppose something supported it."

"Like what?"

"A rock. A branch. A bush."

"Was there anything like that around?"

"I have no idea."

"And even if something did support it," she went on, "what would make it lie flat again?"

"The rock shifts. The branch breaks. The bush dies."

"How likely is that?"

"I have no idea."

"Then all we're doing is guessing here. Isn't there any way we can check this out? Can't we go see the spot where the body was found? Can't we look around for dead bushes and broken branches?"

Nick leaned back in his chair and folded his hands in front of him. "You mean, can't we investigate?"

Kathryn sat quietly for a moment, then picked herself up from the floor. She walked very slowly around the office, carefully considering the choice she was about to make. She came to the large, glass-doored unit in the corner of the room and stopped. Looking in, she saw the collection of plastic containers. Each contained three or four wiggling white maggots hungrily feeding on strips of raw chicken liver—all except for two containers. One contained the infamous Bubba, who was responsible for beginning the entire brouhaha earlier that evening. The other, containing a single specimen of ordinary size, bore the simple label "?".

"What is this thing?" she asked, running her hand along the polished chrome trim.

"It's a Biotronette—a breeding unit," he said. "It allows us to simulate the precise environment in which the larvae were collected. It allows us to rear them to adult flies."

"Why do we need to do that?"

"When they mature, we'll be able to identify their different species."

"And what will that prove?"

"Everything. Nothing. It all depends on what we find."

Kathryn sat down again across from Dr. Polchak. She sat staring at his frosted glasses, trying somehow to connect with the elusive spheres behind them. It was impossible; they darted and evaded her gaze like startled minnows. She knew that she was at a decided disadvantage in this negotiation. He could peer into her thoughts, but she had no access to his.

"If this is not about money," she said cautiously, "then why do you want to finish this investigation? You never wanted to start this in the first place—so why do you want to continue now?"

"I have my reasons. The only thing that matters to you is that I'm willing to continue. A more important question—and one that may have a direct bearing on this case—is why you want to continue."

"I didn't say I did."

He said nothing in response, but slowly raised one eyebrow; it arched up from behind his glasses like a cat rising from sleep. He leaned forward until his elbows rested on his knees.

"What I want to know," he said slowly, "what I need to know—is why this is so important to you. Why do you have to know what happened to Jim McAllister?"

For an instant the elusive eyes came almost to rest on hers. The sudden intensity of his gaze startled her, and she rose so quickly from her chair that she sent it clattering across the linoleum floor. She turned and started for the door—then stopped. A full minute later, without turning, she began to speak.

"My father died when I was seven. For my sixth birthday, he gave me a beautiful sweater. It meant everything to me, especially . . . after. One day the sweater just disappeared. Gone. I looked all over town for it. Did I lose it? Was it stolen? I asked everyone I knew, and a lot of people I didn't. You know, I never found it. Never," she said with a shrug. "At first, all I wanted was the sweater back. But the more I searched for it, the more I just wanted to know what happened to it. By the end, I think I would have given up the sweater itself if only I could know."

"So this is all about a sweater."

Kathryn wheeled and glared at him. She gave her chair an angry shove and it rocketed across the floor toward Nick. He stopped it with his foot, nudged it a few feet away, and motioned for her to sit down. She stood silently for a moment, carefully weighing the potential benefits versus the definite risks of continuing her story.

She straddled the chair and slowly sat down again.

"I told you that the three of us grew up here—Jimmy, Peter, and me." She paused. "There was a fourth. His name was Andy."

"Ah," he said, recalling Mr. Schroeder's inquiry that afternoon. "That would be Andy whose 'body has never been recovered.' "

"You don't miss much."

"That's what people pay me for."

"The three of them were like brothers—too much like brothers. It was always who is the fastest, who is the toughest, who is the best. If one of them went out for football, all of them had to go out for football. And then it was who is the captain, who scores the touchdown, who is first-string." She shook her head. "You know how boys can be."

"I'm familiar with the species."

"They competed for everything."

"Including you?"

Her face reddened slightly but she made no reply. "About ten years ago they all took a drive up to Fort Bragg together—that's where the 82d Airborne is based. One of them decided to sign up and—"

"I've got the picture."

"Andy and Jimmy were assigned to one unit, Peter to another. In the spring of 1990 things were heating up in the Persian Gulf and the U.S. was starting its buildup of forces. The boys got the word that the 82nd Airborne might be deployed to Saudi Arabia—"

"And Andy decided to make sure the cow was tied up before he left the barn," Nick broke in, "as they say in Holcum County."

"We were married in July. Three weeks later they were called up. Andy . . ." She stopped. She couldn't stand to look at Nick any longer. Even if he really needed to know, she couldn't bear to tell the rest of the story to those eyes—eyes that would flit and hover over her words but never care enough to land on any of them.

"Andy was apparently killed in action near Al Salman Airbase in Iraq."

"Apparently killed?"

"Remember Vietnam? By the time it was all over, there were more than eighteen hundred MIAs. It was an unbelievable mess—mothers waiting to hear about their sons, kids praying for Daddy to come home. It's still going on today, thirty-five years later. After Vietnam the Defense Department said 'never again.' They started collecting a DNA sample from every soldier. Now if they find nothing but a finger on the battlefield, they still know it's you. No more eternally grieving mothers, no more Tomb of the Unknown Soldier."

She glanced up to check for telltale signs of inattention or indifference, anything that would give her an excuse to protest and bring her story to a premature end. But Nick sat transfixed, waiting patiently for her to continue.

"Do you know how many MIAs there were in the Persian Gulf? None. Zero. But what they don't tell you is that there were thirteen soldiers who just disappeared. Oh, they know what happened to them—so they say. A Tomcat missed the net and rolled off the flight deck, there was a direct bomb hit, that sort of thing. So they came up with a new category to cover those situations: 'Killed in action, body not recovered.' "

"Andy?"

"He was lucky thirteen—only they had no explanation for Andy. No missing Tomcat, no witnesses to the bomb blast—nothing. All they could tell me is that they were advancing on Al Salman and Andy got ahead of the rest of the unit—probably trying to be the first one there." She tried to force a smile. "Just before nightfall there was a firestorm with the airbase, and Andy got cut off. When the smoke cleared at daybreak, no Andy. No Andy anywhere."

With these words Kathryn dropped her face into her hands and began to sob softly.

"I'm . . . sorry," Nick fumbled. The impotent words fell and echoed like marbles on a slate floor. "Was there a search? Were there no . . . diplomatic channels?"

"It was a little awkward to say to Iraq, 'Can you help us find one of our soldiers?' when they lost a hundred thousand of their own." Kathryn carefully wiped under her eyes with both hands.

"So what am I, Dr. Polchak? A widow or a lady in waiting? I've spent eight years wondering. You want to know what's worse than grieving for a dead husband? Not knowing whether to grieve or not. Living every day of your life with an open wound."

She rubbed her eyes hard with both fists now—forget the mascara. She sat silently, staring at the floor, floating in a sea of numbness and exhaustion.

"I can't get my sweater back," she said quietly, "but I'd give anything in the world—anything—just to know what happened to it. When Jimmy died, I said 'never again.' I want to know how he died, Dr. Polchak. I want to know why he died. I have to know."

Kathryn picked up the check still lying on the floor between them. She opened it and smoothed it out on the table beside them.

"Five thousand dollars is an incredible fee for a single day's work. My offer still stands; take it now and we'll put an end to this. Of course, if you do, you'll miss out on the other fifteen."

"And if I do," Nick returned, "then you'll never know. We can stop now, Mrs. Guilford, but there's only one way to put an end to it."

For the first time that day Kathryn smiled. "I was hoping you'd say that."

CHAPTER
7

O ne of these, okay, Ed?"
Sheriff Peter St. Clair leaned across the bar and pointed to a red and gold plastic tap handle.

"You off duty yet, Pete?" a voice called out from behind him. "We can't have the law weavin' all over the road, y'know."

"Somebody's stickin' his nose where it don't belong," the sheriff called back.

He turned to see three grinning hunters seated at their regular table just below the ceiling-mount TV at the Buck Stop Bar and Grill.

"Speakin' of which," the sheriff said with a nod, "you boys might be interested to know that the investigation into Jimmy's death isn't over after all."

"Not over? How so?"

Pete picked up his glass and stepped slowly to their table. He reached up and clicked off the TV, drew out a chair with his toe, and settled himself across from them. He studied each of the hunters in turn.

"You boys heard about this Bug Man character? Down from NC State. Here to do research at the County Extension Station over near Sandridge."

"We heard." Denny snickered. "We heard he tried to swipe a body off old man Schroeder! What was that all about?"

The sheriff wasn't smiling. "Seems he's been hired to look into Jimmy's death. Thought it might interest you boys—especially you."

Ronny straightened. "Why us?"

" 'Cause you're the ones found the body," Pete shrugged. "Naturally, that makes you suspects."

No one was smiling now.

"I knew it," Denny groaned. "I told you we should keep our noses out of it. Just walk away and let somebody else report it, I said."

"Oh, shut up!" Wayne barked back.

"You . . . you don't believe we had anything to do with it?"

Pete shook his head. "Not me—but then, I'm not the one doing the investigating."

"This Bug Man," Ronny repeated. "You said he was hired. Who hired him?"

The sheriff paused. "Kathryn hired him."

"Kathryn? Your Kathryn?"

"She's not my Kathryn," Pete shot back. "And she's got a right to investigate Jimmy's death or anything else she wants, as long as she stays within the law. She can waste her money any way she chooses."

"But—didn't you tell her how we found him? About the gun and all? And what about Mr. Wilkins? He checked out the whole thing!"

"She knows all about it. She just doesn't want to believe it. She can't believe that Jimmy would ever do himself in."

"Well, we believe it," Wayne growled. "Seeing is believing."

"You say this Bug Man is looking for some other explanation?" Ronny asked. "How? What does he do?"

The sheriff slowly rolled the golden liquid around in his glass. "He looks at the bugs," he said quietly. "He looks at the maggots on the body."

The three hunters stared at one another in disbelief.

"This is just great," Wayne moaned. "We stumble onto a dead guy in the middle of nowhere, a mile away from everybody, with his own gun still in his hand—and now a bunch of maggots are somehow gonna prove we did it!"

"Nobody said we did anything," Denny said with very little assurance.

"Don't you see what's happening here?" Wayne glared back at him. "This whole thing could blow up in our faces! You let one of these 'experts' loose and there's no telling what he'll manufacture! He's being paid, you know—and by somebody who doesn't want it to be a suicide! You think he's going to side with us or with the one who foots the bill?"

The four men sat together in silence.

"Can't you talk her out of it?" Denny whispered to Pete. "You say, 'She's not my Kathryn,' but that's not true. Everybody in town knows she's more yours than anybody else's. She'll listen to you."

Pete pushed his chair back and slowly stood up. He bent over slightly, tucked his thumbs in his belt, and stretched his shirt front tight. "You know Kathryn. She has her own mind about these things."

He tossed a five-dollar bill on the table and nodded to the bartender as he left. At the doorway he looked back at the hunters one last time—first Denny, then Wayne, then Ronny.

"Somebody ought to have a talk with that Bug Man."

Kathryn steered her rented Contour once again into the gravel lot in front of the sea green Quonset, which glowed cobalt blue in the first light of day. The air was still heavy with the night's humidity and the warming hand of the sun had just begun to peel back the thick gauze blankets of morning mist. She rested her head against the steering wheel for a moment. It was much too early to be here, but it had been a long and sleepless night, and she could no longer bear to be alone with her thoughts. She had to go somewhere.

To her left was Dr. Polchak's rusting relic, but Dr. Tedesco's Camry was nowhere in sight. It figures, she thought. Dr. Tedesco was probably at home somewhere, sleeping peacefully in neatly ironed percales. Dr. Polchak was probably in the back room curled up in a terrarium with some of his "kids." She laughed out loud at the thought, a reminder of just how exhausted she really was. It suddenly occurred to her that he must remove those enormous glasses of his to sleep.

She shook off the thought. Images of Dr. Polchak unmasked were too much to bear first thing in the morning.

The screen door was unlocked as she supposed it always was. She knocked; no answer. She cupped her hands and peered inside. The office was empty and silent, except for a constant hum from the banks of fluorescent blue lights.

Kathryn walked around the side of the building and spotted Nick seventy-five yards away, standing in the center of an open pasture that sloped off gradually to the right. He looked up as Kathryn waded toward him through the knee-high grass.

"These are not exactly bankers' hours," Nick said, stepping slowly around to the left to reveal a gleaming white monolith jutting out of the purple-green rye like some forgotten monument. It was surrounded by dozens of whizzing, buzzing black-and-gold honeybees.

Even before Kathryn consciously recognized the object, it triggered a memory deep within her. She felt her heart lurch into her throat, and she began to scramble backward through the wet, clinging grass.

"Stop!" Nick commanded in a low, even voice. "Stay as close as you can"—he raised one arm slowly and pointed to an area to her right—"but stand over there."

Kathryn stumbled obediently to her right and stood, jerking her head left and right to constantly scan the air around her for any trace of the black pestilence.

"Have you ever heard of honey from a jar?" Her voice trembled.

"Have you ever tried spaghetti sauce from a jar? It's just not the same." As he spoke, to Kathryn's utter horror, he began to carefully remove the cover from the hive.

What is he doing?

He was prying off the lid from Pandora's box itself, and any moment a swirling black cloud of malevolence would spew out to consume him, then her, and then infest the entire world with its evil. She started to cry out—but to her astonishment, nothing came out of the box at all.

"That's something you don't have around here," Nick said, reaching gently into the hive. "Good spaghetti. Oh, the menu says 'spaghetti,' but it's not. It's North Carolina spaghetti—noodles and catsup. If you want real spaghetti, you've got to come to Pittsburgh." He carefully grasped the edges of the frame closest to him and lifted it straight up and out, resting it with one hand on the lip of the hive. With his right hand he reached slowly into his pocket and removed a small penknife.

"You know what else you don't have around here? A good Reuben sandwich. A good Reuben is like a symphony, like a work of art." With his bare hand he gently brushed back the black mass of bees from the left side of the frame. "You need really lean, tender corned beef from a good Polish deli—not this horse meat you get around here. You need homemade sauerkraut—piles of it—and a really good Russian dressing. Not Thousand Island—Russian."

With the point of his knife he carefully carved away a piece of comb about an inch square from the upper left corner and set it beside the knife on the lip of the hive. Then he carefully slid the frame firmly back into place.

"Ouch," he said with no emotion whatsoever. "Now, Shirley, what was that for? That hurt you a lot more than it did me." He slowly replaced the lid on the hive, being very careful not to trap any bees lingering on the edges.

"There's a place in Pittsburgh called 'Poli's,' " he said, gently wiping a bee from the corner of his mouth. "It's up north in Squirrel Hill. Now they've got a Reuben that melts in your mouth like butter." He looked dreamily into the sky. "Yes sir. Now that's a Reuben."

He picked up the chunk of comb in one hand and set the knife on top of the hive with the other. "Clean this up for me, will you, ladies? It's a bit sticky." Then he turned toward Kathryn, who was still ashen-faced and trembling.

"I think we've got everything we need," Nick said cheerfully as he passed.

In the lab, Nick removed two cups from the top drawer of a tall file cabinet. "I think this is a morning for Dragon Well Green. The Chinese claim that it banishes fatigue and raises the spirit." He dangled a tea bag into each cup and reached for the steaming carafe of water on a hot plate atop the cabinet.

"So where do we begin today?" Kathryn asked.

"You begin by going with Teddy," Nick replied, "to the site where the body was discovered."

"You're not coming? Why not?"

"You'll find Teddy to be very competent at what he does. I have other clients to attend to here. Remember, Mrs. Guilford, I was sent here this summer to do research. I can't go back to school without my homework, now can I?"

Nick moved briskly about the lab, filling his knapsack once again with empty containers, a Nikon equipped with a macro lens, a microcassette recorder, a small notebook, and various other paraphernalia. Then he headed immediately for the opposite door.

"Now wait a minute," she called after him as he stepped out on to a small deck area. "I'm paying you twenty thousand dollars to investigate this case for me. That's a couple of thousand dollars a day. I think I deserve your full time!"

"You're paying for my full attention," he said as the door began to swing shut, "not my full time."

Kathryn was on his heels in an instant, almost running to keep up with his expansive stride. "That's not good enough," she said firmly. "Who are these other clients? How many do you have?"

"Right now? Two. But I'm hoping to pick up another one any day now."

"Another one? Am I interfering with your recruiting? I'm so sorry!"

"No need to apologize."

They had crossed a narrow meadow by this time and began to follow a dirt path that curved back into the woods.

"Are these other clients paying you more than I am?"

"They're not paying me at all."

"Then why are you charging me?"

"I'm not charging you. You offered to pay me, remember? Besides, you have the means to pay for my services and they don't."

"So I'm subsidizing them?"

"In a manner of speaking, yes."

"Look," she said, working hard to catch her breath, "I'm the paying customer here, so I come first. That's only fair."

"It's not that simple. My other clients have issues that require my ongoing attention."

Nick stopped suddenly and swung the knapsack from his shoulder. He pointed to the ground. Beside the path in a sparse patch of weeds lay a colossal, pinkish-gray lump—the cadaver of an enormous sow. Its mottled skin was stretched taut and almost shiny, causing each hair to stand out like a tiny flagpole. At one end the swollen black tongue protruded from the mouth; at the other, the intestines bulged partially from the anus. And everywhere there were flies—black, blue, and iridescent green—circling, feeding, mating, and laying eggs on this most sumptuous of feasts.

"It's a pig!" Kathryn said in disgust, clapping one hand over her nose and mouth.

"Very good," Nick said. "You know your mammals." He bent down, pulled up a handful of grass and tossed it into the air. "I recommend that you stand upwind—over there."

Kathryn needed no urging, remembering the lesson she learned just a day ago at Schroeder's Funeral Home.

Nick walked slowly around the immense form. Beside the head a small white sign had been posted, noting the date of acquisition less than a week ago and bearing the name Porky. Below the name were penciled the words, "That's all, folks!"

"Is this what happens to all of your clients?" Kathryn shivered.

"Only the ones who don't pay. She came to us about a week ago from a small hog farm near here. She's much larger than most of the ones I get—I like them at about fifty pounds, but you take what you can get. Sad story, really. She was getting old, had a lot of pain, but she had become a kind of family pet—so no Pig Pickin' Buffet for her. The farmer couldn't afford to keep her anymore, so I told the family I'd take her. I brought her here to this lovely spot—and then I shot her."

Kathryn grimaced.

"I sedated her first," he said, "if that helps any. Less than a minute after she fell, the first blow fly arrived—less than a minute. A gravid female, so heavy she could barely fly, looking desperately for some place to oviposit her eggs. She'd been hovering in the air for hours, head into the wind, sniffing, sensing, waiting. Suddenly a cluster of scent molecules from the bullet wound came to her. She found her nursery! She followed the scent cluster by cluster to the source a mile away—maybe more. She landed. She knew she had found the right neighborhood, but now she had to decide on a house. The bullet wound was nice but it was so exposed—no trees, no shade. She checked the anal area. Not bad. She was tempted to stay—but she wanted something better for her kids, so she decided to check out a nostril. It's warm, it's dark, it's moist; impressive entryway, cathedral ceilings, large basement. Perfect! She was home at last, and not a moment too soon. She began to drop her eggs—a long line of tiny white specks, sort of like grated cheese. She did her job well, she fulfilled her biological destiny. She made sure her kids would grow up in a decent neighborhood.

"Within minutes there were dozens more. Soon there were hundreds, then thousands. The first to arrive were all friends and relatives—blow flies and flesh flies like the calliphorids and sar-cophagids, maybe even a few Muscidae—common houseflies. But then strangers began to arrive. One day she looked across the street, and her next-door neighbors were Staphylinidae—rove beetles—and rumor has it they feed on the eggs and larvae of other species. Then things really started to go bad; the parasites moved in. Ants came in and carried off her eggs. Wasps laid their eggs among her larvae, and when they hatch, guess who's coming to dinner?

"Soon the place is a ghetto," he said with increasing passion, pacing and gesturing as he spoke. "All the decent housing is taken. There's crowding and tension and fighting everywhere. As time passes the whole place begins to dry up. As the tissues continue to decompose they emit different odors, attracting new and unfamiliar species. Soon all the blow flies will be gone—moved out to the suburbs. A few carrion beetles will stick around to carry off what's left of the tissue and bury it nearby, but soon there will be nothing but dermestids like common clothing moths to feed on the hair and hide. By the time they've all finished and moved on, this body will be reduced to nothing but a pile of bones and barely enough skin to make a football. Less than a week ago dear Porky departed our world—but she has become an entire world to thousands of others."

Nick shook his head in wonder. "Planet Porky."

His lecture finished, he looked silently at Kathryn for some response, some indication that she, too, cherished the biological marvel that lay before her.

"You," she said slowly, "are a very sick man."

"Mrs. Guilford"—Nick gestured to the swollen mass before him—"this is how a forensic entomologist learns his trade."

"By shooting helpless pigs?"

"By studying faunal succession—the natural order in which different species of arthropods occupy a decomposing body. From studies like this we know the exact order of succession—and we also know exactly how long it takes each species to lay eggs, hatch, and develop to maturity."

Kathryn shook her head. "This is what you do? You go around dropping dead pigs off everywhere, then come back to watch them rot?"

"The hog farmers lost a hundred thousand of them in the floods after Hurricane Floyd. I can get one for you cheap."

Nick removed the notebook from his knapsack and jotted a few notations while Kathryn glanced at the moldering cadaver in disgust.

"So this is your other client," she grumbled.

"This is one of them." He slung the knapsack over his shoulder again. "Would you like to meet the other?"

As they continued down the path, Kathryn glanced from one side of the road to the other, studying each passing clump of brush or grass for a telltale patch of pink or gray . . .

"If you're searching for a body, don't look down," Nick said. "Look up."

Kathryn raised her eyes and looked ahead down the path. About twenty yards ahead the path came to a rise and then disappeared. Just over the rise, to the left, a black cloud of flies hovered in silent circles.

The cadaver lay under a tree in a patch of tall grass. As they approached, Kathryn caught a glimpse of the now familiar pinkish-gray skin stretched taut.

"We try to deposit them in different environments to study the effects of temperature and exposure," Nick said as they waded into the grass. "Porky was deposited in full sunlight. This one we placed in the shade. Someday I'd like to study one left in the trunk of a car. That's where many murder victims are discovered."

They stood directly over the cadaver now. It had the same mottled and swollen appearance, but Kathryn noticed it was much smaller and somehow different in proportion. Her eye followed the bloated contour of the body. The right end was partially covered by the tattered remains of a flannel shirt.

Kathryn gasped and stumbled back out of the grass onto the path behind her.

"That . . . That's a man!"

"That was a man." Nick walked around the cadaver, pushing back the tall grass to expose the body to full view. Just like the sow, a small white sign had been posted to the left bearing the date of acquisition, just over two weeks ago. Beneath it was adhered a blue-and-white nametag that read, "HELLO! My name is—" with the name Bob handwritten below. In the corner was a round, black sticker festooned with pink confetti that said, "This is what 50 looks like!"

"How did you . . . where did you . . . ?"

"Igor brings them to me from the graveyard," Nick said casually—then seemed to reconsider his choice of words. "Actually, they're very difficult to obtain."

"But how—"

"I request unclaimed bodies through the medical examiner's office in Chapel Hill. There's tremendous demand and a very limited supply. Sometimes there's an organ donor whose cause of death renders his organs unusable, or a migrant worker whose family never learns of his death. On rare occasions there's an executed criminal. Everybody wants them. You just have to wait in line."

"Thanks. I'll take a number."

Kathryn stood squinting, slowly shaking her head from side to side. What was she to think of this man? A moment ago he was just a perverse and twisted little boy playing with his cameras and containers and tweezers. But with each new revelation he seemed more sordid, more despicable, like a spook house that grew more macabre around every bend. This was not just another experiment. This was not just another geriatric sow.

"Look at it this way," Nick said. "Bob here donated his body to science. But science didn't want it—at least, not the traditional sciences. So Bob agreed to join me here to advance the emerging science of forensic entomology."

"Did Bob really agree to join you here? Did you say to Bob before he died, 'I'm going to throw your body on the ground and let insects consume you'?"

"Of course not—no more than a medical school would say to him, 'We're going to let ignorant first-year students cut you apart to see what you're made of.' "

"I just don't think he would have wanted to end up like . . . this."

"Like what?" Nick said in disdain. "Decomposed? Decayed? Rotten, putrid, rancid, and rank? What is this 'thing' your species has about death? Everybody ends up like this, Mrs. Guilford." He swept the tall grass to one side and pointed to the swollen abdomen. "This is what happens when you die. Bacteria in the intestine begin to multiply and consume you from the inside out—

first the intestines and the blood and then the surrounding organs. These runaway organisms produce sulfides—gas—that bloats the abdomen and stretches the skin until it splits. If you're here at just the right time, you can actually hear it rip." He released the grass and stepped onto the path in front of Kathryn.

"The way I see it, you've got two choices: You can be eaten by little bugs, or you can be eaten by big bugs. Either way, you're just shoofly pie."

"Nobody should end up as—what did you call it? Shoofly pie. This man deserved a decent burial."

Nick let out a laugh. "What do you think is different if they place you in a shiny copper coffin with a satin lining? Do you think biology stops if they powder your face and fill you with embalming fluid? Did you know that coffins are designed to burp—to let out the gas that's produced inside? They bury the bugs with you, Mrs. Guilford. You can slow things down, but you still end up like this. Insects are just nature's way of speeding things along. The arthropod motto is, 'Don't throw it away—recycle.' "

He took out his notebook once again and began to make notes. Kathryn glared at him as he finished his observations and began to repack his bag. It wasn't the nature of his study that bothered her most, it was his annoying flippancy, his arrogant callousness toward the objects of his study—toward aging sows, and unwanted old men, and Jimmy McAllister, and a young woman with a pathological fear of insects—toward life and death itself.

Nick swung the knapsack over his shoulder and started down the path again. As he passed, Kathryn said, "I just don't think you should treat a human being this way."

He looked around in mock confusion. "What human being?"

"That human being."

"That? That's bug food, Mrs. Guilford—nothing more—and the sooner you understand that, the sooner we can get to work."

Is this the meadow?"

"Yes ma'am," Casey said. "That's the spot where me 'n Griff found him over there." The young man pointed to a rise where a tangle of yellow ribbon fluttered between sticks placed in some unrecognizable geometric pattern. "You need anything else?"

"No thanks," Kathryn said. "We can find our way back from here. Oh, there is one more thing"—She tucked a twenty-dollar bill into his breast pocket and straightened his shirt—"Mr. Schroeder doesn't need to know you helped me today—does he?"

Casey grinned, nodded to Kathryn and Dr. Tedesco, and headed back into the woods.

Dr. Tedesco dropped two bulky black valises and pulled a white handkerchief from his shirt pocket.

"How much farther?" he wheezed, dabbing at his face and forehead with the folded cloth. "It seems like we've been walking for an eternity."

"Why don't you give me one of those?" She picked up one of the black valises and turned toward the open meadow.

"I'm sorry. It's just that I've never truly been a field man. I'm really more of a researcher—a taxonomist, to be precise. Give me a collection of third-instar larvae and a dissecting microscope and I'm as happy as—"

"A bug?" Kathryn finished the sentence for him.

"All of this—the hiking, the exploring, the collecting—this is really Dr. Polchak's forte."

As they walked easily across the open meadow Kathryn looked at him. "May I call you Teddy?"

"I suppose it's inevitable."

"Would you rather I didn't? It's just that I heard Dr. Polchak call you Teddy. "

"That was his little invention. Nicholas just loves to name things. I suppose there's a little taxonomist in his blood as well."

"What's your real name?"

"Eustatius," he said under his breath.

"I'm sorry?"

"So am I. It means peaceful. My family is Pennsylvania Dutch."

"Then you're from Pittsburgh, like Dr. Polchak?"

"What makes you think he's from Pittsburgh?" he said with a wink. "Haven't you noticed? Even his honeybees wear black and gold."

They arrived at the perimeter and set down their equipment. Kathryn wasn't sure what she had expected to find at a death scene, but she was surprised at how completely ordinary everything appeared. In the center of the ring was a small depression where the grass was matted and yellow, indicating the original location of the body—but nothing more to indicate that someone she loved had died here only a week ago.

"Nicholas and I met in graduate school at Penn State," Teddy said, unpacking the first of his valises. "We were both studying entomology, and it was there that we both became interested in the forensic aspects of our field. That's when Nicholas and I became friends."

"Dr. Polchak has a friend?"

Teddy smiled. "Have you ever observed a drone fly? It isn't likely—but if you had, you probably would have thought it was a wasp. A wasp makes a distinctive sound. The buzz of a wasp wing registers at about 150 hertz. The drone fly has learned to mimic the wasp's sound almost exactly—147 hertz, to be precise. Listening to them, you cannot tell them apart. The drone fly sounds like a wasp, and he acts like a wasp—but he is in fact a harmless fly. He has no stinger. If there's one thing I've learned in this field, it's that appearances are often deceiving. That is the first principle of taxonomy: Nevermind what a thing appears to be—what is its true nature?"

Kathryn lifted one leg and began to step across the yellow police line.

"Wait! Don't!"

"What's wrong? Aren't we allowed?"

"We are allowed, but it would not be wise."

Teddy walked slowly around the perimeter eyeing the yellow patch carefully. "Here," he said at last, "we'll approach from here. When approaching a death scene the first order of business is to establish a single line of approach. That protects the surrounding area from unnecessary disturbance. See there?" He pointed to a wide area of bent and broken grass that surrounded the yellow. "That's where our foolish hunters trampled the area while they were observing the body. I'm afraid they didn't do us any favors." He stepped gingerly across the line and Kathryn followed behind, feeling as though she had just stepped out onto a tightrope.

Teddy studied the shape of the yellowish impression. "The head was up there, and the legs here. Notice the deeper imprint left by the torso. That's where we'll focus."

Kathryn's eyes followed the faded area to where the right leg must have rested. She saw no signs of branches or rocks or objects of any kind.

"I see it too," Teddy nodded. "There's no indication of anything that might have held the knee erect prior to fixed lividity. That is most enigmatic."

They carefully made their way back to the valises, and Teddy began to unpack a bizarre selection of devices and paraphernalia. Most of the space seemed to be reserved for a half-dozen quart-sized containers, much larger than any Kathryn had seen yet. He also removed two small hand trowels, some type of long metallic probe, a magnifying glass, and a strange glass cylinder topped with a black rubber cork and a flexible hose.

"I have absolutely no idea what you're doing," Kathryn said.

"How much has Nicholas told you about this whole process?"

"Dr. Polchak tells me nothing—except that he likes to shoot family pets and collect dead bodies." A twinge of remorse came over her as she remembered who she was talking to. "I'm sorry. It's just that—is Dr. Polchak so annoying to everyone? Is it just me or what?"

"Don't take it personally." Teddy returned to the approach point with an armload of gear, depositing it in a heap just outside the fluttering yellow tape. He selected a trowel and a container and stepped carefully across the barrier once again. "Nicholas is not a cruel man. He simply has difficulty relating to . . . your species."

"You mean women."

"No. I mean your entire species."

"What species is that?"

"Kingdom Animalia, phylum Chordata, and class Mammalia; of the order Primate, in the family Hominidae, genus Homo. The species would be sapiens."

"I'm not a taxonomist, but isn't that his species, too?"

"Not if you ask him." He wiggled his fingers in the air as he stretched on a pair of bluish green latex gloves, then gently knelt by the yellow patch and laid down a wooden yardstick with one end positioned at the exact center of the open area. At that spot he began working his fingers deep into the dense thatch.

"What are you looking for?"

"I'm collecting leaf litter." He lifted a handful of decomposing shreds of leaf, bark, and grass and dropped it into an open container. "When a body lies exposed in an open area like this, it is quickly inhabited by a series of arthropods—"

"I've heard this part. First come the momma flies, looking for nice neighborhoods with good schools. But because there's no zoning, the whole place goes to pot and everyone moves out to the suburbs."

Teddy smiled. "I see Nicholas has entrusted you with the technical version. Perhaps I can fill in a few details." He measured twelve inches out from the site of his first collection and repeated the sifting and gathering process again. "When the egg of a blow fly or flesh fly hatches—about eight to ten hours after oviposition—a small larva emerges, perhaps only two or three millimeters in length. As that larva engorges itself on the decomposing tissues, it passes through three distinct phases of development, known as instars. About a week later—depending entirely on the specific species, of course—the third-instar larva ceases to feed and prepares to pupate into an adult fly. It begins to shrink in size, and its skin thickens and darkens into a puparial capsule—a sort of cocoon. Most importantly, the prepuparial larva becomes restless and wanders away from the corpse, seeking a protected site to await eclosion—emergence as a mature fly. Some of these late-instar larvae and puparia will drop off the body and hide in litter close to the ground surface. And those little vagabonds," he said, gingerly depositing his third handful of humus, "are the ones we seek."

"Can I do anything to help?"

Teddy looked up and studied her face thoughtfully.

"Really," she assured him. "I'd like to do something."

"I hope you understand—I thought it best to wait for you to ask." Teddy handed her a magnifying glass and a pair of light tension larval forceps. "Your eyes are better than mine and certainly a lot better than Nicholas's. Let's put them to use."

They both knelt down on all fours near the end of the yardstick. "What am I looking for?"

"Puparia. Tiny brown capsules about the size of a grain of rice."

"Like we did at the funeral home."

"This is a most important part of our investigation. The larvae Nicholas collected from the cadaver were in their third instar. Back at the lab he is attempting to rear those larvae to maturity under the same temperature and humidity conditions we find here. Some of those larvae are now beginning to pupate. We should find specimens here at a similar stage of development."

"And if we don't?"

"Then the infestation of the body is at a more advanced state of development than the infestation of the area where the body was discovered. That raises the possibility—only the possibility, mind you—that the body was placed here sometime after the time of death."

Kathryn's heart raced at the suggestion. "Dr. Polchak told me that the body was moved."

"He told me that the leg was moved," Teddy replied gently. "At this time, we are unable to account for that phenomenon. We must be very careful not to jump to conclusions. For now we must be content to do our homework."

"How far do I have to look?"

"They do have the wanderlust, these little creatures. They may migrate as far as twenty feet away. But concentrate on the circle defined by the yardstick. If there are any puparia to be found, they will probably be found there."

Kathryn began her search with gusto, moving quickly through the crumpled grass. She felt a hand on her shoulder and looked up into Teddy's face.

"Slowly, and very carefully." He patted her shoulder. "We must be careful to see what we see, not what we wish to see."

Kathryn started her work again, reluctantly returning to the place where her search began, carefully separating the twisted blades of grass. She felt like a woman doing a self-examination, searching diligently for any telltale lump or bump while at the same time praying that she would find none. If she found no puparia, that meant Jimmy's body might have been moved. If his body had been moved, then someone else was involved—someone who might have done more than just move the body.

Teddy began to dig small core samples of soil at one-foot intervals along the yardstick and sealed each one in a one-liter cylindrical container.

"Some carrion feeders are burrowers," he explained. "We must look a few inches beneath the soil as well."

Suddenly Kathryn's heart sank. There, lying atop the moldy remains of a red maple leaf, was an unmistakable puparium. Teddy followed her eyes.

"As I expected," he said, "as it should be. Is the capsule completely enclosed, or is a cap missing from one end, sort of like an open medicine capsule?"

"It's closed."

"Light in color, or dark?"

"Light brown."

"Then it's a young pupa. A very important discovery. Place him in here." He handed her a small plastic vial.

Kathryn returned to her search with greatly diminished enthusiasm. What was the point? The larvae on the ground were apparently at the same stage of development as those taken from the body. Perhaps the body had not been moved after all. Perhaps the coloration of Jimmy's leg was just some unexplainable anomaly. Perhaps all this was a waste of time . . . and money.

Teddy seemed to sense her change in mood. "Did you know," he said cheerfully, "that there may be more than thirty million insect species in the world? Far more than all other species combined—

and only about a million have been described and classified so far."

"That's great news," Kathryn murmured.

"Dr. Polchak has studied hundreds of them. He loves to investigate an unfamiliar species—any unfamiliar species. And to do so, he believes that he must remain objective. And how can one be objective if one is a part of the very species he hopes to explore? I believe that is why Nicholas has left our species."

Kathryn looked up. "You're joking."

"Oh, he would admit to being Animalia and to having a backbone—and he's a chordate all right. If he was nursed by his mother, then he certainly can't deny being a mammal. I think he would admit to being a primate—and who knows? On a good day, he might even admit to a common family and genus. But I'm afraid that's where it stops. Nicholas is a man in search of a species."

"I didn't know you could resign from your species."

"Technically you can't, of course. But you can refuse to participate. Yes, that's a very good way to put it. Nicholas has decided that he would rather study our species from outside, as an impartial observer."

"Why? Who hurt him?"

Teddy paused. "Suffice it to say that Nicholas has encountered a number of difficult people in his past. And to be honest, this business tends to acquaint one with the more barbarous tendencies of the human species. Somewhere along the line, Nicholas decided he had more in common with the insect world— and so he has turned the tables on us. Now he holds the magnifying glass, and we are in the terrarium. He studies people; he examines them." He let out a sigh. "Personally, I find that it's much more pleasant if you actually get to know someone."

Kathryn watched this tiny, gentle little man as he worked. The few strands of chestnut hair assigned the duty of covering his balding pate drifted helplessly in the wind, fluttering in rhythm with the yellow police line behind him. His round spectacles continually slid down his nose as he worked on all fours, causing him to pause every few moments and nudge them back into place with the back of his hand. He was an altogether harmless and likeable little fellow. How strange it was to find two men, good friends, both drawn to the same esoteric field of study and yet so completely opposite in nature. One tall, one short; one blind, one seeing; one cold, one caring. Maybe there was something to what Dr. Polchak believed. Maybe they were not the same species . . .

Securing the lid on the last of his samples, Teddy inserted the long probe into the ground near the center of the yellow patch and noted the soil temperature in his logbook. He then picked up the eighteen-inch sweep net and stood motionless, his eyes darting from side to side as if tracking the movement of the wind itself. In one fluid and remarkably graceful motion he swept the net downward and to the left, followed by a sudden upturn that flipped the long tip of the net up and over the metal ring. It was a simple action, something a child could do, but Kathryn thought that he somehow imbued the motion with the mystery and beauty of a fly fisherman's cast. With his left hand he seized the net just below the tip, quickly twisting and trapping its tiny victims inside. With his free hand he opened a wide-mouth Ball jar, empty except for a half-dozen cotton balls in the bottom. He placed the tip of the net inside and quickly sealed the jar again.

"Ethyl acetate," he explained. "It's a killing jar, if you'll pardon the expression. In about two minutes we can transfer them to alcohol."

"What are they?"

"Blow flies. Mostly Calliphora vomitoria, I would guess— they're very common in rural areas and one of the first to arrive after death. We will examine them to determine their species."

"Why?"

"The larvae back at the lab are being reared to maturity for two reasons. First, by determining exactly how long it takes them to reach adulthood, we can work backwards and determine a very precise time of death."

"How can you tell that?"

"Suppose it takes seven days for our specimens to emerge from their puparia. And suppose we know from past studies that this species requires exactly fifteen days between oviposition and final eclosion—to develop from an egg to a mature fly. If we note the exact moment the adult flies emerge from their puparia and count backward fifteen days, we would know the exact time of death.

And we would also know the postmortem interval—the amount of time between the moment of death and the discovery of the body."

"How does that help us?"

"It may not. But there is a second reason we are rearing those larvae to maturity. It's very difficult—sometimes quite impossible—to identify the species of a fly while it's still in its larval form. There are ways to tell—but to be certain, you must wait until adulthood, when species becomes obvious. In this case there seems to be no dispute over the time of death—but the possibility has been raised that the body was moved sometime after death."

He held up the killing jar and tipped it from side to side. A small pile of lifeless black dots lay huddled at the tip of the soft, gray netting.

"These mature flies will tell us what species we should expect to find when our larvae mature. If there are any surprises—and especially if we find any species not indigenous to this area—then our suspicions will be confirmed. We will know that the body was moved. We may even be able to identify the actual place of death."

Kathryn's eyes betrayed the glimmer of hope she felt. "I'm not promising," he reminded her, "but one can never tell. We're not finished yet."

Teddy repeated the sweeping motion three more times, each time exposing the specimens to the deadly ethyl acetate, then emptying the contents into a vial of isopropyl alcohol. One group was deposited into an empty vial—"For dry mounting later," he explained.

Down on his knees again, he searched among the blades of grass for other living specimens.

Suddenly Kathryn sensed the hiss of compressed air. The black valise by Teddy's side exploded inward and then spiraled up into the air, dropping again a few feet away. An instant later a faint cracking sound echoed past them from the distant woods.

Teddy straightened and reached out for the shattered valise, its back panel blasted outward in curling strips of black sheet metal.

"The case . . . my specimens . . . what—?"

Kathryn lunged for Teddy, knocking him flat. She lay stretched across his body, pinning him to the ground.

"Teddy, stay down! Someone's shooting at us!"

Nick snapped the lens cap back on his Nikon, then bent down and shook the leafy green milkweed. Hundreds of tiny black dots rolled off and disappeared into the grass around the decomposing body. They were teneral blow flies, young adults whose wings were still too moist and fragile to allow them to fly. It was a lucky find; they only remain in this transitional state for a few short hours and are seldom photographed. But despite Dr. Ellison's warning back at NC State, Nick's mind was no longer on theoretical research—it was on applied science.

He looked up to see Teddy and Kathryn hurrying toward him from the parking lot. He met them in the middle of the meadow, not far from his alabaster beehive.

"You're late," Nick said, shoving the camera into his knapsack.

Without a word, Kathryn dropped the shattered valise on the ground before him.

"That was careless," he said. "Equipment is expensive, you know."

"Someone tried to kill us," Kathryn said.

Nick turned to Teddy.

"It is possible." Teddy nodded. "This damage was done by a bullet, fired from some distance away."

Nick knelt down and examined the case. "What about the specimens?"

Kathryn's mouth dropped open. "Did you hear what I said? Someone tried to kill us!"

"No one tried to kill anyone, Mrs. Guilford."

"How do you know that?"

"Where did the shot come from? How far away were the woods from your location?"

"A good hundred meters," Teddy said.

"And how far was the case from you when it was hit?"

"Maybe ten feet away," Kathryn said, "on the ground."

"So someone fires at you from a hundred meters and misses you by ten feet? That's pretty bad shooting, Mrs. Guilford. If he wanted to kill you he could have come a lot closer than that. And isn't it coincidental that the bullet would strike the case? What was he shooting at, your ankles? Someone wanted to frighten you, that's all. Now what about the specimens?"

"We were able to replace most of them," Teddy said. "That's why we were late. We had to—"

"Wait a minute!" Kathryn broke in. "Is that it? Someone fired a gun at us! Whether they were trying to kill us or just scare us, what difference does it make?"

Nick raised his glasses just enough to rub his temples in slow circles. "Mrs. Guilford," he said, "what do you want us to do? Did you get a license plate number? Did you get a description? Did you see a car, a truck—anything at all?"

Kathryn said nothing.

"Then all we know is that someone doesn't want us to continue this investigation. Now there's a surprise. The best thing we can do right now is press ahead with the investigation. Time is critical in our discipline, Mrs. Guilford—so why don't you tell me what you and Teddy learned today?"

Kathryn glowered in silence. "First of all," she began slowly, "you were wrong. There was nothing to hold up the leg."

Even before she finished the sentence Nick began to shake his head. "I didn't ask what you believe, Mrs. Guilford. Tell me what you know."

She stopped and reconsidered her choice of words. "We know that there was nothing at the death scene to explain how the leg could have been supported." She paused. "If there was something that once held the knee erect, it must have been removed at a later time."

"Very good, Mrs. Guilford. And if there was such an object, who could have moved it?"

"I don't know. Maybe the two boys, when they took away the body to the funeral home."

"No."

"Why not?"

"Because the object would have been there when the sheriff viewed the body earlier, and he said he found the body flat."

"Then who else?"

"Think."

"Wait . . . how about the hunters who discovered the body?"

"Of course."

"But why would they move the object?"

"Perhaps to make the body more comfortable."

Kathryn blinked twice.

"It's a common phenomenon at death scenes—and a great nuisance to investigators. A passerby finds a body sprawled out on the ground, let's say with one arm bent behind its back. The passerby says to himself, 'That's got to hurt,' and he helps the poor stiff out by making him more comfortable—and possibly ruins the investigation in the process."

"So Denny or Ronny or Wayne might have rearranged Jimmy's body to make him more comfortable?"

"It happens."

"You're only telling me what can happen," Kathryn said, "not what did happen. How can we know if they really did reposition the body?"

"We can't. That is, unless we ask them."

"Someone must have moved the body before it was found in the woods. Maybe that someone was responsible for Jimmy's death. Maybe the murderer."

"It's possible," Nick conceded. "But there is another possibility you've overlooked." He paused. "The sheriff could have moved the body."

"But he said he didn't."

"Yes." Nick looked directly at her. "That's what he said."

They turned at the sound of a car crunching to a stop in the gravel fifty yards behind them. A moment later the dust settled to reveal the sheriff's black-and-white Crown Victoria. The door opened and the sheriff emerged. The obedient deputy was not far behind, carefully adjusting his hat as he straightened his massive body. The sheriff was out of uniform; he wore blue jeans, boots, and a tight navy T-shirt that emphasized the leanness of his six-foot-two-inch frame. He slipped on his Ray-Bans, and they started across the meadow.

"Is this casual day at the sheriff's office?" Nick called out as he approached.

"Thought I'd dress easy today," the sheriff called back. "Sometimes the uniform gets in the way."

"Uniforms often get in the way," Nick said under his breath.

"Saw the razor wire when I drove in. Nice homey touch."

"We like it," Nick said. "It's mostly symbolic, but we do have a legitimate biohazard here."

"I know about that. You caused me a bit of paperwork, you know. I had to sign off on your last acquisition—that old man from over Kensington way. I knew that man."

"You wouldn't know him now."

The sheriff gave Kathryn a peck on the cheek. "Pete St. Clair," he said to Teddy, extending his hand.

"Peter, this is Dr. Tedesco, Dr. Polchak's research assistant."

"The team keeps growing," the sheriff said. "I'd like you all to meet Mr. Benjamin Bohannon, senior deputy of Holcum County."

"Only deputy!" Beanie grinned. He leaned forward and extended his beefy hand, wrapping it around Teddy's slender fingers like a huge catcher's mitt. He took Kathryn's hand gently between his thumb and fingers as he might pick up a rose.

"Hullo, Aunt Kathryn," he said, blushing.

"Hello, Beanie dear." She slipped one arm around his trunklike waist and hugged.

As the deputy reached for Nick's hand, the sheriff said, "Shake the man's hand, Benjamin." The deputy began to tighten his grip, and Nick heard the crack of cartilage and felt a flash of pain shoot up his arm.

"Easy, Barney," he said through clenched teeth, "I need that hand."

The deputy relaxed his grip. "Name's Beanie," he frowned.

The sheriff ducked as a single bee streaked by, narrowly missing him.

"I wouldn't stand there if I were you," Nick said, rubbing the blood back into his hand.

"Too close to that hive?"

"Wrong spot. You've heard the expression, make a beeline? Well, you're standing in one."

"You're kidding."

"There's clover on the other side of that rise behind you." Nick pointed with his head. "When a bee finds a good source of pollen, she comes back to the hive and does a little dance. The dance communicates the exact location and distance of the pollen—sort of like a briefing before a bombing run. The bees check it out, determine the most efficient path to the source, and establish a beeline—and they don't like anyone blocking the way."

The sheriff shrugged off Nick's advice and turned instead to Kathryn. "Now what's all this about someone taking a shot at you this morning?"

"We were in the woods. Teddy and I were investigating the spot where Jimmy was . . . where Jimmy died."

"You were investigating?" the sheriff said with an angry glance at Nick.

"The shot was fired from at least a hundred meters away," Nick said. "Tell me something, Sheriff—could you hit a man from a hundred meters?"

"Firing from a stationary position? With a scope? Anybody could."

"But they didn't. They hit this instead." Nick bent down to the valise and poked his finger into the gaping hole at the exact point where the bullet must have entered. "Could you hit the center of this case from a hundred meters?"

The sheriff estimated the entry point. It was well left of center and near the bottom of the case. "Easy."

"They were aiming at the case, that's for sure," Nick said. "And anyone would naturally aim for the center of the case. But the bullet dropped a good four inches en route. I'd say he fired from more like three hundred yards away."

The sheriff looked at him. "I thought you were a Bug Man."

"I took a ballistics course at Quantico," Nick said. "I'm a big fan of continuing education."

Now the sheriff turned to Kathryn. "The doc is right. Whoever it was wasn't aiming at you."

"Peter, someone wants us to stop this investigation. But who? And why?"

"Now hold on," the sheriff said. "Let's not get paranoid here. It might just have been a prank."

"A prank? I don't see how—"

"Look, the two of you go crawling around in the middle of an open meadow. What do you suppose you look like to a man with a rifle three hundred yards away?"

"A man with a rifle?" Nick raised one eyebrow. "Why would a man be out there with a rifle this time of year? What's in season right now, Sheriff?"

"Nothing," the sheriff admitted. "But a lot of the boys head out that way to work on their deer stands. And while they're out there, they take a little target practice. They'll fire at anything: a stump, a limb—"

"A person?"

"That's why I said it might've been a prank. Some good ol' boy is out taking potshots in the woods; he sees you two, he sees the case . . . pretty hard to resist. I'll bet you two just about jumped out of your skins."

"You don't seem very concerned," Nick said.

The sheriff's mood changed in an instant. He turned to Nick with a cold stare. "I'm concerned," he said. "I'm concerned that you'd let her go out there in the first place. I'm concerned that you put her in harm's way."

"Stop it!" Kathryn said. "Nobody let me do anything. I wanted to go. And no matter why this happened, it's not going to change my mind about anything."

No one spoke for a full minute. The sheriff was the first to break the silence.

"I got to thinking things over last night, and I reconsidered. I think we should cooperate on this. I still think it's a waste of time, but if you're going to go to the trouble—and the expense," he glanced at Nick, "then I'd like to know what you come up with. That way if you do turn up anything, I can take the ball and run with it."

"Thank you." Kathryn squeezed his arm. "That's very thoughtful."

"Yes," Nick said, "I'm sure a great deal of thought went into this. But it has to work both ways, Sheriff."

"How do you mean?"

"I'll be happy to share with you anything I find. But in return I'd like access to some things you've got."

"Like what?"

"Like the photos of the death scene. I assume you took some? And a look at any test results. And most importantly"—he leaned forward—"I want permission to interview the major players."

"Who are we talking about?"

"The hunters, the coroner, the sister of the deceased . . ."

"I already took care of that," the sheriff said. "I can brief you."

"No. I want to interview them. I want a clear field to talk to whomever I want, in any way I want. And in return," he said with a smile, "I'll be happy to brief you."

The sheriff turned to Kathryn with a look of silent complaint.

"Peter," she said, "we just want to talk to them. You've probably already asked all the same questions. Dr. Polchak just wants to make sure there was nothing they missed."

"You mean nothing I missed," he scowled. "Okay, Doc. You're free to ask around—but on one condition." He nodded toward Kathryn. "She goes with you. I want somebody there who knows these people, somebody who knows how far is too far."

Nick looked at Kathryn. "I doubt she would have it any other way."

Another honeybee whizzed by close. The sheriff ducked his head again and swatted at the dark streak.

Nick shook his head. "I would definitely not do that."

Suddenly the sheriff spit out a curse, slapping the side of his neck and batting at the air around him.

"I warned you not to do that," Nick said. "Quick, let me see it."

"I'm fine," he said angrily, brushing him aside.

"Oh Peter, let him look," Kathryn said. "Don't be such a baby."

"Leave me alone," the sheriff growled, rubbing at his eyes.

Nick watched him.

"Please, Peter," Kathryn said again.

"Oh, for the love of . . . There." He turned his head to one side.

"Too late now," Nick shrugged.

"Too late for what?"

"When the stinger pulls out of the bee, it's still surrounded by part of the abdominal muscle wall. The muscle acts like a pump," he said, making a squeezing gesture with his fist. "It continues to pump venom into the wound—unless you pull it out within the first five seconds."

"Big deal," the sheriff sneered. "It's just a bee sting."

"Not to you it's not."

Kathryn looked at Peter, then at Nick. "What do you mean?"

"Tell her," Nick said. "Tell her what you're feeling. Your eyes itch and your breathing is labored. Your pulse is racing, your skin is pale, and you've already got a welt the size of a quarter at the injection site. You're experiencing a considerable anaphylactic shock."

Kathryn felt Peter's forehead and face with the back of her hand.

"When is the last time you were stung by a bee?" Nick asked.

"Beats me. Not since I was a kid, I guess."

"Then you're developing a sensitivity to Hymenoptera venom."

"Is that serious?" Kathryn asked.

"It's serious to about four people out of a thousand. They drop dead from a single sting. You're a lucky guy, Sheriff. You found out about your allergy before the Big One hit. If I were you I'd stop by a drugstore and pick up an epinephrine syringe—and I'd carry it with me at all times."

"I'm not walking around with a needle like some . . . drug addict," he said, glancing sheepishly at Kathryn.

"It's your life. But a little friendly advice. Be careful in the summer, especially on bright, sunny days. I'd stick to the uniform—bees don't like dark colors. And the next time your friendly neighborhood entomologist tells you to step out of a beeline," he said bluntly, "try listening. Ignorance can get you killed—and you've got a bad case."

"Thanks for the friendly advice."

"Now a piece of advice from me," Kathryn scolded. "Go lie down for a while, Peter. You look terrible."

"I got work to do."

"Don't make me pull out your gun and shoot you in the leg."

He cracked a smile. "Okay. But only for you." He kissed her on the forehead, then turned to Nick one last time. "So we're going to cooperate. You get what I get, and the other way around."

Nick smiled. "Just think of us as one big family. I know I do."

CHAPTER 11

The door to the Buck Stop Bar and Grill burst open and Peter St. Clair headed straight for the table of the three hunters. The sheriff grabbed Ronny by both lapels, dragged him from his chair, and jammed him up against the wall; the TV hanging overhead dipped and wobbled, and the screen went black. Ronny stood three inches taller than the sheriff and outweighed him by twenty pounds, but there was no mistaking the alpha male here.

The straight-faced man behind the bar set down a glass and reached below the counter.

"Leave it, Eddie," Pete called over his shoulder. "This is official business." The sheriff locked eyes with his paralyzed prey. "What's this I hear about someone taking a shot at Kathryn?"

"Not at Kathryn," Ronny fumbled. "Never at her. At that Bug Man guy, the one with all the nets and bottles and stuff."

Wayne got up from his chair and edged toward the door; the massive deputy filled the doorway, blocking his way. "We didn't fire at anyone, Pete," Wayne said. "We just aimed at a little suitcase. Thought it would—you know—send a message."

"What message?"

"You know—to leave it alone. To go away and stop making trouble."

Pete dropped his head and let out a rumbling growl. "You idiots! Is that the message you think you sent? That's like standing in front of a candy jar with your hands in your pockets! Your little message told them somebody has something to hide—now they're twice as determined to see it through."

"But . . . you said somebody ought to have a talk with that Bug Man."

"That wasn't the Bug Man! That was just his assistant, some little guy who goes around catching butterflies for him."

Two truckers rose from their table at the back of the bar. They glanced up at the broken TV and let out a curse as they passed and headed for the door.

The sheriff released Ronny and stepped away. "Which one of you fired that shot?"

No one answered.

Pete looked at Ronny again. "You're the one with the Leupold scope." He stood across the table, eyeing each one of them. "Okay." The sheriff nodded slowly. "But no more of this. You could have hit Kathryn."

"C'mon, Pete. From that distance?"

"You could have hit Kathryn. What do you think I would do if that happened?"

No one had the slightest doubt.

The first trucker arrived at the doorway, where the deputy still stood transfixed.

"Move," the man growled.

The deputy just smiled.

"Hey, Sheriff," the second trucker called back. "Tell this idiot boy of yours to get his big carcass out of the doorway."

The sheriff turned and looked at him. "Move him yourself."

The man hesitated. "You mean it?"

The sheriff slid off his star, held it up, then dropped it into his shirt pocket. "Be my guest."

The first trucker shoved Beanie hard with both hands, barely budging his immense form.

"I said move," the man grumbled, backhanding the deputy hard with his right hand. Beanie absorbed the blow and turned back to face the man with an expression not of anger but of hurt and confusion.

The trucker took a second swing at Beanie, then a third.

Beanie slowly raised both arms and tucked his head, as if ducking from an unexpected summer shower.

The trucker's hands closed into fists and he began to rain down a hail of blows. He stepped in and landed a left and a right to the torso, with no apparent effect at all. He swung a roundhouse left that glanced off the top of the deputy's head, then an uppercut that just touched the tip of his barely exposed chin. He finally stepped back and paused, panting, and when Beanie lifted his head like an ill-fated bird at a turkey shoot, the man shot a solid right cross to Beanie's left eye, tearing open the skin and sending blood trickling down his cheek.

"Sheriff!" the bartender said. "Help your boy there."

"The boy can take care of himself," Pete replied.

The man's blows were becoming wilder and weaker and much less frequent. Beanie somehow absorbed each blow, peeking out from under his arms and staring patiently at the sheriff.

The first man finally stepped back in exhaustion, and his partner, sensing his opportunity, stepped up. Beanie remained immobile, blood dripping from his cheek to the wooden floor below.

"Benjamin," the sheriff said quietly, and then made one large nod.

The deputy stepped forward and reached for the first trucker with his enormous hands. The man swung a wild right at Beanie's midsection, much slower than before. Beanie took the blow and swallowed the man's wrist with his right hand; with his left hand he seized his forearm just below the elbow and drew him closer. The man struggled uselessly to pull away, as if ensnared by some great white tar baby. Suddenly Beanie's viselike hands tightened and twisted. There was a crack like the report of a rifle, and then a scream.

Beanie released his hands, and the man stumbled back against his partner, his right forearm dangling at a ninety-degree angle.

The trucker lay sprawled on the barroom floor, clutching his shattered arm across his chest. Beanie stood over him, smiling at the sheriff, no longer aware of the man's existence.

The sheriff glanced at the deputy's bleeding face. "Gonna need a couple of stitches. We better head back to the office and have Agnes take a look at it."

On the way to the door the sheriff poked his toe at the man's dangling hand. The trucker screamed in agony and jerked away.

"Better get that fixed too," he said.

The sheriff turned back to the three hunters one last time. "Think about this, you morons: Now the finger's pointed at you more than ever. What are you going to do now?"

The door slammed shut. The men stared at one another in silence.

"He's right," Denny whispered. "What are we going to do now?"

CHAPTER 12

What is this stuff?" Nick sneered, licking at the little pink spoon. "It tastes like butyl rubber. That's it—it tastes like surgical tubing."

"That's chocolate mousse royale," the man behind the ice cream counter said with a roll of his eyes. His thick southern accent made the word royale sound especially ludicrous.

"What about that green stuff? What's that?"

"Mint chocolate chip," the man said tiredly.

"Okay, give me a sample of that."

The stout little man behind the counter was Hiram Wilkins, known to all but the oldest residents of Rayford as Will, the proprietor of Wilkins's Drug Emporium and the elected coroner of Holcum County. Mr. Wilkins was dressed in his shopkeeper's white shirt and black tie, which he never seemed to change regardless of season or occasion. He had a habit of repeatedly running one finger between his neck and collar and tugging, as if to release the buildup of pressure from his expanding midsection below. He wore a well-stained apron that he donned whenever he stepped behind the ice cream counter, a position he now occupied with diminishing patience.

"Well?" Mr. Wilkins demanded.

"I can't place it," Nick said thoughtfully. "Wait—I've got it. Scope. It tastes like mouthwash."

"Look, you've had five samples. Are you going to buy something or—"

They were interrupted by the jingling of the front door. Kathryn entered and stepped up to the ice cream counter with a smile.

"Hello, Kathryn," Mr. Wilkins beamed. "What can I get for you today?"

"I'll have what he's having." She gestured to Nick.

Mr. Wilkins's face dropped. "He don't know what he's having."

"Then I'll just have a scoop of cookie dough."

"What about you?" Mr. Wilkins glowered.

"Nothing for me, thanks—I was just waiting for the lady. What I would like is to ask you a few questions. I wonder if you would mind joining us for a few minutes," he glanced around at the empty store, "whenever you can find a free moment."

Nick and Kathryn sat down at a round, red Formica table in front of the store window. The chairs had red vinyl seats to match, and the backs and legs were made of thick black wire that twisted and curved to form the shape of hearts. Mr. Wilkins balanced himself uncomfortably on one of these, opposite Dr. Polchak.

"What's this all about?" he said.

"I understand that you are the coroner of Holcum County."

"That's right. Duly elected."

Nick smiled.

"I wanted to have a chance to meet you. I'm Dr. Nicholas Polchak, research entomologist and diplomate of the American Board of Forensic Entomologists." He leaned forward and extended his hand. "I understand we're colleagues."

Mr. Wilkins smiled vaguely and shook his hand.

"Haven't we met before?" Nick continued. "Your name is very familiar. Dr. Wilkins . . . Dr. Wilkins . . . Did we meet at the American Academy of Forensic Sciences convention last year? Or perhaps it was the National Association of Medical Examiners."

Kathryn kicked him under the table.

"No matter." Nick rubbed his shin. "I wanted to ask you some questions about your examination of the body of James McAllister."

"I can't discuss that," Mr. Wilkins said with a wave of his hand. "That's official business. You understand."

"I do indeed," Nick said, "but as Mrs. Guilford will verify, we're here under the jurisdiction of Sheriff St. Clair. That makes this an official inquiry. You can call him if you like."

Mr. Wilkins tugged again at his collar and shifted awkwardly on his wobbling chair.

"What is it you want to know?"

"Mr. McAllister's death was unwitnessed, which in most cases makes an autopsy mandatory—yet you declined to request an autopsy. Why?"

"Because it was definitely a suicide. No doubt about it."

"No doubt?" Nick arched one eyebrow. "In that case, I'd like to ask you to explain something to me. How do you account for the unusual lividity in the right leg? The right foot and ankle were marked, but not the dorsal surface of the leg itself. That indicates that the leg was supported in an upright position at the time of death and then moved several hours later."

Mr. Wilkins blinked hard. "How did you—"

"I had a chance to examine the body—very briefly."

"I never saw that. I never saw the leg."

"Really? Why not?"

"Well . . . he had clothes on."

Nick looked at him blankly. "Did you make any effort to examine under the clothing?"

"The body was in no condition for that sort of thing."

"That's because he was dead. That's sort of the whole point, Mr. Wilkins. As a colleague, may I make an observation? Personally, I find it very difficult to determine the cause of death by looking at someone's outfit."

Mr. Wilkins tugged harder at his collar.

"There's something else you missed," Nick continued. "Something that could be quite important."

Kathryn straightened and looked at Nick.

"The bullet produced two wounds—an entry wound here," he pointed to his right temple," and an exit wound on the opposite side. But there was a third wound—here." He indicated an area on the forehead just to the left of center.

"That could have happened when the body fell."

"When the body fell backwards?"

"What difference does it make? We know that his death was caused by the bullet, so what does it matter if there was another wound?"

"It matters because the wound was infested by larvae. Flies oviposit in traumatized tissues. In other words, they don't lay eggs on unbroken skin—they look for open wounds. It took quite a blow to open that wound—a blow that could cause a man to lose consciousness. The third wound was not caused by the bullet or the fall. That means that the wound was probably present at the time of death. Now tell me this, Mr. Wilkins"—he leaned back in his chair—"how do you suppose Mr. McAllister injured his head?"

"How would I know? A body gets pretty banged up lying around in the woods for a week."

"Yes it does, but only in certain ways. As the eggs hatch into larvae, they begin to consume the tissues outward from the place of oviposition. That explains why the eye sockets grew larger and the bullet wounds increased in size—but it does not explain how an unrelated wound spontaneously opened in the center of the forehead."

Mr. Wilkins said nothing.

"I'll give you a hint: The wound must have been caused by an object."

"But there wasn't no object."

"You see?" Nick smiled at Kathryn. "This is what happens when two professionals put their heads together. Mr. Wilkins has rightly deduced that, since no object capable of causing the wound was present at the death scene, then something—or someone—must have taken the object away. Now, who would have had motive to do such a thing? Perhaps the one who employed the object to strike Mr. McAllister—perhaps his killer."

"But he died from a gunshot wound from his own gun!"

"An unconscious man makes an easy target, Mr. Wilkins. The sheriff says the gunpowder residue test on Mr. McAllister's hand proved negative. That can be explained by the clean firing of the gun—but it can also be explained by someone else firing the gun."

Kathryn sat open-mouthed, staring at Mr. Wilkins. The combined effect of her probing eyes and Nick's accusing questions was more than he could bear. His face grew red and hot, and he tugged at his collar until his tie hung low like a noose around his bloated neck.

"You're only guessing," he said. "You don't know any of this."

Nick said nothing for a moment. "You're right," he said quietly. "I am guessing. Mr. McAllister could have wounded himself prior to entering the woods. Or perhaps he injured himself in the woods—perhaps he bumped his head on a tree limb on the way to the meadow. I don't know, Mr. Wilkins. My point is, you don't know either. Where I come from, we call that doubt."

"And where I come from, when a man has a bullet hole through his head and he's holding the gun, that's a suicide."

"No, Mr. Wilkins, that's an apparent suicide."

"Nobody had any reason to think otherwise."

"You had reason—if you had done your job. You didn't bother to look under the victim's clothing. You overlooked a wound in the center of his forehead. Did you roll the body over? Did you check for indications of other wounds? If you couldn't get a blood or urine sample for toxicology screening, did you take a tissue sample?"

"Don't tell me how to do my job!"

"Mr. Wilkins," Kathryn cut in, "we're not here to criticize you. It's just that the investigation went so quickly, there were some things left—"

"I am the duly elected coroner of Holcum County," he said with all the dignity he could muster. "I work under the authority of the chief medical examiner's office of North Carolina! I submitted my report to the CMEO, and they saw no reason to question my conclusions."

"Your conclusions?" Nick almost laughed. "Almost every county in North Carolina has a medical examiner appointed by the CMEO to a three-year term, appointed from a list of licensed physicians. But a tiny handful of counties—like this one—are still on the old coroner system, where a coroner is 'duly elected' from a list of anybody who wants the job."

The front door jingled again, and an older gentleman stepped tentatively inside. He was stooped, and he wore his light gray trousers well above his waist, giving the impression that his black-and-red suspenders exerted tremendous tension. He glanced around the room with a puzzled expression.

"Krispy Kreme Donuts?"

"Down the way!" Mr. Wilkins thundered, and the old man muttered something inaudible and shuffled out again.

The room was ominously silent—the kind of silence that follows the blast of a concussion grenade. Nick spoke first, in a perfectly pleasant tone of voice. "Do you know what item is shoplifted from drugstores more than any other?"

Mr. Wilkins and Kathryn both stared at him, expressionless.

"You'd think it would be candy or condoms. Or aspirin. Maybe infant formula or cold medicine. Nope. Know what it is?" He leaned forward and looked at both of them. "Hemorrhoid cream."

He sat back in his chair, allowing the profundity of this revelation to have its full impact. Kathryn and Mr. Wilkins continued to stare blankly, waiting—for something.

Now Nick looked directly at Mr. Wilkins.

"But you knew that, didn't you, Mr. Wilkins? You knew that because you own a drugstore. You know all about hemorrhoid cream and insoles and nasal spray and those little foam beverage coolers with NASCAR Racing on the side." As he spoke he leaned steadily forward until he inclined well over the table in Mr. Wilkins's direction.

"But you don't know diddly-squat about forensic pathology, now do you?"

Mr. Wilkins jumped up from his chair and sent it clattering across the linoleum floor. He ripped off his apron and threw it onto the table. His face raged red, and the veins that framed his forehead bulged like purple tree roots.

"I think it's time to go," Kathryn said firmly, grabbing Nick by the arm and pulling him toward the door. In the open doorway Nick turned one last time.

"Is it too late to get a scoop of that butyl rubber royale?"

Kathryn shoved him through the doorway, and the door jingled shut behind them. She hustled him down the sidewalk as the fading roar of obscenities snapped at their heels.

"If there's one thing I can't stand," Nick said, frowning, "it's bad ice cream."

Kathryn turned on him. "Why do you do that?"

"Do what?"

"Every time you talk to someone you almost start a fight!"

"That's true. You seem to have a lot of argumentative people down here."

"I don't see what you hope to accomplish this way. What's the good in giving poor Mr. Wilkins a heart attack?"

"It could do a great deal of good, if it allows a competent professional to take over Mr. Wilkins's job. Look, Mrs. Guilford, don't feel too sorry for poor Mr. Wilkins. What we discovered in our little interview is that he completely botched the original investigation. If that examination had been conducted by a medical examiner, there's a good chance there would have been an autopsy. They would have noticed the unusual lividity, and they would have taken a good look at that third wound—and you might have gotten the investigation you wanted. As it is, Mr. Wilkins signed off on the death certificate without so much as a second look, and they enbalmed your friend before the ink was dry. I only had time to do a ten-minute examination and to collect a bare handful of specimens. That means that we're trying to conduct an investigation with almost no evidence and no chance for a second look—all thanks to your 'poor Mr. Wilkins.' "

"Why didn't you tell me before about that third wound? Is there anything else you haven't told me?"

"That's the question I keep asking you."

Kathryn folded her arms and scowled.

"Well then," Nick said, "I guess we'll both find out what we want to know when we need to know."

"If we have almost no evidence and no chance for a second look, then what have we got?"

"We have doubt," Nick said. "That's a start."

"Okay, we have doubt—but as you would say, what do we know?"

"Very good, Mrs. Guilford. You've been listening." He stopped and thought carefully. "We know that the anomalous lividity in the victim's leg suggests that the body was moved—at least, we've been unable to account for it in any other way. We know there was a wound on the victim's head unrelated to the gunshot wounds that may have required the involvement of a second party. And on top of that, we have specimens from all three wounds—specimens that are approaching adulthood right now in their little puparia back at the lab."

"What will they tell us?"

"Suppose your friend was murdered, with the right leg supported at first in an upright position by some object. Eight hours later, lividity became fixed—and then the body was transported to the site in the woods where it was discovered. That scenario would account for the unusual coloration of the leg."

"Okay . . ."

"If the body was moved, that means the murder could have been committed anywhere. Across town—in the middle of a city—even in another state. Remember, Mrs. Guilford, different flies are unique to different areas. Calliphora vicina, for example, is synanthropic—it lives with people. It's found almost exclusively in large cities and towns. But Calliphora vomitoria is found only in rural areas. Now suppose our flies turn out to be vicinas. How did a city fly get on a body that supposedly died miles from the nearest town? The presence of Calliphora vicina would confirm our suspicion that the body was moved—and that would mean that your friend must have been murdered."

"But how could we prove who murdered him?"

"We couldn't—not with what we have now. But we would have enough evidence to compel Mr. Wilkins to request an order of exhumation—and if he refused, we could go over his head. The remains would be sent to the CMEO where a real, live pathologist who doesn't sell ice cream on the side could perform a decent autopsy. Who knows what might turn up?"

"And what if the flies turn out to be normal? What if we only find the species that are supposed to be there?"

Nick paused. "Then you spent a great deal of money for nothing, and you raised several more questions about your friend's death that may never be answered."

Kathryn stood quietly for a long time. Nick had warned her from the beginning that their investigation might produce nothing. She had known about this possibility all along—but she had never allowed herself to truly consider it before.

"So what do we do now," she asked glumly, "just sit around and wait for a bunch of bugs to grow up?"

"I'm not very good at sitting around. That's what I've got Teddy for. He checks the pupae every hour, and he'll contact us the moment the adult flies begin to emerge. Our time can be better spent asking some more questions. But essentially, yes—we just sit around and wait for a bunch of bugs to grow up."

"Then it all comes down to the flies."

"In my business, Mrs. Guilford, it always comes down to the flies."

CHAPTER 13

Kathryn stared at the ceiling fan that turned slowly and rhythmically above her, slicing a hole through the thick night air. She lay heavy and still, feeling the throb of exhaustion in every limb. She had dropped her things at the front door and headed directly for the bedroom, not even pausing to turn on the lights or check her messages. Why bother? The flashing red light told her there were four, and they would all be from the bank: Margaret wanting to know the whereabouts of some elusive file or Robert John asking exactly how many days she was taking off—though she had told him a half-dozen times—or Anna asking if she could just take a few minutes to review the so-and-so account.

She sprawled on top of the covers exactly as she first lay down, her entire body begging her to just stop moving. And so she lay, feeling the warm woolen blanket of sleep begin to creep up over her, mesmerized by the spinning blades above, spinning around the bright brass hub that gleamed each time it caught the headlights of a passing car through the window. It gleamed and then darkened and then gleamed again. On . . . and off . . . and on.

Kathryn saw herself swing open the screen door and step out onto the porch on a sultry July night almost ten years past. She instinctively banged her fist on the wall below the yellow porch light, which responded by flickering on and then off and then on again.

"When are we gonna fix this thing, Momma?" she called back into the house. Behind her she could hear the sound of *Matlock* on the television and the soft hissing sighs of the steam iron.

"Why don't you get one of those boys of yours to fix it?" her mother called back. "Maybe they're not smart enough."

"They're smart enough, all right."

"Maybe they don't want that bright ol' porch light shinin' all the time. Maybe they don't mind a little dark out there on the porch. Maybe they're too smart to fix it."

"If they're so smart, how come they're all three leaving me alone on a Saturday night?" She flopped down on the porch swing and sulked, watching the ailing porch light as it periodically flickered off and then on.

"Where have those boys been to lately? You think they found themselves a couple of Fayetteville sweethearts what stole their hearts away?"

"Stop it, Momma. Andy says things have been hoppin' at the Fort ever since those Iraqi boys marched into Kuwait. He says the Airborne might have to go over there and take care of it. They could get called up any day now."

"I sure hope not."

"They might could. Andy says he wants to go. Says it might speed up his commission."

"I don't like to hear that," her momma said. "I don't like to hear that one bit."

The screen door opened slowly, and Kathryn's mother stepped out, pulling an afghan tight around her shoulders. She never seemed to step outside without a covering, even on a muggy summer night. "It's the night air," she would always say. She looked older than her forty-five years, and she walked thickly and heavily as if she had physically carried the burden of raising a daughter alone for a decade. She sat down on the porch swing beside Kathryn and began to gently stroke her long, auburn hair.

"You got your daddy's hair," she said, smiling, "and his eyes, too. Thank the Lord, he took those ears of his to the grave." They both laughed.

"Your daddy and I got married just out of high school. Seems like most everybody did back then—that was June of '63. Just a year later his number came up, and he was off to Vietnam. I was worried sick, but he said not to go on about it. They was gonna make short work of it; they was gonna march right up the Ho Chi Minh Trail to China, and he'd be back before I even knew he was gone." She stared vacantly into the darkness as she spoke. "I knew he was gone all right. I was worried sick for three years."

"Andy says we got them outgunned and outmanned and outsmarted. We got the whole United Nations on our side! Andy says it's not like Vietnam."

Her mother smiled and studied her eyes. "Andy says this and Andy says that! How come it's never 'Jimmy says' or 'Peter says' anymore?"

Kathryn grinned and bent forward, flipping her hair up over her head, then straightened again and tossed it back. Her mother leaned forward and kissed her forehead, then stiffly rose, creaking and groaning like the weathered floorboards beneath her feet. She paused at the door and gave the porch light another thump.

On, then off and on, then off again.

"You be smart," her mother said from the darkness. "Most girls don't get to choose."

Kathryn sat rocking in the quiet blackness, pondering her mother's words, when she heard a sharp crack from the woods in front of the house. She stared hard into the darkness, and a moment later a lone figure emerged into the clearing and headed straight for the porch.

"Who's that?" Kathryn called out.

"Who you think?" the figure replied. "Who you expecting?"

"Jimmy!" She bounced down the front porch steps to meet him. "Where you been so long?" she scolded. "I was about to die of loneliness here!"

"Like I believe that," he said, laughing. He slid his arm around her waist, but she pulled away and ran to the porch swing, beckoning him to join her.

"What's goin' on?" she asked eagerly. "I hardly seen any of you."

"Miss me?"

"I miss all of you. Now tell me—what's the word at the Fort?"

"It's gonna happen, Kath," he said solemnly. "Word is we're goin' in. Nobody knows for sure, but everybody thinks so."

"When?"

"A month. Maybe less."

She sat in stunned silence. "All of you?"

The yellow porch light fizzled and switched on again, and for the first time Kathryn could see clearly into Jimmy's face and eyes. There was something there that she hadn't seen before—something her mother had tried to warn her about, something she had denied, something she secretly dreaded and hoped would never come. But it had come. It was here. Jimmy picked up her hand and held it tightly.

"I've known you for a long time, Kath . . ."

The words made her heart feel suddenly sick, and she longed to pull away and run into the house, to keep the words from ever being spoken. But she knew that if Jimmy could summon the courage to speak them, then she owed it to him to listen. She steeled her eyes against the flood of emotions she felt within and waited for the words that would most certainly follow.

"We been friends for a long time. We been more than friends. I been more, that is," he stammered. But there were too many thoughts and too few words, and he jumped up in frustration and slammed the porch post hard with the butt of his hand. The porch light sizzled and went out.

He stood silently in the darkness, then suddenly spun around. "You remember that day we drove way over to Asheville? You was maybe sixteen, no more."

"I remember."

"The day went long, the traffic was bad, we got on the road real late."

"And it was pouring rain. A hurricane, I think. We couldn't see a thing."

"So we pulled under an overpass just outside Greensboro to wait it out."

"And we fell asleep!" She laughed. "We didn't get home till the next morning! Did I ever catch it from Momma," she whistled. "Who knows what she must have thought—what everybody thought!"

Jimmy sat down beside her again. "You fell asleep. You put your head back against my shoulder, and you fell asleep. But I watched. I watched you all night long."

They sat in silence.

"I don't know what everybody else thought," he said with gathering momentum, "but I'll tell you what I thought."

"Jimmy . . . wait—"

"I thought it was the best night of my whole life. I thought that for the first time I was that close to what I wanted. And I knew I wanted a whole lifetime of nights like that."

He took her hand again. It was strangely limp.

"I got to go. But I don't want to leave without telling you . . . I want to . . . I want to ask you to . . ."

The porch light suddenly switched on again and in one terrible instant Jimmy saw what was in Kathryn's eyes—he saw everything: fear, remorse, compassion, pity—and the unmistakable answer to his unvoiced question. He saw it all, and there could be no more mistake than if it were painted on the side of a barn.

He dropped her hand.

"I want to ask you to write to me," he said softly. "I'd kick myself if I left without reminding you."

Kathryn closed her eyes, knowing that they had surely betrayed her. She prayed for the light to go out again so that she could hide, so that they could both pretend that the words had never been spoken and go back to the way they had always been. A thousand explanations and excuses ran through her mind, but she knew that there was absolutely nothing she could say. Her traitorous eyes had said it all, and now things could never be the same again.

Jimmy slowly rose, his stance less confident than it was just a moment ago.

"Don't go," she pleaded, tugging on his hand.

"I better." He pulled away.

"I will write, because I care about you." Good words, kind words, but only fossils of the words he'd hoped to hear. They stung him as he turned and headed down the steps toward the woods.

"Jimmy!" she called after him in tears, "you be careful! I'll write to you, and you write back, okay? Jimmy!"

The light sputtered out.

Kathryn saw herself back on the porch swing, her legs folded and her face in her hands, crying gently in the darkness. Now she understood her mother's words: Most girls don't get to choose. Most girls are lucky, she thought. She didn't want to choose. She only wanted to say yes, but never, ever no. She wanted to be chosen and never have to shatter the hopes of someone who was so close . . . but not quite close enough.

A moment later Kathryn heard another sound from the woods. Why was he coming back, and what in the world would he say this time? But another silhouette emerged into the clearing with a different manner and a longer gait.

"Who's there?" Kathryn called, but there was no response. "Call out, or I'll set loose the dog!"

"Turn that old cur loose," came the reply. "I haven't had a good laugh all day."

Andy!

Kathryn bounded down the steps and met him halfway, throwing her arms around his neck and almost knocking him over.

"I have been away too long." He laughed, pulling back and looking into her emerald eyes.

"Oh, Andy, it's been the worst evening! But I don't want to talk about it—come sit with me." She took him by the hand and led him to the porch swing.

As they passed the porch light, he reached out and gave it a thump. The amber light cast deep shadows across his chiseled face and made his bottomless brown eyes black as the night. Kathryn watched the shadows cut deep rivulets through his wavy bronze hair. His arms were long and muscular, and he was broad-chested. He had the stature and physique of a man, but whenever he faced her he always dropped one shoulder like an awkward boy. His smile was the best of all; when Andy smiled his face lit up like a torch.

"It's happenin', Kath," he said with excitement. "They say the division's gonna be called up any time now—I mean the whole 82d Airborne! They say we're heading for a base in Saudi Arabia."

"I know," she said glumly.

He looked at her. "Who was that I passed coming back through the woods?"

Kathryn said nothing.

"I see." He smiled. "There's been another rooster in the henhouse. Well you know what they say"—he nodded toward the flickering porch light—"where there's light, there's bugs."

"It was just Jimmy."

"And what did Private James McAllister want this evening?"

"Maybe it's none of your business."

"Just wanted to drop by and set a spell with the two old spinsters?"

"He just wanted to marry me, that's all. Oh, Andy, it was awful. I love Jimmy—I've always loved Jimmy, but—"

"But not that way." He finished the sentence for her, and she was glad, because the words sounded so hollow and cheap. "So he asked you to marry him?"

"Not quite. But he was about to."

"What stopped him?"

"I think he just knew, and he backed off."

"No wonder he had his tail between his legs." Andy whistled.

"I guess he'll get over it."

"Maybe. I know I wouldn't." Andy stepped to the light and gave it a thump. It flicked on. "Guess I can't blame him. He's always loved you—ever since we were kids."

"I never knew that!"

"I knew. Pete knew. Even your momma knew. We could all tell." The light blinked off, and he gave it another tap. "I wonder if they all know about me?"

Kathryn felt a lump in her throat.

"I wonder . . . ," he said, "I just wonder what you'd say if I was to ask you the same question?"

"What question?"

"Jimmy's question. The one he never quite got out."

"Well," Kathryn said indignantly, "you'll never know unless you ask."

"Oh, I don't know. Jimmy knew without asking." He wiggled his finger. "Come here for a minute."

Kathryn sat glaring at him. There was something about his arrogance and overconfidence that infuriated her—but there was something else about it that she couldn't quite explain. She stamped over to him and stood, arms folded, nose turned upward.

He wrapped his arms around her waist and stared deep into her eyes.

"What are you doing?" She arched away from him.

"Looking for my answer—just like Jimmy did."

"How do you know what Jimmy did?"

"Something tipped him off, and I'm betting it was your eyes. You say everything with your eyes. Always have. And they never lie."

"So what do you see?"

He pulled her closer and looked again. "I see yes."

"Yes, what?"

"Yes, you love me. Yes, you always have. And yes, you'll marry me."

"You just might be mistaken," she scolded.

"I'm not." He smiled.

"What makes you so cocksure?"

" 'Cause when I look in your eyes this close I see my eyes—and I know what mine are saying."

She looked into his eyes, and he was right. It was all there, and there could be no mistake about it.

He pulled her in tight and they kissed, long and deep.

She slowly opened her eyes again—and Andy's face began to somehow change. It grew longer and more angular. Not less handsome, just . . . different. She had never noticed it before, but he wore glasses. They began as tiny round spectacles like an elf might wear, but as she watched they began to grow to an enormous size, and Andy's beautiful brown eyes began to soften and fade until they floated away like two gray orbs—then they disappeared completely. Still the spectacles continued to grow; now they were the size of windows. In place of the eyes a pair of tiny black-and-gold spots appeared, then two more, then more, until there were thousands crawling and wriggling and pressing against the glass. She frantically struggled to get away, but the arms still held her fast. At last she broke free, but the spectacled figure only laughed and tipped his glasses downward, and the thousands of angry black spots streaked toward her, swarming over her arms and legs, clinging to her face and neck, filling her eyes and nose and mouth . . .

Kathryn shrieked and threw herself from her bed. The lamp from her nightstand crashed to the ground and shattered in a flash of blue light. She stood in the darkness, flailing at the air, trapped inside the black cloud that always hung so near.

She scraped furiously at her legs and arms—and then stopped, panting, gradually recognizing the familiar walls around her and the fan still spinning overhead.

She sank slowly to her knees and began to weep in long, hopeless sobs.

CHAPTER
14

It was just after dawn when Nick came jogging into the parking lot. He wore a gray Penn State sweatshirt torn off at the shoulders and a pair of sagging black running shorts that hung to his knees. He sported a spotless pair of Nike's, the nicest article of clothing he owned. He stopped beside the Dodge and pulled off his cap—the Steelers this time—and tossed it through the back window.

Parked beside the Dodge was a trim black sedan. Nick checked the license plate; in the upper left corner it bore a Holcum County sticker, and below the cherry red "First in Flight" insignia were stamped the words, PAX DEI. Nick headed for the lab.

As he approached the office, Nick could see a figure seated inside. He was a black man, ancient in years and as thin and brittle as a reed. His head was large and seemed to dominate his body, and his magnificent brow overshadowed his sloe-black eyes like a mahogany cornice. He was dressed immaculately in a blue-black suit and a silver tie. Oversized hands projected from slender wrists and rested gently on either side of a large, open book. There was a profound calmness about him; his hands moved slowly and deliberately, with the beautiful economy of motion that comes only with age.

Nick rapped on the office door and stepped inside. The old man looked up and smiled. "I do hope you'll forgive the intrusion. The door was unlocked, and it was a bit muggy outside."

"No problem," Nick said. "What can I do for you?"

"Dr. Malcom Jameson." He extended his hand. "Pastor of Mount Zion African Methodist Episcopal Church."

"Nick Polchak, NC State University." Nick returned the handshake and glanced down at the massive tome that lay open before him. The text was entirely in Latin. It was Jerome's Vulgate, opened to the Gospel of Matthew.

"*Adtendite a falsis prophetis qui veniunt ad vos in vestimentis ovium,*" Nick read aloud. "Beware of false prophets who come to you in sheep's clothing."

Dr. Jameson's eyes brightened. "You read Latin? I can't say I'm surprised. I was admiring some of your specimens in the outer office—especially the Pandinus imperator Koch."

"My Emperor Scorpion."

"A magnificent specimen, with an imperial name to match. But then, you know the old saying: *Quidquid latine dictum sit altum viditur.*"

Nick smiled. " 'Anything said in Latin sounds profound.' No offense, Dr. Jameson, but what's a smart guy like you doing in a town like this?"

Now the old man smiled. "I am a fisher of men. The biggest fish is not always found in the largest pond."

Nick nodded. "I've caught a few in small towns myself."

A look of recognition spread across the old man's face. "You are that Bug Man fellow, are you not? I believe I read about you in the papers. A fascinating discipline, this fo-ren-sic en-to-mol-o-gy of yours." He pronounced the words slowly, delighting in each syllable. "I'm afraid a man of your—how shall I put it—breadth of experience may find life a little dull in a town such as ours."

"Things are picking up," Nick replied. "I've been hired to investigate the death of Jim McAllister."

Dr. Jameson seemed taken aback. "I understood that the young man took his own life. Do you have reason to believe otherwise?"

"Let's just say I'm looking for reasons. How did you hear about his death?"

"I have been requested to preside at Mr. McAllister's memorial service." The old man pulled a folded piece of paper from his coat pocket. "I received a call from a Kathryn Guilford asking me to meet her here today, to arrange any necessary details."

"We had a long day yesterday," Nick said. "It might be best if I had her call you. Did Mr. McAllister attend your church?"

"Mr. McAllister was unchurched," the old man said. "That is, he was not a member of any local congregation. In situations such as this, I am often called upon to perform the services."

"In other words, you get the white trash."

Dr. Jameson looked at him sternly. "There is no such thing. Will you be attending the funeral, Dr. Polchak?"

"Never had much use for them."

"Oh yes, I see. You only handle the clinical side of death. I suppose there's nothing clinical about a funeral."

"Just a lot of fuss over a little shoofly pie."

"Shoofly pie," the old man repeated thoughtfully. "An interesting euphemism. The body dies, it starts to decompose. What remains becomes food for other living things. And what happens after?"

"After what?"

"After you die."

"Your question has no meaning," Nick said. "After you die is like saying after the end. If it's the end, there is no 'after.' "

"You believe there is nothing after?"

"What I believe is irrelevant. I'm telling you what I know. I see a body; it ceases to function; it decomposes. That's what I know."

"Sometimes knowing is not enough, my young friend. Sometimes you have to believe. That is my business."

"Different lines of work," Nick shrugged.

The older man studied Nick. "Perhaps. Perhaps not. We have more in common than you may think, Dr. Polchak. You seek guilty men to administer justice; I seek guilty men to offer grace and forgiveness. But it seems to me that, in our own way, we are both fishers of men."

He closed his book and slowly rose to his feet. He extended his hand to Nick once more.

"I will pray that you find what you are looking for. Much more importantly," he said with a penetrating gaze, "I will pray that you discover what it is that remains when even the shoofly pie is gone."

Nick walked the old man to his car. Just as the black sedan disappeared from view, Kathryn's silver Contour rounded the corner and came to a stop directly in front of the Quonset.

"Was that Dr. Jameson?" she said.

"I told him you'd call. Oversleep?"

"Didn't sleep." She followed Nick to the front door, where she hesitated. "Aren't we doing another interview this morning? What do we need to go in there for?"

"Dr. Jameson wanted me to show you something," Nick said.

Kathryn followed him cautiously, stepping only as far through the doorway as was absolutely necessary. "What is it?" she asked, eyeing the glass cases on either side.

Nick stepped around to the right and removed the lid from a terrarium. He reached in and slid his right hand under something that looked like a black leather glove. He returned to Kathryn with a smile on his face, holding his hand in front of him like a waiter with a dessert tray.

It was not a glove, but it was black—black as coal tar. Two bulbous arms extended before it like the claws of a lobster and a thick knotted tail curved up behind it like a whip—a whip with a very sharp tip.

"This is Lord Vader."

Kathryn began to back away. "Dr. Jameson wanted me to see that?"

"He was quite impressed with him. 'A magnificent specimen,' I believe he said. 'Be sure to show it to my dear friend Kathryn.' "

"I've never met Dr. Jameson."

"Lord Vader is an Emperor Scorpion. He's quite impressive, don't you think? A good eight inches if he's an inch." Nick held his hand at eye level and stepped forward, smiling. Kathryn stepped back.

"I can see it just fine from here."

"From way over there?"

Another step forward, another step back.

"Emperors are very unusual—first, of course, because of their enormous size. But they're also unusual in that they're social. You can keep several together in one tank, like I do, and they get along just fine. But they do like to be alone every now and then, so from time to time I allow Lord Vader to go for a stroll here in the lab."

"You let that thing run loose? It could kill someone!"

"Don't be ridiculous. Lord Vader rarely stings—only in self-defense. He doesn't need to, really, because of these." He stepped forward and pointed to the enormous black projections the scorpion held menacingly aloft.

"Are those pincers?"

"They're called pedipalps. They're remarkably powerful. I feed him mostly crickets and giant mealworms, but every now and then . . . See that metal box under the table? That's a rodent trap—a live rodent trap. Whenever an unfortunate Muridae tries to invade our sanctuary, he must face the wrath of Lord Vader. It is his destiny. It's an amazing battle—arachnid against mammal, invertebrate against vertebrate."

"You let that thing loose on a helpless mouse?"

"A mouse isn't defenseless, Mrs. Guilford. It has teeth and claws. It can crack through a kernel of corn or gnaw its way through a floorboard. But it's no match for Lord Vader, I'm afraid. Would you like to hold him?"

"No. Thank you." She retreated a step farther.

"You'd think Lord Vader would use his stinger. After all, a mouse is the size of a cow to him. But he doesn't. He just grabs hold of Mickey with those pedipalps and tears him limb from limb."

As he spoke, Nick continued to inch forward. He held his hand out to one side and gestured to it as he sidled closer to Kathryn, then swung his hand back slowly in her direction. Each time she would back away, and they would repeat this maneuver, over and over like a kind of waltz, both of them moving slowly down the aisle toward the office door.

"The fact is, his sting is no worse than a wasp's. There's a rule of thumb in the scorpion world: the bigger the pedipalps, the more harmless the scorpion. The little brown ones with the long, slender pedipalps—now those are the ones to watch out for."

"Do you have any of those?"

"Of course. The entire row of cases just inside the door is my Scorpionidae collection. On the right, Lord Vader and his Imperial Stormtroopers. In the middle, common southwestern U.S. species. But on the left, watch out—those are my North Africans."

"For heaven's sake, what do you keep them for?"

"It's a hobby," he said, placing Lord Vader on the floor and nudging him forward until he skittered away. "I think from time to time everybody needs a bit of distraction. Don't you?"

He reached past Kathryn, opened the office door, and stepped inside.

She stood motionless for a moment, realizing in amazement her current location; then she quickly slipped into the office and slammed the door, eyeing the floor behind her as it closed.

"You look much less wrinkled today," Nick said. "Now how about that interview?"

The Dodge rolled to a stop on the shoulder of the dirt road about fifty yards away from the decaying farmhouse. Kathryn heard two completely different hissing sounds emanating from somewhere under the hood, then a mysterious clicking noise followed by a kind of groan. She shifted to keep water from dripping onto her shoes from under the dash.

"We'd have been a lot more comfortable in that rental of yours," Nick said. "Why did you insist on taking my car?"

"I just thought it might be a good idea."

"You know, it's customary to call ahead and set up an appointment before doing an interview. I don't usually just drop by. 'Hello, I'm a forensic entomologist. I collected some maggots from your brother's corpse, and I'd like to ask you a few questions.'"

Kathryn rolled her eyes.

"What if Mr. McAllister's sister isn't home?"

"She's home. She's always home."

Several minutes passed.

"What exactly are we waiting for?" Nick asked.

"I'm just not sure this is a good idea." Kathryn shook her head doubtfully. "I don't see why we need to talk to her."

"Because the difference between a suicide and a murder is one of motive. Motive is everything, Mrs. Guilford—and who might understand the motives of the deceased better than his own kin?"

Kathryn continued to shake her head.

"If I didn't know better, Mrs. Guilford, I'd think you didn't want the lady to see you."

"Amy McAllister and I don't exactly—what I mean is, we have a history."

"Really? I love history."

Kathryn took a deep breath. "Jimmy and Amy came from a . . . troubled family."

"Troubled in what sense?"

"Troubled is a small-town term. It covers everything from minor neglect to outright cruelty and abuse. It's the polite way to say it, and polite is very important in a small town."

"Well, I'm from Pittsburgh. Was Amy abused?"

"In every way imaginable. You could say that she's . . . not quite right. Growing up, Jimmy and Amy kept each other sane. Jimmy was all she had in the world—no mom, no dad, no real friends—she had Jimmy."

"And Jimmy had you."

Kathryn winced. "Jimmy . . . wanted to have me. Nine years ago Jimmy asked me to marry him—the same night that Andy proposed to me."

"Two in one night. Boy, you were on a roll."

"This is not a joke! I had to turn him down, and it broke his heart. Jimmy always walked the line, and I think—Amy thinks—that my rejection is what started him over the edge. He went into a depression after that and started disappearing for long periods without explanation."

"And sometime during that period his drug abuse began."

"Sometimes I wish I had married him," Kathryn said under her breath.

"A rescue marriage." Nick nodded. "Very common. Very noble. Very stupid."

Kathryn glared at him. "Everything is so easy for you, isn't it? It must be so much simpler working with insects that have legs and wings but no feelings!"

"You have no idea how much simpler."

Kathryn closed her eyes and massaged her temples in slow circles. "Amy blames me for Jimmy's depression, for his withdrawal from her, for his anger and isolation. Amy blames me for everything."

"For his death?"

"Especially for his death."

"In other words, one of your motives for this investigation is to prove to Amy that it wasn't your fault. If it was suicide, then you're to blame; if it was murder, you're off the hook."

"Does that matter?"

"As I said, Mrs. Guilford—motive is everything."

Nick peered down the road at the crumbling farmhouse.

"And I thought this was going to be just another boring interview." He smiled, opening his door. "This could be downright interesting."

The dirt road disappeared into the mottled front yard of the aging house. Two Leghorns wandered aimlessly across the grass and one misshapen ligustrum thrived beside the sagging porch stoop. Four wooden columns, each rotted away at the base, supported a rumpled and pockmarked tin roof. The floorboards of the porch were cupped and twisted, long ago worn bare, and the brittle glazing around each window pane curled in like yellow parentheses. The curtains were thin and worn and pulled tight across each window. It was a dark and tired and withered house that had long ago given up hope.

Nick knocked gently at the door.

"No answer," he said.

"She's home."

Nick knocked again, a sharp, rapping, annoying barrage that continued until the curtain jerked to one side and an ashen face suddenly appeared, startling both of them. Kathryn stared at the floorboards and stepped slightly behind Nick.

The door opened, and a woman of almost undiscernable age stepped out. Her features were still young and rounded, but her skin was sallow and pasty, drawn into tiny canyons that drained into the eyes and mouth. Her hair was pulled back in a thoughtless manner, and her dark eyes bore a constant glare. She was still dressed in a faded blue housecoat. She studied Nick, starting with his feet and working her way up, recoiling when she came to his enormous spectacles. She leaned forward and glared harder, as if trying to grab hold of the elusive eyes darting beneath.

"What you want?" she barked.

"Are you Amy McAllister?"

"Depends on who you are."

"I'm Dr. Nicholas Polchak. I'd like to ask you a few questions."

"Don't need no doctor." She dismissed him with a wave of her hand, retreating back into the house. "You tell Family Services I ain't crazy, I just like my privacy."

"I like my privacy, too, Miss McAllister. I'm not that kind of doctor."

She turned as Kathryn reluctantly slid out from behind Nick.

"Hello, Amy," Kathryn said softly.

Amy's eyes widened and then narrowed again until they were only slits. Her mouth began to form a dozen different words, but the only one that emerged was a guttural, "You!" And with that she stormed back into the house and slammed the door behind her.

Kathryn hung her head and muttered, "I told you she still blames me. I told you there was no use in trying to—" But in the middle of her protests, Nick casually opened the door and stepped in.

He walked briskly from room to room, stopping in each room just long enough to make a quick appraisal. On the left was a dining room; the table was thick with dust, and a vase of long-dead flowers sat crumbling in the center. On the right was a kind of sitting room dominated by the smell of mildew and an aging Queen Anne sofa covered in a slick and barren red velour.

But the most noticeable feature of every room was the candles. Tall ones, short ones, on saucers and coasters and tins, lining bookshelves and furniture and dotting the floor like tiny fireflies. Candles smoldered everywhere, scenting the air oppressively and giving the entire house the look of a mausoleum.

At the end of the hall a double doorway opened into a small room completely devoid of furniture. The drapes were drawn tight, and the room would have been black as night if not for the candles. On the far wall was a stone fireplace. On the center of the mantel stood an Olan Mills portrait of James McAllister in full-dress uniform, framed by a pair of thin, white, flickering tapers.

Kathryn was right behind Nick, glancing nervously about as she tiptoed from room to room.

"You can't do this! You can't just march into a person's house and—"

Nick ignored her, continuing on until he finally rounded a corner to find Amy McAllister, squatting on the kitchen floor among several more candles, peacefully stroking a yellow cat. She had let her hair down, and it draped raggedly around her face. Her housecoat spread open at the waist and her pale legs jutted out to both sides. She looked like an alabaster gargoyle as she squatted and stared, mesmerized by the undulating movements of the cat.

She looked up at Nick and Kathryn with no expression at all. Then, slowly, a look of recognition came over her face. She snapped to her feet and opened her mouth to speak, but before she could get a word out, Nick cut her off.

"Miss McAllister, I am investigating the death of your brother. There are some questions that need to be answered—and I need your help to answer them."

Amy glared furiously at Kathryn.

"Why not ask her?" She pointed accusingly. "She knows why Jimmy died!"

"Amy," Kathryn said with a groan, "that was nine years ago!"

"You killed him!" Amy hissed. "You killed him just as sure as if you put that gun to his head! You was the one . . . the one who . . ."

Amy's voice suddenly trailed off, silenced by the sound of pleasant humming and cabinets quietly opening and closing again. Both women stood dumbfounded, watching Nick as he casually searched through the kitchen cupboards and pantry. He pulled out a faded tin of almond mocha, sniffed at it, and with a look of disgust, slid it back in place again. He turned a tall jar with his thumb and finger to peer at the label—instant Nestea, decaf. He shivered and wiped his hands on his pants. On the top shelf he spotted a half-empty box of Celestial Seasonings.

"This will have to do. Miss McAllister," he said, placing the box in her hand, "do you believe your brother took his own life? I'm not sure I do. If you want to talk about it, I'll be in the parlor." He tapped on the box. "I take mine with honey."

He turned and walked out of the room, leaving Amy staring open-mouthed after him. Kathryn glanced at Amy, then lowered her eyes and walked quickly after him. Nick was already stretching out on the Queen Anne sofa when Kathryn entered the parlor.

"I love what she's done with the place." He nodded approvingly. "The candles are a nice touch—sort of a Stephen King motif. I wonder if she decorated Schroeder's Funeral Home."

"Be quiet! Are you out of your mind?"

"You keep asking me that."

"Is this how you conduct an interview?"

"You were doing so well, I hated to interrupt."

"I tried to tell you about her. Amy hasn't been quite right for a long time."

"Quite right? Take a look at this place, Mrs. Guilford—the lady is skating on the other side of the ice."

"She's had a lot on her mind."

"She's had you on her mind, that's for sure."

Kathryn glanced nervously back down the hallway. "I think you had better do the talking this time."

"Gosh. I just hope I can handle it."

The clinking of metal against ceramic brought their conversation to an abrupt halt. Amy cautiously rounded the corner carrying a tarnished metal tray bearing two china cups with mismatched saucers. A single tea bag floated in each; one was still in its package. She stopped in the middle of the doorway, as if uncertain whether to enter or not. Her eyes went immediately to Kathryn. She stepped around to Nick and offered him a cup, then set the tray down on the coffee table and pulled a chair up close. She sat silently, her black eyes darting from the remaining cup to Kathryn and back again.

Kathryn slowly reached to take the cup. Amy immediately snatched it up for herself and redoubled the intensity of her glare. She sat silently sipping her cup of tea, her eyes never shifting from Kathryn's face. Kathryn drew back, red-faced, and stared fixedly at her hands in her lap.

They all sat in silence for several minutes. Kathryn could feel the heat from Amy's eyes, as if she were being prodded with a fire iron.

"Miss McAllister," Nick said at last. Kathryn almost let out an audible sigh of relief. "I am a forensic entomologist from North Carolina State University. I specialize in the investigation of unwitnessed deaths and the analysis of their possible causes." As he spoke he saw Amy begin to shake her head slightly, like a mare trying to force her eyes into focus. Nick paused, set down his cup, and began again.

"Miss McAllister. Do you really believe your brother killed himself?"

She shrugged and shook her head several times before finally speaking.

"They say he did."

"Who says he did? Who are they?"

She shrugged again. "Peter. Peter says everybody thinks so."

"Do you think so?"

Amy's eyes grew darker and more confused. It was obvious to Nick that she had little ability to form her own opinions; those she had could easily have been given to her by someone else. Her only contribution would be her knowledge of her brother's past.

"Miss McAllister, I'm told your brother had a history of depression. Is that right?"

She nodded.

"When did it begin? Do you remember?"

"I remember, all right." She turned her glare to Kathryn again. "It started after her! She's the one who—"

Nick interrupted. "When Mrs. Guilford rejected your brother, I'm sure he was hurt. He was disappointed and angry—that's not the same as depressed. Think carefully. When did he begin to sleep longer hours? When did small tasks begin to seem overwhelming to him? When did he begin to stay to himself and disappear for long periods of time?"

"He always did some of that. But it got worse after the Gulf—lots worse. He went up to Walter Reed for a spell. Didn't help much."

"Walter Reed Army Medical Center? In Washington?"

She nodded.

"Was that the Gulf War Syndrome treatment program?"

"He went for a couple weeks at a time. Didn't do no good."

"Did he have any other symptoms besides depression? Weakness? Fatigue? Memory loss, neurological disorders?"

"None of that." She shook her head. "He just got down on hisself."

"Did your brother see action in the Gulf? Did you ever talk to him about what happened there?"

"I tried—but when I asked about it he just clammed up. Sometimes he brung it up. Sometimes he'd start to talk about what he done or what it was like in the desert or some tight spot him and Andy was in—but then he'd just as soon get quiet again, and no matter what I did, I couldn't bring him out of it. That's when he'd head off by hisself—sometimes for weeks."

"Where did he go during those periods? Do you know?"

"Off in the woods, mostly. To hunt. Jimmy loved to hunt."

"Mostly around here?"

"All over. You go where the game is, where the season is."

Nick paused. "Who did your brother hunt with?"

"Most everybody in town."

"The three hunters who found him? Ronny, Denny, Wayne?"

"Sure, lots o' times."

"Did he ever mention a problem with any of them? One of them he didn't seem to get along with?"

"None in particular. Jimmy didn't take to nobody too well."

"What about the sheriff? Did your brother hunt with the sheriff?"

"Peter, sure. Most of all Peter. Peter got hisself an old hunting cabin just outside of Valdosta. Hunt turkey and hog there."

"Valdosta, Georgia?"

She nodded.

"Miss McAllister, I want you to think very carefully. Who was the last person to see your brother alive?"

Her eyes took on a distant look. "Me, I guess."

"The last time you saw him, how did he act? Was there anything unusual about his behavior? Can you remember anything he said?"

Amy squinted hard, as if staring into a deep darkness. "He was mad as mud—even more than usual. Said he was going to make things right."

"Make things right—what do you think he meant by that?"

She shrugged. "Jimmy said a lot of things didn't make no sense."

"And when he went to 'make things right,' where did he go? Any idea what he did, who he spoke with?"

No answer.

Nick sat quietly for a minute, his searching eyes darting rapidly behind their glass enclosures. Amy's eyes sank to the floor, and

Kathryn ventured her first glance up at Amy's face. She looked so tired, so much older than her twenty-five years. Her entire childhood had been a walking death, and now death surrounded her, suffocated her—perhaps as it had Jimmy.

"Miss McAllister," Nick spoke again, "I'd like to ask you one last question—one that I asked you before: Do you really believe your brother killed himself?"

Amy's face began to twist and contort. Half a dozen times she seemed as if she would speak, only to shake her head or shrug and start again. At last she managed just a single word.

"No."

"Why not?"

"Because I'm still here," she whispered. "And Jimmy wouldn't leave without me."

Kathryn let a single sob escape.

Amy slowly rose from her chair and silently left the room.

It was all Kathryn could do to contain herself. The utter wretchedness of it all almost swallowed her alive.

Nick slapped his hands on the sofa and stood up. "I think our interview is over," he said, stretching. "She gave us a lot to think about." He headed for the door, and Kathryn slowly followed. A part of her wanted to stay behind, to find Amy and hold her, to stay with her.

At the door a quiet voice stopped her.

"Wait."

Kathryn turned to see Amy holding a small Bible and a faded cigar box bound together with a cracked and brittle rubber band.

"These are Jimmy's things," she said. "His personal things. They might as well go with you." She held out the bundle, and Kathryn saw the briefest flicker of light in Amy's eyes—then darkness again.

"I can't see you again," Amy whispered. "I can't."

"Amy—I want you to know—" Kathryn stopped midsentence.

Over Amy's shoulder Kathryn saw thick gray smoke rolling toward them down the hallway ceiling from the back of the house. She spun around. Nick was already halfway back to the car.

"Nick! Fire!"

By the time she turned back again, Amy was halfway down the

hall. She ducked into the living room just long enough to grab her brother's portrait, then raced toward the kitchen.

"Ariel! Here, Ariel!"

"Amy! Leave the cat! We've got to get out of here now!"

Amy hesitated in the doorway, silhouetted against a rising amber glow, then disappeared into the roiling cloud.

"Amy!"

Kathryn started forward when she felt a powerful hand grab her by the arm and jerk back. "We've got to get out of here!" Nick shouted, dragging her back toward the open doorway. "We can't find her this way, the smoke's already too thick! We've got to head around back and find a shorter way in!"

They raced across the porch and around the left side of the house. Flames were visible from three windows, and individual panes cracked and exploded outward from the expanding gases. The vinyl siding began to brown and curl like frying bacon.

The end of the house was already engulfed in fire. Flame belched out from the kitchen window like a blowtorch. Less than a yard from the house, in the very center of the inferno, was a hulking silver capsule.

A propane tank.

They both saw it simultaneously.

"Back the other way!" Nick shouted. "Go, go!"

They raced back down the side of the house through blasts of flying glass and heat, around to the front of the house where the raging remains of the house might shelter them from shrapnel. Above the flames they could hear a shrill whistle that steadily rose to a deafening shriek.

"The ditch!" Kathryn screamed. "Into the ditch!"

They both dove headlong into the shallow water of the drainage ditch and threw their arms over their heads and necks.

There was a thundering roar, and a great orange fireball rolled into the sky.

Nick and Kathryn clutched coarse woolen blankets around their shoulders and watched the Holcum County Fire and Rescue team kick apart the remaining embers that an hour ago formed the house of Amy McAllister. Somewhere in the smoldering ashes lay the remains of Amy herself.

Sheriff Peter St. Clair stood with his arm around Kathryn as the fire chief approached.

"What can you tell us?" the sheriff called out. "How did it start?"

"Are you kidding?" the fire chief said. "You tell me. All I can tell you is what you already know: It hit the propane tank. There isn't enough left of the house to tell us anything else. Man, the heat inside that fireball must have been like a hog roast on the Fourth of July."

Nick felt the stubble on the back of his left arm, where the heat from the blast had singed it almost to the skin. "My guess is she started the fire herself. She went to make us some tea—probably left the gas on. The woman wasn't dealing off the top of the deck."

"I can tell you how the fire started," Kathryn grumbled. "Somebody set it."

Both men looked at her.

"What makes you think that?"

"First somebody takes a shot at us in the woods; now they try to burn us alive."

The sheriff squeezed Kathryn a little tighter and shook his head to the fire chief, who turned and headed back toward the EMT truck.

"Kath," Peter said softly, "they were two separate things."

Kathryn twisted away from him. "Are you going to tell me that this was just a prank too?"

"No. I'm going to tell you it was an accident. C'mon, you saw the condition of the place—the bare wood, the brush, the debris piled next to the house. You saw how many candles she had burning in there, like it was some kind of shrine. It's a wonder the whole place didn't go up a long time ago. Like the Doc said, she probably set the fire herself."

"But it didn't go up a long time ago, Peter. It went up while we were in it."

"That is a bit coincidental," Nick joined in. "The fire started in the back of the house, probably in the kitchen. But we were in the kitchen less than half an hour before we saw smoke, and the place went up in minutes. It's hard to see how a spontaneous fire could spread that fast."

The sheriff glared at him. "So now you're the Fire Man too?"

"Okay, so I'm out of my league here. All I'm saying is it seems a little odd."

"You said it yourself, everything about the place was odd. Including Amy."

Kathryn turned to face Peter. "Someone wants us to stop this investigation, Peter. If Jimmy's death was such an obvious suicide, why would anyone care if we take a closer look? It looks to me like someone has something to hide."

"Now wait a minute. Slow down—"

"Maybe this was an accident. Maybe Amy burned her own house down. Maybe she decided to set fire to it herself when she first saw me at the front door! But Amy didn't take a shot at us in the woods. And when you put the two together . . ."

"Hold on," the sheriff began—and then he stopped abruptly. He kicked at a piece of charred debris and smothered a curse. "I know who fired on you in the woods."

Nick poked his head around Kathryn and stared at the sheriff. "Excuse me?"

"It was Ronny. Or maybe Denny or Wayne—one of those three."

"The three hunters? The ones who discovered the body in the meadow?"

Peter nodded. "I had a hunch about it, so I stopped by the Buck Stop the other night—it's a bar over in Elkhorn where some of the boys like to hang out."

"And?"

"Look, put yourself in their place. Three good ol' boys stumble across a body in the woods. They know the man's problems, they see the gun in his hand, they put two and two together. So they do their civic duty and call the authorities. Next thing they know, some witch doctor comes to town saying he's gonna find out what really happened. And the boys get worried that somebody's gonna point the finger at them. So they fired a shot to try to scare you off. They weren't trying to hurt anybody."

"That's it?" Nick said.

"That's it," the sheriff said. "Now you know. Don't worry, I put the fear of God in all three of 'em. There won't be any more of that nonsense."

Kathryn looked at the charred remains of the house and wondered.

Nick turned to the sheriff. "Do you believe their motive? That they were only trying to protect themselves from false accusation?"

"They saw the O. J. trial, Doc. They know how screwed up the law can get."

"Did it ever occur to you that they might be covering up a deeper motive? They discovered the body, Sheriff; they certainly had the opportunity to manipulate it before you saw it. Any one of them could have played a role in Mr. McAllister's death."

"Maybe. But you're forgetting something, Doc—something you can't understand because you're not from around here. I know those boys—and I knew Jimmy. That plays a big part in knowing what did and didn't happen."

"You're forgetting something," Nick responded. "Mrs. Guilford knew Jimmy too—but she holds a different opinion. You put a lot of faith in your knowledge of people, Sheriff."

"Jimmy was an accident waiting to happen," the sheriff said.

"You're sure about that? Absolutely positive?"

"You see a blind man walking toward a hole, you watch him walk right up to the edge, then you turn away for a split second—

and when you look back, he's lying at the bottom of the hole. Do you ask who pushed him?"

"No," Nick said. "I ask, 'Who's the blind man here?' "

Kathryn could contain herself no longer. "Why didn't you tell us this before, Peter? Yesterday or the night before? You said you were going to cooperate!"

Peter pointed to the smoldering ruins of the house. "Because that's you. You're a fire out of control. First you thought somebody was tryin' to kill you in the woods, and it was just a couple of boys tryin' to cover their own backsides. Now you think somebody wants to burn you alive. Pretty soon you'll be finding conspiracies under every rock! Jimmy killed himself, Kath—I'm sorry you can't accept that. I just don't want to see you wasting any more of your time and money. I don't want to fuel the fire."

"If I'm wrong," Kathryn seethed, "then I'm only wasting my own time and money. But if you're wrong"—she pointed to the house—"then that was another murder!"

Kathryn picked up the small pile of Jimmy's personal belongings and began to brush off the dried mud and soot.

"What's that?"

"Jimmy's personal things—what's left of them anyway. Amy thought I should have them."

"Mind if I have a look?"

The sheriff slid the crumbling Macanudo cigar box out from under the rubber band and handed the Bible back to Kathryn. He flipped open the lid. Inside was a scattering of personal items: Jimmy's Airborne insignia and campaign ribbon, a small Buck pocketknife, a pair of shiny onyx cuff links, and a banded deck of Aviator playing cards. There were also a half-dozen letters and papers of various shapes and sizes.

"Mind if I hang on to this for awhile? I'll go through the papers, see if I find anything that might help." He leaned toward Kathryn. "I don't expect to."

"If you don't expect to find anything, then give them back," Kathryn said.

"We said we'd cooperate," the sheriff said gently. "You got to let me do something."

Kathryn shrugged the blanket from her shoulders and

dropped it at Peter's feet. She spun around and stormed away toward the car.

Nick let the embers cool for a few moments before saying, "It is her time, you know. Why don't you just humor her?"

The sheriff glared at him. "It's time that could be better spent."

"Better spent . . . on you?"

The sheriff leaned in close and spoke in a low, rumbling voice. "There are lines, Doc." He turned and stomped off toward the waiting patrol car.

"There are lines," Nick whistled. "And I think I just found one."

CHAPTER
17

Ten o'clock, hon. League play just ended; it's open lanes now."

"Thanks." Nick sat at the snack bar at the Strike 'N Spare Lanes, watching three men in matching gray Loungemaster shirts with the name Buck Stop chainstitched in red across the back.

"Can you give me lane twelve? The one beside those three there."

"Sure thing. Friends of yours?"

Nick shook his head. "What can you tell me about them?"

The waitress eyed him suspiciously. "Why you asking?"

"I'd like to do a little business with them."

"Ronny, Denny, and Wayne," the waitress said, pointing. "Three peas in a pod, those boys."

"What do they do—for a living, I mean?"

"Denny—he's the little one—still works for his daddy at the Feed & Supply. Don't worry, he'll tell you more'n you want to know. Never stops talkin', that one. Wayne—the one that used to have hair—he drives a truck for Ferrellgas. Ronny's the big, quiet fella. He's got hisself an office over on Dalrymple. He's the success of the three."

"What's his business?"

"Insurance, I think. Something like that. Always seems to have money anyway." She glanced up just in time to see Denny chest-thump Wayne after picking an easy split. "If you ask me, none of 'em's a bargain."

Nick picked up his plate of pork ribs and potato salad and headed for the alleys, stopping by a rack of multicolored spheres just long enough to fit his fingers into a coal black, sixteen-pound Ebonite.

"You need shoes?" the waitress called after him.

Nick shook his head. "Not for this game."

The three men recognized him even before he sat down. They had never seen Nick before, but they had no doubts about his identity; his massive spectacles were already legendary in the little town of Rayford. They watched as Nick silently added his ball to the return rack and set his plate down on the scoring table.

"Mind if I join you?"

"Can you bowl?" Wayne snickered. "I mean, can you see the pins?"

Nick lifted his ball and turned to the alley. He held the ball chest high, paused, then took three quick steps forward. His backswing rose above his head, and the black shape floated weightless for an instant before arcing down again. The ball met the alley without a sound and rocketed forward along the right gutter, spinning like a gyroscope on its side. Two-thirds of the way to the target lateral rotation overcame forward momentum, and the ball broke, curling in perfectly just behind the headpin. Ten pins exploded and ricocheted inside their black frame.

Nick turned to the three hunters. "Did I get any?"

"You're that Bug Man," Denny said. "Settle a bet for us. What's the deadliest insect in the world?"

"Who are the nominees?" Nick asked.

"I say it's the female black widow spider."

"A naughty lady, but not even in the running."

"Your turn, Wayne. Tell the doc what you said."

"It's a definite fact," Wayne stated with all the authority he could summon, "that the daddy-longlegs, if eaten, is the deadliest spider in the world."

"Anyone stupid enough to eat spiders isn't likely to live very long, but he won't die from the Phalangida. That's an urban legend. Any other votes?"

The third and largest of the three cleared his throat and spoke a single word. "Scorpions."

"That's right," Denny said, "I hear there are scorpions that can kill a man in less than a minute!"

"Not that fast." Nick shook his head. "But you're getting closer."

"Okay then," Wayne said with a generous dose of contempt, "what is the deadliest insect in the world?"

"You've got one on your arm."

All three men jumped back, and Wayne wiped frantically at both arms, sending a single black fly buzzing back toward the snack bar. Ronny and Denny erupted into laughter. Not Wayne.

"That was close," Denny hooted. "Good thing we got a doctor nearby!"

"Funny," Wayne grumbled. "Real funny."

"I wasn't joking. Less than 3 percent of insects can harm a human being, but that little Musca domestica—a common housefly—is at the top of the list."

Nick raised his plate up to eye level. There sat a second fly, motionless, leisurely feeding atop a heaping mound of creamy white potato salad.

"Flies can't chew. They can only suck up liquid. So when they land on solid food, they spit. They eject saliva, and the saliva dissolves the food—dinnertime. The problem is, the fly always leaves a little saliva behind wherever he goes. Now if this fly only visited potato salad it might be okay—but the fact is, he was raised in a manure pile, and he stopped off for lunch on a decomposing rat."

He carefully lifted a hefty forkful of potato salad, fly included, and brought it to his open mouth. He paused.

"Or maybe he stopped on one of the cadavers over at my place." The fly buzzed away at the last possible moment before its meal disappeared down the dark, gaping cavern.

"Flies carry cholera, typhoid, leprosy, and polio," Nick said through his generous mouthful. "They've killed millions." He held out his plate to the four men. "Say, this is really good. Try some?"

"You really got cadavers over at your place? What for?"

"I'm a forensic entomologist. I study the way necrophilous insects can indicate the time and the manner in which someone died."

"What kind of insects?"

"Necrophilous. Dead flesh eaters."

"What these scientists won't come up with," Denny said.

"What I do is nothing new. The first book on the subject was written seven hundred years ago by a Chinese investigator named Sung Tz'u. He called his book *The Washing Away of Wrongs*." Nick cocked his head to one side. "Great title, don't you think?

"Back in 1235 some good ol' boy got angry with one of his drinking buddies and decided to express himself with a sickle. The authorities questioned everyone in the village but got nowhere, so they sent for Sung Tz'u—the local Bug Man. Sung Tz'u didn't bother with questions; he just had all the villagers bring their sickles and lay them side by side in the hot sun. Then he waited."

Nick casually took another bite of potato salad. "Mmm. You're sure you don't want to try this?"

"Waited for what?"

"Flies."

"What flies?"

"On the sickle. Necrophilous flies were attracted to traces of blood and tissue left on the killer's sickle."

"What did they do to him?" Denny asked.

Nick shrugged. "I suppose they Washed Away the Wrong. So you see, I'm part of an ancient tradition. There's only one way to learn about death, fellas—you have to study the dead."

"Disgusting," Wayne muttered.

Nick arched one eyebrow. "Oh, come now. I thought you boys were hunters. Surely you're not squeamish about seeing something dead."

"Animals," Denny said. "Not people."

"That's not what I heard. Weren't you the three that found Jimmy McAllister's body in the woods?"

Nick looked down and picked at his plate just long enough to allow each of the men to exchange awkward glances. Then he casually set his plate down on the scoring table and wiped his hands on his shirt.

"I answered your questions—how about answering a couple of mine?" Nick smiled at each of them. "I'm investigating the murder of James McAllister."

No one smiled back.

"You got to be kidding," Denny said. "It was an obvious suicide."

"Oh? How so?"

"The gun was still in his hand—his own gun."

"And the way we found him," Wayne joined in, "flat on his back. All his stuff was there. No sign of a fight, no struggle."

"And his history," Denny added. "You know, the cocaine thing and all."

Nick stopped. "What cocaine thing?"

"Didn't you know? It turns out Jimmy'd been doing the stuff. For a long time—since back in the Gulf. That stuff can make a man do things he might not do in his right mind."

"It can indeed," Nick nodded. "Where did you hear about this?"

"From Ronny."

Nick turned to Ronny.

"Pete told me," he said with his usual economy of words. "I told these two."

"When did Pete tell you? How long ago?"

"A few days."

Nick paused.

Denny suddenly felt the weight of two sets of eyes. He glanced awkwardly at Ronny and Wayne; one rolled his eyes, the other shook his head and turned away.

"Okay," Denny grumbled. "Maybe I wasn't supposed to tell anyone."

"And maybe you were," Nick said quietly. "Where do you suppose Jimmy got his cocaine?" There was no response. Nick smiled. "Maybe it's not so hard to keep a secret in a small town after all . . . Let's change the subject. Tell me how you found the body. How was it lying?"

"Sort of like . . . this," Wayne pantomimed, standing with his arms and legs spread wide.

"Show me." Nick pointed to the maple floor.

"What—here?"

"Why not? Who's going to notice?"

Wayne looked around cautiously, then spread out uneasily on the glossy surface. "Like this," he said, and quickly started to rise again.

"Not yet." Nick knelt at his side. "Think carefully. Could one of the arms have been like . . . this?" He lifted Wayne's right arm and dropped it across his chest.

"Uh-uh." Wayne shook his head. "It was definitely out to the side." Ronny nodded his agreement. Denny kept silent, still smarting from his earlier indiscretion.

"How about the legs?" He lifted Wayne's right knee and pulled his foot in tight against his buttock. "Could the right leg have been more like . . . this?" He let go, and Wayne's leg flopped out to the side.

"How could it? It won't stay up like that."

"No, it won't," Nick said. "Not without help. Were there any objects around the body, anything that might have temporarily supported a limb in a position like that?"

They all shook their heads.

"Did you boys move anything? Take anything? Did the three of you adjust the body in any way?"

There was a long pause, then Wayne jumped to his feet. "I don't like this," he snapped. "Are you saying we did something wrong? 'Cause if you are, say so."

"I'm not saying you did. I'm saying you could have. Let's be honest. You three came across the body in the meadow. You could have put it there."

"Now why would we do that?" Denny growled.

"You tell me."

"Jimmy'd been dead a week when we found him!"

"When the three of you found him, yes. But any one of you could have put him there the week before, then accidentally 'discovered' him a week later with the other two. By the way—which one of you suggested that you work on your deer stands that day?"

The three men looked at each other nervously.

"It was Denny, wasn't it?"

"Me? I'm the one who said to go have a beer and wait for better weather!"

"Now I remember," Wayne said. "It was Ronny . . ."

Nick picked up his ball again and stepped up to the line. This time, the ball hit the headpin square-on and left the seven and ten pins standing.

The hunters stared warily at Nick. They were downwind now, heads held high, straight and alert and ready to run.

"Settle a bet for me," Nick said. "Which one of you is the best shot?"

No one dared to answer at first—then Denny spoke up unexpectedly. "Probably Ronny. He's got a Weatherby Mark V Crown Custom. It's got a Leupold scope on it, and—"

"Shut up, Denny!" Ronny roared. "Can't you ever keep your mouth closed?"

Nick turned to Ronny. "A Weatherby Crown Custom? Business must be good. Then I assume you're the one who tried to kill my assistant?"

"We didn't try to kill anybody!" Wayne spluttered. "We only wanted to scare you off!"

"That's what the sheriff thinks," Nick said. "He said you boys only did it to protect yourselves. To protect yourselves from what?"

"From this!" Denny shouted. "From some long-nose trying to make out like we had something to do with Jimmy's death!"

"How could anyone get that idea? Did any of you have any reason to want Mr. McAllister dead?"

Silence again—but now the air between them was electric.

"Did you boys hear about Amy McAllister? Just this afternoon. I was there, did you know that? Quite a close call—I barely made it out of the house in time. There was a fire, and the fire hit the propane tank. It went off like a bomb. Would you believe her propane tank was right against the back of the house? But you knew that, didn't you, Wayne? You work for Ferrellgas, don't you?"

Wayne scrambled to his feet and charged at Nick. Nick spun to face him. Wayne drew back his right arm, then glanced at Nick's huge spectacles and hesitated.

In that instant Nick swung a roundhouse left. It was smooth and sure, and it came from the floor. It caught Wayne square on the jaw; there was a click and a dull smack, and Wayne crumpled to the floor like a stringless puppet.

Denny jumped to his feet, while Ronny sat and watched. Nick glared at both of them. "Anyone else want to try?"

Wayne lay on his back on the hardwood floor, just as he had done a few minutes ago; this time, his imitation of the dead was much more convincing. Nick reached down with one hand and grabbed Wayne's belt where it curved around his side. With one smooth motion he flipped him over onto his face, a skill he had mastered by rotating the decomposing carcasses of countless swine.

He reached into Wayne's back pocket and pulled out his wallet. He flipped it open, took out two twentys, and tossed the empty billfold at Ronny's feet. "To cover the cost of my equipment," Nick said. "You boys can work it out between you."

He glanced down at Wayne's motionless form. "When he wakes up, tell him I don't believe the three of you are responsible for Jim McAllister's death. But one of you might be—and one of you just might know who it is. Think it over—all three of you don't have to take the blame. If you want to talk, you know where to find me."

Nick backed slowly away toward the exit. He glanced one last time down the alley at the two remaining pins.

"A split," he whistled. "Tough one to pick."

CHAPTER
18

You did what? You punched him?"

"It seemed the thing to do at the time," Nick said.

"You can't go around getting into fistfights," Kathryn scolded. "You of all people!"

"Why is that?"

She cocked her head and stared at his enormous spectacles.

"What, these? Actually, I've found them very helpful. I find that most people hesitate to take a swing at a man wearing glasses." Nick smiled. "I don't have that problem."

She shook her head. "You'd think a blind man would have learned not to go around throwing punches."

Nick shrugged. "Where I grew up, you learned to swing first."

Kathryn glanced around the cavernous room; the Idle Hour Café looked more like a hunting lodge than a nightclub. A score of pedestal tables were scattered randomly across a floor half the size of a skating rink, and a handful of couples eagerly spun and two-stepped among them. On the table sat a half-dozen empty brown bottles, courtesy of the Carolina Brewing Company of Holly Springs, North Carolina.

"So you beat up Wayne just to get the money back for your equipment? I guess I'd better be careful to pay you on time."

"We know the hunters want this investigation to stop," Nick said. "What we don't know is why. The sheriff thinks they were just covering their backsides. Maybe—or maybe they're trying to cover something more. I wanted to divide them, Mrs. Guilford. Three peas in a pod—that's what the waitress at the bowling alley called them. They're a team, and as long as they act as a team they'll protect each other. I wanted them to know they're all in danger so each of them will start looking after his own backside. Now we'll find out if they have anything to hide or not."

Kathryn rubbed at her face with both hands. "I can't stop thinking about poor Amy. Peter said it was just an accident."

"Could be. She could have caused the fire herself—she was capable of it. But I find the timing a little too coincidental, and the fire spread awfully fast. No way to check for arson though. The propane took care of that."

"Do you think it was one of the hunters again?"

"Hard to say; this was more than just a warning shot. What can you tell me about Ronny?"

"Why Ronny?"

"He's the one who fired at you in the woods. What business is he in?"

"Investments, I think."

"The waitress said insurance."

"I'm not sure. But he seems to do pretty well."

Nick paused. "The waitress said the same thing—and Ronny owns a very high-end weapon. Don't you find it a little strange that a man could be so successful in a town this size and no one is sure what he does?"

Kathryn shrugged. "People don't know everything in a small town."

"Really? I wonder." Nick flagged down a passing waitress. "I'm a little new around here," he said. "Everybody's talking about this Jimmy McAllister character. What's the story?"

The waitress glanced over her shoulder. "Jimmy was a home boy, grew up right here in Rayford. Shot hisself in the woods just a week ago. And no wonder—turns out he been doin' a little . . ." She held her little finger up to her nose. "For years, they say. Guess it finally caught up with him." A man at another table signaled her, and she moved away.

Kathryn was stunned.

Nick looked at her. "Who did you tell about Mr. McAllister's cocaine habit?"

"Are you kidding? Why would I tell anyone?"

"The three hunters knew," Nick said. "The sheriff told Ronny a few days ago. Ronny told Denny and Wayne. By now the whole town knows."

"But—why would Peter tell anyone? Why those three, especially a loudmouth like Denny?"

"There's an old saying, Mrs. Guilford. If you want a secret kept, keep it yourself."

Several minutes passed. Suddenly, for the first time that evening, Kathryn became aware of the intimacy of the couples around them. A young couple to her right leaned together across a table with no more than a handbreadth between their faces. On the dance floor a man and woman were entwined like kudzu, swaying eagerly with very little regard for the rhythm of the music.

"I'm not going to call you 'Dr. Polchak' anymore," she said abruptly. "It takes too much energy. From now on I'm going to call you Nick."

Dr. Polchak—Nick—said nothing.

"Okay?"

"Are you asking for my approval?"

"For twenty thousand dollars I think I should be able to call you Nick."

"For twenty thousand dollars you can call me Queen Latifah."

She looked at Nick, who sat quietly rapping the rim of his bottle on the table in time with the music.

"Would you like to dance?" Kathryn blurted out—then quickly glanced around as though the words might have come from another table.

Nick looked over both shoulders, wondering if he had accidentally intercepted a message intended for someone else.

"I really don't dance—except at weddings."

"How often do you go to a wedding?"

"Never."

They sat in awkward silence again. Nick inspected the roof trusses and ventilation shafts that lined the ceiling while Kathryn carefully removed the paper labels from four of the empty bottles.

"Dancing is a strange phenomenon," Nick said suddenly.

"Excuse me?"

"Dancing. It's one of the ways your species and mine are very much alike."

"This I've got to hear."

"Look at those two women standing at the bar. They're dressed in bright colors; they're wearing makeup—too much makeup—and probably perfume. Those are their attractants. Watch . . . they seem to be friends, don't they? They're not. They have to compete with one another for the available males, just as members of my species do. Watch their movements. The one on the left keeps tossing her hair back—see? Each woman knows what her most desirable feature is and tries to draw attention to it. This allows her to choose between better males."

"Why does everything have to be about males? Did you ever think that maybe she did it for her own self-esteem?"

Nick rolled his eyes. "Look at her, Mrs. Guilford. See the way she swings her hips as she talks? I'm sure that enhances her self-esteem. And look at the way they both smile and laugh and try to look as animated as possible. No, this is typical courtship behavior."

"You seem to be an expert on female behavior."

"I am. Did you know that in one study a caged female pine sawfly attracted more than eleven thousand males? Now that's what I call perfume."

"I thought we were talking about females of my species."

"I've studied a few of them too—purely in the name of science, of course."

Suddenly Kathryn noticed that Nick's elusive eyes had come to rest on some object behind her, just across her left shoulder. She turned. At the jukebox stood a young woman with a body as sleek as a hornet, swaying seductively from side to side as she studied the selections. Kathryn turned slowly back to Nick with a broad smile.

"Aha."

"Aha what?"

"Nothing." She raised one eyebrow. "Just 'Aha.' "

"Don't be annoying, Mrs. Guilford."

"You seem to have taken more than a clinical interest in a member of my species. Down here, that's what we call eye-eatin'."

"Nonsense," he said casually. "I was merely observing."

Kathryn leaned forward. "Liar."

"Well," he took a second glance, "it's hard not to appreciate an outstanding example of any species."

Kathryn watched as Nick's floating eyes turned back to her again, studying, analyzing, searching for something. She had the distinct impression she wasn't going to like what came next.

"I suppose your attraction to someone can keep you from seeing things clearly," he began. "Sometimes it takes a third party to help you see what's going on."

Kathryn hesitated. "Who are we talking about?"

Nick rocked back in his chair and folded his hands in front of him.

"Let me ask you a question. It appears quite possible that your friend's body was moved—and if it was moved, he was most likely murdered. The body could have been moved just a few feet—or many miles. The murder could have occurred anywhere—in another county, even in another state. Suppose the murder occurred far away; why would the killer choose to return the body to Holcum County? After all, an apparent suicide could be staged anywhere."

Kathryn shrugged.

"The killer would return the body here because Holcum County is one of the only counties in North Carolina that still operates under the old coroner system—where the death investigation would be conducted by the ice cream man. Here he would have the best chance of faking a suicide and fooling the authorities. Now—who would know such a thing? Not the hunters. The coroner would know, of course—and anyone else who is familiar with medico-legal procedures in your county. Now, who might that be?"

The hair began to stand up on Kathryn's neck.

"Of course, even if the killer fooled the coroner, the police might figure it out." Nick looked directly at Kathryn now. "Unless for some reason the police didn't want to figure it out . . ."

Kathryn's eyes narrowed to a fiery glare. She brought both fists down hard on the table and sent two bottles clinking to the floor. The couple on her right stopped and turned. She glanced awkwardly over at them, then turned back to Nick and lowered her voice to a growl.

"Are you saying you suspect Peter? You think he might have done it?"

"Could have done it," Nick corrected. "Of course, there is one other possible suspect . . ."

"Who?"

"You."

Kathryn slumped back in her chair and threw both hands in the air.

"Me? You think I would pay you twenty thousand dollars to investigate a murder I committed myself? Are you out of your mind?"

"You know your problem, Mrs. Guilford? You're naive—and in this business that can be a fatal error. This sort of thing happens all the time. Here's the scenario: A beautiful young woman decides to do away with her friend, or boyfriend, or lover—whatever—and then she comes to me to investigate the death for her. She knows that there's little chance I'll be able to find anything, but her eagerness to investigate and her willingness to sacrifice her hard-earned money convinces everyone in town of her innocence. Twenty thousand dollars is a small price to pay for that kind of public support."

Kathryn sat in stunned silence, shaking her head in disbelief. "Do you actually suspect me?"

Nick paused. "No. I don't."

"Then why—"

"Because I want you to open your eyes. No, I don't suspect you of murdering your friend—but I'm willing to suspect you. I'm willing to suspect you and the hunters and the Sunday school teacher and the president of the PTA. I'm willing to suspect anyone—including your old friend the sheriff. My concern is that you're not."

"Peter offered to cooperate with us in this investigation."

"I believe his words were, 'I'd like to know what you come up with.'"

"And in return, he said he'd give us everything he has."

"Which is nothing. An interesting form of cooperation."

"Then why did you agree to go along with him?"

"First, because like it or not your friend is the law, and it's within his power to demand our cooperation. Second, because I'd rather keep him where I can see him. And third," he said with a tilt of his head, "because I have no choice, do I? This is your investigation—and wherever you are, I have a feeling the sheriff won't be far away."

Kathryn could barely contain herself. "Let me tell you something about Peter," she seethed. "When I lost Andy he was the first one there. He stayed with me. He held me while I cried."

"What a terrible burden for him."

"He helped settle Andy's affairs. He fought with the Department of Defense about searching for Andy's body. He took care of the finances. He washed my car, he cut my grass, he did my shopping for me—he kept me from losing my mind."

"That reminds me of a joke," Nick said. "A man lies dying on his bed with his faithful wife sitting beside him. He says to her, 'You've always been there, Margaret. When I lost the business, you were there. When I had the accident, you were there. When I suffered the nervous breakdown, you were there. And now that I'm dying, you're still there. It just occurred to me—you're bad luck.' "

"That's not funny," Kathryn glared. "I owe Peter everything."

"Apparently not."

"What's that supposed to mean?"

"You don't love him."

"How do you know? Maybe I do."

Nick raised both eyebrows and peered at her over the top of his glasses. "You're a very poor liar. Take it from an expert."

"What makes you so sure Peter loves me anyway?"

"Oh, come on," he groaned. "Mother bears are less protective."

"Oh, really. It just so happens Peter has a girlfriend, you know."

Nick stopped. "Now that's interesting. And what might her name be?"

"Oh no you don't," Kathryn shook her head. "The last thing I want to do is turn you loose on Peter's girlfriend."

"I'm not going to eat her, Mrs. Guilford. I'd just like to ask her a few questions."

"What kind of questions?"

"Like, 'When the sheriff holds you, are you aware that he's thinking about someone else?' "

"You are way out of line!"

"In my business, Mrs. Guilford, there are no lines."

"I am not paying you to suspect Peter!"

"Oh? Who are you paying me to suspect?"

"Anyone else, but not him!"

"Why? Because he's not capable of killing anyone? You know better, Mrs. Guilford. Because he had no reason to? Take another look behind you."

Kathryn turned to see the woman with the hornetlike body still smiling and swinging hypnotically from side to side. Two eager young drones now circled around her, vying for her attention and flashing increasingly angry glances at one another.

"She could settle this right now if she wanted to—but she won't. She'll let them fight over her. In another ten minutes they'll be out in the parking lot. If it goes badly, one of them may even die. That's why your species kills, Mrs. Guilford. That's all the reason they need."

"Not Peter."

Nick adjusted his glasses. "And you thought I was blind."

Kathryn jumped to her feet. "Why don't you drop this 'your species' and 'my species' routine? Like it or not you're a part of this species, mister! You can withdraw if you like—you can hole up in that perverse little laboratory of yours and spend your life staring at bugs, but you're still one of us. You can look down your nose at everyone and distrust everyone and pick fights with everyone—but that doesn't make you more of a bug, it just makes you less of a human! You say I'm naive—well maybe I am, but you're a cynic! You think you're above it all, standing outside and staring in the window at the rest of us—but you're not! You're just the pathetic little boy with the big funny glasses who got tired of being hurt and ran to his room and slammed the door!"

Kathryn suddenly realized that she was standing and that her voice had inadvertently risen to a shout. Half the room had grown silent, watching, and several couples now stood motionless on the dance floor. As if in response to the change of atmosphere, the music segued to a slower beat.

She sank awkwardly into her chair again and sat staring at her reflection in the amber bottle closest to her. There was a long, long silence—so long that Kathryn began to wish that Nick would shout or scream or even throw something—anything would be better than the awful silence.

"You know," Nick said suddenly, "I believe I'd like to dance after all."

He rose and stepped a few paces away from the table, then turned and held his arms out for Kathryn. She sat stunned, blinking in disbelief, her mouth gaping open—until she noticed her reflection in the bottle. She slowly rose from her chair and stepped toward him. She stopped a few feet away and held her own arms out, almost with a shrug, as if to say, "It's your move."

Nick stepped forward and slid his right arm around her waist, pulling her closer than she expected. He held her right hand against his chest and put his cheek almost against hers, his lips just a few inches from her right ear. They began to move with the music, far more smoothly than Kathryn would have imagined possible—for someone of his species.

Minutes passed.

"So you're convinced that the sheriff couldn't have done it," Nick said softly.

"I'm absolutely sure."

"Then the next time you see him, will you ask him something? Ask him why, after nine years of silence, he suddenly chose to make your friend's cocaine habit public knowledge."

"He only told one person," she reminded him.

"Yes. But he told the right person."

Kathryn thought about his words. "All right. I'll ask him."

Nick spotted the waitress working her way toward them across the dance floor. He stopped and looked into Kathryn's eyes. At this distance, his eyes seemed truly enormous.

"Promise? The next time you see him?"

"I promise."

"Your ride is here," the waitress said to Kathryn.

"Hope you don't mind," Nick said. "I have a few things to take care of."

"Thanks for thinking of me." She patted him on the chest.

She turned and headed toward the door. Halfway there she recognized the figure of Peter St. Clair standing by the entrance, grinning, holding a handwritten sign that said, KATHRYN GUILFORD.

Kathryn spun around and glared back at Nick, but Nick had already turned away, busily studying two angry young men hustling one another out the side door.

CHAPTER
19

Looked like quite a party back there." Peter smiled without taking his eyes from the road. A burst of static and an indistinguishable voice broke through momentarily on the police scanner. He reached down and switched it off.

"It wasn't a party," Kathryn said, her eyes transfixed by the endless telephone poles blinking past her window. "It was work."

"You needed a ride home from work? You got a better job than I do."

"I didn't need a ride home," she said irritably. "This was Nick's idea."

"So now it's Nick."

Kathryn looked at him for the first time since she got in the car. His face flashed lean and angular in the stark headlights of each passing car, and his eyes sparkled like blue ice in the glare of the cold halogen beams.

"How is Jenny?" she asked softly. "You never say."

Peter paused. "She's fine."

"She's fine," Kathryn repeated. "That's all men ever say. This is fine. That's fine. I'm fine, thank you very much. 'She's fine' just means, 'I don't want to talk about it.' " Kathryn paused and looked at him again. "How are you two doing?"

Peter turned and looked at her. "Fine."

She shook her head, and they sat in silence for several minutes. "Do you love her?"

Peter said nothing.

"I saw you dancing with the doc," he said lightly. "Looks like you're keeping your employees happy."

"That was his idea," she lied. "We had an argument, and I think he was trying to patch things up."

"An argument about what?"

This time Kathryn said nothing.

"I thought we were going to cooperate on this investigation of yours. How come I'm not invited to these 'work sessions'?"

"It's Nick. He likes to work alone."

"He didn't seem to want to work alone tonight."

Kathryn winced.

"So when am I going to hear something? After all the hours you two have spent together, you must have come up with something."

Kathryn hesitated. "Nick says he wants to wait until he's sure."

"C'mon, Kath, this is me. I know when I'm being stonewalled. I expect that kind of runaround from the doc, but not from you." He reached over and squeezed her arm.

Kathryn looked out the window again.

What's wrong with me? Why am I hesitating? Nick suspects everyone—he said it himself. Why am I allowing him to plant doubts in my mind about Peter, of all people?

"Peter, I need to ask you something."

"Go for it."

"Why didn't you tell me about Jimmy's cocaine habit?"

Peter sighed. "Put yourself in his place, Kath. Life isn't going the way you wanted. You got baggage from the past, you got a sister who belongs in the loony bin, you even got dumped by the girl you wanted to marry."

"Thanks."

"One day you find yourself in the middle of some nameless desert, about to fight the Mother of All Battles. They say you could get nuked or gassed or infected with who-knows-what. You could use a little confidence. I suppose that's how it started for Jim."

"But the war wasn't as bad as everyone thought it would be."

"That's right—so when it's over, you feel a little silly about the whole thing. Never again, you tell yourself. You'll just stop—nobody has to know—you'll beat this thing all by yourself. So you quit. But then you do it just one more time—in a moment of weakness, maybe on a bad day. So what? You beat it before, you can do it again. And you do—until the next time. You beat it for a couple of years, and you tell yourself it's over. Then you can only hold out for a few months. Pretty soon you can only go a week, but every time you tell yourself that you're in charge, you can handle it. Fact is, you can't handle it—but you're not about to admit it to anyone. You won't even admit it to yourself."

"I don't get it. I would have told someone. I would have asked for help."

"You're not Jim," he said. "Call it a guy thing."

"Then how did you find out?"

"From Andy. They were in the same unit, remember? Andy walked in on Jim one day. Caught him in the act. If he hadn't, believe me, Jim would never have told anyone."

"But why didn't you tell anyone else?"

"I did what Jim wanted me to do. I did what I would have wanted him to do for me."

"Couldn't you have at least told me?"

Peter glanced at her. "Think about it, Kath. He asks you to marry him. You say no—so he figures for some reason he doesn't quite measure up in your eyes. But maybe he can do better, maybe he can make you wish you had said yes—and then you hear that he's got this little drug problem? I couldn't do that to him. The thought of having a second chance with you is what kept him alive."

Kathryn smiled at him and took his hand. "You're always protecting someone, aren't you, Peter? Andy and Jimmy and now me. Most of all me."

"Just doin' my duty, ma'am." He smiled. "We aim to serve."

Kathryn hesitated. She felt foolish, she felt faithless asking her next question—but she had to ask. A promise is a promise.

"You didn't even want me to know," she said softly. "So why did you tell Ronny? Ronny told Denny—Denny, of all people. Now everybody knows."

Peter slowly shook his head. "You don't believe Jim killed himself. I do. All the evidence points that way, especially when you figure in the cocaine—but nobody knew about the cocaine. So along comes your Bug Man friend, and he starts to stir things up, starts people talking. Maybe Jim didn't kill himself, maybe it was murder, he says. He talks to Amy, he talks to Ronny and Denny and Wayne. He tells the coroner he didn't do his job—next thing you know, maybe I didn't do my job. I wanted to put an end to it— so I let people know the rest of the equation." He paused. "Maybe I shouldn't have."

"No, you shouldn't have—not until we find out the truth."

"The truth." Peter rolled his eyes. "Is that what you and the doc are finding? Admit it, Kath, all you've got is questions. You've got no answers."

Kathryn studied his face carefully and took a deep breath.

"Peter," she whispered. "Jimmy's body was moved."

She waited for his reaction . . . there was none. Not a word, not a questioning glance, not even the rapid blink of a startled eye. He sat rigid, staring straight ahead, as if the words had never been spoken. They had been spoken, and he had certainly heard them— but whatever Peter St. Clair thought of those words he was not about to reveal it.

"What do you mean moved?" he said slowly. "Moved how?"

"Do you know what 'fixed lividity' is? Do you know about that?"

Peter nodded, then glanced at her. "Do you?"

"I do now. Jimmy's right leg was different—not the way it was supposed to be. Nick says he died with his leg like this." She lifted her foot onto the seat and pulled it tight against her thigh. "But everyone agrees that when they found him, his leg was flat out again. That means that somebody moved him." She longed to add, "And that means somebody killed him"—but she remembered Nick's constant admonition to say only what you know.

Peter groaned. "That could be explained a hundred ways."

"For instance."

"Maybe the leg just stayed up on its own."

"It can't do that." She shook her head. "Try it yourself."

"Then maybe something held it up."

"What? Did you find anything? Everybody else says there wasn't anything around. If there was, somebody had to move it. Who would do that?"

Peter grew more impatient with each of Kathryn's questions. "Do you know about rigor mortis?" he said irritably. "Where the body stiffens up? Did the doc tell you about that too?"

Kathryn frowned. "I've heard of it."

"It usually takes a few hours to set in—but there's a thing called 'instant rigor mortis' too. It happens when the victim is exhausted just before death, and when the death is real sudden—like in a suicide," he said pointedly. "The whole body goes into an instant spasm—it locks up on the spot. I've seen it happen on the battlefield. A guy takes a bullet to the head and you have to pry his fingers off his rifle."

"That can't be it."

"Why not? Tell me."

"I don't know why. It just can't, that's all!"

Peter pulled the car into Kathryn's driveway, shifted into park, and turned off the ignition. They sat side by side in the silent shadows for an eternity. Kathryn performed the crucial task of wiping dust from the creases of the dashboard while Peter squeezed and relaxed his grip on the steering wheel in rhythm with his pulse.

Peter turned and reached into the backseat. "You'll want these," he said, handing Kathryn the crumpled cigar box. "Jimmy's things."

"Did you find anything?"

"Just what I thought I'd find," he said. "Just what you see there."

She opened the lid and removed a small bundle of paper. There was a torn and ragged birth certificate, a Social Security card, and a few outdated and irrelevant financial records. There was a yellowed clipping from the *Courier* proudly announcing that no less than three of Rayford's finest had enlisted together at Fort Bragg, and that the world was sure to be a safer place as a result. There were faded letters from Amy during the deployment in the Gulf. There were two letters from Kathryn as well—just two—and the sight of her own handwriting stabbed her through the heart. It seemed pathetic that a human life could be ultimately reduced to such a tiny collection of memorabilia.

She looked at Peter. "What are you thinking?"

"You don't want to know."

"Yes I do."

"I was wondering why you always seem to prefer the dead to the living."

Kathryn turned away.

"First it was Andy," he said. "I know you loved him—I mean, I know how hard it must have been to lose your husband."

"No you don't. You can't know."

"Maybe not. But I tried to help in every way I could think of. I was there for you every day—in person, in the flesh. I'm the soldier who came home," he said, "but you wanted the one who didn't. I knew it would take time for you to get over Andy—but I hoped that . . . over time . . ."

"We talked about this, Peter," she said awkwardly. "It was hard to let go—not knowing what happened to Andy. It's like he was never really gone. I never felt free."

"That was almost ten years ago, Kath. Aren't you free yet?"

She said nothing.

"Now it's Jimmy. Now you spend all your time trying to figure out what happened to him. I think I got sore about this investigation of yours because it started to look like Andy all over again! I was sorry about Andy—and now I'm sorry about Jim. But life goes on, Kath. They're dead—we're alive. It's time to stop living in the past and start looking ahead."

Kathryn tried to look at him but couldn't.

"It's true. I know it is. I couldn't let go of Andy—and now I can't let go of Jimmy either. I can't let go because they're all I ever had."

"You've still got me."

"I know, but . . . it's like that story in the Bible, remember? If you lose one sheep, you leave the other ninety-nine and go look for the one you lost."

"You don't leave the ninety-nine forever," he muttered. "Sooner or later you come back. Sometimes I think the only way to get any attention from you is to die."

"Don't say that! Not even joking."

They sat in silence again. Kathryn leaned back against the headrest and searched carefully for her next words.

"I know you won't believe this," she said, "but I do love you."

"Then why—"

"I don't know why—and I know it's not fair to you." She looked at him hopelessly. "Why don't you marry that nice Jenny McIntyre and start a family? She deserves you."

"And I deserve you. But that doesn't seem to matter."

A car rolled by behind them. The sweep of the headlights lit Peter's face for a few seconds, and Kathryn caught a glimpse of his gray-blue eyes. She had always thought that his eyes were the color of deep river ice or perhaps winter fog. To her amazement, she suddenly realized that Peter's eyes were very much like Nick's— both seemed somehow elusive and unapproachable; both seemed to hide behind a thick wall of glass. Somewhere behind that flat gray wall, a soul floated and darted but never really came to rest.

Peter spoke quietly now. "You say you love me. For me, it's more than that. Have you ever felt like you were made for someone? Like you were meant to be together? I don't know how to explain it, but that's how I feel—that's how I've always felt about you.

So far things have gotten in the way—but those have only been delays. It has to happen, Kath. I know that we're supposed to be together—now, always, forever."

They were the most endearing words Kathryn had ever heard. Once again she dredged the depths of her heart for some token of longing or passion for Peter. She found none. She had done the exercise a thousand times, and each time that she hauled the net to the surface she found only the scattered debris of gratitude or pity. She hated herself for her coldness, for her inability to respond to such a loving, loyal, and patient man. He was right—he deserved her love. He had earned it. She ought to love him. And yet . . .

Kathryn looked at Peter with tears in her eyes.

"Was it my fault?" she whispered.

"What?"

"Jimmy's death. Was Amy right? Did I send him over the edge? Did he kill himself because of me?"

"It wasn't you," he said. "It took more than that."

"How do you know?"

Peter smiled and took her hand. "He was disappointed over you. But if disappointment was enough to kill a man, I would have been dead a long time ago."

Kathryn put her face in her hands and began to weep, and Peter began to softly stroke her hair.

CHAPTER
20

L ay it over there on the grass, upside down." Nick turned from the hive and handed the lid to Kathryn, who took it with her thick, gloved hands.

Kathryn watched as Nick picked up a tin smoker and sent a single blue puff from the smoldering pine straw into the hive opening, then two more puffs across the open top. He lifted off the entire top super, a drawerlike unit laden with more than forty pounds of amber honey. Row after row of thin wooden frames projected down into it like air filters in a furnace. Each frame was spanned by a section of chicken wire, and the wire was almost obscured by thick golden comb in a quilt of hexagonal cells. On each frame hundreds of bustling bees raced about, darting into empty cells and out again.

"The bees don't look . . . angry," she said in wonder.

"Bees don't get angry—or jealous or cruel or spiteful. Those are qualities of your species, Mrs. Guilford, qualities you project on other species to justify your own irrational fears. They do share one quality with you, however. They will fight to protect their home, just as you would."

Nick followed Kathryn to the selected site and gently placed the super on top of the inverted lid, then returned to the hive and prepared to remove the second super. Kathryn studied this strange ritual in silence.

"You've barely said two words all morning," Nick said. "Something on your mind?"

"I'm mad at you," Kathryn said.

Nick peered deep inside the hive. "I think I've got varroa mites," he said. "That's bad."

"Don't you want to know why?"

"You expect me to ask? That's like volunteering to be shot. You'll tell me when you're ready."

"You called Peter to drive me home last night. You set me up."

"I arranged an interview for you. As I said, it's customary to call first."

"I thought you were concerned about me. I should have known better."

"I'm concerned about completing this investigation. I thought that was your concern too."

Kathryn said nothing.

Nick peered at her over the top of his glasses. "So . . . did you have a nice drive?"

The third super was about ten inches deep. Nick carefully hoisted it and lugged it to the growing stack of supers just a few yards away.

"I told him," Kathryn said. "I told Peter that the body was moved."

Nick said nothing for a few moments but continued about his work. "The point of an interview," he muttered, "is to gain information, not to give it away."

"He deserved to know. We said we would cooperate. Fair is fair."

"By all means let's be fair," Nick said under his breath. "So tell me, how did the sheriff react?"

"I told him about the leg and he said—"

"No—how did he react? What did he do in the first five seconds after you told him the body had been moved?"

"Nothing."

"Nothing at all? No exclamation, no look of surprise, no comment of any kind?"

"No. He just . . . sat there."

"Did he turn to look at you?"

"He just stared straight ahead. I don't see what difference it makes."

"I know you don't. Now tell me what he said about the leg."

"He told me about something called 'instant rigor mortis.' He said the body might have locked up instantly, and that might have frozen the leg in place."

"Very clever." Nick smiled. "It's actually called 'cadaveric response.' It happens because adenosine triphosphate disappears from the muscles. ATP is the compound that allows muscles to contract—without it, the muscles stiffen until decomposition accelerates about a day later. Rigor first appears in the jaw and neck and works its way toward the feet. That means it might take several hours to affect the right leg under normal conditions. But if there's been violent exertion just before death—as in the case of a struggle, for example—the ATP is already depleted and the muscles stiffen rapidly. In the case of sudden death, rigidity may occur instantaneously. That's a 'cadaveric response.' "

"Peter said that can happen in a suicide."

"It can—but it didn't happen to your friend."

"How do you know?"

"Because we have to account for the bent position of one leg, not two. Remember, the spasm is instantaneous. Was your friend standing or lying down at the time of death?"

"There's no way to tell."

"Then let's suppose he was standing. To stand, both legs have to be straight; to crouch, both legs must be bent—but you can't have one straight and one bent. For a cadaveric response to leave your friend's leg in the position we're looking for, he would first have had to somehow exhaust himself, then stand on one leg and raise the other one like a whooping crane—then put the gun to his head and pull the trigger. Very strange behavior, even for a manic depressive like Jimmy."

"What if he was lying down?"

"It's a similar situation. Your friend runs all the way to the woods, thus exhausting himself; then he lies down, raises one knee in an uncomfortable position, takes out his gun and fires. Do you believe that? Besides, if he was lying down we might have found some blood spatter on the grass around the exit wound. Teddy found none. I'm afraid the sheriff's theory doesn't hold up to scrutiny. The best explanation for the leg continues to be that the body was moved."

The look of relief was evident on Kathryn's face. Nick studied her closely.

"What else did the sheriff have to say? What about my question?"

Kathryn looked back at him awkwardly. "It's a little complicated . . ."

"Translation: I find it embarrassing to talk about. Look, Mrs. Guilford, can't we get past this 'it's too personal' thing? Repeat after me: 'Peter loves me. I don't love him. He won't give up. He wishes Jimmy and everyone else would get out of the way so he can have me all to himself. He wants this investigation to be over—so he purposely spread the word about Jimmy's drug addiction to put an end to the rumors and help seal the verdict of suicide.' "

"He wants the investigation to be over," she said, "because he thinks I'm obsessed with Jimmy's death."

"And he foolishly assumes that when Jimmy's death is behind you, your attention will turn to him."

Kathryn glared at him. "He answered your question. Now do you understand why he told Denny about the cocaine?"

"I understand that he wants the investigation to be over," Nick said. "And I understand the reason—the reason he gave you anyway. But there may be another reason he wants things wrapped up so quickly. That's a possibility we still have to explore." He leaned toward her. "That is, if you're willing."

Kathryn shook her head in exasperation. She looked at the shrinking hive, which now had only two deep supers remaining.

"What in the world are you doing?" she asked.

"I thought we'd do something very special today—and something even more special next time. Come over here."

Kathryn didn't like the sound of his invitation, but she also knew by now that it wasn't really an invitation anyway. Nick slid one of the frames from the exposed super and studied it closely, then carefully plucked a single wriggling insect from among the swirling masses. It was slightly thicker and darker in color, with eyes much larger than the rest.

"There are three kinds of honeybees in a hive," he said. "The vast majority are infertile females—workers. Their job is to build and maintain the comb and to care for the brood of young bees. They provide, they nurture, and they defend—they're the ones who can sting you. Then there's the queen, the only sexually productive female in the hive. Her only job is to lay eggs—one every twenty seconds, about fifteen hundred a day. But for those eggs to produce new workers, you need one of these." He held up the wriggling creature between his thumb and forefinger. "This is a drone—a male."

"Why doesn't it sting you?" Kathryn shuddered.

"Because it has no stinger. He's helpless—he has to be fed and cared for by the females."

"Just like in my species."

"In many ways bees are very much like your species—and in other ways they're different. The male's single goal in life is to mate with the queen. He has to compete with other males for the privilege, and he often dies in the act of mating."

"How are they different?"

Nick smiled. "There are only a couple hundred of them in the hive. The ladies will keep him around until autumn and then drive him away. There's nothing more useless than a tired old stud." He turned to Kathryn. "Hold out your hand."

Kathryn hesitated, then slowly extended her gloved left hand.

"Good," he said. "Now—take off the glove."

Kathryn began to pull away, but Nick quickly caught her hand in a firm handshake. He loosened his grip and began to pull—slowly, gently, all the time smiling and looking into Kathryn's eyes. The glove began to slip away. She stared wide-eyed at the growing patch of soft, pink flesh at the end of her sleeve.

"I . . . I can't . . ."

"You can," he said firmly. "This is just a little bit of yarn—a piece of carpet fuzz."

"With legs."

"With legs, yes, but no stinger. He can't hurt you. He likes you—after all, he's a male. He's thinking to himself, 'That's the most remarkable female I've ever seen! I'd sure like to mate with that!' Very much like the males in your species."

"Don't make me laugh!" she said nervously. "What do I do?"

"You do nothing. You just hold still."

Nick held her by the wrist and gently set the drone on the palm of her hand. It had six fragile, finely haired legs. The twin forelegs seemed to pat their way along as the tiny creature crept a few steps, fanned its wings, then moved on. She could see the individual mouthparts, the threadlike veining of the cellophane wings, and the bulbous compound eyes that protruded on either side. The striped abdomen waggled from side to side as it moved.

"It . . . tickles." Kathryn stared at the tiny life form in her hand and marveled at its complexity—but even more she marveled at the experience itself. She was actually holding an insect—and not just any insect, but the ancient demon from the pit of all her fears. For an instant she allowed her memory to slither back to that day in the Chevy long ago—then she looked again at the tiny bee in the palm of her hand. Her fingers trembled slightly, not from fear but from the rush of pure adrenaline. She felt exultant, she felt redeemed—for the first time since she could remember she felt free.

The drone lifted off from her hand and buzzed away, and Nick released her wrist. Kathryn continued to stare at her bare hand, astonished at its vulnerability and at her simultaneous absence of fear. A moment later the bee returned and landed once again on her open palm.

"I guess he does like me." She grinned broadly.

"By the way," Nick said, bracing himself to hoist the fourth super, "you might be interested to know that I did a little interview of my own last night."

"Who did you punch this time?"

"I was at the Glam-O-Rama Coin Laundry, and who do you suppose I happened to run across? Jenny McIntyre."

"That is a coincidence."

"I think she's in the market for a new relationship," Nick said, looking directly at Kathryn. "Things don't seem to be going well with her current boyfriend."

"Oh?"

"It's very odd. She says he seems distant, distracted—as if his mind is always someplace else. He takes her to public places, but doesn't care to spend time with her alone—as though he were only interested in the appearance of a relationship. And she said, 'He never touches me.' That's very strange with such an attractive woman, don't you think?"

"So you find her attractive?" Kathryn said casually. "Do you think you'll be seeing her again?"

"I doubt it. She already told me everything I need to know."

"And what did you need to know?"

"Why a man who loves you so single-mindedly would dabble in another relationship."

Nick waited, but Kathryn said nothing. She stood silently, arms folded, looking as indifferent as possible.

"Well?" he said. "Don't you want to know why?"

"You'll tell me when you're ready."

Nick smiled. "Have you ever seen a reduviid? It's commonly known as an assassin bug. It carries a long, curved beak underneath its abdomen like a sheathed sword. It stalks its victim with incredible patience. Sometimes it will run after its prey and then suddenly stop, almost as if it's lost interest. And that's what the victim thinks, too, until the assassin bug slowly raises that beak and—"

"I'm getting fed up with all these bug analogies," she broke in. "We're talking about my species, remember?"

"The sheriff is not interested in Jenny McIntyre," Nick said. "He's interested in you. Jenny knows it—and according to her, so does everybody else in town—except, apparently, you. My bet is that he was pressing in on you, and he sensed you were getting nervous—why is your business—so he decided to take the pressure off by acting disinterested. And what better way than by appearing to have another relationship?"

"That's what you believe," she said crossly.

"That's what you believe too—if you'll open your eyes."

"Why are you so suspicious of Peter?"

Nick shrugged. "He smells funny."

"He what?"

He turned and looked at her. "Did you know that a male lasiocampid moth can detect a female from more than two miles away? Two miles. Do you know how he does that? By smell, Mrs. Guilford. Insects navigate the world by smell. Only a few of the so-called 'higher life forms' are limited to sight and reason."

"So you have no real reason? This is nothing more than a hunch?"

Nick smiled at her. "Maybe we're not so different after all."

By now, the hive was reduced to a single super covered by a thin sheet of metal perforated with small holes.

"Are you having fun playing with your blocks?" she said. "One more and you'll have a brand-new hive over there."

"We're not moving this last one," he said, lifting away the sheet of metal. "We're looking for something."

"What?"

"Her royal highness, the queen."

Kathryn looked again at the tiny piece of fuzz that wandered harmlessly over her hand. "What does the queen look like?"

"She's huge," he said ominously. "Didn't you see *Alien*?"

"How do you know she's in there?"

"Because of this," he said, leaning the sheet of metal against the base of the hive. "This is a queen excluder. The small holes allow the workers to pass between the supers, but keep the larger queen below in the brood chamber. That restricts her egg laying to the lower level and reserves the top ones for honey. That makes it a lot easier for the keeper."

He removed the outermost frame and set it aside, then began to work his way toward the center, examining each frame carefully and moving it toward the outside.

"These are the brood frames. The comb is exactly the same, but instead of honey each cell contains a single egg. Take a look." He held one of the frames up for Kathryn. Some of the cells appeared empty, some contained a single plump, white larva, and still others were capped off with wax.

"This is the queen's domain. Her job is to wander over the comb looking for open cells. When she finds one she inserts her abdomen and deposits an egg. All we have to do is search these frames carefully, and . . . bingo."

There in the center of the frame was one bee that was clearly different. She was larger overall than the surrounding workers and her egg-producing abdomen was twice as long as any other.

"Watch her for a minute," he whispered. "She even moves differently."

The queen wandered quickly from cell to cell, searching determinedly for the empty nursery she would require in the next few seconds. Her wings, long unused, were folded back along the top of her thorax. Nick reached down and gently pinched her wings together, plucking her from the comb.

"Can she sting?" Kathryn shivered.

"As many times as she wants. Her stinger is straight, not barbed like the workers. But she only uses it to kill other queens. We can't have anyone usurping the throne, now, can we?"

Nick picked up a piece of screen wire rolled into the shape of a tube about the size of a roll of quarters. A wooden plug sealed each end, and in one plug was a hole no wider than a pencil. He started the queen into the hole headfirst. She seized the edges with her forelegs and willingly proceeded inside. Nick sealed the hole behind her with a rubber cork, then held the contraption and its prisoner aloft by a string attached to each end like a kind of living necklace.

"No thanks." Kathryn shook her head. "It's not exactly my style."

"It is a necklace," Nick said, "but it's not for you. It's for me."

He turned to a small cage about the size of a thick briefcase. It was framed in thin cypress, but the sides were covered with fine screen wire. In the top panel was a hole a baseball could just fit through.

"This is a bee crate. This is how bees are shipped—you can order them by mail, in case you're interested. Now, the first thing we do is put in the queen." He dangled the queen's wire cage into the bee crate until she hung suspended, halfway to the bottom, like an ousted ruler condemned to the gibbet. He secured the shoestring with a thumbtack, then inserted into the hole a large funnel rolled from galvanized sheet metal. From the stack of relocated supers he selected a frame thick with workers and held it above the funnel. With one well-practiced flip of the wrist he shook off a fist-sized clump of bees into the funnel and down into the throne room below.

"Will they just stay there?" Kathryn asked.

"They'll stay. That's where the queen is. The queen constantly emits a pheromone from her mandible. It's sort of like a powerful perfume that tells the workers, 'I'm the queen. You're safe here. This is where you belong.' For a honeybee, the hive is not home; the queen is home. Wherever the queen is, that's where they belong—and they'll follow her anywhere."

Nick continued to fill the bee crate with the inhabitants of a second frame, then a third, continuing on until several thousand honeybees huddled around the queen in her tiny cage and wandered over the wire sides of the box. Satisfied with the size of his collection, Nick removed the funnel and sealed off the hole with a simple wooden plug. Then he picked up a plastic spray bottle and began to wet the screened faces of the box with a clear, viscid liquid.

"Sugar syrup," he said. "Bees love any source of sugar. For the next day or so the bees will engorge themselves on it. It makes them fat and happy, and when they're fat and happy they forget about little things—like stinging you."

"I still don't get it. What exactly are we going to do?"

"We're going to make a bee beard, of course."

Bee beard. Kathryn remembered hearing the phrase only once

before, at the age of nine, when her mother took her to the state fair in Raleigh. She had accidentally wandered into a demonstration by the North Carolina Beekeepers Association where a man had purposely covered his face and neck with thousands of wriggling bees—and she had to be carried screaming from the pavilion.

"You're going to make a bee beard," she corrected him. "Look, Nick, I know what you're trying to do. And I appreciate it, really I do—"

"No, you don't."

"And I've already got the message: Insects are your friend. I believe you, okay?"

"No, you don't. Mrs. Guilford, you don't just have a fear of insects, you have a pathological fear of insects. The most effective form of therapy for that kind of phobia is immersion therapy."

"You want me to immerse myself in bees? You're out of your mind."

"No, I'm going to immerse myself in bees. I just want you to watch—and maybe help a little. It's a remarkable experience. It's a therapeutic experience."

Kathryn looked at him doubtfully. "How exactly does this bee beard work?"

"You've probably guessed most of it. We've removed the queen from the hive and placed her in a kind of collar. We've gathered two or three pounds of workers around her and we'll sedate them for a day or two on sugar water. The bees have been removed from the hive so they have no honey to protect or brood to defend. Their instincts will tell them to stick to the queen. So in a couple of days I'll pull out the queen and I'll tie the collar around my neck—and then all the bees come to Mama."

"And you won't get stung? Not at all?"

"Maybe once or twice, but only by accident. You have to be careful, of course."

She looked down again at the single bee that still clung tenaciously to her hand. She slowly rotated her wrist this way and that. Each time the bee simply crawled to the upper surface and remained.

"I think I've made a friend."

Nick reached out and gently took Kathryn by the wrist again.

"I wouldn't get too attached," he said. "You've been holding a female."

Before Kathryn could jerk her hand away Nick clamped a paralyzing grip on her arm.

"Or is it? Maybe it's a male, too, just like the first bee. Or maybe I was lying to you all the time—maybe there never was a male. Maybe they're impossible to tell apart. Or maybe this is the queen, and she can sting you as many times as she wants. Think about it, Mrs. Guilford. A moment ago you thought you had made a new friend, and now you feel that old bogeyman crawling up your spine again. What changed? Your enemy is not out here," he said, pointing to her hand. "It's in your head."

He gave her wrist a quick flip and the bee soared away, back to what remained of the hive.

Nick began to reassemble the hive from the nearby stack of supers, while Kathryn stood rubbing the white imprints of his fingers from her wrist. He picked up the lid and began to reposition it atop the hive. At the last moment the lid slipped from his fingers and dropped, crushing two workers lingering on the edge. The faint smell of smashed bananas floated up to Kathryn, triggering an ancient, haunting memory.

"We'd better wrap things up," Nick said. "That alarm pheromone will make them more aggressive, and I'm a wee bit underdressed for that party."

He collected the smoker, the funnel, and the other tools of their morning's work, then headed back toward the lab.

"Well?" Kathryn called after him. "Aren't you going to tell me what it was? Was it a drone or a worker? A male or a female?"

Nick stopped. "What do you think it was?"

"It doesn't matter what I think it was," she said irritably. "What was it?"

"On the contrary, Mrs. Guilford. It makes no difference what it was; it only matters what you perceived it to be."

Kathryn watched as he turned and walked away.

"Meet you at the car," he called back. "We've got a long drive ahead of us."

We need gas." Nick nodded toward his fuel gauge. He draped his left arm out the window in a halfhearted signal as Exit 83 approached.

"How can you tell?" Kathryn shouted above the hot afternoon wind that rumpled past the open windows. She pointed to the bottom of the fuel gauge where the red needle indicator had long ago fallen and lain to rest.

"It's an intuitive thing for me. You live with someone long enough, you get to know their needs."

"You two make a great couple."

He turned off I-95 just north of Richmond, Virginia, and steered the smoking Dodge into the Parham Road Texaco. Kathryn was glad for the break. They had been on the road for over three hours now, and she felt half-beaten by the combination of pummeling wind, stifling heat, and bone-jarring vibration. The thirty-five-year-old Dodge had no suspension left at all and handled each dip and pothole like a bowling ball on a stairway. The wind constantly whipped wisps of auburn hair across her face where it clung to her lipstick. She took a tissue from her purse and wiped her face clean, then pulled her hair back in a thick ponytail.

The car shuddered several times and lurched to a stop at the pump, followed by an angry complaint of hisses, clicks, and groans. Nick turned and looked at Kathryn.

"You expect me to pump the gas?" she asked.

"Of course not." He tossed aside his seat belt. "I expect you to pay. 'Plus expenses,' remember?"

Kathryn enthusiastically slammed the door and flashed a look of mock remorse back at Nick before heading toward the service center. She set a Mountain Dew and a convenience pack of Extra-Strength Tylenol on the counter.

"Pump six," she muttered to the cashier, who glanced out the window and slid a quart of 10W-40 and a paper funnel across the counter.

"It's on the house," he said with a note of genuine sympathy in his voice.

"How far to D.C.?" she asked, tearing through the foil of her Tylenol.

"An hour and a half—that's just to the Beltway. Where you headed?"

"Walter Reed Hospital." She rolled the capsules to the back of her tongue. "On the north side—almost to Maryland."

"Then add forty-five minutes. Double if you hit the traffic."

As they pulled back onto I-95 North, Kathryn slid a yellow foil-wrapped sausage biscuit across the seat to Nick. He peeled back the foil with his teeth and took a bite.

"What's this?"

"Plus expenses. Eat hearty."

Nick reached down by his feet and took a chocolate chip cookie from a plastic bag. "They're from Teddy," he said through a mouthful. "He made them for you."

"How am I enjoying them?"

The Dodge slowly accelerated to cruising speed like a jet approaching the sound barrier. It vibrated and shook until Kathryn was sure the frame would come apart beneath her—but then it somehow settled into a relatively smooth and even ride.

"She just has to hit her stride," Nick said, and Kathryn wondered silently why unreliable equipment is always referred to in the female gender.

They had passed most of the journey in silence, neither one wanting to expend the energy to shout above the constant roar of the wind, but by this point the ennui was becoming more stifling than the heat. Kathryn stopped rubbing her temples and glanced up at Nick.

"We could have taken my car, you know. It has this new thing called 'air conditioning.'"

"I thought my car would fit the image better."

"What image?"

"The image of a down-and-out Desert Storm veteran and his poor wife, their lives plagued by his lingering Gulf War Syndrome—mysterious rashes, fibromyalgic symptoms, chronic fatigue, and memory loss."

"How long have we been married?"

"You're asking me? I'm the one with memory loss."

Kathryn smiled in spite of herself. "And why is this little charade necessary?"

"I've been doing a little research. It seems Walter Reed Army Medical Center is the premier treatment unit for Gulf War Syndrome in the entire U.S. Several years ago they opened a Specialized Care Program for Gulf veterans and their families. It's a three-week outpatient program. According to Amy, her brother took part a couple of times."

"What are we looking for?"

"Our interview with Amy raised some interesting questions. Who was the last one to see Jim McAllister alive? Amy didn't know—no one in Rayford seems to know. It may have been someone up at Walter Reed."

"Is there some prize for being last in line?"

"The last one to see your friend alive may be able to give us some insight into his state of mind just before the time of death. Was he angry again? Did he seem out of control? Did he say where he was going or what he planned to do? Did he appear in any way suicidal?"

Kathryn felt a knot tightening in her stomach. "I don't like all this pretending. Can't we just request Jimmy's medical records or something?"

"Sure, if you're the next of kin. I suppose you could tell them you almost married him . . ."

Kathryn shot him a look. "I just don't want this to turn into another Schroeder's Funeral Home. All right? Okay?"

Nick smiled. "Did you bring the things I asked for?"

"I packed an overnight bag, if that's what you mean."

He paused. "Does the sheriff know we're making this trip together?"

"Yes. Why?"

"Does he know we're staying overnight?"

She narrowed her eyes to tiny slits. "Why shouldn't he know?"

"Good," he whistled. "Good, good, good."

Kathryn turned to the backseat. "I brought you this." She held up a faded gray T-shirt with the words "82d AIRBORNE" in black block letters across the top with Master Parachutist's wings beneath. "It's the only thing of Andy's that I thought would fit you."

"It might be a little tight in the chest."

"You wish."

"What else have you got for me?"

Kathryn hesitated.

"Come on, Mrs. Guilford, let's see them."

She turned slowly to the backseat once more and removed an accordion letter file with a brown shoestring wrapped around it. She opened it and carefully removed a small stack of well-worn envelopes, each bearing her name and address in a coarse handwritten script. Some bore large and foreign-looking stamps; some had no stamps, but several different postmarks; some were so badly worn that the pages within poked through the crumbling corners of the envelope.

"There aren't many of them," she said. "Not as many as I would have liked—not many at all before September of '90, when the postmaster announced that the soldiers could send letters home for free. Andy said he'd go to mail a letter but the whole book of stamps would stick together because of the heat. The truth is, he wasn't much of a writer."

She flipped through the crumbling papers like a rabbi handling the Torah. She turned to Nick.

"I'm not sure I want you to touch them."

"I don't want to touch them. I want you to read them to me."

Kathryn looked aghast. The words of these few letters were more than personal; they were sacred. Was she supposed to casually recite each one as though it were nothing more than an interesting tidbit from this morning's *Holcum County Courier*? And how was she supposed to read them? Should she simply relay each word, or should she make a real performance out of it—should she put some feeling into it? The worst part was that she knew this Bug Man was oblivious to all of these concerns. To him these sacred writings were nothing more than miscellaneous bits of evidence—perhaps insignificant bits of evidence—to be tagged and filed away for possible use. Her blood ran cold at the very idea. She felt incensed; she felt insulted; she felt violated.

Nick interrupted her thoughts.

"Mrs. Guilford, we're trying to understand the cause of your friend's depression. Your husband and Jim McAllister were in the same unit—that means they camped together, they ate together, they probably fought together. Jim's depression may have been triggered by a specific event in the Gulf, and that event may have taken place before your husband was killed. If so, his letters may provide some clue as to what it was. I'm sure you've read them a hundred times; maybe there's something you overlooked."

"Maybe what killed Jimmy was my husband's death," she snapped. "Did you ever think of that?"

"I doubt it."

"Why?"

"Because you survived it, and no one felt his loss more than you."

It was a minor acknowledgment of her feelings, no more than a nod in her direction, but Kathryn appreciated it nonetheless.

Nick began to slowly shake his head. "There had to be something else—something more. Mr. McAllister felt that there was something wrong that needed to be made right. Maybe your husband knew what it was."

Kathryn slowly picked up the first of the precious envelopes and carefully removed the letter within. With the first glimpse of her husband's handwriting a wave of grief overtook her. These were more than words, they were strokes made by Andy's hand—a hand that no longer existed anywhere in the universe. The script was rough and uneven, and the left margin of his letters was never straight. He dotted every "i" with a tiny circle because Walt Disney did, and he liked that. Whenever her name appeared—always as "Kath," never "Kathryn"—it began with a printed "K" simply because he had never mastered the cursive letterform. Every jot and loop and curve reminded Kathryn of the man. It was almost like hearing his voice again, and she longed to weep. Instead she felt sick to her stomach.

She turned to Nick. "Roll your window up," she said. "I'm not going to shout this."

He took one look at her and complied without question. She began to read clearly and evenly.

August 8, 1990

Dear Kath,

Well, by now you know it wasn't just another alert. Got to the base just before midnight—it was pouring rain. Most of the boys were betting that this was just another emergency deployment exercise and after a day in the woods we'd be back home. Then a Red Line came down from brigade HQ and we found out the whole 82d was called out! That's when I knew it had to be the Middle East.

Spent the night at the Corps Marshalling Area. Slept on the concrete floor—sure wished I was back in bed with you. Most of the unit made it for lock-in but I bet they had to search all the bars in Fayetteville to round up some of the boys. Pete and Jim both made it in, but I was in first. The 2d Battalion split off and that's the last we saw of Pete.

The next day was just squat and hold. Tried to find out what we could about the mission, but nobody knew much of anything except that we're headed for someplace called DARAN (can't spell it) and we're not jumping in. Then we got the word that the 2d Brigade would be first to deploy and Jim and me were on the first chalk out. We were slotted to leave on a DC-10 but we drew a C-141 instead. It was crowded—forty boys, two Hummers, and a M-105 trailer. We had wheels-up less than fourteen hours from call-in—good thing we were the DRB. Stopped to refuel in Goose Bay, Canada, then again here at Torrejon AFB in Spain. I'm mailing this from the USO post. Free mail!

Can't tell you much about the mission except nobody thinks we'll be here long. Sorry I didn't get to say a proper good-bye—you were sleeping sound and I didn't want to wake you. Wish you hadn't been too tired when we went to bed! NOW how long do I have to wait? When I get home let's set the day aside and—

Kathryn looked away. She folded the letter and gently returned it to its envelope.

"I followed most of that," Nick said. "What's the 'DRB'?"

"The Division Ready Brigade. The 82d Airborne is the army's rapid-reaction force, and they have to be ready to deploy anywhere in the world in just a few hours' time. The division is made up of three infantry brigades. They take turns being the DRB, each one for six to eight weeks at a time. It's like a doctor on call. When you're the DRB, you're on two-hour recall and you have to be ready to have wheels up on the lead aircraft within eighteen hours of call-in. Andy and Pete and Jimmy were all in the 2d Brigade, and they were the DRB when the call came in."

"They were all in the same unit?"

"Not exactly. You were never in the army, were you? A brigade is broken up into battalions. Andy and Jimmy were in the 4th Battalion, Peter was in the 2d. The 4th Battalion was designated DRF-1—Division Ready Force 1—that's why Andy and Jimmy were the first ones out."

"Two-hour recall—that's pretty short notice."

"Andy left so fast he took the car keys with him. I couldn't drive because the keys were in Saudi Arabia." Kathryn stared out the window. "I never even woke up," she whispered. "Maybe that's why I never sleep now."

Without looking down she opened the second envelope.

"The next one's dated two weeks later."

August 24, 1990

Dear Kath,

We made it into Dhahran. Me and Jim marched out the back of the Starlifter in full combat gear and camo paint ready to go to war. It was the middle of the night and there was nobody around anywhere. We felt like idiots! Some buses met us on the tarmac and took us to our command post out in the middle of nowhere, an old Saudi air-defense base near a place called al-Jubayl.

Got your first letter last week along with three more. Jim was jealous as a jay—write more! Took a while for the mail to catch up with us here. Thanks for the picture but guess what? The Saudis

*blackened out your arms and legs. Seems that's pornography
around these parts, young lady! I'll have to fill in the rest from
memory. Thanks for the* County Courier. *It's a few days old,
but the papers are our only source of news around here. Send a*
Fayetteville Times *if you can.*

*You wouldn't believe how hot it is here! We picked a great
time to fight with Iraq. Yesterday we deployed into the desert for
the first time, mostly to start getting used to the heat. By 0800 it
was 95 degrees—it can hit 130 in the afternoon. We started NBC
training—nuclear, biological, and chemical—and we're learning to
spot Iraqi land mines.*

*Most of all we're learning how to see. Sounds crazy, doesn't
it? In the desert, distances are really tough to judge. That's risky
when you're trying to call in fire. Sometimes the rocks heat up and
they look like enemy patrols through our thermal sights. We got a
lot to learn fast—the 82d's last deployment was in the jungle in
Panama!*

*Nobody knows when the enemy might come. We keep hearing
about terrorist threats but we haven't seen a single wog since
we've been in country—but they tell us there are 250,000 of them
just a hundred miles north! We have to wear our helmets and
carry our weapons and masks at all times, even at mess. Got to be
ready when the balloon goes up.*

*You'd love it here, Kath. They've got the biggest black flies you
ever seen! The joke around here is that this is where the army's
helicopters are born—the flies are really baby Chinooks. They love
our food so we have to eat fast. Had our first scorpion casualty too.
Your kind of place—wish you were here.*

*Word is we might redeploy soon. Rumors everywhere—none
of them reliable. I'll write when I can. Jim says hello.*

Miss me?
Andy

"I know those flies," Nick whistled. "They're tabanids—
probably Tabanus arabicus. Very large, very nasty."

"Is that all you're getting out of this? Observations about the
local insects?"

"Not at all," he said calmly. "So far we have a lonely soldier eight thousand miles from home, uprooted on a no-notice call-out, adjusting to a strange and hostile desert environment, and living under the constant threat of enemy attack."

"Two lonely soldiers," Kathryn corrected.

"But only one with a loving wife waiting for him back home."

The traffic began to slow and came almost to a standstill where the HOV lanes had been closed after the morning rush. With the windows rolled up and the breeze no longer forcing its way through the vents, the car became more and more unbearable.

Kathryn resisted the urge to wipe a bead of sweat rolling down her forehead.

"The next letter didn't come for over a month."

October 15, 1990

Dear Kath,

Sorry it's taken so long to write—you know me. The first of the month we redeployed to a place called Ab Qaiq. It's the home of a huge ARAMCO oil complex and we're here to protect the pumping station from attack—a ton of Arab oil flows through here to the Gulf.

It's about a hundred miles farther away from the enemy—bet you're glad to hear that, but I can't say I am. We were the first troops into Saudi Arabia and now it seems like we're being told to move over and let the heavy forces do their stuff. I didn't come here to squat and hold, Kath. I want a front-row seat when the show gets started. It looks like we could be at Ab Qaiq for a long time and nobody likes it.

The 4-325 is in an area called Camp Gold, nothing but a huge piece of desert surrounded by concertina wire. We've built a tent city there—it's really something to see. Pretty rough—no lights, no mess facility, no wash basins, no laundry. We shower together outside—no stalls. It's okay now but they say it gets cold in December! There's no privacy at all. We each have a small corner we call our own and everybody's starting to stockpile stuff sent from home. We stash it in our MRE boxes we keep under our cots. *That's my whole world right now—one cot and the stash underneath.*

Caught a glimpse of Pete yesterday. 2d Battalion is in Camp White, an old warehouse across the way behind the motor pool. I waved but I don't think he saw me.

Three weeks ago we lost our first man—a truck overturned on a paratrooper from the 505. Somebody wasn't paying attention. Last week some grunt gave himself the "million dollar wound"— shot himself in the foot just to get back to the States. The waiting and the crowding are starting to wear on all of us. I think the cracks are starting to show. I'm handling it okay but I think it's driving Jim nuts. You know he likes to get alone sometimes, and there is no alone here—not anywhere. No alcohol either—that was one of the Saudi's rules. I'd give a week's pay to be able to take Jim out for a couple of brews. He looks like he could use it.

Write to him, Kath. The mail comes in every day on two or three forty-foot tractor trailers. Some of the guys get piles of letters and all Jim gets is some hen scratchings from that sister of his begging him not to get killed. He's taken to reading the unopened "To Any Soldier" mail—stuff from some grade-school class from who-knows-where. I think it's getting him down. I used to show him all the great stuff you send, but not anymore—it just makes him angry. Write to him.

I miss you.
Andy

"So did you?" Nick asked.

"Did I what?"

"Write to him."

Kathryn shifted uneasily.

"Why not?"

"I did a couple of times, but I didn't want to give him—you know—the wrong idea. So I kept writing, 'Andy and I this,' and 'Andy and I that.' But Andy said it only seemed to make things worse, so I just stopped."

They sat in silence for a few minutes before Kathryn reached for the next letter.

"So we know that Jimmy's getting discouraged," she said.

"Yes," Nick said under his breath, "and we know that he's getting angry."

"The next letter wasn't until January. Andy called home at Christmas—both MCI and AT&T offered free three-minute phone calls to all the troops. It was wonderful to hear from him, except that an NCO was listening in the whole time to make sure we didn't pass along anything confidential. I got a video from Andy too—every soldier got a free videotape and the chance to record a fifteen-minute message for the folks back home."

"Did you bring it along?"

"Of course not."

"Too bad. I guess it's ESPN tonight."

There was a long pause that followed.

"I got a video from Peter too. I suppose you'd love to see that one."

Another pause.

"It was nothing." She shrugged. "Really. It was just about where he'd been and what he'd done and how he hoped he'd be home soon—that sort of thing."

"What could be more harmless than that?" Nick intoned.

"Exactly."

"So why did it make you feel uncomfortable?"

"Who said it made me feel uncomfortable?"

Nick slowly turned and looked at her.

At last they began to move again, slowly and relentlessly gathering speed as they approached the Capital Beltway. The traffic didn't open up, it simply began to accelerate together in one vast, irresistible herd. Kathryn had visited Washington several times, and she always felt as she approached the city that there was a kind of suction, a vortex that seemed to draw her toward some mysterious end of its own.

January 25, 1991

Dear Kath,

 I know you've been following the news so you know where things are going. Some UN bigwig went to Baghdad on the fourteenth to try to get Iraq to pull out by the deadline the next day—no luck. Iraq's got the fourth largest army in the world and they're itching to try it out. For our part, the 82d is happy to oblige them.

Now the air war has started and that means more waiting—but at least we got our marching orders. The entire brigade has moved into attack position. I can't say where, and you won't hear about it on the news, but I'll tell you this—I can see the border from here. At night I can hear the bombers pass overhead and when the strike zone is close enough I can hear the bombs. On the way back home they dump their excess ordnance in the desert not far from here, and I can feel the ground rumble. The Iraqis fired their first SCUD at us but a Patriot brought it down. We started taking our PB pills every eight hours—they're supposed to stop anthrax and nerve gas, but nobody knows for sure. They make some of the boys sick.

Two soldiers from the 3rd ACR were wounded yesterday in a firefight across the border. The Iraqis are only six miles away. They know we're here and they can reach us with artillery if they want to. The pressure's building. Everybody knows we're going in but nobody knows when. Not much time to talk to Jim—everybody's busy digging in.

I plan to write again before G-Day. The mail caught up with us here so you can still write to me.

Andy

They took the exit for 495 North to Rockville, Maryland, where I-95 dumps into the Capital Beltway in a violent confluence of horns, engines, radios, and tires. Hulking gray rigs and flatbeds lumbered along belching puffs of smoke, while Porsches and BMWs honked and darted between them like angry mosquitoes. They all pushed, shoved, and jammed their way toward their destinations, some chatting on phones or dabbing at makeup as casually as if they were still parked at home.

The next envelope was a medium-sized manila padded mailer. Kathryn squeezed it open and peered deep within, as if she were searching for a bucket in the bottom of a well. She reached in with two fingers and removed a folded letter on ordinary notebook paper, then carefully tipped the mailer over. A golden band rolled out into her left hand.

She sat silently staring at the ring for several minutes. The folded letter still lay on her lap.

"May I?" Nick said gently.

She barely nodded.

He propped the letter against the steering wheel and began to read.

February 17, 1991

Dear Kath,

I can write this now because by the time you get it everyone will know anyway. A few days from now the ground war begins. G-Day.

The 82d has been attached to the French 6th Light Armor Division. We'll be under their command when the battle begins. Our job is to do what the Airborne always does—push in fast and deep, secure a foothold, and clear the way for the heavy forces behind us. Our objective is to seize Al Salman Airbase about 90 miles north of here. At Al Salman we'll go up against the Iraqi 45th Division—three infantry brigades and two artillery battalions. They got a tank battalion, too, if there's anything left of it. They're not the Republican Guard, but they're no pushovers.

The French will lead the way in AMX-10RCs—small, fast six-wheeled tanks with 105mm guns. Our boys will follow in five-ton trucks, stopping to clear enemy positions along the way. We'll wear our NBC suits—they're awkward, but nobody knows what to expect from the Iraqis. At Al Salman the real party begins.

The 4-325 was the first to deploy, the first in country, and now we have the honor of being the first into Iraq. I tell you the truth, Kath, I can't wait. I'm sick and tired of being a target—I want to do what I came to do—what I joined the Airborne to do. Try not to worry—I won't do anything stupid—but they don't give battlefield promotions to the ones who sit on their hands. I plan to do the deed. I'll make you proud.

*I'm enclosing a little something for you. What with the heat
and sweat and all I was afraid I might lose it in the desert. It might
be a good idea if you hung on to it for me. Don't worry, I'll tell all
the Iraqi girls I'm married.*

*Went over to the 2-325 to see Pete today. Wanted to wish him
luck—and I needed to talk to him about Jim. We had a big blowup
the other day—can't tell you about it now. I guess everybody's
been a little nuts lately. All I can say is, he better straighten
himself out fast. We sure need to be on the same team in a few
days.*

*I'm not going to say good-bye—by the time you read this it
will all be over and I'll be writing you another letter. But I want
you to know how much I—*

"Don't," Kathryn snatched the letter back again. "Don't read
that part."

He looked down at her hand. "That's the ring?"

"A lot of the boys mailed them home. The wives all panicked,
of course. The Family Support Group at Fort Bragg had to call
us in and assure us that this was perfectly normal and that we'd
all be slipping them back on our husbands' fingers in no time
at all."

She held up the ring and slowly examined it. "I've still got
mine."

Nick let several minutes go by before he spoke again. "Andy
said he had a 'big blowup with Jim'—something he didn't want to
talk about."

"Something he didn't want to write about. Until the ground
war began, all the letters home were read by censors."

"So you think that's when your husband discovered Jim's drug
habit?"

She nodded. "He wouldn't take a chance on putting that in
print."

"So—what happened on G-Day?"

Kathryn removed the last envelope, the only official-looking
document among them. The letterhead bore the address of the
United States General Accounting Office.

B-260898
April 7, 1995

The Honorable Jesse Helms
United States Senate
Dear Senator Helms:

In response to your request, this report presents the results of the GAO's investigation of events leading to the apparent death of PFC Andrew Guilford of the 82d Airborne Division; and an assessment of the adequacy of U.S. Army investigations following the incident.

On the night of February 26, 1991, PFC Guilford's unit, under OPCON of the French 6th LAD, encountered heavy resistance at the Al Salman Airbase. In pursuit of the enemy PFC Guilford became separated from his unit in a position exposed to both friendly and hostile fire. Hostilities ceased near daybreak, at which time a search was immediately conducted for PFC Guilford. Despite considerable effort, no identifiable trace of his body or equipment was discovered.

Two soldiers of the 6th LAD were killed in the same hostilities, and ten were wounded. It is assumed that PFC Guilford was the victim of indirect fire of either friendly or hostile origin. Within hours the 82d Airborne began an AR 15-6 fratricide investigation of the incident. No disciplinary action was recommended.

Supplemental investigations yielded no further evidence; all available diplomatic channels with the Iraqis were exhausted. The Forces Command Staff Judge Advocate recommended that PFC Guilford be officially listed as Killed in Action, Body Not Recovered. He was posthumously awarded the Bronze Star for his actions.

GAO has briefed U.S. Army representatives and the deceased serviceman's immediate family on the content of this investigation.

Yours,
Richard C. Stiener
Director

Kathryn carefully returned the file of letters to the backseat, then rolled her window down again. She leaned her head back on the seat and let the wind engulf her, washing away the stinging words and the broken promises and the haunting memories—lifting her out of the past and setting her gently back in her own world again.

"What about Jim?" Nick said. "Did he have anything to add to the official account?"

"Jimmy said nothing. He could never bring himself to talk about Andy. I think it hurt him almost as much as it hurt me."

She looked at Nick, who sat motionless behind the wheel. She knew by now that even when his body was at rest, his mind was in constant motion. "I'll probably hate myself for asking this, but . . . what are you thinking?"

"Nothing you haven't thought of before."

"What does that mean?"

Nick glanced over at her. "Jim McAllister asked you to marry him. You not only turned him down but accepted another man's proposal the same night. Think about it, Mrs. Guilford. How does that make a man feel?"

"I don't know," she mumbled. "Hurt, I suppose."

"No. How does that make a man feel?"

She said nothing.

"Come on. You know the answer to this one."

"Angry," she said slowly. "It makes him feel angry."

"Angry at whom?"

"At me, of course."

"Wrong. He loved you."

Kathryn looked at him. "Where are you going with this?"

"You spurned Jim McAllister for another man, Mrs. Guilford. What do you suppose Jimmy told himself—that you didn't love him or that you loved another man more? Jim McAllister had every reason to resent your husband, even hate him. He had everything to gain if your husband was removed from the picture."

"That's ridiculous."

"Is it? Who was the last one to see your husband alive, Mrs. Guilford? Odds are it was someone on the battlefield—someone in his unit. Why is it that Jim McAllister could never bring himself to talk about what happened in the Gulf? Sounds like a man wrestling with his conscience to me."

"Stop it!" she shouted. "You didn't know Jimmy or Andy, and you have no idea what they felt or what they might have done! You have no right to accuse Jimmy this way! I am not hiring you to investigate the death of my husband!"

They drove on in silence. It was several minutes before Nick glanced over at her again.

"Like I said," he whispered. "It's nothing you haven't thought of before."

CHAPTER 22

What can we do for you, Mr . . . ?"

"Call me Nick. And this is my wife, Darlene."

Kathryn glared at Nick as hard as she dared, then turned and smiled at the man and woman before them.

"Nick, Darlene—welcome to the Specialized Care Program."

Kathryn sat beside Nick in a comfortable reception room on Ward 64 of the Main Hospital at Walter Reed Army Medical Center. The man across the desk from her was the program administrator, a pleasant-looking man in his midfifties, himself a veteran of over thirty years in the infantry who traded in his uniform for a pair of comfortable khakis and a navy button-down. The trim woman who leaned against the desk to his right was the social worker, who said she always sat in on the initial interviews.

"Exactly what kind of information are you looking for?" the man asked, folding his hands before him.

"I heard about this program from a friend, another Gulf War vet. He came here a couple of times, and he said it did him a world of good. He said I should check into it myself, so here we are."

"You really should have made an appointment, Nick. To tell you the truth, I shouldn't be talking to you at all, but the receptionist said you were very . . . persistent."

"I appreciate that, I really do," Nick nodded. "It was a last-minute thing—call it a whim. The little woman dragged me up here to see the Gowns of the First Ladies exhibit over at the American History Museum, so I said what the hey! It's just a stone's throw to Walter Reed. Might as well drop by."

He smiled at Kathryn and put his hand on her knee. She smiled back, lifted his hand, and put it in hers while the social worker watched.

"I need to ask you for a last name, Nick, and what branch of the service you were in. We need to verify that you are in fact a Gulf War veteran. Just a formality."

"Well now, that's the thing," Nick said uneasily. "I'd rather not say. Not just yet."

"Why not?"

"It's my job. I've been calling in sick a lot at the factory, and people are starting to wonder. I get these joint pains and headaches, and I'm tired all the time. And I have trouble remembering things. If word gets back to them that I have some kind of 'syndrome' or something, it could be bad for me."

"Nick—your employer cannot legally discriminate against you just because you have Gulf War Syndrome."

"Not legally—but you and I know it happens in other ways. They forget to ask you if you want overtime, you get passed over for a promotion, whatever. There's always some other explanation, but you know why."

The social worker stepped in. "Nick, you mentioned pain and fatigue and memory loss. Are there any other symptoms?" She glanced at Kathryn. "What about your relationship with Darlene?"

Nick looked forlorn. "I don't mind telling you it's not what it used to be. I mean, Darlene used to be a regular ball of fire . . . you know. But lately—"

"We don't like to talk about it," Kathryn cut in abruptly. "It's very personal."

"But we need to talk about it, Darlene," Nick implored. "If we can't talk to these nice people, who can we talk to?"

Kathryn glowered at him hard, since it was appropriate to the part she played, hoping that her deeper meaning would come through. But it was obvious that Nick was enjoying his little game and that he was not about to give it up for something as insignificant as her dignity.

"Perhaps some general information about the program would be helpful," the administrator offered, sliding an information packet across the desk. "The Specialized Care Program serves Gulf War veterans of all branches of the military. It's a three-week outpatient program that runs continuously throughout the year. At any given time there are from seven to ten personnel joining us—spouses are welcome too." He smiled at Kathryn.

"On the first day we take the group on a tour of the hospital. After that they're introduced to the program staff. Each patient works closely with an internist and our staff psychologist. The rest of the team includes myself, Mrs. Andino here, a physiatrist, an occupational therapist, a physical therapist, a fitness trainer, a wellness coordinator, and a nutritionist. We meet Monday through Friday, 7:30 to 4:30."

"How long has your psychologist been here?" Kathryn asked.

"Ten or eleven years. I assure you, Darlene, he's very experienced."

"I'm sure all conversations with your psychologist are confidential," Nick said with emphasis, glancing over at Kathryn.

"Absolutely. All of our clinical records are confidential. You need have no fears about that."

"Tell me more about the group," Nick said. "I imagine they get to know each other pretty well after three weeks together."

"They become very close," the social worker said warmly. "They spend a lot of time discussing their experiences in the Gulf, the impact of their symptoms, areas of personal struggle—what we call 'life stressors.' "

"Do you find that some of them stay in touch after the program has ended?"

"Some of them become lifelong friends."

Nick nodded thoughtfully. "What if three weeks doesn't do it? Can I come back?"

"As many times as you like," the administrator said. "We teach vets how to manage a chronic illness. Some of them have returned several times over the years."

"Do groups ever return—together, I mean?"

"We've never had a whole group return. But we sometimes find that two or three group members become so close that they agree to return together from time to time to sort of renew their friendship."

Nick leaned forward. "That friend," he said quietly, "the one who told me I should check you out? The last time he came here he met some other fellows—well, they really hit it off. He never stopped talking about them, and the more he talked the more I realized those are just the kind of guys I'd like to get together with."

"I'm sure you'll have just as much luck with the group you're assigned to, Nick." The social worker smiled reassuringly.

"I don't put much faith in luck," Nick said. "What I want to know is, can I meet with those fellows? Can you put me in touch with any of them so I can see if they'd like to meet together?"

The administrator shook his head. "Can't do that, Nick. It's a privacy issue—you understand. I can't reveal the names of any past members of our program. I'm sure you can appreciate that."

"Suppose I gave you my number and you passed it on to the fellows in that group. All you'd have to do is say, 'If you're interested, give Nick a call.' "

"Sorry, Nick. The groups are formed randomly, and we facilitate no outside meetings between group members. That's our policy."

Kathryn squeezed Nick's hand hard. She knew they had reached a dead end; if Nick pushed any harder it would only generate suspicion.

"You said the day ends at 4:30. What do people do in the evenings?"

"Whatever they wish. Some of them take the Metro downtown and see the Capitol. Most of them just hang around the Mologne House and talk further."

"The Mologne House?"

"We have a wonderful hotel right here on the base," the social worker beamed. "The Mologne House is open to all military personnel, active and retired, and to their extended family as well."

"That's where all the group members stay?"

"Unless they live close enough to commute from home. If you'd like to check it out, it's just a five-minute walk from here—just past the Institute of Research on Fourteenth Street."

"We don't have accommodations for tonight yet—any chance of us getting a room there?"

"I can call over for you and find out," the administrator said. He reached for the phone while the social worker turned to Kathryn.

"Our couples often use the evening hours to work on their relationships." She winked, and Kathryn managed a faint smile in return. "Do you two have children?"

Kathryn shook her head, "No," while Nick nodded, "Yes."

There was a pause.

"None at home," Nick explained. "Military school."

"Then you should have an uninterrupted evening." The social worker winked again. "Trust me, Darlene—that can make a world of difference."

"I'm not sure we're ready for that," Kathryn said. "I'm not sure Nick is ready—if you know what I mean." Two can play at this game.

The administrator interrupted. "They have one room left with a queen-sized bed."

"No!" Kathryn shouted.

There was an awkward silence from all parties. Nick turned to Kathryn and took both her hands.

"You know how I feel about you, Darlene—and I know how you feel about me. If we just had this one night—at the Mologne House—I think it could make a big difference for us. A big difference . . ."

Kathryn flashed her most compassionate smile and dug her fingernails into the back of Nick's hand.

"We'll take it," she smiled to the administrator.

"They want to know how you'll be paying."

"She'll be paying in cash," Nick said.

CHAPTER 23

The Mologne House was a four-story structure of the same Georgian brick and stone that comprised all the original buildings at Walter Reed. Off the main lobby was a restaurant—the Rose Room—and there Nick and Kathryn sat at a table in the exact center of the room.

"I could move you to a nice booth," the waitress offered, "if this is a little too public for you."

"This is perfect," Nick replied. "Do you have any kind of buffet? Something where you have to get up and get your own food?"

"Don't you army boys ever get tired of the chow line?"

"What makes you think I'm an army boy?"

The waitress rolled her eyes and pointed her pencil at his gray 82d Airborne T-shirt.

"Oh yeah," he said. "Forgot I had that on."

Kathryn ordered a dinner salad, and the waitress left them alone. A handful of other couples filled most of the booths while servicemen in twos and threes dotted the rest of the room.

"Did you have fun back there?" Kathryn asked with more than a little sarcasm.

"I did. I enjoyed myself very much. But," he said as he leaned forward and put his left hand on hers, "the night is still young, Darlene."

Kathryn tapped his ring finger, now bearing Andy's gold wedding band. "Lose this and you die."

"Lose it? It's like part of my hand."

Kathryn paused. "Ever wear one before?"

"Briefly," he said.

"You seem to have lost that one."

Now it was Nick's turn to hesitate. "I lost her."

"Different species?"

"That's as good a way as any to explain it."

"Don't tell me she was from the South!"

"Be reasonable, Mrs. Guilford. We were both from Pittsburgh. I grew up in a hill town on the north side called Tarentum. She was from across the river in New Kensington."

He ended the sentence as though the story was finished, but Kathryn's insistent gaze told him she was not yet satisfied. He took a deep breath and continued.

"Where I grew up you went to high school, you got a job, you got married, you had babies—not always in that order."

"But you decided you wanted something more."

"No. She did."

He took a roll and tore it in half and reached for a pat of butter. Kathryn felt suddenly ashamed. It had never occurred to her that the Bug Man could at one time have been just a human being. This man who caused her so much frustration and embarrassment could have been—could still be—hurt by someone else. She wondered what the woman looked like, what qualities she possessed that actually caused him to love—maybe for the one and only time. She watched him as he ate, head down, his huge spectacles hanging from his ears like a pair of glass scales weighing in the balance everything that passed before them. She wondered how long he had worn those glasses and how much pain they had caused him.

"Plus twenty diopter," he said without looking up.

Kathryn started. "What?"

"Plus twenty diopter. You were looking at my glasses."

Kathryn opened her mouth to deny it but quickly realized how silly and unconvincing the words would sound. Nick was right—she was a very bad liar.

"Don't let it bother you," he said. "There comes a time in every relationship when I know they're looking at my glasses. It was just your time."

"What does 'plus twenty diopter' mean?"

"I'm hyperopic. I'm farsighted. I see things better at a distance—not good, just better. 'Plus twenty' means that up close I'm blind as an earthworm."

Kathryn wondered what the world looked like through those massive lenses. She wished she could try them on, but she couldn't bring herself to ask. How do you ask a blind man if you can try out his cane?

"You may," he said, and carefully removed the spectacles from his head.

Kathryn started again. "I hope you use these psychic powers wisely."

"I'm not psychic. I just know your species."

As he held out the spectacles, she saw his face for the first time whole and complete. She had imagined that his real eyes would be tiny, molelike dots; in fact, they were larger than normal and very dark. They were beautiful eyes, really, and it seemed very sad that such eyes could only be viewed in a mirror dimly.

"How do I look?" She smiled.

"I have no idea. Go across the street and let's have a look at you."

Kathryn's mouth dropped open. Looking through the bulky lenses was like staring into a cloud through wax paper. She raised her right hand and flexed her fingers; she saw a pink feather boa curl across her field of vision, undulate at one end, and then disappear. She looked at Nick; she saw nothing but amorphous blobs where features should be, as though a painter had roughed in areas of color where a final portrait would follow. It was a world without particulars of any kind, and Kathryn felt her own eyes darting back and forth just as Nick's did, searching through the mists like a rock climber groping for a solid grip.

She handed the glasses back, placing them carefully in Nick's open hands. "How long have you worn these?"

"Forever. When I was in first grade my teacher thought I was an idiot. Numbers, letters, they were all just blurs to me. I thought that's just the way the world looked. Then one day my mother took me to an optometrist. When I walked out I was wearing these, and for the first time in my life I saw details. I looked down at the ground and saw an ant mound." He shook his head. "I must have sat there for an hour. Then my mother thought I was an idiot."

"And you've been staring at ant mounds ever since."

"My folks both worked for Allegheny Ludlum Steel. Pittsburgh was a steel town when they were growing up, and they always figured their boy would grow up to work at the plant just like they did—just like everyone in Tarentum did. But then the Japanese started dumping cheap steel in the '60s, and the mills all started to close down. No one knew if Pittsburgh would even survive. That's when my folks decided they'd better save up and send their baby boy to college."

"And you decided to study entomology. What did they think of that?"

"They didn't even know what it was," he shrugged. "So I graduated with a B.S., and the only job I could get was driving a pickup truck with a big cockroach on top. That's when I decided to go to graduate school. My folks were thrilled. The only thing they heard is that their son was going to be a doctor. So I finally came home—Doctor Polchak—and all the relatives start dropping by. My Aunt Edna said her hip was bothering her. What should she do? I told her, come back and see me when you're dead."

Kathryn laughed out loud—a genuine belly laugh. It was the first time she had made that sound around Nick, and she stopped a little short. But she couldn't help herself. Images of a grade-school Bug Man and exterminator trucks and an ailing Aunt Edna were more than she could contain.

At that moment three men in civilian clothes passed by on their way to the buffet line.

"Excuse me," Nick said. "It's been fun, but I'm late for work."

He stood up from the table and stretched, rotating left and right from the waist to display his T-shirt to the widest possible audience. He walked slowly around the entire restaurant, occasionally bumping into a chair and stopping to excuse himself. He finally arrived at the buffet line, picked up a plate, and nodded a greeting to the enlisted man across from him. A few minutes later he returned to the table with one small plate of food.

"It looks like the Gulf War Syndrome has affected your appetite," Kathryn said.

"I plan to go back several times."

"Why?"

"To show off this T-shirt. Somewhere in this hotel there may be a man who knew Jim McAllister—or knew someone who did. We have exactly one night to find him."

CHAPTER 24

It was just after midnight when Sheriff Peter St. Clair stepped through the screen door into the darkened lab. The bright light glowing from the office beyond cast streaks of blue fire across the faces and edges of glass throughout the room, but still left the inhabitants of each terrarium a dark mystery. The sheriff walked slowly down the aisle, stopping to peer uselessly into each shadowy case. He tapped on the face of one and heard a quick skittering sound. He ran his fingernails across the screen wire atop another and a menacing hiss shot back.

What in the . . .

He avoided the rest of the cases and made his way to the office door, stopping for a moment to observe the excited little man with the cell phone pressed against his ear. The sheriff rapped sharply on the window.

Teddy looked startled; then his face erupted into a broad smile. He folded the cell phone and set it on the counter.

"Thank you for hurrying," he spluttered, shaking the sheriff's hand and pulling him into the room. "I'm sorry to call you so late. I hope I didn't catch you at an inopportune moment."

"What have you got back there, some kind of snake?" The sheriff nodded back toward the darkness.

"Ah! You must have disturbed our giant hissing cockroaches—they let out a loud hiss when they sense danger. Impressive, aren't they?"

"Impressive," the sheriff muttered.

Teddy stopped abruptly. "You didn't reach into any of the cases, did you?"

He shook his head.

"Thank heavens," Teddy whistled. "That could be serious—quite serious indeed."

"So"—the sheriff glanced around disdainfully at the incredible disarray of paper and equipment—"what's this big news?"

Teddy grinned from ear to ear and held up one finger, then turned to the Biotronette environmental unit and removed a single plastic container. He held it with both hands as one might hold a bulging water balloon.

"The big news," Teddy beamed, "is this!"

The sheriff bent down and peered into the container. Inside was a single black fly clinging to the plastic wall, motionless except for the sporadic fanning of its tiny wings.

"It emerged less than fifteen minutes ago. We expected it to be a Calliphora vomitoria or a sarcophagid—perhaps even a stray Muscidae—but I'm fairly certain that it's a Chrysomya megacephala, a species not indigenous to the Carolina piedmont at all."

"Whoa!" The sheriff interrupted with a wave of his hands. "Slow down! What are you talking about? Is all the excitement over one lousy fly?"

Teddy turned and set the container carefully on the worktable, then took a few moments to calm himself and collect his thoughts.

"When Mr. McAllister died, certain species of flies deposited eggs on his body. We call these necrophilous flies—flies whose larvae feed on the tissues of decaying animals. Now certain flies are indigenous to certain areas," he said slowly and precisely. "That means if an animal dies in one area, its body will be infested by one species of fly; but if it dies in another area, it may be a different species of fly entirely. Dr. Polchak collected specimens from all of the observable wounds on Mr. McAllister's body, and we have been rearing them here in our environmental chamber, waiting for them to mature so that we could accurately identify each species. Over the last several days each specimen has reached eclosion—the moment when the adult fly emerges from its puparium—and each has turned out to be precisely the species one would expect in this area. That is," he said with a grin and a nod toward the worktable, "all except that one. That specimen emerged just a few hours ago, and I am quite certain that it is a Chrysomya megacephala—a species not found anywhere in North Carolina."

"Where does that one come from?" the sheriff asked.

"From a place with warmer winters. This species is found only in Florida and southern Georgia."

The sheriff said nothing.

"That means," Teddy continued, "that Dr. Polchak was correct in his suspicions about the unusual lividity of the left leg. The body must have been deposited here—but death actually occurred somewhere in Florida or southern Georgia. And if the body was transported"—his eyes widened—"then in all likelihood you have a murder on your hands."

The sheriff turned away and began to slowly pace around the office. He stopped and stood motionless, staring at the floor. He took a few steps more and put his hands on his hips, staring at the bare wall ahead of him. After a few moments he turned back to Teddy again.

"You're saying that Jim's death was not a suicide at all. You're saying he was murdered—in another state—and his body was only dumped here."

"Precisely!" Teddy said with obvious satisfaction.

"But the coroner's report—"

"The coroner's report indicated that it was an apparent suicide, and so no autopsy was ordered to verify the cause of death. But now that we have contravening evidence, we have every reason to obtain an order of exhumation to examine the body in detail. Further forensic study may provide any number of clues to the manner of death—and perhaps even to the killer."

The sheriff nodded slowly. "We got to be careful here—this could rock a lot of boats. You're sure you can prove all this?"

"Oh yes," Teddy assured him. "Forensic entomological evidence is considered quite reliable by our courts, and species identification is my specialty."

The sheriff turned away again. "Does the doc know yet?"

"I haven't been able to reach him," Teddy said. "They're up in Washington, you know, but they never checked into the hotel where they made reservations. I asked the front desk to check under other names, and I asked them to check with their other hotels in the area, but no luck. That's why I called you, Sheriff. You must have some connections, some way of tracking him down."

"What about his cell phone?"

"I just tried it—no answer. Maybe his phone is off, or maybe he's outside of a digital area. I was just about to leave him a voice mail when you came in."

The sheriff stepped to the worktable and gently lifted the plastic container. "This is the one? The only one?"

Teddy nodded. "We must be very careful. Its wings will be dry soon, and it will be capable of flight. In the morning I'll kill it and prepare it for positive identification."

"Identification? I thought you said you already knew."

"I do; I mean, there are ways I can already tell—but legally it's not considered a positive identification until certain procedures are followed."

The sheriff carefully set the container down again. "Then let's wait till morning to fill in the doc. No sense getting his hopes up if this whole thing turns out to be smoke. They oughtta be back first thing, and you'll know for sure by then."

"Is there anything else I can do?" Teddy offered. "Any way I can help?"

"There is something you can do. You can go home and get some rest. I need you alert. Come tomorrow, I have a feeling it's all gonna hit the fan."

CHAPTER 25

Y ou must be Nick," a tired voice said. "I'm Vincent—Vincent Arranzio."

Nick looked up from his lukewarm tea to see a tall, gaunt figure wearing an open fatigue jacket over a sagging gray T-shirt. His clothing seemed loose and ill fitted, as though he had lost a considerable amount of weight. Nick extended his hand and then motioned for the man to sit down opposite him. The man slid into the booth and sat quietly, moving only occasionally to scratch at both arms.

"I wish I could offer you something"—Nick gestured to his tea—"but the place closed down a long time ago."

The man shrugged. "Looks like you don't sleep any better than I do."

Nick glanced at his watch—2:45 a.m. "I appreciate you meeting me here. I know it's a bit late."

"It was either this or stare at the ceiling for another couple of hours." The man leaned forward. "How did you say you got my name?"

"From a marine I met in the lobby a couple of hours ago. He was with the 4th Marine Expeditionary Brigade in the Gulf. Said he knew you from a group you were in together a couple of years ago. He said we might have a friend in common—Jim McAllister."

The man nodded. "How is Jim?"

Nick paused. "He's dead, Mr. Arranzio."

The man slumped back against the booth. "How?"

"I was hoping you could help me find out."

The man glanced at Nick's 82d Airborne T-shirt again, then glared at him suspiciously.

"You were never in the Airborne," he said, nodding at Nick's enormous spectacles. "Not with those. Now what's this all about?"

"Mr. Arranzio, I am a forensic entomologist—a kind of investigator—and I am helping a very dear friend of Mr. McAllister look into the circumstances surrounding his death."

"How did he die?"

"According to the coroner's report, he shot himself in the right temple with his own service sidearm. Do you believe that?"

"What do you mean do I believe it? If that's what happened, I believe it."

Nick looked at him. "I understand you knew Mr. McAllister quite well."

"We were in a couple of groups here together. He was with the 82d Airborne—I was with the 101st. The 82d attacked on foot with the French at Al Salman—we went in by air in Apaches on their right flank. You could say we had a lot to talk about."

"Mr. Arranzio, do you believe Jim McAllister was capable of taking his own life?"

The man paused and scratched at both arms again. "How much do you know about Gulf War Syndrome?"

"A little. In the Gulf our forces were subjected to a series of potentially toxic substances—petroleum smoke, depleted uranium, nerve agents—no one knows what long-range effects those substances might have, especially in combination."

The man leaned toward Nick.

"Want to hear an interesting fact? Since the Gulf War ended, about three-quarters of 1 percent of all Gulf War veterans have died. If you compare that to all the troops who didn't deploy to the Gulf, it's less. The vets are doing better than everyone else! We're not dying from Gulf War Syndrome—we're just going nuts." He stopped scratching at his arm and pulled up his sleeve. "Look. I've got a rash that never goes away. Why? I get headaches, night sweats, swollen glands. From what? I forget things—and I don't know whether I was gassed by the Iraqis or I'm just getting old. It can get you down, Nick—it got Jimmy down—and believe me, it gets pretty dark always looking up from the bottom of the well."

"Mr. Arranzio, did you ever talk with Mr. McAllister about his experiences in the Gulf? I don't mean actions and troop movements—I mean the way things affected him."

"That was a big part of the group. Some people think the Gulf was a cakewalk just because our side didn't suffer many casualties. I saw men starved, fried, shot to pieces, and blown all over the countryside. It was no picnic."

"Did Mr. McAllister ever single out any special event—anything that seemed to cause him special anguish or remorse?"

The man dropped his head and began to rub his temples in slow circles as if he were trying to coax an elusive thought up to the surface of his mind.

"Sometimes the group would swap stories about what we saw. One guy kept talking about Khafji. The Iraqi tanks rolled in with their turrets backward like they were going to surrender—we lost twelve marines that day. Another fella lost a buddy to friendly fire. Remember the Apache that fired a Hellfire at one of our own trucks? Another guy kept talking about Highway 8, where we trapped the Iraqis retreating from Kuwait and it turned into a shooting gallery. They called it the Highway of Death."

"And Jim?"

"Jim had a few stories, too, but he kept coming back to this one. There was this guy—what was his name? Something happened with this one fella. His name was . . . Man, I've got holes in my head like a Swiss cheese."

"Did he say what happened?"

"Funny thing. It got pretty nasty over there, but Jim could always talk about it, he could describe it—except when it came to his problem with this one guy. He'd always start into it and just shut down. I figured whatever it was, it must have been a pretty serious business."

"You said he would 'start into it,' as if he wanted to talk about it, but couldn't. What did he say at those times? Did he give you any idea what had happened between them?"

The man continued to massage his temples in long, slow circles.

"Mr. Arranzio, did he ever mention anyone named Andy?"

Arranzio squinted hard.

Nick looked down into his teacup and noticed the small flecks of black leaf resting on the bottom. The Chinese believed that the remains of tea leaves formed symbols that could reveal hidden knowledge. The rim of the cup foretold the immediate future, the sides of the cup revealed more distant knowledge, and the bottom of the cup contained the darkest secrets of all.

"Mr. Arranzio," Nick said without looking up, "did you know that Jim McAllister used cocaine?"

Silence.

Nick leaned forward. "I'm not with the DEA, if that's what you're thinking."

The man shook his head slowly. "You must think I'm some kind of idiot to ask me a question like that."

Nick raised both hands. "You're right—I apologize. Let me put it another way. I know Jim McAllister used cocaine—I examined his body shortly after death. And I know his cocaine use started in the Gulf. What I want to know is, do you think it had anything to do with this problem he kept talking about?"

Mr. Arranzio sat quietly for a moment, glaring at Nick. He took a long, slow, backward glance over both shoulders, then leaned in again.

"It was part of it," he said quietly, and when Nick opened his mouth to speak again the man added sharply, "and that's all I'm going to say about it. Clear?"

Both men sat back in their seats and studied each other for a moment. Mr. Arranzio shook his head and made a kind of snorting sound.

"What kind of an investigator did you say you are?"

"A forensic entomologist."

He sneered. "Seems to me you're asking the wrong questions."

"I'm listening."

"When did Jim die?"

"Less than two weeks ago."

"And Desert Storm was over eight years ago. You keep asking about what happened in the Gulf. I'd be a lot more interested in what happened after."

"Go on."

"What's the street price of cocaine these days?"

Nick shrugged. "I suppose a hundred, a hundred-and-fifty bucks a gram. Why?"

"What do you suppose a moderate user like Jim would consume in a week—four, five grams? Well, the last time I saw Jim he was flat busted—not a dime to his name, no job, no prospects. Now where does a guy like that come up with seven-hundred-and-fifty bucks a week for flake?"

"You tell me."

"You beg, you borrow, or you steal. It's as simple as that."

Mr. Arranzio slid to the edge of the booth and stood up. "I hope you find what you're looking for. Answers are pretty scarce these days."

Nick handed him his card. "That guy you mentioned—the one that Jim McAllister had the big problem with. If his name ever comes back to you, drop me a line, will you?"

Nick looked down once again at his teacup and the random bits of stem and leaf that still clung to the bottom. He stared long and hard—and then a pattern began to emerge.

Kathryn heard the key in the lock and opened her eyes. The door opened and Nick entered, stopping to observe her motionless form before stepping into the bathroom.

"Too much tea," he said. "Did you get any sleep?"

Kathryn raised her head and looked at the clock—4 a.m. She lay diagonally across the queen-sized bed with the bedspread pulled roughly over her, exactly as she lay down three short hours ago. She heard the sound of rushing water, and Nick stepped out, wiping his hands on a coarse white towel. He dropped it on the carpet and looked at her again. He stepped slowly to the bed and sat down, his hip touching hers. He said nothing for a moment, watching, then leaned forward and gently straightened the bedspread stretched across her. His eyes were truly enormous at this distance, and they hung above her like chestnut moons.

"Mrs. Guilford," he said quietly. "I want to ask you something."

"Yes?"

"Did your bank ever grant a substantial loan to Jim McAllister?"

Kathryn blinked hard and worked to clear her mind.

"Are you asking me if I ever approved a loan to Jimmy?"

Nick nodded.

"No. Never."

"If I checked the bank's records, is that what I would find?"

Kathryn paused. "Did you just ask me if I'm lying?"

"I've been wondering how your friend managed to come up with several hundred dollars a week to finance his drug habit."

"I work in commercial lending," she reminded him. "Jimmy would never have qualified for a personal loan either—he had no income, no collateral . . ."

"If you don't beg, and you don't borrow," he said thoughtfully, "then you steal. Did your friend have any criminal record? Burglary, breaking and entering, assault?"

"Absolutely not."

Nick raised one eyebrow and Kathryn rolled her eyes.

"None that I know of." She sighed. "If he did, Peter would have to know."

"Yes," he said. "That's what I keep telling myself—Peter would have to know."

He sat for another minute staring straight ahead at the wall, then slapped his hands down on the mattress.

"Let's go."

"Go? Go where?"

"Home, of course."

Kathryn glanced back at the clock. "Right now? It's four o'clock in the morning!"

"Okay." Nick shrugged. "Then roll over."

Kathryn sat upright. "I'll get my things."

As Teddy turned his Camry down the secluded dirt road, his headlights flashed across a pickup truck half-hidden by a grove of trees, then onto a single-wide trailer a hundred yards ahead. The trailer was long and roomy enough but it was mud-ugly. Despite Teddy's best efforts to add a touch of decoration or landscaping here and there, it was still essentially a tin shoebox with a propane tank attached. Its one redeeming virtue was that it was cheap, and that made it the perfect residence for a research assistant on temporary assignment.

He parked in front of the trash cans, which had been plundered for the third night in a row by the local raccoons—that was the problem with living so far from the main road. He tidied up and fastened the lids down securely, took two sacks of groceries from the backseat, and headed for the door. A single cinder block step led up to the doorway, which was covered by a twisted aluminum screen door that long ago ceased to serve any useful purpose. He went through the gesture of entering the key in the lock, though the door fit so loosely in its frame that all it really needed was a good push to open it. He stepped in and fumbled for the light switch.

He flicked it on.

Nothing.

He turned left into the shadows, feeling his way carefully toward the kitchen counter. The sagging plywood floor creaked with every step. He stopped to hoist the paper sacks higher, and the floor creaked behind him—a deep, groaning sigh—and Teddy stood erect, straining to extend his senses out into the darkness. He felt exactly like the Blattidae, the cockroaches that lined his cupboards and pantry, whose tiny hairs search the air for the slightest vibration and allow them to react ten times faster than the human eye can blink. Teddy saw nothing, he heard nothing, but he sensed something—a weight, a presence, a shifting shape in the blackness behind him.

He felt something cold touch the base of his skull and through the back of his eyes saw a blinding white flash of fire.

CHAPTER 26

We're here." Nick gently nudged Kathryn's shoulder. "You slept like a brick."

She shook her head and felt the deep mists of sleep begin to evaporate from her mind. They were back in Rayford, parked directly in front of her house. She looked at her watch: 9:30 a.m.

"I feel like I slept on a brick," she groaned, stretching and rubbing her backside.

"I thought I'd drop you off." He nodded toward the house.

"What are you going to do?"

"I've got one quick stop to make, then I'm headed to the lab to check in with Teddy. That last specimen should be ready to pop any time. I should have heard from him by now. I checked my cell phone just outside of Raleigh; it said One Call Missed from Teddy's cell phone, but there was no message. I called the lab—no answer."

"I should go with you."

"No need," he said firmly. "You get some rest. I'll call you as soon as I know anything."

Kathryn reluctantly walked to the house. At the door she turned back.

"As soon as you know anything," she called after him as he pulled away in a billow of blue smoke.

He drove less than a mile and parked again on Dalrymple Street, two full blocks from the sheriff's office where he could clearly see the Crown Victoria patrol car parked in front. It was almost an hour before the figure of the sheriff emerged from the office, followed closely by a second and much larger figure ambling behind. The patrol car pulled slowly away from the curb, and Nick reached for his door.

"Excuse me, is Sheriff St. Clair here?"

A stout-legged woman about fifty years of age sat staring intently at a glowing computer monitor. A shapeless blue dress hung haphazardly over her trunk, and short, tight curls hugged her head like a salt-and-pepper shower cap. Her left hand held open an instruction manual while the thick, blunt fingers of her right hand occasionally pecked at a key.

"Just missed him." She nodded toward the door without breaking her concentration. "He went on rounds—should be back in about an hour."

Nick cocked his head to one side and looked at her.

"Wait a minute. You must be Agnes, the one Pete talks so much about."

She glanced up from the flickering screen.

"I'm Dr. Nicholas Polchak." He rolled up a chair across from her and casually straddled it. "But you can call me Nick. I'm working with your boss on an investigation. Has he mentioned me?"

"Can't say he has."

"Well, he talks about you all the time. It's always, 'Agnes does this,' or 'Agnes takes care of that.' Sounds to me like you do most everything around here."

"You name it, I do it," she said with increasing enthusiasm. "I'm the secretary, accountant, and dispatcher. I'm the first one here every morning and the last one out at night. See this?" She pointed to a cheap wood-burned plaque above her desk that proclaimed, "IDEA girl." "That's me—the IDEA girl. That stands for I Do Everything Almost."

"I can tell you one thing. They sure don't pay you enough."

"Who you tellin'?" she said with a backward glance. "I swear sometimes I'm nursemaid and mother to those two boys!"

Nick nodded sympathetically. "What about time off? Do you ever get a vacation around here?"

"It's just the three of us. I take vacation when they take vacation. I can't make rounds or take calls without them, and they can't do nothin' without me—so we just close up shop for a few days. The Harnett County boys come over and take our calls."

"When was your last vacation, Agnes?"

"I got three days back in February—no, January. Went to see my sister—she lives up Edenton way, you know? She got this disk problem, gets laid up real bad, pain shoots all down her legs and—"

"Six months ago? Six months with no vacation?"

"Till a couple weeks ago, that is."

Nick leaned forward and smiled. "Well, it's about time. So—the whole office shut down just a couple of weeks ago?"

"I went back again to see Rayleen—not that it did much good, not this time. That disk of hers, it just pops out on her one day and then right back in the next. She never—"

"And the boys," he cut in. "Where did they head off to?"

"Down to Myrtle Beach. Spent a few days in the sun."

Nick paused. "That's funny. I thought Pete said he did a little hunting—down in Georgia. You're sure they didn't go to that place of his in Valdosta?"

"It was Myrtle Beach all right. See? They brought me this." From the corner of her desk she slid a small, paste gray sand dollar.

Nick turned the sand dollar over slowly.

"I guess it must have been the beach then. Where else could you get one of these?" He handed it back to her. "Did they bring you any pictures?'

"Can't say as they did."

"No pictures?"

"Do you take pictures on vacation?"

He smiled. "You must have had a couple of sunburned boys to take care of when they got back."

She paused. "That's funny . . ."

Nick rose from his chair. "Agnes, you've been a big help—and I'm glad to hear your sister is doing better."

"Want me to tell Pete you stopped by?"

"No need. He'll know soon enough."

Nick slumped a little lower in his seat as he turned onto County Road 42, headed back toward the lab. He was tired—bone tired—but he was not about to rest. This was the way he preferred to work, driving himself day and night, never stopping to rest until his mind was no longer able to focus—and his mind was clearer than it had been in days.

The sheriff and his deputy were out of town just a week ago, contemporaneous with the death of James McAllister. They went to Myrtle Beach—or so they told their secretary. They brought her back a sand dollar—maybe from the beach, maybe from any gift shop between there and Miami—but no other evidence of their stay. And no tan. A few days at the beach and no sun?

Got to check the meteorological records for Myrtle Beach last week.

Nick began to drum his fingers on the steering wheel in time with some imaginary tune. Behind the great glasses, his dark eyes darted from thought to thought like worker bees.

He rolled to a crunching stop in front of the green Quonset.

That's odd. Teddy's car is not here.

Nick headed straight for the office. He opened the door—and then froze. The left exit door stood wide open.

He glanced quickly around the office. Nothing seemed to be missing, nothing was broken, but the exit door had been left open—an error that Teddy would never make. Too many predacious species could be allowed in, or . . .

Allowed out.

He ran to the Biotronette and began to search through the specimens. Left ocular . . . thoracic . . . right temporal . . . right ocular . . . They were there. They were all there.

Wait. Where is . . . Where could it possibly . . .

He searched desperately around the room. There in the center of the worktable was a single plastic container—with the lid removed.

Nick ripped a cardboard box from a shelf and dumped its contents onto the floor, fumbling frantically for another lid. He found one and slammed it down on top of the open container.

Too late.

Inside the container was nothing but a tiny, empty capsule about the size of a grain of rice.

He lunged for the open door and jerked it shut. He stood silently, his eyes searching every inch of the ceiling and walls in the desperate hope that the fly had not yet escaped the lab. He began to step slowly around the office, waving his arms in great circles over every table and shelf, straining every sense to detect a quick streak of black or a telltale buzz.

Nothing.

Nothing but a handful of moths drawn to the stark fluorescent ceiling lights the night before.

The door was left open last night.

Nick searched the worktable near the Biotronette and found Teddy's log, the one he used to record changes in the specimens at fifteen-minute intervals. He fanned through the pages, scanning the entries—almost nothing had been entered for more than a day now, when the rest of the specimens had emerged from their puparia.

1515 Left ocular specimen reaches eclosion
1530 No change
1545 Second temoral specimen reaches eclosion
1600 No change

He flipped forward to yesterday's entries—it was an endless list of "No change" notations penned in Teddy's flawless script. He ran his finger down the list, turned the page, and continued until he came to the final entry:

2356 inal specimen eclosion

He closed the book. At 11:56 last night the final specimen emerged from its puparium, and Teddy faithfully noted the event in his log—but what happened next? How did the specimen come to be left out of the Biotronette and allowed to escape? Why was the lab left open and unsecured?

Nick glanced down again at the cluttered counter.

Teddy's cell phone.

Nick flipped it open and jabbed the TALK button twice; the

auto-redial activated, and a number appeared on the tiny LCD screen—Nick's number. Teddy did try to call—but if he couldn't get through, why didn't he leave a message? Nick pulled out his own phone and checked again: No New Messages.

It never occurred to Nick for even an instant that these events could be accidental. Teddy was a consummate professional who took pains with the slightest details of his work. The idea that he would leave a door open or allow a critical specimen to escape was more than impossible, it was unthinkable. No, someone else had been here, someone who had purposely left the office door open— someone who had an interest in allowing this specific specimen to escape. But how did they get in? How did they get around Teddy? And why was Teddy's cell phone still there?

Where is Teddy?

Nick grabbed the logbook, threw open the lab door, and ran for the parking lot.

CHAPTER
27

Kathryn sat cross-legged in front of the coffee table, working her way through accumulated junk mail and stopping to pay an occasional bill. She hadn't been able to "get some rest" as Nick had suggested, but that came as no surprise. Sleep was a rare and delicate bubble for Kathryn, and once disturbed it was impossible to restore. Her night's rest consisted of the few moments of sweet oblivion she had managed to snatch between bone-jarring potholes on I-95 South.

The muted television in front of her flashed images of chatty news anchors exchanging smiles and nods. Kathryn stared at it blankly for a few minutes, then reached for the remote and switched to channel four. The screen turned bright blue. From the bottom drawer of the entertainment center she took a videotape marked OUR WEDDING and slid it into the machine. She sat back down on the floor and pulled her legs up tight against her chest, resting her chin on her knees.

The church custodian had reluctantly agreed to shoot the video, and he seemed to spend the first fifteen minutes learning to work the camera. A random shot of the church ceiling was followed by a shot of his own shoes, followed by a series of nauseating pans and zooms to nothing in particular. There were broken sound bites of music and laughter interspersed with a few colorful words from the custodian himself. The cinematography slowly began to improve, however, and soon a shot of the front of the sanctuary revealed two bridesmaids and the groom—with Peter and Jimmy at his side.

Finally the bride herself appeared in the double doorway leading down the center aisle. A crude facsimile of the "Wedding March" began to blare from the organ—even worse than she remembered it—and the dozen-or-so guests scattered throughout the pews rose and turned toward Kathryn as she entered the sanctuary. She walked alone, no father to give her away.

She arrived at Andy's side and turned to face him. Words were spoken—the sound was indistinguishable—then the camera jostled, cut off, and started again several yards closer to the bridal couple. It was a tight shot on their faces, and at the sight of Andy's smile her tears began to flow.

From somewhere beyond the wedding party a voice began, "Dearly beloved, we are gathered together today in the sight of God and man . . ." Kathryn watched her own face, then his, then hers again. She saw nothing in their eyes but hopes and dreams and possibilities.

How long ago was this? It seems like forever.

"Repeat after me," the voice continued. "I take you, Kathryn, to be my lawfully wedded wife, knowing in my heart that you will be my constant friend, my faithful partner in life, and my one true love."

"I take you, Kathryn, to be my lawfully wedded wife . . ."

For some inexplicable reason the custodian chose this moment to pan slowly across the members of the bridal party. There was

Amelia on the left, who constantly hitched up her slip throughout the service, followed by dear cousin Rose who married shortly
thereafter and moved away to ... Where was it? Colorado?

The voice boomed out again: "I affirm to you in the presence of
God and these witnesses my sacred promise to stay by your side as
your faithful husband for better or for worse, in joy and in sorrow,
in sickness and in health."

"... my sacred promise to stay by your side ...," Andy
repeated, while the camera suddenly jumped to the other end of
the row and settled on Jimmy. Smiling Jimmy, always happy—
maybe not so happy, Kathryn thought, but always a smile on his
face. The camera panned slowly to the left, stopped briefly on
Peter, and finally came to rest on the groom once again.

Kathryn suddenly stopped. She reached for the remote and
backed the tape up to the image of Jimmy, then watched again as
the camera rolled past Peter. What was that? What was he doing?
She rewound the tape again and let it go, moving closer to the
screen this time.

"I promise to love you without reservation," said the preacher,
and after each phrase Andy repeated his words. "To honor and
respect you, to provide for your needs, to protect you from harm,
and to cherish you for as long as we both shall live." Was it just
her imagination? No—there it was again! Each time Andy spoke,
Peter's lips also moved. He was repeating the vows himself, but in
silence.

"... for as long as we both shall live," Andy finished solemnly,
and Peter ended at precisely the same instant.

Kathryn turned off the tape. What did she just see—and why
had she never noticed it before? Was Peter simply empathizing
with Andy, willing him to remember his lines like a bowler
urging a ball back into the center of the lane? Or was it something
else ... something more?

She got up and angrily ejected the tape. Why was she even
wondering about this? What was so unusual about Peter's
behavior? Peter hadn't done anything a thousand other best
men hadn't done before him. The only reason she found herself
considering some deeper motive was the ridiculous suspicions
Nick had planted in her mind.

But somewhere inside her a voice whispered: Is it really so ridiculous?

She tossed the tape back in the drawer and kicked it shut, then flopped down on the sofa and reached for a paper. Her life was complicated enough right now without searching for hidden meanings.

The phone rang and Kathryn unconsciously reached for it.

"Hello," she said absently.

"Mrs. Guilford."

The voice on the other end was thin and hollow, almost a whisper. It sounded strangely distant, as though it came from somewhere very dark and very far away.

"Who is this?"

"Nick."

Kathryn sat up in alarm. Something was wrong—terribly wrong. Whatever it was had produced a tone of voice that she never dreamed she would hear from the unflappable Nick Polchak—and it terrified her.

"Where are you? What's happened?"

There was a long pause on the other end. "Do you know where Teddy lives?"

"He lives in a trailer, doesn't he? Off Lead Mine Road?"

"How soon can you be here?"

"Fifteen minutes. Why? Nick, what is it?"

"It's Teddy," came the whisper. "He's dead."

CHAPTER
28

The bullet had entered at the base of Teddy's skull and passed easily through the soft tissues of the brain, exiting through the left eye with sufficient velocity to penetrate the flimsy trailer wall and escape. Death was instantaneous. He fell headlong, his arms still curled around the two crumpled sacks of groceries. The bags still seeped a variety of liquids, but none was as horribly stark and vivid as the red-black pool that lay directly beneath his face.

Kathryn sat on the cool trailer floor with her legs drawn up tight and her head down on her knees, staring at the curled and yellowed linoleum beneath her. She had wept until her soul was empty, and now there was nothing to do but sit and nurse the pounding ache inside her head. Each time she glanced up at Teddy's body sprawled before her, she felt another wave of grief. It angered her that already each wave had begun to diminish a little, like the wake of a distant boat.

Teddy had fallen facedown. The force of the fall shattered the nose and incisors and forced the jaw back into the skull. He lay in this grotesquely comical position with a bag tucked neatly under each arm, looking somehow trim and tidy even in death.

Kathryn raised her eyes and looked across at Nick, who sat opposite her in exactly the same position—arms wrapped around legs and head resting on knees—except that his eyes never left Teddy's body. It was the first time Kathryn had ever seen his huge, dark eyes completely motionless, almost lifeless. They no longer darted and evaluated and analyzed; they just gaped open like two black sewers, draining the image before him of all horror and misery and pain. Kathryn wanted to say something, but she knew from experience that sometimes sorrow is so profound that speech is blasphemous. She just looked at him, using her eyes as best she could to comfort and soothe and hold.

"I did this," Nick said in an almost inaudible voice. "This is the result of my foolishness—my sloppiness—my stupidity."

Kathryn shook her head. "You couldn't possibly have—"

"I should have seen it coming. I should have recognized the danger. I should have warned him to be careful."

"Nick, this is not your fault."

Nick met her gaze. "You haven't asked me how I happened to discover Teddy's body."

Kathryn said nothing.

"This morning I went to the lab. Teddy wasn't there, and the door was open. The office door. The final specimen, the one we were waiting for—it was allowed to escape. Someone removed the container from the Biotronette and took the lid off. It's gone,

Mrs. Guilford, along with any hope of proving that Jim McAllister was murdered. Who left that door open? Who took the lid off that container?"

"It had to have been Teddy."

"Never."

"But it's possible that he—"

"Listen to me!" he shouted. "You came to me to investigate the death of Jim McAllister because you believed he would not take his own life—and you believed this in the complete absence of any evidence or witnesses to support your opinion. You believed not because of logic, but because you knew him—and you knew this was something he would never do."

Kathryn nodded sadly. "I also found out that sometimes people don't act the way you expect them to."

"Then why are you still here, Mrs. Guilford? Why did you choose to continue this investigation? Have you changed your mind? Have you decided that suicide is something your snow-blowing friend just might have done?"

"No. Never."

"And I'm telling you, Teddy would never have made such amateurish mistakes. When I saw that open container I knew—I knew to come here—and I knew what had happened to Teddy before I ever opened the door to this trailer."

Kathryn paused. "You think someone released the fly on purpose? And you think Teddy was murdered to cover it up? But why?"

"Because Teddy saw the fly before it was released." He held up the brown leather logbook. "Teddy's log. His last entry indicated eclosion at 11:56 last night—that's when the mature fly emerged from its puparium. Teddy saw it. I'm betting he knew what it was—and where it came from. Someone wanted to make sure he didn't tell anyone else."

"Who?"

"You already know the answer to that question—we both know—you just don't want to believe it."

Kathryn closed her eyes and began to slowly shake her head.

"We have some very expensive equipment in that lab," Nick said. "But nothing was stolen. In fact, the only thing disturbed in the entire building was one plastic container. Whoever opened it had to know what it was and why it was significant. Who else does that leave but Peter St. Clair?"

"Nick, that makes no sense."

"He left the door open to make it appear that the fly had escaped by accident. But Teddy would never have left the container uncovered and he would never have left that door open—and at that hour of the night the fly would never have left the lab on its own. It would have remained inside, attracted to the light. Your friend released the fly outside, then left the door open to make it look like it was all an accident."

"If Teddy saw the fly, why in the world would he call Peter?" Kathryn asked. "Peter wouldn't understand what it was or why it mattered. You had your cell phone with you last night—why wouldn't Teddy call you?"

"He did try to call—but he didn't leave a message."

"And even if Peter did drop by the lab for some reason late last night, why in the world would he want to let the fly escape?"

Nick looked at her. "There's only one possible reason, Mrs. Guilford—because your friend Peter has something to protect. Because he was in some way involved in Jim McAllister's death."

She opened her mouth to protest, but he cut her off.

"Look. Andy, Jimmy, and Peter all loved you—but Andy won the prize. Then they all went off to war. Andy was killed; that left just two. Both of them came home hoping to fill Andy's shoes, but only one could win. Two men vying for the love of the same woman, Mrs. Guilford—that's called motive. And in my world, motive has a powerful smell."

"He didn't have a motive to commit murder."

"Didn't he? In Jim McAllister's mind something was terribly wrong, something that his sister said he wanted to make right, remember? Maybe he found out Peter was about to propose, maybe he felt that he should be next in line. Maybe what Jim wanted to make right was Peter—but maybe Peter made it right first."

Kathryn looked at him sadly. "You say I'm unwilling to believe—it sounds to me like there's something you're not willing to believe."

"What's that?"

"That Teddy—dear, wonderful Teddy—was only human, and that he might have just made a mistake. That his murder has nothing to do with the fly or the lab or the Gulf—or with Peter. Admit it, Nick—it's possible."

Less than five feet away was the brain that could answer all of their questions—but it was not a brain anymore. It was just a lump of convoluted tissue with a black tunnel torn through the center, three hundred billion lifeless cells already shrunken and ashen gray since the life-giving blood had ceased to flow. His extremities were blue, and lividity was evident in the face and arms where the purplish blood had already settled.

Nick reached out to press the skin to see if it would blanch.

"Did you know that a body begins to cool at a rate of one-and-a-half degrees per hour?" he said in a distant voice.

"Nick . . ."

"The sphincters relax, and the bowel and bladder void. The skin becomes waxy and translucent, and the head begins to turn a greenish-red. The eyes begin to flatten and the corneas become milky and opaque. Rigor mortis begins in the face and lower jaw and then spreads lower and lower and—"

"Nick. Stop it."

Nick suddenly noticed a sound above him. He lifted his head; in the air above Teddy's body a single black-and-gray fly drifted. It slowly descended in an erratic pattern until it came to rest on the moist tissues of the entry wound at the base of Teddy's skull.

Nick lunged forward and swung at the fly. It darted away and hovered momentarily, then began its erratic descent again. He swung a second time, then a third, each time with growing rage—and each time the gravid female waited patiently for this minor annoyance to subside before pursuing her biological destiny.

Nick jumped to his feet swinging wildly, chasing the black speck higher and higher into the air. He whirled to the right and grabbed a wooden chair from the dinette.

"Nick . . . don't!" Kathryn screamed, rolling onto her side and shielding her head with both arms.

The first wild arc caught nothing but air. The second tore off a cabinet door and sent plastic plates and cups clattering across the floor. The dazed fly, disoriented by the cyclonic winds, tumbled to the ground—and Nick was on top of it in an instant. He swung the chair high overhead and brought it down with a deafening crash again, and again, and again, until he was left holding nothing but a single splintered spindle.

He dropped to his knees, panting, the adrenaline slowly beginning to withdraw its talons. Kathryn lay on her side, staring at him wide-eyed, her arms still covering her head.

"Go ahead," he muttered. "Say it."

"Say what?"

"That's a lot of fuss over a little shoofly pie."

CHAPTER 29

From outside the trailer came the sound of an approaching engine. Nick glanced up to see the black-and-white patrol car and a bronze Ford LTD crunch to a stop, followed by a rolling cloud of dust. A moment later the screen door opened, and in stepped the sheriff, followed by Mr. Wilkins. The tiny trailer suddenly seemed impossibly crowded.

"Thanks for hurrying." Nick glowered at the sheriff. "Stop for donuts?"

"It's been a busy morning."

The sheriff surveyed the trailer quickly, stopping abruptly when he noticed Kathryn crouching in the corner and the dark, red circles under her eyes.

"Did you have to bring her in on this?"

"I came because I wanted to," Kathryn said angrily. "I came for Teddy's sake."

The sheriff looked down at the pile of kindling at Nick's feet and the broken spindle still in his hand.

"I shouldn't have to tell you this, Doc; this is a crime scene.

Until Mr. Wilkins here is finished with it—until I'm finished with it—you don't touch anything."

Nick looked at the coroner. "I see you brought the ice cream man. I didn't know you deliver, Mr. Wilkins."

Mr. Wilkins looked as indignant as possible and turned to the sheriff. "Sheriff, do I have to conduct my investigation in this unprofessional atmosphere?"

"I'm afraid so," Nick said, "unless you leave."

"You are way out of line," the sheriff said. "Mr. Wilkins is the official coroner of Holcum County. Now step aside and let the man do his work."

Nick stood up and dusted himself off. "Before you proceed with your evaluation of the crime scene, may I make a couple of observations? I think you may find them helpful."

The sheriff nodded doubtfully, while Mr. Wilkins folded his arms and said nothing.

"This is Teddy's laboratory log," he said, handing the brown journal to the sheriff. "His last entry was made at 11:56 last night, placing the time of death sometime in the last eleven hours. You'll notice there is some lividity, which takes about three hours to begin, narrowing the window somewhat more."

He knelt down and pointed carefully to the entry wound at the back of Teddy's skull. "Probably not a suicide," he said in the general direction of Mr. Wilkins. "The entry wound is star shaped, indicating a contact wound. That means the gun was in contact with Teddy's head when it fired. The gases escaping from the barrel ripped the skin open in a star-shaped pattern. Someone stepped up behind Teddy and fired execution-style. That indicates to me that someone was waiting for Teddy."

Kathryn interrupted. "But how could anyone have gotten that close without Teddy seeing?"

Nick stepped to the wall switch and flipped it on. Nothing happened. He stepped around Teddy's body to the single light fixture that hung in the center of the ceiling. The white glass bowl had been removed and one bare bulb stood out like a pearl thumb. He picked up a dishtowel and covered his hand, then reached up and gave the bulb a quarter-turn to the right. The brightness of the light caused all of them to wince and turn away.

"That's how," Nick replied. "It looks to me like someone made sure the room was dark and then stepped out behind Teddy when he first entered the trailer." He pointed to the two crumpled grocery sacks. "He never even made it to the counter."

"I don't buy it." The sheriff shook his head. "The way I see it, your friend just picked the wrong place to live. This is the cheapest part of town all right—it's also the worst part of town. We get a lot of lowlifes passing through this way looking for a quick buck. Did your friend own a TV? A VCR?"

"No," Nick said, "but he did own an exceptional sound system."

"Where?"

In the corner of the room a small particle-board cabinet lay overturned, and a bare extension cord snaked across the floor.

"Looks like a drug-related murder to me," the sheriff continued. "Some pothead breaks in and grabs the first big-ticket item he can find—but before he can run, your friend comes to the door. The killer backs into the corner and waits for him to step inside. Your friend goes to set his bags down before he hits the lights—the killer steps in behind him, and . . ." He formed a gun with his right hand and made a recoiling motion. "If your friend had gone for the lights first, he'd still be dead. He just would have got it from the front—like old Mrs. Gallagher did."

Kathryn spun around. "Mrs. Gallagher? What happened to Mrs. Gallagher?"

"Like I said, it was a busy morning." He looked at Nick. "Mrs. Gallagher lived just a quarter-mile from here, on the other side of that windbreak. Lived in a trailer just about like this one. Last night somebody walked in and put a bullet through her head too—the front of her head—and then walked off with the TV and VCR. Her boy stopped by to look in on her. Found her early this morning."

No one said anything for a few moments. They had all known Mrs. Gallagher for years—for decades. She was a kind and gentle woman who had outlived her beloved husband by thirty years and quietly and patiently awaited their reunion in the seclusion of her little trailer.

"Was there any sign of forced entry?" Nick asked.

The sheriff looked around at the flimsy trailer. "In these things?

There is no forced entry—just entry. Anybody can walk in who wants to."

"Or who is asked to," Nick said. "What about the light bulb? How do you explain that?"

"I can explain that"—the sheriff looked at him—"but I don't think you want to hear it."

"Try me."

"Okay. I think you did it."

Nick slowly smiled.

"You know," the sheriff said, nodding to the floor, "your boy here called me last night."

The smile disappeared from Nick's face. "What time was that?"

"About midnight. He was all excited, said he had some big news for you—but he couldn't find you. You two left a hotel number for him, but apparently you never showed up. Find better accommodations?"

Kathryn flushed. "We were at the Mologne House at Walter Reed, not that it's any of your business. It was a last-minute change of—"

"Did you go over to the lab?" Nick broke in.

"At midnight? I got better things to do. I told your boy to let it wait till morning. I told him the two of you would be back then, if you hadn't run off together."

"Shut up, Peter."

The sheriff turned to Kathryn. "If your friend here had a little more company last night, he might still be alive. Ever think of that?"

Kathryn glared at him hard. "I don't deserve that."

"I've tried to humor you as long as I can, Kath, but it's time to wise up. Have the two of you come up with any answers yet—any real answers? 'Cause if you have, I haven't seen 'em. I think what you've got here is one desperate Bug Man. He's on your payroll; he knows he's got to produce something, so he leads you around on a wild goose chase. Says you need to do research, collect evidence, conduct interviews—but where are the answers, Kath? Now he loses his friend—and he still doesn't have any answers—so he makes his friend's murder part of the story, part of the conspiracy.

Only he needs things to look a little more sinister, so he unscrews the light bulb. Now he's got an execution, not just some senseless killing."

"I don't believe it," Kathryn said. "I don't believe Nick would do that."

"Really?" the sheriff looked at her. "Did the two of you arrive together or did the doc get here before you did?"

He turned back to Nick now. "That's how I explain the light bulb. Now here's a question for you: If your friend was executed, if someone purposely waited here for him, then how do you explain Mrs. Gallagher? How does she fit into all this?"

Nick said nothing. There was an explanation for Mrs. Gallagher's death—a simple and obvious explanation—but it was so monstrous that it would have sounded absurd. There were only two possible explanations for Mrs. Gallagher's death: Either it was nothing more than a random and unrelated act of violence, or the sheriff had committed a double murder last night. He had chosen a second victim, an innocent old woman, for no more reason than to draw attention away from Teddy's death. It was possible—but Nick knew he could never give voice to such a possibility. Even to him it sounded almost unthinkable . . .

Almost.

Nick slowly turned to Kathryn again, studying her anew as though he had never looked at her before. Here was a woman who had led one man to the altar, another to depression, and a third to pathological devotion—and possibly murder. One loved her, one lost his mind over her, and one killed for her. What was the power this woman possessed? Nick suddenly felt like Odysseus, longing to understand the seduction of the Sirens' song, begging his shipmates to unlash him from the mast. He looked again at the graceful curves of her hips and thighs, the thick mane of fiery auburn hair, the glistening emerald eyes—but there was something different about her eyes now, something he had never seen before. For the first time there was a strange darkness—it was a look of confusion or hesitation or uncertainty. Then her eyes met his, and he knew in an instant what it was.

It was doubt.

"I should go," Nick said quietly, "and leave you two

professionals to your work." He stepped to the door and pushed it open, passing Kathryn without a word.

"Don't go far, Doc," the sheriff called after him. "I'll need to ask you a few questions about all this."

Well done, thought Nick as he slid into his car and started the engine. You not only got away with murder, you managed to shift the suspicion to me. Not even Mrs. Guilford knows who to trust now.

Well done, Sheriff. Well done indeed.

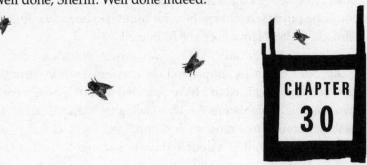

CHAPTER 30

The memorial service of James and Amy McAllister was held on an unusually pleasant June morning. An unexpected cold front had driven out the two-headed monster of Carolina summer—the oppressive heat and the clinging humidity—and had left in its place a flawless spring day.

Kathryn felt cheated. She didn't expect everything to stop for Jimmy and Amy, but it would have been nice if the world had at least tipped its hat in the form of a drizzling rain, or perhaps a dramatic haze over the cemetery grounds. Instead, the skies were a crystalline azure blue.

The change of climate was not overlooked by the people at Mount Zion A. M. E. Church, who all seemed a bit more cordial and cheerful than usual—and in Kathryn's view, a good deal less mournful than the occasion required.

Long folding tables hauled from the church fellowship hall were now draped in white and lined up in long fluttering rows. People stood for the most part, while the older folks sat on folding garden chairs and picked halfheartedly at sagging paper plates. The adults mingled in small groups and did their best to shush the smaller children, who found it impossible to contain themselves on such a day.

Kathryn worked her way through the considerable crowd, patting a shoulder here and accepting a heartfelt condolence there. Conversations seemed to center on the spectacular nature of Amy's demise or the dark curse that hung like a shroud over the McAllister family. And did you hear about old Mrs. Gallagher? Shot through the head just two nights ago—and in her own trailer!

Not a single soul mentioned the death of Dr. Eustatius Tedesco.

Kathryn looked up to see Nick slowly approaching from across the yard, dressed exactly as he was the last time she saw him at Teddy's trailer the day before. She hurried to meet him halfway. He seemed stooped and disheveled and profoundly tired, but there was still an unquestionable alertness in his eyes.

"I wasn't sure you'd come," she said.

"Why not?"

"I know you're not big on funerals. A body ceases to function, it decomposes—what's the point, right?"

Nick smiled faintly. "A wise man once told me: Sometimes, you have to believe."

"I wish all this was for Teddy. I wish there was something—"

"He's on his way back to Lancaster County," Nick said quietly. "Back to family. Ever been there? It's beautiful country."

Kathryn reached up to straighten his collar. "When was the last time you slept?"

"My species doesn't require much sleep," he said. As he spoke his eyes searched across the sea of heads until he located one familiar face.

"Come on," he said to Kathryn, "I feel like mingling."

The sheriff and deputy stood together near the center of the throng. As they approached, Kathryn flashed Peter a lukewarm smile; the two men exchanged no greeting of any kind. Kathryn reached up and hugged Beanie, then brushed back his wild brown hair and straightened his tie. He hardly seemed to notice; his eyes were fixed longingly on a half-dozen children playing at a picnic table thirty yards away.

Kathryn looked at Peter. He nodded his reluctant approval, and Beanie frolicked off to join his waiting friends.

"I was wondering," Nick spoke up, "now that the investigation is over, would you mind if I asked you a couple of questions? Just out of curiosity."

The sheriff glanced at Kathryn. "Why not?" he said pleasantly. "Fire away."

Nick rubbed hard at his chin. "What was Jim McAllister's problem anyway?"

"What problem is that?"

"You know—in the Gulf. Everybody says he had some kind of problem—it seemed to bug him constantly. He never got over it—thought it was worse than anything that happened to him in the war. Imagine that—worse than the war! What was the problem anyway?"

The sheriff folded his arms and looked at the ground. "The 82d was based at a place called Ab Qaiq," he said. "Andy and Jim were in the 4-325, assigned to Camp Gold. It was a temporary deployment, a tent city. Everybody got packages from home, and we used to stash the good stuff under our cots—and we'd raid each other's stuff from time to time. One day Andy was digging through Jim's stuff, and he found a little container of white powder. Got it?"

Nick squinted hard. "I ran across an old friend of Jim's up in Washington. He seemed to think Jim's big problem was with some guy."

"Jim was afraid Andy was going to turn him in."

Kathryn broke in. "Andy would never have turned Jimmy in!"

"Of course not," the sheriff grumbled. "But Jim was afraid he might. That stuff can make you a little paranoid, you know."

"You know what they say about paranoia," Nick said. "Just because you're paranoid, that doesn't mean someone's not out to get you."

The sheriff rolled his eyes.

"How do you know all this?" Nick asked. "Did Jim tell you?"

"I never saw Jim in the Gulf. We were assigned to separate units, remember? Andy came to see me a few days before the ground war began. He wanted me to know."

Nick stared thoughtfully into the sky. "So this big problem was that his old friend found out he had a nasty habit—and that was worse than the war? Worse than bombs and tanks and dead people? So bad that he could never even talk about it—even years later?"

The sheriff shrugged. "You'd have to ask Jim about all that."

"Yes," Nick nodded. "And that's not easy to do."

The sheriff grew impatient. "Anything else?"

"Yes," Nick said. "Where did Jim McAllister get all his cocaine? In a small town like this, for all those years?"

"Beats me."

Nick did a double take. "You don't know? You knew your friend was a user when he came back from the Gulf. You knew he must have had a supplier. You mean there were drugs being sold in your nice little town for all those years, and you never even knew about it?"

"Not in my town. Maybe his connection was up Fayetteville way. That's a rough town, an army town. There'd be plenty of connections up there."

"You knew your friend was a user, and you didn't like it. Didn't you ever think about cutting him off from his source?"

"I didn't know the source, okay?" the sheriff said angrily. "Jim stuck to himself a lot. Disappeared for weeks at a time. Nobody knew what kind of people he was hanging around with—nobody," he said with a glance at Kathryn, then turned back to Nick again. "Any more questions, Doc?"

"Just one more." He paused. "The night before last—the night Teddy was murdered—where were you? I checked the phone records. Teddy didn't call your office, and he didn't call your home; he called your cell phone. Where were you when he called?"

The sheriff shoved his hands deep into his pockets and kicked furiously at the dirt. He muttered something to himself and glanced quickly up at Kathryn—but it was a full minute before he finally answered.

"I was . . . with Jenny McIntyre," he grumbled.

"After midnight?"

"After midnight."

"How long were you there?"

"Most of the night."

"All night?"

"All night, okay?"

Nick smiled.

Kathryn stared at Peter in embarrassment and confusion, and Peter did everything he could to avoid her gaze. "Will you excuse me?" she said awkwardly, and the two men watched in silence as she walked away.

"Okay, Doc." The sheriff turned to Nick. "It's just the two of us now, just you and me—so why don't you drop the act and tell me what's on your mind? I'd like to know how you've got this whole thing figured."

Nick studied the sheriff's face carefully.

"I figure you're in love with Kathryn. It's not really love, of course—it's more like a pathological obsession—but it's the closest thing you've got. It must have really popped your cork when she decided to marry Andy. But then you got a lucky break when he was killed in the Gulf, and you had a second chance. You played the knight in shining armor to the grieving widow—you were her savior, her deliverer. You couldn't win her love, so you tried to earn it—but it didn't quite work, did it? I think she wants to love you, but for some reason she can't—maybe because deep down inside she sees through you, just like I do. You kept pursuing her, but somewhere along the line she started to feel the heat, so you backed off. Like they say in these parts: If you send in the dog too fast, you flush the bird. That's where Jenny McIntyre comes in. The sheriff got himself a girlfriend—in name only, of course—and that took the pressure off Kathryn. Now you two could be buddies again. That was a neat bit about spending the night with Jenny. Boy, I would have loved to be a Diptera on that ceiling. You should have seen the look on Kathryn's face when you told her—but then, you were staring at the ground at the time, weren't you?"

The sheriff stared at Nick with the eyes of a shark—eyes gray and flat and impenetrable; eyes capable of masking an entire ocean of rage and wrath with utter, absolute coldness.

"You seem to enjoy pushing me, Doc," he said with no hint of emotion. "Why is that?"

"It's hard to say," Nick said thoughtfully. "You seem to bring out the worst in people."

"I'm not a fool, Doc."

"Believe me," Nick said, "I never took you for one."

There was a long, icy silence.

"Something really bothered Jim McAllister after the Gulf," Nick went on. "I call it guilt. I think ol' Jimmy knew more about what happened to Andy than he let on. They served in the same unit, went into battle side by side . . . I think Jimmy saw an opportunity to have a second chance at Kathryn—and I think he took it.

"So he wrestled with his conscience—but it wasn't bad enough to stop him. He still had to deal with you—after all, only one of you could have her. That's where you come into the picture. I'll bet the two of you had a very interesting competition going over the years—vying for position, trying to outdo one another in service to the grieving widow.

"About a week ago it finally came to a head, and that's when you murdered him. I'm not so sure you planned to. Maybe the two of you had an argument, and it got out of hand. Maybe he wanted to kill you; after all, he had his gun with him. Maybe you just meant to hit him, and he fell backward—with his right leg propped up. Then you saw your opportunity, so you shot him in the head with his own sidearm and then placed the gun in his hand. No gunpowder residue, remember?

"Not very sophisticated, was it—a phony suicide? I mean, for a professional like you who's seen enough murders to know how to do it right. So sloppy, so many potential questions. Now what do you do? How would you ever get away with it? It took you several hours to figure that one out—time enough for the lividity in the left leg to become fixed. Then it suddenly dawned on you—what better place to bring the body than your own backyard, where the county coroner is the ice cream man! You knew that Mr. Wilkins's incompetence would allow you to avoid an autopsy and all the nasty questions that would go with it. So you dumped the body here—with the leg flat this time—in a meadow where you knew hunters would stumble across it in just a day or two. Very neat. But the ironic thing—the funny thing—is that your plan was spoiled by the only person in the world you care anything about."

The sheriff shook his head. "You're in the wrong business, Doc. You should be writing those detective stories."

"Truth is stranger than fiction, Sheriff. Two nights ago the final specimen emerged from its puparium, and Teddy called to let you know; the poor guy was actually naive enough to cooperate with you. There could only be one reason to make a fuss over that last specimen—it must have been indigenous to some other area, verifying our suspicions that the body had been moved. But there was only one fly, and Teddy was the only one who knew about it. So you sent poor Teddy home, then released the fly—and left the door open to make it look like an accident. And then, for the coup de grâce, you somehow made it to Teddy's trailer ahead of him and waited. Very tidy; no evidence, and now no witness."

Nick began to slowly shake his head. "But the thing I find incredible—the one real shining moment in all of your pathology— is when you put a bullet in the face of an innocent old woman just to help cover your tracks. Her death wasn't even essential. You could have gotten away with Teddy's murder without it. It was that extra little touch that shows what a truly demented individual you are."

The sheriff said nothing at all for a moment. Then he began to smile and finally laughed outright.

"So that's your story?" he said through his laughter. "If I spent all that time at your lab that night, how could I beat your partner to his trailer? And how could I murder your partner and poor old Mrs. Gallagher if I was with Jenny the whole night? And most of all, why would I want to kill my own best friend? Why would I need to? To win Kath? I've been first in line for Kath ever since Andy. It was never about Jimmy, Doc."

"There are still a few missing pieces to the story," Nick said. "I don't suppose you'd care to help me with the details?"

"What are you going to do with a cockamamie story like that? You've got no evidence or witnesses at all. You think you can take a fairytale like that to the law?"

Nick smiled and leaned forward. "I'm not a fool either, Sheriff. The evidence is gone—you're in no danger from the law. The only way I can hurt you, the only thing that really matters to you, is if I can sell my story to Mrs. Guilford."

The sheriff stopped abruptly. He stood silently for several moments, expressionless once again, and then he began to smile once more.

"You hang on like a tick. I got to give you that. She must be paying you a fortune."

Nick shook his head. "This isn't about money. This is for Teddy."

"Go ahead," the sheriff shrugged. "Try to sell your story to Kath. There's one piece of the equation you're overlooking, Doc: You're the outsider here. She's known you for, what—a week now? Kath and I grew up together. She loves me."

"Like a brother," Nick needled.

"Maybe so—but that still makes me the brother and you the blind geek from Pittsburgh. Who do you think she's going to believe?"

"You, of course. Unless."

"Unless what?"

"Unless one of those missing pieces turns up."

"So long, Doc." The sheriff waved. "I'll be seeing you around."

Nick gazed after him as he moved away. "I'll be watching for you."

CHAPTER 31

Nick headed slowly across the churchyard, the sheriff's questions kept returning to him.

How could the sheriff murder Teddy and Mrs. Gallagher if he was with Jenny McIntyre all night? Was he really at Jenny's, or was it just an empty alibi? He must have been there at least part of the night—the story would be too easy to check out. But if the sheriff came and went during the night, Jenny would certainly know. Would she lie to protect him—maybe to win him away from Kathryn?

He approached the picnic table lost in thought when the glint of sunlight from something on the table caught his eye. Beanie stood beside the table like a towering totem with a band of tiny worshipers gathered about him. The deputy held them back from the table with his trunklike arms. The children were oohing and aahing over Beanie's police sidearm, shining in the hot afternoon sun.

"Don't touch," Beanie said with great authority. "Everybody look, but don't touch."

Nick stepped closer and peered over the heads of the solemn assembly. "What kind of gun do you have there, Deputy?"

"A police gun," Beanie said proudly.

"It looks a little like the sheriff's gun."

" 'Zactly like Unca Pete's gun."

It was exactly like the sheriff's weapon—a 9 millimeter Beretta 92F, the civilian equivalent of the standard army sidearm. They were identical except for the absence of the engraved emblem of the All American Division.

"I think Uncle Pete's gun is bigger."

" 'Zactly the same!" Beanie repeated with obvious irritation.

Fifty yards away and thirty feet in the sky, a single black Calliphora vomitoria hovered in the breeze, head into the wind, sensing and sampling the air as it rushed past. Suddenly, the blow fly detected an airborne cluster of blood molecules—and then another. She eagerly followed the elusive scent forward, drifting down from cluster to cluster, the scent leading it irresistibly onward until it finally came to rest on the handgrip of the deputy's gun.

Nick spotted the fly even before it landed. "That's enough," Beanie said. "I got to put it away now."

"No!" Nick grabbed his arm as he reached for the gun. "Tell me more about your gun, Beanie. Do you ever get to use it?"

The fly wandered over the serrated grip, its extended proboscis in constant motion—probing, sensing, tasting.

"Can't talk about that." Beanie shook his head.

"Do you ever clean it? You can tell me that."

"I wipe it off sometimes."

The sun bore down on the gleaming chrome pistol, and the

metal grew steadily warmer. The fly worked its way slowly over the Beretta, first to the trigger guard, then the frame, then the slide, its senses leading it inerrantly toward the muzzle of the gun.

"But do you ever really clean it? Take it apart? Clean the barrel?"

Beanie shook his head. "Wipe it off, mostly. Makes it shiny."

Nick held his breath as the fly hesitated for a moment at the very tip of the muzzle—then disappeared into the deep blackness of the barrel.

Nick stood paralyzed, watching as Beanie carefully picked up the weapon and slid it neatly back into its leather holster—exactly as he had done two nights ago after firing a bullet into the base of Teddy's skull.

Nick turned and drove his right fist into the center of Beanie's face. The nasal bone shattered beneath the blow, and blood spurted from both nostrils. The children scattered like startled doves. Beanie staggered backward from the force of the blow, and Nick was on him like a spider on a fly, driving his massive body to the ground with a thundering whump. With his left hand he grabbed for Beanie's bulbous throat, and he brought his right fist back for a crushing blow—and then he stopped. For one split second he met Beanie's eyes, and there he saw . . . nothing. There was neither malice nor anger nor cruelty of any kind. There was nothing but confusion and sorrow and pain. They were not the eyes of a killer—they were the eyes of a little child. Nick lowered his fist. In his rage at the puppet master, he had attacked the puppet.

He felt an explosion of pain in his left side, and the force of the blow threw him off of Beanie and onto his back. His wind was completely gone, and he writhed on the ground in agony, staring into the searing white sky above. The figure of the sheriff stood towering over him, the blinding sun flashing out from behind him like light from the face of Moses. An instant later he felt Kathryn's body drop across his like an interceding angel—covering him, protecting him.

"Stop it, Peter!" she screamed. "You didn't have to kick him that hard!"

"Look at Beanie!" he shouted back. "I should have shot him!"

Beanie stood calmly a few feet away, hands on knees, blood draining freely from his nose.

"Nick doesn't know what he's doing! He hasn't slept for days!"

"He knows what he's doing, all right. He knows exactly what he's doing!"

The sheriff circled menacingly around Nick's body while Kathryn stretched out over him, keeping her body between him and the avenging angel above.

"He's under arrest!" he jabbed his finger at Nick's body.

"Leave him alone! He's had enough!"

"He assaulted an officer of the law!"

"He hit Beanie. Don't be so stupid, Peter! Whose side are you on?"

"Not his!"

Kathryn rose up to her knees now and put her hands on her hips. There was an unmistakable fire in her emerald eyes. "Then how about my side? You always say you're on my side, Peter, well how about it? For me?"

Peter scowled at her and cursed under his breath. "Get him out of here," he growled, "and keep him away from me!" He turned and stormed off, leaving the deputy still doubled over behind him.

Kathryn immediately began to drag Nick to his feet. "We'd better get out of here before he changes his mind."

He put his right arm around her shoulders and braced his left hand against his aching ribs, and they staggered off together toward the parking lot. She deposited him against the hood of his car, then carefully lifted his shirt.

"Let me see that," she said. "You may have some broken ribs."

The site was already turning a greenish shade of purple. She began to feel gingerly along the contour of each rib. He winced and pulled away.

"Don't be a baby," she snapped. "You're lucky you're not dead. What in the world got into you back there? Why did you hit poor Beanie?"

"Because 'poor Beanie' murdered Teddy."

Kathryn stared at him in utter astonishment.

"The entry wound on the back of Teddy's skull was a contact wound, remember? That means the gun was placed against his skin and then discharged. In a contact wound, the gases

escape the muzzle at such tremendous velocity that they create a temporary vacuum in the barrel—and that vacuum sucks
blood back into the barrel. It's known as blowback. I watched
a Calliphora vomitoria land on Beanie's gun and crawl into the
barrel. That fly is attracted to blood, Mrs. Guilford; fresh blood.
It found some."

Kathryn shook her head in disbelief. "There must be some other
explanation."

"Give me an explanation. Tell me any other way the deputy
could have gotten blood into the barrel of his gun."

"Nick, this is Beanie we're talking about. Beanie isn't capable of
killing anyone."

"He isn't capable of hating anyone, Mrs. Guilford—I'm not even
sure he's capable of anger. You still want to believe that the deputy
is a gigantic Pinocchio, and your friend the sheriff is just kindly old
Gepetto. But this Pinocchio is capable of crushing a man's hand or
firing a bullet into a man's brain or anything else Gepetto tells him
to do."

Kathryn's legs felt weak, and her head began to swim.

"Didn't you find it interesting that the sheriff suddenly
developed a passion for Jenny McIntyre the other night? Didn't
you find it a little surprising? I'll bet Jenny was surprised."

"That's none of my business."

"It is your business, Mrs. Guilford. Don't you see? When the
sheriff told you he spent the night with Jenny McIntyre, he was
telling the truth. He couldn't have murdered Teddy and Mrs.
Gallagher, but that doesn't mean he couldn't send someone else to
do the errands for him."

"Nick—do you know what you're saying?"

"I'm saying that it wasn't passion that led the sheriff to Jenny's
door. He needed an alibi. The sheriff was in some way involved
in Jim McAllister's death. When that last specimen emerged, it
proved that the body was moved—and maybe it proved more than
that. The sheriff had to intervene, but he knew that I would suspect
him—so he sent his boy around to murder Teddy and to knock off
Mrs. Gallagher just to throw us off the scent.

"I know exactly what I'm saying, Mrs. Guilford, and so do you.
I'm saying that if your friend the sheriff wasn't a murderer before,
he is now."

The crowd at Mount Zion A. M. E. had long ago dispersed. All that remained from the morning's elaborate funeral reception were two folding tables draped unevenly in stained and wrinkled linens.

Nick sat by himself on a sagging picnic bench. He picked at the splinters of decomposing wood; it was made of cedar, a wood whose natural resins were supposed to protect it from decay. Everything decomposes, Nick thought. Some get a little more time than others, but sooner or later everything breaks down.

He lifted his shirt and gently tested his aching ribs. He was lucky; they were bruised, but not broken. A scarlet hematoma the size of his fist throbbed an angry reminder of how the world works: Blood vessels rupture under the skin. The blood pours into the surrounding tissues, and the stranded blood cells begin to die. The skin turns purple or blue or black. Black, the color of death; your own little piece of death to carry around with you.

His thoughts were interrupted by the closing of a car door. He looked up to see Kathryn remove a small casserole dish from the backseat and turn in his direction. Her gait was slow and halting; it was obvious that she was very much preoccupied with thoughts of her own.

"I have no idea why I brought this," she said absently, setting the casserole down to secure the edge of a fluttering tablecloth.

"Because there's nothing else to do," Nick said. "People have been bringing food to funerals for centuries." He lifted the foil from the edge of the dish. "Tuna puffs . . . I love these things."

"I've been thinking about what you said this morning—about Beanie and Teddy. About Peter."

"And?"

"Nick, you've got to try to see all this from my perspective. We're talking about Beanie—a little boy in a man's body. And Peter, a man I've known and trusted all my life. You come to me with eggs and maggots and flies that can smell blood from miles away, and you ask me to weigh those things against the things I know."

Nick leaned his head back and drew a long, deep breath through his nose. "Smell the air," he said to Kathryn. "Go ahead, give it a try. What do you smell?"

She sniffed at the air. "Not much. Tuna, mostly."

"Come on, you can do better than that."

She sniffed again. "I can smell the pines. And the asphalt heating up in the driveway. And . . . I don't know . . . some flowers, maybe."

"Amazing, isn't it?" Nick said. "Here we are, supposedly the highest form of life on the planet, and yet the only odors we can detect are so powerful that they would overwhelm a lower life form. We're thinking beings," he said, "but our senses have grown dull."

"Where are you going with all this?"

"I find that sometimes a situation becomes clearer when you do more than think—when you use all of your senses. You say that the evidence I've shown you seems unconvincing compared with what you know about the sheriff—but what do your other senses tell you? How does he smell? How does the whole situation feel? What do your instincts tell you?"

"You're asking me to weigh what I smell against things I know?"

"There are different ways of knowing," Nick said. "Sometimes what we call 'knowing' is just a form of prejudice."

"So now I'm prejudiced?"

"Of course you are. Look at it from my perspective, Mrs. Guilford. I see three men who all fell in love with you—and in your own way, you loved all three of them. You lost the one you loved the most; a week ago, you lost the second. Now you have only one left."

"And if I accept what you're telling me, then I've lost Peter too. I've lost everything."

"You said you had to know, Mrs. Guilford. The truth doesn't care."

"Well, I care," Kathryn said, "and I still have to know. Before I give up on Peter, I have to be absolutely sure. I'm not like you, Nick. I can't just smell things."

"Can't you? While we were interviewing Amy McAllister, her house just happened to burn to the ground. Then Teddy committed an unthinkable blunder, and that same night was murdered in a random act of violence. A day later, I watched a fly in search of blood enter the barrel of the deputy's gun. Come on, Mrs. Guilford—if you can smell asphalt, you can smell this."

"Can you tell me for certain—absolutely for certain—that there's no other reason that fly might have crawled into Beanie's gun? Did you ever stop to think that if you hadn't hit Beanie, we might have found a way to get hold of his gun? We might have been able to have it tested to see if there really was any blood—and if it was Teddy's?"

Nick said nothing.

"And there's something else, Nick—if Peter spent the night with Jenny, how did Beanie get to Teddy's trailer? He can't drive, Nick—Beanie can't drive. I'm sorry," she said, "I need proof."

"Wish I could help you," Nick shrugged. "But the only proof we might have had is gone—flying around somewhere, looking for a body of its own."

A small white door at the back door of the church opened, and the figure of Dr. Malcolm Jameson emerged, carrying a familiar black book at his side. Nick turned to Kathryn as he approached.

"About all this," Nick said with a wave of his hand.

"You're welcome. I just wish more people could be here."

"I wish Teddy could be here."

Dr. Jameson greeted them both with a solemn nod. "This seems an inappropriate location," he said with a frown at the littered surroundings. "Perhaps Dr. Polchak could suggest something more apropos."

Nick quickly scanned the terrain; at the edge of the church property, through a break in the tree line a golden green meadow rose up and away from them, brilliant in the full noon sun.

"There," Nick said. "Teddy would like that spot."

The three of them walked toward the meadow together. Dr. Jameson's pace was slow and deliberate, and Nick had to rein himself in to stay in step.

"So tell me," Dr. Jameson said, "how is the fishing?"

"Not good," Nick shook his head. "I had a big one on the line, but he got away."

"Nonsense. No one gets away, my friend. As the apostle said, 'Some men's sins go before them, and some follow after.' If your fish needs to be caught, he will be caught—sooner or later."

"I was hoping for sooner," Nick said.

"Patience. You are still a young man, and young men do not make good fishermen. Young men discourage too easily; they give up after the first false strike. The old fisherman knows he must wait."

"Wait for what?"

"For Providence." The old man smiled. "There is more to fishing than meets the eye."

At the crest of the meadow they halted. Nick and Kathryn stood side by side, and Dr. Jameson turned to face them. He opened the great book and slowly searched through the fragile pages; then he stopped, closed his eyes, and raised his face to the June sun.

"God our Father," he began, "Maker of heaven and earth—we gather today to deliver into Your hands the soul and memory of Dr. Eustatius Tedesco . . ."

He said the name without fumbling—no moment's hesitation, no awkward glance at a written reminder. He said the name as though it was worth knowing, and Nick was grateful for the offer of dignity and respect.

"We remember today the life of a man well-loved, a man who spent his life in the service of others and in the pursuit of justice. This man has been cruelly taken from us, O Lord, and our hearts are darkened—Your world is darkened by his loss! 'Help, Lord, for the godly man ceases to be, for the faithful disappear from among the sons of men.' "

The old man spoke in slow, thundering waves. He began almost in a whisper; then his voice swelled to a rumbling crescendo, then broke, receded, and slowly rose again. Almost a song, Nick thought, just like the cicadas in the woods.

"We bring our complaint before you today, for our friend was taken from us by murder most foul. Our hearts cry out for justice, O Lord—and our brother cries out to You from the grave! Nothing is hidden from Your sight, O God, 'For there is nothing covered that will not be revealed, and hidden that will not be known.' "

The deputy can't drive, Nick thought. Then how did he get to Teddy's trailer and back again? The sheriff couldn't have dropped him off, there wasn't time. He had to take care of things at the lab, and then he had to get to Jenny's to establish his alibi. Then how did the deputy get there?

"You are no stranger to killing, O Lord. You have witnessed the taking of countless innocent lives. You were there at the first, at the slaying of righteous Abel. You looked down upon wicked Cain; You knew the burning jealousy in his heart. 'Why are you angry?' You said to him. 'And why has your countenance fallen? If you do well, will not your countenance be lifted up? And if you do not do well, sin is crouching at the door; but you must master it.' " The old man glanced down at the ancient text and translated the Latin effortlessly as he read.

Would the fly have gone into the barrel for any other reason? Not likely—not that species of fly. The deputy killed Teddy, Nick thought. He could smell it. But that's not enough for Mrs. Guilford—she wants proof.

"But Cain did not master his jealousy; he did not contain his rage. He slew his own brother and thought he could hide his sin from You . . . From You, who sees all the inward workings of the heart! 'And the Lord said to Cain, "What have you done? The voice of your brother's blood is crying to me from the ground." ' "

Nick stopped. "What did you say?"

The old man slowly looked up from his text.

Nick snatched the book from his hand and scanned the facing pages. "Where were you reading?"

"The Book of Genesis," Dr. Jameson said quietly, "chapter four."

Nick ran his finger down the text, searching. "Here it is," he said. *"Vox sanguinis fratris tui clamat ad me de terra . . .* The voice of your brother's blood cries out to me from the ground."

"What is it?" Kathryn asked.

Nick turned and raced toward the parking lot. "I'll be back in a few hours," he called back. "If everything goes well, you'll have all the proof you need!"

"Nick! Where are you going? Nick!"

Kathryn watched the Dodge belch out of the driveway. She turned back to Dr. Jameson and stared at the leather-bound volume in his hands. "What was it? What did he find?"

The old man smiled. "I believe the young man is going fishing."

CHAPTER 33

Nick steered his Dodge into the impossibly crowded parking lot at North Carolina State University and double parked behind two university service vehicles. His faculty parking permit had long ago expired, and he had long ago ceased to care. He had come to enjoy this ongoing game of eluding the University Safety Patrol—or the "Parking Gestapo," as he referred to them. He plucked a small, clear plastic vial from the passenger seat and held it up to the light. He tipped it gently from side to side, searching for its tiny occupant.

He walked briskly across the Brickyard, the central plaza of the North Campus, an acre-wide mosaic of rose-and-cream masonry punctured intermittently by an ancient red oak or a stately wax-leafed magnolia. The western end of the Brickyard was bordered by Gardner Hall, a nondescript monolith of red Carolina brick and limestone-ledged windows, each choked with its own pulsing air conditioner. The second, third, and fourth floors are home to the NCSU Department of Entomology—and on friendlier days, home to Dr. Nick Polchak as well.

The meandering summer students seemed to sense the urgency

in his gait and stepped aside as he strode through the entry door and swung left into the open doorway of the departmental office. A middle-aged woman looked up at him from behind an almond steel-case reception desk.

"Where is Noah?" Nick demanded.

The woman smiled politely. "Why, Nick! It's been quite a while since—"

"Where is Noah? Does he have a class? Do you have his teaching schedule?"

The smile quickly disappeared from her face. She glanced at the summer schedule tacked to the bulletin board in front of her. "He has ENT 502," she said dully. "It's in 3214. Do you want your mail? You've got several letters."

Nick turned without a word and headed for the doorway.

"Nice to see you again," she called after him.

He stopped in the doorway and turned back, staring at her curiously.

"Who are you?" he asked, and without waiting for an answer he wheeled around again and was gone.

The heels of his loafers clacked and echoed down the hollow corridors of Gardner Hall, largely empty during the hot summer months except for the ever-present graduate students who slumped lethargically in front of computers and laboratory tables. Nick sprinted up a flight of stairs, then down a long, white hallway veined with pipes and ducts and electrical conduit. The floor was a glossy checkerboard of aging brown and black linoleum, and a single row of rectangular fluorescent dashes lined the center of the ceiling. It was an altogether quiet and sterile environment in the summer, and Nick preferred it that way. He enjoyed the teaching profession most when he wasn't saddled with the annoying distraction of students.

He paused before the door to room 3214 and peered through the translucent glass at the silhouette of a single figure standing motionless behind a lectern. He rapped sharply on the glass, and without waiting for a response, he invited himself in.

The door crashed open, and a half-dozen startled students awakened from their heat-induced torpor. The ancient figure behind the lectern stood oblivious, completely immune to interruption after more than fifty years of teaching—but as he continued with his lecture on Insect Systematics he gradually became aware that his students' focus had been thoroughly diverted. He rapped his knuckles sharply on the wooden lectern and flashed his sternest look. A student in the first row helpfully gestured toward the door. The old man reluctantly turned and studied Nick without any sign of recognition whatsoever—and then a light went on somewhere in the vast, endless library of his mind.

He smiled.

"Why Nicholas," he said with delight.

"Noah." Nick extended his hand. "I need your help."

Dr. Noah Ellison was one of the most venerated entomologists in the world. His research on the systematics of medically important arthropod species was legendary. During World War II, Lieutenant Ellison pioneered mosquito-control strategies for the Allied forces in the jungles of the South Pacific, and he almost single-handedly tripled the specimen collection of the Smithsonian Museum of Natural History, where he was now one of only three curators emeritus. After major field studies and surveys on five continents, he was a veritable encyclopedia of knowledge on the 85,000 species that constitute the order Diptera: mosquitoes, gnats, midges, and—most important to Nick—flies.

Despite the summer heat Noah was dressed as always in a crisp white button-down and scarlet bow tie. Regardless of temperature or humidity, he always dressed the same. He never seemed to chill or sweat; he was timeless, changeless, a mathematical constant in a universe of variables. But age was beginning to take its inevitable toll on Noah Ellison, and in the last few years his colleagues had sadly noticed the first decline in his remarkable intellectual powers. Nick had consulted him many times in his investigations and had always thought of Noah as a kind of timeless reference work that would forever stand on ready reserve. Now Nick thought of him more as a priceless, ancient manuscript, filled with wonders of knowledge and wisdom but rapidly crumbling to dust— which fueled all the more Nick's sense of urgency in seeking his assistance.

"Class," Dr. Ellison said warmly, "allow me to introduce Dr. Nicholas Polchak, a colleague and member of our faculty. His face may be unfamiliar to you because he was recently exiled to the wilderness for dabbling in the black arts. Dr. Polchak, you see, is a forensic entomologist. So be on your guard"—he glowered at the most sleepy-eyed of the students—"or you may turn up as one of Dr. Polchak's field studies."

The students smiled and nodded their greeting. Nick ignored them and reached into his pocket for the precious plastic vial.

"Noah, I need your help—with this."

Noah adjusted his glasses and peered at the impossibly small occupant of the vial.

"Nicholas"—he nodded slightly toward the students—"I'm in the middle of something right now—"

"Noah, Dr. Tedesco is dead. Teddy was murdered, Noah, and I'm after the man who did it. I need you to make a species identification for me—I need to be absolutely certain—and all I can give you to work with is this."

Nick held up the vial containing a single brown speck the size of a grain of rice—the puparial capsule left behind when the final specimen was released.

As they headed down the hallway toward the stairwell, Nick had to double back twice to keep pace with Noah's ambling shuffle.

"Let's take the elevator, Noah—just this once."

"Nonsense," Dr. Ellison grumbled and began his slow ascent of the twenty-four steps leading to the fourth floor. The Gardner Hall elevator bore a bronze plaque officially denoting it the "Noah Ellison Memorial Elevator," in honor of the fact that Noah Ellison had never once in more than fifty years employed it.

Room 4321 housed the Insect Collection, a warehouse of gray metal specimen cabinets and shelves that always smelled of mothballs, necessary to protect the thousands of dried specimens from dermestid attack. Noah seated himself with a sigh at a laboratory table bearing a single gleaming microscope. He removed a neatly folded handkerchief from his shirt pocket and spread it on the table before him.

"Now then"—he turned to Nick—"let's have the little fellow."

Nick carefully inverted the plastic vial and the tiny brown speck rolled out into the center of the handkerchief. Noah selected a pair of light tension forceps and turned to the specimen, widening his eyes and craning his head forward and back in an attempt to bring the diminutive object into focus. His hand shook like the tremens of an alcoholic; it seemed laughable that he would ever be able to pinpoint the single elusive speck. Nick held his breath, with visions of the precious specimen flipping onto the floor and disappearing into a vent or crack. To his astonishment, Noah seized the puparium on his very first attempt.

"You seem nervous, Nicholas," he said acidly, somehow managing to place the puparium in the exact center of a glass specimen slide. "You must learn to relax if you ever wish to reach my age. Now—tell me about Dr. Tedesco," he said as he adjusted the microscope.

"A body turned up in the woods near our research station just over a week ago. The local coroner botched the examination completely, and I was hired to do an independent investigation—without the permission of the authorities."

Noah glanced up. "Nicholas, is this your idea of staying out of trouble?"

"I only had time to collect a handful of specimens. We've been rearing them in the lab to identify the species. This one came from an isolated wound above the left eye—the kind of wound a good right cross might make. I have reason to believe that the body was moved postmortem, and I was hoping this specimen might confirm that suspicion."

"And the mature fly?" Noah peered into the lens again.

"Teddy was on watch. He indicated in his log that eclosion occurred the night before last at about midnight. I arrived at the lab several hours later. The back door was open and the fly was gone. I went straight to Teddy's trailer—"

"Tragic," Noah said solemnly. "Dr. Tedesco was a fine systematist and an even better human being. I shall miss him."

"I believe Teddy identified the species, and I think he made the mistake of notifying the wrong person—someone with a motive to cover it up."

"Someone quite ignorant of our discipline," Noah murmured. "Someone under the assumption that species can only be determined by the mature specimen and not by the puparial sac it leaves behind." He rocked back from the microscope. "Take a look, Nicholas. Tell me what you see."

Nick groaned. "Noah, please. I'm in a hurry here."

"Nicholas," he repeated sternly, "tell me what you see."

It was Noah Ellison's most endearing habit, and his most annoying as well. He was, above all, a teacher—and he never gave a simple or direct answer when he could invite the student to learn for himself. Neatly framed above his office desk were the words of E. M. Forster: "Spoon feeding in the long run teaches us nothing but the shape of the spoon." Nick knew it was useless to resist. Noah moved aside, and the student took his place at the master's knee.

"Now then. As you know, the puparium is formed by the skin of the third-instar larva. This means that the puparium is a kind of shrink-wrap around the maturing fly which retains many of its identifying features—and some of its own morphological uniquenesses as well. Notice first of all the microsculpturing on the cuticle—quite characteristic for this species."

"I see it."

"Look at the bubble membrane. Do you see the little globules? Now examine the dorsal lateral surface of segment five."

"What about this rupture?"

"It is caused by the aversion of the pupal respiratory horn—its location is significant. Now notice some of the other structural features: the scalelike texturing, the tiny projections and processes—"

"I see it." Nick looked up. "I see it all, Noah—but I need an identification. What species are we looking at here? Can you tell me?"

The old man closed his eyes for several moments and then slowly began to shake his head.

"I cannot," he said sadly.

Nick's heart sank.

Noah leaned forward and spoke almost in a whisper. "It shames me to say this, but—" He stopped and glanced back over his shoulder toward the door. "I am going to have to refer to a book." He stood up without a word and shuffled out into the hallway, with Nick on his heels.

Three doors down Noah rounded the corner into the tiny room that served as his office. It was sparsely decorated, almost empty except for the tidy metal desk and the vinyl visitor's armchair resting beside it. The one remarkable feature about the room was the complete absence of paper. It was impossibly neat for the office of a scientist—but that was simply because, over the years, Dr. Ellison had carefully transferred the contents of each book and monograph into his formidable memory.

"Now where did I put that book," he mumbled, wandering about the office. "Ah!" He spotted a single green volume atop the lone filing cabinet. Nick wasn't sure the old man could even lift the massive tome; he stepped over and took it down for him, wiped the dusty cover against his shirt, and spread it open on Noah's desk.

Nick agonized as Noah slowly leafed through page after page of crowded text.

"Now this is interesting," he would say from time to time—and then point out some obscure tidbit of entomological trivia that had nothing at all to do with their quest. Nick's impatience grew more and more obvious, but Noah was unflappable.

"You must learn to enjoy the journey, Nicholas," he said without interrupting his reading. "You must learn not to weary the soul by longing only for the destination."

Endless, agonizing minutes passed.

"Here it is," he said at last. "Exactly as I suspected. These references are organized very poorly, very poorly indeed. There really should be a cross-index of morphological features. I must speak to the publisher about this, I—"

"Noah!"

Dr. Ellison looked at him implacably. "It is a Chrysomya megacephala, Nicholas—commonly known as the Oriental Blow Fly."

"I know that species," Nick said. "It has anterior spiracles. It's greenish blue with purple highlights, and the posterior margin of the second and third abdominal segments is jet black."

"Precisely. Megacephala is an immigrant species that was introduced into Florida sometime in the eighties. It prefers the warmer winters, and so its range is limited—but it seems to be adapting and slowly moving north."

"How far north?"

"Central Georgia. No farther."

"Not North Carolina?"

Noah looked at him with disdain. "The last time I consulted an atlas, Nicholas, Central Georgia was about eight hours from North Carolina."

"And you're positive?"

Noah raised a single eyebrow. His meaning was unmistakable.

Nick extended his hand. The old man took it and gripped it tightly until they both made eye contact.

"I wasn't joking about the black arts, you know. Be careful, Nicholas. I've lost one colleague this week—I wouldn't care to lose another."

Nick hurried down the hall, stopping at the insect collection just long enough to retrieve the crucial specimen.

"Your mail!" the secretary yelled to him as he raced past the doorway of the departmental office. "Don't you want your mail?"

Nick snatched the rubber-banded stack of envelopes without a word and sprinted across the Brickyard to his car. He pulled the pink square of paper from under his windshield wiper, crumpled it, and threw it into the car, then roared out of the parking lot with a clatter of valves and a trademark puff of blue smoke.

Nick picked up his cell phone and punched in Kathryn's number.

"Mrs. Guilford," he said. "I need you to do something for me. I need you to call the sheriff and invite him over to your house. That's right, your house. Because I need to take a look at his patrol car, that's why; and I can't very well do it while it's parked in front of the sheriff's office. I figure I need about thirty minutes—thirty uninterrupted minutes, Mrs. Guilford—I don't think my ribs can stand another encounter with the sheriff just yet. Whatever you do, keep him in the house for thirty minutes. Got it?

"What? I don't know. Tell him you want to talk. Tell him you want to cry on his shoulder. Tell him you're having second thoughts about him—that should do it. And once he's inside, well . . . you think of something.

"I've got to stop at the lab first, but I can be at your place by a quarter to four. Tell him to meet you at four o'clock. I'll park down the street and watch for his car. What? There's no time now, I'll explain everything when I . . . Hello? Mrs. Guilford, are you there?"

Nick looked down at the phone. The green LCD panel flashed the words, SEARCHING FOR SERVICE. He looked out the window; he was east of I-95 now, well outside the city. He thought about Walter Reed and its location at the northern tip of Washington, almost to the Maryland border.

Nick reached over for the stack of mail and tugged off the rubber band with his teeth. He pinned the rumpled envelopes against the steering wheel and rifled through them: a departmental notice, a schedule of summer classes, a past-due notice from the University Safety Patrol . . .

Mr. Vincent Arranzio, Washington D.C. PERSONAL.

He tore off the end of the envelope and fumbled open the single sheet of paper inside. In large letters was scribbled a single sentence:

THE GUY'S NAME WAS PETE.

Nick slammed the pedal to the floor.

CHAPTER 34

'll see you at four then. Thank you, Peter."

Even before Kathryn hung up the phone, she felt a familiar tightening in her stomach. Nick said Beanie must have killed Teddy. Could it be true? Was it even possible? If Beanie really did it, then Peter had to be behind it. But why would Peter want Teddy dead, unless . . .

Did I just invite a murderer over to my house?

There was no evidence. There was no proof. She had no way to know—but Nick was right. Somehow, there was the strangest smell.

The knot in her gut began to grow.

What was she supposed to do with Peter for thirty minutes? She told him she wanted to talk—about what? What would she say to him, "I invited you over to tell you again that I don't love you?"

She checked her watch: 3:15. Forty-five minutes until Peter would arrive. What was she supposed to do until then? She glanced around the house: The coffee table was stacked with unread newspapers and unpaid bills, the kitchen counter was dotted with spills and stains and articles of glass and plastic, and the carpet was cluttered with everything dropped there in the last week and a half.

She decided to clean up. It was a lesson she had learned from her mother, which her mother had gleaned from her mother before her and so on back to the beginning of humankind: When the world makes no sense, clean up. Sometimes the truth is simply buried beneath the clutter.

She started with the paper: the magazines, the flyers, the junk mail that seemed to accumulate like falling leaves. She dumped a mound of unfolded laundry onto the bed, then made a sweep of the house with the laundry basket gathering shoes and books and a score of other wayward items.

She picked up the ancient Macanudo cigar box from the coffee table and carried it into the kitchen. There on the kitchen table sat Jimmy's black leather King James Bible, still bound by an ancient rubber band and stamped in gold by the Gideons International. Kathryn smiled. It was just like Jimmy to include among his possessions a copy of the Book of Righteousness—one that he had stolen from a motel room.

She set the Bible on top of the cigar box and stretched the rubber band around them both—but the brittle rubber band snapped, and the Bible fell to the floor. When she lifted it, the leather cover came loose and slipped away. To her surprise, the text within was not Scripture at all; it was some kind of diary in Jimmy's own broken handwriting. The first entry was dated August 3, 1990—the week before the 82d Airborne was called to active duty. It was more than just a personal diary—it was Jimmy's war journal, his own record of what happened to him in the Gulf. What went wrong, what depressed him, what he could never bring himself to say aloud.

Kathryn scolded her imagination for running ahead of her, and with trembling hands turned the first fragile page.

August 3, 1990

> *2d Brigade had inspection today. In a few days we start our rotation as DRB. Six weeks on two-hour recall. So what—I got no place to go anyway.*
>
> *Lots of talk about Iraq and Kuwait and all. Where IS Kuwait anyway? Word is the 82d might get called in to clean things up just like in Grenada and Panama. If the balloon goes up on our shift, 2d Brigade will be first to go.*
>
> *Can't stop thinking about Kathryn, but I got to try—she's married and gone now. If it couldn't be me, I'm glad it was Andy. Better Andy than Pete. What's the difference? Pete, Andy, either way she's gone. Gone for good.*
>
> *Can't believe I ever had the guts to ask her. What was I thinking—that she'd take me just because I was first in line? Who am I anyway? Nobody, that's who. I'm nobody and I got nothing. Hi Kathryn, I'm nobody. Will you marry me? You can have half of my nothing. Now you're Mrs. Nobody, with nothing.*

Kathryn could hardly bear to read on. She knew that she had hurt Jimmy, but she had only experienced his heartache through the protective buffer of others: through a letter from Andy or a comment from an acquaintance or a scathing look from Amy. But here were Jimmy's own words, the distilled putrescence of all his anger and pain. It was almost too much to endure.

Almost.

August 28, 1990

> *Arrived in Saudi Arabia, someplace called Dhahran. Lots to do, lots going on. Desert training, trying out our biological suits. Hot as Hades in those suits, but I guess we'll be glad enough if the Iraqis try to gas us like they done to Iran.*
>
> *Tough schedule. First call at 0430. Hot, crowded, grunts everywhere. 1500 of us so far, twice that many soon. Food stinks.*

Burgers and fries from Hardees today, twice last week too. They got Hardees over here! Everything was cold.

Some of the boys get mail by the truckload. I get nothing. Tough to watch Andy get so much from Kathryn—cookies, boxes, good-smelling letters. Pictures too. Look at me in my swimsuit, look at me with my hair up. Makes me crazy sometimes. I guess if you win the chicken you get the eggs.

Kathryn began to read faster now. The words seemed to fly from the pages, and the pages seemed to turn by themselves. She felt like a little girl careening downhill on a bicycle, out of control, thrilled by the ride but terrified of what might await her at the end.

October 12, 1990

Redeployed to Ab Qaiq 80 miles southeast—80 miles farther away from the action. Started drawing imminent-danger pay two weeks ago, but nothing to spend it on. One day off each week, but nothing to do. Plenty of training—thank God for the training. Keeps me busy, keeps me from sitting around and thinking.

Somebody said the 82d will head home once all the heavy forces arrive. I hope not. I didn't sign on just to clear the way for somebody else to get the medals. I got to have my chance to show what I can do, I got to prove myself.

Prove myself to who? I got nobody to impress. I got nobody back home. Truth is, I still want to prove myself to Kathryn. But why? So Kathryn will say Boy did I make a mistake, Boy did I get the wrong guy. Then she'll say Sorry Andy, I made a mistake, I got the wrong guy.

Sure she will.

November 3, 1990

Got a letter from Kathryn today. Not a fancy letter, not a good-smelling one, just a white envelope with white paper from the Ramada Inn Beaufort where Andy took her on their wedding night. So she sends it to me. Dear Jimmy, I'm married, how are you, I'm married. I bet Pete got one too. I wonder who else got one? Maybe she made copies for everybody.

November 21, 1990

I swear I'm going nuts. Nothing but tents everywhere like some kind of shantytown. No space, no room to breathe. Everybody keeps their stash under their cot. Cookies and cake and soap and toilet paper from home. From girlfriends and wives and lovers back home. But I got nobody back home, so I got nothing to stash. I keep empty boxes under my cot so nobody will ask.

November 28, 1990

No beer here because the Saudis want it that way. The Saudis want it! Somebody needs to tell the Saudis we came over here to keep the Iraqis from whipping them and taking their oil. Who's protecting who here? Why do we care what the Saudis want?

Some of the boys do a little snow from time to time. Put it in a nasal spray, mix it with a little vodka and water. Like they got allergies or something so nobody knows, nobody cares. They say it's like a couple cups of coffee. Doesn't sound so bad. One thing I know—a soldier got to kick back sometimes or he loses his edge.

What do they expect anyway? No beer!

Kathryn felt as though she were staring through the window of a burning building at a confused and frightened child. But there was no way into the building and no way out. All she could do was watch the flames grow higher and hotter, knowing how the story had to end.

December 16, 1990

More waiting. Four months in country and nobody knows what's going on. First we're supposed to be guarding marines, next we're guarding oil wells. Where are the bad guys?

Made a new friend—best one I've had for a while. Don't know

*what all the fuss is about. I hardly even feel it. Helps me relax a
little, gives me a little lift—no big deal.*

　　*No more letters from Kathryn. Just as well—great girl, but I
got a little shopping to do before I buy.*

December 25, 1990

　　*Andy called Kathryn today. Free phone calls, three minutes
to anyone in the States. Who are they trying to fool? The line is
bugged—somebody listens in the whole time. I told them to take
their phone call and shove it.*

　　*Why are they after me? What do they want to know? Andy
said it's no big deal, said I was acting crazy. No big deal for him,
maybe. They don't care about a man with family—they think a
family man can be trusted, they know he's got something to lose.
They save their worry for grunts like me. We're the dangerous
ones, we're the ones who got to be watched.*

　　Why is Andy helping them? Can't trust anyone anymore.

She could trace the effect of the drug from entry to entry. Jimmy
seemed to rise like a phoenix to heights of supreme confidence and
then plummet into confusion and paranoia in the course of a single
page. But gradually each high became a little less convincing, and
each low brought him closer to the flames.

January 20, 1991

　　Saw Pete again today.

Kathryn stopped. Saw Pete? But didn't Peter say that he never
saw Jimmy in the Gulf?

Saw Pete again? A single visit Peter might have forgotten—but
more than one?

　　*I was talking about Kathryn again, about how much I miss
her—Pete blew up! Said I should stop whining, said I wasn't
the only one who loved her, who wanted to marry her. Who else?
I said.*

Turns out Pete's got it worse than me. He's not just sorry about Kathryn, he's mad at Andy! He thinks Andy just got there first, thinks he took Pete's place. What about me? I said. I got there before Andy—before anybody. Doesn't matter, he said—it was HIS place, like Kathryn belonged to him or something. I told him he was nuts. I told him Kathryn would take me before she takes him. That's when he took a swing at me. Not a little poke, either—they had to pull us apart.

And all this time I thought I was the only one.

Kathryn read the words again and again: Pete's got it worse than me . . .

What made Peter angry enough to attack poor Jimmy—and what in the world did he mean that Andy had taken his place? The very idea should have enraged her—but it didn't.

It chilled her to the marrow of her bone.

February 18, 1991

I'm in trouble. I'm in big trouble.

Andy found my stuff. He was digging through the MRE boxes under my cot—said he was looking for something to eat. He found the mirror, the razor, the straws—everything. I thought he'd blow a gasket but he didn't. Said he understood. Said he wanted to help. Andy is a straight arrow. Andy is an okay guy.

But he told Pete.

Pete said he was going to turn me in! I asked him not to, I threatened him, finally I begged him. They'll discharge me, they'll wash me out. I'll miss the show! You should have thought of that he said. It's rules, it's regulations, it's the honor of the outfit. Don't do this to me, I said. This could mean court martial, this could mean jail. I'm on his heels, I'm begging, I'm running after him like some sniveling mutt. We got all the way to the door of the HHC before he stopped. Okay he said, I won't turn you in.

Not now anyway. Not NOW he said.

He was going to do it if I didn't stop him. What if he gets steamed at me again, what if we have another fight? Pete gets mean sometimes, he gets REAL mean. I won't beg anymore and I won't go licking his boots.

Not now he said—but maybe tomorrow or the next day . . .

I'm going nuts, I'm going nuts, I swear I am going nuts.

February 22, 1991

Word came down today, we're going in tomorrow. Thank God—anything but this waiting. Haven't seen Pete for three days. What is he doing? Who is he talking to? Had chow with Andy. Good luck tomorrow he says, good luck Jim. Yeah Andy you got the good luck. You got the girl, you got the good luck. Tomorrow I'm a hero and they give me the medal of honor—then Pete turns me in. I hope I take a bullet tomorrow, that's the only way out of this mess. That's MY luck Andy, you get the girl and I get a bullet.

Kathryn's hands shook so badly she could barely turn the page. She prayed that there would be no further entry, that the three boys simply went to war and Andy was lost and Pete and Jimmy came home. She thought she wanted to know everything, that there was nothing worse than the agonizing uncertainty of not knowing. But now she understood for the first time that there was something infinitely worse—learning what you wished you never knew and could never again forget. The truth doesn't care, Nick told her. Part of her still wanted to know—and part of her was sorry she had ever asked.

The boys she had loved since childhood, the boys who held her hand on the front porch swing, the boys with the bright, clean uniforms and the shining hair were dissolving before her eyes like wet sugar candy.

February 27, 1991

God have mercy on me a sinner. What have I done? I didn't know. God forgive me. I didn't know what I was doing.

We attacked Al Salman last night. We were with the French going in at night. We called in fire from the big 155 mms in back, then we huddled and waited till the smoke cleared. That's where we ran into Pete's unit, and there he was.

God what happened—what went wrong? We moved too fast, we got overextended. They warned us, they told us no heroes, but it went so fast. It was so dark, it was so easy. Andy ran forward and took a position behind a berm—then it all came apart. We thought they were all dead, we thought all we had to do was walk in and raise the flag. They were there all right—a whole brigade of the Iraqi 45th. There was a firefight. Man, what a show—tracers and shells everywhere like fireflies like the 4th of July. Andy got cut off, there was nothing we could do except duck for cover. We could see him fifty yards ahead, but we couldn't move, couldn't get to him.

I poke my gun up over the wall and start firing high, firing to keep them away from Andy. I'm firing and firing and I look over at Pete. He's aiming his gun but not firing. Now he's aiming low, he's adjusting his thermal site. He's aiming at Andy!

Andy is waving to us, waving us forward. Come on he says, it's okay now. I'll cover you. Come on, why don't you come? You can make it.

Pete fires.

I cover my head and I start to cry like a baby. I cry just like a little baby.

Pete looks at me. "I tell you what," he says. "You help me bury my problem and I'll help you bury yours."

Kathryn stumbled back from the table, sending the chair clattering across the floor. She stood struggling for breath, not knowing what to do next, not knowing what to think or feel.

He's aiming at Andy, the little words said, and Pete fires. Such simple words, such harmless words, but they tore through her soul like a bullet—like the bullet that killed Andy. Like the bullet from Peter's gun that killed Andy! And now she knew, now she knew what she longed to know for eight long years—and she would give anything in the world not to know again.

He lied to me about Andy and about Jimmy and about everything every day since. He held me, and he watched me cry, and he told me that he loved me. I could have married him and had children with him—the man who murdered my own husband.

The unfolding reality engulfed her like a series of thundering waves, each more powerful than the last, pounding her and tossing her about like flotsam and depositing her exhausted body at last on the cold kitchen floor. Kathryn drew a deep breath and prepared to weep, prepared to summon forth the keener's wail that comes from the blackest corner of the soul.

But before she could make a sound, the doorbell rang.

It was four o'clock.

CHAPTER 35

The doorbell rang again.

Kathryn tried to struggle to her feet, but a wall of nausea slammed her down again. She forced herself up, gagging, and tried to straighten herself as best she could. Her legs would not support her the entire distance to the door; she stumbled to the sofa and collapsed. She quickly wiped her eyes and waited, staring silently at the door.

The doorbell rang a third time.

What do I say? What do I do?

The man she invited to her house a hundred times before was a faithful and trusted friend, a man she had known and loved for three decades. But that man was dead now, gone forever, destroyed just minutes ago by a handful of words scribbled in a soldier's diary. The man outside the door was a man she had never seen before, a liar and a murderer, a monster capable of unspeakable evil. Was she supposed to greet him with a kiss? Should she sit with him and hold his hand, the same hand that squeezed the trigger and casually put an end to her husband's life? Should she chat with him about the future—about their future—as though he had not single-handedly engineered the destruction of Kathryn's entire world?

A moment later she heard the sound of a key fumbling in the lock. The door swings slowly open.

"Didn't you hear the bell?" Peter said.

Kathryn said nothing. It was all she could do to keep her composure, to keep from vomiting or screaming or gasping for air. She felt like a child standing petrified in a dark room, overwhelmed by a sense of approaching evil. No, it was more than that.

She felt like a seven-year-old girl helplessly trapped in a '57 Chevy.

Peter stepped closer and looked at her—at the pallor of her face, the emptiness of her gaze, and the rigidity of her posture. He whistled softly.

"Hey," he said. "Who died?"

Nick watched the sheriff enter the house from a block away where he carefully hid his car behind a pair of rusting construction Dumpsters. His '64 Dodge had become something of a landmark in Rayford, and this was one time he couldn't afford to be recognized. He waited several minutes before approaching on foot, sticking close to trees and shrubbery in case he had to make a last-minute dive for cover. He would only need a few minutes to raise the hood of the sheriff's car, take care of business, and be on his way. Five minutes had already elapsed. If Kathryn managed to keep the sheriff occupied for even half of the thirty minutes he asked for, he would still have time to spare.

The driveway rose sharply toward the house, and the black-and-white Crown Victoria was parked to the right of Kathryn's car. He approached almost casually from behind—but twenty yards away he suddenly recognized a second figure in the car, a hulking silhouette on the passenger side.

Nick took several quick steps back, afraid that the deputy might have already spotted his legs in the rearview mirror—but there was no sign of motion or recognition from the car.

Nick glanced at the patrol car, then at the house—then at his watch.

"I'm sorry I kicked your Bug Man friend, if that's what this is all about." Peter searched in vain for the cause of Kathryn's gloom. "But he had it coming."

By sheer force of will Kathryn raised her eyes and looked at a face she had never seen before. For the first time she noticed the barracudalike jut of his jaw, the awkward spacing of his empty gray eyes, the spatter of cratered pockmarks on his mottled skin, and the wiry coarseness of his sallow hair. It was evil. It was all evil. Why had she never seen it before?

"I know you must be upset about the shooting," he ventured. "You know, Dr. What's-his-name."

"Teddy," she managed a trembling whisper. "His name was Teddy."

"Whatever. That must have been tough for you. Sorry you had to see that."

Kathryn looked into his hollow, soulless eyes.

"Why, Peter? Why did anyone have to die?"

"It's a shame." He shook his head. "Sometimes it comes to that."

Kathryn stared at him. "What's it like? To kill a man, I mean."

"I don't like to talk about it."

"But I want to know. Do you look at his face, or do you avoid his eyes so you won't hesitate to pull the trigger? Do you try to think of him as just a target—like one of those big silhouettes at the firing range—or do you think about where he came from, who might love him, who he might be leaving behind?"

He looked at her. "Boy, you're in a mood today."

"I want to know," she repeated, holding back her tears.

"There's no time to think. In my line of work, sometimes you have to make a split-second decision. There's no time to think about things like that."

"I'm not talking about your line of work—I'm talking about murder. What do you think about when there is time? What do you think about when you know you're going to kill someone?"

He hesitated. "I don't suppose a murderer thinks about any of those things."

"Sometimes killing is necessary," she said. "Sometimes it's your duty. You can always tell yourself later it was my job, I had to do it, he deserved to die. But what does a murderer think later? What does he tell himself? How does he explain it all away?"

A pause. "I suppose he tells himself he had to do it too."

"He had to do it," she repeated. "But of course he didn't have to. He chose to. It was just his selfish, stupid, cowardly way of trying to fix things—trying to make things go his way."

"I . . . I guess so . . ."

"Do you suppose a murderer thinks of himself as a good person who just had to do a bad thing? Because that's a lie, you know. But maybe it doesn't matter—maybe he's gotten so good at lying to himself that he can't tell the lies from the truth anymore."

He shifted uneasily. "How should I know?"

She stared into his eyes. "Don't you think about these things, Peter? I do. I think about them all the time."

"How would you guys like to make ten bucks?" Nick smiled at the three bored youngsters draped across a buckling swing set.

"You guys?" the first boy mocked. "Where you from, mister?"

Nick eyed him. "I'm from a place where the kids have got guts."

"What do we gotta do?" the second boy asked indignantly.

"You boys know Beanie? Beanie, the deputy sheriff?"

All three nodded.

"He's a friend of mine, and I want to play a little joke on him. He's sitting right over there in the squad car, see him? The sheriff told him to stay in the car, and I want to sneak up and surprise him. All you have to do is distract him—keep him occupied for, let's say, twenty minutes."

"How do we do that?"

"How should I know? Talk to him, tell him some jokes, show him your baseball cards. What am I paying you for? You think of something. But remember—twenty minutes."

The third boy cocked his head to one side. "Each. Ten bucks each."

"Ten bucks even," Nick replied, "and I'll give each of you a scorpion the size of your hand."

The three boys raced to Beanie's window.

"Hey, Beanie!" the first called out. The deputy turned to them, displaying a broad, white swatch of gauze plastered across the center of his face.

"Wow!" the second boy stopped. "What happened to your nose?"

"I got hit," Beanie sulked. "Go 'way."

"Is it broke?"

"Nope." Beanie brightened a bit. "Agnes says my head's too hard. But it sure did bleed! You shoulda seen it."

"You got two black eyes," the third boy joined in. "Cool!"

Nick swung to the left and approached the car obliquely, hoping to remain in Beanie's blind spot. When he reached the tail of Kathryn's car he ducked down and crawled forward along the left side, then right across the front of the car, staying low and tight against the bumper and grill. At the right front corner he paused, then dropped to the ground and rolled across the gap between the two cars, stopping on his back directly in front of the Crown Victoria.

He heard a sound. He glanced to the right to see one of the boys smiling and watching him. Nick jabbed at his wristwatch and then gestured angrily for the boy to move away. The boy shook his head, held up both hands and flashed the number "twenty."

Twenty, Nick nodded furiously, and I'll put the scorpion in your bed.

Peter leaned back and stretched his arms across the top of the sofa.

"This is all about Jimmy, isn't it?"

"What do you mean?" Kathryn could feel his eyes on the back of her head, and it made the hair stand up on her neck.

"I tried to warn you. You got your hopes up. You thought you could prove that Jim was the victim of some sinister plot, so you hired some fancy Bug Man—but it wasn't as easy as you thought."

"No," she whispered. "It turned out to be more complicated than I ever imagined."

"I should have stepped in. I asked the doc not to take your money, but he wouldn't listen. I knew he was the wrong sort from the beginning. I know it's hard when you trust someone and they let you down."

She turned and stared at him. "You have no idea."

"So you've had enough? You're willing to listen to reason now?"

Kathryn turned her head to one side and studied him thoughtfully.

"People commit suicide in different ways, don't they, Peter? Some people put a gun to their head and pull the trigger, and it's over in an instant. But others hang themselves, and I imagine that takes quite a bit longer. Some people poison themselves or even starve themselves, and then it could take weeks or months to die. But it's all still suicide, isn't it?"

"I suppose so," the sheriff shrugged.

"You can help someone commit suicide, can't you? What do they call it—'doctor-assisted' suicide? You aren't actually killing anyone, they can't convict you of anything, you're only assisting— but you still make the suicide possible. You don't pull the trigger, but you buy the gun. You don't make him take the poison, but you hand him the pills. There must be a thousand ways to help kill a man, and it's all still suicide."

The sheriff said nothing.

"It gets confusing, doesn't it, Peter—the question of who's to blame, I mean? One man ties the noose, another puts the rope around his neck, and someone else kicks the chair away. Who did the actual killing? It isn't necessarily the one who took the final step, you know—sometimes it's the one who was thinking the clearest or the one who had the most malice in his heart. It's strange, isn't it? You drive a man to depression, you take away all of his hopes and dreams, and then you hand him a gun and he pulls the trigger. It's suicide. But who really killed him?"

The sheriff glanced at his watch. So did Kathryn.

"You were right, Peter. I can see now that you were right all along. Jimmy was responsible for taking his own life—but I think someone helped him. I think someone handed him the gun. And I know who did it too."

She stared hard into the depths of the thick, gray ice.

"I did it," she said. "I killed Jimmy when I didn't love him enough to see how much he was hurting."

Kathryn studied Peter's eyes, praying for some telltale shift in the ice, some glimmer of guilt or remorse, some flickering recognition of the utter damnation of his own soul. But the ice remained immovable, impassable, and that's when Kathryn knew beyond all doubt that the soul of Peter St. Clair was beyond redemption.

He put his hand on her shoulder and squeezed. "Don't be too hard on yourself, kiddo. You didn't know."

A swell of revulsion and utter contempt heaved up from her stomach into her throat and she struggled to hold back the rage that surged up within her.

"I've had enough," she said through clenched teeth. "I'm ready to listen to reason now. I want you to give me a reason, Peter, just one reason . . ."

Kathryn rose from the sofa. "I want you to tell me the reason you murdered my husband."

CHAPTER
36

Nick lay with his head directly underneath the radiator of the Crown Victoria. It was darker than he had hoped. This would be a lot easier if he could simply raise the hood, but that was hardly something the deputy would consent to. He pulled a white handkerchief from his shirt pocket and spread it open on the ground by his right ear. He fumbled through his pockets for a pair of light-tension forceps, then squeezed his left forearm up into the narrow gap between the radiator and grill. He felt delicately along the surface of the radiator until his fingers arrived at the first tiny lump stubbornly wedged between the fragile metal fins. Then he brought his right hand up to the same location and maneuvered the forceps into position, carefully plucking out the specimen and dropping it onto the handkerchief to his right. He repeated the process again and again, as quickly as possible, until he could feel no more telltale projections at all.

"Show us your gun, Beanie!" one of the boys entreated.

"Yeah!" another chimed in. "Show us your gun!"

Beanie shook his head sadly. "Unca Pete took it. Says he gotta clean it real good. You got to have a clean gun."

Nick smiled. It didn't take the sheriff long to figure out the reason for his assault on Beanie at the picnic table. By now the Beretta was clean as a whistle—or gone entirely, and with it any chance of matching the blood in the barrel to Teddy's. "I'm not a fool, Doc," the sheriff had warned him.

No, Sheriff, I've got to hand it to you—you're no fool.

He rolled onto his right side and carefully pulled the dotted handkerchief up close. He quickly discarded a variety of Lepidoptera and various scarabaeid beetles—the moths and June bugs that abound in the thick summer skies, and the occasional honeybee that had drifted across the road on its way to gather pollen. All that remained on the handkerchief was a tiny pile of Diptera, an assortment of flies of various colors and sizes.

From his left pants pocket Nick removed a photographer's loupe. He raised his glasses and pressed the tiny magnifier tight against his right eye, then one by one began to pluck up the remains of each insect and examine it like a jeweler appraising a precious stone.

"Who hit you anyway?" one of the boys asked Beanie, staring at the white bandage plastered across his face.

"I dunno. A doctor. A doctor hit me."

"A doctor? Why would a doctor hit you?"

"I dunno," Beanie repeated irritably. "But he hit me—hard. And then he jumped on me, and he was gonna hit me again, but Unca Pete stopped him."

"What did he look like, this doctor that hit you?"

Beanie scrunched up his face and thought long and hard. "He didn't have no eyes."

"No eyes?" one of the boys laughed. "He was a blind doctor?"

"I mean glasses." Beanie scowled at them. "Big, funny glasses."

The three boys looked at each other.

Large body, red eyes, gray-checkered abdomen—it's a sarcophagid.

Nick tossed it aside.

Broad head, flattened body, multicolored eyes—just a big old horse fly.

He quickly glanced at his watch—only five minutes left. He pulled his glasses back down and began to rapidly sort through the remaining specimens—the metallic green and blue calliphorids here, the common Muscidae over there—soon only two specimens remained and they appeared to be identical. He seized the most intact specimen with his forceps and held it up to the loupe.

Greenish blue with purple reflections. The lower squamae are brown, the posterior margins of the second and third abdominal segments are jet black—and it has anterior spiracles!

He rotated it forward and searched the bulbous, dome-shaped head for the final indicator. Sure enough, the upper eye facets were greatly enlarged. It was a Chrysomya megacephala—the same species that Noah identified from the puparium left by the fly on Jim McAllister's body. Jim McAllister was in southern Georgia or Florida just over a week ago—and so was this car.

Means, motive, and opportunity, Sheriff. Three strikes and you're out.

Nick was startled by the sound of a door closing and the scatter of children's feet. He quickly placed the two megacephalae in the center of the handkerchief, folded it carefully, and stuffed it into his shirt pocket. He reached up for the bumper and began to wriggle out from under the car when a pair of massive hands grabbed on to his belt and shirt and jerked upward. His body rose from the ground as if weightless. His forehead smashed against the bottom of the grill, stunning him, but the impact barely even slowed his upward ascent. He continued to rise up into the searing, blinding sun—and then an instant later came crashing back down onto the hood of the car, knocking the wind from his lungs. He felt the two massive hands release him for an instant and then fasten again on the front of his shirt, pinning him against the scalding metal.

Nick's mind was a blaze of fire, and he felt a trickle of blood run down into his left eye. He shook it out and looked upward into the smiling face of the deputy sheriff.

Peter sat in stunned silence.

Kathryn rose and walked to the kitchen. She returned a moment later holding Jimmy's journal in her hands. She held it open to him like a lectern, like the Book of Life revealing all that he had ever done or thought. Without a word she dropped it into his lap and backed away.

Peter began to flip slowly through the pages, and wave after wave of agonized realization swept across his face.

"Where did you—"

"He hid it inside the Bible—a place he knew you'd never look."

He read one entry and winced. He read another, then rubbed his neck and rolled his head in great circles.

"You coward!" she seethed. "You thought you had been cheated; you thought someone had taken something that was rightfully yours. But I was never yours, Peter. I was never yours!"

"I can explain—"

"So can I! I can explain everything now! You found out about Jimmy's drug habit, and you went to turn him in—but you didn't, did you? You realized there was a better way to use that little piece of information, didn't you?"

"Kath, wait—it wasn't like that—"

"Then when you ran into Jimmy and Andy at Al Salman you saw your chance. Andy got ahead of you, he got separated. It was dark, it was crazy, there were bullets flying everywhere—and Andy started waving to you. He wanted you to come to him, Peter, he wanted you to help him. He was calling you—he was calling his friend."

Tears were streaming down her face. Her voice trembled with rage, and her legs shook as if they might buckle at any moment. Peter started to rise from the sofa to reach for her.

"Don't!" She forced herself to stand erect. "Not ever again!"

He sat back again.

"Why did you have to bury him? Why didn't you just shoot him in the back and claim it was an accident? Why didn't you blame it on 'friendly fire'? I would have believed you—everyone would have!

"What was it like when you saw later that I couldn't let go

of Andy? What did you feel when you realized that when you buried Andy, you buried any chance that I could ever love you? Did you wish you could go back? Did you wish you could do it all over again? You did it to yourself, you little coward! When you shot Andy in the back, you shot yourself too!"

Peter said nothing.

"And then you made poor Jimmy help you bury Andy. You got rid of Andy's body, but Jimmy could never get him out of his mind. Jimmy wasn't like you, Peter. He had a conscience—he had a soul. He remembered what he had done and it ate him alive."

She stopped abruptly. A sudden look of realization came over her face.

"That's why you overlooked Jimmy's drug habit all those years, isn't it? You didn't want him getting clean and straight and dealing with his conscience—you wanted him hooked. But Jimmy had no money for drugs. . . . But that means . . . you must have . . . You supplied him, didn't you?"

She shook her head in disgust. "You didn't kill one man at Al Salman, Peter, you killed two—and they were both better men than you'll ever be. Jimmy was right, you know," she said with utter contempt. "I would have taken him before I'd take you."

Peter sat quietly staring at the pages of the journal. He lifted a page, looked it over front and back, then slowly ripped it from the binding and lay it on the sofa beside him.

"Since the day he married you," he said without looking up.

"What?"

"Isn't that the question you were going to ask me next? 'How long did you think about killing Andy?' Since the day he married you."

Kathryn watched in horror as he tore away a second page. Nick said he hoped to bring back proof—but that proof, whatever it was, would only tie Peter to the death of Jimmy. The journal was the only thing on earth that linked Peter to the death of her husband—and Peter was shredding it before her eyes.

"Give me back my journal!"

"Jimmy's journal," he replied quietly.

He gathered the remaining handwritten pages together and removed them, then tossed the journal on the floor at her feet.

"There you go. All yours."

He collected the handful of scribbled pages and carefully folded them, placing them in his front shirt pocket.

"It doesn't matter," she choked. "You can destroy those pages if you want to—but I still know what you did. Maybe I can't have you arrested or send you to jail, but I can hate you for the rest of my life. You've lost, Peter. You did it all for nothing. You will never marry me, and I will never, ever love you. Take a good look— because I never want to see you again."

Peter rose slowly from the sofa. He bent over slightly, hooked his thumbs inside his trousers, and hitched them up an inch or two. Then he straightened, stretching his shirt front tight again.

"Do you believe everyone has a perfect match? I do. I think God made one perfect person for everyone, and your job is to search the world over until you find her—and then you get married. But what if there's a mistake—what if someone else marries my perfect person? Not on purpose, not out of meanness, but just because they didn't know any better. Then there's something wrong with the world—something that has to be fixed, don't you see? They can't be happy together, because there's someone better for both of them out there somewhere, and I can't be happy because they're keeping me from my perfect match."

He shook his head. "How can I make you understand? I didn't hate Andy, and I don't blame you for marrying him. You were just . . . confused, that's all, and I just had to straighten things out."

He began to step quietly toward her. Kathryn heard a buzzing sound slowly begin to rise. She started to tremble.

"I don't expect you to love me. Not right away. It's going to take time. There's been so much pain and disappointment, and we have so much to talk about . . ."

The angry buzz grew louder as he drew nearer. He held out one hand as he approached, like a rider trying to steady a skittish mare. He was only an arm's length away now, and the buzz in Kathryn's mind was almost deafening.

He took her gently by the shoulders.

"I told you before, Kath. I told you all along. We were meant to be."

With every bit of strength left within her she swung her right foot up between his legs. He crumpled to the floor.

She stumbled back and stared wild-eyed at the figure writhing on the ground—and then she turned for the door and ran, ran as fast and as hard as she could run. She had to run, she had to get away, because the swirling black cloud was right behind her, and she knew that it would follow.

Nick could barely breathe under the weight of Beanie's hands. He had to break that grip; he had to get away. He knew he was in no immediate danger from the childlike deputy, but at any moment the sheriff would emerge from Kathryn's house, and then with a single word the harmless deputy could become the sheriff's executioner. Nick grabbed the pipelike wrists and strained, but he was no match for the deputy's incredible strength. He felt along the back of Beanie's right hand for the exact spot where the bones of the thumb and first finger joined in the base of the massive hand; he made a knuckle with his own right hand and drove it hard into Beanie's ulnar nerve. The deputy winced in pain and momentarily released his grip. Nick rolled hard to the left, pulling his right arm from his shirt, then his left. The startled and confused deputy stood motionless, still pinning an empty shirt to the hood of the patrol car.

The realization that his prisoner had escaped began to slowly dawn on him. He dropped the shirt and slowly started toward Nick with outstretched arms. Nick ducked his head into the patrol car for an instant, jerked the hood release, then began to backpedal quickly around the car until they faced each other from opposite sides. He continued to circle, Beanie slowly following, until he had maneuvered the deputy to the trunk of the car. Then with one quick motion he raised the hood, grabbed two spark plug wires and ripped them from the car.

At that moment the front door exploded open and Kathryn raced out. She saw the shirtless Nick with Beanie in frustrated pursuit, and Nick saw the look of absolute terror in Kathryn's eyes. They both knew that escape was the only thing that mattered now.

"We'll take yours!" He pointed to her car.

"The keys are in the house!" she shouted. "Where's yours?"

Nick pointed down the street toward the two rusting Dumpsters. Kathryn spun to face the deputy.

"Beanie, Uncle Pete is hurt! He's in the house, Beanie, and he needs you! Do you understand? Uncle Pete is hurt!"

Beanie stared blankly, then he nodded slowly and lumbered off toward the open door. Kathryn and Nick raced across the driveway and down the street toward the waiting Dodge.

They scrambled into the car and slammed the doors. Nick fumbled for the keys.

"Go, go!" she shouted.

"What's your hurry?" He grinned as he tossed the two spark plug wires into her lap. "They're not going anywhere without these."

She held them up and then looked at him.

"Is this it? Is this all you got? Just two?"

"I thought I did pretty well, under the circumstances."

"Nick—don't you know anything about cars?"

Nick shrugged.

"A Crown Victoria has an eight cylinder engine! You can't just pull out two spark plug wires, you need three or four! The engine will run rough on six cylinders, but it will still run! All you did is make their car run as badly as yours! You bought us a few minutes, that's all—now get this pile of junk moving!"

They roared out from behind the Dumpsters as the patrol car lurched down the driveway behind them.

CHAPTER
37

got it, Mrs. Guilford," Nick shouted over the roar of the engine. "I got all the proof you need."

"What proof?"

"When the sheriff released our specimen, he thought he had covered his tracks, but he was wrong. The fly left behind a puparial capsule, and from that capsule we were able to identify the species.

The fly from Jimmy's body doesn't come from North Carolina, Mrs. Guilford—not anywhere in the state. It's found only in Florida and southern Georgia. Did you hear me?"

"Southern Georgia . . . Peter's hunting cabin!"

Nick nodded. "Sometimes a car is an entomologist's best friend. The radiator acts like a giant butterfly net, collecting specimens wherever it goes—and leaving a record of where it's been. I checked the radiator of the patrol car—guess what? I found the same species of fly. That means the sheriff spent his vacation in Georgia, not Myrtle Beach—and Jim McAllister was with him. They drove back together—only your friend came back in the trunk with one leg propped up. A microsearch of the trunk will verify it. We've got all the proof we need, Mrs. Guilford, we've got—"

Suddenly Nick slammed his fist against the dashboard.

"What is it? What's wrong?"

"My shirt! I left the radiator samples in the pocket!"

Kathryn said nothing.

Nick glanced over at her. "Mrs. Guilford—you've got to believe me."

"I believe you," she said evenly. "I believe everything you've said all along. I believe he killed Jimmy. I believe he killed Teddy. I believe he killed poor old Mrs. Gallagher."

She turned and stared at him.

"I found Jimmy's war journal. It wasn't in the papers Amy gave me—Peter went through them himself. It was hidden inside that Bible. It told about the Gulf, about the drugs, about the conflict. It told about everything." She closed her eyes hard. "It told how Peter shot Andy in the back."

Nick said nothing. He knew he should reach out and comfort her; he knew he should take the time to express his outrage and sympathy—but his mind was too busy racing, fitting together the remaining pieces of this fascinating puzzle.

"Where is this journal?" he asked.

"He destroyed it," she said without emotion. "It doesn't matter."

Nick groaned. "It matters, Mrs. Guilford. Without the specimens from the radiator, we can't tie the sheriff to the death of your friend. And without that journal, we can't prove that he had anything to do with the disappearance of your husband. We know what happened, but we can't prove anything. We've got nothing, Mrs. Guilford, we've got—"

He stopped abruptly.

"The puparium!" he shouted. "It's at the lab—I dropped it off on the way back from the university. We've got to get it, Mrs. Guilford, it's all we've got left. With that puparium I can at least prove that your friend didn't die in North Carolina. That's enough to convince the medical examiner to reopen the investigation, and anything can happen from there."

Nick raised the sagging rearview mirror and stared into the distance behind them. Through the billowing oil smoke he could see glints of black and white. The patrol car was gradually gaining on them—now less than two hundred yards away.

"They're right behind us—and they're getting closer. At this rate they'll catch us before we reach the lab."

Kathryn twisted the mirror and looked. "In this car we're about as hard to spot as a forest fire!"

"I thought I slowed them down more than that."

"Part of the problem is the car," she said, "and part is the driver. Switch with me!"

"What?"

"Switch with me!" she shouted again, and without hesitation she grabbed for the wheel. Nick rolled to the right and dragged himself into the backseat, and Kathryn slid into the driver's seat after him.

"The fence with the razor wire," she shouted. "Does it have another gate?"

"On the west side. There's a service entrance."

"Then I know a shortcut. It should be right about . . . here!"

She jerked the wheel to the right, and the Dodge slammed into the curb. The car lurched crazily left and right, then once again as the rear wheels followed after. There was a bone-jarring clank of metal as the rims cut hard into the concrete through the aging tires, and Nick was slammed weightless into the ceiling. He came crashing down again beneath a hailstorm of paper, notebooks, and debris. Instantly there was a second clank, then a third and much louder one as the muffler tore away and did a rusted dance on the pavement behind them.

The hood of the car blasted into a thick screen of privet and viburnum and then nosed suddenly downward, careening down a steep bank and into a small fence. A single strand of barbed wire stretched across the windshield and snapped like an old guitar string. The car cratered hard in a dry red gully before nosing up again into a vast field of shimmering yellow-white and green.

"When you said shortcut"—Nick struggled up from the floor of the backseat—"I assumed you meant a road."

The car bounded across the open meadow like a charging water buffalo. A sea of roof-high reed and feather grass whipped and stripped across the windshield as they plunged ahead.

"How in the world can you see?"

"You just have to know where you're going," she shouted. "I know this field—I used to race here with the boys all the time when we were teenagers!"

"Who used to win?"

For an instant Kathryn actually smiled.

"Then the sheriff knows this field too?"

"He knows." She nodded. "Take a look behind you!"

Nick whirled around and saw the patrol car not more than thirty yards behind them, drafting in their wake like a stock car at Rockingham.

"He'll be even with us soon! He'll try to pass us, to cut us off!"

She shook her head. "He's gaining on us because the grass is slowing us down! If he pulls out from behind us he'll lose ground! He knows he doesn't have to catch us—he just has to stay with us until we finally have to stop!"

Suddenly Kathryn began to slow down, narrowing the gap between the two cars.

"What are you doing?"

She watched until the patrol car filled the rearview mirror with a thundering blur of black and white.

"Do you have anything valuable in the trunk?"

"Do I what?"

She jerked the wheel hard to the right and jammed the brake pedal to the floor. The Crown Victoria braked an instant late, slamming head-on into the Dart's right fender. The patrol car windshield blazed white as twin air bags exploded into the driver and passenger, and before the shock of impact could wear off she stomped on the gas again and spun away, spewing a cloud of red dust behind her. She veered hard right, dragging the crumpled remains of a fender as she disappeared into the tall grass.

Nick was thrown forward like a toy, hurtling almost into the front floor, then rebounded back once again amid the paper and debris.

"It would help if you told me what you were going to do before you did it."

"You'll get used to it," she said. "I did."

She steered the car in a wide circle until she was at a three o'clock position to the patrol car, no more than twenty yards away. She slammed the brakes down hard again, shoved the stick into reverse and looked back over her shoulder.

"I'm going to back up now," she said to Nick. "Just thought I'd let you know."

"You're going to what?"

"Didn't you ever go to the Demolition Derby when you were little? Oh, that's right . . . you're a city boy."

She jammed the accelerator to the floor. The car fishtailed left and right, and the grass behind them began to divide slowly, then faster and faster like an endless parting curtain. They both braced themselves . . .

A split second later they saw the black-and-white cruiser flash past them on their right. They had missed the front end by less than a foot.

As they raced past they saw that the hood was crumpled and bent down and back, and the grill and right headlight were shattered. They saw the face of the deputy frozen in shock and confusion.

But the driver's seat was empty.

Kathryn curved left away from the car and sped backward thirty yards or more. She braked hard and sat silently for a moment, the engine idling but her mind still racing. She felt a hand on her shoulder and heard a voice near her right ear.

"He's on foot, Mrs. Guilford. He can hear our engine—and he has a gun. For crying out loud let's get out of here!"

Kathryn stomped the gas and veered hard left—then slowly began to curve right again in a wide circle around the patrol car.

"The other way, the other way!" Nick jabbed frantically over his shoulder.

She shook her head furiously.

"Was their engine still running? I couldn't tell. We've got to make sure or they'll be on us again in no time!"

She circled wide, counting the hours off a mental clock as the car roared on.

Three o'clock . . . four o'clock . . . five o'clock . . .

She knew the chance she was taking. In her mind's eye she saw Peter crouching invisibly in the tall grass, waiting for her to pass again, waiting with gun in hand and shell in chamber for the moment of impact when the car stood still, waiting to rise up and rapid-fire into the backseat—and then into the front? Peter had already done the unimaginable—was anything beyond him?

Nick crawled into the front seat again.

"When you think you're lined up, let me know. I'll poke my head up and guide you in. We only get one shot at this."

"Better poke your head up fast," she warned. "Peter loves a turkey shoot."

Eight o'clock . . . nine o'clock . . . ten o'clock . . .

From the corner of her eye Kathryn caught a glimpse of khaki and steel flashing through the grass to her right. An instant later the sheriff stood motionless less than ten yards ahead of them, gun raised and ready, aiming directly at the driver of the car.

He raised his head from the line of sight with a look of shocked recognition, then jerked the gun aside and tried to steady his aim on the passenger's seat—but the car was almost on top of him now and he had to lunge to the left, firing two shots wildly as the right fender brushed past his leg. The first shot shattered the windshield into a mosaic of a thousand green and white tiles, and the second exploded into the backseat in a puff of grayish oatmeal.

Nick twisted to the right and hunched down into the seat, and with all of his strength shoved the passenger door open. It caught the sheriff full on, knocking him from his feet and sending him tumbling away—but the force of the impact slammed the door back on Nick. The crumbling door wobbled for a moment, then broke completely away from the car and bounded end over end into the tall grass.

Stunned and senseless, Nick lurched forward and rolled out of the car.

Kathryn screamed and lunged for him—too late! Twenty yards ahead she skidded to a stop and turned to the rear window. There was no sound, no motion in the tall reeds. Nothing. She reached for the horn—and then stopped.

She threw open the door and leaped up onto the searing hood. Her right foot punched through the shattered remains of the windshield as she scrambled up onto the roof. Thirty yards to the left she saw the gleaming white roof and red signal bar of the Crown Victoria. To the right, to the left, behind her—nothing. Then a single figure slowly staggered up out of the sea of green. It was Nick.

And he was wearing no glasses.

Kathryn started to shout and then caught herself. She waved her arms frantically—but what good would it do? What could Nick see without his glasses? Was she anything more than a blur to him, just a mysterious white smudge against the blue summer sky?

Then a second head rose up above the tall grass.

Peter turned slowly, dazed, still shaking off the effects of the collision—and he was limping. He stared toward the patrol car, then behind him, and finally turned to Kathryn, who seemed to be somehow standing on the very tips of the blades of long grass just thirty yards away. His mind began to clear. Kathryn looked in horror at Nick, still stunned, standing out like a tombstone on a prairie.

Peter followed her eyes. He raised his gun.

"Nick, get down!"

Nick disappeared into the grass like a trout with a captured fly. A gunshot echoed across the open meadow.

"Run!" she screamed. "But stay down!"

She watched the brush crumple and bend beneath the feet of an invisible figure, and she saw a path began to open—directly toward the sheriff.

"No, the other way!"

The grass stood still for an instant, then began to bend and open rapidly in the opposite direction. The sheriff limped forward, following, searching. Suddenly he stopped, dropped from sight for a moment, then straightened up again.

"Looky what I found," he said, holding up a pair of enormous spectacles. He dropped them at his feet. There was a crunching sound, and then he began to hobble in Nick's direction again.

Kathryn's heart leaped into her throat.

"Is that all you're looking for, Peter?" she shouted. "A blind Bug Man? Well, go ahead if that's what you want—but by the time you find him I'll be long gone!" She forced herself to laugh.

Peter stopped. He looked out across the vast, glistening meadow. Then he looked back at Kathryn.

He turned.

Kathryn took a last mental fix on Nick's speed and direction, then jumped down from the car. She threw open the door, stretched her right leg in, and revved the engine twice. Then she slammed the door hard and loud, doubled over, and vanished into the meadow. An instant later she reappeared, ducked into the car, and ripped out the keys.

She scrambled off into the thick grass, the blind in search of the blind.

CHAPTER
38

"Can you see the Quonset from here?" Nick whispered.

"It's about two hundred yards away," Kathryn whispered back. "I thought you were farsighted."

"I said I can see better at a distance—I didn't say I can see."

They lay exhausted at the outer edge of the meadow. They had scrambled and clambered a half-mile or more, Kathryn leading the way and Nick struggling to follow the blurred flurry of arms and legs ahead of him. They lay facedown, panting, the heavy feather grass bowing and tickling at their arms and necks.

"Okay." Nick hoisted himself up again. "Let's go for it."

"Nick, wait. It's open ground—we'll be sitting ducks. Maybe we should wait here until it gets dark."

Nick shook his head. "We have to get to the lab before he does. He knows we're going there for a reason. If he finds that puparium and destroys it, we're sunk."

"Nick—what if he destroys us?"

"He can't be far behind us. He's going to find us anyway. You said he was limping—our only advantage is to stay ahead of him."

She looked at him. "He may be limping, but you're blind."

He squeezed her arm. "But I've got eyes. Look, the sheriff had a chance to shoot you while you were driving and again when you were standing on the roof of the car. But he didn't. Don't you see? If we stay close together he won't take a chance on shooting and hitting you—not at a distance anyway. If we can get to the lab before he does, we can grab the puparium and head out into the woods. If we can make it to the woods we've got a chance."

Kathryn felt a wave of panic sweep over her.

"Let him have it. I don't want you to die. It's not fair. Let him have the evidence."

"I appreciate that," Nick said softly, "but I'm afraid it's a little late. You see, Mrs. Guilford, I am the evidence now."

They rose side by side, still cautiously doubled over, one arm wrapped around the other's waist like yoked oxen. Behind them in the distance they heard the sound of thrashing grass. They glanced at each other silently and took off running.

They ran frantically, desperately at first—then Nick tightened his grip on Kathryn's waist and reined her back.

"Easy. Pace yourself. Long way to go still."

Nick ran wide-eyed, feeling for the ground ahead of him with every step. Misty shapes and blurs of color streaked by on all sides.

He stumbled and fell headlong. Kathryn hurried him to his feet again, cursing herself for failing at her duty so badly. She looked back over her shoulder—no sign of a figure emerging from the meadow. She looked ahead to the Quonset—no more than fifty yards to go. She felt a sudden surge of energy.

"Come on! We're almost there!"

Only thirty yards to go, then twenty. They approached the building from the side circled around toward the front. They rounded the corner with a sense of elation, exhausted but exuberant.

There on the front step stood the deputy.

They stumbled to a halt. Kathryn jerked Nick back abruptly. "What is it?"

"It's Beanie," she said, panting. "Blocking the door!"

Kathryn released Nick and charged forward. "Beanie!" she waved her arms in a menacing arc. "Go away! Let us in!"

"Can't."

"Beanie, it's me!" she said almost in tears. "Please let us in!"

"Can't," he repeated. "Unca Pete said not to."

"What else?" Nick called out. "What else did Uncle Pete tell you to do?"

"Said I should catch you. Hold you till he comes."

"And if I don't want to be held?"

"Said I should break you."

Kathryn threw herself at him, pounding at his simian chest. "Beanie, this is Aunt Kathryn! Aunt Kathryn is telling you to go away and leave us alone!"

Beanie smiled down at her, oblivious to the tickling blows.

"It's no use," Nick said. "Rock beats scissors, Mrs. Guilford— Uncle Pete overrules Aunt Kathryn. Besides," he said, nodding toward a blur at the edge of the meadow, "I think we're out of time."

Two hundred yards away, just washing ashore from the rolling sea of green, the sheriff came limping toward the Quonset.

"We've got to separate," Nick said urgently.

"I won't leave you!"

"Listen to me!" he thundered. "He's not interested in me, he wants you! All he's ever wanted is you! He sent Pinocchio here to deal with me—to hold me, remember? That means he plans to go after you first, then come back for me. If we stay together they'll catch us both at once. Our only chance is to deal with them one at a time. We've got to separate!"

"What happens when he comes back for you?"

"One thing at a time, Mrs. Guilford. You've got to go!"

She took one faltering step away, then glanced back at the meadow. The sheriff was just a hundred yards away now. His left hand supported his wounded thigh, and his right hand rested on his holster. She turned in terror to Nick.

"But you can't see," she pleaded.

"You can't help me now, and I'm afraid I can't help you either. But believe me, Kathryn," he said with a smile and a nod, "you're more than a match for any man I know. Now go!" he thundered again, and she turned and ran weeping toward the far meadow.

Nick watched for a moment, tormented by the thought that his final image of Kathryn Guilford might be nothing more than a streak of blue and a smear of dancing auburn.

He turned back to the building. He saw nothing but a blurry green semicircle, like a slice of lime beneath a sheet of waxed paper. He could make out the shadowy shapes of the windows on each side and a dark rectangle in the center dominated by an enormous, khaki-colored smudge. He had to get into the lab. Everything he knew, everything that might help him was inside.

"So, Deputy," he called out. "I thought you were supposed to hold me."

The khaki smudge shifted uneasily.

"You can't hold me from over there. You're not doing your job, Benjamin. Uncle Pete's gonna be awful mad!"

The shape began to stretch and grow until it covered the shadow of the door. Nick started to back away.

If he gets those hands on me again, I'm finished.

He dropped to his knees and began to feel the ground all around him. He scuttled back on all fours constantly reaching, searching, until he came upon a small branch about three feet long. He grabbed the very end, stood up, and pointed it at his approaching foe like Peter Pan attacking a pirate ship.

The khaki blur was almost on top of him now. Nick stood staring, blinking, sensing. Suddenly he saw a streak of pink and felt the branch swept aside. He jumped back a step and shoved the branch in the deputy's face again. Once more it was brushed aside, and once more he repeated the strange maneuver. The deputy grew impatient—this time he grabbed the branch, and at that instant Nick pulled hard. The childlike deputy instinctively joined this little game of tug of war and pulled back even harder, drawing Nick close—dangerously close. Nick jerked the branch again, this time with his full strength—and then he waited. He waited for that instant when the deputy would pull back again with his full strength.

And when he did, Nick let go.

The deputy toppled backward and sprawled in the gravel parking lot with a huff and a crunch. Nick turned toward the lab—he had bought himself thirty seconds, maybe less, and he would need all of it. He fixed his eyes on the blurry rectangle in the center of the Quonset and ran toward it, ran as fast as he possibly could with his arms extended straight ahead like a frantic sleepwalker.

I see the door—but how far away is it? Can't afford to slow down—and I sure don't have time to go searching for a doorknob.

An instant later his right ankle caught the edge of the wooden step, and he stumbled headlong into the screen door. His arms and head punched through the screen wire like tissue paper. The center strut caught him across the ribs, and the wooden frame shattered and folded inward like an umbrella. For an instant he lay trapped, surrounded in a tangle of wood and wire like a Lepidoptera in a butterfly net. He leaped to his feet thrashing, flailing, kicking himself free. He turned back to the door and saw the khaki blur rise from the ground, straighten, and then begin to grow larger once again.

Twenty seconds . . . I've got twenty seconds, no more.

He stumbled back against the glass cases. Nick whirled around and slapped his hands against the cool glass. He paused for a split second, thinking—then he stumbled to the left, feeling his way along the glass fronts until he came to the corner, to the last case on the bench, to the fragment of signboard he had once taped to the glass that cautioned unknowing visitors: BUTHIDAE—DO NOT REACH INTO TERRARIUM with remaining hand.

He tore off the cover, grabbed the huge case by the lip, and dragged it over onto the floor. It landed in a thundering crash of glass and rock and sand, and then there was silence.

Except for the tiny, brittle sound of a hundred skittering legs.

Nick leaped backward, feeling rapidly along the glass cases to his right until he came to the case at the opposite end. He backed around the corner, positioning himself behind the massive terrarium.

"Sorry, Lord Vader, there's a disturbance in the Force."

The deputy arrived in the doorway, picking his way through the tangled wreckage of the screen door.

"Hello, Deputy," Nick said with a nod. "Welcome to my world."

The deputy started forward. Nick waited, seeing nothing, estimating the seconds required for the deputy to reach the corner—and then with one great shove smashed the terrarium onto the floor at his feet.

"Look out!" Nick pointed at the floor. A dozen glistening black-knuckled hands with bulbous claws and arcing tails reached out for the deputy's feet. Beanie staggered backward in terror, back toward the open doorway, stumbling blindly into the entangling heap of wood and wire and mesh.

He fell like a giant redwood on the shattered remains of the other terrarium.

He lay stunned for a moment, arms and legs wallowing in the debris—and then there was the skittering of legs again, the flash of slender pedipalps, and the lightning whip of needle-tipped metasomas.

"Ow," he said dully, and then "Ow!" again.

He raised himself to his elbows. "Ow!" He jerked his right elbow up and rolled onto his left side.

"Ouch! Ouch! Ow! Bees or sump'n!" He slowly rolled to his feet.

Nick felt his way down the aisle toward the office door, listening. If he counted correctly the deputy had just taken a half-dozen stings from the Androctonus australis—the north African fat tail scorpion—one of the deadliest scorpions in the world.

He found the door. He fumbled for the doorknob, slipped inside, and slammed it shut behind him. He turned to the lab.

The puparium. Got to find the puparium.

He had left it in a folded handkerchief resting in the center of the worktable—or was it by the microscope? He swept the room with his useless eyes. He saw wispy streaks of green and white, mounded blurs of black and chrome, and flashes of fluorescent blue and shadowy gray. How could he possibly hope to find a puparium the size of a grain of rice?

My extra pair of glasses!

He lunged forward and crashed into a rolling stool, sending it rocketing into the corner. He bumped blindly into the worktable and began to work his way to the right, patting his outstretched hands over the cluttered surface, his darting fingers detecting only textures of vinyl and paper and plastic.

They're in the desk drawer. Or on top of the bookshelf. No—they're in the filing cabinet with the hot plate. He began to slow down. *Or in the glove compartment of the Dodge. Or in my trailer. Or in Pittsburgh . . .*

He stopped. If he couldn't find his extra glasses when he had perfect vision, what were the chances of finding them now?

Behind him the office door burst open. Nick spun around. He could hear the sound of the deputy's shallow breathing and repeated swallowing. His footsteps seemed to shuffle, almost stumble into the room.

The deputy already had systemic effects; his adrenal gland was dumping catecholamines by the truckload. A single sting from a fat tail can kill an average-sized man in a few hours—how long would it take the venom of six to work its way through this mountain of flesh?

One thing's for sure—I can't wait around to find out.

"Beanie, listen to me. Those weren't bees that stung you, they were scorpions. Do you know what a scorpion is?"

Nick eased slowly to the left as he spoke, edging his way toward the exterior door. He stared wide-eyed at the blur before him, watching for the slightest change in shape or size.

"It's like a wasp, only worse—much worse. More like a snake."

"Weren't no snake," said a whimpering voice.

"Like a snake. Like a copperhead, or a rattlesnake—even worse than that! You've got to sit down, Beanie; you've got to rest."

"Unca Pete said to catch you. Unca Pete said to hold you."

It's no use—whatever Uncle Pete wants, Uncle Pete gets. If I can't get him to slow down, then I've got to get him to speed up—I've got to speed the circulation of the venom through his system. I've got to make him run!

Nick whirled around and groped for the doorknob.

"Well, come on then, Deputy!" he called back over his shoulder. "Catch me if you can!"

He threw open the door and lunged out. He took two quick steps forward, caught the wooden deck rail across the groin, flipped head over heels and fell five feet to the ground below. He lay stunned, winded, the sky circling above him in screaming streaks of blue and white.

Suddenly a khaki thundercloud loomed overhead, and Nick heard the heavy clump of boots on the wooden stairs.

Can't breathe ... no time ... got to get up ... got to get moving!

He struggled to his feet and started to run—but which way? The last time he ran, he was yoked to Kathryn; the last time he ran he had her eyes. This time he was on his own. He did a quick mental inventory of the hazards and barriers around the lab—the coils of razor wire, the half-buried posts, the rusted pump housings, the overgrown sinkholes. But there was no time, no time to plan a strategy, no time to chart a path or course. "One thing at a time," he had told Kathryn—and right now the thing was to run.

There was only one direction to go—wherever the deputy was not. He spun around until he spotted that imposing silhouette, then launched out in the opposite direction.

The deputy started after him. He ran slowly at first, toddling like a child, then lumbering like an awkward foal, then galloping like a Great Plains buffalo. Nick listened to the pounding footsteps behind him. They grew heavier and more erratic, and the breathing was increasingly labored—but the deputy was still matching him step for step, even gaining on him. With his sight he could have easily outdistanced the clumsy, plodding deputy—but now he was forced to run like a child himself, shortening his stride and checking each uncertain step. He felt like a circus clown jammed onto a tiny tricycle, his long legs jabbing up and down like pistons, pedaling furiously but going nowhere fast.

He looked up ahead. He could see no trees, no bushes, no details of any kind—but he could at least distinguish where the dark ground ended and the glowing sky began, and it rose sharply to the left.

If I can't beat him with speed, I have to beat him with endurance. I've got to make his heart pump; I've got to make his blood flow. I've got to go up!

He veered left and began to climb. The steep hill cut his own speed in half, but it slowed the struggling deputy even more. The upward climb forced Beanie's thundering heart to pump, to push, to strain . . . and with every gushing pulse the deadly neurotoxins spread.

Suddenly the footsteps behind him stopped. Nick turned, panting, listening. He heard the deputy double over and retch. He staggered forward, halting every few steps in crippling convulsions.

"Can you feel it, Deputy?" Nick called back. "Can you feel the poison spreading through your system? Does it hurt where they stung you? Are your arms and legs swelling yet? Are your eyes watering, does your tongue feel thick and fat, is your throat closing up? Next comes the cramping and then paralysis—that means you can't move, even if you want to. And then you die, Deputy, you die—just like Teddy died when you put a bullet in the back of his head!"

The deputy looked up, forced himself erect, and started toward Nick again.

Nick began to backpedal, easily maintaining the distance between them now. "Come on then," he shouted. "Come and get me, Beanie boy! Uncle Pete said to hold me, remember? Uncle Pete said to break me! Well come on then, break me! I dare you! Come on, Beanie, don't let Uncle Pete down!"

Nick turned to run again—he saw a horizontal flash of purplish brown and then an explosion of fire and light.

He ran head-on into the limb of a tree.

He lay on his back, nauseous from the impact. He felt his forehead—a jagged ravine lay open across the center, and blood poured into his eyes. He squeezed them shut, rubbed them with knotted fists, and forced them open again. He saw nothing but blotches of light through streaks and stains of red. He was blind now, really blind.

And he heard footsteps.

Heavy, dragging, desperate footsteps. And breathing like the sound of ripping canvas, like hissing steam and gurgling tar.

And it was close.

Nick rolled onto his stomach. He felt a tree root coursing under him like a vein. He felt his way along the root, crawling forward until he came to the trunk. He circled around to the opposite side, then reached up and felt for the lowest limb. He pulled himself up and stopped, his own stomach in convulsions, every heartbeat exploding in his head like mortar fire.

He reached up—he pulled—he rested. Waves of dizziness and nausea almost washed him from the tree.

He reached up—he pulled—he rested. He dragged himself up limb after limb—how far had he climbed? How high was high enough?

"Come on!" he shouted below him. "Come after me, you pathetic puppet! Climb! Work! Pull yourself up!"

Below him he heard the rattle of fluid-filled lungs and the crackle of crumbling twigs. The deputy was climbing after him.

An instant later a ham-sized hand clamped his left ankle in a grip of iron.

Nick reached up—he pulled . . . no more. He had nothing left. He threw his arms around the tree and held on.

Now the deputy began to pull—slowly, firmly, until it felt to Nick as though the deputy's entire weight was suspended from his ankle. Nick tried to kick his leg free—impossible.

Now Nick's own grip began to give way. He dug his fingers desperately into the trunk, but he continued to slide helplessly to the left. There was fire in his knee and left hip socket, and the coarse bark raked across his naked chest like burning coals.

The limb began to bend . . .

"Beanie!" Nick raged through grinding teeth. "Will—you— hurry—up—and—die!"

The huge hand began to tremble, then loosen, then slip away, taking Nick's tennis shoe with it. There was an instant of silence, then a great rustle of leaves, and a snap like the crack of a rifle— then silence again.

Nick looked down. Somewhere far below him a smear of brown and green and khaki lay perfectly still.

"Shoofly pie," Nick whispered.

He threw his arms around the tree again, and everything went black.

The sheriff limped to the open doorway and glared in. He saw the twisted wreckage of the screen door and the floor littered with dirt and rock and shards of broken glass. The door to the blue-bright office stood open, and within the office one exterior door swung slowly on its hinges.

From seventy-five yards away he had watched Kathryn turn and flee toward the far side of the building. He hobbled forward, clutching his left thigh where the door handle caught him just below the hip. The impact had knocked him twenty feet and left a throbbing fist-sized knot of purple and green. He never lost consciousness, but it had been a full minute before he struggled to his feet and spotted the despectacled head of Dr. Polchak bobbing like a buoy above the sea of yellow-green. He drew his sidearm and leveled it—but Kathryn's shout made him rush his shot, and he fired harmlessly overhead, cursing himself for his lack of discipline.

He stopped and swept the field with eyes as dark as blood.

There.

A hundred yards away in the center of an open meadow Kathryn stood perfectly still. She faced away from him with her head slightly bowed, and her arms seemed to disappear at the elbow as though her hands might be folded in front of her. She looked to him like that goddess in the picture book at the Holcum County Library, majestic and holy and alabaster-pure, but without arms—because the goddess reaches out for no one, but waits eternally for someone worthy to reach for her.

But he was unworthy . . . he knew that now.

He limped forward. She heard him approach like the slink of a jackal.

Ten yards away he stopped.

"Kath," he said softly. "We got to talk."

She never moved—not a twitch, not a nod, not even a breath. She stood motionless, implacable, and mute. Her auburn ponytail hung down, tied by an artist into a thick sable brush, swaying from side to side and painting a masterpiece of soft curves and perfect forms—a masterpiece that he would never touch again. Her jeans were spotted and soiled but still crisp and tight. Her T-shirt draped between her shoulder blades with sweat.

And two white shoestrings met in a bow at the center of her back.

"Okay," he said. "Then just listen. I know you're mad at me—hey, I don't blame you. I'm not asking you to forgive me. I just want you to try to understand—about Andy, about Jimmy, about everything."

He took a step forward.

"Yes, I was mad when you married Andy. But what could I do? I knew Andy loved you. I knew Jimmy loved you too—we all did. But when I saw you and Andy together, I knew you loved him back. And that was okay—really. I figured it was just sort of his turn."

He stepped forward again.

"Remember what I told you? I always knew we were meant to be together. I never knew when—I just knew it had to be. Finally, eventually, someday. And I figured lots of things would probably happen before that day. Like I might go off to the service or you might move away—but it didn't really matter, because I knew that someday, somehow, we would both end up together. It just had to be.

"I wish I could tell you why I'm so cocksure about it. Some things you don't just think with your head, it's something deeper—something way down inside. It's like when I hunt way back in the woods—you can blindfold me, you can spin me around, but when I take the blindfold off I can always find my way out. I got no map, I got no compass, but it doesn't matter—'cause I've got something inside that tells me which way the arrow points, that tells me which way is up. I see the sun, I see the stars, I can see the big picture in my head—and I know where I fit in the picture.

I can't explain it, but that's how it works—and that's how it works with you too. I know how my life is supposed to go—I can see it—and you were supposed to be part of it."

Another step closer still.

"When you married Andy I figured, 'Okay. Not yet.' So I waited. I waited real patient. I waited like a gentleman because it wasn't my turn yet. But I knew that someday things would have to change—I could see it in my head.

"So every day I expected something to change, something to happen. Every time Andy crossed the street, I thought a truck might pop out of nowhere and run him down. Every time the 82d did a training jump, I thought his chute might not open, that he'd be the one we'd bring back in a bag. But it never happened. Things just kept going the way they were, all wrong and needing to be made right.

"Let me tell you, it wasn't easy to just sit and wait for things to straighten themselves out. It's like when you see old Mr. Jenks sleeping night after night on the bench outside the True Value. Don't you ever get tired of waiting for him to get sober, to straighten up and get himself a job? Sometimes the church gives him a new set of clothes or takes up a collection and gives him a few bucks—and then he goes and drinks it up again. They can't make him change, but they can help him change. Sometimes I got tired of waiting, sometimes I thought maybe I should help things change. Maybe I should be the one driving the truck, maybe I should help him pack his chute.

"But I never did. I just kept waiting, giving him his turn like a friend should do—but things kept going on all out of kilter. And then that day that Andy came to see me in the Gulf, he said, 'When we get back, me and Kath are gonna have kids. Time to start a family,' he said. And that's when I knew that things had to change right away. He wasn't being fair, don't you see? His turn was almost over, and he was planning to take what was mine. My turn. My kids. My family."

He spoke gently and calmly, and he moved constantly forward as he spoke.

"I'm still not sure what happened at Al Salman. I didn't plan it, that's for sure. Andy got ahead of us just like Jimmy said. Tryin' to be the first one across the line, I suppose; he was like that. He was backed up against a berm, and there were hostiles on the other side. Jimmy started firing over the berm, trying to hold them back. I stuck my head up too. I was planning to do the same, I really was. Jimmy was firing away, firing at nothing, wasting ammo like a fool. I played it smart, I sited across the top of the berm and waited for some dumb wog to stick his head up—and then my site crossed Andy's head . . .

"You want to know the truth, Kath? I'm not sure if I shot him on purpose or not. I thought about killing him—I don't deny that— but I don't remember ever saying to myself, Do it, Pete. Pull the trigger. Kill him now. It just . . . happened. But after it happened, I knew that the world was closer to the way it was supposed to be.

"I'm not saying it was right—but sometimes the world doesn't care if things are right, it just shakes things up and puts them back in order. You see a baby bird on the ground because the nest got too crowded and Mama kicked him out to let him die. Is that right? You see a little girl with no hair 'cause she's got some kind of gut-rotting cancer or something, is that right? It doesn't much matter, does it? The world has a path it follows, and when it gets off course it just fixes things and jumps back in line again. And if you're one of the things needs fixing—well, you're just out of luck, that's all."

He stood just behind Kathryn now, little more than an arm's length away. A bee buzzed by, and he dipped his head to let it pass.

"I don't think you're really mad at me," he said softly. "I think you're just scared. You're scared because no one has ever loved you like this before. No one else ever could—the kind of love where the whole world will change its course to make sure it happens. You know what, Kath? Sometimes it scares me too—knowing that no matter what I do, no matter what anybody does, we got to end up together. Together forever."

He flipped up the leather hasp on his holster and slid out the gun. The M9 Beretta held fifteen rounds.

He pulled on the slide and quietly ejected four shells.

"Now about Jimmy." He took a deep breath. "Yes, I found out he was using cocaine in the Gulf. And no, I wasn't going to turn him in—but I sure told him I was. I thought the threat of it might do him some good; I thought it might scare some sense into him. It didn't—because he was weak. Jim was always weak. That was his problem, and that's why I knew he could never have you.

"Sure he helped me bury Andy—why shouldn't he? He had just as much reason to want Andy dead as I did—maybe more. You think he didn't lie awake at night just like I did and think about accidents and things that might go wrong? You think when the three of us shipped out he didn't hope that only two of us would come back—or maybe only one? And that night at Al Salman, when Andy got cut off—you think he really wanted Andy back safe and sound? He didn't go after Andy, you know. He just sat there safe and snug behind his little wall hoping and praying that some Iraqi bullet would do the job for him. And then he stuck his rifle over the wall and started firing—firing at what? You know what I think? I think he hoped one of his own stray shots might find the mark.

"But life doesn't work that way. You can't just hope for things, Kath, you got to make them happen; you got to be the man. Jim looked over at me, and he knew what I was thinking—he knew because he was thinking it too. The only difference was I was willing to do it. So I pulled the trigger. I did what he could never do; I did what he could only wish and whine and snivel about. And you know what he did then? He started to cry, he started to blubber like a baby—because he saw that I was strong and he was weak, that I did what he could never do, and that I was the only one who deserved to have you."

As he spoke he drew back the slide again and again. Four gleaming brass cylinders tumbled through the air and disappeared into the thick meadow grass.

"Who knows? Maybe I was weak too. Maybe I should have sent Jim after Andy and then finished both of them off. I didn't; now I wish I had. So we came home, Jim and me, and he was weaker than ever, he was hooked on that stuff for good. The only time he felt strong, the only time he felt good about himself was when he was flying high. He'd whimper and wail and moan about what we done, about what happened to 'poor Andy'—and then he'd do a little fluff, and all of a sudden he was strong; he was in control again. And then he'd always say, 'I'm going straight, I'm getting off this stuff. And when I do, I'm going to the authorities, I'm turning you in for what you done.'

"But I knew he never would, because he was a coward. Because the next day he'd be down at the bottom of the well again, and he'd be craving the stuff—just once more, just one line, just this last time, and then that's it. He knew that if he really went to the authorities they'd make him go straight, and we both knew he couldn't live without it.

"But I figured, what if he can't get the stuff? Then he'd have nothing to lose, then he just might turn me in. So when he ran out of money, I began to supply him. I struck a bargain with Ronny. Did you really think he made that kind of money just by selling burial polices to old ladies? Don't worry about Ronny—he won't be turning up in any meadow. He won't be turning up anywhere.

"And that's how it went for years. I looked the other way when Ronny did business in Holcum County, and Ronny kept Jimmy happy. I knew Jim would never turn me in. He needed me—he needed the stuff.

"Then a couple of weeks ago I was at my place in Valdosta, and one day Jim showed up—hitchhiked the whole way down. Said he had a change of mind, a change of heart. Said he had to clear his conscience; he had to come clean and make things right. I told him I would make things right just like I always did—that all he needed to do was keep his mouth shut—but he kept saying he was going to turn me in, that this time he really meant it. I didn't believe him at first—I thought it was just the cocaine talking again—but the longer I listened, the more I believed he just might do it this time. He really meant business; he even had his gun with him.

"So I hit him. Just once. Right between the eyes. Not hard enough to kill him, just hard enough to shut him up. I needed some quiet, I needed some time to think. And then I looked at him lying there on the ground, and I knew what I had to do. It was just like Al Salman again. I didn't plan it; I didn't want it to happen—life just gave me the chance to straighten things out again, and I had to choose. I couldn't just wish and hope that Jim would keep his big mouth shut, I had to make it happen. I had to be strong again.

"So I pulled out his gun, and I put it in his hand. And I was strong.

"But I didn't have a plan, so I had to think. I went back in the cabin, and I thought—I thought for a long time—and I figured it all out. I loaded him in the trunk of my car, and then I laid him in the meadow back here in Rayford. I knew some hunter would find him, and I knew they would call it a suicide. And I knew you would weep and wail and mourn, and then you would get over it. And then everything would finally be the way it was supposed to be."

Then, for the first time, the statue spoke. Without turning, without even moving, a tiny voice drifted up from Kathryn, half whisper and half-moan.

"Amy . . . You murdered Amy, didn't you?"

"That wasn't murder," he grumbled. "I just put her out of her misery like her old cat. I had to. I didn't know what Jimmy told her before he left; I didn't know what she might tell you."

"You killed Teddy too. And Mrs. Gallagher. Oh, Peter, Mrs. Gallagher."

"You made me do that!" the sheriff snapped back. "You made me do it when you wouldn't listen to me, when you got that Bug Man involved in all this."

"You knew what that fly would prove," Kathryn said. "That Jimmy died in Georgia and not in North Carolina. Then it wouldn't be a suicide—then there would be questions."

The sheriff said nothing.

"Do you know why it didn't work, Peter? Because you were weak—weak in the mind, just like you've always been—weak in the mind and sick in the soul. When you went to the lab and let the fly escape, you thought you had fixed everything. But you didn't. The fly left behind a little capsule, a kind of cocoon, and from that Nick still figured out where the fly came from. And when you were at my house, guess what Nick was doing? He was checking the radiator of your car, looking for flies just like the one he found on Jimmy's body. He found them, Peter, he found them. And when he shows them to the authorities, there'll be all kinds of questions. You're going to have a lot of explaining to do."

"I wouldn't worry about the doc," he shrugged. "I don't think he'll be showing anything to anybody. I stopped in at the lab on the way over—quite a mess. I don't think Benjamin had a very hard time catching up with a blind man, do you?"

Kathryn began to tremble.

"You're right about one thing," he said. "After the doc's death there'll be a lot of questions asked around here—more than I'll be able to explain. That's why I can't go back. That's why it all has to end here."

The sheriff pulled the slide twice more. Now only two bullets remained.

"I'm not asking you to forgive me. I just want you to understand—all this has happened because I love you. Because I was willing to be strong, because I was willing to do the hard thing for both of us." He looked down at the gun. "And I'm going to do the hard thing again, Kath—for both of us."

"You can kill me," she trembled, "but we still won't be to-gether. Because I'll be in heaven with Andy, and you'll be frying in hell."

"Don't know much about hell," he said. "But I figure there's no heaven if I can't be with you."

He reached out and stroked her hair. A pair of bees circled her head once and buzzed away.

"I would never hurt you, Kath. I know how to make this quick and easy. I hope you understand that I can't leave you behind. If I did someone else might have you—and that can never be. We were supposed to be together, Kath—and if we can't live together, then . . ."

He slowly raised the Beretta and placed it at the base of her skull.

"Let me turn around," she whispered. "Let me see you one last time."

He lowered the gun.

She slowly turned.

In front of her she held a small, square crate covered with fine wire mesh. It was a bee crate—and it was empty.

She dropped it. It bounced away at her feet.

Around her torso, suspended by two white shoestrings, was a piece of screen wire rolled into the shape of a small tube. Inside was a single honeybee with an abdomen twice the size of an ordi-nary bee.

It was the queen.

And on the queen, on the wire tube, on Kathryn's waist and breasts and arms and neck, three thousand honeybees swarmed in one buzzing, roiling mass of black and gold.

The sheriff gasped. His arms went limp, and the gun slipped unnoticed from his hand. He stared in utter disbelief—yet there she stood, her soft, pink skin swarming with thousands of wriggling, crawling creatures of her own private hell.

Kathryn slowly raised her arms above her head and then stopped. Her face was pale and rigid, her lips were pressed tight shut, and her eyes were fixed in a scream of terror and rage and indomitable will.

And Peter knew that she was right, that he was weak, and that he had never been worthy of this woman. He lowered his eyes and opened his mouth to speak, but nothing came out. There was nothing left to say.

An instant later Kathryn threw her arms around his neck and squeezed.

There was a muted roar.

There was a muffled crunch.

And there was an overwhelming odor of smashed bananas.

CHAPTER
40

Kathryn drifted in a velvet void. She turned without turning and looked about. It was black, everywhere black, nothing but black. She strained her eyes to stare deeper into the darkness, but she had no eyes to strain. She raised her hand to feel for her face, but she had no face, and no hand either. She was only a mind, floating free in the starless night of sleep—or was it death? There was no pain, there was no care, but she was somehow still aware. And somehow she knew that the darkness had an end, that if she had hands to reach out with she would find walls not far away—cool walls, smooth walls, curving up like a vaulted dome above her. And somehow she knew that she was staring at the inside of her own skull.

Then a buzzing sound whizzed by very close, a sound that some ancient instinct told her should evoke fear—but there was no fear, not here. There was a second buzz, then another, and each one struck the wall of her skull with a bright white spark and ricocheted back even louder and closer than before. The buzzing grew louder, and the sparks flashed brighter until it all blended together into one blinding, sizzling light. And suddenly the walls were gone, and the light came streaming in.

And the light brought back the pain.

Now a face appeared above her in the light. It was an odd face but nevertheless a strong and good face, and it was strangely familiar. The face began to soften and come into better focus. In the center was a pair of enormous spectacles.

She reached out her hand to touch the face, and she had hands again.

"Hello, Dorothy." Nick smiled down at her. "Welcome back to Kansas." He sat beside her on the edge of her hospital bed and cradled her right hand in his.

She looked up into the familiar brown orbs that bobbed and floated behind the glass—only now they floated in a storm of red and black that spiraled out from under his glasses like the fingers of a hurricane. Across his forehead was a long white bandage spotted with dots of scarlet.

She reached up and touched his cheek.

"Are you . . . alive?" she whispered, her lips barely moving.

"More or less—if you call this living."

"You look terrible."

"Look who's talking."

Her eyes drifted from his face, to her hand, to her arm. The hand looked normal enough, but on her forearm she saw a spatter of reddish spots and blisters that increased in size and number until her entire upper arm seemed to erupt in a cascade of fleshy bumps and moguls. She reached up and felt about her face and neck. Her neck was a continuous mass of lumps and welts. Her cheeks were puffed and bloated, and her bloodshot eyes peeked out from their swollen sockets like two cranberries from a muffin.

"How do I look?"

"Lumpy is the word that comes to mind. But on you it looks good." He leaned back for a moment, taking a better view. "You look like one of those Cabbage Patch Dolls, remember?"

She slowly rolled her eyes, then closed them.

"Those were very popular, you know."

"How long have I—"

"Been away? About three days. Not bad considering you took about a thousand stings, mostly to the torso. The doctors stopped counting at seven hundred, but I counted more."

She raised one eyebrow.

He shrugged. "I had some time to kill. A thousand stings is nowhere near the record, but still very impressive." He leaned forward and gently brushed a stray wisp of auburn from her forehead. "I'm afraid your friend the sheriff didn't fare as well."

"What happened?"

"Are you sure you want to know?"

She hesitated for an instant—only an instant—and then nodded.

"My guess would be he was unconscious before he hit the ground and dead within a minute—two at the most. You were very thorough. He took about as many stings as you did, but it didn't take a thousand to kill him, just two or three. I warned him to stay away from bees. I should have warned him to stay away from women who wear them."

She smiled, and it hurt.

For a minute he said nothing more. He just sat staring, slowly shaking his head. "Well," he said abruptly, "I'd say your entomophobia has improved considerably."

Another smile, another shooting pain.

She touched his face again. "He told me you were dead."

"He told you that?"

"He saw the lab. He said it was a wreck."

"Well that's true. Of course, it was a wreck before. I think he was referring to the screen door. I had a little trouble finding the doorknob, so I had to run through it." He paused. "Or maybe he was talking about my scorpion collection. I'm still looking for a few of them."

Kathryn's eyes widened.

"I was a little careless on the way to the office," he said. "It seems I accidentally spilled my collection of north African fat tails on the floor—and I'm afraid the deputy had the unfortunate experience of falling down on them."

She winced.

"It was heart failure or possibly respiratory collapse—probably both. He lasted less than an hour, but it was a very long hour."

"Poor Beanie," she whispered.

"The deputy's cousins have already claimed his body."

"And Peter?"

Nick shrugged. "No wife, no family, and no friends left, either. Nobody seemed to want the sheriff's remains. Don't worry, it's all been taken care of."

She took a moment to close her eyes and rest.

"Ronny," she said suddenly. "Ronny was the supplier."

"I figured. If the deputy couldn't drive himself to Teddy's trailer, somebody else had to do it—somebody who also had an interest in seeing Teddy dead. The sheriff was occupied; that left only one other interested party: the supplier. After all, if the sheriff went down, he could take Ronny down with him. I'll bet Ronny was more than happy to drive. We'll have to see what we can do about Ronny."

"I don't think anyone's going to find Ronny."

"The sheriff?"

She nodded.

"Very thoughtful of him. Saved us a lot of trouble."

She pointed to Nick's bandaged forehead.

"This? I was attacked by a Quercus falcata," he said solemnly. "That's a red oak to you. I ran into a tree—a very hard one. Which reminds me . . . I passed out in the tree. They never would have found me if you hadn't made it back to the lab and given the police my general direction. After all you went through, you were still able to make a phone call?" Nick let out a whistle. "In Pittsburgh, you are what we call 'one tough chick.' "

Kathryn looked up at him. "So what happens now?"

"You mean the investigation? We take the evidence we have to the authorities—not the ice cream man this time, the real authorities. The puparium should still be in the lab, and I'm betting the sheriff didn't have time to dispose of my shirt, so we can recover the specimens I collected from his radiator, too. That should be enough to request an exhumation, and then the medical examiner's office in Chapel Hill will look for further evidence."

"So now I know," she said sadly.

"So now you know. How does it feel?"

She said nothing.

"If it's any consolation," Nick said, "we proved that your friend didn't take his own life. It turns out your hunch was right after all."

"So was your sense of smell. About Peter, I mean."

"And you're off the hook. You may have hurt your friend's feelings, but you didn't drive him to an early grave. Too bad Amy's not around to hear that."

She paused. "And I found out something I thought I never would. I found out what happened to Andy."

He squeezed her hand.

"Most important," he said brightly, "you avoided a possible marriage to a deranged megalomaniac."

"What? Did you propose too?"

"Not likely." Nick smiled. "Proposing to you seems to be a definite health risk."

Kathryn looked thoughtfully at the ceiling. "All in all, it was a good week's work."

"We worked pretty well together," he nodded. "Which reminds me . . . Now that Teddy's gone I'll be needing a new assistant, and . . . well, I was just wondering . . ."

She blinked.

". . . if you'll be paying me anytime soon. It takes a lot of money to hire a research assistant, you know."

She glared at him. "I'll pay you," she said crossly. "I said I'd pay you and I will. Twenty thousand dollars."

"Plus expenses," he reminded her.

"What expenses?"

"My car. Destroyed in the line of duty. Destroyed by you personally, I might add."

"I barely scratched it!"

"The windshield is gone. The right door fell off. The rear fender is missing. There's a bullet hole in the backseat. And after you left it, with the sheriff's assistance it burned to the ground."

She covered her face and let out a snort like a startled mare.

"I find your lack of respect for the dead alarming," Nick said. "I have no choice but to bill you for the full replacement value of the vehicle. That brings your current total to twenty thousand and thirty-seven dollars. That might seem a little high, but I had a half of a pizza in the backseat."

She laughed in spite of herself. It was agonizing, healing laughter.

"And I don't take checks," he frowned. "Not from your bank anyway."

They sat in silence for a minute.

"You called me Kathryn," she said quietly.

"What?"

"In front of the lab. When you said we had to separate, you called me Kathryn—not Mrs. Guilford."

"That's right, I did, didn't I?"

"I remember something Teddy taught me. The first principle of taxonomy is: Never mind what a thing appears to be, what is its true nature? Well now I know for sure that I'm not 'Mrs. Guilford' anymore. I'm Kathryn again. Just plain Kathryn."

"Kathryn," he repeated. "That will take some getting used to."

"Try it out from time to time. It'll grow on you."

He smiled again, and then he rose to leave.

"Do you have to go?" she said.

"I'm afraid so. I have another client who requires my attention."

"Another client? Already?"

On the extreme western boundary of Holcum County, in a remote area of old abandoned home fields, a pale green Quonset hut sits at the end of a winding gravel road. Behind the hut, across a short meadow, a dirt path disappears into the woods. Down the path, past the sagging hulk of a decomposing sow, past a mottled cadaver dressed in shreds of flannel, lies the burned-out skeleton of a '64 Dodge Dart.

The windshield is gone. The rear fender is missing. The right door gapes open. But the trunk remains closed.

And inside the trunk, flies buzz, eggs hatch, and a thousand wriggling maggots engorge themselves on a bloated figure still wearing a sheriff's star.

CHOP SHOP

BUG MAN NOVEL 2

For my father-in-law Bill Burns,
my research assistant in Pittsburgh and Tarentum,
who once climbed across a burning bony pile
and lived to tell the tale.
Thanks, Dad.

And for Joy—always for Joy.

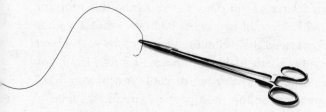

University of Pittsburgh Medical Center, 1973

T he young man set his glasses down beside the sink, then bent down and cupped handfuls of cold water against his face. He fumbled for a strip of coarse, brown paper towel, straightened, and studied himself in the mirror. *You can do this,* he said to himself. *There's a first time for everybody. Come on, Julian, you did a PhD in bioethics at twenty-five. You can do this.*

"Good morning!" he said aloud. "I'm Dr. Julian Zohar."

Too eager. For crying out loud, their daughter died thirty minutes ago! He replaced his glasses and turned back to the mirror.

"I am Dr. Julian Zohar," he said solemnly. "First of all, let me say how sorry I am . . . how very sorry I am . . . how terribly sorry I am to hear about little Angela"—he picked up a file folder, flipped it open, and ran his finger down the page—"little *Angelita.*" *Nice work, Julian. At least get the kid's name right.*

He took a deep breath, composed himself, and began again.

"I am an organ procurement coordinator for the Center for Organ Procurement and Education." *Man, what a mouthful.* He flipped open the file folder and scanned it again:

Father: Tejano Juarez, age 31, landscape maintenance.

Mother: Belicia Juarez, age 26, domestic services.

"I'm Dr. Julian Zohar," he mumbled, "and you two are probably a couple of wetbacks who barely finished the sixth grade before you squeezed under a fence somewhere in west Texas. Organ procurement coordinator. Organ pro-cure-ment. *Comprende* 'procurement'? Sure you do."

He tossed the folder beside the sink and began to pace back and forth in the rest room, gesturing in the air as he spoke.

"Well, hello there! I'm Julian Zohar. I was just passing by, and—what's that? Your four-year-old daughter drowned this morning in a drainage ditch? Say, that is a bit of bad news. But speaking of people who don't need their vital organs anymore—can I have hers? Oh no, not all of them, just her kidneys. *Riñones,* I think you call them. I can? Well, that's very big of you! Now, if you'll just scratch your names here on this multipage release form, I'll be on my way. And so sorry about Angie, or Amy, or whatever her name was."

He stood silently in the center of the rest room for a moment, then turned back to the sink. He opened the spigot, plunged both hands under the stream, and watched the water run off. Minutes went by.

Finally, he looked up at his image once again, slowly leaned forward, and pointed at his own face.

"I am Dr. Julian Zohar," he said deliberately. "I learned less than an hour ago about the tragic loss of your daughter. I cannot tell you how sorry I am. I have no way to comprehend your feelings of loss and grief. But I came here today to tell you that your daughter's death does not have to be in vain. Even now, even in death, she has the ability to save another little girl's life. Just a few miles away from here, over at Children's Hospital of Pittsburgh, there is a little girl dying of end-stage renal disease. Your daughter is the right size, the right blood type, and they are reasonably histocompatible. I am asking you to release your daughter's kidneys for transplant. Without them, that other little girl will die—and you have the power to prevent it. One little girl died this morning. Please don't let there be two."

Just then the rest-room door swung open with a pneumatic sigh. In stepped the figure of a priest.

"Please forgive the intrusion," he said. "I'm looking for Julian Zohar."

"You've found him."

"I'm Father Anduhar," he said, extending his hand. "I received a call this morning about the Juarez family—about their loss."

"I didn't call you," Julian said.

"The family services coordinator called. I understand that you're preparing to approach the family about organ donation. In such cases, it's often helpful if a member of the clergy is there to assist."

"No thanks." Julian stepped past the priest and pressed the hand blower with the butt of his palm.

"May I ask why not?" the priest said above the low roar.

"Sorry," Julian said, rubbing his hands smoothly one over the other.

The priest waited patiently for the roar to subside. "Why not?" he asked again.

Julian turned to him. "I'm about to ask a mother and father to allow a surgeon to cut out their daughter's kidneys. Their daughter is dead. They know that, but they don't feel it yet. Clinically speaking, there's a very fine line between life and death; emotionally, there's no line at all. The last thing I want is a priest talking to them about 'the resurrection of the body unto life everlasting.' "

The priest shook his head. "You misunderstand. The Catholic church wholeheartedly endorses organ donation—"

"It's not what you endorse; it's what you represent," Julian said. "You tell the family, 'Angelita lives on! She can hear you, she can see you. Talk to her, pray for her.' I tell the family, 'Angelita is dead. She cannot hear, she cannot feel—so give me her kidneys. Let someone use them who is alive.' You encourage people to dwell on the dead; I want them to think about the living. No thank you."

The priest shook his head. "If you fail to care for the dead, you fail to care for the living."

Julian stepped toward the door. "You go ahead and sprinkle your water and wave your incense. Say your prayers for the dead—me, I work with the living."

The priest stared after him in astonishment. "Remarkable. You have no faith at all, do you?"

Julian turned back again. "Let me tell you what I have faith in," he said. "One year ago, a Swiss biochemist named Jean Borel discovered an amazing immunosuppressant called cyclosporine. It's made from a common soil fungus. Up until now transplants have been hit or miss, but when cyclosporine hits the market, it's going to revolutionize transplant technology. No more massive tissue rejection, no more 20 percent survival rates. Can you imagine? People living ten, twenty, thirty years longer; people surviving cancers and overcoming genetic defects; people extending the duration and quality of their lives because they can get *parts*. And not just kidneys and the occasional liver; I'm talking about intestines, lungs—even hearts. *Hearts!*

"And when all this happens, Father whatever-your-name-is, you know what the greatest barrier to transplantation will be? People like you: people who encourage others to focus on the past instead of the future. Because even with all that wonderful technology, people will still have to be *willing* to give up their organs—and that has to change."

"What do you mean?"

"Not all cultures are as individualistic as we are in the West. Here, we assume that each individual should possess sovereign rights over his own body—even after death. In more communal cultures—more *enlightened* cultures, in my view—they believe that the community should assume the rights to your body at the moment of death, and the community should then be free to use your body for the greater good."

"That's frightening."

"You think so? What frightens me is the idea that the dead should have power over the living. That's your world, not mine. I want to make people understand that it's not just a privilege to donate an organ, it's an obligation."

"You're going to tell this family that they're obligated to surrender their daughter's kidneys?"

"I'm going to tell them whatever it takes," Julian said.

"That is immoral and unethical."

Julian smiled. "I have a PhD in bioethics," he said. "You want to talk ethics? What's the greater good here: that a family should be permitted, through ignorance or selfishness or superstition, to allow perfectly good organs to perish, or that those organs should be used to save another human being's life? What do you think, Father? Should one little girl die today or two?"

The priest said nothing. Julian turned and pulled open the door.

"I think you are a very great fool," said the priest.

"I am the future. You are the past. Now if you'll excuse me, I have a life to save."

Julian peered through the waiting-room window at the grieving Juarez family. There were six of them huddled loosely around an orange vinyl sofa in a tableau vivant; Julian studied the setting the way a painter would analyze the composition of a painting.

Seated in the center was a gray-haired woman; she held her head in her hands and bobbed back and forth, wiping at the corners of her eyes with the tips of her fingers.

Grandmother. The beloved matriarch. The tent peg of the family, the one with the strongest sense of loyalty and tradition. She can turn the whole family if she wants to.

A younger woman sat stroking the old woman's back, reaching across to pat the face of a crying sibling, stopping only to cover her own face and let out a shuddering sob.

Mother. The backbone of the family, the one who holds everyone else together. No matter what she feels, she'll do what she thinks is best for the rest of them. She's the lever, the one who can move them all.

Three children orbited the grieving women like little satellites. The oldest, a girl, stood weeping beside her mother. Her younger brother cried more gently, grieving more over his mother's pain than over a death he could not yet comprehend. On the floor, an even younger boy sat blissfully flipping through the pages of an activity book.

Daughter. The only one of the three who's really a player. She's the catalyst; she holds the family's heart. If she trusts me, the rest will follow. I can reach them all through the daughter.

To the left, standing at a distance and facing away from the rest of the family, stood a small, sinewy man with a copper face and a tangled mustache. He was dressed in work clothes: sagging denims that hung down over mottled gray boots, and a faded gray T-shirt with a gaping collar. He stood with his hands jammed deep in his pockets, pacing back and forth in quick steps like a stallion that wants to bolt but has nowhere to run. His eyes alternated between confusion, grief, and rage—but rage was winning out.

Father. The alpha male. He has all the anger; he's the wild bull. I can ride him, or he can trample me. He has the ego; he's the one to stroke.

Julian took a deep breath, tucked the file folder under his arm, and rapped on the glass.

"Good morning," he said as evenly as possible, "I'm Dr. Zohar."

The father stopped and looked at him, his eyes brightening.

"There is news?" he said excitedly. "Something has changed?"

Suddenly the entire tableau broke apart before Julian's eyes. The mother sprang to her feet and rushed toward him, grasping Julian's forearm with both hands. The children swept in behind her like flotsam in the wake of a boat. The father charged forward and then halted, staring in wide-eyed anticipation.

And then, worst of all, Julian saw the grandmother struggle painfully to her feet and shuffle forward. He had made the old woman rise—and for nothing.

A terrible moment of silence followed.

"No—there's no change. Angelita is still . . . I mean, I'm not that kind of doctor."

Julian felt the mother squeeze his arm again, and then release. He saw three pairs of youthful eyes turn to her for explanation. He watched the older woman's shoulders round and her body sag as though she might drop right where she stood. Worst of all, he saw the rage returning to the father's eyes. Julian bit his lip. By raising their hopes, even for an instant, he had caused them to look backward. Now his job would be twice as hard.

"Then what do you want?" the father growled. "Leave us!"

"I just stopped by . . . to see if . . . if there's anything I can do," Julian stumbled.

"What can you do? You can bring my little Angelita back to life. Can you do this? No? But you are not that kind of doctor."

The women had returned to the sofa now, weeping freshly and glancing resentfully back at Julian.

"I came to tell you that your daughter's death does not have to be in vain."

The father turned to his wife and shrugged. "*¿Qué quiere decir?* 'In vain.' "

"*Inútil*," she translated. " 'Useless.' "

The father whipped around in a fury. "Angelita's death was not useless. What do you want from us? Is this how you help?"

"No. I'm sorry. Please—let me explain." He stepped to the sofa, smiled, and rested his hand on the little girl's head. She ducked away and leaned against her mother.

"There is another little girl. She is very sick. She is in a hospital right now, not far from here. Angelita can help her."

"Angelita can help no one. Angelita is dead."

"She can still help. A *part* of her can help."

The mother squinted at Julian in confusion—until a look of horrified recognition began to spread across her face like gangrene.

Julian saw it. Seconds were critical now; he plunged ahead.

"We want your permission to remove your daughter's kidneys. The doctors want to transplant them—place them—into the little girl who is sick. This can save her life."

The father turned again to his wife and mother. There was a flurry of Spanish between them: *"Angelita . . . los doctores . . . sus riñones . . . trasplante."*

The old woman groaned.

The father stumbled back as though he had been punched in the gut.

"Is this why Angelita is dead?" he said. "Did the doctors even try to save her?"

"Mr. Juarez, of course they did. The doctors here did everything in their power to—"

The father charged forward, jerked the file folder from under Julian's arm, and handed it back to him. "The girl in the hospital," he said. "What color is she?"

"Mr. Juarez, it makes absolutely no difference—"

"What color is she?"

Julian fumbled open the folder and ran a finger down the first page, focusing on nothing at all. He knew the answer before he opened the folder.

"The little girl . . . this particular little girl . . . seems to be of Caucasian descent."

"Anglo!" the father spluttered. "Angelita is dead so an Anglo can live!"

"Mr. Juarez, this has nothing to do with race—nothing whatsoever." Julian listened to the sound of his own words. The harder he protested, the more hollow the words seemed to sound.

"Mr. Juarez, listen to me. Angelita is dead. She feels nothing."

"I feel! I feel!"

"You have the power to save a little girl's life."

"And you! You had the power to save my little girl's life!"

"Mr. Juarez, try to think of the other girl's family."

The father stared at Julian in amazement. "My Angelita is dead less than one hour. You come to me and say, 'Please! Give me her *riñones!* We will cut her open! And then you ask me to think of *another* little girl? Get out! Get out of here!"

Julian turned silently to the door and stepped out. As it closed behind him, he looked one last time at the family of Angelita Juarez, a little girl whose perfect little kidneys, through a series of chemical changes, would soon be reduced to two lumps of decomposing waste.

Waste.

Angelita was dead—and so was the little girl across town.

North Carolina State University, May 2003

Nick Polchak stood with his nose less than twelve inches from the blackboard, his right hand waving a stick of chalk like a conductor's baton. From time to time he stopped abruptly, and the chalk would tap out a hypnotic staccato; then he would suddenly arch away from the blackboard, study his most recent series of scratchings, make a few quick edits with his left hand, and begin again. He spoke directly to the blackboard, as though students might somehow be trapped behind it. In fact, they were behind him, fighting off heat-induced slumber and cursing the fate that had forced them to take General Entomology during a summer session while more fortunate classmates were right now stretching out on the sands at Myrtle Beach.

"While all bugs are insects, not all insects are bugs," Nick confided to the blackboard. "True bugs belong to the suborder Heteroptera; these include lace bugs, squash bugs, chinch bugs, red bugs, water bugs. The tips of their wings are membranous, but only the tips—insects with entirely membranous wings belong to the suborder Homoptera, which includes cicadas, treehoppers, aphids, and lantern flies. Both orders, of course, are characterized by sucking mouthparts—"

"Dr. Polchak," a weary voice interrupted, "will this be on the final?"

The chalk stopped tapping. Nick turned slowly and looked over the class as if he were shocked to discover someone sitting behind him.

"Who said that?"

The soft shuffling of papers and shifting of bodies abruptly stopped; all eyes turned to the blackboard. Nick Polchak was a legend among students at NC State. He was a professor who had been censured by his own department so many times that he had achieved an almost mythical status. Nick was a forensic entomologist in a department of horticulturalists and livestock specialists, a man whose private research on human decomposition had spawned a dozen campus legends about missing undergraduates and shallow graves deep in the Carolina woods. But the best-known thing about Nick Polchak, the thing that every student knew about, was his eyes. Nick wore the largest, thickest glasses anyone had ever seen, and they made his chestnut eyes appear enormous. But it was more than size—it was the way the eyes moved. They floated and darted like synchronized hummingbirds; they scanned and penetrated like orbiting probes; they disappeared completely when Nick closed his eyes, then suddenly reappeared twice as imposing as they were just a moment ago.

Nick's entomology courses were among the most popular on campus. Everyone wanted a chance to look at him—but no one wanted Nick to look back; those eyes were just too much to bear. Whenever Nick turned from the blackboard—an event that was mercifully rare—every head was bowed and every pen was busy. Everyone knew that Nick Polchak loved insects more than anything in the world. He was the Bug Man—and someone just asked the Bug Man if bugs would be on the final exam.

A young man in the second row, squeezing himself down into the recesses of his writing desk, looked up to see twin moons rise in the sky above him.

"It seems a bit *premature*," Nick said, "to be asking in the first week of a course whether 'this will be on the final.' It shows tremendous . . . *foresight*."

Nick blinked, and the brown moons vanished—then they flashed open again, even larger than before.

"What you're really asking me is whether *this*"—he gestured to the blackboard—"is worth *knowing*." Nick cocked his head to one side and studied the young man's face as though he were searching for those sucking mouthparts. "Insects comprise the largest class in the animal world," he said. "Ninety-five percent of all animal species are insects. There are about a million known species; there may be *thirty* million more waiting to be discovered. They are distributed from the polar regions to the rain forests, from snowfields in the Himalayas to abandoned mines a mile underground. They flourish in the hottest deserts, on the surface of the ocean, in thermal springs—even in pools of petroleum. The smallest insect is less than a hundredth of an inch long; there is a kind of tarantula that weighs a quarter of a pound and measures eleven inches toe to toe. It has fangs an inch long. It eats *birds*. Is any of this worth knowing?

"Did you know that ants and termites alone make up 20 percent of the entire animal biomass of our planet? Did you know that one out of every four animals on earth is a beetle? Your little town of Raleigh has a population of what—a quarter of a million? There may be two million insects in a single acre of land. Insects eat more plants than all the other creatures on earth. Without insects, we would be living in an ecological nightmare—mountains of rotting organic matter everywhere. Without insects, half the other animal species on earth would probably perish—yours included. My species rules this world; you are a member of an annoying minority group. When you ask me if this is worth knowing, you're asking me if life *itself* is worth knowing."

Nick studied the young man's face. Like all undergraduates, he knew how to look suitably repentant; it was one of their most basic survival skills. This one looked like a cocker spaniel that got caught peeing on the rug. He was sorry—so *very* sorry—that even phys ed majors like him had a three-hour science requirement.

Nick let out a sigh. "Let me bring it down to your level," he said. "The kissing bugs of Central and South America can consume twelve times their body weight in blood. That's the equivalent of a Sigma Chi drinking two hundred gallons of beer at one party."

The entire class let out a cheer.

Nick turned back to the blackboard. "I should never have turned around," he said. But before he could return to his private lecture, another student, sensing the opportunity, spoke up.

"Dr. Polchak, what are your office hours? I can never find you."

"My office is here in Gardner Hall, room 323. Knock on my door; if I answer, those are my office hours. If you really need to whine about something, talk to me after class."

"But I can never *catch* you after class. Am I supposed to talk to your back while you're running down the hall toward your lab?"

Nick nodded. "That works for me. Now can we get back to this? I've got a lot of material to cover. And *yes*," he said with a nod in the direction of the cocker spaniel, "this *will* be on the final. The only thing I will not require you people to remember is *useless* knowledge—and in case you're wondering, there is no such thing as useless knowledge."

But as the classroom quieted once again, an unusual sound drifted forward from the back of the room. Heads began to slowly turn—Nick's last of all. There, spread-eagled atop a cool, black laboratory island, was a student fast asleep. He lay on his back, mouth open, with a little pool of spittle beside his face.

A piece of chalk snapped in two.

"Did I ever tell you," Nick said slowly, "about a case I had several years ago? It was in Colorado, in an area near a meat-processing plant. The men who worked there carried an unusual type of knife, something like a boning knife, and they were very adept with it."

As he spoke, Nick started back through the classroom toward the sleeping student.

"They found one of their employees in the bottom of a nearby ravine with his gut sliced open. The body had been there for several days. After seventy-two hours, forensic entomology is the most reliable way to determine postmortem interval, so the local medical examiner asked me to come in before they moved the body."

As Nick passed each row of students, he gestured for them to follow.

"I could see the body from the top of the ravine, lying in an opening between some small trees. It looked as if they had painted a chalk line around the body, like they do to mark the placement when a body is finally removed—only the body was still there. When I got closer, I realized what it was. The long gut wound had allowed a massive maggot infestation in the abdomen, and the maggots had completed their third instar—they had eaten all they could hold, and they were leaving the body, looking for a safe place to pupate. There were so many maggots exiting all at once that they formed a white outline, slowly moving outward toward the trees."

Nick was standing over the lab table now with the rest of the class gathered silently around. He spoke quietly, glaring down at the oblivious student. Nick opened a drawer and removed a scalpel and a pair of forceps. With the forceps he gently lifted the boy's shirt near each button, and with a quick flip of the scalpel sent each button tapping across the table. Now he used the forceps to peel back the shirt, leaving the bare chest and abdomen exposed. The student brushed an imaginary fly from his nose, licked his lips, and let out a long, moaning snore.

"I examined the abdomen. The wound stretched from the breastbone to the groin—just the kind of incision a man would make who's used to gutting Herefords. The maggot mass was enormous, the largest I've ever seen. I wanted to measure the temperature at the core of the mass. I slid in a probe—it was almost 120 degrees at the center! But maggots can't regulate their own body temperature, and that's about the point where thermal death occurs, so the maggots were circulating away from the core as fast as they could. The cooler ones were wriggling their way toward the center while the overheated ones were struggling to get out, venting their excess heat on the surface like tiny radiators. It was amazing! The entire mass looked like a pot of boiling ziti.

"Then all of a sudden, I felt something land in my hair. I brushed it off without thinking about it—then it happened again. Then something hit my arm . . . then my back. Finally, something landed on my neck, wriggled for a minute, and rolled down my back. I looked up . . ."

Nick stood beside the boy's head, leaning ever closer as he spoke. He held the gleaming scalpel directly in front of his face, and the volume of his voice began to slowly rise.

"When maggots flee a body, they instinctively look for a drier place to pupate. To a maggot, dry means high, so they climb anything they can find: a rock, a bush—even a tree. Thousands of maggots had inched their way up the surrounding trees, crawled out to the tips of the lowest branches, and now they were dropping off. It was raining maggots, and they were landing on my neck and rolling down my back. And there's only ONE thing in the WORLD that I HATE more than MAGGOTS DOWN MY BACK . . ."

The boy's eyes popped open. Two great brown meteors crashed down on him, mere inches from impact, led by the flash of surgical steel.

Nick spoke in a low, rumbling tone: "DON'T-EVER-FALL-ASLEEP-IN-MY-CLASS."

With a quick flip of his hand Nick placed the cold, blunt butt of the scalpel on the boy's breastbone and drew it firmly down the center of his abdomen. The boy shrieked, clutched at his chest with both hands, and rolled off onto the floor. Nick looked up at the rest of the stunned students.

"Now then. Does anyone else have a question?"

Dr. Noah Ellison, chairman of the NC State Department of Entomology, tapped his spoon against the side of his coffee cup; the various members of the faculty committee took their seats and shuffled into silence.

"We have a number of items on our agenda this evening," Dr. Ellison began. A man directly across the table raised his hand slightly and, without waiting for recognition, plunged ahead.

"Perhaps I might suggest an appropriate starting point," he said with a dripping Southern lilt in his voice. "Let's see now. We could begin with research reports from our various agricultural extension stations. Then again, we might consider the budget allocations for new equipment in the graduate laboratories. Now, what was that other item? It escapes my mind just now—oh yes, now I recall." He shot a glance toward the end of the table, where Nick Polchak sat slumped in his chair with a copy of the *Journal of Medical Entomology* open on his chest. "We could discuss Dr. Polchak's decision to dissect a student in his class this morning. Yes, let's begin with that."

Nick closed his journal. "I didn't actually dissect him," he said, "though the idea does open up some interesting research possibilities. Some of these undergraduates, I'm sure no one would miss."

"Why, Dr. Polchak," the man replied, "rumor has it that you have an entire woodland forest filled with decomposing undergraduate students. Whatever would you do with another?"

The man glaring at Nick was Dr. Sherman Pettigrew, tenured professor of Applied Insect Ecology and Pest Control. Dr. Pettigrew had several years of seniority on Nick, and he had strongly opposed the decision to hire Nick in the first place—but his "foresight went unheeded," as he liked to put it, and now he took every available opportunity to remind Nick that he was not, and never would be, welcome. He despised Nick's arrogant iconoclasm; he was horrified by the very idea of *forensic* entomology; and most of all—though he would never admit it—he resented Nick's popularity with students.

For Nick's part, Sherman Pettigrew represented everything he hated about academia, traditional entomology, and the South. Sherman Pettigrew was a large man, in his midfifties, but with the face of a child: round, soft, and still bulging in places that should have long ago turned to muscle and sinew. It gave his face a look that Nick found hard to take seriously, even in an argument. He had the old Southern habit of always wearing white: white shirts, extra starch, with the cuffs buttoned tightly about his wrists; white cuffed pants with knife-edge pleats; white socks; white shoes—that's what irritated Nick the most—and an ever-present white linen handkerchief for mopping beads of sweat from his pudgy forehead. His choice of apparel did his physique no favors, and only added to his babylike appearance. "Light colors make a room look bigger," Nick once said to him. "Don't they have decorators in the South?" Nick had an entire collection of nicknames for Dr. Pettigrew—the Great White, the Bulgy Bear—but since their very first faculty meeting together, Nick had addressed him as "Sherm"—not Sherman, not Pettigrew, and never, ever Dr. Pettigrew.

"Perhaps you find this amusing," Dr. Pettigrew replied. "I, for one, fail to see the humor in it. Even as we speak, there is an aggrieved family meeting with the university's counsel, deciding whether or not to take legal recourse—legal recourse as in *lawsuit*, Dr. Polchak. While your colleagues are submitting papers to academic journals, you may find yourself submitting to a deposition."

"I read *your* last paper," Nick said. " *'The European Corn Borer: Larval Parasitism in Selected North Carolina Hosts.'* What a snoozer."

"Dr. Ellison, I really must protest—"

The aged chairman of the entomology department knew that it was time for a judicious intervention, but he hated to interrupt. For Dr. Ellison, the ongoing verbal volley between Dr. Polchak and Dr. Pettigrew was the highlight of these endless committee meetings, and he resented the role he was forced to play as peacekeeper and hand-slapper.

"Nicholas, Dr. Pettigrew does have a point. We really cannot make a habit of attacking our students with surgical instruments."

"He fell asleep in my class," Nick said sullenly.

"Perhaps there is a reason for that," Dr. Pettigrew offered.

Nick glared at him. "I'm sure the European Corn Borer has them bouncing off the walls in your classroom, Sherm."

"Gentlemen," Dr. Ellison said. "I think we're all in agreement that Dr. Polchak's disciplinary action this morning, while memorable, was a tad . . . extreme. We are now in the position of having to decide what to do about it."

"There is only one thing to do about it," Dr. Pettigrew said. "I move for the immediate dismissal of Dr. Polchak."

A groan arose from the entire faculty committee.

"A failed coup attempt." Nick whistled. "How embarrassing."

"That also is a tad extreme." Dr. Ellison frowned at Dr. Pettigrew. "However, some form of punitive action is necessary. I'm sure you understand, Nicholas, that to avoid legal action, the university must be able to demonstrate that you have been chastised in some appropriate way."

"You could make me take one of Sherm's classes," Nick suggested.

"Nicholas, you're not helping."

Suddenly, Nick took on a look of deep remorse. "There's only one alternative," he said. "Official censure. I'll have to give up my classes for the summer and go away somewhere."

"This is patently unfair," Dr. Pettigrew interrupted. "Everyone here knows that Dr. Polchak hates teaching. And every time he is 'officially censured,' he goes off to do whatever he pleases while the rest of us are forced to assume his class load."

"What else can we do, Sherm?" Nick said solemnly. "After this kind of tragedy, can we all just go back to business as usual? What would it communicate to the grieving family if today I vivisect little Bobby, and tomorrow I'm back teaching as usual? No, something must be done. I say we send me away. I say we apologize to the boy's family. And I say we send him to Sherm's class and let him sleep as much as he wants to."

Dr. Ellison wanted to smile, but his role required him to maintain a sober countenance. "I think there is something to what Dr. Polchak has suggested," he said. "Very well, Nicholas, you will once again be officially censured by this department and by the university proper—"

"*That* hurts," Nick moaned.

"And you will forfeit your summer classes—and all remuneration associated with them."

Nick winced. That did hurt.

"And if I may make one more suggestion," Dr. Pettigrew smiled. "It seems to me that Dr. Polchak could put some of this free time to good use—perhaps in some constructive activity that will help him to reconsider his errant ways."

"Such as?"

"We all know the priority our department places on community service activities—especially our K-12 educational seminars. So far, Dr. Polchak has avoided them like the proverbial plague. There's almost a month before the public schools dismiss; perhaps his involvement in this area would have a redeeming effect—a *calming* effect on him."

Under the table, Nick rolled his journal into a tight scroll and squeezed. Dr. Pettigrew smiled, taking special delight in this particular torture.

Dr. Ellison turned to Nick. "Nicholas?"

"Agreed," Nick said through clenched teeth.

With the issue settled, the committee adjourned briefly for refreshments. As Nick passed Dr. Ellison, he bent over and whispered in the old man's ear.

"So I have to go away," he said. "Does anybody care where I go away?"

CHAPTER 2

Pittsburgh, Pennsylvania, May 2003

Riley McKay's heels clicked and echoed down the hollow corridor of Fairview Elementary School. The shoes hurt. She curled her toes and wriggled her feet from side to side in a vain attempt to stretch out the unbroken leather. She longed for the comfortable Nikes she wore at the Allegheny County Coroner's Office each day, but there were strict rules about the appearance of pathologists participating in community educational programs. It was Health Day for the second-graders at Fairview Elementary School, and in the opinion of her supervisor, such an auspicious occasion was no time to be a slouch.

The blue glow from the windows at the far end of the corridor created a tunnel-of-light effect. It reminded Riley of the hallway that led to the autopsy room back at the coroner's office: worn linoleum endlessly buffed to a dull shine; cinder-block walls layered with so many years of thick, glossy paint that the texture of each block had almost disappeared; and heavy oak doorposts and lintels that bore the scars of hundreds of daily collisions. The walls were dotted with odd-sized bits of paper too—but at Fairview Elementary the papers were chalk and crayon drawings, not headshots of trauma victims and reminders from the histology lab.

Riley shook her head. She expected her pathology fellowship program to include some extracurricular duties—evening hours, extra weekend rotations, additional paperwork, and administrative chores—that just came with the territory. But why ask an MD with five years of pathology residency to conduct a seminar that any of the deputy coroners could do? Why ask her to—

Just then a classroom door burst open, and a young boy ran directly into her, straddling her with his arms like a blind man walking into a pole. He instinctively wrapped his arms around her waist, then recovered and looked up at her sheepishly. Riley looked down into his beautiful eyes and brushed the sandy hair back from his face.

"I got to go to the bathroom," he said.

Riley smiled. "When you got to go, you got to go."

He grinned back. Riley hoped for one more hug before he left, but he slid past her and raced off down the hall.

"Where's room 121?" she called after him.

"Next one down!" he shouted back. "Ms. Weleski!"

Riley rapped on the thick glass panel embedded with a cross-hatch of black safety wire. A pleasant-looking woman sprung up from a seat in the back of the room and pushed open the door.

"Ms. Weleski? I'm Dr. Riley McKay from the Allegheny County Coroner's Office. You asked for someone to speak about our 'Cribs for Kids' program?"

"Yes! Yes!" She took Riley by the arm and pulled her inside, effervescing with an enthusiasm perfected by twenty years of daily exposure to seven-year-olds. "Thank you ever so much for coming! But I'm afraid we're running a bit behind. Our first presenter showed up a bit late," she said with a roll of her eyes. "He's just getting under way now."

"No problem. I can wait," Riley said with a smile and a wink. She wedged herself into a chrome-and-plastic desk beside the teacher, squeezed off her shoes, and reached down to massage her aching arches.

"My name is Nick Polchak," said a voice from the front of the classroom. "I am a forensic entomologist. Can anybody tell me what that means?"

Silence.

"OK," Nick said, "how about just the entomologist part? Does anybody know what an entomologist does? I'll give you a hint: it comes from the Greek word *entomos*, meaning 'one whose body is cut into segments . . .' "

Still nothing.

Riley looked up to see a tall man with angular limbs and large hands. His appearance was casual, as if he had just stopped off on the way to a Pirates game. To Riley it looked as if he dressed quickly, and once dressed forgot what he had put on. *No one's setting a dress code for him,* she thought. He wore a faded plaid oxford, sleeves rolled up to the elbows, over a gray Penn State T-shirt. His shorts were weathered and worn, the ragged edge more the result of wear than style. Everything about him seemed to say, "It's not about how I look; it's about what I do." Riley smiled in agreement.

Then she noticed his eyes.

Nick Polchak wore the thickest eyeglasses Riley had ever seen. Behind them his brown eyes floated like two buckeyes, flashing off and then on again as if they might be communicating some mysterious code.

"Dr. Polchak," Ms. Weleski said in a pleasantly pleading tone. "Perhaps you could make it more—" She held both hands palm-down and made a patting gesture in the air. Nick looked at her blankly, then slowly turned back to the class.

"When you finish with a soda can, what do you do with it?"

"You throw it away," came a voice from the second row.

"Wrong," Nick said. "That's what your parents did with it. What do *you* do with a soda can when you finish with it?"

"You recycle it," said another voice.

"Why do you do that? Why do you recycle it?"

"So you don't waste stuff." The pace was quickening now.

"Exactly. Now—who can tell me what happens to you when you die?"

There was a long pause here. The class was suspicious, wondering if the man with the buckeyes might be trying to trick them.

"They . . . bury you," one brave soul ventured. "Or they burn you up. That's what they did with my grandpa."

"Ah!" Nick held up one long index finger. "But what if they can't *find* you?"

"Why can't they find you?"

"What if you're in the woods, and no one knows you're there, and you have a heart attack? Or what if someone shoots you four times, dumps your body in a drainage ditch, and covers it with debris? I had a case exactly like that, where—"

Ms. Weleski made a sharp coughing sound in the back of the room.

"Or what if you're in the woods, and no one knows you're there, and you have a heart attack?" Nick said again. "What happens to your body then?"

No one had the slightest idea.

"Then you're *recycled*," Nick said triumphantly, "because nature doesn't like to waste stuff either. And what do you suppose recycles you?" Nick swept the classroom with his huge brown eyes.

"Insects do," he said. "They *eat* you."

There was an audible gasp from the classroom, most notably from the corner where Ms. Weleski sat. It was all Riley could do to keep from laughing out loud.

Suddenly Nick clapped his hands together and the entire class jumped in unison. "Let's do a little demonstration. I need somebody to be a dead guy." He turned to a small, doe-eyed boy in the front row. "How about you?"

"Don't want to be a dead guy," he grumbled.

"Not a real dead guy—just pretend. Come on up here and lie down on the teacher's desk."

Ms. Weleski tried to quickly stand, but the little desk rose up with her like a hoop skirt. "Dr. Polchak," she protested, "please be careful . . . I don't think it's a good idea if you—" But by now the boy was sprawled out across the desk, staring mournfully at the ceiling above.

"OK, we got a dead guy," Nick said. "Now, how did he die? Anybody?"

"He got his head chopped off," one little girl offered cheerfully.

The little boy propped himself up on one elbow. "Do I look like I got my head chopped off?" Nick put one hand on his head and pushed him back down.

"OK, he got his head chopped off," Nick said. "Now, as soon as he hit the ground, certain kinds of flies began to—"

"What happened to his head?" said a voice in the front row.

"Forget the head. A raccoon carried it away."

"Raccoons eat heads?" someone whispered.

"Yes—and hands and feet too—but that's another story. Now, certain kinds of flies will land on the body, and what do you think they do?"

"They eat you?"

"No. They lay eggs on you so their *babies* can eat you."

Riley had to cover her face with both hands. She let one long snort escape, which she did her best to disguise as astonishment.

Nick picked up an eraser and held it over the boy. "Here comes the momma fly. She smells blood, she lands, she lays her eggs—thousands of them, and they look just like that cheese they sprinkle on your food at Olive Garden."

The boy on the desk lifted his head. "I like Olive Garden."

Nick pushed him back down. "You have no head, remember? Now, when each of the eggs hatches, it becomes a maggot. And each maggot has two little hooks on one end, like this." Nick held up two curled fingers like quotation marks. "They try to eat you, but you're too darn tough—so they puke out this digestive fluid, and it dissolves the tissue that's in front of them."

Ms. Weleski was free of her desk now. "Thank you, Dr. Polchak! Thank you, thank you for coming to see us today—"

"And then the maggots begin to scrape, and scrape, and—"

"Class, can we all say a nice thank-you to Dr. Polchak for visiting our health fair today?"

Nick blinked at her. "But I haven't explained the life cycle of the maggot yet, and how we use it to determine postmortem interval."

"Thank you, Dr. Polchak! Thank you!" Ms. Weleski led the stunned class in a chorus of appreciation, while at the same time beckoning Nick cheerfully toward the door.

"OK." Nick shrugged. He turned to the class one last time. "Don't forget, when it's time to go to graduate school, remember NC State. Go Wolfpack."

Riley watched as the door closed behind Nick, and Ms. Weleski momentarily braced herself against it as if to prevent a forced reentry. She turned to Riley with a look of utter despair. "Dr. McKay," she said, "what is your topic?"

A tiny voice inside of Riley longed to say, "The Autopsy: A Guided Tour." But her kinder self got the best of her, as it always seemed to do with Riley, and she simply said, "Cribs for Kids, Ms. Weleski. How your second-graders can help contribute cribs to underprivileged families with infants."

Ms. Weleski heaved an audible sigh and stepped away from the door, but Riley stared at the door a moment longer.

He's the one, she said to herself.

Tarentum, Pennsylvania, June 2003

Riley knocked on the front door of the tiny brick-and-siding split-level, then turned and stood with her back to the door. Before her, row after row of gray shingled rooftops descended away from her, down toward the mountainous coal pile and the railroad tracks that snaked along the Allegheny River.

There was no answer. She followed the sidewalk around the left side of the house and there, tucked back among the sycamores along the steep hillside, she saw a lovely old greenhouse that must have been constructed decades ago. The frame was made of flaking iron once painted a pale shade of green. The panels looked to be the original glass, spotted and speckled and smoky around the edges, as though only the centers were ever wiped clean. Down the center of the ridge line ran a pair of hinged panels that could be opened or closed to control the temperature inside. Riley thought it looked very much like the town that contained it: once a thing of beauty, now just a skeleton, a monument to better days and more bountiful times.

In the midmorning sun, the glare from the glass was blinding. Riley lowered her sunglasses, ducked her head, and stepped inside. Even with the ridge vent wide open, the heat was sweltering and the humidity even worse. Standing in the center of the greenhouse, oblivious to her presence and to the tropical climate around him, was the man with the enormous glasses. Beside him stood a man of similar age and of Indian descent, who mopped constantly at his dripping brow.

"This is oppressive. Worse than Kolkata in May," the man complained. "Nick, why don't you open a window?"

"There are no windows," Nick said.

"This is a *house* of windows. Do they have no hinges in Tarentum?"

In the doorway, Riley reached out and rapped against the glass wall. "Dr. Polchak? I'm Dr. Riley McKay. I'm a pathology fellow at the Allegheny County Coroner's Office. May I come in?"

"You are in," Nick said. "Dr. Riley McKay, meet Dr. Sanjay Patil: molecular biologist, Pitt Panther, and part-time whiner." Nick turned back to his overheated companion and handed him a plastic container. "Tuesday," he said. "No later."

"Impossible," Sanjay replied. "You have given me half a dozen specimens, and you want an RFLP on each of them by Tuesday? I tell you it is not possible."

"Let's ask her," Nick said, nodding toward Riley. "When you order a DNA typing at the coroner's office, how long does it take to get lab results?"

"Two weeks," Riley said. "And that's only if you flirt with them."

Nick looked at Sanjay. "Do you want me to flirt with you?"

Sanjay placed the container in a black specimen case, exactly like the one Riley held at her side, and headed for the door. "It was a pleasure," he nodded to Riley as he passed. "See what you can do for him; it is truly a job for a pathologist."

Nick turned to Riley. "Thanks a lot, Dr. McKay. Sanjay used to do the impossible for me all the time because he didn't know any better; now you've told him it's impossible. What am I supposed to do now?"

"I guess you'll just have to start being reasonable," she said.

Nick cocked his head and looked at her. When he did, Riley saw his eyes begin to dart and roll—like the BBs in a little puzzle, she thought, only infinitely larger. The soft brown orbs first traced the contour of her body, then slowly scanned her vertically from head to foot, halting momentarily at special points of interest. Suddenly they slashed back and forth across her, as if making a series of surgical incisions; then the eyes made a sequence of slow, sweeping motions over her, wiping up after the procedure, coming to rest at last on her face.

Riley exhaled sharply, unaware that she had been holding her breath. No one had ever looked at her—no one had ever looked *through* her like that before. It was like having a CAT scan. No—it was like having an autopsy. He was taking her apart and reassembling her with his eyes. She felt that somehow Nick Polchak knew her now, knew her inside-out, and she had some catching up to do.

"You look . . . familiar," Nick said.

"I should. I was in Ms. Weleski's class the other day at Fairview Elementary School."

Nick let out a groan.

"I thought it went very well," Riley assured him. "Especially the part about the little hooks on the maggots that scrape and scrape."

"What was *your* topic? What's the coroner's office handing out these days?"

" 'Cribs for Kids.' "

"See, that's not fair," Nick said. "You probably use PowerPoint, don't you? With slides of pathetic little toddlers sleeping on tile floors. Let's see what you can do with a maggot infestation."

Riley smiled. "You know, I had a little trouble finding this place."

"What, you mean Tarentum? Second star to the right and straight on 'til morning."

"It's a little . . . tucked way."

" 'Tucked away' as in 'buried.' Dead things deserve to be buried, Dr. McKay. Tarentum is almost a ghost town—but you should have seen it seventy-five years ago, before the steel mills and glass factories began to close down."

"Riley."

"Excuse me?"

"You're a doctor, I'm a doctor. We cancel each other out. Let's make it Riley and Nick, OK?"

Nick nodded. "I assume you didn't come all the way from Pittsburgh just to critique my classroom presentation. What have you got for me?"

"Red off that table and I'll show you." She stepped forward and lifted the black valise.

"Wait a minute," Nick said. He carefully moved a glass terrarium containing a single black spider, rearing up on its hind legs like a lion.

"What's that?"

"An *Atrax robustus*—a Funnel Web Spider. It's one of the two deadliest spiders on earth. It's killed thirteen people in Australia, one in less than two hours."

She stared at him, blinking.

He shrugged. "I just thought you might not want to knock it over."

"Good idea. Thanks." Riley looked the table over a little more carefully this time, then set down the valise and began to remove a series of containers: the smaller ones were made of glass, the larger ones plastic; some had screw-on lids, and others had snap-on tops with holes punched in the center. Nick picked up each one and examined it carefully. In the bottom of each glass vial was a pile of paste-white larvae of different sizes and shapes. He carefully pried back the lid from one plastic container and peered inside. In the bottom was a layer of brown-and-white vermiculite; on top of it rested a piece of aluminum foil folded up on the sides and crimped at the top like a little lunch sack. Nick didn't have to open it; inside would be a small square of damp paper towel, a palm-sized slab of beef liver, and a handful of maggots eagerly scraping and scraping . . .

"This is very good," he said. "Who did the collecting?"

"I did."

"No kidding? Hats off to your fellowship program. You wouldn't believe some of the garbage I get from coroners and crime-scene investigators: unlabeled specimens, leaking jars, containers full of dead larvae because they had no air holes, completely desiccated specimens . . . and then they say, 'Analyze this for us!'"

Nick held one small glass vial up to the light. In the bottom of the ethanol lay a half-dozen plump, white maggots. A neat, handwritten label encompassed the vial, and a second label stuck out of the fluid inside.

"You even double-labeled." Nick smiled. "Smart girl."

"And I wrote the labels in pencil so the ethanol doesn't eradicate the ink."

"Well, thank you for coming all this way to show me your Diptera collection," Nick said, handing the vial back to her. "Is there anything else?"

"Yes." Riley smiled. "Analyze this for us!"

Nick smiled back. "For us? Or for you?"

The smile disappeared from Riley's face.

"The Allegheny County Coroner's Office is a big operation," Nick said. "Forensic entomology isn't new to your people. Who's your regular bug man? Who do you use?"

Riley set the vial down with the rest of the containers. "Sometimes Neal Haskell out of central Indiana. Sometimes Steve Bullington from Penn State."

"I know them both," Nick nodded. "Good men. So tell me, Dr. Riley, why does a pathology fellow go outside of regular channels to request an entomological evaluation? And why does she drive twenty miles all the way from downtown Pittsburgh just to deliver the specimens herself? Don't they have UPS at your office?"

Riley said nothing.

"And why do I bet that you'll be paying me by personal check, and not by a bank draft from Allegheny County?"

"Those are good questions," Riley said. "Do you need answers before you'll do my evaluation?"

Nick paused. "Not as long as you have two pieces of identification with your check. So what are you looking for—a postmortem interval?"

"I'm looking for . . . anomalies."

"Anomalies—as in, 'something out of the ordinary.' I assume you collected these from a dead person? *Something* was out of the ordinary."

"I want to know everything an entomological evaluation can tell me. Time of death, place of death, manner of death."

"All of which can ordinarily be determined by the coroner's office."

"Ordinarily."

Nick studied her intently. "I have so many questions," he said.

"So do I. Will you help me?"

"Three hundred and fifty dollars," Nick said. "I'll need a week. Maybe two."

"That long?"

"I'm just being *reasonable*. It's the new me."

"Can't your assistant help out?"

"You mean Sanjay? He can't make larvae grow any faster. Besides, Sanjay is not my assistant. We went to grad school together at Penn State. Now he's a research biologist at Pitt. He's helping me with a little research project: We're doing DNA fingerprints on flies of forensic significance. In their larval form, most flies are impossible to tell apart. The DNA sequences will let us distinguish different species even in their earliest stages of development. Cutting-edge stuff."

Just then there was a sound from the doorway. Riley turned to see the figure of a short, stout woman in a screaming floral dress, beaming from ear to ear. She was—*loud,* that's the only word Riley could think of. Her lipstick was too red, her pearls were too large, and her hair was too high—but she had an altogether warm and inviting manner. The woman cleared her throat a second time.

"Nicky, aren't you going to . . ." She gestured to Riley.

Nick said nothing.

"Nicky! Who is this lovely woman? Tell your mother."

"Mama, I'd like you to meet Dr. Riley McKay. Dr. McKay, the flashing siren standing in the doorway is Mrs. Camilla Polchak, ruler of all Poland—or at least all the Polish people living in Tarentum and Natrona Heights."

"Mama?" Riley whispered to Nick.

"Four hundred dollars," Nick whispered back. "Keep it up."

"A doctor," Mrs. Polchak beamed. "And not just one doctor, two doctors, in fact! Just look at the both of you!"

"Mama," Nick said. "Why don't you just throw rice on us and get it over with? We'll try to produce a grandchild by Christmas."

"What are you talking about, grandchild? Did I say grandchild? I just like to have a pretty face to look at sometimes, not just those two big portholes of yours." She dismissed Nick with a wave of her hand and took Riley by the arm. "Such a pretty face," she said. "And what do I have to look at around here? Bugs. Flies and spiders and things I don't want to tell you."

"Mama . . ."

"Nicky is blind," she said, ignoring him. "The glasses—did you notice? A small thing. But let me tell you, under those glasses is a very handsome man. You stay for tea."

"What? Oh. I would love to, Mrs. Polchak, but I have a very busy day."

"Always a busy day," Mrs. Polchak scolded. "Too busy, maybe. Too busy to have a cup of tea with a lonely old woman?"

Nick rolled his eyes. "You should go into real estate, Mama. You could make a fortune."

Mrs. Polchak glared at him. "Why should I work? I have a rich doctor for a son! But no, you have to be a doctor for dead people—a doctor who makes no money. I ask you, what kind of person wants to be a doctor for dead people?"

"Ask her," Nick said. "I'm a bug man myself."

Mrs. Polchak looked at Riley in silence.

"I'm a forensic pathologist," Riley explained. "Just a fellow, actually."

Mrs. Polchak did a double take. "No man worth a zloty would call you a 'fellow.' Nicky, I ask you—is this a fellow?"

Nick looked her up and down. "Looks like a fellow to me."

"*This* is why I have no grandchild," Mrs. Polchak said. She turned and headed back across the yard toward the house.

Riley looked at Nick. "You live with your mother?"

"I'm just visiting," Nick replied. "Honest. I have my own car and everything."

"We'll have tea another time," Mrs. Polchak called back from the house.

"Another time, Mrs. Polchak. Thank you."

"Promise me. Promise me another time."

"I promise," Riley said, smiling at Nick. "I have so many questions."

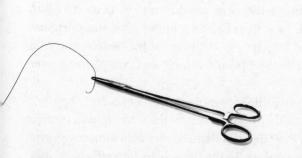

CHAPTER
4

Cruz Santangelo crawled on his belly across the damp limestone surface. He reached forward with both arms and then pulled, pushing forward at the same time with his toes, propelling himself slowly forward like a swimmer. A hundred and fifty feet above him, rainwater trickled down through cracks and fissures, leeching carbonic acid from the soil, dissolving layers of calcium from the limestone, leaving behind foot-high fissures and cracks that run three miles long and four hundred feet deep through the Pennsylvania hills.

Santangelo watched the green reflective strips on the soles of three other cavers ahead of him. Suddenly the light on his helmet blinked off; he raised his head slightly and tapped his helmet against the rock only inches above. The light flashed on again, and the long shadows reappeared on the rolling ceiling and floor that undulated together like two stone blankets.

"What's the problem back there?" one of the forward cavers called back, his voice thin and strained.

"No problem," Santangelo said quietly.

"Well, keep that thing on! We're in a hurry here—you know the weather forecast!"

Santangelo shook his head. They should be back with the women in the Tour Cave, standing erect on the nice wooden boardwalk, oohing and aahing over theatrically lit stalactites and flowstone and soda-straws. They had no business tackling a virgin crawlway; they had no business caving with *him*. But he had been forced to suffer their presence all day long, a safety requirement of the Laurel Cavern authorities: *caving in groups only.*

One of the men wore nothing but a simple pair of blue jeans and a thin flannel shirt. Another actually wore shorts—*shorts!* The fool had no idea that despite the summer temperatures above, fifty feet below ground the cave would stay an even fifty-two degrees year-round. Less than fifteen minutes after their original descent the man had begun to grumble about the penetrating cold and dampness, and he had been whining and complaining ever since.

All three men wore ordinary tennis shoes—not a decent pair of climbing soles among them—and none of them thought to bring a watch. Santangelo never did; but then, he was a veteran caver, and he knew how to compensate for the time-distorting effects of utter darkness—that is, except when he was distracted by the constant chatter of three anxious neophytes. Now none of them knew how much time had elapsed, and they were hurrying back toward the cave entrance just as fast as the unyielding stone would allow.

"Can you believe this?" one of the men laughed nervously. "We sure know how to spend a Saturday!"

"I tell you one thing, you're buying tonight!" said the man to his right.

"You're on!" his friend shot back.

"You guys can do what you want," the third man shivered. "I just want to get *warm*. I swear, I'm numb from the waist down!"

Their voices crackled like electrical wires; they spoke with ever-increasing energy and volume. They were venting fear, Santangelo knew, bouncing their voices off the stone the way bats do. But the stone gave nothing in return, and the absolute stillness—the absence of even the tiniest echo—was shredding the nerves of all three of them. Santangelo despised them; their incessant blabbering violated the perfect blackness like arrogant tourists shouting across the aisles of a great cathedral. *They're whistling past the graveyard, he thought, and if you're not at home in a graveyard you have no business being down here.*

"Quiet," Santangelo whispered.

"What? Who said that?"

"I did. Listen."

From the darkness beyond the narrow cone of their lights came a soft, shuffling sound. It was a kissing sound, a rubbery sound, like the sound of wet soles on a hardwood floor. It grew no louder, but it came steadily closer.

"Hey!" One man arched up suddenly, forgetting his narrow confinement; there was the dull crack of plastic on stone, and his light disappeared. "Something ran across my hand!"

"What was it?"

"I see it! There's another one!"

Santangelo tipped his headlight down at the limestone floor. A small, greenish gray form wriggled past his left hand. He watched it pass; it had four fingers on each foreleg, each ending in a tiny suction cup. Its body was slender and tapered, and mucous-covered skin stretched smoothly over the head where eyes would ordinarily be.

"Lizards!" one of the men shouted. "There must be a hundred of 'em!"

"They're cave salamanders," Santangelo said quietly. He

reached forward with both arms, compressing his shoulders as tightly as possible, and began to roll onto his left side; his shoulders wedged between the ceiling and floor. He closed his eyes and exhaled slowly, relaxing, elongating his body. He felt his right deltoid scrape past the coarse stone ceiling, and he rolled over onto his back.

"They're everywhere! Where are they coming from?"

"Rocks. Cracks. They don't like to be seen." Santangelo slowly rotated his helmet from side to side, studying the rippling ceiling. Ten feet to his left the stone rose abruptly and then descended again, forming a sort of bubble six inches higher than the ceiling directly in front of his face. He began to work his body toward it.

"Why are they running toward us?" a panicky voice shouted back.

Centered under the bubble now, Santangelo pulled both heels under him, wedging his knees tightly between the ceiling and floor—then he reached up and switched off his lamp. "They're not running toward you," he said. "They're running away."

An instant later the wall of water hit them. The water itself reached them almost before the sound, and the flood caught the three men before their minds even had time to comprehend the nature of their impending deaths. Santangelo heard a half-scream, a muffled shout, and then the cavern was silent again.

The water hit Santangelo's helmet hard and cold. His knees scraped across the stone ceiling, but the force only wedged his legs tighter, and his position held. He arched his back and let the force of the water lift him up toward the bubble. He lay perfectly still, the water caressing his back in pulsing gushes, his arms waving at his sides like drifting seaweed.

He felt his right arm brush against denim, and then a series of kicks and jabs from a pair of flailing legs; seconds later they passed. He saw quick beams of light sweep across the ceiling like searchlights, and then disappear into the darkness. Suddenly he felt the full weight of a body jam against his back, forcing him even tighter up into the air pocket above. The body was rigid and desperate—kicking, groping, clawing—and then just as suddenly the current pushed the body off to the left and away. But as it washed past, one frantic hand caught his left forearm and held on, clutching at the last remnant of life in the subterranean graveyard. The hand jerked hard twice, and Santangelo imagined a voice saying, "Can't you help? Are you just going to let us all die?"

He felt the grip slowly release, and then all was still and quiet again.

He pursed his lips and breathed slowly into the air pocket, in through his nose and out through his mouth. He floated in the dark water, feeling gusts of current and bits of debris wash over his back, grateful that the blackness had at last swept through the cathedral and washed its sacred floors clean.

It was more than an hour before the water subsided, draining silently away into even deeper and darker recesses of the earth. Santangelo lay motionless, slowing his pulse and controlling his breathing just as he had done a thousand times on the firing range, waiting for the telltale pause between heartbeats before squeezing off a round at a silhouette of a man's head three hundred yards away. When the receding waters at last lowered him gently back to the stone floor, he switched on his light and swept the crawlspace from side to side. It was completely empty. He rolled onto his stomach and began to work his way back toward the cave entrance.

An hour later, Cruz Santangelo stood by the cavern opening, unzipping his sodden coveralls and peeling them down to his waist. He removed the ascenders from his nylon line and dropped them into a duffel bag. He took out a towel and began to blot at his wrinkled skin. He looked into the sky; to the south, lumbering gray thunderheads rolled off toward the West Virginia border.

Behind him, a mud-splattered SUV crunched to a stop. Windows rolled down, and three anxious faces peered out.

"We're looking for three men," the women said. "Have you seen them? Can you help us?"

"We went down together," Santangelo shrugged. "Last I saw them, they were headed the opposite direction."

The car slowly rolled away.

There was a beeping sound from the duffel bag. He pulled out his pager and checked his text messages. The single memo read: ZOHAR: MANDATORY: THURSDAY 2300: FOX CHAPEL YACHT CLUB.

Dr. Jack Kaplan sat slumped behind the wheel of his Porsche 911 Turbo, drumming his thumbs on the steering wheel in time to the thundering pulses of two fifteen-inch subwoofers. Half a block ahead he watched two squad cars, lights flashing, a thin band of yellow tape fluttering in the breeze between them. One officer restrained a weeping mother and daughter; another knelt beside a reclining body, while a third reached through the window of his black-and-white cruiser.

It was almost 2:00 a.m.; Kaplan's shift at the UPMC Trauma Center had ended at midnight, and adrenaline still coursed through his veins like jet fuel. He had spent the last two hours slowly cruising the city, listening to his police scanner, hoping for some medical emergency that might keep him from having to return home to yet another sleepless night.

He looked impatiently at the two officers; they seemed to take forever. "C'mon, boys," Kaplan grumbled. "It's the Golden Hour."

At last, he heard his police scanner crackle.

"Scene secured. Med One can approach."

A block and a half ahead, a pair of headlights blinked on, and an orange and white EMS rig began to roll slowly toward the scene. Kaplan revved his own engine, shoved the stick into gear, and pulled away from the curb. His silver Porsche and the cube-shaped EMS truck arrived simultaneously.

A paramedic and two EMTs scurried over the rig, gathering equipment from a series of side compartments: a bright orange backboard with nylon restraining belts, a torpedo-like oxygen tank, a trauma kit, a Kevlar med bag, and Advanced Life Support equipment.

Kaplan approached the scene at a jog, neatly scissors-kicking the yellow barrier tape, holding his credentials in front of him like a shield.

"Dr. Jack Kaplan," he said to the kneeling officer. "I'm a trauma surgeon at UPMC Presbyterian. What have you got?"

The officer reached up, steadied the credentials, then nodded to Jack. "Male, Caucasian, twenty-eight," he began. "He's a local resident—"

"I don't need his life story," Kaplan said. "I want to know why he's lying here in a pool of blood."

"Multiple stab wounds to the chest."

"Pulse?" Jack opened his medical bag and began to pull on a pair of greenish blue latex gloves.

"Yes—at least, I think so."

"You *think* so. That's kind of important."

Kaplan ripped open the shirt. He wiped a sterile pad once across the bloody chest and watched; three small scarlet fountains reemerged through horizontal slits just below the rib cage.

"The attacker was a big man," Kaplan said. "See the angle of the wounds? That's a thrusting stroke. If he came at him overhead, the ribs would have stopped at least one of them."

The EMS team approached now; the officer rose and stepped back away from the body.

"Do you mind?" the paramedic said to Kaplan. "We got a job to do here."

"Your job is to assist *me*—I'm signing off on this one."

"And just who exactly are—"

"Ask him." Kaplan nodded to the officer. "We're old pals. Now, backboard this guy, block him, whatever you've got to do to get him on the truck—but get a cuff on him and get me a pulse *fast*."

The EMS crew went to work. Within a minute the body was restrained, lifted to a stretcher, and headed for the truck.

"We've got an erratic pulse," the paramedic said, "and his BP is dropping off the charts."

"Keep the straps clear of the chest area," Kaplan said. "On the truck I want you to tube him, and I want two IV lines. You've got ALS equipment? Good—get a heart monitor on him right away."

The stretcher rolled in head-forward and locked into place. The paramedic turned for the driver's door—Kaplan stopped him.

"Uh-uh. You're in the back with me."

"Wait a minute, this is *my* rig—"

"And you've got the most medical training. You're in the back." He turned to the two EMTs. "Who's the third man here?" he said. They glanced at one another, and the man on the left sheepishly raised his hand. "You're out," Kaplan said. "You bring my car—I'm not leaving it in this dump. The keys are in it. Touch the radio and I'll remove your spleen—scratch it and I'll use a chain saw." Kaplan turned to the remaining EMT. "You do know how to drive?" The man nodded. "Then do it. UPMC Presbyterian," he called back to the officer. "Let the family know."

"Hold it," the paramedic broke in. "Presby is ten minutes farther away."

"Keep talking and it'll be fifteen minutes. Get in the truck."

The doors closed solidly like the doors of a meat locker; bright overhead lights flickered on, and the siren started its keening wail. The truck rolled slowly forward and then rapidly accelerated. The paramedic slid down the long vinyl bench on the right, connecting and adjusting the heart monitor; it was on less than five seconds before emitting a high, even tone.

"Cardiac arrest!" the paramedic shouted. "I'm going to defib!"

"No you're not," Kaplan said. "Not with a penetrating injury. Betadine the chest area—all of it, from the clavicle down."

"Why? What are you going to do?"

"A thoracotomy."

"A what?"

"I need you to switch places with me—now!"

The paramedic worked his way around the head of the stretcher. "What's a thoracotomy?"

"I'm going to make an incision right here," he said, drawing a line with his finger between two ribs. "I'm going to spread the ribs, open the pericardium, and repair any damage to the heart and coronary vessels. I'm going to clamp off the descending aorta to redirect blood flow to the lungs and brain, and then I'm going to reach in and massage the heart by hand until we get to UPMC."

The paramedic swallowed hard. "Have you done this before?"

"Nope. Always wanted to try it, though."

"Dr. Kaplan, we're not set up for that kind of surgery—our job is to stabilize and transport. We've got no instruments—one little tracheotomy scalpel, that's all, and maybe a forceps."

"Get them out. I need your trauma shears, too, and anything we can use for suction. I've got most of what I need with me—for the rest, we'll improvise."

"Will this work?"

"The survival rate is somewhere between 0 and 4 percent."

"Dr. Kaplan, we're *two minutes* from Allegheny General."

"I need more than two minutes. Don't you guys have a radio? Hey, driver! Give me something to work by back here."

"Allegheny General is set up for this kind of thing. Please— don't do this."

Kaplan said nothing. He placed the gleaming point of the scalpel near the sternum in the fifth intercostal space and drew it firmly down.

"You're killing him," the paramedic said.

"He's dead now," Kaplan shrugged.

Eight minutes later the twin doors of UPMC Presbyterian Trauma Center burst open, and the stretcher raced in. The paramedic was at the head, pushing and guiding, while an EMT hurried along at his side, steadying the IV bag and line. On the opposite side, Jack Kaplan walked quickly and evenly, with both hands extending into a gaping scarlet hole.

A tall, thin woman in a white lab coat swept in behind them. "Jack, don't you ever go home? Isn't a twelve-hour shift long enough for you?"

"I was gone for two hours," he said. "I got bored."

"What did you *do*?" she said, staring into the wound.

"A resuscitative thoracotomy."

"In the back of an ambulance? What were you thinking?"

Three more ER staff came alongside now, and the paramedic and EMT passed off the stretcher like a baton in a relay race.

"He's got multiple stab wounds to the chest," Kaplan announced to the group. "He was in arrhythmia at the scene and went into cardiac arrest in the ambulance. I opened him up and checked for cardiac wounds—the vessels were all intact, but I sutured one atrial laceration. I displaced the heart and searched for posterior wounds—there were none. And I've been massaging this thing for ten minutes now, and my hands are cramping—somebody want to take over for me here?"

Kaplan stepped away as the stretcher disappeared into the OR. He stepped to a waste receptacle and began to strip off his dripping gloves.

"Hey, Rosa," he called to a passing nurse. "You're looking good tonight. When are you going driving with me?"

"When I feel like putting a gun to my head," the nurse said without turning.

He was at the sink, scrubbing, when the paramedic and both EMTs approached.

"I just want to say one thing," the paramedic growled. "You didn't have to do that. You can explain it away to the family, maybe even to your doctor friends, but *you* know and I know. We were two minutes away from a fully equipped ER. You did it the hard way, and you did it just for the doing." The paramedic shook his head in disgust. "Don't ever ride on my rig again."

Kaplan looked at him without expression, then turned to the EMT at his side. "How did it drive?"

The EMT dropped the keys on the floor. All three men turned and left.

Kaplan stepped into the waiting area. In the center of the room, two women stood embracing and weeping. The older woman was fiftyish, heavy and thick-limbed, her eyes bloated and red. Kaplan's eyes moved quickly to the daughter, who looked twenty, maybe twenty-five, with the face and body her mother might have had a very long time ago. Both women looked up as he entered.

"I'm Dr. Kaplan," he said solemnly. "I was the surgeon in charge tonight. I took responsibility for your—" *Husband? Brother? Jack never even got a name. No matter.*

"It's lucky I happened along when I did. I just want you to know, I did everything I could, and he's in the best of hands now."

At this, both women began to weep openly. The mother turned to Kaplan with a look of infinite gratitude, her arms outstretched. Kaplan brushed past her and took the younger woman in his arms, comforting her as best he could.

There was a beeping sound at his belt. He glanced down at the luminous green LCD. It read, ZOHAR: MANDATORY: THURSDAY 2300: FOX CHAPEL YACHT CLUB.

CHAPTER 6

The Allegheny River cuts a three-hundred-mile channel from New York state across western Pennsylvania to the city of Pittsburgh. The Allegheny's riverbed is solid rock, smoothed by some ancient glacier, and the water that flows across its siltless bottom is a clear greenish blue. To the south, the Monongahela River wallows its way toward Pittsburgh through a hundred and twenty-five miles of mud and clay, pumping its red brown water through the old Steel Valley that once belched out so much smoke and soot that the streetlights had to be turned on at noon. Both rivers were once choked with debris and industrial effluent; now both are clean again, lined with marinas and private quays dotted with weekend pleasure boats. The two rivers join to form the mighty Ohio at a place simply known as the Point, at the tip of downtown Pittsburgh.

Nick Polchak stood with his toes overhanging the concrete ledge, staring into the churning waters. To his right the water flowed clear green; to his left, muddy brown; straight ahead, the two colors swirled together in a watery palette and disappeared into the distance. The Point is one of the most dangerous places to swim in all of Pittsburgh; the two rivers collide like angry storm fronts to spawn tornadolike undercurrents—but the Point is also the most tempting place to swim in all of Pittsburgh, and each year a handful of the brave and the foolish surrender to temptation at the cost of their lives.

"Thinking of jumping in?" a voice said behind him.

"Every time I come here," Nick replied.

Riley McKay's hair was straight and whitish blond, cut off above the shoulders and pulled back from her face with a thin, tortoiseshell band. Nick cocked his head and took her measure, comparing this new image with the one burned into his memory just a week and a half ago. Her cheekbones were high and her skin was fair—the Scots blood in her, Nick thought. Her shoulders were broad, well-boned, and her lean arms hung down from them like stockings from a coat hanger. Her fingertips broke just below midthigh, a bit longer than usual; her hands were long and slender, and her fingernails were cut to the quick like a concert pianist—no, like a forensic pathologist.

She wore a straight, knee-length skirt with a back vent. Nick looked at her legs; they were tight and sinewy. When she shifted her weight from side to side, he could see the cut between the gastrocnemius and the soleus. Her ankles were slightly thicker than normal—a little swollen, Nick thought—and on her feet she wore a pair of bright white Nike cross-trainers. Her hair, her dress, even her simple jewelry—everything about her was less a matter of style than expedience. Riley McKay was a woman with somewhere to go and something to do.

Nick's eyes returned to her face. A spray of freckles lay across the bridge of her nose, the product of countless unguarded hours in the sun, and her eyes—Nick stopped abruptly. Her eyes were two distinctly different colors: one brown and one green.

"Like them?" Riley smiled. "My dad used to call me Three Rivers." She leaned forward and peered at Nick's enormous glasses. "What did your dad call you?"

"Blind," Nick said.

"Oh. Sorry."

Nick shrugged and handed her a manila envelope. Riley turned and stepped to the edge of the great round basin that occupies the center of the triangular Point. She raised one hand in the air, testing for overspray from the fountain, then sat down. Nick took a seat beside her.

She opened the envelope and removed the brief report. The title read, "Forensic Entomology Investigation: Report of Diagnostic Laboratory Examination." Underneath, the traditional demographic information—name, sex, age, case number—was all left blank. Under "Requesting Agency," Nick had written, "Personal Request."

She flipped through the few sheets of paper. "You can sit here and watch me read this," she said, "or you can tell me what it says. Do you have a postmortem interval for me?"

"No."

"Did you find any indicators regarding the cause of death?"

"No."

Riley looked at him. "Dr. Polchak, is this a social call?"

"I can't give you a reliable PMI until I rear the last of the blowflies to maturity. That could take another two weeks. As to cause of death, you've given me very little to work with. I can do a toxicology screening—but then again, so can you. You're from the coroner's office, aren't you?"

"Then why did you call me?"

"As I recall, you said you were looking for anomalies. I could have waited another two weeks to give you my final report, but I thought you might want to hear what I've found so far. After all, a woman who goes outside of regular channels might also be a woman in a hurry."

"You found something?"

"Yes. But if you'd rather wait for the final report . . ."

Riley waited, but Nick said nothing more.

She frowned. "Did anyone ever tell you you can be really annoying?"

Nick nodded. "Dad called me that too. I was just wondering: Why didn't we meet at your office today? It's just five blocks away, right up Fourth Street there. You've got reserved parking; you've got air conditioning. It's so hot in Pittsburgh this time of year, don't you think? Why meet outside? Why in such a public place? Why sit here by a fountain, where it's so hard to hear?"

"You have a lot of questions," Riley said.

"So do you—*time* of death, *place* of death, *cause* of death. Hey, I've got an idea: I'll answer one of your questions, and you answer one of mine."

"I'm paying you to answer my question," Riley glared.

"You're right, that's hardly fair. I know—how about a discount? I tell you what, I'll knock my fee down to *two* hundred dollars. That's got to help—how much does a pathology fellow make? And after all, this is a *personal* expense—"

"*One* question," Riley said. "But you answer mine first—and it better be a two-hundred-dollar answer."

Nick smiled. "You told me that the man's body was discovered in Butler County—that's a good twenty-five miles from metropolitan Pittsburgh."

"That's right."

"He didn't die there."

Riley's eyes widened.

"Is that worth two hundred dollars?"

"That depends," she said. "Keep going."

"The maggots you collected represent four different species of blowfly. You were lucky. All four can be distinguished in their larval form—I didn't have to wait for them to mature. The first was *Phaenicia coeruleiviridis*—a green bottle fly. It's a common carrion fly, one of the first to arrive after death. The second species was *Phormia regina*, the black blowfly. They usually arrive twelve to twenty-four hours after death. Both species are very common, very predictable, exactly what you'd expect to find in a rural setting."

"And the other two?"

"*Phaenicia sericata* is another type of green bottle fly. It's sort of the city cousin of *Phaenicia coeruleiviridis*. It's not unusual to find a few in a rural setting—maybe 5 percent of the specimens—but sericata made up half of the maggots you collected. You're sure you took a representative sampling of all the maggots that were present? You didn't give preference to any particular size or shape?"

"I was careful to include the largest specimens," Riley said, "but I also included a sampling of everything I saw, all sizes and shapes. That's the way they taught us."

Nick nodded. "The clincher was *Calliphora vicina*, the blue bottle fly. Blue bottles like shady places and urban habitats. Find a body in a basement, and you'll find blue bottles. The funny thing is, they make up 10 percent of your specimens. The presence of *sericata* in such high numbers might have been a fluke—I doubt it, but it's at least possible—but when you add the presence of blue bottles, there's no other explanation. Your boy spent some time in the city—some time *after* death. What was the cause of death listed on the autopsy report?"

"Is that your one question?" Riley asked.

"C'mon, that's hardly worth two hundred bucks. It's just a simple question."

"AMI—acute myocardial infarction," Riley said. "He was only thirty-five."

"Statistically unusual, but not unheard of," Nick said. "Here's the real problem: either the victim perished in an urban area and was later moved to the country, or he died in the country and was transported to the city and back again."

"Why would anyone do that?"

"Beats me." Nick shrugged. "That's the sort of thing the coroner's office investigates, isn't it? One thing is for sure: someone else was involved in the circumstances surrounding this man's death, and that seriously calls into question the diagnosis of 'death by natural causes.' I'd take another look at that AMI if I were you."

Riley said nothing. The wind shifted slightly, and mist from the fountain drifted down on them like a descending cloud.

"And now for my question," Nick said brightly. "The category is 'Nagging Suspicions' for two hundred dollars, and the question is: Why don't you trust your supervising pathologist?"

Riley turned. "I never said I didn't trust—"

"You're a pathology *fellow*," he said. "That makes you low man on the totem pole at the Allegheny County Coroner's Office. These questions you're asking, they're very good questions—the kind of questions you should be asking the pathologist in charge of your fellowship program. But for some reason, you don't want to ask your senior pathologist. You don't *want* him to know you're asking these questions at all, do you? So you collect your own evidence— entomological evidence, the kind no one will miss. Very shrewd, Dr. McKay. Then you find your very own bug man, and you offer to pay him out of your own pocket. It looks to me like you want answers, but for some reason you can't find them in your own office. For two hundred dollars, my question is: Why not?"

Riley paused.

"Look," Nick said. "You went outside of normal channels to get an expert opinion. OK, here I am. I'm an outsider. I don't know anyone at the coroner's office, they don't know me, and I report only to you. If you can't talk to me, who else can you talk to?"

Riley looked at Nick's eyes, as if hoping to take some reading on the soul behind those enormous lenses.

"It started about three months ago," she began. "I was barely into my fellowship program. A man passed away at Allegheny General, a head trauma victim. When the call came in, the pathologist on rotation was my supervisor, Dr. Nathan Lassiter. He ordered an autopsy. That was strange enough, since it was a physician-attended death. But then he denied me access to the autopsy—he gave me some nonsense about its utter simplicity having 'no instructive value.' He practically shut the door in my face."

"Is this your first experience with arrogant authority figures?" Nick said. "Welcome to my world."

"The thing is, the victim was carrying a valid organ donor card, and a request was made for his kidneys while he was still at Allegheny General—but Lassiter refused to release the organs for transplant. That happens from time to time: a pathologist can refuse to release organs for transplant when she thinks removal of the organ could destroy forensic evidence. But denying a *kidney* over *a head trauma*?"

"And when you asked him about it, he said . . ."

"That I was still in my residency, that I had a lot to learn. That some of these judgments require years of experience, et cetera, et cetera. It was all bluster and bravado. So I went over his head; I appealed to the coroner himself."

"I'll bet that went over big."

"My supervisor threw a fit. He started throwing around terms like *lack of respect, professional courtesy, and a track record of incontestable judgment*—that was my favorite. What was the coroner supposed to do, side with a wet-behind-the-ears resident over one of his senior pathologists? He backed his homeboy, of course, and I had to eat crow. It's been a steady diet ever since."

"There are other means of appeal," Nick said.

"Question the *coroner's* judgment?" Riley groaned. "Now there's a career move for you. Look, Nick, the Allegheny County Coroner's Office is one of the top five in the nation. Two of our senior pathologists are former fellows themselves, and—"

"And when you finish your fellowship, you're hoping to land a job there. I don't blame you. It would be nice, you being from Pittsburgh and all."

"How did you know—"

"You said, 'Red off that table,' remember? That's Pittsburgh talking."

"Dr. Lassiter has shut me out of a couple of autopsies," Riley said, "and he keeps pushing me out of the office, sending me out on errands or to do those community educational programs."

"You'll learn to love those," Nick said. "I know I did."

"It was a mistake to go over Lassiter's head. At least, I *think* it was a mistake. When he didn't back down at all—not even an inch—that's when it hit me that either he's hiding something, or he's just a sexist, egotistical, scum-sucking pig."

"Which is a very real option," Nick said. "Trust me, I know that species."

"I don't know what it is, but there's just something about him . . ."

"He smells funny."

"What?"

"Do you know how blowflies are attracted to a body? The decomposing tissues emit a kind of chemical indicator—no one knows exactly what it is. The blowflies lay eggs, the eggs become larvae, the larvae pupate and produce a new generation of flies. But the next generation will not be attracted to the same body. Do you know why? Because the tissues have been breaking down and drying out, and now they're emitting a different indicator. Blowflies find bodies because of the smell—something only they can detect—and it only lasts for a short time."

"You're saying that I should act quickly? Or that I remind you of a blowfly?"

"I'm saying that smells are reliable indicators of decay. And yes, Dr. McKay, you do remind me of a blowfly; after all, aren't you both forensic investigators in your own way? If Dr. Lassiter smells funny to you, I'd go with your instincts—the rest of the animal world does."

Nick watched Riley slide the report back into the manila envelope, then stare off toward the confluence of the two rivers. He looked into her eyes, one green and one brown, and he wondered what sort of turbulence lay behind them.

"I have another question," Nick said.

"The deal was for *one*."

"I'm willing to pay for it. The category is 'Hidden Motives' for a hundred dollars. The question is: Why does this bother you so much? What's in it for you? What do you care if an arrogant pathologist makes a bad call?"

Riley paused for a long time. "I'm not ready to answer that question," she said at last. "I don't know you that well."

"That's a fair answer," Nick said, "but hardly worth a hundred bucks. How about one more try? My final category is 'Occupational

Hazards' for a hundred, and the question is: How far are you willing to go with this?"

"I don't know," Riley said. "I guess it depends on what I find."

"Then you plan to go on looking?"

"Would you?"

"I once dissected an undergraduate student just to get out of teaching," Nick said. "I'm not the best person to ask about boundaries."

"I'm not very good at knowing when to quit either," Riley said. "But what am I supposed to do next? So I've got an anomaly. Am I supposed to run back to the coroner's office and start blowing the whistle again? That would finish me."

"I agree, timing is very important for you. The next time you blow that whistle, you better have something substantial to show for it. You better have *proof.*"

"That's the problem," Riley said. "Proof is the product of evidence, and Lassiter controls all the evidence. When he locks me out of an autopsy, all I can do is read the report when he's finished—and the report says whatever he wants it to."

"You could urge the next of kin to request a second autopsy. They can do that, can't they?"

"Yes—but what do I say when they ask me *why*? Who pays for it? And worst of all, what if it turns up nothing? Then word would get back to the coroner's office for sure."

"At least you have a couple of things going for you."

"Like what?"

"Like the fact that Dr. Lassiter is your supervisor, so you have ongoing access to him. Like the fact that you're part of a fellowship program, so you're expected to ask questions around the office—you're not nosy, you're a *resident.* You have knowledge of this anomaly—knowledge that Dr. Lassiter doesn't know you have. And doesn't Lassiter work a scheduled rotation? Then you'll know when he's up for an autopsy, and you can poke around and see what you can find."

"See what I can *find.* Nick, I have a medical degree, and I've done a five-year residency in pathology. I'm an experienced pathologist, but I still know next to nothing about forensics. I'm not exactly sure *how* to 'poke around.' "

"Whereas I am experienced in forensics," Nick said, "but I

know far less about pathology. Maybe it would help if we formed a partnership: I'll do the forensics, you provide the pathology. Together, we'd make one mean forensic pathologist."

"Thanks," Riley said, "but to be honest, I can't afford to pay for your ongoing services. This is a personal expense, remember?"

"My prices are very reasonable. Didn't I just give you a 100 percent discount on my first bill?"

Riley looked at him. "You don't know me, Nick. I could be a crackpot for all you know. This whole thing could be just my imagination."

"The blue bottle flies weren't your imagination."

"Why would you want to do this? Why would you want to help me?"

"Because you remind me of me: you're smart, you're good-looking, and you're broke."

"I'm serious."

"OK," Nick said with a sigh. "If you must know, it's my mother. She's been after me to join the Sons of Poland. She keeps trying to feed me pierogies—I hate pierogies. I'll pay *you* if it gets me out of the house."

"Nick. *Why?*"

Nick returned her gaze at last. "Bottom line?" he said.

"Bottom line."

He shrugged. "I like the way you smell."

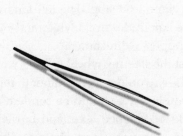

CHAPTER 7

He pulled out of the driveway at exactly seven o'clock, the same time he did every Thursday night, after the same old argument with Melissa over his one night out with the guys. It's not like he did this every night—didn't he skip a poker night just a couple of months ago? Didn't he take the boys to a Penguins game?

So Melissa's got the kids all day. So what? What was he doing at PPG all day? And besides, a man needs to stretch his legs once in a while. Once a *week*, for crying out loud! Melissa's got her girlfriends; she's off to Starbucks at the drop of a hat—is one night a week too much to ask? Once a week is a bargain. For once a week, she oughta be *grateful*. He straightened a little and took a firmer grip on the steering wheel.

He took a left on Franklin, then a right on Kittanning, just as he did every Thursday night. He passed the same endless parade of indistinguishable row houses, all lined up like books on a shelf, each with its own overcrowded porch, overhanging roof, and tiny rectangle of neatly trimmed ryegrass.

Two blocks down, the neat little houses gave way to a different kind of neighborhood. Porch roofs began to dip and sag, long streaks of gray peeked out through peeling flecks of paint, and the occasional gutter drooped to the ground like a dying limb. After another two blocks the houses crumbled away entirely, leaving nothing behind but a graveyard of pawn shops, convenience stores, and razor-wired storage yards. In the stark mercury vapor lights, the early evening shadows cut like straight razors, and everything that wasn't black glowed the same electric blue.

He unconsciously leaned his elbow on the door lock, just as he did in this exact location every Thursday night.

At the end of Kittanning he would turn left again, away from the porn shops and the boarded-up churches, and into a better neighborhood. But at the end of Kittanning he did something he had never done before—he came to a stop. The left lane was blocked off by a flashing orange barricade, and a white-and-black detour sign pointed him in the opposite direction.

He slammed his hand against the steering wheel. What's wrong with those idiots at PennDOT? Why would anyone bother to repair a road in this shell hole? The whole place should be condemned; the whole neighborhood should be scraped level and buried in some landfill. He was the only car on the road—he was *always* the only car on the road. Do they think one lousy car merits road work? Go figure—your tax dollars at work.

He looked to the right. Just a block or two, then he'd take a left on the best-lit street he could find; two more quick lefts and he'd be back on track again. He shrugged and turned the wheel slowly to the right.

Two blocks down, a second detour sign beckoned him to the left. He turned up a narrow, lifeless, two-lane road walled in by empty back porches and buckling garage doors. In the dusk ahead, his headlights discovered a cherry red BMW, barely off the road, that leapt out from the shadows like blood on a newspaper. The trunk was open, and the car sagged limply to the left.

Beside the left rear quarter panel, holding a tire jack, stood a beautiful young woman with long, auburn hair. Her V-neck blouse was pristine white. As his car approached, she swept back her hair with the back of her hand, locked on to his eyes, and mouthed the words, "Help me—PLEASE."

He felt a rush of excitement. He pulled his car over just ahead of hers and looked quickly around the area the way a man does when he comes across a twenty-dollar bill on the sidewalk. He got out of the car, tucked his shirt front in tight, and approached.

"Need some help?"

"I feel like such a *girl*," she said. "I should know how to change this thing myself, but—it's so sweet of you to stop." She stood with one leg just in front of the other, like the women in the catalogs always do. She wore black stiletto heels, and her skirt was tight around her knees. He tried to imagine her squatting down to wrestle off a set of stubborn lug nuts. He smiled.

"You picked a heckuva place to get a flat tire."

"Didn't I, though?"

"Look," he said, considering their surroundings for the first time, "maybe I should drive you to the nearest Tire and Auto. They can help you out."

She turned up her lower lip. "It's just that I'm running so late," she said, holding the jack away from her like a dripping umbrella. "I was hoping you'd be one of those big, strong types—you know, the kind who has a whole garage full of tools back home. I guess that was kind of stupid of me."

He hitched up his pants. "Let me take a look at it," he said, taking the jack from her. He squatted down and began to pry off the hubcap with a rusted squawk.

"Is your spare in good shape?"

"I really don't know. I guess I should check that from time to time."

He glanced up at her. "Doesn't your boyfriend help you with these things?"

She winked. "Maybe that's what I really need—a spare boyfriend."

He started to say, "Are you from around here?" But then he looked at her again: smiling down on him like his very own moon, leaning back against the driver's door in that long S-curve. Whoever she was, whatever she was, she was not from around here.

He felt electrified. He felt feverish. His head was covered in a cold sweat, and he could almost feel his own pulse. She was so close to him, so completely present, that his senses allowed room for nothing else: not the tug of the shirt that clung to his back, not the grainy grit of the grease on his fingertips, not the weight of the tire in his hands—not even the sound of quiet footsteps that approached him from out of the shadows.

He glanced up at her again. He saw the smile disappear from her face, and he saw her cover her eyes with her left hand.

He felt himself slump forward against the tire, and then he felt nothing at all.

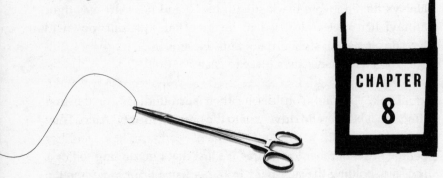

CHAPTER 8

Good morning, Dr. McKay."

Nathan Lassiter was dressed in sea green scrubs, ready for the morning's round of autopsies. The Allegheny County Coroner's Office averages two or three autopsies every day of the calendar year. With luck they would finish by lunchtime, leaving the afternoon to review histology slides and begin the autopsy reports. Riley glanced at her watch: it was almost nine-thirty. She had already been there for an hour, reviewing the day's cases and arranging assignments with the autopsy techs and assistants. By now she was used to Lassiter's utter disregard for schedule—*her* schedule—but it still never ceased to irritate her.

"Good morning, Dr. Lassiter. I was looking over the chart—I've had a little time to kill. We've got three today: One is a drowning victim, a little four-year-old girl from Penn Hills. That's a sad one."

"I hate floaters," Lassiter said. "I'll leave that one to you. What else have we got?"

Riley looked up at him. Lassiter was fifteen years her senior. The hair coloring he used was two shades over the top, a kind of glaring chestnut brown that contrasted badly with his colorless face. The skin along his jawline was beginning to sag and pouch, and faint brown liver spots already dotted his temples. He dressed the way middle-aged men do when they lose touch with the times—when they lose touch with women. "We've also got a peri-operative death from Allegheny General," she said, "plus a homicide—gunshot to the back of the head. I assume we'll do the homicide first."

"*I'll* do the homicide first," he said. "You're heading over to the University of Pittsburgh Medical School."

"What? Why?"

"You're giving a lecture there today on the proper way to fill out a death certificate."

Riley tossed her clipboard onto the counter. "You've got to be kidding."

"Not at all. There's not a single class in all of medical school that teaches doctors how to fill out a death certificate. You wouldn't believe some of the garbage we get here: nonmedical terminology, indistinguishable causes of death—it's a serious problem."

"Dr. Lassiter, surely one of the deputy coroners could—"

"Not a chance," Lassiter said. "I've done the lecture; so have all the other pathologists. Why should you get special treatment?"

"This is bogus," Riley said. "My fellowship program requires participation in two hundred and fifty autopsies."

"Your fellowship program requires participation in all the activities of the coroner's office: crime scene investigation, toxicology, ballistics, *everything*—including community and educational activities."

"Come on, Dr. Lassiter. I did a hundred autopsies on natural deaths during my residency. Today we've got a homicide. Isn't that what I'm here to learn about?"

"You're here to learn about lots of things."

"Look, I've done *five years* of postgraduate training in both anatomical and clinical pathology, and I did a subspecialty in renal pathology—yet you keep sending me out on errands a schoolgirl could do. Why is that?"

"Because around here you *are* a schoolgirl—unless you want to take your five years of training and get yourself a nice job in a hospital lab somewhere. You're a pathologist, Dr. McKay, but you're not a *forensic* pathologist—not until you finish this fellowship program and take your boards."

"Then *let* me finish it! Let me stay here and do autopsies—that's what this fellowship program ought to be—"

"Don't tell me how to run your program!" Lassiter barked. "You think that med school lectures and community seminars are somehow beneath you—well they're *not*, Ms. McKay, and as long as I'm your program supervisor, you'll do anything and everything I assign you to do. Is that clear? Maybe in the process you'll learn that there's more to being a forensic pathologist than just performing autopsies. Maybe you'll learn a little *humility*."

Riley bit her lip hard. To have to stand there and listen to this man preach on the need for humility. It took all of her resolve to say nothing in reply. Lassiter was, after all, a senior pathologist and a member of the coroner's office staff. She knew that if she ever hoped to work there she had to hold her tongue—but not her imagination. In her mind's eye, she imagined Lassiter lying on his back on the cold, stainless steel autopsy table. She saw herself make the classic Y-shaped incision, from both collarbones to the sternum and then straight down the abdomen.

"I think we both have our assignments this morning," Lassiter said. "The sooner you leave to do yours, the sooner I can get started on mine—unless you have any *more* objections?"

Now Riley made the circular incision around his skull, applied the bone saw, removed the skull cap, and found . . . nothing at all.

"Then get moving," Lassiter said. "The day isn't getting any younger."

Riley ran her tongue across her lower lip and tasted blood.

She wheeled around and charged down the hallway and up the stairs, ignoring a morning greeting from the chief deputy coroner. She headed for her tiny second-floor office, intending to stop just long enough to drop her lab coat and grab her purse—but on the way she passed the open doorway of Lassiter's office.

She looked back at the stairway. In a few minutes the autopsy would begin, and then Lassiter would be occupied for at least two hours—three or four if there were abnormalities. She glanced across the hall at the cubicles that filled the center office. She saw the tops of heads just visible above the fabric-covered panels. No one looked up; no one met her eyes; no one was watching.

She stepped back into Lassiter's office and quietly shut the door behind her.

She turned and rested against the door, surveying the office. Her anger had somehow left her, replaced by a strange sense of exhilaration. She felt lightheaded, almost giddy, the way she felt as a teenager playing a midnight game of Capture the Flag—but this was no game. She had acted impulsively; she had acted out of anger; she had entered Lassiter's private office without even knowing what she was looking for. *You'd better figure it out fast,* she said to herself. Her exhilaration was quickly giving way to gnawing fear.

And then she remembered—*autopsy dictations.*

During every autopsy, the senior pathologist wore a headset microphone and kept a running verbal commentary on a voice-activated digital recorder. These were his notes, the observations and details he would use to refresh his memory as he composed the final autopsy report. The recording sounded nothing like an organized presentation; it was always broken, choppy, filled with the pathologist's off-the-cuff remarks and unconscious reactions. Riley had heard comments made about a victim's attractiveness, or ethnicity, or even about his obvious guilt or innocence—comments that would never appear in written form. In the course of a two-hour autopsy, who knows what Lassiter might have said? His dictations might reveal evidence that never made it to his final reports.

Riley stepped around the desk and sat down at Lassiter's computer. She knew that the digital recordings were downloaded onto the pathologist's computer, where the session could be audibly reviewed or the file could be e-mailed to an outside vendor for transcription. On the monitor, a screen saver of a cherry red Dodge Viper was displayed. Riley jiggled the mouse and the image instantly vanished, replaced by the Windows Desktop. She quickly hunted through the dozens of icons, searching for the medical dictation program.

And then she heard the doorknob turn.

A pure panic-reflex caused her to jump to her feet just before the door opened wide. Nathan Lassiter stood looking at her without expression.

"Can I help you?"

Riley's brain flooded with adrenaline, and a thousand lame excuses and ridiculous explanations competed for her approval. But none of them was adequate—none was even close—and Riley stood there looking guilty and ashamed, like a little girl caught with a quarter pressed tightly in her hand and her mama's purse at her feet.

From the corner of her eye Riley saw the computer monitor, and she almost audibly gasped. The screen saver was gone; the Windows Desktop was still in view.

Lassiter charged forward. Riley quickly stepped out to block him from circling the desk.

"I came in to . . . leave you a note," she stumbled.

"You couldn't leave it with my secretary?" He moved forward again. Riley stepped as far forward as she could and still keep the screen in her peripheral vision.

"It was . . . personal in nature," she said.

Lassiter softened a bit. "Oh?"

"It was . . . an apology." She stood uncomfortably close to him now, but it was the only way to keep him from the computer screen.

"Well, here I am. Let's hear it."

Riley winced. "I just wanted to say . . . I'm sorry."

"Sorry for what?"

"For . . . for my attitude." Riley felt her stomach turn. She felt as though she were vomiting up each detestable word. "You're my supervisor, and I was . . . disrespectful." She eyed the monitor; how long does it take for a screen saver to reappear? Thirty seconds? A minute? She didn't know how much more of this sniveling she could endure. She was sure of one thing: Lassiter could listen to it all day.

"Well, I appreciate that," he said beneficently. "It takes a little perspective to see these things clearly, and I suppose that comes from experience." He reached out and placed one hand on her shoulder. It had all the warmth of a cadaver. From the corner of her eye, Riley saw a flicker of light and a change in hue from Windows blue to cherry red. She felt an overwhelming rush of relief, but she had no idea how to break off this touching encounter.

"OK," she said abruptly. "Gotta go." She stepped under his arm and headed directly for the door, exiting without looking back. She stopped briefly at her office, hung up her lab coat, and collected her purse. Then she hurried out of the building, looking for a suitable place to scream.

CHAPTER
9

There was a steady, insistent rapping on the metal fire door that opened onto the parking lot at the Allegheny County Coroner's Office. Riley hurried to the corner of the autopsy room and pushed it open. There stood an expressionless Nick Polchak, a canvas backpack slung over one shoulder.

"Nick, what took you so long? I called you thirty minutes ago!"

"I live thirty minutes away," Nick said.

"You said you were going to be 'on call.' "

"You mean just sitting around day after day, waiting for you to call? And they say men are demanding."

She grabbed him by the arm and pulled him inside.

"Where is everybody?" Nick said. "The place is dead—no pun intended."

"It was a quiet night—there were no calls coming in—so I gave them some money and sent them all out for pizza and beer."

"You seem to personally fund a lot of interesting ventures. Remind me to tell you about a certain grant proposal."

"Nick, they left twenty minutes ago. They could be back any moment now."

"Then we'd better get busy. What have you got?"

"We had a body come in this morning. It was a gunshot wound to the rear of the head. He was apparently changing his tire, and they found him slumped over against his car—he picked a bad place to get a flat. Nothing was taken from the victim or his car; it looks like a drive-by shooting, possibly gang related."

"And the autopsy? I assume it was Lassiter's rotation."

She nodded. "I offered to assist, as always—this time he sent me to Pitt to teach medical students how to hold a pen. I reviewed the police report just before I called you. Estimated time of death was yesterday, around dusk. They talked to the victim's wife—he left home at exactly seven p.m. He was due at a poker game by seven thirty, but he never showed up. Lassiter did the autopsy late this morning."

"And?"

"The procedure is to issue a death certificate immediately after the autopsy, but all it indicates is the primary cause of death. The details of Lassiter's autopsy report won't come out for a week or two—but I talked to one of his autopsy techs. He said the cause of death was a single bullet through the occipital bone. There was an entry wound, but no exit—it was a small-caliber weapon. The size and shape of the wound suggest a short-to-intermediate firing distance, and it was straight-on—just what you'd expect from a drive-by."

"Nothing out of the ordinary?"

"Nothing the tech could see—nothing he was *allowed* to see. The only way we'll know for sure is to check for ourselves—that is, if you're still willing to help."

"What can I do?"

"I need a second pair of eyes. We can't reopen the body—we can't even use the autopsy room. We can't send any tissue samples to the histology lab, and we can't draw any fluids for a toxicology screen. All we can do is work from the outside. I can check for contusions, abrasions, additional wounds of any kind—I need you to look for evidence of insect activity. I'm looking for anything, Nick—anything that doesn't look consistent with a drive-by shooting. But whatever we do, we've got to do it *fast*."

The cooler door opened with a soft click, and a wall of icy air greeted them. The cooler was a single large room, long and deep, with a series of utility shelves and wire-rimmed, circular fans lining the far end. The walls looked like panels of Reynolds Wrap imprinted with poultry wire, a dull silver gray, and three stark incandescent bulbs dotted the midline of the ceiling. Packed in the center of the room were a half-dozen aging gurneys with white Formica tops and large, narrow wheels. Each one supported a human cadaver, sealed in a glossy blue body bag with a long black zipper directly down the center.

Riley pulled the door shut behind them and wheeled a single gurney into a small, open area.

"We have to do our looking in here," Riley said. "Sorry it's a bit chilly."

"My mom has no air conditioning," Nick said. "This is heaven." He pulled the zipper all the way to the feet and began to tuck the vinyl back away from the torso.

Riley started with the soles of the feet and worked her way up, searching for any telltale mark or scratch that might reveal a struggle, an antemortem wound, or a posthumous relocation of the body. Nick began at the opposite end, checking the eyes, ears, and nasal passages for infestation. He pried open the lower jaw and peered into the mouth with a penlight.

"This is interesting," Nick said.

"What?"

"There are eggs in the back of the mouth; blowflies go for the natural orifices first, and they often oviposit well back in the passageway. You said the time of death was after seven o'clock, around dusk? Blowflies usually knock off after dark, when the temperatures begin to fall. That would put the time of death as close to seven as possible. Looks like these ladies just got in under the wire."

"Hurry, Nick," Riley said. "We can debrief later."

Riley worked her way up toward the neck and cranial area, while Nick headed for the lower orifices; they stumbled into one another at the center of the body. When they bumped against the gurney, a tiny, paste-white object dropped into the crease at the bottom of the body bag.

"Now that is interesting," Nick said, smoothing the crease and lifting the edge of the body bag closer to his face.

"Do you need a magnifier?"

Nick tapped his glasses. "Got one—it's one of the perks." Under the powerful lenses, a single, barely moving larva came into focus.

"It's a first-instar maggot," he said, "the earliest stage of larval development. There are two possibilities: Either the temperatures remained warm enough last night to allow a blowfly egg to hatch, or it's a sarcophagid—a flesh fly. Blowflies lay eggs; flesh flies give live birth. They sort of squirt the maggots out, sometimes without even landing on the body. The big question for us is: where did it come from?"

"You already found eggs in the oral cavity."

"Yes—*deep* in the oral cavity. Flesh-eating flies are attracted to openings in the body—usually the natural orifices first, because that's where the gases are released that are the by-product of decomposition. But there are no orifices in the middle of the body, and yet we seem to have dislodged this little guy from somewhere."

Nick stooped down and grasped the thorax with both hands, hooking his thumbs under the lower back, rolling the body slightly onto its left side. On the back, just below the rib cage, was a long, curving wound that was roughly sutured shut. In the center of the wound, wedged tightly between the lips of flesh, were two more tiny maggots.

"Bingo," Nick said.

Just then they heard the click of the cooler door. Nick released the body, which settled thickly onto its back again. Riley lunged for the zipper, tugging it shut. She gave the gurney a shove with her hip, sending it rolling into the others. The cooler door began to swing open.

Nick turned to Riley, took her roughly in his arms, and kissed her.

Riley was so astonished that for the first instant she stood with her eyes bulging, her arms thrust down and back like a gymnast finishing a dismount, as rigid as one of the cadavers around her. Then, just as suddenly, she realized what was taking place and understood her part in it. She swung her left arm up around Nick's neck, closed her eyes, and kissed him back hard.

She heard a kind of snort from the doorway behind her, and then a giggling sound from out in the hall. "Sorry," a voice said. "Bad timing."

She turned to face them. Two deputy coroners and the dispatcher stood in the doorway holding a white cardboard box.

"We brought you back some pizza," one of them said. "Guess we should have brought extra." There was a smothered laugh and a trading of elbows.

"You two better take it easy," said another. "We can't have the stiffs thawing out in here."

Riley's face felt flushed and hot—something she hadn't experienced in a long, long time. She felt like a schoolgirl who had been caught behind the lockers with her boyfriend. She despised their adolescent snickering, and even more her temporary loss of hard-earned status—but there was nothing to do now but play her part out to the end.

"We'll be through here in a minute," she said.

"Doesn't look like it to me," someone whispered.

"Do you mind? Close the door on your way out."

The door closed firmly, abruptly cutting off the sound of rising laughter.

Riley glanced at Nick, peeled off her glove, and wiped her index finger across her lips.

"Well," Nick said. "I'd say this was very productive time."

Riley stepped through her apartment door, pausing to wrestle her keys from the deadbolt. Nick stepped into the doorway behind her and stopped, his eyes taking in the room in broad strokes.

"Nice place," he said. "It's a little Spartan."

"That's because I don't live with my mother."

"Ouch."

As Nick stepped into the room, he shoved his hands deep into his pockets, like a little boy cautioned not to break anything. He stood in the center of the room, turning and looking.

"You almost lost me on the way over here," he said. "You drive pretty fast. Why doesn't that surprise me?"

"I couldn't lose sight of *you*," Riley said. "There was a big blue cloud of smoke behind you. What in the world are you driving?"

"A car," he said.

"What *kind* of car?"

Nick frowned. "I really don't know."

Riley flopped onto the sofa and folded her legs underneath her. She straightened stiffly and grimaced, massaging her lower back with her thumbs.

"Back trouble?" Nick said, taking a seat across from her.

"Too many hours on my feet," she said. "What about that dorsal wound? I barely got a look at it."

"Very strange. You said Lassiter listed a gunshot wound as the primary cause of death. On the autopsy tape, there was no mention of any other major wounds?"

"None at all."

"Would a pathologist neglect to mention a wound just because he thought it had nothing to do with the cause of death?"

"Of course not. For a pathologist, the issue isn't simply the *cause* of death, but all the circumstances *surrounding* death. The very presence of a secondary wound makes it important. It would take the world's worst pathologist to make that kind of omission."

"Do you know what they call the guy who graduates last in his class in medical school? *Doctor*."

Riley shook her head. "I don't suspect Dr. Lassiter of incompetence."

Nick leaned forward. "What do you suspect him of?"

Riley said nothing.

"I know," Nick said. "You're 'not ready to answer that question.'"

She smiled slightly.

"There are three things that are significant about that wound," Nick said. "First of all, it was more of an incision than a wound—the edges of the tissue were too smooth to have been caused by any street weapon. Second, the wound was sutured closed—not surgically, like in a hospital, but the way your people do after an autopsy—just enough to hold it shut. Finally—and most important of all—Dr. Lassiter didn't make that incision."

"How do you know that?"

"Because there were larvae in the wound—we dislodged one of them, remember? I found two more still intact. If Dr. Lassiter made the incision during the autopsy, there would be no maggots present."

"Could the maggots have moved there from some other part of the body?"

"Not a chance. The only other infestation was still in the egg stage, and even if there were other larvae, maggots stay very close to where they're deposited—they don't go wandering around the body."

"Then the incision must have been made earlier—before our office picked up the body—and before dark, because you said flies cease activity at night. But, Nick, that pushes the incision all the way back to the time of death."

Nick nodded.

"Could it have been made even earlier? Say, the day before?"

"It's possible, but highly unlikely. For the wound to be infested, it had to be exposed. Don't forget, when flies approach a body they have a choice of egg-laying locations. All they need is warm, dark, and moist—that's why they like the mouth so much. But the only maggots on this body were on a wound near the center of the back. At some time after death, that wound was as open and available as the eyes, ears, or mouth."

"Then I have some questions," Riley said. "What role did this wound play in the overall death scenario? Why would anyone bother to suture a wound on a dead man? And most of all, why would Dr. Lassiter choose to overlook it?"

"Good questions," Nick said.

Riley slumped back against the sofa. "Then we're right back where we started from—we've got a bunch of questions and no answers."

"We've got a *different* set of questions," Nick said. "Now you have a second anomaly—an actual, physical anomaly—and now it looks much more certain that Lassiter's apparent negligence is intentional. I call that progress."

"So what do we do next?"

"It's a question of access. We can't go back to the crime scene, and we can't re-examine the body, so we go with Lassiter. Let's see what we can dig up about his possible motives."

"And the way we do that is?"

"I've got a couple of ideas."

Riley shook her head. "Why doesn't that surprise me?"

Neither one said anything for a minute.

"You kissed me," Riley said suddenly.

"What?"

"In the cooler. You kissed me."

"Are you just noticing this now? I've got to work on my technique."

Riley squinted at him. "The way I see it, Nick, there are only two options: either you're incredibly quick and able to think on your feet, or you're a big, fat coward."

Nick stared at the ceiling for several seconds, then slowly began to nod his head. "Yes," he said, "those would be the options."

CHAPTER 10

Nathan Lassiter stepped out his front door and tiptoed barefoot down the herringbone brick sidewalk that led to his driveway and the morning *Post-Gazette*. He wore a fading Penn T-shirt tucked into the powder blue surgical scrubs he always used as pajamas. The shirt did nothing to conceal his sizable paunch. His shoulders were narrowing and rounded, and his once-prized pecs—no longer able to be sustained by a dozen monthly bench presses—were fast becoming nothing but nipples. He was unshaven, uncombed, and thanks to Dr. Atkins, his breath reeked of ketones.

He stopped abruptly. In the center of his driveway was a bright orange pickup truck with a generic black insect on top, smiling and doffing its hat to passersby. The truck was empty, and the windows were rolled down. Lassiter looked around and noticed that the gate to his backyard hung open.

Halfway down the side of the house, Nick Polchak knelt beside the open door to the crawlspace that ran underneath the house. He wore blue coveralls with an embroidered logo representing a company called "Bug Off," and he was busy making notations on a silver metal clip box.

"Hey, you," Lassiter said, picking his way across the dewy grass. "What do you mean by just walking in here and—"

"You want the damage report?" Nick said. "You paid for it."

"What? I didn't pay for anything."

"Are you Nathan Lassiter? You got a five-year service contract with our company." Nick waved the paperwork in the air and then tossed it facedown on the grass. "Once a year we check under the house for termites, whole house wood bores, the whole shebang."

"I've never seen you here before."

Nick shrugged. "You never had a problem before. You think we'd knock on your door just to say, 'Everything's peachy'? If you got no problem, we're invisible—just like your termites."

"I never paid for any service contract."

"Is there a Mrs. Lassiter?"

Lassiter closed his eyes.

"Well, there you go," Nick said. "A smart woman, Mrs. Lassiter."

Lassiter glared at him. "What's this about termites?"

"Not just termites. You got carpenter ants—those are really tough to get rid of. I found powderpost beetles—with beetles you got to kill the eggs too, 'cause baby beetles can raise themselves, not like kids these days, huh, Nate? And then you got brown recluse spiders—I never seen so many of 'em. You ever seen someone bit by a brown recluse? I heard about a guy up in Blawnox, he crawled under to check his furnace, took a bite right here on his thumb. They say it looked like a gunshot wound, the whole hand practically rotted away—"

"Look, do I really need to deal with this right now?"

"Not if you don't mind your house being eaten out from under you. Hey, you got a floor joist down there that looks like a twenty-foot loofah."

Lassiter muttered a colorful phrase to no one in particular. Nick watched him. His toes were hanging over the edge; all he needed was one more push.

"If it makes you feel any better, you already paid for it."

"What? When?"

"It's part of your service contract. You know how it works, sort of like a homeowner's warranty. You pay the cash up front; we cover the service if you need it. Some people win, some people lose—you're about to win big time."

"OK then," Lassiter shrugged. "Go ahead and spray."

Nick threw back his head and let out a laugh.

"Go ahead and *spray*? You look like a smart guy—what are you, a nurse? Let me explain something to you. A termite queen can lay thirty thousand eggs a *day*. Down along the Gulf Coast, Formosan termites can consume an entire house in just eighteen months. You have an *infestation*, my friend. You can only spray the ones you can see. The only way to kill them all is to fumigate."

"Fumigate? How does that work?"

"We tent the house. We wrap it up top to bottom with big yellow tarps—you should see it, Nate, it's really something—then we tape all the seams and lay sand snakes around the bottom to seal it up tight. Then we fill the whole thing up with *Vikane*—sulfuryl fluoride gas."

Lassiter groaned. "How long does all this take?"

"Not as long as you'd think. We can wrap a little place like this in, say, half a day. We blow in the gas—that doesn't take long—and then the whole thing sits for maybe a day. We pull off the tarps, open all the windows to air it out—that's it, you're done. A day and a half total. And there's hardly any prep work for you to do. Just be sure to remove the plants and the pets—'cause that Vikane will kill every living thing under the tent. A couple years ago in Tampa, a woman committed suicide that way. Do you have a cat? You look like a cat person to me."

"I can't do this now," Lassiter said. "Maybe in a month or two."

"It's your call," Nick said. "I can fit you in late December."

"That's six months away!"

"The whole thing works on a big computer schedule. You know how it is. When we set up the service contract, we schedule the inspections and the repairs together. If you want to reschedule, you got to take what's available. I'll put you down for the weekend after Christmas."

Lassiter hesitated.

"Or I can do it tomorrow," Nick said. "A day and a half, the whole thing's out of your hair by the end of the week. Whaddya say? You head off to work tomorrow morning, but you get a hotel room tomorrow night. Or you could just find an empty bed at the hospital—hey, who's gonna know?"

"I'm a *pathologist,* you idiot!"

"It's OK," Nick said softly. "Hey, my wife's on Zoloft."

Lassiter turned and stormed off toward the driveway. "Do it tomorrow," he shouted back, "but I don't want to see any sign of your crew by the following afternoon!"

"Trust me," Nick called after him, "you'll never know we were here."

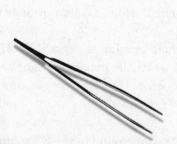

CHAPTER 11

Nick and Riley sat at a corner table at the Common Plea, just a short walk from the coroner's office at Fourth and Ross. The eatery was first-rate, one of Pittsburgh's finest, an authentically Italian establishment without a trace of checkered vinyl tablecloths or wax-rimmed Chianti bottles. The pecan-stained walls were trimmed in ornate moldings and lined with elegant candelabra sconces and glossy oil paintings framed in gold. Riley looked at Nick, dressed just as casually as ever, looking as out of place as a fly on a china platter. He busied himself with a plate of veal Veneziana while Riley looked on.

"You like Italian?" she said, picking at her own plate.

"I like food."

"Funny. Somehow I figured a bug man would be a vege-tarian."

"Why? Insects are some of the biggest carnivores on the planet. Did you know that in Chile they have a spider that eats *mice*?"

She pushed her plate away. "Nick, I'm trying to eat here. Do you want to hear about my last autopsy?"

"OK by me."

"Look," she said, "I need you to explain this whole thing again. We go to Lassiter's house tomorrow, and the whole thing will be covered with tarpaulins. Then we just walk in dressed like exterminators and take our time looking around. Is that it?"

"Not too much time," Nick said. "We should be out by dark. It wouldn't do to have lights visible beneath the tarps."

"What about the sulfuryl fluoride? The gas is toxic."

"What gas?"

"I get it—you wrap the house, but you never fill it with gas. But then, how do you get rid of his termites?"

"What termites?"

Riley shook her head in disbelief. "How did you arrange all this?"

"I know a guy—an old classmate of mine at Penn State. He's doing pretty well for himself—he's actually making a living with an undergraduate entomology degree. He owns a pest control company in Oakmont. We worked out a deal."

"What's in it for him?"

"They don't tent and fumigate much around here—it's more of a Southern thing. When my friend wraps up a house with those big yellow tarps of his, it's practically a media event. He hands out cards all over the neighborhood. He tells them, 'See? This is what can happen if you don't do regular treatments.' It works out for both of us."

"Nick, has it occurred to you that this is slightly illegal? It's called *breaking and entering*."

"Why? Lassiter signed a release form that allows the exterminators access to his home."

"We're not exterminators! We're masquerading as exterminators in order to do an illegal search of his home."

"Details."

"Nick—have you ever been in trouble with the law before?"

He paused. "Define 'trouble.' "

"Do you know what a risk this is for both of us?"

"For both of us? Or for you?"

"OK," she grumbled. "For me. If I got caught, this would be the end of my career. It would end my fellowship—and even if they let me finish, who would hire a forensic pathologist who's a part-time burglar?"

"Not me."

"You seem to be taking this all pretty lightly."

"Look," Nick said. "I respect the law. We have the same goal in mind—I just find it necessary to take a different path to the goal sometimes. I like to think I keep the *spirit* of the law."

Riley rolled her eyes. "I'll bet the prisons are filled with people who kept the 'spirit of the law.' "

"I'm open to legal alternatives. Got any ideas?"

"No," Riley said sullenly. "I told you what happened when I tried to search his office. I guess this is not my specialty."

"Well, it's *my* specialty. I've taken risks with the law before, and let me tell you, this is a pretty good one. When you tent a house, people know that toxic chemicals are involved and they steer clear of it. The next-door neighbors generally clear out for the day, and you won't see a kid outside for a block in any direction. There's virtually no chance that Lassiter will return unexpectedly like he did at his office—and even if he did, what would he see? A house wrapped in plastic and a company truck in the driveway. And once we're inside—well, that's the best part. Lassiter knows that the exterminators need access to the house, and he'll expect a certain amount of disturbance—doors left open, objects rearranged, that sort of thing. As long as we don't do anything stupid, our tracks will be covered. It's a terrific setup. Personally, I'm hoping he has an indoor hot tub."

Riley's eyes widened.

"Hey, lighten up."

"Lighten up," she groaned.

"Look, if you feel this way, maybe you shouldn't come along."

"You mean let you do it alone?"

"Like you said, it's not your specialty. You almost got caught once; if something goes wrong this time, you'll be in the clear."

Riley watched him wipe a slice of bruschetta around the edge of his dish.

"Nick, why would you do this? You barely know me. I'm not even paying you. You're not just offering to take a risk with me, now you're offering to take a risk *for* me. Why?"

Nick looked at her. "I'm not ready to answer that question," he said.

She shook her head. "Thanks, but I can't let you do this alone."

"I know you can't—I just wanted to see how loyal you are. I suspect that's what's driving this whole investigation of yours: some sense of betrayal on your part. As I suspected, you're a fiercely loyal person. You could never let me go alone."

"So your offer was just a test?"

"I think of it more as an experiment," he said. "Would you care to comment on my observations?"

"No," she said. "It just has to be the two of us."

"The three of us."

"What?"

Nick nodded toward the door.

Riley turned to see a short, barrel-chested man in a lambskin blazer and a white, ribbed crewneck. His narrow forehead supported a thick crop of shining, coal-black hair. His face bore a smile—no, his face *was* a smile, casting warm light wherever he turned like the glow of a miner's lantern. His eyes were dark and shining, squeezed tight by his constant smile until they glowed like black amethysts. He drifted from table to table, halting momentarily to squeeze a hand, rub a shoulder, or revivify a boring conversation.

"Does he own the place?" Riley asked.

"He owns every place—at least, you'd think he does. Brace yourself, here he comes."

He stopped beside their booth with both arms spread wide, smiling and nodding like a salesman presenting a new line of cars.

"*Buona sera,* my friends! Ah, what an evening, what a city, what a life!"

"Riley McKay, meet Leonardo Lazzoli, known to his friends as Leo. Leo, this is Riley McKay."

Leo turned to Riley and did a dramatic double take. He looked stunned, astonished, and for a moment he said nothing at all; then the smile once again relit the lamp of his face, and he gestured toward her with outstretched arms.

"Now *this*," he said. "*This* is a wonder. *This* is a thing of beauty. This is . . . *perfection*." He turned to Nick with a look of contempt. "And what did you tell me? 'We're meeting with a *woman*.' A *woman*," he spat. "You're a dead man, Nick. You have the soul of a goat. You spend too many hours poking around in dark corners. You need to look *up* once in a while, you need to see the beauty around you. Have you told this angelic being that she has the face of the Delphian sibyl and the grace of Michaelangelo's *Pieta*?"

"I was just about to," Nick said. "Grab us some dessert menus and sit down."

He took a chair next to Nick, still beaming and nodding at Riley with a look of profound satisfaction. "What a pleasure," he kept repeating, "what a very great pleasure." Riley smiled back, but could think of nothing at all to say.

"What the heck is *mascarpone*?" Nick said, flipping over the menu.

"Give me that, you peasant," Leo said in disgust. He beckoned to the waitress.

"Leo's coming along tomorrow," Nick said to Riley.

"Thanks for letting me know," Riley glared back. "Leo, are you an exterminator?"

"An *exterminator*," Leo said with delight. "I've never thought of it quite that way before. Yes, you might say I'm an exterminator—I help people eliminate bugs. Nick tells me that you have one or two of your own."

"Leo has a doctorate in electrical engineering," Nick said. "He's a software engineer and a network specialist. Basically, he's your all-around tech head."

"All lies," Leo said with a wave of his hand. "I am an artist, a connoisseur of beauty, a lover of the finer things in life. But, like all artists, I must suffer—so I teach Information Technology at Pitt."

"Leo's a handy guy to have around when you're looking for *information*."

Riley looked at Nick again.

"He knows," Nick said. "I could hardly ask him to become an accessory to the crime without telling him why."

"It seems like everyone is taking chances for me tonight," Riley said. "Leo, has Nick told you the risks involved in this?"

"I doubt it. When Nick tells you there's no danger, he's lying. When Nick says there will be no problems, expect problems. This much I know about Nick Polchak."

"How's your sister?" Nick asked. "Does she still mention me?"

"Yes—when she has a high fever, or when she shuts the door on her hand."

"I should call her."

"I offer to help you, and you threaten me?"

"How do you two know each other?" Riley cut in.

"We grew up together, in Tarentum," Nick said.

"In different neighborhoods, of course," Leo added. "He grew up in the degenerate Polish section, while I was raised in the more fashionable Italian section. His family attended Holy Martyrs, whereas mine attended the more sublime Saint Peter's—where the pope himself would attend, given the choice."

"Not this pope," Nick said. "He can't wait to get back to Krakow."

"Your singular claim to glory—but in general, my people were launching the Renaissance while yours were still painting bison on cave walls."

"We met as teenagers," Nick said.

"After several encounters, we discovered that we shared the same penchant for . . . *adventure*."

"In other words: same high school, same detention hall."

"Hold it," Riley said. "This is not high school—and if anything goes wrong, they won't be sending us to detention hall. Leo, I have to ask you again: do you know what you're getting yourself into?"

"Do you?" he said. "If you're working with Nick, you probably don't."

"Then why do you want to come along?"

"Why, for the adventure, of course. Nick promised me a dragon to slay."

The waitress arrived at the table now, and Leo turned his attention to her. "Your tiramisu," he said to the waitress. "It's not the kind with custard, is it? It has the layers of mascarpone? And then we'll need something chocolate—something with ganache and a sprinkling of cocoa powder. You have cheesecake, of course; bring us a slice with some white chocolate slivers, or perhaps fresh strawberries. We'll need a nice dessert wine—perhaps a Vin Santo or a black Muscat? That would be wonderful. And now," he said with a wink, "tell us your secrets. What are you holding out on us? You have something special back there, don't you, something you haven't told us about yet?"

The waitress smiled and winked back. "We do have a nice panna cotta with fresh raspberries," she said.

Leo groaned. "Please hurry—life is brief. We don't want to die before we taste your panna cotta."

"I usually skip dessert," Riley said.

"Skip dessert?" Leo looked around as though the voice had come out of nowhere. "Did someone say 'skip dessert'?"

"I don't eat very much."

"We don't *eat* dessert," Leo said. "What are we, gluttons? We *taste* dessert. The entrée feeds the body, but dessert feeds the soul. Dessert is for pleasure, and pleasures are meant to be tasted, not consumed. When you skip dessert, you leave with a full belly but an empty heart. Animals eat meat and vegetables, my dear Riley. Dessert is what makes us human."

"Life is dessert," Nick said. "You should hear his sermon on pasta."

"The goat-man speaks," Leo said with a toss of his head. "You know, I have watched him swallow an entire meal without even tasting it."

The waitress returned with four small plates, each a swirling patchwork of colors and textures and sheens. She arranged them in a square in the center of the table, and set out four gleaming forks.

"Where is the fourth?" the waitress said.

Leo picked up a fork and handed it back to her. "Should we take pleasure from you and give none in return? The first taste is yours."

The waitress smiled a sheepish grin, glanced over her shoulder, and took a quick mouthful of panna cotta before hurrying back to the kitchen.

Leo opened the black Muscat and poured the rich, dark liquid into three small glasses. "And now, I'd like to offer a traditional Italian blessing."

"Here we go," Nick said.

"Do you mind?" Leo cleared his throat and stood up.

"May those that love us, love us.

And those that don't love us,

May God turn their hearts.

And if He doesn't turn their hearts,

May He turn their ankles,

So we will know them by their limping."

He held his glass out to each of them.

"That's a traditional Italian blessing?"

"Sicilian, actually. When Nick is around, it comes in handy."

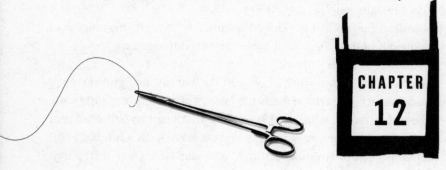

CHAPTER
12

Leo sat on the passenger side of the BugOff van, staring up at the two-story house wrapped completely in bright yellow plastic.

"Like an enormous baby Gouda," he said. "Marvelous. Truly."

"Put these on before you get out of the van," Nick said, handing gas masks and hard hats to Leo and Riley.

"I thought there was no gas," Riley said.

"It just completes the disguise. This way, your own mother wouldn't know you."

Nick took a large toolbox and a plastic garden sprayer from the van, and they all went around to the back of the house. Nick searched the tarps, locating all the seams; at one point, just to the right of the patio, the duct tape stopped six feet above the ground and a vertical seam flapped loosely in the breeze.

"That should be the door," Nick said. "Good boy, Freddie."

They slipped inside and removed their masks and helmets. Nick opened the toolbox, took out a black garbage bag, and handed it to Riley.

"Start with the trash," he said. "Go room by room and round up everything, especially from the bathrooms and the study, if he has one. We'll spread it all out on the floor in the garage. Leo, you know your domain."

"I'm on it. I hope he wasn't too cheap to buy a decent computer."

"I'll look for files and other records," Nick said. "If anybody finds anything good, shout it out."

Nick wandered through the downstairs rooms, drawing general observations from the overall layout. It was clearly the house of a divorcé, and definitely a divorced male. The furniture, though contemporary in style and of a very high quality, had been selectively removed from each of the rooms, leaving gaping holes and awkward asymmetries everywhere. The family room was the most desolate; it contained nothing but an old recliner that faced off with a thirty-six-inch Toshiba resting on the carpet in the center of the room. On the wall, a rectangle of contrasting paint marked the spot where an armoire or bookshelf once stood. The mantel above the fireplace was barren, and every print and photograph had been removed except for one framed medical diploma that stood out on the empty wall like a beetle on a windshield. The dining room contained a table, but no chairs; there was a breakfront, but every cup and dish had been removed. It was still a functional house, but no longer a home. Every trace of warmth or humanness had been negotiated away in the final settlement.

"There is no trash," Riley said. "I checked the garage cans too. It must have been taken out."

Nick frowned. "I should have checked the collection day."

"What would we find in the trash?"

"Everything. Pay stubs, bills, phone numbers, credit card numbers, purchase receipts—if you own it, it eventually ends up in the trash."

"Now what?"

"Upstairs," Nick said. "It's obvious Lassiter doesn't live down here anymore—the place looks like an empty museum."

The upstairs hallway branched off into four smaller rooms. On the left was the master bedroom and bath; near the center, a second bedroom contained nothing but an abandoned bedframe and three empty corrugated boxes. Farther down, an even smaller room housed a Landice treadmill, a wobbly workout bench, and a mismatched set of black iron dumbbells. Nick flipped the treadmill on and off quickly and watched the dust line move to the center of the roll.

At the end of the hallway, Leo sat smiling behind a black-and-mahogany computer workstation crammed with software boxes, user manuals, and other esoteric documentation. His fingers moved in a blur. Every few seconds he would stop, hum or whistle something to himself, and then his fingers would skitter off again like scorpions on a tile floor. On the floor beside him sat a squat, two-drawer file cabinet with brushed aluminum handles.

"You start in the bedroom," Nick said to Riley. "I'll go through this file cabinet."

"Why don't I start on the files?" Riley countered. "His bedroom gives me the creeps."

"Have it your way." Nick turned and headed down the hallway.

In the bathroom, he opened the mirror-front medicine cabinet. The top two shelves were conspicuously empty; the bottom contained the expected toiletries along with a bizarre assortment of vitamins and herbal supplements. Nick searched first for antidepressants or signs of any questionable prescriptions or illicit drugs; there were none. Next, he carefully picked up each bottle and examined it, being careful to note the facing of the label before he removed it from the shelf. There was red yeast rice extract for his rising cholesterol, Ginkgoba biloba for his fading memory, and saw palmetto for his aging prostate. There was ginseng root for extra energy, creatine for muscle growth, and Horny Goat Weed for—Horny Goat Weed? This guy's trying way too hard, Nick thought. It looked like a salvage shop for middle-aged men.

In the bedroom he checked the dresser and nightstands for

journals, phone lists, or personal letters. There was very little of a personal nature anywhere. Was that the cause of his divorce, or the result? Many men, failing in love, choose to pour their entire lives into their work; Lassiter had obviously chosen this path. The only indication that his wife had ever existed was her conspicuous absence, and the fragmented home she left behind.

Nick headed back down the hall.

"Any security problems?" Nick said to Leo.

"Security, but no problems," Leo replied. "I was in in less than three minutes."

"How about you? Finding anything?"

"Bits and pieces," Riley said, the floor around her scattered with manila folders. "Most of this is obsolete financial records, old tax returns, auto repair histories . . ."

"Anything current? Anything that would tell us about his income or his financial situation?"

"I know what he makes," Riley said. "A pathologist in our office makes about sixty thousand a year."

"Sixty thousand? You people put in four years of medical school and six or seven years of residency just to take home sixty grand? And I thought professors were crazy."

"That's not all of it," Riley said. "Most of our pathologists have private autopsy practices and consulting services that can be very lucrative. The smaller counties can't afford to keep their own pathologists, so they hire ours on a case-by-case basis. And sometimes, when a local medical examiner gives them a verdict they don't agree with, they hire one of ours to get a second opinion. An autopsy here, a consulting fee there—it all adds up."

"No, it doesn't," Leo said. "That's the problem."

Nick and Riley stepped behind him and looked over his shoulder at the screen.

"Our friend does his personal finances and business accounting in Quicken and QuickBooks," Leo said. "Doctors are notoriously bad with money; his expense records are very spotty, but he does manage to keep track of his salary and receivables. He's not incorporated, so he's treating his private practice as part of his personal income. Riley, do you have his most current tax return?"

"Got it."

"OK, check his 1040 for total income. Does it come out to about . . . that?" he said, pointing to the screen.

"That's about right."

"Really? Then how do we explain . . . this?" Leo clicked on Quicken's Investing Center icon and switched to Portfolio View. There, in front of them, was an inclusive listing of Lassiter's investment holdings, complete with a record of individual transactions.

"Last year, his investments were modest and unfocused. A few shares of a tech stock, a little money in a high-yield fund—just your average dabbling day-trader. But this year all his investments have focused on a single company. And last year, his investments were roughly consistent with his earnings. But notice this fiscal year. Look at this transaction . . . and this one . . . and this one here. See? Those three transactions alone total a quarter of a million dollars. My friends, that's more than his entire income."

"Where is he getting that kind of money?" Riley asked.

"Is there any record of a loan, a second mortgage, anything like that?"

"There's no indication of where the money came from," Leo said. "However, we do know where it went." He pointed to the Security line within each of the three transactions. Each one read, "PharmaGen, Inc."

"Now look at this," Leo said, switching to Internet Explorer and pressing the History icon. "This is a record of all the Web sites he's visited in the last three weeks. There are the usual hits: eBay, Google, ESPN, plus a few that reveal a serious lack of character. But notice all these: *PharmaGen, PharmaGen, PharmaGen*. What's the old saying? 'Where a man's treasure is, there will his heart be also.' "

"What do we know about this PharmaGen?" Nick asked.

"I've heard of it," Riley said. "It's a Pittsburgh-based biotech startup in the field of personalized medicine. It's known as *pharmacogenomics*. Very new, very cutting edge."

"They're talking about this in my department," Leo said. "It involves a groundbreaking information field known as *bioinformatics*—taking genetic or biological information and putting it on a computer for comparison and analysis."

"Has this PharmaGen gone public yet?"

Leo opened a separate window. A few quick keystrokes took

them to the Web site of the Securities and Exchange Commission and its EDGAR database. "They haven't filed with the SEC yet," Leo said. "It looks like the company is still privately held."

"Then our boy isn't buying stock," Nick said. "He's trying to get in on the ground floor of this company *before* it goes public. Looks like he's betting the farm on it."

"He's betting the farm and then some," Leo said. "The question is, where is the farmer getting the extra money? And why this one company? This is not what one would call a 'diversified portfolio.' He's taking an enormous risk."

"Maybe," Nick said. He leaned forward and took the mouse, guiding it to the PharmaGen folder in the History list. He tapped the mouse, and a dozen specific links appeared underneath.

"He's been all over this Web site," Nick said. "What's the big interest?" He clicked on the link titled "PharmaGen.com: Welcome," and the screen went suddenly black.

The Web site opened with a low, tremulous tone, followed by a woman's voice as smooth and mellow as amber honey. "Welcome to the world of personalized medicine," the voice cooed. "Welcome to the future. Welcome to PharmaGen." In the right corner, a tiny Skip Intro icon appeared, and Leo instinctively reached for the mouse.

"Don't," Nick said. "This is what they want the public to see."

In the background, music began to rise: first the rumbling percussion, then the soaring woodwinds, then the stentorian brass proclaiming "The World of PharmaGen" in clarion tones. Now vibrant images began to flicker past like flashcards: a baldheaded child with dark, sunken eyes and a pleading smile; handsome men and women in white lab coats and gleaming silver stethoscopes; backlit vials and flasks of bright, multicolored liquids; crowded laboratories and computer rooms dotted with intense, concerned faces; and a stunning panorama of the Triangle taken from the exit of the Fort Pitt Tunnel.

"PharmaGen," the voiceover said. "The medicines of tomorrow from the knowledge of today."

Now the screen dissolved to black again, and the image of a multihued double helix appeared. The image began to tip and rotate, and the viewer's eye soared like a falcon over the connecting shafts and curling banisters that comprise the DNA molecule.

"Nice graphic," Nick said.

"Nice Web site," Leo added. "This was not cheap."

"Pharmacogenomics is the application of recent discoveries about the human genome to produce a bold, new world of pharmaceuticals, specifically tailored to individual needs. Environment, diet, age, and lifestyle all influence an individual's response to medication—but an individual's unique genetic makeup is the key. By tailoring medicines to individual genetic profiles, we can achieve far greater efficacy and safety than we can through the 'one size fits all' methods of today."

The image of a young girl was suddenly superimposed; she was seated on an examination table, draped in an oversized hospital gown.

"A child is diagnosed with leukemia. As part of her treatment, she will receive a standard protocol of chemotherapy drugs. But a small percentage of Caucasian children lack a crucial enzyme that keeps those drugs from building up to toxic levels in their bloodstreams. Will her medications heal or harm? The drug that saves the life of one patient may take the life of another. Adverse reactions to medications kill an estimated hundred-thousand Americans every year and hospitalize two million more.

"Researchers at PharmaGen are studying the inherited variations in genes, known as 'snips,' that determine drug response in each individual. With this knowledge, we will be able to predict whether a medicine will have a helpful effect, a harmful effect, or no effect at all; we will be able to produce stronger, better, safer drugs and vaccines; we will enable doctors to determine dosages with much greater accuracy; and, by reducing the number of adverse drug reactions, we will play a major role in decreasing the soaring costs of healthcare.

"But it all begins with research. To accomplish these goals, PharmaGen faces a daunting challenge: we must identify as many of the genetic variations in the human genome as possible and trace them to specific diseases. To make this vision a reality, PharmaGen is forming a vital partnership with the people of western Pennsylvania. These visionary volunteers, half a million strong, are joining with us to accelerate our knowledge and help make the future a reality today.

"Won't you join with us? Visit the PharmaGen Web site now to find out how you can contribute, invest, or become a member our Keystone Club volunteer program.

"PharmaGen: the medicines of tomorrow from the knowledge of today."

At the tagline, the music rose once again, crescendoed, and ended with a clap of muted cymbals. The final image morphed to form a sleek, elegant, corporate front page.

No one said anything for a minute.

"Impressive," Leo said, breaking the silence.

"Lassiter thinks so," Nick said. "But how much of all this is just vaporware? Do they actually have a product yet?"

"I haven't heard of one," Riley said, "but they seem to have a great PR department. They're in the news all the time, talking as if the big breakthrough is just around the corner."

"They probably have an IPO coming up," Nick said. "You think all the talk is just smoke and mirrors?"

"There's no way to tell," Riley shrugged. "Pharmacogenomics is a promising field, but the problem is in doing the original research. Even with DNA micro array technology, looking for specific gene variations is a slow process. Then it's hard to determine which genes are involved with each disease or condition—it's hard to get the big picture. But the biggest problem is that, for their data to be reliable, they need an enormous population base to study. No one can afford to pay for it, so it all has to be done on a volunteer basis—that must be the Keystone Club they mentioned. PharmaGen's success depends on the sheer goodwill of half a million Pennsylvania residents."

"That's a lot of goodwill," Nick said. "Leo, check his e-mail. See if you can find any correspondence that might explain some of this."

"I already did," Leo said. "His e-mail has been selectively encrypted. I checked his installed program list; he's running PGP. It's a high-end encryption program. Without his key, we're not going to get into it."

Nick frowned. "I thought you guys could just type a few keys and hack your way into anything."

Leo mirrored his expression. "I thought you guys could just ask the flies and they'd tell you how long they've been there."

"So now what?"

"We can't see what he's e-mailed in the past," Leo said, "but we can see what he sends in the future. In fact, we can see a lot more than that." He took out a single, unlabeled disk and loaded it into the CD/DVD drive.

"What's that?"

"For want of a more honorable term, it's called spy ware. It hides on his computer, and it records every keystroke he makes. It records everything—e-mails, chats, instant messages, passwords—and it e-mails it all to us in tidy little reports. What's more, we can even set up a remote screen connection that allows us to see what he's seeing in real-time."

"You can do that?" Riley said.

Leo smiled. "I've impressed you! A most satisfying achievement. Yes, dear Riley, you can do that. Welcome to the world of corporate surveillance. Employers want to know how their employees are spending their office hours, and this is their answer. A lot of suspicious spouses and jealous lovers are finding applications for it too."

"But isn't this . . . illegal?"

Leo glanced around at their surroundings. "A moot point, don't you think?"

"So we can get his e-mails now? But won't they still be encrypted?"

"E-mails are encrypted when they're sent or stored. We won't be intercepting his messages, we'll be watching them as they're being typed, key-by-key."

"It sounds great," Riley said, "but what do we do now, just sit around and watch Lassiter surf the Web? Do we just wait until the right e-mail comes along?"

There was a long pause.

"You know," Nick said suddenly, "I feel a sudden surge of goodwill coming on. I don't know about you two, but I think I'll join the Keystone Club."

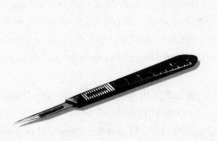

Mr. Polchak? Mr. Nicholas Polchak?"

"That's me," Nick said, dropping his magazine on the side table and rising to meet the smiling young woman.

"Welcome to PharmaGen, Mr. Polchak. My name is Kelli. Thank you so much for your call."

Her expression was warm and welcoming, and her eyes were round and bright. She extended her hand; her long fingers, tipped in a perfect French manicure, came almost to a knifepoint. Nick took the hand. It was as smooth and soft as Ultra suede, and he felt an almost irresistible urge to rotate it and study the surface more closely. Most impressive of all, she looked him almost perfectly in the eye. There was almost no hesitation at his enormous glasses, almost no fractional blink or subtle widening of the eye.

Almost.

"I'm a clinical research coordinator here at PharmaGen," she smiled. "Will you follow me, please?" She placed one foot behind the other and pivoted with perfect balance, heading for a doorway beside a smoky glass-and-chrome reception desk.

Nick watched her as she walked ahead of him. Her deep umber hair was pulled back tightly, except for one casual strand that curled across her right eye, creating the perfect synergy of professionalism and sensuality. Her immaculately tailored jacket was wide and sharp at the shoulders, tapering tightly to the waist before a deep back vent allowed it to curve around her hips. She was, like the lavish waiting room around her, a calculated image of precision and professionalism. She was the glossy cover on a soon-to-be bestseller, a story of imminent success.

They entered a small sitting room, much warmer and more intimate than the futuristic reception area. The lighting was all eye-level, without a trace of hospital-blue fluorescence anywhere. Golden light poured through textured lampshades, casting fireside shadows across the lush green plants and overstuffed furniture. On the walls, pastoral landscapes completed the image of friendship, trust, and security.

"Please have a seat, Mr. Polchak. Oh no, not there—try this one. It's full grain calfskin. Now, isn't that nice?"

"Like a big catcher's mitt," Nick said, settling back. He gave a quick thought to the ballpoint pen in his back pocket, but let it go.

"So—where did you come in from today?"

"Tarentum," Nick said.

"Tarentum. I don't believe I've heard of—"

"It's about twenty miles up the Allegheny, across the river from New Kensington and Lower Burrell." Nick leaned forward. "You have heard of Lower Burrell, haven't you?"

"Of course," she lied. "You know, you didn't have to drive all the way down here."

"You have offices in Tarentum?"

"We have offices in twenty-nine western Pennsylvania counties."

"That's remarkable for a company as young as yours," Nick said. "I hope you plan to buy stock."

"I'll be first in line," she said with a wink. She opened the chocolate-colored folder in her lap. "So you're here to join our Keystone Club."

"I'm here to learn more—this is all very new to me. I know the basics, of course: PharmaGen's goal is to develop personalized medicines by identifying disease-causing genetic variants in the general population."

"That's very good, Mr. Polchak."

"My mom says I have an aptitude for science. Tell me, does PharmaGen have a marketable product yet?"

"Not yet, but we're very, very close. Currently, we're focusing most of our resources on our population study. That's the Keystone Club."

"Half a million strong," Nick quoted. "That's an enormous research base. Do you have anywhere near that number signed up?"

"We will—with the help of people like you."

Nick nodded. "Tell me, how does one go about enlisting the cooperation of half a million people? They can't get that many people to vote."

"By making it easy to do, Mr. Polchak—that's the key. PharmaGen has formed a partnership with the University of Pittsburgh Medical Center. UPMC is the largest healthcare system in western Pennsylvania. Their facilities include twenty hospitals, four hundred doctors' offices and outpatient centers, fifty different rehab facilities—they even do in-home care. There are five thousand physicians in the UPMC network, and every one of them can sign you up for the Keystone Club. It's as simple as going to the doctor—even people who don't vote have to go to the doctor."

"Very clever," Nick said. "And what's in it for UPMC?"

"A big chunk of the company I'll bet—but you didn't hear that from me."

"OK, so I go to the doctor for my yearly exam. What happens then?"

"First of all, you'll find our brochures in every waiting area and exam room—brochures like this one." She handed Nick a slick four-color trifold with many of the same images and graphics from the Web site. "We also train nurses and phlebotomists to introduce our program to their patients, so you're very likely to hear about us face to face."

"And if I agree to participate? What happens next?"

"Here's the beauty of it, Mr. Polchak. All it requires of you is a signature, a blood draw, and a brief interview."

"The blood gives you the DNA sample—what about the signature? What exactly am I signing?"

"A simple release form, allowing PharmaGen access to your personal medical history."

"Whoa," Nick said. "I'm signing over my entire—"

"*Anonymously,*" she interjected with surgical precision, anticipating the objection. "Your name is removed from all medical records and replaced by a numerical code—the same code is attached to your blood sample. Our researchers never know who you are, Mr. Polchak; they only need to know that *this* blood sample goes with *this* medical history. Complete confidentiality is assured."

"And the interview—what's that about?"

"It's a family history questionnaire. We want to know about your environment and background, especially the incidence of certain diseases and conditions in your family—but once again, the information is encoded and remains completely confidential."

"So PharmaGen has my blood, my personal medical record, and the history of disease in my family—and that allows them to search for predictable variants in my DNA."

"Variants that could predict diseases like asthma, diabetes, hypertension, and certain cancers—those are some of the ones we're working on first."

"Let's go back to the subject of confidentiality for a minute."

"Everyone does," she said with a reassuring smile. "It's perfectly understandable. Let me tell you this: The results of your DNA analysis will not be revealed to employers, insurance companies, or anyone else who doesn't have a legal right to know. In fact, PharmaGen has obtained a Certificate of Confidentiality from the National Institutes of Health. That certificate prevents our researchers from revealing any information that might identify you, *even if subpoenaed by a court.*"

Her presentation was polished, and her enthusiasm was genuine. Nick smiled.

She was, without a doubt, a future stockholder.

"You're very good," he said. "Would you mind if I asked a couple of . . . *harder* questions?"

She gave him a mischievous grin. "I'm ready for you. Fire away."

"When is my name removed from my medical records—before they leave the doctor's office or after they arrive at PharmaGen?"

"Well, I . . . I have to admit, I've never been asked that—"

"Think it over. The doctor's role is merely to release the medical records and to obtain the blood sample. Who assigns the confidential numerical code?"

She knew this one. "PharmaGen does that."

"That means my records are *not* confidential when they leave the doctor's office, and not when they first arrive at PharmaGen."

"Perhaps—but immediately after arrival, they—"

"How *long* after arrival? And who specifically removes the name and assigns the numerical code? Do you know?"

The young woman said nothing.

"Let me try a different question. We have an aging population in the United States. In the future, the demand for safe and effective pharmaceuticals will continue to skyrocket. I can see how PharmaGen is poised to make an enormous amount of money—*if* they can come up with a product. My question is: just how far away is the first *personalized medicine*?"

"We're very, very close—"

"It wasn't a fair question," Nick said, ignoring her stock response. "That's PharmaGen's deepest secret, now, isn't it? You haven't gone public yet, so you're surviving off venture capital and up-front investments—and to keep those investments coming in, success *has* to seem very, very close. This company survives on the promise of success, and you're very good at promising. The waiting area, this room, even you, Kelli—everything about this place says, 'I promise.' "

She did her best to maintain her confident smile, but she seemed to grow awkwardly self-aware.

"PharmaGen survives on trust," he said. "It's worth more to you right now than any amount of venture capital. For you to succeed, the public has to trust you. What I want to know is: can you be trusted, Kelli?"

The young woman closed the folder in her lap. "I think your questions are a little over my head," she said. "If you'd care to speak to my supervisor—"

"Better yet," Nick said, "who runs the company?"

She did an obvious double take now, the first real crack in her flawless image.

"Well . . . I . . . our founder and CEO is Tucker Truett, but—"

"Where can I find him?"

"Mr. Polchak, you can't just—"

"Is he here? Is his office in this building?"

"No. I mean yes, but you can't possibly see him without—"

"You never know. Let's give it a try," Nick said, rising from the chair and heading for the door. "Let's see: We came from that direction, so the offices must be . . . *this* way."

"Mr. Polchak! Wait!" As Nick disappeared out the doorway, she grabbed for the phone and dialed a single number.

Just a few yards past the reception area the cosmetic image of success suddenly fell away, revealing underneath the raw flesh and driving pulse of an ambitious young company. Nick picked up a coffee mug from the first unattended desk and walked confidently past a series of crowded desks and buzzing cubicles.

"Hey, Bob," he called to a man at a computer screen, snatching the appellation from a desktop nameplate.

"Hi, Jenny. Great sweater," he smiled at a passing woman. If you can't look familiar to them, he thought, make them think they look familiar to you. Nick could fake it with the best of them, but he knew this is where his eyes worked against him; the guy with the funny glasses never blends in. It was only a matter of time before someone called his bluff.

He moved quickly through the maze of cubicles and file cabinets, seeking the nerve center of the office, following his instincts like a blowfly tracing the scent of blood in the air. The CEO of PharmaGen would not have a cubicle; he would enjoy the privilege of an enclosed office. Tucker Truett would have a window; not just a window, a corner window; and not just any corner window, but the window with the best panorama of downtown Pittsburgh. Nick headed directly for the opposite corner, where a break in the surrounding buildings allowed an impressive overlook of the Allegheny River and PNC Park. He stopped at the administrative assistant's desk directly in front of the closed door.

"Is he in?" Nick said casually.

The young man cocked his head and squinted at Nick. "And you would be—"

"Just a quick question. I know he's busy today."

At that moment, a security guard hustled up behind Nick, with an anxious Kelli following a safe distance behind. Inquisitive coworkers began to fill in behind them, seeking the source of the disturbance. The security guard stepped squarely in front of Nick, then craned his neck backward to get the full effect of Nick's imposing spectacles.

"Can I help you *sir*," he said, the last word dropping like a flatiron. It wasn't a question at all; it was a shot across the bow.

"I'm a potential investor," Nick said. "I had a couple of questions Kelli couldn't answer, so she suggested I take them up with Mr. Truett."

The guard glanced over Nick's shoulder; Kelli vigorously shook her head.

"I only need a minute," Nick said. "What's the big deal?"

"Do you have an appointment?" the guard said, folding his arms.

"For one simple question? He said if I ever had a question, I should just drop by."

"You're acquainted with Mr. Truett?"

"With Tuck? I've known him for years."

There was a long pause.

"No one calls him 'Tuck,'" the guard growled. "No one. Ever."

Nick nodded. "I thought that was probably over the top—but it was worth a try. Are you required to throw me out, or can I walk?"

The guard pointed firmly to the door. Nick turned to the crowd of onlookers and handed one of them the coffee mug. "If you people can find a variant in thirty thousand genes, why can't you make a decent cup of coffee?"

The crowd shuffled aside as he passed through.

"I'll be out of the office today, Bob," he called back. "Tell Jenny I meant what I said about the sweater."

CHAPTER 14

"This isn't how I thought I'd be spending the Fourth of July," Riley said.

Nick pulled hard on the oars, urging the skiff silently forward on the black waters of the Allegheny River. Each time he leaned back and pulled, Riley watched the lights of the city flash blue or white or yellow off the face of his glasses. The Boardwalk Marina disappeared into the shadows behind them, and they passed under the lights of the Sixth Street Bridge and out into the darkness of the river.

"Where *did* you expect to be on the Fourth of July?"

Riley shrugged. "Not on a rowboat in the middle of the Allegheny, that's for sure. Maybe up on Mount Washington, standing on the platform at the top of the incline, watching the fireworks at the Point."

"Then this is a definite improvement. You're going to have the best view of the fireworks you've ever seen."

Two hundred yards downstream, a fleet of boats large and small basked in the afterglow of the Bucs-Astros game earlier that day at PNC Park, dotting the river like a gaggle of geese. Within the hour the lights would die entirely, and the annual Fourth of July fireworks display would erupt from a series of barges opposite the Point at the mouth of the Ohio River. Nick pulled for the shadowy flotilla.

"That platform on top of Mount Washington," Nick said. "Did you expect to be there alone, or with someone else?"

"What?"

"You know, to watch the fireworks."

"With someone else, of course."

Nick said nothing for a minute. "Someone else like a boyfriend, or someone else like a family member?"

"Yes," she said. "Those would be the options."

Riley looked down at her feet. A half-inch of water puddled in the bottom of the boat, sloshing toward her shoes each time the oars caught the water and the boat dipped forward. She lifted her feet; they were her newest shoes, patent-leather slides, and she was not about to get them wet. She smoothed the front of her black silk spaghetti-strap dress, straightened her pearls, and shifted to the exact center of the bench. She picked up her beaded purse and set it on her lap, glancing over the side of the boat at the inky water.

"Nick, why this fixation on PharmaGen? Why are we going to so much trouble just to meet Tucker Truett?"

"You said you were interested in anomalies. As far as we know, PharmaGen is the only other anomaly in Lassiter's life. A quarter of a million invested in one company in a single year—don't you find that interesting?"

"So he's a lousy investor. What does that have to do with PharmaGen?"

"I can see why Lassiter might be interested in PharmaGen—but why is PharmaGen interested in Lassiter? A quarter of a million is a lot of money to your boss, but it's chump change to a group like PharmaGen. This is a high-stakes game; you don't sit down at this table unless you've got *millions*. Yet PharmaGen is letting Lassiter in on the ground floor. I'd like to know why. Besides," he said, filling his lungs with the night air, "this is a lot more fun than waiting for something to show up on the spyware."

"Is this your idea of fun?"

"Cheer up," Nick said. "You could have been stuck with some loser up on Mount Washington."

Riley turned and peered down the river. "Where is this yacht?"

"We can't miss it. It's seventy feet long, and it says *PharmaGen* across the stern. They say it's the biggest thing on the river from here to Cincinnati. Truett keeps it up at the Fox Chapel Yacht Club."

"Why couldn't we meet them at Fox Chapel and sail down together? I feel like an idiot rowing around in this little dinghy."

Nick said nothing.

Riley narrowed her eyes. "Nick—if there's something you haven't told me, this would be a good time."

"Did you know that it's exactly 443 feet, 4 inches from home plate to the river? A strong left-hander can reach the water on the fly—Daryle Ward did it just last year. If we had come earlier, and if we were in just the right spot—"

"Nick."

"You're a very suspicious person," Nick said. "It's very unflattering."

"I'm a pathologist. I'm paid to be suspicious. You're *here* because I'm suspicious."

"You have a point there."

They were approaching the rust-yellow trusses of the Roberto Clemente Bridge now, and the stadium loomed large on their right. Just past the bridge was the first circle of boats, the smaller craft dotting the perimeter of the flotilla like cruisers around ships of war. They could hear the rising sound of music and laughter now, and they could make out individual forms against the glowing deck lights.

"You told me we would spend the evening on Tucker Truett's corporate yacht," Riley said. "You told me you had arranged a meeting with Truett, and that we would get the chance to ask some questions about PharmaGen, and maybe get some insight into Dr. Lassiter's involvement."

"All true. The rest is just details."

"I want to hear the details."

Nick let out a heavy sigh. "OK," he said, "I arranged a meeting with Truett, but . . . he didn't exactly arrange a meeting with me."

"Oh, Nick. Oh, Nick, please . . . don't tell me that Truett doesn't know we're coming."

"What's a party without a few unexpected guests?"

Riley's jaw dropped. "You lied to me! You said we were invited to spend the evening on his yacht!"

"Actually, I said that we were *going* to spend the evening on his yacht. And we are—we just have to figure out how to get on his yacht."

They passed the first of the boats now, and Nick nodded a friendly "Evening" to the captain and his crew of one. He rowed a little closer than necessary to the next boat, hoping to keep Riley's temper in check. Like a lighthouse, her expression flashed between forced smiles at fellow seafarers and furious glances at Nick.

"Turn the boat around. Turn it around *right now!*"

"After we've come all this way? Come on, the hard part's over. We're almost there. See?"

As they passed the last row of medium-sized sport cruisers, they saw it. There, a respectful distance away, the gleaming hull of the *PharmaGen* stabbed up through the dark water like a white bowie knife. Its hull was so sleek and angular that it appeared to be in motion even at rest. A shining stainless steel railing outlined the contour of the deck from the tip of the bow to the stern. Three elliptical portholes poured orange light from the staterooms below deck, and a half-dozen extremely well-styled figures held champagne flutes and chatted on the sun pad and aft deck.

"Nick, we can't just row up and knock on the side of the boat!"

"That would be silly, now, wouldn't it?"

"You must have *some* kind of plan."

"Of course I have a plan. I wouldn't row all the way out here without a plan."

She waited for him to continue, but he said nothing. They

were almost alongside the boat now. Riley looked up at the yacht towering above them; she saw cream-colored skin showing through the draped back of a scarlet evening gown. She turned back to Nick.

"You're going to humiliate me, aren't you?"

"I'm going to get you on the boat," Nick said. "Whether or not you're humiliated is up to you."

She gave him a searing stare.

"Let's look at this thing logically," he said. "As you pointed out, we can't just knock on the side of the boat. And we can't very well throw grappling hooks over the side and climb aboard either. One way or the other, they have to invite us to join them. Now I asked myself, what would make them do that? There are boats all around here, and no one's inviting them to join the party. And then it occurred to me: What if we were in distress? It's the first rule of the sea: Boaters always stop to help others in distress."

"What kind of distress? You mean like losing an oar?"

"That hardly qualifies as 'distress.' They could just hand us a spare oar."

"What are we supposed to do, set the boat on fire?"

"A fire? On a boat with no engine? That makes sense. 'Excuse me, can you help us out? We seem to have spontaneously combusted here.' "

"Then what?"

"It has to be genuine *distress*. Our situation has to be desperate, immediate, irreversible."

"Nick—are you suggesting that we jump in the water?"

"Of course not—If we fell in the water, we could climb right back into the boat again. Unless, of course, the boat wasn't here anymore."

Riley looked at him in horror. "Nick, do you know what you're saying?"

He nodded. "You're going to lose your fifty-dollar deposit at the marina."

For the first time, Riley looked at Nick's clothing. He wore a beaten pair of loafers broken down toward the insteps, and he had no socks. He wore a crumpled pair of khakis and a faded navy sports coat that showed white threads around the sleeves and collar.

"Look at you! The water would *improve* that outfit! But look at me—I'm wearing silk! Do you have any idea what this thing would look like wet?"

"It'll give us just the right touch of pathos. After all, who would help us if we fell in in our swimsuits? It's only fifty yards to shore."

"Turn the boat around," she demanded.

Nick released the oars, folded his arms across his chest, and cocked his head to one side. "I think it's time for my 'Commitment' speech," he said. "Whose cause is this anyway? Who's helping who here? How is it that I seem to be more committed to your cause than you are?"

"I am committed—but not like this. There must be other options."

"I'm all ears."

"We can meet with Truett some other way."

"How? I tried to make an actual appointment—not a chance, unless you've got an extra million dollars in your back pocket. I tried to drop in on him yesterday morning—he's got tighter security than the governor. We have to catch him when he's standing still, and a man like that is rarely standing still—except when he's on this boat, where he was certain to be on the Fourth of July. So here we are, and there he is. What do you want to do, Riley? It's your call."

She said nothing.

"OK," Nick said, "I didn't want to have to resort to this, but you leave me no choice. I *dare* you, Riley. You gutless pretender, I double-dog *dare* you."

Riley's eyes narrowed to slits. She shoved her purse between her legs and grasped the sides of the boat with both hands. "I had to hire *you*," she growled.

Nick held on too. "You get what you pay for," he said.

On the count of three, they turned the boat over and plunged into the darkness.

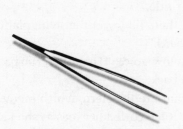

Hey! A little help down here!"

Nick and Riley bobbed in the water beside the PharmaGen yacht, just out from under the shadow of the hull, where they could be easily spotted by any of the guests on board. Beside them the overturned rowboat still floated, its ribbed aluminum bottom level with the surface of the water. Riley kicked, and one of her slides slipped off and disappeared beneath her.

"What if nobody hears us?" Riley said.

"Remember Cortez," Nick said. "There's no turning back now."

"Ho there! Need some help?"

Nick slowly turned in the water; behind them, a sixteen-foot Sylvan bass boat nodded in the water like a small bar of soap.

"Take us in a little closer, Doris! Move that cooler and make room for these folks!" The one barking orders, a large-bellied man with a full beard, reached over the port side and extended an aluminum gaff.

"No thanks," Nick said.

"What? You're kidding. Grab ahold now."

"No, really. We're OK."

"You just felt like taking a swim? What about your boat there?"

"Look, do you mind? We'd like to be rescued by a better class of people."

Doris shrugged and gunned the engine, drowning out the big man's colorful farewell as the bass boat motored away.

"What's the problem down there?" came a voice from above them.

"We had a little accident," Riley called back.

"Are you both all right? Is anyone injured?"

"We're OK—we just lost our ride."

"Swim around to the stern, then. I'll lower the swim platform. Climb on and I'll bring you aboard."

"There, now," Nick said in a low voice. "That wasn't so bad."

"Shut up," Riley whispered back.

They worked their way around to the stern, which seemed to take forever in the dark water. Riley curled her toes as she kicked in a vain attempt to hold on to her remaining shoe, but it was a hopeless task, and she finally allowed it to drift away in search of its mate. They could hear the hiss of a hydraulic lift; by the time they reached the stern, the swim platform was level with the surface of the water.

Nick grabbed one of the projecting handles and pulled himself up into a sitting position, facing away from the boat. Riley looked up at the small crowd gathered on the aft deck to observe their entrance. She glanced down at the front of her silk dress, then reached for the handle and dragged herself onto the fiberglass facedown.

"That was graceful," Nick said. "You look like Shamu."

"Do you mind? I'm trying to salvage a little dignity here."

"Good luck with that."

The platform immediately began to rise, and after a few seconds it locked into place again. The gate to the aft deck swung open, and a young man slid down the railing to the platform below.

"Everybody OK? What happened out there?"

"We were hoping to see the fireworks," Nick said. "I warned her not to stand up."

"You can watch the fireworks with us," he said. "I'm Tucker Truett, and you're my guests. Let's get you out of those wet clothes."

"Nick Polchak," Nick said, shaking Truett's hand. His grip was fast and powerful. Truett stood eye to eye with Nick, but he was even broader in the shoulders and much thicker in the arms and chest. "This is Riley McKay." Truett turned and smiled at Riley, who stood with her arms pinned across her chest. He did not extend his hand.

Truett's face was square and very lean; when he turned, Nick could see the veins in his temples and the sinewy lines of his jaw. His eyes were a pale cerulean blue, and his tight, wavy hair glistened under the last of the stadium lights. He was barefoot, and his long toes seemed to almost grip the deck. He wore crisp white slacks with knife-edge pleats, and his black poplin shirt hung open to reveal a single strand of gold. Black and gold—the symbolism wasn't missed by Nick, nor would it be by anyone else in Pittsburgh. Tucker Truett was handsome, powerful, and he exuded confidence. He was an electrified, neon billboard for the city of steel—and for a rising new company called PharmaGen.

They were joined now by some of the other guests, who gathered around them with towels and long terry bathrobes monogrammed with the PharmaGen logo. Three elegantly clad women ushered Riley below deck. Nick stripped off his own dripping jacket and shirt, pulled on a bathrobe, then dropped his khakis around his ankles and kicked them away. He followed Truett up the steps to the aft deck and exchanged brief pleasantries with two other men, who then descended to the salon to check the satellite TV for the starting time of the fireworks display. Truett stepped to a refrigerator in the cockpit, opened it, and handed Nick an Iron City Beer.

"Thanks," Nick said. "Nice boat."

"It's a yacht," Truett said. "Technically, a yacht is any vessel that carries another boat on board. We carry a spare."

"I could have used a spare tonight. Is this yours?"

"It belongs to my company—PharmaGen. Ever heard of it?"

"Who hasn't? As a matter of fact, I stopped by your office the other day to join your Keystone Club—but you'd have no way of knowing that, would you?"

"Nope. I'm proud to say, you're just a number to us. But thanks for helping out."

"A population study of half a million—that's a researcher's dream."

"It's an IT's nightmare—but that's part of the challenge. This company is built on information."

"Funny," Nick said. "I would have said your company is built on trust." He ran his hand over the cool white fiberglass hull. "What's a boat—sorry, what's a yacht like this worth anyway?"

"With the extras? About two million."

"That must have taken a sizable bite out of your venture capital. What did your board of directors have to say about it?"

"It was their idea." Truett cocked his head and looked at Nick more closely. "What do you do for a living, Mr. Polchak?"

"It's Doctor Polchak—I have a PhD. Technically, a PhD is anyone who carries a student loan the size of a yacht. I'm just a lowly professor from the backwater state of North Carolina."

"My, aren't we humble," Truett said.

"Humility is a nice quality, don't you think?"

"Not in my business. This yacht is almost twice the size of anything on the three rivers, and that's no accident. Been to a Bucs game lately, Dr. Polchak? What do you suppose it cost PNC Bank to put their name on that stadium? This yacht sits right here every weekend, and especially for every home game. We always turn the stern to face the park, and there hasn't been a game yet where the JumboTron didn't show the PharmaGen logo to thirty-eight thousand fans."

"When was the last time the Pirates had thirty-eight thousand fans?" Nick peered into the cockpit. The Euro-styled captain's chair looked like something from the bridge of the starship Enterprise. The instrument console was covered in high-gloss mahogany burl, and a soft blue light glowed from the radar and navigational monitors. "So this is all for advertising? Wouldn't a billboard have been cheaper?"

"This yacht is worth twice what we paid for it. The *PharmaGen* doesn't just sit in the river, Dr. Polchak; it dominates the river. We own the river, just as we will soon own the field of personalized medicine. As you said, this business is built on trust—on public confidence. You don't ask a man to invest by telling him, 'Someday we hope to be successful.' You tell him, 'We're successful *now*, and if you don't get on board you'll be left behind.'"

"*Are* you successful now? Where exactly are you in your population study? How close are you to your goal of half a million volunteers?"

"The research doesn't have to wait for half a million volunteers," Truett said. "Are you familiar with the Marshfield Clinic in Wisconsin? They're doing similar research, and their goal is only forty thousand volunteers—that's enough to produce statistically significant results. We have eight times that many now, and our research is well under way. It's a progressive effort: as the population study grows, so do the scope of the research and the reliability of the conclusions we draw. Once again, Dr. Polchak, it's all about *confidence*. Our study is so massive, so far beyond anything anyone else has attempted, that we will virtually *swamp* the competition."

"Big yachts swamp little boats," Nick said. "But size isn't everything; quickness counts. What if one of the little guys beats you to market with a product? And what about FDA approval, how long will that take? Just how far *are* you from a marketable product, Mr. Truett?"

Truett smiled.

"I know," Nick said. "Very, very close."

Just then, Riley emerged from the stateroom below. She was still barefoot, but she was now dressed in loose-fitting slacks and a breezy, open blouse with a camisole underneath. The clothes were casual, but very expensive; she was better dressed now than before her dive into the Allegheny. She stepped onto the aft deck, rubbing at her hair with a white terry towel. "Thanks for the hospitality," she said.

"Feeling better, Ms. McKay?"

"Much. I appreciate the clothes; I'll get them back to you."

"Keep them. Dana has plenty—I make sure of that."

"By the way," Nick said, "it's *Doctor* McKay."

"Another doctor? With all that education between you, you'd think you two would be better sailors."

"We all have our specialties," Nick said. "What's your specialty, Mr. Truett?"

"Vision, Dr. Polchak. I am an evangelist."

"And just what is your vision?" Riley asked.

"I see a world where no one ever dies from an adverse drug reaction; where physicians have an entire range of medicines to choose from to treat a deadly disease; where medications target tumors like smart bombs and leave surrounding tissues unharmed; where genetic susceptibility to disease can be determined in childhood, and possibly even prevented."

"Right out of the brochure," Nick said. "Where are the fireworks when you need them?"

"Why, Dr. Polchak—you sound like a cynic."

"Cynicism is the ugly cousin of humility, Mr. Truett. I don't think much of myself, but then I don't think much of anyone in *your* species either."

"My species?"

"What about you?" Riley cut in. "Surely you have a little *personal* vision in all this somewhere?"

"You bet I do. I see a world where patients think of medicines the way they think of coffee: they want it strong, they want it made their way, and they want it now—and PharmaGen will be there to serve the coffee. I see a world where aging baby boomers will pay anything to have the latest, strongest, and most *personal* medication. In other words, Dr. McKay, I see dollar signs—and I'm not ashamed to say it. I raised seventy million dollars to start this venture, and I plan to make a whole lot more in return. My goal is not to make money; my goal is to succeed—but if I succeed, the money will follow."

Nick watched him as he spoke. Truett would talk about PharmaGen all night, Nick thought. He was the genuine item, a true believer. He had willingly answered each of their questions, ignoring his invited guests for the opportunity to defend his dream to a couple of perfect strangers. His conviction and enthusiasm were hypnotic; he cast vision the way a dog sheds water, catching everyone within his reach. Maybe the yacht was worth two million, who knows? One thing was for certain—Tucker Truett was worth a whole lot more.

"I wonder if you know an associate of mine," Riley said. "Dr. Nathan Lassiter?"

"One of our early investors," Truett said. "A visionary himself."

"Oh? How so?"

"Most people invest their money in bits and pieces, a little here and a little there. They're trying to avoid risk—but that's investing out of fear, Dr. McKay, and that's no way to live. Life is a gamble, and you have to roll the dice. Dr. Lassiter is a visionary, he can see the future—*our* future. He placed his money on PharmaGen, and he was wise to do so."

"The dice don't always come up the way you want."

Truett smiled. "It's my job to see that they do."

One of the other guests emerged from the stateroom now, a

young woman almost as long and as sleek as the yacht itself. She was the lady in red, the one they had glimpsed from the water below. Nick watched her; she moved smoothly, silently, flowing like the river around them. She leaned up against Truett, slipped an arm behind him, and nuzzled his ear—but Truett showed no awareness of her presence. *She's an early investor too,* Nick thought, but the return on her investment wasn't yet clear.

"Speaking of risk," Nick said. "What about this Keystone Club?"

"What about it?"

"You're asking people to give you a sample of their DNA—but no one really knows just how much information is locked up in the DNA molecule. We can read a certain amount of it today, but tomorrow we may find a way to unlock an entire library of genetic information about the individual."

"That's what we're hoping for; it means that even more extensive research will be possible."

"It also means that people have no way to know what they're really giving you. It's like asking them to sign a blank check."

"But the check is not from their personal account. Don't forget, Dr. Polchak, they give this gift anonymously. No one knows who you are."

"Yes—'PharmaGen promises complete confidentiality.' That's a big promise, Mr. Truett."

"As you said, this whole thing is built on trust."

Nick slowly folded his arms across his chest. "So I give you infinite knowledge of my genetic makeup, and in return you promise to keep it a secret—is that the trade? You called yourself an *evangelist*—if I remember my Latin, the word means 'messenger of good news.' You definitely are a messenger, Mr. Truett, the best I've ever seen. My question is: are you sure this is good news?"

Truett let out a laugh. He pulled the lady in red in close and planted a kiss on her, as though he just now became aware of her existence. She was a prop, Nick thought, just a visual aid in his presentation, and this was his way of making a transition. He was sprinkling pixie dust on everyone, trying to lift the ship out of troubled waters.

"I understand that you two might have some cautions about all this," he said. "I find that better-educated people often do. That's why, early on, PharmaGen established an ethics advisory board to advise us on controversial issues like genetic privacy."

"Your own ethics advisory board? Isn't that like asking senators to vote for term limits?"

"Not at all. These are professional bioethicists, very accomplished and well-respected in their fields. They are not employed by PharmaGen, nor are they remunerated by us in any way."

"Who sits on this advisory board?"

"Our founding member was Dr. Ian Paulos. He's a professor of ethics at Trinity Episcopal School for Ministry over in Ambridge. He's been with us from the beginning—he helped us shape all of our privacy policies. If you really want to pursue this issue of genetic privacy, you should take it up with him."

"Thanks," Nick said. "I just might do that."

To the west, in the distance, there was a cannon retort followed by a booming echo. Three seconds later a brilliant red starburst illuminated the sky, dropping sparkling silver tentacles on every side. It was the signal flare, the opening volley in the Zambelli Family's annual fireworks extravaganza at the Point. On board the *PharmaGen* it was all hands on deck now, and the whole group pressed against the starboard railing to witness the aerial display. Each couple pressed tightly together, holding hands and standing side by side or cheek to cheek. Nick glanced at Riley standing stiffly beside him, and he wondered what would happen if he put his arm around her. Not an all-out embrace, not even a perceptible squeeze—just his left hand resting on her left shoulder. What would she do? He took a mental accounting of the night's activities: he had lured her out to the middle of the Allegheny River in a rowboat, then dumped her in the water; he had caused her to lose her shoes and purse, and had ruined her dress; and he had forced her to stand almost naked and dripping in front of better-dressed women. Nick could imagine her taking out a scalpel and severing his hand at the wrist.

He glanced at her again. *I dare you,* Nick said to himself, *I double-dog dare you.* He lifted his arm and rested it gently across Riley's shoulders.

Riley did nothing.

Nick smiled. "I love fireworks," he said.

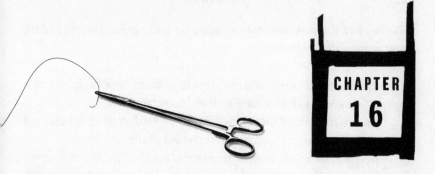

The *PharmaGen*'s twin diesels rumbled patiently, holding the boat steady in the water as the lower gates to Lock Number 2 slowly opened upriver. In the cockpit, Tucker Truett watched a handful of pleasure boats cautiously emerge, then gun their engines and curl off, leaving white streaks of foam in the black water behind them. Truett waited for a dozen or so smaller craft to enter the lock before him. It was more than civility that caused him to hold back. When the lock was filled and the great upper gates opened northward, the wake from the *PharmaGen*'s twin screws could turn smaller boats behind him into floating bumper cars.

Truett heard the lockmaster's go-ahead on his marine band radio. He nudged the throttle forward and pulled slowly into the lock, the great swan and her cygnets returning to roost upstream at the Oakmont and Fox Chapel marinas. He tossed a bow and stern line up to the lockmaster to secure his position, and then came the low, grinding sound of hydraulics as the lower gates swung closed behind him.

Truett had taken the *PharmaGen* up and downriver through the Allegheny's locks a hundred times. The process was as second-nature to him as riding an escalator. But this time when the lower gates locked shut behind him, sealed tight by the pressure of the rising water, a strange thought wormed its way into Truett's mind: Can the doors be reopened? Can the process be reversed? If he lay on his air horn, if he signaled the lockmaster, could he open the massive doors again and allow the *PharmaGen* to gently back out onto the peaceful lower river?

When is it too late to change your mind?

Truett sat alone in the cockpit now, staring silently ahead at the warning pattern on the black upper gates, watching the yellow stripes slowly dip into the water and disappear as the level began to rise. For the next twenty minutes, he had nothing to do but sit and stare and remember.

"To the ethics advisory board," Truett said, raising his glass in a toast. "May you keep us on the straight and narrow."

"And to fortuitous meetings," Zohar replied, raising his glass in return. " 'When comets cross, do the skies illumine.' "

The two men sat across from one another at the S-shaped conference table in PharmaGen's newly commissioned boardroom. The flowing curves of the table accented the soft, organic shapes of the chairs and other furnishings, all washed in tones of olive and gold and sienna. On the walls, a row of stark black frames featured digital photographs of Heinz Field, PNC Park, and, largest of all, the *PharmaGen* yacht.

"I want you to know how much I appreciate your joining our board," Truett said. "I know what a busy man you are."

"I consider it a great privilege." Zohar smiled. "I'm never too busy to help with a strategic new venture. Perhaps you could tell me a little more about your vision for this board."

Truett leaned back in his chair and folded his hands across his stomach. "Ultimately, I'd like to have a dozen or so members— well-known, highly respected ethicists like yourself, from all different philosophical perspectives."

Zohar smiled. "Then you see this board as largely a public-relations effort. I'm disappointed."

"No, not at all," Truett said. "Our efforts here at PharmaGen are going to raise a lot of concerns about genetic privacy and bioethics. I want to meet those concerns head-on, and I want the ethics advisory board to spearhead that effort."

Zohar ran his index finger gently around the rim of his glass. "Have you ever served on an ethics panel yourself?"

"Can't say as I have."

"Let me tell you how they operate. They always begin very politely, everyone sharing the same goal, colleagues all. Then individual differences in perspective begin to appear—not superficial differences, mind you, but disparities in fundamental philosophical assumptions. Soon each member becomes entrenched in his own position, defending his own precious *a priori*, becoming more and more intractable and defensive.

"They're like a group of travelers who came to a fork in the road long ago, and each chose a different path. Now all they can do is shout to one another to abandon their path and join them on their own. No one is willing, of course; they've all traveled far too many miles to turn back now. Soon the members tire of all the bickering and the backbiting, and the panel begins to cool down and collapse like a dying sun. The truth is, Mr. Truett, asking a diverse group of ethicists to form a panel is like asking Congress to have a discussion about politics."

Truett rocked slowly back and forth in his chair. "Then what do you suggest?"

"As I see it, Mr. Truett, I have two things to offer this wonderful venture of yours. First of all, you were very wise to form this ethics advisory board. There will be many concerns, and it will be a tremendous advantage to be able to assure the public that you are addressing them. And you need to address them—but not by collecting a smorgasbord of ethical opinions. As a leader, Mr. Truett, I doubt that you make most of your own decisions by committee; that would bring your company to a grinding halt, now, wouldn't it? So there's the dilemma: you need to address ethical concerns, but you need to get things *done*. May I suggest a simple solution? You need to work from a single ethical perspective."

"*Your* perspective?"

Zohar smiled and spread his hands. "Why not? I think you'll find we have much in common, Mr. Truett—a vision for the future, an appreciation of technology, and most of all, a certain *force of will*. Like you, I like to make things happen. That's the first thing I can do for you, Mr. Truett—I can help you make things happen."

"And the second thing?"

"I can help you refocus your vision."

"Does my vision *need* refocusing?"

"If you'll forgive me, I believe it does. Do you know the difference between a dreamer and a visionary? Focus. Any child can conceive some grandiose scheme or utopian future; it takes a visionary to recognize the attainable part of that dream and bring together the necessary resources to make it happen. You are more than a dreamer, Mr. Truett. You've proven that already. But visionaries need to learn to *refocus* their visions, or their visions may end up nothing more than dreams."

"*Refocus* as in keeping a single-minded purpose? Keeping your eye on the prize?"

"Just the opposite, actually. You see, there's also a difference between a visionary and a fanatic. A fanatic focuses only on the destination; a visionary learns from the journey. The true visionary understands that, though he has a clear destination in mind, other opportunities may present themselves along the way that have even greater potential. The visionary must be determined, but he must remain flexible. How does the proverb go? 'The mind of man plans his way, but the Lord directs his steps.'

"Perhaps an example will help. When automobiles first appeared in our country, the railroad barons were kings—they had enormous wealth and power. When the automobile industry began to grow, the railroads were in a perfect position to buy them out—but they didn't. Do you know why? Because of a simple lack of vision. The railroad owners told themselves that they were in the *railroad* business—and what does a railroad have to do with automobiles? If they had only had the foresight to say, 'We are in the *transportation* business,' today we would all be driving Union Pacific Town Cars and Santa Fe SUVs."

"Interesting," Truett said. "So how does this apply to us?"

"I'd like to encourage you to think outside the box, Mr. Truett. Regardless of your current mission statement, despite what it says in your annual report, you are not in the business of personalized medicine."

"Oh? What business am I in?"

"The business of *applied genetic information*."

Truett let out a laugh. "I'm sorry, Dr. Zohar. That sounds like semantics to me."

"I assure you it's not. Your ultimate goal is to develop personalized medicines—but along the way to that goal, I think you've generated some other very lucrative possibilities for PharmaGen to explore."

"Such as?"

"Applied genetic information," Zohar said again. "You know, I really have to congratulate you on what you've already accomplished here."

"I wouldn't break out the champagne just yet. We need a salable product first. We need a clear path to cash."

"But you have a salable product right now. Don't you see? It's the genetic information you've collected from over a quarter of a million residents of western Pennsylvania."

"That information is strictly confidential."

"I couldn't agree more. The information you collect should never be sold, transferred, or released to any second party. However, the good people of Pennsylvania have entrusted PharmaGen with this information, which allows the possibility of certain secondary applications *within* your company."

Truett shifted uneasily in his chair. "What sort of *secondary applications* are we talking about?"

Zohar looked at him penitently. "I must confess something to you, Mr. Truett. Our introduction last week at that reception was not, strictly speaking, *fortuitous*. I intended to meet you there. You see, I've been observing the progress of your company from the very beginning. It's just the sort of pioneering venture I might have attempted myself, as a younger man. I've collected quite a bit of information on PharmaGen—not just from your brochures and glowing press releases, but from other sources—external sources. I have contacts among your major investors, and they tell me that PharmaGen has all but exhausted its original venture capital. The cost of your population studies has been enormous, and it's now a race against the clock to see if you can produce that salable product before your company goes the way of so many other promising tech startups. How many ambitious young entrepreneurs have faced the same dilemma? To attract ongoing investment, you have to promise success. But to deliver that success, you require ongoing investments. And so, like so many other young companies, you find yourself out of cash—and you're doing your very best to hide it, aren't you?

"The financial cost of failure would be enormous for you—but the *personal* cost would be even greater. You see, Mr. Truett, I've also looked into your past business ventures; this isn't your first attempt at a visionary startup, now, is it? There was that rather innovative multilevel marketing effort you attempted, followed by a most ambitious Internet venture. Each time you raised several million dollars in venture capital to get your project under way, and each time you failed."

Truett's face grew red. "That was not my fault."

"Of course not. There were unforeseeable market forces, unpredictable actions on the part of your competitors, but investors rarely bother themselves with such details, do they? Despite all their financial sophistication, investors tend to operate by a rather simple rubric; *three strikes and you're out.* To borrow a metaphor from your beloved Pirates, Mr. Truett, you are standing at the plate for the last time. If PharmaGen fails, *you* fail, and it will be time for you to retire to a nice, safe, *conventional* job—perhaps as an entry-level investment banker. That's a nice little career—though I doubt it comes with a yacht."

Truett looked at Zohar as though he had never seen him before. He had misjudged the man's abilities, and that was an error he rarely made. He ran his eyes over the old man again, quickly revising all of his initial impressions. Zohar was small in stature and unassuming in appearance—but he carried himself like a man much older than his actual years. Truett saw now that Julian Zohar was not old, he was cunning; he was not polite, he was calculating; he was not weak, he was restrained. Truett had thought of the man as little more than a doddering old academic, someone who could lend a scholarly aura to his company's sterile image—but now he saw him in a different light. Zohar was a serpent—a cobra—and Truett was unsure of his reach, his speed, or the power of his venom.

The old man reached across the table and gently patted Truett's hand. "My young friend," he said softly, "you're in such a fragile position. A virtual sword of Damocles hangs above your head—and I would hate to see that sword fall, Mr. Truett. I would deeply regret the demise of this visionary venture. I would do anything in my power to help keep this company alive. That's why I wanted to meet you; that's why I sought you out. I want to show you that *path to cash.*"

Zohar smiled warmly. "Would a million dollars a month help? Tax free, of course."

The grinding of gears from the lockhouse brought Truett back to attention. There was a crackle from the marine band radio. In the smaller boats ahead of him, captains and their crews scurried over their vessels, coiling ropes and preparing for the remaining journey upriver. Truett glanced over the side of the lock at the lower river far below. When is it too late to change your mind? The question seemed strangely foreign to him now, a product of the black water and the darkness of the lock, and he cast the thought aside like a clinging bow line. There was nowhere to go but forward—and Tucker Truett was not a man to look back.

The water was at pool stage now, and the black-and-yellow upper gates began to groan open away from them. Truett stared at the warning pattern and watched as it disappeared into the dark of night.

CHAPTER
17

Dr. Ian Paulos ambled down the hallway at Trinity Episcopal School for Ministry, surrounded as always by an eager group of students who hovered around him like tugboats on a barge—a fitting image, since Dr. Paulos himself was built something like a barge. He was much too stocky to fit the expected image of a scholar, and he walked more like a longshoreman than a doctor of divinity. His uneven mustache completely obscured his lower lip, and his gnarly salt-and-pepper hair looked as though it could shatter any mortal comb. He wore half-spectacles on the tip of his nose, causing him to constantly tip his head back and forth, depending on whom or what he wanted to include in his range of vision. Wherever he went, at any time of the day, his left arm seemed to be forever curled around a stack of books, and his right hand always carried an ancient brown leather briefcase.

His introductory ethics courses, intriguingly entitled "Right and Wrong 101" and "Telling Good from Evil" were the most popular in the seminary curriculum, and they were impossible to contain within four walls. Dr. Paulos had a habit of ending each lecture by simply turning and exiting midsentence; anyone curious enough to know how that particular sentence might end would simply follow after him. Discussions invariably ensued down hallways, across courtyards, through parking lots—sometimes even in crowded rest rooms, much to the chagrin of the female students.

"I still say love is the highest of all principles," one student passionately contended. "The most *loving* thing to do is the *right* thing to do. 'You must love the Lord your God with all your heart, all your soul, and all your mind,' he quoted. "This is the first and greatest commandment. A second is equally important: 'Love your neighbor as yourself.' "

"Read the book and saw the movie—loved them both," Paulos said. "So this 'highest principle' of yours, this 'love'—what exactly is it?"

"What is *love*? Doesn't everybody know that?"

"Do they? What about that woman a few years ago who backed her car into a lake and drowned all her kids? When they interviewed her later, she said, 'I loved my kids. No one ever loved their kids more than I did.' Do you think she loved her kids?"

"Of course not."

"How do you know? Are you able to somehow get inside her head and tell me what she did or didn't feel?"

"Maybe she felt the *feelings* of love," another student said, "but she didn't act in a loving *way*."

Without breaking stride, Paulos turned to the student, tipped his head forward, and peered at her over the top of his glasses. Trinity students learned to read Paulos the way a hunter reads a bear: When he leaned back and squinted at you through his lenses, that was good; it was a sign of consideration or even respect. But when he leaned forward and looked at you full on, it was time to climb the nearest tree.

"*A loving way*," he repeated. "Whatever does that mean?"

She shrugged. "You know."

"I don't know—and I don't think you do either."

"A way that's . . . you know . . . loving." That merited a laugh from the entire group.

"*Love* is a ruined word," Paulos said. "It's been gutted like an old trailer—stripped of objective meaning. When you say 'act in a loving way,' what you mean is 'act in a way that *feels loving* to you.' Isn't that right?"

"I guess so . . . yes."

"That's an *emotivist* ethic," Paulos said. "Start with David Hume and then read A. J. Ayer's *Language, Truth and Logic*—then we'll talk again. You see the problem here? The woman who drowned her kids *felt* loving. She *feels* she did the loving thing; you *feel* she did an unloving thing. Is that all we've got here, Ms. Stuart, a difference of feelings? Then how do you ever tell her she was *wrong*?"

Paulos arrived at his office door now. He shifted his briefcase to his already overloaded left hand, reached for the doorknob, then turned to face the group.

"Let me give you a BB to roll around in your puzzle: Five centuries ago John Calvin wrote, 'Love needs law to guide it.' In other words, the highest principle is not love, but God—because without God, love *has* no meaning. Think it over."

Paulos turned the knob and stepped forward, bumping into the door with a resounding thud. He stepped back again and fumbled in his pocket for the key.

"A truly great exit ruined," he grumbled.

He tried the knob again, pushed open the door with his hip, and backed inside.

"Does this mean the lecture is finally over?" one student quipped.

"The lecture is *never* over. Education is not a preparation for life, my young friends, education is life. Now take what I've taught you and get out there and do some serious good."

Paulos nudged the door shut behind him, turned, and stopped. Standing at his bookshelf was a tall man with very large glasses, leafing through one of his books.

"I hope you don't mind," Nick said, motioning to the open volume.

"Mi libro, su libro," Paulos said, dumping his own stack on the edge of his desk. "The way I see it, no one really owns a book."

"My students would agree with you," Nick said. "That's why the books keep disappearing from Ready Reserve."

Paulos smiled. "A fellow member of the Divine Order of the Underpaid? Welcome, brother."

"Nick Polchak," he said, extending his hand. "I teach entomology at NC State in Raleigh."

Paulos took his hand. "Oh yes—Tucker Truett's assistant called me about you. How do you know Truett?"

"We met on his yacht the other night."

"Lucky you. I got the tour once, plus a nifty PharmaGen windbreaker. Did you meet his girlfriend?"

"I saw a woman. Do you think she was the same one?"

"I doubt it. Please, have a seat—just dump those books off on the floor. Sorry about the mess. I could tell you that you caught me on a bad day, but as an ethicist I'm obligated to tell the truth: it's always like this."

"You should see my lab," Nick said.

"I like you already. Can I get you something? A Coke, some tea?"

"Nothing, thanks."

"I'm an Episcopalian—I can get you something stronger."

Nick shook his head.

Paulos took a seat behind his own desk, leaned back, and put his feet up on the corner. "So you have questions about PharmaGen," he said. "Fire away."

"I understand you're a member of PharmaGen's ethics advisory board."

"*Ab initio*," Paulos said. "From the beginning. I'm the founding member of an esteemed panel of—let's see, how many of us are there now? Oh yes—two."

"Truett says you guys don't get paid."

"I'm supposed to serve as a kind of ethical watchdog for this company, Dr. Polchak. I could hardly be expected to bite the hand that feeds me, now, could I?"

"Then what's in it for you? That is, if you don't mind my asking."

"I'm an ethicist. PharmaGen is creating one of the first industries based entirely on genetic information. That raises questions about genetic privacy, questions that up until now have been largely theoretical. This whole area fascinates me—and it worries me too. I want a voice in all this."

"And what is your voice saying?"

Paulos smiled. "I'd like to hear a little of your voice first. Why the big interest in PharmaGen?"

"I was considering becoming part of their population study. I've got some of those questions about genetic privacy."

Paulos tipped his head down and peered at him over the top of his glasses. "First you corner the CEO, and now you track down the ethics advisory board? I smell a journalist, Dr. Polchak—or maybe a competitor?"

Nick said nothing.

"OK," Paulos said. "Ethically speaking, withholding information is not the same thing as actually lying."

"Why did Truett decide to form an Ethics Advisory Board? What's the watchdog watching for?"

"That's easy enough. Ever since the Human Genome Project, there's been a growing concern about the possible misuse of genetic information: employers refusing to hire because of future health risks, insurance companies charging higher premiums for certain genetic types, that sort of thing. *Genetic discrimination*, that's what they call it. That's why the Project formed the Ethical, Legal, and Social Issues in Science group—to help develop guidelines for the security and proper use of genetic information.

"Now along comes PharmaGen, asking half a million people to give away their genetic information free of charge—that's what you call a problem of confidence, Dr. Polchak. People want to know if PharmaGen can be trusted—after all, there are guidelines about genetic privacy, but there are very few laws. PharmaGen anticipated this concern by volunteering to police themselves; they formed their very own watchdog group, and they make sure everybody knows about it. You should have seen the press conference when this board was first formed—quite the gala event."

"Are you saying the board is just for the sake of appearance?"

"I'm saying that appearance is a very big part of it. Don't misunderstand, we have a very real function—but to be honest, our biggest function is simply to let people know we exist. We're the dog that watches the henhouse. We help create the public confidence that makes PharmaGen work."

"Why you? Why were you asked to join this board?"

"Who better? I teach at a seminary, Dr. Polchak. Who better fits the image of guardian of the public welfare and enemy of moral turpitude? I'm an Episcopal priest *and* an ethicist—that makes me twice as nice. All modesty aside, I'm a well-educated and well-published ethicist—but I'm not kidding myself about my real value to PharmaGen."

"You're a very humble man."

"I'm a very realistic man. PharmaGen is a corporation, not a discussion group. They have places to go and things to do—they have money to make. They need my presence, but they hope I'll sit in the corner and act like a good little boy. But I've been a bad boy—I've forced them to ask some hard questions about the risks involved in what they're doing."

"Have they listened?"

Paulos shrugged. "I watch the henhouse from outside the fence. I have no physical presence at PharmaGen. I serve as an advisor; how they implement my suggestions is up to them."

"What about the other guy? Who's the second member of the panel?"

Paulos folded his arms across his chest. "Now there's an interesting bird," he said. "His name is Julian Zohar. He's the executive director of COPE—the Center for Organ Procurement and Education here in Pittsburgh."

"Organ procurement?"

"You know, for transplants—hearts, lungs, livers, that sort of thing. The United States is divided into fifty-nine regions by the federal government. Each region has its own not-for-profit organ procurement office. Their job is to make the connection between potential donors and patients awaiting transplants. If you run your car into a bridge abutment, and if you've got a little red heart on your driver's license, then they call Zohar. Zohar checks the waiting list, takes the first guy on the list who matches your blood type, and zingo—you left your heart in Pittsburgh. Zohar runs our regional procurement office. It covers western PA and West Virginia, too, I think."

"So why Zohar? Why not another Episcopal priest?"

"You'd have to ask Truett that one. Maybe for variety—different ethical perspectives."

"Are your perspectives different?"

"Like night and day."

"How so?"

Paulos got up now, stretched, and walked around to the front of his desk. "Ethics is not just about right and wrong," he said. "It's about how you get to right and wrong. As an Episcopalian, as a Christian, I believe in the need for a grounded ethic—an ethical system that has its roots in unchanging values of right and wrong. I believe those values are found in the nature of God himself."

"And Zohar?"

"Like I said—a strange bird. Zohar did a doctorate in bioethics when the field was first emerging. He was very smart, very passionate, and very persuasive. He's an internationally respected bioethicist—or I should say, he was."

"What happened?"

"Transplant people are very concerned about definitions of death—they can't save a life until somebody else loses his, and the sooner he does, the better the odds of an effective transplant. The definition of death we use in America is a view known as whole-brain death: death is not pronounced until there is irreversible cessation of all functions of the brain and brain stem.

"But all the functions that make us really alive—personality, consciousness, memory, reasoning—they all involve the cerebrum, the so-called higher brain. If you lose all consciousness and personality, are you really alive? And if not, why should we wait around for all the lower-brain functions to cease as well? That was Zohar's position. He began to champion this view, known as higher-brain death."

"And that got him into trouble?"

"Not really—lots of people hold that view. He was just a little ahead of the curve on that one. It was what happened next that sank his boat. Zohar began to push an ethical view of organ procurement known as *routine salvaging,* a view that grants the state the right to harvest needed organs after death without the individual's permission."

"Wow."

"I agree. But think about it: when you set your garbage out on the curb, it's no longer your property. Anyone who wants to go through it can do so. Your rights over your garbage end at your property line. The routine salvaging view makes the same case for the human body: when you die, what's left over is garbage, and you give up your rights over it at death.

"You can see why a transplant person would love this view. His biggest headache is that he has to ask permission, and almost half the time he gets turned down. Wouldn't it be easier if he didn't have to ask?

"Zohar threw everything he had into this fight, but it was a no-win situation. In the Western world we place too high a value on the rights of the individual. We believe we have the right to control our own bodies, and that those rights continue even after death. To the Western mind, ideas like routine salvaging call up images of Dr. Mengele and Nazi medical experiments. When Zohar argued for a new definition of death, he was able to blend in with the crowd. But when he began to really push for routine salvaging—not just as an ethicist, but as a transplant officer—people recognized him for what he was: a pure utilitarian. The harder he pushed, the harder everybody else pushed back, until he finally gave up in disgust and just disappeared."

"Disappeared?"

"Dropped out of the ethical arena. Withdrew from panels and ceased publication. It's too bad, really. I used to read some of his stuff—very insightful. I lost track of Zohar completely until he suddenly turned up on PharmaGen's advisory board."

"Did that surprise you?"

Paulos shrugged. "I guess you can't expect burnout to last a lifetime. I was glad to see him again, actually—at least at first."

"The Christian meets the utilitarian," Nick said. "How has that worked out?"

"It hasn't exactly been a marriage made in heaven. Zohar is a big fan of PharmaGen—why wouldn't he be? PharmaGen is a utilitarian's dream: *the greatest good for the greatest number of people.* I don't get a lot of warm fuzzies from Zohar when I remind him about the rights of each individual, made in the image of God."

"You have concerns about where Zohar is taking the company?"

"I have concerns about a utilitarian approach to ethics. 'The greatest good for the greatest number of people'—what exactly does that mean? What is good, Dr. Polchak, and whose good are we talking about? I fear an ethical system that isn't tied down."

"Tied down?"

Paulos held up three fingers. "Three cowboys ride into town.

The first cowboy ties his horse to the second horse, the second ties his horse to the third, and all three horses run off together. Why? Because none of the horses was tied to the hitching post. That's the problem with an ungrounded ethic, Dr. Polchak—no hitching post. Things have a way of running off without you."

"And who are these cowboys?"

"I suppose they change in every generation. In our day and age? I'd vote for information, technology, and efficiency—but that's just my opinion. There are a lot of new frontiers—and there are plenty of cowboys out there."

Nick slowly rose from his chair and extended his hand again. "Thanks for your time," he said. "Lots to think about."

"You might want to follow up with Dr. Zohar. You know—talk to the cowboy in person."

"I just might do that."

"So tell me—have you decided to participate in the population study?"

"Would you?"

Paulos grinned. "You're asking the watchdog if the henhouse is safe. All I can tell you is, I haven't seen a fox so far."

Nick returned the smile. "What if the fox is already inside?"

CHAPTER
18

Riley pulled off the oven mitt and opened the door to her apartment. There stood Nick Polchak, his head buried in an open book.

"What do you know about organ transplantation?" he said without looking up.

"Nice to see you too," Riley said, heading back for the kitchen. "Do you want to come in, or are you going to finish the book first?"

Nick stepped slowly inside, leaving the door wide open behind him. He drifted toward the sofa like a sleepwalker and sat down, his eyes still glued to the pages.

"Water or wine?" Riley called from the kitchen.

"With what?"

"Food."

"Wine."

"I talked to Leo," she said. "I had him check the spyware reports from Lassiter's computer—"

"And there was nothing out of the ordinary," Nick cut in. "A few innocuous e-mails, visits to the usual Web sites . . . nothing we haven't seen already. I talked to Leo too—he said you called him twice today and three times yesterday. Give it some time, Riley. Have a little patience."

She poked her head around the corner and glared at him. "I spent the Fourth of July treading water in a Donna Karan because you couldn't wait to meet Tucker Truett. Are you going to stand there and lecture *me* on patience?"

Nick thought it was a good time to change the subject. "I saw Paulos today."

"And?"

"A very interesting guy."

"I should have come with you," Riley grumbled.

"We talked about this—you need to be at the office. You can't start disappearing all of a sudden. What would Lassiter say?"

"A senior pathologist is only on rotation eight days a month," Riley said, "but a fellow is on five days a week and every other weekend. How am I ever supposed to get away? When do I get to go with you?"

"*You never take me out anymore . . . All I do is work.* Didn't I just take you out on the Fourth of July?"

An oven mitt sailed through the kitchen doorway.

"What did you find out from Paulos?"

"I'm not sure yet. Did you ever hear of a guy named Julian Zohar?"

"I don't think so."

"He's the executive director of your local organ procurement organization."

"COPE? I've never met Zohar, but we work with COPE all the time."

"Really? Why is that?"

"There are about sixteen thousand deaths per year in Allegheny County, but we only do autopsies on about twelve hundred of them. Drug-related deaths, homicides, suicides, deaths in prisons or nursing homes—those are the ones that fall under the coroner's jurisdiction. Some of those people are potential organ donors—but our office has to view the body and sign off on it before COPE can claim the organs. You like garlic on your bread?"

"Sure."

Riley glanced at him as she set the plate down on the table. "You're not planning on kissing me again?" She paused. "Or putting your arm around my shoulder?"

Nick looked up from the book. Riley had already turned away and was headed back to the kitchen.

"Do you know how to tell male and female blowflies apart?" he called after her.

"What a fun evening this is going to be."

"It's their eyes. A male's eyes are very close together, almost touching. But a female's eyes are always spread wide apart."

Riley poked her head around the corner. "I'm waiting."

Nick shrugged. "I think females see more than males do."

"You needed a PhD to figure that out? Most males of all species are clueless."

Just then, a coal gray cat jumped onto the sofa and padded its way up onto Nick's lap, stretching and settling itself comfortably across his legs. Nick arched stiffly back and frowned down at the intruder. Riley returned from the kitchen, setting two glasses and a deep burgundy bottle on the table. She glanced at Nick's frozen posture, and at her cat contentedly stretched across his lap.

"Problem?"

"Your mammal is sitting on me."

"Nick, it's called a cat."

"Why do people keep mammals? What fun can you have with a mammal?"

"You keep poisonous spiders."

Nick looked up at her. "My point exactly."

Riley shook her head. "C'mon, time for dinner."

Nick looked down at the slumbering feline, its legs tucked invisibly under its overfed body. It seemed almost lifeless to Nick, except for the radiant warmth and the rumbling sound that came from somewhere deep inside. Nick frowned again; it looked like one big, amorphous, fur-covered blob.

"How do I pick it up?"

"How do you pick up an insect?"

"I use a sweep net, and then I drop it in a killing jar."

"That's a little hard on a cat," Riley said, scooping it off Nick's lap with one hand and dropping it onto the nearby recliner.

They sat together at the tiny dinette. Nick propped the book open against a stack of napkins, weighting down the curling signatures with the salt and pepper shakers.

"Tell me about organ transplantation," Nick said. "How does the system work?"

"I thought a forensic entomologist would know all this."

"Why? My species regenerates its own organs."

"Your species also gets stepped on a lot."

"That is a downside," he said. "This is good chicken. It needs salt."

Riley gestured to the salt shaker holding down the verso side of Nick's book.

Nick used it liberally, then extended it to Riley.

She shook her head. "I don't use salt."

Nick nodded slowly. "Tell me how the transplant system works," he said.

"Well, let's say you have a serious liver problem—"

"Let's say it's a kidney problem."

Riley paused. "OK, you have a *kidney* problem. So you go to a specialist, and he verifies that you need a transplant. Your medical information is entered into a database, and you're put on the national waiting list."

"Who runs that waiting list?"

"There's an organization called UNOS—the United Network for Organ Sharing, down in Richmond. They have the federal contract to administer the waiting list."

"Does that list include everyone who needs a transplant of any kind? All over the U.S.?"

"That's the whole idea. The list was created as a result of the National Organ Transplant Act of 1984. The goal was to ensure a fair and efficient system of organ allocation."

"How do you know all this?" Nick asked.

"People underestimate pathologists. We have to know something about every realm of medicine and surgery. We have to be familiar with every kind of procedure and its risks, and we have to be able to diagnose diseases by both tissue and fluid. Besides, in my residency I did a subspecialty in renal pathology."

"A national waiting list," Nick said thoughtfully. "All that information in one place. Who has access to that list?"

"Nobody."

"Nobody?"

"Not if you're talking about calling up the list and just looking it over. Nobody gets to do that. It's very private, and it's extremely secure."

"Then how is it used?"

"Suppose you have a motorcycle accident, and at the hospital you're pronounced brain-dead; that's when the local organ procurement organization goes to work. In western Pennsylvania, it's called COPE—the Center for Organ Procurement and Education. The hospital keeps you on a ventilator—they keep your *body* working—while COPE talks to the next of kin to request your organs for transplant."

"Do they always have to ask the family?"

"Not if you're over eighteen and you're carrying a donor card. But if you're underage or your wishes were never made clear, then somebody has to grant permission. So let's say they do—that's when COPE sends your medical information to UNOS, and UNOS sends back a matching donor list."

"And who's on that list?"

"Everybody in your local area that's a potential match, in order of priority. COPE calls the transplant surgeon in charge of the first person on the list and offers the organ; if he wants it, it's his; if not, it's offered to the second person on the list, and so on until the organ is placed. If no one wants the organ locally, it's offered regionally; if no one wants it regionally, it's offered nationally. That's how the system works."

"How is your place on the list determined?"

"The placement protocol is different for every organ. For kidneys, it's done by body size, tissue compatibility, medical urgency, and time spent on the waiting list."

"How long can you stay on the waiting list?"

"Forever," she said. "Some people are harder to match than others."

"So how do you beat the system?"

"You can't."

"Come on, Riley. What about our own governor a few years ago—what was his name?"

"Robert Casey," she said. "I was an undergraduate at Pitt at the time. Casey had a heart-liver transplant here at UPMC. He was on the waiting list less than a day, when the average wait for a liver was two months—six months for a heart."

"So it doesn't hurt to be first citizen of the state."

"It doesn't help either. They reviewed that case, Nick. Six people were ahead of Casey for a heart, and two for a liver. Casey jumped to the top of the list because he needed a multi-organ transplant—that's the only reason."

"You're telling me there's *nothing* the rich and powerful can do to manipulate the system in their favor?"

"Oh, there might be a couple of things. They could move to the transplant hospital with the shortest waiting list—the wealthy can afford to do that. Their surgeon could put them on the waiting list earlier than necessary, just to increase their seniority. And their surgeon could hospitalize them early, too, in order to make their need appear more urgent. But those are small things, Nick; none of them really tip the scales your way. For the most part, the rich and powerful have to just sit tight and wait—just like the rest of us."

Nick said nothing for a few minutes, busying himself with his dinner. Halfway to his mouth with a forkful of pasta and mushroom sauce, he stopped and set the fork down again.

"You said COPE sends the donor's information to UNOS."

"That's right."

"And COPE gets the matching donor list back."

"Right—all the potential matches in your local area."

"The size of that list would change from area to area. What about this area? They must do a lot of transplants in Pittsburgh."

"UPMC Presbyterian does. It's a huge transplant center."

"So when COPE gets a matching donor list, it could show most of the people at UPMC Presbyterian waiting for that organ."

"It could, yes."

"Think about it," Nick said. "Nobody gets to browse the waiting list, but every time COPE submits a donor's name, they get to see a *piece* of that list."

"In a way, yes."

"So if COPE wanted to, they could compile a list of all the people awaiting a kidney transplant in this area. And by comparing those lists over time, they could know how long each person has been waiting for their kidney."

"I suppose so—but why would they want to?"

"Listen to this," he said, turning to his open book. " 'The French law on organ procurement adopted in 1976 is one that presumes the consent of persons who do not, during their lifetime, expressly refuse to have their organs taken on their death. The law states that "an organ to be used for therapeutic or scientific purposes may be removed from the cadaver of a person who has not during his lifetime made known his refusal of such a procedure." ' According to this book, laws like this exist in Austria, Belgium, Finland, Italy, Norway, Spain, and Switzerland."

"It's called 'presumed consent,' " Riley said. "They *presume the consent* of the donor unless he says otherwise."

Nick frowned. "I thought I was going to impress you. OK, smart girl, try this one: 'Within the United States, at least two states have considered laws that would, if enacted, have properly been called presumed consent laws.' Maryland is one of those states; for one hundred dollars, name the other one."

"Pennsylvania," Riley said without looking up. "It didn't pass." She pushed her plate away and looked at him. "Where are you going with all this? Why the sudden interest in organ transplantation?"

"Julian Zohar," Nick said. "Executive Director of COPE. He's the guy who pushed for this law in Pennsylvania."

"Why wouldn't he? That kind of law would make COPE's job a whole lot easier."

"He's also a member of PharmaGen's ethics advisory board."

"So? What's the connection?"

"Ian Paulos told me that the ethics advisory board exists mostly to instill public confidence—to convince people that PharmaGen can be trusted to do the right thing. Paulos was brought on because he has the perfect image—he's an Episcopal priest. But Paulos gave me the feeling that his ethical input is not really valued. Paulos wants to talk about ethical concerns, and Truett wants to build a company.

"Then PharmaGen brought on a second ethicist: Julian Zohar. Zohar is philosophically much more to PharmaGen's liking—he likes to get things done. So the ethics advisory board stops with just two members, Paulos and Zohar. Publicly, they serve their function as symbols of moral uprightness. But privately, they butt heads. Zohar says 'go,' Paulos says 'slow.' I wonder who really has Truett's ear?"

"Where is all this taking us, Nick? We start with Lassiter, then we drop in on Truett, then you go to see Paulos, and now it's this Zohar guy. Aren't we getting off track here? What's the tie-in with all this?"

"Remember the blowfly," Nick said.

"The clueless one or the female?"

"The female. She finds a body by tracking molecules of blood in the air. First a single molecule, then a small cluster, then an even larger one, back to the source of it all. The blowfly follows the path of increasing concentration—that's what we're doing here. Follow your nose, Riley. We started with the anomalies in Lassiter's autopsies. Then we found that he's investing enormous amounts of money in a single company—PharmaGen. That's more than a wild investment. What gives Lassiter his confidence in PharmaGen? And why is PharmaGen willing to take on such a small-time private investor?

"Next we visited Truett. PharmaGen is about to make a ton of money—*if* they can keep public confidence long enough to produce a marketable product. But when we asked about things that could get in the way, pesky little things like ethical concerns over genetic privacy, who did he direct us to? Not Zohar, but Paulos—he never even mentioned Zohar. But Paulos tells me that he's mostly a figurehead, and that Zohar may be the real conscience behind the company."

"My head is spinning," Riley said, rising from the table. "I need to lie down for a minute—it's been a long day." She moved to the sofa and stretched out facedown. Nick turned in his chair and watched her. She seemed especially weary tonight, and she moved more slowly than usual. There was a sort of heaviness about her. She straightened slightly and grimaced, rolling her shoulders from side to side.

"Want me to rub your back?"

"What?"

"Your back seems to give you a lot of trouble. Want me to rub it for you?"

"It won't help."

Nick picked up his chair and carried it to the sofa, setting it down beside Riley. "Want to hear a wild idea? What if Zohar and Truett and Lassiter have found a way to create a black market in human organs?"

Nick watched Riley closely. She blinked once but said nothing.

"You're still not impressed. Now I'm really disappointed."

"The idea occurred to me," Riley said, "but it's crazy."

"Is it? There have been attempts before—in the Philippines, in India, even in England. We know that Julian Zohar is a big fan of 'routine salvaging' or 'presumed consent,' or whatever you want to call it. What if he found a way to pull it off? What if Lassiter refused to release that first kidney for transplant because he had some other use for it? What if you're being shut out of autopsies because Lassiter doesn't want you to see what's happening behind closed doors? What if Lassiter is 'salvaging' organs from cadavers for Zohar, and PharmaGen is acting as some sort of go-between?"

"C'mon, Nick," Riley said, sitting up slowly. "That's an old urban legend. It's just not possible."

"Why not?"

"There are a dozen reasons. How many people would it take to pull off something like that? Where would the organs be removed? At the coroner's office? We don't get bodies until hours after they're dead, and the organs would no longer be viable. And what does Dr. Lassiter do, just drop a kidney in a cooler and walk out like it's his lunch? Where would these organs get transplanted? What doctor would do that? What hospital would allow it?"

"What if—"

"Nick—there are a *dozen* reasons, and I'm just too tired to go into them all tonight." Riley stood up and stretched painfully.

Nick looked at her again. He saw the droop in her shoulders, and he heard the dullness in her voice. Riley McKay was strong and she was stubborn, but her exhaustion was showing through like the bones behind her lucent skin.

"I'm worried about you," Nick said.

Riley stopped and looked at Nick. "I like you too," she said. "You can be a very sweet bug man. You don't know what your help means to me."

"No, I don't. I wish you'd tell me."

She put one hand on his chest and spoke slowly and deliberately. "Nick, I think it would be better . . . if we *both* tried . . . to keep this on a professional level."

Nick paused. "Want to know what *I* think?"

"No," she said. "I'm sorry, Nick. I'm just telling you the way it has to be. Now if you'll excuse me, I really need to get some rest. Can you let yourself out? Just lock the door behind you when you leave."

Nick watched her turn and shuffle slowly down the hallway toward the bedroom.

"I've got a long drive home," he called after her. "Mind if I use the bathroom?"

She reached in an open doorway and flipped on a light switch, then continued silently down the hallway, closing the bedroom door quietly behind her.

Nick shut the bathroom door and turned on the water in the sink. He quietly opened the white porcelain medicine cabinet and looked inside. There were three shelves containing cosmetics, deodorants, lotions, and a predictable array of items for personal hygiene and first aid. On the lowest shelf, front and center, were three prescription medicine bottles. Nick took out a pen and copied down the information from the label of each.

He flushed the toilet, turned off the light, and quietly let himself out.

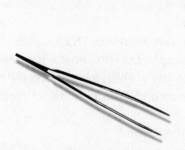

"Let me get this straight," Leo said. "Somebody dies, the coroner's office gets the body, and somebody strips it for parts before they release it for burial. Right?"

"Wrong—somebody strips it *before* it gets to the coroner's office."

Nick raised his head to get the waitress's attention. It wasn't difficult; she had been periodically glancing over at the man with the funny glasses for the last half-hour. Nick pointed to his coffee cup.

"Remember I told you about the guy in the cooler and the wound on his back, just below the ribs? It was tack-sutured shut. That's not a wound, Leo, it's an *incision*—and I found two maggots in that incision. That means it was made out of doors, and it was made sometime before dark—because blowfly activity tends to stop at night. The time of death was around dusk the night before the body was discovered; that means the incision was actually made at the time of death."

"Made by whom?"

"I don't know."

"Made *why*?"

"I think it was made to remove the kidney."

"For what purpose?"

"Again, this is just a theory: to offer the kidney for transplant."

"How? By selling it on eBay?"

"A guy actually tried that once, remember? I don't have all the details worked out, Leo, but look at the pieces. Zohar is the director of an organ procurement office. He knows who's waiting for a transplant locally, he knows how desperate they are, and with a little additional research he knows what they can afford to pay. PharmaGen collects genetic information from people all over western Pennsylvania. Truett could easily provide a match with someone on Zohar's waiting list."

"A *match*?" Leo glanced over both shoulders. "Nick, Truett isn't collecting information on *dead* people. Do you know what you're saying? If Truett is making matches with living donors, they're not just following these people around until they die of natural causes."

"No," Nick said. "They're killing them."

Neither man said anything for a minute.

"Nick, this is more than slightly illegal. Why would Truett risk such a thing?"

"Maybe to keep a startup afloat. He's got to keep the cash coming in until they get a product to market—and he's got an expensive lifestyle. Then there's Lassiter—he's a pathologist, he works in the coroner's office . . . If a kidney was removed at a death scene, who would be in a better position to cover it up? Think about it, Leo: This explains Lassiter's investments in PharmaGen—and where he's getting the money to make them. Lassiter's making sure that PharmaGen succeeds—and when they do, he'll be in a position to cash in big time."

"And Zohar? What would be his motivation?"

"That's what I want to find out," Nick said. "Leo, listen: Riley told me that no one has access to the UNOS waiting list. Do you think *you* could break into it?"

"Not likely. It's a federal database—a *medical* database—and privacy would be a huge priority. I would anticipate several layers of redundant security."

Nick thought for a minute. "Riley says that most of the transplants in our area are done at UPMC Presbyterian; wouldn't they keep a list of their own people waiting for transplants?"

"That would make sense."

"And isn't it likely that a single hospital's database would be easier to break into than the one at UNOS?"

"I would think so. Of course, I won't know for sure until I try." He lowered his voice. "I assume you're asking me to try?"

"I need a list of everyone at UPMC Presby who's waiting for a kidney transplant—no other organs, just kidneys. And if you find that list, Leo, I want you to look for *past* lists. Can you do that?"

"I can check for archived files," he said, "or for backups of the whole system. It could take a couple of days. What are you looking for?"

"I want to find out who used to be on the transplant list who isn't anymore. I want to know why they dropped off the list."

"Either they died, or they got their kidney. What other reason could there be?"

Nick shrugged. "Maybe they got a better offer."

"I don't know," Leo said. "This whole idea seems too fantastic to be possible. That guy in the cooler—are you positive his kidney was missing?"

"No."

Leo raised both eyebrows. "A minor detail."

"We didn't have time to check. The three deputy coroners came back with the pizza, and I had to kiss Riley."

Leo did a thoroughly Italian double take. "You kissed Riley? Where?"

"On the lips, of course."

"No—*where* did you kiss her?"

"In the cooler. At the coroner's office."

Leo leaned forward and thumped Nick on the forehead with the butt of his palm. "Let me explain something to you. A woman like Riley should be kissed over the Salmon Wellington at the LeMont, looking out over Mount Washington at the lights of the Golden Triangle. A woman like Riley should *not* be kissed in a cooler, at the coroner's office, surrounded by dead people in plastic bags."

"I had to think fast."

The waitress arrived and lifted the carafe to Nick's cup. "Bring my friend decaf," Leo said. "He's been thinking too fast."

"I put my arm around her too."

"Where? At a landfill?"

"No, on a seventy-foot yacht in the Allegheny, watching the fireworks display at the Point."

Leo looked at him. "How did you get access to a seventy-foot yacht?"

"We rowed up to it in a dinghy and then flipped the boat over."

Leo thumped him on the forehead again.

"Would you cut that out?" Nick said. "That hurts."

"It ought to hurt—I'm trying to knock a hole in it. Do you know your problem, Nick Polchak? You spend your whole life *up here.*" He tapped hard on Nick's head with his index finger. "You're trapped inside this . . . this *charnel, this sarcophagus.* Your whole life is spent thinking; you have no senses—no sense of touch or taste or smell. And do you know why you have no senses? It's this business of yours—all these flies and maggots and decomposing bodies! You've shut down your senses, Nick—you've had to, just to survive."

"That's ridiculous."

"Is it? Let me ask you something: what does Riley McKay smell like?"

Nick paused. "Well, since she works at the coroner's office, I suppose she would smell like—"

Leo reached out to thump him again, but Nick ducked away.

"You see? Even when you try to use your senses, you're still *thinking.* Listen to me, Nick. Riley McKay smells like lavender. Have you ever noticed? And she uses Trésor from time to time, but she lets it wear off—it leaves just the slightest hint behind. Have you ever listened to the sound of her voice, Nick? Not the words themselves, but the *sound*?"

Nick's eyes floated upward behind the huge lenses. "It sounds like . . . a wind chime," he said distantly. "Even when she's angry."

Leo looked at him, then leaned forward and spoke softly. "Nick, let me ask you something: are you experiencing ordinary human emotions toward this woman? Because from you, I find that frightening."

"So do I," Nick said. "It's been a long time for me."

Leo paused. "You're serious?"

Nick said nothing.

"This complicates things."

"It gets worse. I was at her apartment tonight. I've been noticing some things about her. Her back seems to bother her a lot, and she tires out easily."

"She's a pathologist. What did you expect?"

"But I've noticed swelling in her ankles—she's too young for that. And she never uses salt; isn't that a little odd? So I checked her medicine cabinet for prescriptions."

"An excellent start to a relationship," Leo said. "Always check their meds."

"Leo, I stopped by a pharmacy on the way over here. Riley has some kind of kidney disease. It could be serious."

"How serious?"

Nick shook his head.

"This waiting list from UPMC Presbyterian," Leo said. "Is there any particular name you're looking for?"

Nick said nothing.

"Nick, if this black market theory of yours is correct—if Riley's name is on that waiting list—then which side do you think she's on in all this?"

"I don't know," Nick said. "But I'd better figure it out. I need to know which side *I'm* on."

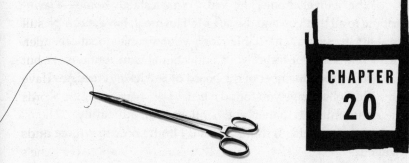

CHAPTER 20

Julian Zohar ran his hand across the thick hardwood mantel, admiring the hand-carved woodland scene on the frieze that supported it. The fireplace beneath it was at least fifteen feet wide; the chocolate gray flagstone that covered it was hand-picked from the fields of Pennsylvania. Above the mantel, a formidable-looking man stared out from a full-length portrait framed in burnished gold. Twenty feet higher, the ceiling sprawled like the roof of a cathedral, a soft white canopy ribbed with thick veins of inlaid wood. The room below was awe inspiring. One corner was dominated by a Steinway concert grand, another by a life-size bronze; in between, rich upholstery and elegant furniture settings dotted the floor like luxuriant oases.

There was a sound at the doorway. Zohar turned to see a late-middle-aged woman in a motorized wheelchair approaching, escorted by a private nurse.

"Mrs. Heybroek," he smiled, "how nice to see you."

She extended her hand to him. He cupped it in his own right hand and patted it gently with his left.

"Have we met?" she said, cocking her head slightly.

"We have not; my misfortune. I'm Dr. Julian Zohar, executive director of the Center for Organ Procurement and Education here in Pittsburgh."

The woman's eyes widened. "Have you found a match? Is that why you're here?"

"Perhaps we could speak about that—in private."

The woman dismissed the nurse with a quick wave of her hand and watched until she disappeared through the archway into the darkness of the adjoining room. Then she turned to Zohar again—but Zohar was now occupied admiring an ornate mahogany breakfront.

"What a lovely home," he said. "What a stately home—a fitting tribute to all that you and the late Mr. Heybroek have accomplished in your lives: your charitable work, your sizable donations to the arts—and let's not forget your educational contributions. Wasn't Mr. Heybroek a member of the board of Sewickley Academy?"

"Mr. Zohar, have you found a *match*?"

Zohar turned to her and smiled sympathetically. "There's no match," he said. "I think you and I both know that there never will be."

He turned away again and continued his tour of the room, running his hand over the surface of a plush sofa, sampling the scent of a lavish flower arrangement, or stepping back to admire a particularly fine oil painting.

"This rural scene—it's an original, isn't it? A Pissarro, if I'm not mistaken."

"Mr. Zohar, what is the purpose of your visit? If this is not about my kidneys—"

"Oh, this is definitely about your kidneys," Zohar said. "It's an amazing thing, isn't it, the way our current transplant system works? Or perhaps I should say, *doesn't* work. Did you know that there are more than eighty thousand people just like you, hoping and praying for a kidney or a liver or a heart? Sixteen of them die each day without receiving it. It's tragic; but I don't have to tell *you*, now, do I?"

Zohar walked slowly back across the room now, taking a seat on a settee beside the woman's wheelchair. He leaned back, folded his hands neatly in his lap, and gazed intently into the woman's eyes.

"Do you know *why* this problem persists, Mrs. Heybroek? Do you know why you'll never get your kidneys? Because, despite all of the advances in medical technology, the current transplant system still requires us to ask *permission* to obtain an organ. Here you sit, waiting for a statistically improbable event—waiting for someone with your rare blood type to fall off a motorcycle or suffer a stroke—and even then, we have to ask. The fact is, Mrs. Heybroek, half the time the family will say no.

"And did you know that, even if a matching kidney is discovered, the law requires it to be offered regionally first? That means if someone in, say, Philadelphia falls off that motorcycle, his kidneys must be offered to someone in that region first, even if that person's need is less critical than your own—even if that person is less *deserving*. So many inconsistencies," he said sadly. "So much injustice."

Zohar stood up, put both hands in his pockets, and began to slowly wander around the room again, this time shaking his head sadly over each piece of furniture or work of art. "It's ironic," he said. "Despite all your power and influence, despite all your contributions to society, you will have to die along with the rest of them. Your money is of no help to you now. You're the victim of an arbitrary, outmoded set of bureaucratic regulations."

"Stop this!" the woman shouted. "Don't you think I know these things? Did you come here just to gloat?"

A look of profound compassion came over Zohar's face. "Is that what you think? No, Mrs. Heybroek, I didn't come here to gloat. I came here tonight to offer you your kidneys."

She looked at him in astonishment.

"I'm an ethicist," he said. "In my ethical system, organs would be allocated on the basis of *utility*—who would benefit from them most? Who could use them for the greatest good? In my ethical system there is a concept known as *social worth*. Look around you, Mrs. Heybroek. Who could seriously argue that your life is worth no more than that of, say, an indigent? Or a criminal? Someone who has spent his life taking from others, instead of making a contribution? You've contributed so much to this world, Mrs.

Heybroek, and you have a lot more still to give. I want to help you make that contribution."

"How?" she said in almost a whisper.

"I believe you have the right to obtain a new pair of kidneys. And since you've worked so hard to amass a personal fortune, I believe you should be able to use that fortune to obtain them. Why not? You've *earned* the right."

"Stop these riddles," the woman said. "If you really have something to offer me, let me hear it."

Zohar smiled. "You are currently on the waiting list for a kidney transplant; you've been on that list for almost three years now. Next week you will announce to your physician that you have lost hope, and that you wish to be removed from the waiting list and simply go home to die in peace. And you will go home, Mrs. Heybroek, but you will not die. I will provide you with your pair of kidneys. Your transplant surgery will take place in a state-of-the-art surgical center. You will then return home to convalesce in seclusion for the next twelve months, during which time you will experience a miraculous 'recovery' from your end-stage renal disease."

"*You* will provide my kidneys? How? Where will they come from?"

"As an ethicist, I insist on a policy of strict confidentiality. I will not reveal the source of your organs, nor will the donor's family ever know who has received them."

"But you must be going outside the legal system."

"The *legal* system? I'm going outside the *unethical* and *unjust* system, Mrs. Heybroek; a system that's more than happy to let you die to protect the rights of someone with virtually no social value."

"I can't be a party to something like this."

"Can't you?" Zohar turned to the painting suspended over the fireplace. It was the focal point of the entire room. Two recessed halogen lights illuminated the painting, creating a fiery glare in the center of the glossy canvas. "James Ludlum Heybroek," he said. "Quite a man. He foresaw the decline of Pittsburgh's steel industry in the sixties, and he helped pioneer the transition from an industrial to a technological economy. He was a leading figure in Pittsburgh's second Renaissance, wasn't he? Three Rivers Stadium, the USX Tower, PPG Place, the Mellon Bank Tower . . . so many men were indebted to him—and he called in a few of those debts, didn't he? Debts that ruined other businesses, debts that even resulted in a couple of notable suicides."

"How *dare* you—"

"Don't misunderstand, Mrs. Heybroek. I have the greatest respect for your late husband. I'm simply pointing out that people of power and influence are accustomed to making hard decisions. I didn't just show up on your doorstep tonight. I've spent a good deal of time researching you and your family's history. You're an impressive person, Mrs. Heybroek, no less so than your husband. You didn't get where you are today through timidity and caution, now, did you?"

The woman narrowed her eyes and lifted her chin. "How much?" she asked.

"Three million dollars. By electronic transfer to a series of offshore accounts."

"Three million—"

"A small price, considering. Look at it this way, Mrs. Heybroek: I'm not really charging you, I'm empowering you. Money is power, that's what they always say, but right now your money has no power. You're about to die with three million dollars in your pocket, and it will be of no value to you then. I'm giving you back the chance to get something for your money."

"I could have you arrested for this."

"You could—but you'd be signing your own death warrant, wouldn't you? I'm not offering you an option, Mrs. Heybroek, I'm offering you your *only* option. Where else will you get your kidneys?"

"I . . . I need to know where the kidneys will come from."

Zohar sat down beside her again, picked up her left hand, and cradled it gently. "Where did that lovely dress come from? Paris? New York? Where did your wheelchair come from? Mexico? China? Do you know? Do you really care? When you purchase a product, Mrs. Heybroek, you don't concern yourself with the process of production and distribution. That's what you pay other people for."

She said nothing but stared straight ahead.

Zohar reached into his coat pocket, took out a business card, and placed it in her hand. He rose and stepped to the doorway, where he stopped and turned back.

"You are a woman of great power," he said. "Please—exercise that power. I want you to live."

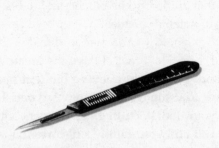

Smoke poured from the toaster oven. Nathan Lassiter pawed the piece of blackened toast onto the counter, spit out an expletive, and shoved all four fingers into his mouth like his infant son used to do. He stood at the sink, scraping off the layer of crumbling carbon with a knife, when his cell phone rang. He dropped the toast into the sink and picked up the phone.

"Lassiter, what is it? Oh . . . it's you." He jabbed at the remains of the toast with the point of his knife until it folded like a little umbrella and disappeared into the garbage disposal.

"I'm fine, Margaret. No, I'm fine—I'm just a little busy, that's all." He felt the glass decanter in the coffee maker; it was cold. He pulled it out and stared at the thin layer of dark liquid in the bottom. He swirled it around twice, then sniffed it.

"Look, you didn't call just to see how I'm doing. What's on your mind? You got the check, didn't you? I know I wrote it." He pulled a cup from the stack of dirty dishes and examined the inside. He set it down and picked up another, then a third. He pinned the phone against his shoulder and wiped the rim of the cup with the tail of his shirt. He emptied the decanter into it, set it in the microwave, and punched a button. Nothing happened.

"I'm not starting something. I just asked about the check, that's all. I'm not arguing. Who's arguing?" He opened the fridge and scanned the barren shelves. There was a bulging, half-empty milk bottle with a thick yellow layer on top, and a series of opaque plastic containers all jammed to the back to the shelves. He slid one forward and began to pry off the lid, then thought better of it.

"What? No, I don't know why we always fight. I guess that's why people get divorced, isn't it?" He opened the pantry door and removed a promising-looking box from the shelf. He shook it and heard nothing; he dropped it on the floor and tried another. Behind one box he spotted a single granola bar wrapped in green and silver mylar. He took it.

"Look, can we get to the point? I've got a lot going on here. What is it you want? What?" Lassiter pulled the phone away from his ear and let out a laugh.

"You've got to be kidding. You got the bedroom suite, you got the oils and the Wedgwood—now you want the *plants*? Why don't you take the carpet too?" He flipped through the *Pittsburgh Post-Gazette* on the island, pulled out the sports and financial sections, and headed for the family room and his favorite recliner—his *only* recliner.

"No, I don't *need* the plants—I just don't think you'll want them anymore. Because they're dead, that's why. No, I watered them all right—*you* killed them. That exterminator you hired. That's right, he tented the house and fumigated. The gas killed every living thing in the house, including your plants. What? Yes, you did—you bought a service contract. I saw the paperwork. Well, maybe that's the problem, Margaret. You don't remember where the money goes. Anyway, the plants are yours if you want them—help yourself. Uh-huh. Well, I've got to go. Talk to you later. Yeah. Bye."

Lassiter dropped the cell phone on the carpet and leaned back in his recliner with a look of satisfaction. He set the paper on his lap and opened the sports page. As he scanned the headlines, his eyes drifted above the paper and focused on a mahogany plant stand near the doorway, supporting a leafy Boston fern.

It was in perfect condition.

The silver Porsche roared into a parking space in front of the Fox Chapel Yacht Club and killed its lights. Jack Kaplan turned to the beautiful young woman sitting silently beside him and smiled.

"You know, Angel, when I saw you leaning up against that red Beamer the other night, I almost stepped out and helped you myself. I don't know who first spotted you, but you were the perfect choice for this job. I mean the face, the dress, the body—baby, you are the total package. Looks to die for, you might say."

"I didn't ask your opinion," the woman said.

Kaplan reached across and stroked her long, auburn hair. "I love this," he said.

She swung around and knocked his hand away. "Let me make something clear to you, Dr. Kaplan: This is a business relationship. I don't like you, I don't trust you, and I certainly don't need your help. Have I made myself clear?"

Kaplan thrust an imaginary dagger into his heart and twisted it. "You're killing me, Angel. But then, that's your specialty, isn't it?"

"One more thing: when we're out of sight, don't you ever touch me."

Jack looked her over once more and shook his head. "Your loss," he said. "Are you ready? It's showtime."

Kaplan stepped out of the car, fastened the top button of his sports coat, and moved around to the opposite side of the car. He opened the passenger door and extended his hand. Angel reached down at her feet and picked up a glossy black handbag and a bottle of champagne; she swung her slender legs from the car, then rose up to meet him, smiling and kissing him lightly on the cheek. They walked arm in arm down the sidewalk on the right side of the building, avoiding the glare of the streetlamps, heading directly for the marina and the wooden docks that projected into the river like gray piano keys.

Behind them, a second car rolled to a stop beside the Porsche. Two men sat silently, watching Kaplan and the woman called Angel work their way down the pier toward the farthest slip.

Nathan Lassiter turned to the driver. "I want to ride with Angel next time," he said. "I just got divorced, you know. What does this look like to people?"

Santangelo ignored him. "We'll give them another minute," he said evenly. "No sense crowding them."

Moments later, the two men emerged from the car and followed the same secluded path to the wooden quays lined with gently rocking sailboats, catamarans, and sport cruisers of all shapes and sizes—but none of them compared in size or luxury with the corporate yacht in the final slip, the seventy-foot *PharmaGen.*

There were hearty laughs and eager handshakes as the last two men stepped aboard, completing the party of six. The bow and stern lines were quickly cast off, the *PharmaGen's* twin diesel inboards gave a guttural growl, and Tucker Truett backed the yacht slowly out of the slip and into the darkness of the Allegheny River.

As soon as the yacht passed out of range of the bright marina lights, the jovial pretense was dropped and the party fell silent. They traveled just over a mile upriver, to an isolated spot where Nine Mile Island and Sycamore Island lay side by side, dividing the river into three separate channels. They dropped anchor in the central channel, where the wooded islands blocked them from view from either bank.

Julian Zohar stepped into the center of the group and cleared his throat.

"Mr. Truett informs me we have refreshments tonight—please, help yourselves." They took seats on the U-shaped leather sun bench—all except for Truett, who remained seated in the captain's chair in the adjoining cockpit.

"I don't like this," Santangelo said. "All of us meeting together is a risk."

"We've been over this," Truett said.

"I still don't like it. I've got a lot to lose here."

"We've *all* got a lot to lose."

"Mr. Santangelo," Zohar said calmly, "I wouldn't take the risk of bringing this group together if it were not an absolute necessity. I am not simply a contractor handing out tasks to individual vendors. We're creating this venture *together*, and we need to learn from one another."

"We never should have met in person," Santangelo said.

"I considered other means of bringing this committee together, but all of them involved equal or greater risk. Mr. Truett entertains a different group of people on this yacht almost every evening—who would notice one more assembly? I decided that our safest course of action was to 'hide in plain sight,' so to speak."

"I don't like these people knowing who I am," Santangelo said, gesturing to the group. "Knowing my name, knowing what I do for a living."

"You are Mr. Cruz Santangelo," Zohar replied, "special agent of the Federal Bureau of Investigation. I am Dr. Julian Zohar, executive director of the Center for Organ Procurement and Education. If something goes wrong, we all know where to find one another, don't we? I think that creates a certain incentive for *loyalty*, don't you? We've all cast our lots together, Mr. Santangelo. Why not just accept it?"

"This is old ground," Angel said. "Can we get down to business?"

Zohar nodded. "The first item on our agenda is to review our prior endeavor. We're on a learning curve here, and it's critical that we benefit from our mistakes and improve our performance with each effort. Mr. Santangelo, you control the first phase; let's begin with you."

"The setup went off without a hitch," Santangelo said. "I scouted the location for a week—it was perfect for us. Homewood is a war zone. In that neighborhood I could have fired an assault rifle without anyone raising a blind. One thing," he said, looking at Angel. "Don't cover your eyes—never look away. He saw you, remember? One break in character is all it takes."

"Sorry," she grumbled. "I'm not a professional."

"Lady, you are now."

"I thought she was great," Kaplan said. "You guys should have seen her, standing beside that car all helpless and pouting—Please, won't somebody stop and help me? Man, a monk would have pulled over."

"That's another thing," Santangelo said, turning to face Kaplan. "If you ever crack another joke while we're waiting for the target, I'll kill you myself."

"Hey, lighten up."

"I will not lighten up," Santangelo said, enunciating each word with icy precision. "You are undisciplined and unrestrained. I despise your sloppiness. It has no place in an operation like this."

"Take a valium," Kaplan said. "Doesn't the Bureau offer any therapy for ex-snipers?"

Santangelo began to rise, but Zohar put a hand on his forearm and prevented him. "Mr. Santangelo's comments merit consideration," he said. "Discipline and precision play a crucial role for *all* of us. Dr. Kaplan, perhaps you would like to report next."

"Well," Kaplan grinned, "doing the removal on-site was a real rush—but surgically speaking, it's a risk. The 'donor' has no worries, of course—he's a flatliner, thanks to the Terminator here—but there's an increased risk of contamination of the organ. I transferred it into sterile ice as fast as I could, but—hey, kids, I'm doing surgery on the side of a road here."

"There are bigger risks," Santangelo said, "like exposure. In our first attempt, I was out of there in two minutes. Kaplan did the removal at the other end."

"Very handy," Kaplan said. "Not as much fun, but very convenient. I had the donor in one room, and the recipient in the next. I'll bet that was the fastest kidney transplant on record."

"Now that we're doing the removal on site," Santangelo said, "there's more of a chance of being spotted. There are more variables that are out of our control."

Zohar turned to Kaplan again. "Is there any way to speed up the procedure?"

"Are you kidding? Not unless I reach down his throat and yank it out. This is still surgery, guys—I'm in and out in record time now. Nobody I know could do it faster."

Now Lassiter spoke up. "This is all a moot point. The first time, Santangelo and Angel drove halfway across town with an unconscious man in the trunk. What if they had a wreck? What if a cop pulled them over? And the surgical site was in a populated area, remember? Even late at night, sooner or later someone's going to spot you lugging bodies in and out of your trunk. Besides, there's the forensic side to consider. It's always risky to move a body from the place where death occurs. There are ways to tell."

"I thought you were taking care of all that," Santangelo said. "You cover the autopsies, don't you?"

"It's not that simple," Lassiter said. "We schedule these things when I'm on rotation, and only when our two boys are there to pick up the body—but there are police on the scene too, you know. The coroner has jurisdiction over the body, but the police have responsibility for the scene itself, and they collect their own forensic evidence. There's always a chance that somebody will spot something."

"Dr. Lassiter is correct," Zohar said. "We have no choice. Despite the potential risks, on-site removal is currently our best alternative. Mr. Santangelo, the onus is on you to find suitable locations and scenarios for these procedures. The last one seems to have served quite well."

"Angel and I are working on it."

Zohar looked at the group. "Suggested improvements for our next procedure?"

Lassiter turned to Santangelo. "These things have got to look like *accidental* deaths," he said. "You set the last one up to look like a drive-by shooting. That was acceptable, because our people don't expect to find a perp in a drive-by—but in the future it's got to look like an accident. A murder sets a whole different set of wheels in motion. We don't want investigators sifting through the evidence, trying to find some nonexistent killer—that's asking for trouble. And each scenario needs to be different; the police have people looking for crime trends, like serial killers and rapists. If you do two or three of these things the same way—even *close* to the same way—that raises a flag, and they'll be all over it. I hope the FBI taught you better than that. We can't afford that kind of screwup."

Santangelo narrowed his eyes.

"There will be no 'screwups,'" Zohar said, "simply because there can *be* none. We each need to do our job well, and we must encourage one another to do the same. Let me say again: This committee, this group, it's more than an organization—we are a team. A family, that's the way I like to think of it—we happy few, we band of brothers. We depend upon one another for our very survival. Think of this committee as a body; if one member suffers, we all suffer. It's in the body's best interest to make sure that each member contributes to the welfare of the whole."

There was the sound of a smaller boat approaching on the port side. Truett stepped to the railing, smiled, and waved as it passed. The rest of the group turned their faces away and waited until the drone of the engine disappeared into the night.

Zohar leaned back in his seat again and smiled. "On a more positive note," he said, "our previous client's payment has been received in full, and the appropriate transfers have been made into each of your offshore accounts, as you can verify as of noon tomorrow. And on a personal note, I'm happy to report that both of our prior clients are recuperating quite nicely in the seclusion of their homes. My congratulations to the entire team.

"Looking to the future, I'm pleased to announce that we are actively pursuing additional clients. Mr. Truett, I continue to be grateful for your organization's ever-expanding population data. I'll forward our potential clients' medical information to you tomorrow. If you will compile the potential donor lists, we can discuss our final selections."

Truett nodded.

"I suggest we spend our remaining time meeting as subcommittees. Mr. Santangelo, you and your team have donor scenarios to discuss. Why don't you remain on deck and enjoy the evening? Dr. Lassiter, I have an issue I would like to discuss with you and Mr. Truett in the salon below."

Lassiter nodded nervously.

Zohar smiled and looked at each member of the group. "The word *committee* comes to us from Latin," he said. "Its original meaning was 'one who has been entrusted'—one to whom something valuable was *committed*. That's what this committee is: a group of people who share a great responsibility. This bold venture of ours has the potential to be enormously lucrative; may I encourage you all to constantly remember the responsibility we share. We are *committed*, my friends. Please don't forget it."

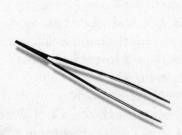

Truett pulled the hatch door shut behind him and descended the handful of steps to the salon below. Dr. Zohar was already seated in the center of the L-shaped sofa, his legs decorously crossed and his folded hands resting lightly on one knee. Truett checked both the forward and aft staterooms, and glanced in both heads as well. Satisfied, he took a seat on Zohar's left.

Lassiter started toward the sofa himself, then reconsidered. The remaining seat placed him much too close to Zohar, and it blocked his view of Truett. The two men watched silently as Lassiter stepped back again, folded his arms clumsily, and leaned against the galley counter.

"So?" Lassiter said as indifferently as possible. "What's this all about?"

Zohar said nothing for a full three seconds; the silence had the impact of an air horn. After three decades of impromptu appeals to bereaved and grieving families, Zohar understood the power of both speech and silence, and used both with surgical precision.

"A problem has come to my attention," he said evenly.

"A problem? What sort of problem?"

"A potential breach of security. I hate to bring this subject up . . . again."

"That wasn't my fault!" Lassiter protested. "The first donor you picked was carrying a uniform donor card! When the coroner's office reported the death, his organs were requested by your own organization! What was I supposed to do, release the body and let them find a kidney missing? That would have ended this whole project! The best I could do was to refuse to release the organs for forensic reasons."

"As you say, it was the best you could do—but your method attracted undesirable attention. That's the last thing we want."

"Well, talk to *your* people about it. They requested the organs."

Zohar smiled. "Remember, Nathan, no one at COPE knows about this project of ours. Their business is to procure organs for people on the traditional transplant waiting list. I trained them myself, and they're very good at it. I can hardly stop them from doing their jobs now. But as a result of that first little mishap, I have made two corrections to our system: I will no longer select donors who carry traditional donor cards, and whenever we select a donor for our purposes, I will personally contact the next of kin to 'request donation'—and I will make certain that they decline. Those two steps should keep us from any further conflicts of interest with the traditional donor system."

"You'd better be right," Lassiter said. "I bluffed my way out of that one; I can't do it again. They'd be all over me—and like you said upstairs, I know where you live."

Truett began to speak, but Zohar gently placed a hand on his arm with a sideward glance, then turned back to Lassiter again.

"The issue I wanted to speak to you about is a different matter entirely. It appears, Nathan, that you are once again attracting undesirable attention."

"What? How?"

"As you so eloquently pointed out, the members of this committee depend upon one another—we live or die together. That kind of mutual dependency creates the need for a certain amount of *accountability*. In our case, the left hand must know *exactly* what the right hand is doing. For that reason, when you agreed to join us, Mr. Truett took the liberty of installing a type of surveillance software on your computer, both at your home and at the coroner's office. This software records every keystroke you make on your computer, and it reports the activity to us."

Lassiter opened his mouth to object, but Zohar raised his hand.

"You were not being singled out, Nathan. We took the same measures with every member of the committee. It was a necessary precaution, as I'm sure you'll recognize after proper reflection. You can see why this discussion needed to be held privately; you are the only member of our group who knows about this, and we're counting on you to keep it in the strictest confidence."

Now Truett joined in. "Last week, Dr. Lassiter, we noticed some unusual activity on your home computer. It appears that someone did a very thorough search of your personal records."

Lassiter blanched. "Which records? What sort of a search?"

"Everything, top to bottom. It was very careful, very thorough, very professionally done. Special attention was paid to your financial records."

"My ex-wife," Lassiter hissed. "She's looking for hidden assets."

Truett shook his head. "We don't think so."

"Why not?"

"If it was your ex-wife, she had help. They even searched for *steganography*—files hidden within other files, like child pornography files sometimes are. Does your wife have that kind of computer expertise?"

"Margaret? No way. E-mail and basic Internet, that's her limit."

"Well, here's the kicker, Dr. Lassiter: Before leaving, whoever it was installed another version of the same surveillance software that we use. They're not just interested in your finances, they're interested in your ongoing activities. Does that sound like your wife to you?"

"But—if it's not Margaret, then who? The IRS, maybe? Can you tell?"

Truett shook his head again. "The spyware uploads the reports of your activities to a server, and they're forwarded from there to the interested party. That's why it's called *spy*ware; we can track the reports to the server, but no farther. It's like a Swiss bank account: we know where the deposits are going, but there's no way to know who's making withdrawals."

Lassiter was beginning to pace now, growing more agitated by the minute. Suddenly he stopped and turned to Truett. "What day did this happen?"

"Last Tuesday, about midmorning."

Lassiter's eyes darted back and forth like two bees in a jar. "The plants weren't dead," he whispered.

"What?"

"The exterminator. He said he found termites; he said he needed to fumigate. He tented the whole house—wrapped it up in plastic and filled it with gas. He said the gas would kill every living thing—but I forgot to remove the plants, and the plants weren't dead."

Truett glanced at Zohar, then back at Lassiter again. "What was the name of the company?"

"I don't know. I mean, I didn't look. He said my wife hired him—some kind of service contract or something . . ." His voice trailed off as he spoke.

Zohar spoke up. "Nathan, listen to me. Do you know this exterminator? Have you used him before? Did you recognize him?"

Lassiter shook his head dumbly. "He was a tall guy with huge glasses."

Truett started. "Did you say *glasses*?"

"Big, thick lenses. Made his eyes the size of walnuts."

Truett slumped back against the sofa. Zohar turned and looked at him.

"I met this man," Truett said. "He had a little boating 'accident' on the Fourth of July, and we dragged him out of the water. He had a lot of questions about the company—questions about genetic privacy. He was with a woman."

"A woman," Lassiter said breathlessly. "Was it Margaret?"

"What does your ex-wife look like?"

"She's . . . she has . . . she's sort of . . ." Lassiter struggled to provide the most basic details about the woman he shared a bedroom with for seventeen years. "She has brown hair."

Truett shook his head. "This woman was a blonde."

"Did you get names?" Zohar asked.

"I didn't catch them. They were both doctors, I remember that. He said he was a professor somewhere in the Carolinas."

"And her?"

Truett squinted hard, searching for faded bits of memory. He shrugged. "All I remember is, she had remarkable eyes: one green and one brown."

Lassiter drew a sharp breath. He staggered forward, groping

for the edge of the sofa. He sank down on trembling legs and sprawled backward, blinking at the ceiling. "Riley . . . McKay," he said in two gasps.

Zohar glanced at Truett, and Truett nodded.

"She's the one," Lassiter panted. "Pathology fellow . . . called me on the carpet . . . asked too many questions . . . had to get her out of the office . . ."

"Calm yourself," Zohar said sharply.

"*Calm* myself?" Lassiter struggled to an upright position. "Are you out of your mind? Do you know what this means?"

Zohar said nothing for a moment, staring directly ahead. "It means that someone's asking questions—questions about you. She's enlisted someone's assistance—or vice-versa—and they've gone so far as to break into your home and tap into your computer. That suggests a very high level of . . . *interest*," he said, his voice trailing off into silence again.

"I'm out of here," Lassiter said, struggling to his feet. "We have to fold this thing right now."

"Sit down and be quiet."

Lassiter stared at him in astonishment. "Julian, someone is on to us. Somebody *knows*."

"Someone is asking questions—what we don't know is the answers they've come up with. We all have a great deal invested in this program, Nathan. It would be premature to abandon it over the first breach of security. Agreed, we have to take action—but remember, *whatever* action we take has its risks. We need to find out what they know, who knows it, and how they learned it. With luck, we'll be able to close those loopholes and have an even stronger system than before. What we have here is an unparalleled opportunity to learn."

Lassiter sank down again and buried his head in his hands.

"This exterminator," Zohar said. "You mentioned paperwork."

"I've got it—somewhere."

"Find it. When you do, we'll have Mr. Santangelo look into it."

Lassiter looked up. "Why him? Why does he have to know about this?"

"Now, Nathan," Zohar said with a minimum of reassurance, "Mr. Santangelo is a part of our team. He's on your side. Remember,

Mr. Santangelo is an active FBI agent, and that allows him to do a certain amount of *investigating* without arousing suspicion."

"He's an assassin," Lassiter said.

"He's an authorized representative of your own federal government. Where's your patriotic spirit?"

"I'm leaving town. I've got vacation time coming—"

"You'll do nothing of the kind. Someone in your office is asking questions; this is hardly the time to do something out of the ordinary. You'll return to work tomorrow just as you always do."

"I've got to get that program off my computer—"

"You'd never find it," Truett said. "It takes a professional."

"Then *you* guys remove it."

"No," Zohar said. "It might prove useful. For now, I want you to use your computer as you normally would—but you are not to send e-mail, and you are to make no attempt to locate or remove that surveillance program. Do you understand, Nathan? If you do, they'll know—and so will *we*. You're to return to your regular daily routine, and you're to act as though nothing is out of the ordinary."

"I . . . I don't think I can do this."

Zohar looked at him. Beads of sweat dotted his forehead like dew on a leaf. The blood had drained entirely from his cadaverous face, and the pallid skin surrounded his eyes like two purple sinkholes.

"Nathan," he said evenly, "let me reiterate what I said earlier: this committee is a *body*. As you well know, there are times when a part of the body becomes diseased, and then surgery is required to remove the diseased member. It may be painful, it may be costly, but otherwise the disease could spread—and that wouldn't be fair to the rest of the body, now would it? Mr. Santangelo and I want you to understand: we are not above doing surgery, should it become necessary. Do I make myself clear?"

Lassiter said nothing.

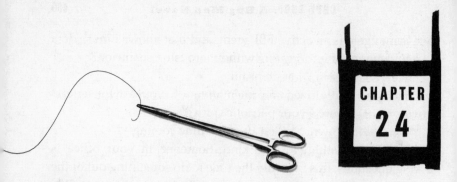

Nick held the pole of the aerial insect net in his left hand, with the wire hoop parallel to the ground. With his right hand he pulled up on the tail of the net, holding it open like a giant gauze cone. Below the net, a forty-pound sow lay decomposing in the July sun, swarming with hundreds of cream-colored larvae, each vying with its neighbor to see which would reach the breakfast table first.

Nick watched the black dots hovering above the decaying sow. He lowered the net slightly, causing their instinctive escape behavior to lead them up and into the waiting net. Then he brought the net down with a swatting motion, finishing the stroke with a quick flip of his wrist. The net swung up and over the hoop, confining the tiny occupants in the tip.

The long meadow sat like a green cap atop the steep ridge comprising the town of Tarentum. The view from the field was spectacular; as a boy, Nick had spent many an afternoon here, gazing at the panorama of the Allegheny River below and watching the cars that crossed the Tarentum Bridge until they disappeared into the town of Lower Burrell. Down the hill, through the tips of the trees, he could almost see the back of his house. Nick thought of this field as his private property. His neighbors, aware of his strange entomological studies, were more than happy to let him have it to himself. Above the houses, exposed to the clearing winds, it was perfectly suited for some of his more malodorous experiments.

He opened a wide-mouth killing jar and draped the tip of the net inside. He sealed it again, allowing the ethyl acetate to do its work. Nick had already sent most of the predictable specimens to Sanjay for DNA analysis; he was hoping for something a little more unusual today—perhaps a *Phormia regina* or a Holarctic blowfly. In a few minutes, he would drop the specimens into an opaque jar of 95 percent ethanol to preserve them, and to prevent ultraviolet light from degrading their DNA.

From his backpack came a high, trilling sound. Nick took out his cell phone and opened it.

"Yes?"

"Nick? Nick Polchak?"

"Who's this?"

"Nick, it's Freddie, over at Bug Off."

"Hey, Freddie, how's the bug business? Did you pick up any—"

"Nick, we got a problem."

Nick paused. "I'm listening."

"The FBI paid me a visit this morning. Did you hear me? Not the police, Nick, the *FBI.*"

"That's interesting. What did they want?"

"He wanted to know about a fumigation we did at 1874 Branchwater Trail. Sound familiar? It seems the FBI did a follow-up inspection and guess what? No termites and no sign of wood damage."

"Another satisfied customer," Nick said, swinging his net at a passing secondary screwworm fly.

"Nick, this is serious. He knows the job was a scam. He wants the names of my people who did the job—he wants to look at my service log. And if he does, guess what he'll find? All my people were on other jobs that day. How am I supposed to explain the extra crew?"

"Times are good. You hired on for the summer."

"Sure, and then he'll want to see employment records. I've got no tax IDs on you guys, no social security records . . . and get this, Nick: He checked with neighbors, and he found somebody who *saw* you guys. He asked me about one of my employees, a tall guy with *big glasses.* Who have I got who looks like that?"

"That's your problem, Freddie. You don't hire enough good-looking people."

"Look, this is not a joke. He's threatening to pull my license. Did you hear what I said? *My license.* I did you a favor, and now the whole thing's blowing up in my face. Nick, what did you do? This is the FBI!"

"What does he want, Freddie?"

"He wants names."

"Did you call me on your cell phone?"

"Yeah. Sure."

"Then he's probably got my name—you've used it about a dozen times. Like you said, Freddie, this is the FBI."

"Nick, I've got until tomorrow morning to cooperate. He's coming back, and he says he's going to—"

"I'll take care of it, I promise. Did he leave a card?"

"I got it right here."

"Then give him a call, and let him know you'll be happy to cooperate."

"What do I tell him?"

"Tell him my name—and tell him I want to meet him." Nick paused. "Better yet—tell him he wants to meet *me.*"

CHAPTER 25

Dr. Polchak? I'm Special Agent Cruz Santangelo. Mind if I join you?" Nick and Riley sat side by side on the upper deck of the *Majestic,* the premiere riverboat of the Gateway Clipper Fleet. The wooden deck was scattered with tables, mostly empty on this early morning excursion that offered a panoramic one-hour tour of the Ohio, Allegheny, and Monongahela Rivers. The deck was surrounded by a white spindled railing, trimmed with touches of red and blue. Two black smokestacks protruded through the deck, completing the picture of a patriotic showboat from a bygone era. They sat in the full sun near the port paddlewheel; it was the noisiest spot on the upper deck.

Nick nodded toward the wooden bench opposite them, and Santangelo took a seat.

"I assumed we would be meeting privately," Santangelo said without taking his eyes off Nick.

"I think this is someone you'll want to meet. Special Agent Santangelo, this is Dr. Riley McKay of the Allegheny County Coroner's Office."

"Cruz," he said. "It'll save us ten minutes." Santangelo looked at Riley for the first time. Medium build, short blond hair, fair skin—and the unmistakable eyes. "Dr. McKay, it's a pleasure to—"

"May I see your credentials?" Riley extended her hand. "I'm the suspicious type."

Santangelo smiled. "We've noticed." He handed her the small leather folder. Riley laid the credentials open on her lap, took out her cell phone, and punched an autodial number.

"Sheila? Riley McKay. Yes, I know I'm late—I left a message for Dr. Lassiter. Look, I need a number for the FBI office over on East Carson."

"If I'd known you were coming, we could have met at your office," Santangelo said. "We're just across the river."

"Thanks, Sheila." Riley dialed the number and waited. "Good morning. Do you have a Special Agent Cruz Santangelo? No, don't connect me—he's sitting right here. I'd like to describe him to you: He's about six-foot, maybe six-one." Santangelo nodded at the latter number. "Midthirties, lean build, Hispanic mix, black hair, well-tanned, dark eyes. Sound familiar?"

Santangelo motioned for the phone. Riley hesitated, then handed it to him. "Stephanie? Cruz. Everything's OK. Go ahead, answer the lady's question." He covered the phone and held it out to Riley. "We're suspicious too," he said. "Those kind of questions can set off a lot of bells and whistles."

Riley listened intently, fixing her eyes on Santangelo's. "Thanks," she said simply, folding the phone and returning it to her purse.

"Well?"

"She says not to go out with you."

Santangelo let out a laugh. "They warned me not to date coworkers."

"Would you like to see *my* credentials?" Riley asked, lifting her gold coroner's badge from her purse.

"I trust you. I think trust is important, don't you?"

"I think trust has to be earned."

Santangelo turned and looked at Nick. "Dr. Nicholas Polchak," he said. "BS, MS, and PhD from Penn State University. Professor of entomology at North Carolina State University, member of the American Board of Forensic Entomology. It's a pleasure to meet you, Dr. Polchak. Man, do we have a colorful file on *you*."

"Shucks," Nick said, "those are just my federal offenses. How long have you been with the Bureau, Mr. Santangelo?"

"I've been a field agent for five years. Before that, I spent six years at Quantico."

"Six years at Quantico? That's too long for the academy."

"I was with the Hostage Rescue Team."

Nick sat up a little straighter. "I'm impressed," he said. "Dr. McKay, we're looking at a former member of the FBI's very own Delta Force, trained in urban warfare, special weapons tactics, close-in combat—even aerial assault. The HRT is the bad boys of the FBI."

"The *good* boys," Santangelo corrected. " 'The minimum force possible, the maximum force necessary'—that's our motto."

"Five years as a field agent, and six years before that. Why, Mr. Santangelo, you must have been at Waco."

Santangelo barely nodded.

"I remember reading about that," Nick said. "It was almost a two-month standoff, wasn't it? There were three hundred FBI agents, including your own elite hostage rescue team, against a handful of ex–Seventh Day Adventists. You guys brought in snipers, tear gas, even a tank. By the time the smoke cleared, there were eighty people dead—including a bunch of kids. Not exactly a high point for the FBI, was it, Mr. Santangelo? I've always wondered: Where does an HRT member go after Waco?"

Santangelo paused, but his expression never changed. "Pittsburgh," he said simply. He turned his attention to Riley now. "And you, Dr. McKay—you must be the woman."

"What woman is that?"

"It seems we three share a common interest: a certain Dr. Nathan Lassiter."

Nick and Riley said nothing.

"OK," Santangelo nodded, "then let me get things started. On Monday of last week a pest-control service tented the home of Dr.

Nathan Lassiter for fumigation—a fumigation that was entirely unnecessary and that did not, in fact, occur. The following day, a crew posing as exterminators illegally gained access to Dr. Lassiter's home, at which time they performed a thorough search of Dr. Lassiter's computer—including the installation of a surveillance program to allow ongoing monitoring of his investments and activities. How am I doing so far?"

"Impressive," Nick said. "How did you learn all this?"

"We watched them do it. The Bureau is conducting its own investigation into Dr. Lassiter's affairs; not long ago, we installed the same surveillance software on his computer. We watched every keystroke as it occurred."

"What does this have to do with us?" Riley asked.

Santangelo narrowed his eyes. "I figure you for a real smart woman, Dr. McKay. I'd appreciate it if you'd give me a little credit in return. We talked to one of Lassiter's next-door neighbors; she had a brochure from the Bug Off Exterminator Company. Yesterday, I interviewed Mr. Frederick Krubick, the proprietor of said company. That's where I got your name, Dr. Polchak. That same neighbor observed three figures enter the back of the house. She said one of them walked like a woman."

"I resent that," Nick said.

Santangelo looked at Riley. "By your presence here today, I'm assuming that woman was you."

Riley hesitated, then slowly nodded. "Why are you investigating Dr. Lassiter?"

"Funny. I was about to ask you the same question."

"You first."

"Now wait a minute—let me explain something. The two of you are interfering with a federal investigation. You're already guilty of breaking and entering and illegal wiretapping—that's just for starters. I'm not here to answer *your* questions—got it?"

Nick shook his head in disapproval. "It's way too early for the fastball. Your curve ball was doing just fine."

"I could have you two brought up on charges."

"But you won't," Nick said. As he spoke, the riverboat began to pass under the span of the Smithfield Street Bridge, and the cool, gray shadow crept over the upper deck like a mist. Nick leaned back against the railing and stared into the sky. "This is my favorite part," he said, gazing up at the hundred-and-twenty-year-old maze of rusted trusses, pins, and eyebars less than twenty feet away.

"Why not?" Santangelo said.

Nick spoke without looking down. "If you charge us, our interest in Dr. Lassiter will become public knowledge—and that will tip off Dr. Lassiter himself, the very thing you want to avoid. If he looks for *our* software on his computer, he'll find yours too—and you don't want that, now, do you? You can end our investigation, Mr. Santangelo—but in the process you'll end your own."

The bridge passed overhead now, and the midmorning sun streaked the deck again with blinding yellow light. Nick squinted hard and turned back to Santangelo. "Besides," he said, lifting his glasses and rubbing his eyes, "you didn't come here just to tell us to back off—a phone call would have accomplished that. You're here because you want to know what we know."

"You're a hard man to intimidate, Dr. Polchak."

Nick looked at him. "I thought you read my file."

Santangelo turned to Riley. "Why is a pathologist investigating her own colleague? What would motivate you to break into his house? And how did the two of you get together on this?"

Riley glanced at Nick. He nodded.

"I'm in a fellowship program at the coroner's office," Riley said. "Dr. Lassiter is my supervisor. A few months ago, I began to notice some strange anomalies in his work—and when I asked about them, he became extremely defensive. He 'protested too much,' you might say, and it made me suspicious. I met Dr. Polchak at a . . . professional function, and I asked him to help me look into it."

"I'm good at peeking through keyholes," Nick said.

"What sort of 'anomalies' are we talking about?"

"Lassiter refused to release organs for transplant due to a head trauma—that was the first one. Then I asked Dr. Polchak to do an entomological evaluation on an acute myocardial infarction victim."

"And?"

"The body had been moved," Nick said, "shortly after death. It was transported from the city to the country, where it was later discovered."

"So it was dumped," Santangelo said. "It happens."

"It happens to murder victims," Riley said. "Lassiter wrote it off as a death by natural causes."

Santangelo nodded. "Any more?"

"Just one. Dr. Polchak helped me reexamine one of Lassiter's autopsies—the victim of a drive-by shooting in Homewood. The cause of death was a gunshot to the back of the head, but we discovered another wound—an incision on the lower back, just below the rib cage."

"An incision?"

"It was sutured shut," Nick said, "and it all happened at the murder scene."

Santangelo did a double take. "You can tell that?"

"You'd be amazed what I can tell. For example: I can tell that you already know most of this—maybe all of it."

"I'll bite. How do you know that?"

"Because you're a federal agent. The FBI wouldn't get involved with a simple medical misadventure—that's for the local authorities to take care of. Your very presence here indicates the violation of some federal statute or regulation—say, the National Organ Transplant Act, which makes it a federal crime to buy or sell human tissues."

Santangelo sat motionless.

"Thanks," Nick smiled. "Now I know for sure."

Santangelo held up both hands in protest. "I'm not at liberty to discuss details of an open investigation. All I can tell you is, your observations are . . . consistent with our own discoveries. What else can you tell me?"

"Like you said, we searched his computer, and I'm sure we found the same thing you did: Lassiter has been investing enormous sums of money in a company called PharmaGen—money that he never earned. Where's that money coming from, Mr. Santangelo?"

"Sorry."

"Come on, *Cruz,* I thought we were all friends here. We answered some of your questions; you can answer one of ours."

"I'm asking you to help confirm details of the Bureau's investigation, Dr. Polchak, but I'm not free to answer your questions in return. You know how it works—a need-to-know basis."

"Some friend you are."

"So what about this PharmaGen? Has he mentioned the company at work, Dr. McKay? Can you explain his heavy involvement?"

"No," she said. "At this point, all we have is speculation."

"I'm open to speculation. Let's hear it."

Riley took a deep breath. "PharmaGen has collected genetic information on a few hundred thousand people in western Pennsylvania. They have a man serving on their ethics advisory board—his name is Julian Zohar, the director of western Pennsylvania's organ procurement organization. We think he . . . it's possible that . . ." Her voice trailed off here, and Nick leaned forward.

"We think he could be creating a black market for organs, using PharmaGen's database to facilitate matches between donors and recipients."

Santangelo looked at both of them, then slumped back against the bench.

"Like we said, it's only speculation."

"Can you *prove* any of this? Do you have anything tangible for me?"

Nick shook his head. "You look surprised, Mr. Santangelo. Was your investigation taking you in a different direction?"

"I . . . I can't say," Santangelo stammered. "I'm just . . . amazed that you've . . . made these connections."

No one said anything for a minute.

"That's all we've got," Nick said at last.

"I can't tell you how much we appreciate your cooperation," Santangelo said, his mind still racing.

"So what do we do now?"

Santangelo looked at both of them. "I can tell you this much: We have several people under surveillance. We suspect the involvement of a number of parties, and we won't do anything until we identify all of them and have enough physical evidence to prosecute—that's when we'll close the net."

"What do you want us to do?" Riley asked.

"You've already done it. You've told me what you know, and you've turned the investigation over to the FBI—right? Here's what I *don't* want you two to do: no more breaking into houses, no more tapping into computers, and no more poking around in Dr. Lassiter's affairs. The worst thing you could do is let Lassiter get wind of you—or of *us*. The minute somebody lets out a yell, everybody scatters. We don't want anyone to get away, understand? You need to let us complete this investigation our way, on our timetable. If you do, we'll both be satisfied."

"Just what is that timetable?" Nick asked.

"You'll know when we know. In the meantime, Dr. McKay, you go back to the coroner's office and finish that fellowship program. Talk to *no one* about what we've discussed here. And if you do observe any more irregularities in Dr. Lassiter's conduct—if you even have further speculations—you're to call *me*, understand?" He handed both of them a business card embossed with the black-and-gold seal of the FBI. "One more thing—Dr. Lassiter's neighbor reported seeing *three* people enter the house. Who was the third party?"

They said nothing.

"You're a pathologist, and you're an entomologist," he said, looking at each of them. "I assume the third party was your computer expert."

"An interesting assumption," Nick said.

"The Bureau would really like to know."

"Like you said, Mr. Santangelo—a need-to-know basis."

Santangelo glared at him. "Enjoy your stay in Pittsburgh, Dr. Polchak. Take in a few ball games. Work on your tan—you could use it. Like I said before, you know how the system works: your government thanks you for your cooperation; now keep quiet, stay out of the way, and let us do our job."

Santangelo rose from the bench, shook hands with each of them, and headed off across the deck. Nick and Riley watched until he descended the opposite stairway and disappeared from view.

Nick turned to Riley. "He didn't read my file," he said.

The curving hull of the *PharmaGen* lay in the black water, drifting slightly in the gentle current. The three men sat in a circle on the aft deck, staring in opposite directions at the moonless sky.

"So what do you think?" Santangelo said.

Zohar sat in silence for another moment. "I think we've had an epiphany," he said. "We've learned three crucial lessons from your interview today, Mr. Santangelo: first, we've confirmed Dr. Lassiter's complete ineptitude; second, we've learned that Dr. McKay is a very bright woman indeed; and third, we've learned that we must make a concerted effort to disguise the link between the coroner's office, PharmaGen, and myself. Now that our relationship is well established, Mr. Truett, I think it might be prudent for me to resign from your advisory board. I suggest that you recruit instead more members with Dr. Paulos's reassuring image."

"Never mind the future," Truett said, "what about now? They *know,* Julian—they figured it out."

"What do they really know? Think carefully. They know about Lassiter's foul-ups, but they are unaware of the reason behind them. They know about Lassiter's investments in PharmaGen, but they don't know the source of his funding. And as for the connection to me, that's the weakest correlation of all. As they said to Mr. Santangelo, they're only guessing."

"But they're guessing *right*," Santangelo said. "They don't have to be able to prove anything. They just have to raise the right questions."

"I agree," Zohar said. "But I believe we took care of that today. Where would they raise those questions? To the authorities, of course, and today they did exactly that. They spoke to the authorities—and not just any authority, a federal authority—the FBI. They now believe that their concerns have been heard, that a federal investigation is under way, and that they have no reason for further involvement."

"That's good for now," Truett said, "but what about later on? Cruz promised them an end to the investigation. What happens when six months or a year goes by and it's still business as usual? They won't wait forever, Julian; they're going to want closure."

"And closure they shall have. Please understand me, gentlemen. This situation will have to be dealt with. All I'm suggesting is that we proceed with caution and that we take advantage of this opportunity while we have it."

"What opportunity?"

"Mr. Santangelo made it quite clear: if they learn anything else, they are to call *him*. Don't you see? If there are any more holes in our system, they will find them—and they will report them directly to us. These people are our very own U.N. inspection team! I think we should regard this as a divine opportunity."

"When *do* we deal with the situation?" Santangelo asked. "The sooner the better in my book."

"I think that would be wise. But one thing is crucial: We must identify the third member of their party. As you told them today, Mr. Santangelo, we don't want to close the net until we have identified all parties involved. If we act prematurely, whoever remains will most certainly return to haunt us. Can you do this? Will you be able to identify the remaining accomplice?"

"It could take a few days," Santangelo said reflectively. "I don't have the resources of the FBI for this—I'll have to do it the hard way."

Zohar nodded. "As you said—the sooner the better."

"What about the next procedure?" Truett said. "Do we go ahead, or do we call it off and lay low until this situation is taken care of?"

"I say call it off," Santangelo said.

"I agree," Truett nodded. "The risk is too great."

"Gentlemen," Zohar said in his most reassuring voice. "We must be careful not to let our fears cloud our usual acumen. If we are to test our system for flaws, we must continue as planned with our next procedure. Besides, we must remember that our waiting client also poses a risk. How are we to raise her expectations, only to suddenly postpone without explanation? Believe me, her courage is fragile; if we show the slightest sign of caution or hesitation, she will back out of our arrangement, and then we'll have a risk of a different kind. The only safe client is a satisfied client—and she will not be satisfied until she gets her kidney. We have a week before the next procedure; let's see what Mr. Santangelo can learn in that time."

The men grew silent again, lost in thought. Truett sat slumped forward, his forearms resting on his knees, rolling an amber bottle back and forth between his hands.

"What about Lassiter?"

"What about him?"

"He's been paid well for his part in all this—*very* well. But that wasn't enough for him; he had to invest that money in the company, he had to try to make an even bigger killing. It was his greed that allowed them to make the connection to PharmaGen. It was his stupidity that got them asking questions in the first place. From where I sit, Dr. Lassiter is becoming a greater liability than an asset."

"Lassiter is a loose cannon," Santangelo agreed. "He makes me nervous."

Zohar nodded thoughtfully. "A contact within the coroner's office is a necessary part of this process—but Dr. Lassiter does not have to be that contact. I share your concerns, gentlemen. This situation just might prove a double blessing. I think I see a way to improve our system and to replace our weakest link at the same time."

Zohar reached down to the table in front of him and lifted his wineglass. He glanced at each man, then held the glass aloft. "Any man makes a sailor in calm seas," he said. "Into the storm, gentlemen. Our port awaits on the other side."

CHAPTER 27

Riley parked her car beside the river and took the winding, rust-red walkway over West Carson Street to the lower station of the Duquesne Incline. She loved the hundred-and-twenty-five-year-old building, with its rose-red brick and violet slate roof with gingerbread trim. Nineteen inclines once lined Pittsburgh's formidable hills, transporting workers, vehicles, and coal up a thirty-degree pitch that even horses couldn't master. Now only two inclines remained, the Duquesne and the Monongahela, both offering passengers a silent ascension from the river's southern edge to the peak of Mount Washington. As a little girl, Riley's father brought her often to ride the inclines, but by then they had been reduced to little more than tourist attractions. But it never failed to take her breath away when the red-and-yellow car rose out of the station and the three rivers came into view below.

She always took a seat at the very front of the car, turning to face the glass in anticipation of the stunning panorama—but this morning she moved directly to the rear of the car and took a seat beside a beaming, wavy-haired man.

"The lovely Riley McKay," Leo said. "Truly, the Golden Triangle offers no more beautiful vista than you."

Riley leaned over and gave him a peck on the cheek. "Let's make this a regular thing," she said. "Every time I'm having a bad day, I'll meet you right here."

"I will be your incline, lifting you from the depths of despair to the celestial heights where a woman like you belongs."

There was a small jolt as the incline's twin cables drew taut, and the car began its silent climb up the long track. The lower station began to shrink away, leaving a square, black hole where the car had been.

"I got your call," Riley said. "Sorry if this seems a little cloak-and-dagger, but after our meeting with the FBI, I thought it might be wise if we tried to be a little more . . . discreet."

"Just the way I like things," Leo said. "Discreet."

"What's on your mind?"

"Nick Polchak is on my mind. Is he on yours?"

Riley hesitated. She began to speak but stopped short. She glanced around the empty car, then back at Leo again. All the while, Leo watched her eyes.

"I see," he said.

Riley felt the rush of blood to her face. "What do you see?"

"I see that you care about Nick. But I sense that things are . . . complicated."

"You have no idea."

"Pour out your soul to me; I am your confidant."

"I wish I could, Leo, I really do. But—"

He nodded. "I think you should know, Nick cares a great deal for you. I tell you this because he will have a great deal of difficulty telling you himself."

"Did he tell you that?"

"He said your voice reminds him of a wind chime."

Riley smiled. "That's kind of sweet."

"In a sixth-grade sort of way, yes. But you have to start somewhere, and for Nick, that's really quite remarkable."

"I've tried not to . . . encourage him."

"Nonsense—you've encouraged him by your very existence. You're beautiful, you're intelligent, and you're comfortable with your arms up to the elbow in human viscera. You're Nick's kind of girl."

"Nick is a wonderful man. But he's kind of—"

"Strange? Twisted? Demented? Take your pick. Nick Polchak is all of these and more."

"Leo—I thought you were Nick's friend."

Leo looked affronted. "I love Nick Polchak like my own brother. What am I saying—I *hate* my own brother. I love Nick Polchak like no other man in this world."

Riley grinned. "Leo, is there anything that you just . . . *like*?"

"What would be the point? That's like stopping halfway up the incline. Italians have two emotions, Ms. McKay: we love, and we hate. Everything else is just pasta."

Riley let out a laugh. "Well, I hope you don't hate *me*."

"I adore you—and so does Nick, which brings us back to the subject. Nick is like a man trapped in a great ship, staring out two giant portholes at the world passing by. I believe he wants out—but I don't think he knows how to get out. For that, he needs the help of someone else—someone like you. Nick Polchak, you see, is a tortured soul."

"I was always warned not to get involved with a man like that."

"There is no other kind. But why should that discourage you? We're *all* tortured souls—aren't we, Riley?"

She looked down at her feet.

"Leo, what happened to Nick? What hurt him?"

"I think he should answer that question for himself. But I can tell you this much: Tarentum was a very tough town when Nick and I were growing up. The mills and factories were all closing down, people were out of work. Lean times can make mean-spirited people; Nick's father was one of them. He abandoned the family early, but he kept on returning like a plague—seemingly just to torment Nick. And then there was Nick's obvious visual impairment—people can be very unkind, can't they? That's the world Nick grew up in, Riley. Early on, he discovered two things: that he had a most unusual intellect, and that—once he got his glasses—he could see things other people couldn't see."

"What sort of things?"

"My family liked to do jigsaw puzzles. We had lots of puzzles, and we would assemble them again and again—but over time we lost the boxes, and then we would store the pieces in plastic bags. So when we began a puzzle, we had no idea what the final image would be. Is it the lighthouse? Is it the old mill? It was always a kind of competition to see who could recognize the subject first. One evening Nick came over for dinner, and after dinner he joined us to start a new puzzle. Nick watched us lay down the first three pieces, and then he said, 'It's a clipper ship with three masts.' And you know what? He was *right*. And after that, my family didn't want Nick to help with the jigsaw puzzle anymore. Do you know why? Because Nick takes all the fun out of it. He sees things that other people can't see, and that puts him in a world of his own."

"Does he really think of himself as an insect?"

"He has no love for the human species—at least, not the members of it *he's* met. Human beings can be so unpredictable, so irrational—so *hurtful*. I think Nick came to appreciate the orderliness and predictability of the insect world. I believe there's a cure for his malady—but I don't think it will come in the form of a pill or a therapy. I think it will have to have a human face."

"Leo, I need to ask you something: what do you think of Nick's theory, this whole idea of a black market in human organs?"

"I would call it absurd," Leo said, "except for the fact that it's *Nick's* theory. Remember the clipper ship, Riley. Nick has a kind of intuition that he borrows from the insect world; he makes connections in a most remarkable way. He may be wrong about this, but I would not discount his instincts."

Now Leo took Riley's hand and looked her full in the eyes. "I want to tell you why I really called," he said, lifting a folder from the wooden bench beside him. "Nick asked me to see if I could hack into the patient database at UPMC Presbyterian."

"What? What for?"

"Because you told him that most of the organ transplants in this area are performed there. He asked me to find a list of patients awaiting kidney transplants there. He also asked me to search for *old* lists; he wants to compare them, to see if anyone has dropped off the list without having their surgery. If anyone has, he plans to check them against the obituaries. Nick is putting his theory to the test, Riley. If anyone is still alive who shouldn't be, he wants to know why."

Riley said nothing. Leo squeezed her hand a little tighter.

"How long have you been on the waiting list, Riley?"

She turned to him with a look of both sadness and relief. "Six years, eight months, and seventeen days."

"That's a long time to wait—a long time to *hope*."

"I have a rare compatibility problem, Leo. There's very little chance a kidney will ever turn up for me."

"And if it doesn't?"

"I was diagnosed with chronic kidney failure; when my kidney function fell below 10 percent, it became end-stage renal disease. Dialysis can buy you some time, but a transplant is the only cure." She turned to the window. "The word among doctors is that kidney failure is a pretty good way to go. Your blood becomes more and more polluted, and you just sort of run down like a battery. My battery is pretty low."

"Are there no family members who can help?"

"I have one sister; she's not a match."

Leo put his arm around her, pulled her close, and kissed her hair. "I can see why things are complicated."

"I think Nick suspects anyway."

"Nick knows you're ill. When he was at your apartment the other night, he looked through your medicine cabinet and found your medications."

Riley straightened. "He had no right!"

"Breaking and entering, hacking into patient databases—the question of 'rights' here is a little slippery, don't you think? The point is, Riley, when I hand Nick this list, he's going to see your name on it. He's going to know the full extent of your illness. He's going to *know*, Riley. Is that what you want?"

"What choice do I have?"

Leo opened the folder and took out several sheets of paper. "As a friend—as someone who *loves* you—I'm offering to remove your name from this list."

Riley stared at him. "Would you be willing to do that?"

"I might—but first you have to answer some questions for me: Why are you involved in all this, Riley McKay? What's your true motivation? And what does this have to do with your own need for a kidney transplant?"

Riley took a minute to collect her thoughts. "When Lassiter refused to release that man's organs for transplant, I thought, 'Those could have been *my* kidneys!' And even if they weren't, they could have saved *someone's* life. People die on the waiting list every day, Leo. Someday soon, I will. I had to know why Lassiter would do that. It just triggered something inside me; I didn't know where all this would lead." She looked into his eyes. "Do you believe me?"

"Without question," he nodded. "Nick lives in a world of the mind—but I happen to know hearts. If you were lying to me, I would have known it before you finished your first sentence. Now, about this list—what do you want me to do?"

"What do you think I should do?"

"If Nick knows you're dying, he'll either throw himself at you or run away. Either way, it could no longer be an ordinary relationship—and that's what I want for him most. The time may come when you have to tell him yourself, Riley, but I want you to have the freedom to make that choice."

Leo tore the top sheet of paper in half and put it back in the folder.

She kissed him on the cheek again. "That's the nicest thing anyone has ever done for me."

They looked out the back window; the car was approaching the end of the steel track. Their piece of the jigsaw puzzle was about to slide into place, completing the picture of the upper station with its white beveled siding and twin towers with violet caps. Riley began to turn toward the door as the car came to its final stop—but Leo held on to her hand until she turned back to him again.

"I don't know if you'll be the cure for Nick," he said, "but I hope you won't contribute to his disease."

"I'll try not to."

"You know, Riley, it isn't enough for you to be Nick's cure—he has to cure something in you as well."

"Oh, Leo—I don't know if that's possible."

Leo kissed the back of her hand. "You never know," he said. "Love heals all kinds of wounds."

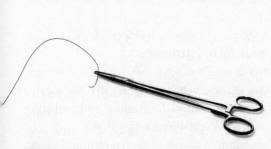

M ake a right on 19," Riley said, studying the MapQuest directions.

Nick pushed harder on the gas as they started up a long hill; the engine made a whining sound, coughing and wheezing like an old man climbing stairs. Each time one of the four cylinders missed, another puff of blue smoke belched out behind them, punctuating the still morning air.

"Nick, I've heard model airplanes that sound better than this."

"That's because they cost more. I got a deal on this."

"Somebody got a deal. How old is this thing?"

"Car talk bores me. Which way at this intersection?"

"Left." Riley sipped her Starbucks and glanced at her watch: *five-thirty*. She was giving up her every-other-weekend-off for *this*? Her only consolation was that Nick had no way of flipping the car over and dumping her onto the roadway—but looking at the shuddering car around her, she wasn't entirely sure. She picked up a half-eaten croissant from her lap, nibbled at it, then wadded it up in her napkin and turned to Nick. "What do I do with this?"

"There's a place for trash in the backseat."

She turned and looked. The backseat and floor were piled high with faded textbooks, drab-looking journals, and glutted three-ring binders spewing disheveled papers. There were two knapsacks, wadded-up articles of multicolored clothing, and a strange assortment of lidded plastic and foam containers.

She looked back at Nick. He took the napkin from her hand and tossed it over his shoulder. It bounced off something that looked like a butterfly net and came to rest under the rear window.

"Has anyone ever told you you're a slob?" she said.

"Only rude people."

Riley folded her arms tightly and settled back in her seat, trying her best not to touch anything around her. "You sure know how to treat a girl," she grumbled.

"Stop complaining. Aren't I taking you to Upper St. Clair? It's the classiest neighborhood in all of Pittsburgh."

Riley looked out her window. Through breaks in the tall hedges she began to catch passing glimpses of sprawling private estates with manicured shrubbery, sculptured fountains, and winding driveways paved in sulfur-gray Pennsylvania flagstone.

"Look at this place," she said. "I've never seen anything like it."

"You're not from around here?"

"Hardly. I grew up about forty miles south of here—a little coal-mining town called Mencken. My father was a coal miner from the time he was old enough to go to work until the day he died."

"What did he die of?"

Riley shrugged. "A coal mine is a toxic place—so are the towns that grow up around them. There's coal dust, fly ash, cadmium, iron oxides—take your pick. My father just began to waste away one day. A month later he was dead. The cause of death was never determined. I think that's one of the reasons I went into pathology: it's nice to know why someone you love died."

"Mencken—why does that sound familiar?"

"Probably our underground coal-mine fire; it's been burning for forty years now."

"Forty years?"

"There are places where the coal vein comes right up to the surface. The miners' families used to go there to gather our own coal to use in our furnaces. People dumped their trash there too, and years ago someone got the bright idea to burn it. That set fire to the coal seam, and the fire's been smoldering underground ever since."

"That's bizarre."

"There are underground coal-mine fires all over Pennsylvania— five in Allegheny County alone. Of course, what makes Mencken so special is that we've got a bony pile fire too."

"A what?"

Riley looked at him. "You're from Pittsburgh, and you've never heard of a bony pile?"

"My family was in steel," he said. "The Carnegies and the Polchaks."

"A coal mine produces a lot of scrap—shale, coal tailings, old timbers, stuff like that. In the old days, when the miners came out of the shaft, they just dumped it all beside the mouth of the mine. Over the years those piles grew to enormous sizes. The Mencken bony pile is two hundred feet high and half a mile long; it went right past our back door. The problem is, those piles contain a lot of low-grade coal, and sometimes they catch fire just like the mines do. Our bony pile has been burning for years now."

"Like a giant pile of charcoal briquettes?"

"Only it burns from the inside out. To look at it, you wouldn't even know it's on fire. I used to play on it all the time as a little girl."

"You used to *play* on it? Isn't that a little dangerous?"

"It is if you don't know where you're going. A man from the Department of Environmental Protection came out once. He climbed halfway up the bony pile and stuck a temperature probe into the ground by his feet. A foot and a half below the surface it was eight hundred degrees. He came down off that pile *fast*."

"And you used to *play* on it?"

"Like I said, you just have to know where you're going. Every winter, when it snowed, the bony pile looked like a ski area. The snow would melt off all the hot spots, and stick to all the cold ones. It made a sort of map; it told us where it was safe to walk."

"And you just hoped it stayed that way until the following winter."

"I'm a coal miner's daughter. We didn't have it soft like you steel tycoons."

"So the mine is on fire, and the bony pile is on fire. That's got to be a little hard on property values."

"My sister and I still own the house, if that's what you mean. How could we sell it? Mencken is a ghost town. The basements collect carbon monoxide, smoke seeps out of cracks in the ground, and after it rains the bony pile steams like a giant compost mound. It's not exactly Upper St. Clair."

"So you and your sister are blue collar girls. Somehow I thought the blue was in your veins."

"Why's that?"

"You're a doctor. I don't imagine many Mencken High graduates went on to medical school."

"Sarah and I both went into medicine. We thought it's what our father would have wanted."

Nick looked at her. "Your father would have been very proud of you."

She met his eyes. "What about your father? Was he proud of you?"

Nick turned away. "Boyce Street. What do we do here?"

"This is it. Make a right—it should be just a couple of houses down."

They passed a series of tall brick posts capped in limestone finials the shape of chess pawns. The posts were connected by sections of intricate wrought-iron fence; in the center of each was a flowering fleur-de-lis. After the sixth post there was a wide, arching gate that spanned an immaculate crushed-stone driveway. Nick pulled to the center of the gate and stopped the car. At the end of the long driveway, visible between a colonnade of stately elms and poplars, was the seemingly endless English Tudor estate of Mr. Miles Vandenborre.

"Five million at least," Nick whistled.

"Nick—don't stop here!"

"Why not?"

"Look at that place—and look at this car."

"OK . . ."

"Do I have to spell it out for you? Their garbage is worth more than this car!"

"I hope so," Nick said. "That's the whole idea." He stepped out of the car and lifted the trunk with a rusty groan. To the right of the gate, two thirty-gallon garbage cans stood sentry, surrounded by a series of smaller white plastic bags neatly twist-tied at the tops. He flipped the lid off each can, pulled out the black cinch-top bags, and carried them to his trunk. He rounded up the white bags in a single armload, and in less than two minutes they were under way again.

Nick glanced over at Riley, who was slumping even lower in her seat. "Now you know why I wanted to bring *my* car—the right tool for the right job."

"Just drive," she said, cupping her right hand over her eyes.

"Your first time Dumpster diving? I guess you've never been a teacher."

"What are we going to do with all this stuff?"

"We're taking it to Leo's. Mr. Vandenborre is a rich man in need of a kidney transplant, but for some reason he removed himself from the waiting list—yet he's still alive. I want to know why."

"And you think his trash is going to tell us."

Nick glanced at the backseat. "You can tell a lot about a person by his trash—don't you think?"

They parallel parked in front of Forest Hills Apartments. Riley took the two black bags; Nick gathered the assortment of white bags and closed the trunk behind him. They disappeared through a stone archway and up a flight of stairs.

Across the street, Cruz Santangelo set his binoculars on the dashboard, took a pen from his coat pocket, and jotted down the address.

CHAPTER
29

Set them there, on the kitchen floor," Leo said.

Riley set the two black bags side by side on the linoleum. Nick was right behind her with an armload of bulging white plastic.

"Don't get them mixed up with your own trash," Nick said. "Mr. Vandenborre could turn out to be *really* weird."

"I'll get the door," Riley said, crossing back across the living room.

"Don't bother," Leo called after her. "I never close the door—to my apartment or to my heart. It helps with the electric bills."

"You have an electric heart?" Nick said.

Leo turned to Riley with a look of disgust. "Have you spent the entire morning with . . . *this*?"

"I had to ride in his car too."

Leo grimaced. "How could you tell it from the trash? Why didn't you drive the whole thing up here?"

Riley looked around the apartment. The entry door was braced open by a small entertainment center; she wondered if he ever closed it at all. The windows were open too, and the summer breeze caused the drapes to flutter in like flags. The room was sparsely furnished, but the walls were crowded with framed reproductions of the masters of the Italian High Renaissance. Along the far wall was a long workbench covered with computers, monitors, storage drives, scanners, and devices that Riley had never seen outside the coroner's own forensics lab. In the center of the workbench, a flat-screen plasma display hung under a copy of Titian's *Sacred and Profane Love*. Behind a high-speed optical scanner stood a marble reproduction of Michelangelo's *Bacchus*. The entire room was an endless anachronism: it was a computer lab within an art museum, a brave new world under the watchful eye of the old.

At the end of the workbench, a charcoal gray flat-panel monitor displayed the PharmaGen logo. As Riley watched, the image changed to the company's most recent corporate report.

"Why are you watching the PharmaGen Web site?"

"I'm not," Leo said, "Lassiter is. I have our spyware configured for remote viewing; whatever Lassiter is looking at, we're watching in real-time. You're seeing what he's seeing right now."

"That's a little creepy," Riley said. "Anything out of the ordinary? I tried not to call for a few days—Nick said to give it a rest."

"He should talk—Nick never gives anything a rest. Don't worry; I check the keystroke logs every hour. There's been nothing of interest to us so far."

Riley stopped, took a deep breath, and bent over slightly.

"Are you all right?"

"I carried those bags up three flights of stairs," she said, stretching her back. "I have to be careful about that kind of exertion."

"Do you need to sit down?"

"I'm OK. I just needed to catch my breath."

In the kitchen, Nick gently patted the sides of the white plastic bags until he came to one. "Bingo," he said, tossing it to Leo.

He tested it himself. "I think you're right." He laid the bag down on the kitchen counter and carefully slid a knife up the side; a tangle of paper strips bushed out through the slit. Leo turned and gave Nick a beaming thumbs-up.

"But it's shredded," Riley said. "What good is that?"

"Shredding is good," Leo replied. "Shredding tells you that they have something they want to hide—something that might be worth looking at." He reached into the slit and carefully pulled out a handful of paper. "See this? This is approximately five documents, and they can be reassembled manually in about ten minutes. That's the beauty of strip-shredders, Riley. They only create the *illusion* of security. They separate a document into narrow strips, then they drop them side by side into the waste receptacle. It doesn't take a genius to put them back together again. It doesn't take a computer specialist either," he said, turning to Nick. "You can do this yourself."

"Come on, Leo, I've got things to do. Don't you have some work-study kids you can give it to? Besides, we're definitely going to need you for *this*." He handed Leo a second bag. He felt along the bottom; it was filled with paper, too, but it was much heavier and more compact. He carried this bag to the kitchen table and carefully slit along the bottom. Thousands of tiny white-and-black squares poured out in a soft mound of paper confetti.

"Don't tell me you can put *that* back together," Riley said.

Leo looked up at her with a pained expression. "Still you doubt me. Still I must prove myself to you. Of course I can put this back together. It just takes a little longer—and it does require a computer specialist. Fortunately for you, I just happen to be one." He shook the bag until no more came out, then carefully searched the inside of the bag for tiny pieces clinging to other objects. Then he began to spread the bits of paper evenly on the table so that no two were touching.

"Next I lay down sheets of a special transparent plastic," he said. "The bits of paper adhere to them. Then one by one I place the sheets on an optical scanner and scan both sides of each sheet. The program does the rest."

"What program?"

"I originally developed it for the FBI. It looks at the image on each bit of paper, and it also notes the exact shape of every edge. Then the computer goes through millions of permutations, matching images and edges until the original document is restored. It's like working a hundred-thousand-piece jigsaw puzzle at warp speed."

"Your family would be proud of you," Riley said.

"But even at warp speed, this will still take a little time."

"How much time?" Nick asked.

"The rest of the day should do it. And what if this should turn up something—something that confirms this theory of yours? What happens then?"

"Then we call Special Agent Santangelo. We tell him what we've learned, and we turn over the physical evidence—that should speed up his investigation."

"He's not going to like it," Riley said. "He told us no more poking around."

"He said no more poking around in *Lassiter's* affairs—I always listen very carefully when people are threatening me. And we're not poking around in Lassiter's affairs anymore."

"We're still monitoring his computer activity."

"Yes, but the FBI has no way of knowing that—all we're doing is watching, just like they are. And all we did this morning is snatch someone else's trash. That's perfectly legal, as long as the trash is curbside."

"Nick, we're reassembling shredded documents. What would the FBI say about that?"

"They're using Leo's program—what could they say? Look, Riley, you're the boss here. We can stop what we're doing right now and leave the rest to the FBI. Would you be happy with that?"

Riley thought for a minute. "No," she said. "With the FBI, it's always going to be a 'need to know' basis—even when their investigation is over. They might not ever tell us what was really going on here."

"I don't want to interfere with a federal investigation," Nick said. "I just want to finish what we've started. We can't call the FBI with every little detail we come up with; if we do, they'll tell us to back off for sure. I think we should finish what we're doing here, and *then* turn over what we have—because the next time we call Santangelo, we're finished."

Nick and Riley stood by the table, watching Leo sort and

arrange the thousands of bits of paper into an enormous, miniature mosaic. He looked up at them.

"Don't you two have things to do?"

"Right," Nick said. "I should get going."

"It is my day off," Riley nodded. "What's left of it anyway."

Five minutes later they were still watching.

Leo walked around the table, took both of them by the hand, and led them to the open window.

"Look out there," he said to Nick. "What do you see?"

Nick shrugged. "Pittsburgh."

He shook his head in disgust and turned to Riley. "Please, rescue this lost soul. Look out the window and tell him what you see."

"Life," Riley said.

Leo threw both hands in the air. "A heartbeat! Faint, but barely audible. For you, there's hope. Your friend here has no pulse at all—he may be beyond resuscitation. You know the problem with you two? Your whole existence is work, and you've forgotten entirely how to *play*. You find you have a few precious hours off, and still you hover around my table like two old prisoners afraid to leave their cells. Go on, get out of here while there's still some hope of redemption for both of you. And *you*," he said, pointing a finger at Nick. "Don't come back here until you *feel* something. Help him with this," he said to Riley, "even if you have to defibrillate him."

He ushered both of them to the doorway, gave them a solid push toward the stairwell, and returned to the apartment.

They stood in awkward silence for a moment.

"He gets like this," Nick said. "He won't let us back in for a while."

"How long?"

"It's hard to tell. Maybe the whole evening."

Riley nodded. "Might as well go, then."

"Might as well."

They slowly turned to the stairwell, with no idea where they were going next.

You make a mean *kielbasa*, Mrs. Polchak," Riley said, pushing away her plate.

"All Polish food is mean," Nick said. "Just give it a few hours."

Mrs. Polchak looked at Riley's half-finished plate. "This is how you eat?" she said disapprovingly. "No wonder they think you are a *fellow*."

They took their coffee in the tiny family room. Mrs. Polchak settled into an upholstered rocker that dominated the room like a throne. On her left was a small taboret, a maple magazine rack, and a portable writing table; on her right was an end table and a reading lamp with a moveable arm. The only other seat in the room was a small love seat directly across from the recliner. Nick and Riley took a seat side by side and stared silently into their cups. Mrs. Polchak turned the reading lamp until it cast its light directly on them.

"So tell me," she said to Riley, "how are things going with you two?"

"Uh—" Riley looked at Nick for help.

"No way," he said. "She asked *you*."

"Oh . . . well, things are . . . they're sort of . . . things are kind of—"

"She doesn't like me, Mama," Nick said. "God knows I've tried."

"That's not true," Riley said. "I do like him."

"Nicky," Mrs. Polchak smiled, "there is a nice lemon torte in the refrigerator. Go and fetch it for us, that's a good boy."

"Why don't we wait awhile before we—"

"Fetch it for us. Slice it up for us in nice little pieces. Take your time."

"Mama, Riley doesn't really like—"

"Nicky!" she said with a quick glare. "Go away so I can talk about you behind your back."

Nick set his cup on the coffee table. "I'll get the dessert," he said. "I may never come back."

They both watched until he disappeared behind the swinging door, then Mrs. Polchak turned to Riley again.

"We have a nice walnut tree," she said. "Do you like walnuts?"

"Walnuts? Yes, I—"

"Walnuts are a lot of trouble. The shells are very thick, and they stain your hands. But they are worth the trouble, don't you think?"

"Mrs. Polchak, it isn't your son, it's me—"

"It's him," she said, shaking her head. "Women take too much blame. When a man does not love us, we say, 'It's me.' When we cannot love a man, we say, 'It's me.' Sometimes it's *them*. Nicky is hard to love. I know; his father was hard to love."

Riley set her own cup down. "Mrs. Polchak, what happened between Nick and his father? Can you tell me?"

"Nicky's father was a very strong man, but he was *ignorancki*—he was not very bright. Nicky was just the other way; he was very smart, but he was weak—his eyes, you see. It is hard for men to have sons; they are like little mirrors. I think Stanislaw did not like what he saw in Nicky's eyes."

"That's so very sad."

"What about you? Do you like what you see in Nicky's eyes?"

Riley slowly nodded.

"Me, I like walnuts," Mrs. Polchak said. "But it takes time to open them up. It takes a big hammer too."

"I wish I had the time," Riley said softly.

"You young people! Is your time so short?"

"I'm afraid it is."

"Then use the time you have."

"Mrs. Polchak, I want to be fair to Nick. I don't want to lead him on."

"And why not?" she said indignantly. "I led three men on, and then I picked the best of them. Stanislaw was the lucky one, and the others survived. What do you think men are, little pastries? Life is not fair; love is not fair; but time, as you say, is short."

Riley considered her words. "You know, I think you're right—Stanislaw was the lucky one."

Just then Nick reentered the room with a small tray containing plates, forks, and a badly mauled lemon torte.

"Why do you embarrass me?" Mrs. Polchak said, grimacing at her beautiful dessert. "You can slice open those little worms of yours, but you can't find the center of a lemon torte? What did you cut this with, your elbow?"

"It's OK, really," Riley said. "I don't think I could touch another bite right now. I could use a walk first."

Mrs. Polchak brightened. "A walk is just the thing. Why don't you two take a nice walk, while I go in the kitchen and throw two hours of hard work in the garbage?"

"This is what's known as a 'guilt trip,' " Nick whispered to Riley. "C'mon, let's get out of here."

They left by the back door. Twenty yards away, tucked in the trees against the hillside, the greenhouse glittered like a faceted jewel in the passing moonlight. They followed a well-worn path toward the greenhouse door.

Nick glanced over at Riley. "So what did she say about me?"

"She said you're a nut, and if I want to open you up, I'd better have a big hammer."

"That's better than I hoped for," Nick said. "Wait here a minute." He stepped into the greenhouse and emerged a moment later with two shining objects. He handed one to Riley; it was a small mason jar with the lid ring holding a coffee filter in place across the open mouth.

"Come on," he said. "I want to show you something." He turned and headed for a second path that curved slowly uphill and disappeared into the woods. Riley followed him to the edge of the trees, stopped, and peered into the darkness.

"Where are we going?" she called after him.

"This way. You've got to see this."

Riley took a deep breath and plunged into the shadows after him, where strips of bright moonlight illuminated the path in a zebra pattern. She caught up to him at a place where the trees suddenly gave way to a great, open meadow.

They walked together to the top of the rise. "Welcome to my world," he said.

The hill sloped gently away from them to form a vast, shadowy meadow that seemed to rise and fall like the ocean at night. Thin pockets of mist lay in the hollows, and around the edge of the woods, thick stands of locust and maple stood guard in uniforms of deep blue and violet. And everywhere, as far as the eye could see, were the gentle, silent, floating green lights of a thousand fireflies.

"It's beautiful," she whispered.

Nick reached slowly into the air and clapped his hands together once.

"Look." He opened his hands to show a glowing smear of light across his palm. "Luciferase. It's the enzyme that produces their light. Did you know that 95 percent of the energy used by an incandescent light bulb is given off as heat? A hundred years of technological advancement and that's the best that your species can do. But this little guy gives off almost 100 percent *light*. Incredible!"

He reached his arm into the air again and a moment later brought it back, holding out the edge of his hand to show a single black insect, tipped with orange and glowing with soft green light. "You're looking at the state insect of Pennsylvania," he said. "New Mexico's is a *wasp*. Fireflies are really beetles, not flies at all. In a few weeks, they'll all be gone." He slowly extended his hand to her. She held out her own hand, and Nick took it, allowing the tiny creature to crawl off of his hand and onto hers. But Nick held her hand a little longer.

They waded forward into the ocean of soft green lights.

"I'll bet I know how to tell the males from the females," Riley said. "It's the eyes. The females see everything going on around them, and the males are all clueless."

"Nice try. The truth is, every one you see is a male. Most people have never seen a female firefly." Nick dropped to his hands and knees and began to search through the thick grass. "Look—here's a female."

Riley saw a tiny green glow coming from the tip of a blade of grass.

"The females stay on the ground. Each species of firefly has its own flash pattern. The females flash their signal, and the males fly overhead and flash back. When there's a match, that's *amore*—most of the time."

"Most of the time?"

"See that one?" He pointed across the meadow. "That's a Big Dipper firefly—a *Photinus pyralis*. He lights his lamp, dips, and then curves up again—see? He writes the letter J over and over again. Now, somewhere in this meadow is a female *Photinus*—but there are also a few *Photuris* ladies too. They're much larger than the Dippers, and they've learned to mimic their flash pattern perfectly. If the male *Photinus* picks the wrong lady, it's dinnertime—and he's dinner."

"Love is a risky business in the insect world," Riley said.

"In the human world too. Get attracted to the wrong female and you can get eaten alive."

"Is that your personal experience or just a scientific observation?"

Nick removed the lid from his jar and began to move among the tiny lights, reaching and bending and scooping at the air.

"At the beginning of the firefly season, there are hundreds of males for every female. The male soars over the meadow, flashing, searching, like Diogenes with his lantern. He spots females everywhere, but none of them are for him. Suddenly he sees it—can it be? Yes! It's *his* signal! After endless miles of flying and thousands and thousands of flashes, he's found his ladylove. He soars down into her waiting arms," he said, with arms extended, "and she bites his head off."

"Why do you think they keep trying?"

"Because they have brains the size of pinheads," Nick said. "What's *our* excuse?"

Riley sat down now and watched Nick as he moved about the meadow. Sometimes he stretched and sometimes he stooped. Sometimes he stood perfectly still and waited. Then he would start again, almost running across the field, arms sweeping back and forth before him. Riley smiled, imagining that even after the fireflies were gone he might come to this field late at night and run, like a child, for the sheer joy of movement.

The moon was bright, but the sky was littered with clouds. At one moment she could see him perfectly, a cobalt figure with a gleaming glass jar. An instant later he was only a silhouette, barely visible at all.

"Riley," he called out. "Where are you?"

Riley sat perfectly still.

"Riley!" he called louder.

Silence.

"So *that's* the game," he said, and began to retrace his steps back across the field toward the rise. There was a flash of moonlight and he whirled around, taking a quick accounting of every potential shape and shadow—then darkness again. Riley sat in a small hollow, blending almost perfectly with the ground around her. He was now very near, and once he passed so close that she could hear his breathing, so close that she felt the hair stand up on the back of her neck. Still she said nothing.

He stopped and turned. He was looking almost directly at her. He stepped forward, stopped, and stared more closely, as if by concentrating he might somehow draw extra light from the coal black sky. He stepped closer; closer; now he was only a few feet away, and the air seemed supercharged between them. Riley held her breath and stared up at him. Another step, and then he bent slowly forward, staring into the strange shadow before him.

At that moment the moon slid out from behind a black cloud, and Nick found himself staring into Riley's green and brown eyes, ablaze in the blue white moonlight. They both found themselves strangely short of breath. Riley rose to her knees; Nick dropped to his and took her in his arms. She blinked hard once, and he instinctively blinked back.

"It's been a long time," Nick said. "What do I do now?"

"I think you're supposed to kiss me."

Nick hesitated. "I think I forgot how."

"They say it's like riding a bicycle."

"I was never any good on a bicycle—I used to fall off a lot."

"Like you said—love is a risky business."

And then they both remembered.

They were interrupted by the sound of Nick's cell phone. He slid it out of his pocket and opened it. "What?" he said with obvious annoyance.

"Nick, it's Leo. Have you felt anything yet?"

"I was starting to. What do you want?"

"Is this a bad time?"

"The worst. Hang on a minute." He motioned to Riley; she edged up beside him, and he held the phone away so she could hear as well.

"I finished the shredding," Leo said. "The program just ended and printed out a copy of all the original documents. Most of them were ordinary financial records—a Visa charge summary, a mutual-fund statement of activity, health insurance explanation of benefits—that sort of thing. But there were a few items in the confetti shredding that I thought you should know about. One was a brochure from an outpatient surgery center in Penn Hills. You don't suppose your boy had a knee repaired or a wart removed, do you?"

"It's possible. What are the other items?"

"Three prescriptions from a Canadian online pharmacy. The drugs are called Neoral, Immuran, and Orasone. I have no idea what they are."

Nick looked at Riley.

"Neoral is a cyclosporine," she said. "Immuran is an azathioprine, and Orasone is a corticosteroid. They're all immunosuppressants, and they're commonly prescribed together—after transplants."

CHAPTER
31

How can I help you, Mr. Polchak? The receptionist tells me you have some concerns."

"Are you a doctor?"

"No, sir. My name is Allen Reston. I'm the COO—more like an office manager, really. You could say I run things here at Westmoreland Surgery Center."

Nick glanced around at the office. The room was precise in every detail, lit with the same antiseptic fluorescence as a procedure room. The desk was a curving slab of white maple with a contoured laminate base. The desktop was bare except for a matching black desk set and a flat panel monitor. The computer itself, like all other functional components of the room, was tastefully hidden from sight.

The walls were dutifully adorned with three sterile landscapes, which provided about the same warmth and assurance as the teddy bears on a phlebotomist's smock. Nick's plum-colored chair, ergonomically designed, forced him to sit more erect than he liked; it made him feel as though someone were pushing him from behind.

"I blew out an ACL on the tennis court," Nick said. "Now my doctor says I need laparoscopic surgery."

"Did the same thing myself," Reston said. "I guess it's the weekend warrior thing; you think you're still twenty-five, but your knees have other ideas."

Nick nodded. "I'm a little uncomfortable about having the procedure done here."

"Oh? Why is that?"

"Well, it's not a hospital. I mean, if something goes wrong in a hospital, you've got state-of-the-art medical facilities."

At this, the man broke into a smile. "You're a little behind the times, Mr. Polchak. How much do you know about freestanding surgery centers?"

"Very little, I'm afraid."

"These places started popping up everywhere about a dozen years ago. Hospital ORs were increasingly overcrowded, and they realized they could lighten the load considerably if they began to conduct minimally invasive surgeries off site."

"That's what I was afraid of—I get bussed to relieve someone else's overcrowding problem. I get second-rate care."

"There's nothing second-rate about Westmoreland Surgery Center," Reston said. "A decade ago, ambulatory surgery centers only performed the simplest procedures: endoscopies, breast biopsies, lesion excisions—and that's all that some centers still do. But more aggressive facilities—like this one—developed into full-fledged, freestanding surgery centers. At Westmoreland, we now do an entire range of surgical procedures: gynecological, urological, vascular, and orthopedic. We're constantly increasing the number of procedures we can perform."

"But you can't compete with a hospital for quality of care."

"Why not? Our surgeons are on the staff of several local hospitals; if you choose to go to a hospital, one of our surgeons may perform your procedure there."

"But surely hospitals have better facilities—the equipment and all."

"Westmoreland Surgery Center has two state-of-the-art surgical suites. They are identical to the ORs in any major hospital—except for the instrumentation, of course."

"The instrumentation?"

"The cost of medical equipment is enormous—a single surgical laser can cost almost a hundred and fifty thousand dollars. Hospitals have the funding to purchase their equipment outright; we avoid the capital outlay by using an equipment outsource company. Suppose you need a procedure that requires the use of that surgical laser; instead of buying one—and charging your insurance company for it—we can lease it for a single day. The outsource company can provide blood bypass equipment, instrument trays—anything we require, depending on the procedure we're doing."

"Clever," Nick said. "That would allow you to do almost any procedure a hospital can do."

"Almost."

"Just out of curiosity, what keeps you guys from going all the way? What keeps you from performing, say, brain surgery?"

Reston leaned as far back as his ergonomic chair would allow and considered this. "In theory, we could—that is, we could at least set up to perform the procedure—but what we're not set up for is long-term convalescent care. No intensive care unit, no month-long hospital stays. This is an *ambulatory* center, Mr. Polchak—strictly outpatient."

"So you knock out a wall and add a few beds. Surely brain surgery is more profitable than vasectomies."

"You'd think so—but the problem is liability. Surgery centers can only expand as far as liability insurance will allow them to. Think about it: We do a brain surgery, something goes wrong, and the attorneys all scream, 'Inadequate care! It wouldn't have happened in a hospital!' One suit like that would be the end of us."

"The end of who? Who owns this place anyway?"

"It's privately owned; that's all I'm allowed to tell you."

"By individual doctors?"

"Sorry. But I can tell you that doctors commonly own these places. Let's be honest, Mr. Polchak, there's a second reason these facilities began to develop: doctors took a good look at the fee structure in hospitals and realized they were missing out on a lot of money. Check a hospital bill—there are professional fees, and there are hospital fees. The professional fees go to the doctor, but the hospital gets the rest. Doctors realized they would never get the lion's share until they owned the facility itself—and outpatient surgical centers were born."

Nick glanced around the room. "I imagine these places are very profitable."

"There's a very definite profit motive behind these places—and I don't mind telling you, because it's to your advantage. Those profits allow us to compete with any other kind of healthcare facility—hospitals included. At Westmoreland you get state-of-the-art facilities, top-of-the-line surgical staff, privately employed nurses, and a lot more attention than you're going to get in a hospital ward with a hundred beds. You have nothing to fear here, Mr. Polchak. We're on the cutting edge."

Nick steered his car onto the Penn Lincoln Parkway and waited until he emerged from the Squirrel Hill Tunnel before punching the button on his cell phone.

"Riley McKay, please." He waited. "Riley—Nick. Can you talk? I just stopped off at Westmoreland Surgery Center and asked a few questions. What? Yes, I was tactful—aren't I always tactful? The COO at Westmoreland told me that they can set up to perform almost any technical procedure there. The only thing that limits them is liability—but if there is no liability, then there are no limits, are there? I think we've got the last piece of our puzzle—and I think it's time to call Santangelo. Are you OK with that? Then you make the call and tell them everything we've found—but keep Leo's name out of it, will you? Right. I knew you would.

"What's your caseload like today? When do you get off? Then let's meet tonight at Leo's, and we'll put a few notes together and collect all the physical evidence. Ask Santangelo what he wants us to do with it, and we can drop it off. Maybe the three of us can grab dinner together—you know, to celebrate. I'm afraid it'll have to be Italian.

"Hey, about last night. That talk you had with my mom seemed to do some good. What did she tell you? What? Well, pity is underrated. No, I'm not proud—I'll take pity any day.

"You know, it's been a long time since I've . . . ridden a bicycle. We sort of got interrupted. Too bad—it was just beginning to come back to me."

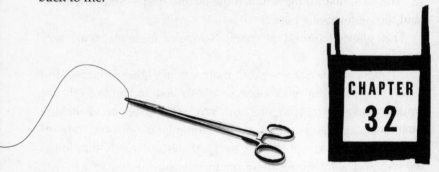

CHAPTER 32

The yacht's twin diesels had barely rumbled to a stop before Cruz Santangelo leapt to his feet.

"They know everything," he said. "They hacked into UPMC's patient records and got a list of transplant patients. They picked the ones who dropped off the list and compared them against death records. They took the richest guy and searched his trash. They've identified a client, Julian—they found Vandenborre."

"Ingenious," Zohar said. "Really quite impressive."

"Did you hear me? They know everything!"

"What *don't* they know?"

"What difference does it make? They've found a client! All they have to do is—"

"What *don't* they know?" he repeated patiently.

Santangelo sat down hard. "They don't know about my involvement. They still believe there's a federal investigation going on. That's why they called me."

"As we expected," Zohar nodded.

"And they don't know about Kaplan or Angel—but those are just details, Julian. They've made the connection between Lassiter and Truett and you. They know enough to put us away for life— what difference does it make what they *don't* know?"

"It makes a great deal of difference. Remember, Dr. Polchak and Dr. McKay are helping us to identify vulnerabilities in our system. They're working for us, not against us—not yet anyway."

"Santangelo is right!" Truett shouted, charging from the cockpit. "These people can destroy us with a single phone call."

"Which they already made—to the FBI, just this afternoon."

"But all it takes is one word to somebody else. I say it's time to shut them down—I've got too much at stake here."

"You have everything at stake here; we all do, Mr. Truett."

"Then we deal with this *now*."

"I agree!" Santangelo said.

Zohar paused to allow their emotions to subside. Then he smiled and spoke even more softly than before. "I agree. I think it's time, as you say, to *shut them down*—assuming, of course, that we know who *they* are. Mr. Santangelo, have you been able to identify the third member of their party?"

"I have—and I know where he lives."

"You've reviewed his vita? You've considered his education and background? You're convinced he was capable of providing the necessary computer expertise?"

"He's the one, all right. This guy has even developed software for the Bureau."

"And you're satisfied there's no one else? No fourth member?"

"There will be if we don't get moving. Who knows who else they might involve in this? The more time we spend here talking, the greater the risk."

"On that point I disagree; the more time we spend here talking, the *smaller* the risk. Remember, gentlemen, we're talking about 'shutting down' three human lives. If Dr. Lassiter were here, he would remind us that a careless course of action now will 'raise all kinds of flags' with the authorities."

"We don't have time for this," Truett said. "We've got to do it *now*!"

"We do have time for this," Zohar corrected, "but I agree that we should not delay. All I'm suggesting is that we proceed just as we've always done—according to *plan*, not out of passion. Mr. Santangelo, you know what to do?"

"I'm ready."

"Please keep me posted on your progress."

"What about the next procedure?" Truett said. "It's coming up fast. Are we still on?"

"Of course. I'll inform the rest of the committee about the details. Remember, we have a client who's depending on us—and I think Mr. Santangelo can guarantee that there will be no more prying eyes."

"You got it," Santangelo said.

Zohar smiled and looked at both of them. "Our last two meetings on this beautiful vessel have been so . . . *depressing*. May I suggest that our next gathering here be a kind of celebration? The end of one era and the beginning of another. What do you say, gentlemen? I'll bring the champagne."

CHAPTER 33

A toast," Leo said, raising his glass. "To the finest team of forensic exterminators ever assembled."

They touched their glasses together and drank. Leo's kitchen table was crowded with paper: strip-shredded documents reassembled into tiny woven mats, thousands of bits of confetti sandwiched between plastic sheets, and one neat stack of computer-generated reproductions. Beside the table, a mound of black-and-white garbage bags still rested.

"And now," Leo said with a flourish, "I would like to invite both of you to join me in a triumphal feast."

"Great idea," Nick said. "There's a little Polish deli just around the corner."

Leo twisted from side to side, as if searching for a place to spit. "How have I offended you? How have I sinned, that you would assign me this penance?"

"OK then, we'll let Riley decide."

They turned to her. Riley folded her arms.

"Has it ever occurred to you two that I'm *Scottish*?"

Nick squinted at her. "You want to go to McDonald's?"

She turned up her nose to him. "Just for that, I vote for Italian."

Leo raised his hands to the sky. "I promise you an unforgettable evening. Cost is no object, thanks to the good Mr. Vandenborre."

"Mr. Vandenborre?"

Leo picked up the top sheet of paper from the table. "Mr. Vandenborre has been kind enough to loan us his Visa card for the evening. I find this to be a poetic justice not even the FBI can attain."

Nick turned to Riley. "That reminds me: How was Santangelo when you told him?"

"Stunned. He didn't say anything at all for a minute—I thought we got disconnected at first. Then he kept asking me to repeat myself, asking for more and more details. Boys, I think we flat-out wowed the FBI."

"No complaints? No rebukes? No requests to give up your trivial pathology career and join the FBI?"

Riley laughed. "I wish I could have been there when he reported this to his superiors. I hope we didn't embarrass him too much."

"All authorities need to be embarrassed from time to time," Nick said. "It keeps them humble."

"I hate to change the subject," Leo said, "but I need my kitchen table back. What do we do with all of this?"

"I told Santangelo I'd call him again once we had time to organize it. Is this everything?"

"I should include a copy of the entomological evaluation I did for you," Nick said. "I need to polish the report and get the specimens mounted."

"This is everything I've got," Leo said, "except for the keystroke logs from Lassiter's computer. I saw no reason to include those, since the FBI has been monitoring them as well."

"We should throw those in too," Nick said. "We want them to know we're holding nothing back; better to give them too much than too little."

"It will only take a minute." Leo sat down at the computer and began to call up the spyware reports and send them one by one to the laser printer. Suddenly, he stopped and studied the screen. "Nick," he said. "Is this what I think it is?"

Nick stepped up behind him and peered over his shoulder. "What have you got?"

"An encrypted e-mail Lassiter sent less than an hour ago. Take a look."

The message read:

NEXT PROCEDURE AS SCHEDULED
DONOR: SARAH JEAN MCKAY
3162 ROCKFORD AVE APT 17/ MT.
LEBANON
O POSITIVE

"Riley," Nick called back to the kitchen, "isn't your sister named Sarah?"

"What's she done now?" Riley said, grinning as she stepped into the living room—but her smile instantly vanished when she saw the look on both of their faces. She charged to the computer and pushed Nick aside.

"Oh no," she whispered. *"Sarah!"*

"Was your sister part of PharmaGen's population study?" Nick asked.

"She's a *nurse*—half the medical people in the city are a part of it!"

Leo examined the screen again. "It says next *procedure*. She's referred to as a *donor*, and even her blood type is listed. There can be no doubt what this is."

Riley covered her face and turned away from the screen.

"Easy," Nick said. "Everything's OK."

Riley spun around. "Everything's OK? Dr. Lassiter did autopsies on three people who are *not* OK—three people who walked into the wrong alley or stopped to change a tire or felt a little needle prick in the back of the neck—and they never woke up again! Well, my sister is *not* going to be the next one!"

"Riley, listen to me," Leo said. "The FBI is monitoring Lassiter's computer just like we are. They've seen this message too."

"Have they? What time do federal agents knock off for the evening? You got this message less than an hour ago—what if they *haven't* seen it yet? The message says, 'Next procedure *as scheduled*'—scheduled when? What if it's scheduled *tonight*?"

She rushed to the kitchen counter and shoved her hand into her purse, fumbling for her cell phone. She turned the purse upside-down and dumped its contents onto the counter. She flipped open her wallet and pulled out a business card with a black and gold seal.

"Who are you calling?"

"Special Agent Santangelo. I'm going to make sure they've seen this message." She dialed the number and waited an eternity for it to connect.

"Hi there," the voice on the other end said.

"Special Agent Santangelo?"

"Mmhmm."

"This is Dr. Riley McKay."

"Of course it is. I've been expecting you to call."

"Mr. Santangelo, are your people still monitoring Lassiter's computer? Did you intercept the e-mail message he sent out tonight?"

"Can you hang on a minute? Coffee's ready."

"No! Wait a minute, you idiot! This is urgent!" She pulled the phone away, stared at it in disbelief, and shoved it against her ear again. It was a full thirty seconds before the voice came back on the line.

"There we go. I find it gets bitter if you brew it too long. Now, you were saying something about a message. What message would that be?"

"A message from Dr. Lassiter—*Next procedure as scheduled—Donor: Sarah Jean McKay! That's my sister, Mr. Santangelo!* These people are targeting my sister next!"

"Dr. Lassiter sent that in an e-mail? That was awfully careless of him, wasn't it? And he probably thought that was a safe thing to do because it was *encrypted*. But you saw the whole thing because you were watching his keystrokes, weren't you? Well, I guess that's what I get for working with morons."

Riley froze.

"I really do want to thank you for your cooperation. Why, without your help, I would have had to *guess* what you kids have discovered—but you were kind enough to keep me informed every step of the way. As a way of saying thanks, Dr. McKay, may I give you a piece of advice? I wouldn't worry about the 'next procedure' if I were you—I'd worry about my own health."

Riley began to tremble so hard that she dropped the phone. She stumbled back away from the counter and into Leo's arms. Nick picked up the phone.

"Santangelo? Nick Polchak."

"Oh yeah, our Bug Man friend. You know, Dr. Polchak, I really didn't appreciate your comments about Waco. The whole thing started when those idiots killed four ATF agents searching for illegal firearms. The truth is, no FBI agent fired a single shot at Waco—did you know that? But I wanted to, believe me. I would have killed them all if I had been given the order—but no, we had to let them set fire to the compound and burn themselves to death, then take the blame for everything."

"So you're the bad boy of the FBI after all," Nick said. "Tell me something: just how many bad boys are there?"

"It's not nice to talk about other people; let's talk about me. You asked me where HRT members go after Waco, remember? Well, I went looking for a more lucrative way to apply my hard-earned skills. And I found one, right here in Pittsburgh."

"You're the one who's been killing these people," Nick said. "The phony cardiac arrest, the drive-by shooting in Homewood. You were trained for this. You're an assassin."

"An *assassin*," he said thoughtfully. "Really, that's like calling Mozart a 'piano player.' No, Dr. Polchak, I'm much more than that—as you and Dr. McKay are about to discover."

"What happened to 'the minimum force possible'?"

"Sorry—this time the maximum force is necessary."

There was a click, and the line went dead.

Nick slowly turned and looked at Riley. "We told him everything," he said. "What was I thinking? Why didn't I see it? We thought we were shutting them down—we've been helping them."

Riley grabbed the phone from his hand and started punching numbers.

"Who are you calling?"

"The *real* FBI."

"Stop," Nick said, pulling the phone from her hand.

"What are you doing? Give me my phone!"

"Riley, he is the real FBI. Remember when we first met Santangelo on the *Majestic*? You called the local FBI office to check him out. Santangelo is an actual field agent, Riley. We have no idea who else in his office is involved."

"We can't just sit here! Sarah's life is in danger!"

"Maybe—maybe not. When you told Santangelo about Lassiter's e-mail, what did he say?"

"He acted like he knew nothing about it. He said Lassiter shouldn't have sent it, and he called him a moron. Why?"

"Santangelo has been working *with* Lassiter; that message may have been nothing more than a plant."

"But why would they plant a phony message? What would they have to gain? They already know what we know, and they know where to find us—why feed us information about another procedure? And why Sarah, of all people?"

"Exactly—why Sarah? Doesn't the coincidence bother you?"

"Nick, listen to me. Lassiter *is* a moron—we know that. We've both witnessed his past mistakes. Maybe he *wasn't* supposed to send that message—maybe Sarah is the next victim. If we assume the message is phony, and we're wrong, then Sarah *is* dead. We can't take that chance—I *won't* take that chance." She took the phone from his hand and opened it again.

"No," Nick said, covering the phone with his hand. "There's no one to call. Think about it, Riley: The FBI? We've been there. The coroner's office? Hardly. The police? They work closely with the coroner's office—who would be safe to call? You're right about one thing: we have to assume that the message is legitimate—but whatever we do about it, we have to do it ourselves."

"What do we do?"

"We get your sister to safety, that's the first thing—and we get *ourselves* to safety at the same time. Now that Santangelo knows everything, he'll come after us. That's his next order of business."

"Where do we go?"

"You can stay here," Leo said. "My house is your house."

"Not a chance," Nick said. "Santangelo referred to 'you and Dr. McKay.' He still doesn't know who you are, Leo, and we've got to keep it that way. There's no sense in endangering you, and we may need your help back here. In the meantime, get the rest of this evidence organized as fast as you can. Somebody's going to want it—we just don't know who yet."

"We can't go to my place," Riley said. "They'll know where I live for sure."

Nick shook his head in frustration. "They're a step ahead of us—they've been a step ahead of us all along. What we need most is time to *think*."

"Nick—we don't know how much time we have."

"How far is it to your sister's place?"

"Ten minutes, maybe less."

"Let's go. First we grab Sarah, then we find some place where we can figure this thing out."

"Here they come," Santangelo said, pointing at the two shadows emerging from the arched doorway into the yellow glare of the street-lamp. Riley climbed into her car, gunned the engine, and pulled away from the curb; Nick followed close behind in his own car, marking his parking space behind him with a glistening black puddle.

"Third floor," Santangelo said. "Down the hall, on the right— look for an open doorway. You know what to do?"

She nodded. "Away from the door and away from the windows."

"Good girl, Angel. I'll be right behind you."

CHAPTER
34

Riley knocked again, this time harder. The apartment door opened until the chain stretched tight, and a single eye appeared in the crack.

"Riley?" a woman's voice said. "Is that you?"

"It's me, Gabriella. Can we come in?"

The woman peered around the door's edge and discovered Nick, glaring impatiently at her from over Riley's right shoulder. Her eye widened at the sight of Nick's enormous eyes.

"It's late," she said uneasily. "I'm not exactly dressed for company."

"Gabriella, please. This is important."

The chain made a scratching sound and then dropped away. The door slowly swung open with Gabriella still behind it, peering around the edge at Nick, who followed Riley quickly through the open door.

"Sarah!" Riley called out, hurrying toward the hallway and the two back bedrooms.

"She's not here," Gabriella said.

"Where is she?"

"Why? What's wrong?"

"Gabriella—*where is she*?"

"Sarah's at the grocery store. What is it? What's happened?" She shut the door and chained it again, then hurried over to Riley, making a wide arc around Nick.

"It's a little late for grocery shopping," Nick said.

She jumped. The combination of Nick's deep voice and over-powering eyes had an unnerving effect on Gabriella. Riley stepped close, put her arm around her shoulders, and squeezed her tight.

"Gabriella, I want you to meet Nick Polchak. Nick is a friend of mine—a good friend. Despite those big buckeyes of his and his terrible taste in clothing, he's a nice guy, really."

"Does your roommate always do her grocery shopping at night?" Nick plunged ahead, ignoring Riley's attempt at warmth and reassurance.

Riley rolled her eyes. "Nick, Gabriella is Sarah's roommate. They're both nurses at UPMC—they often work late."

"Do you know anyone around here?" Nick said. "Family? Friends? Somewhere you can go for a few days?"

Gabriella stared at Nick. "You guys are scaring me. I need to know what's going on."

Riley turned her away from Nick and led her to the sofa. They sat down side by side, and Riley took her by the hands. "Gabriella, you know that I work for the coroner's office, right? Well, something has come up—something that I can't tell you about right now. There's a chance that Sarah is in danger—and you could be in danger too, because you share this apartment. We think it's best if you get away from here for a few days. Can you do that? Give me your cell phone number, and I'll call you when it's OK to come back. Is that OK?"

Nick sat down on the other end of the sofa. "What store does your roommate shop at? Does she go at the same time each week? Does she follow a predictable route to the store? Does anyone else know that route?"

"*Nick*," Riley said with a quick glare.

"When should I leave?" Gabriella asked nervously.

"The sooner the better," Riley said gently.

"First thing in the morning?"

"*Now*," Nick said. "The longer you stay here, the greater the risk."

Gabriella scrambled to her bedroom; Riley followed her to the doorway, then then turned back to Nick.

"What's wrong with you? Do you want her to jump out the window?"

"That would be a little counterproductive; I just wanted to hurry her along. Do you know where your sister shops?"

"There's a Giant Eagle just a couple of miles from here. Should we go there and look for her?"

"We can't both go—if we missed her she'd come back here, and then she'd be alone in this apartment. I can't go by myself—I don't even know what she looks like. And *you* can't go."

"Why not?"

"What if you find Sarah and she's in trouble?"

"What if *you* find Sarah and she's in trouble?"

"Better me than you," Nick said. "Besides, if you leave me alone with Gabriella, she *will* jump out the window."

Riley picked up her purse from the sofa. "Stop trying to protect me."

Nick stepped between her and the door. "Isn't that the whole point here?"

"The point is to protect Sarah first. Get out of my way."

"The point is to protect all of us."

She took a step closer. "Don't make me walk over you. I will, you know."

Nick raised both hands. "You wouldn't hit a man with glasses, would you?"

"This is my sister, Nick. You don't know how it is for me."

Now Nick stepped closer. "You don't know how it is for me."

Just then, there was the sound of a key fumbling in the lock. The door opened a few inches and then stopped, with a paper grocery sack wedged in the opening.

"Gabriella, get the chain!" a voice called from behind the door. "I'm losing this bag!"

Riley unlatched the chain and swung the door open wide. Sarah stood in the doorway, mouth open, blinking at her sister. "You look like someone I know," Sarah said. Then she looked at Nick. "Whoa—who's the big guy?"

Nick stepped forward and lifted both bags from her arms.

"Watch that one," Sarah said. "It's got eggs."

"Get in here!" Riley said. "Where have you been?"

"Is this a double date? You could give a girl a little more notice."

Riley gave her a quick embrace, pulled her into the apartment, and shut the door.

Sarah watched Nick as he disappeared into the kitchen. "Cute," she whispered. "Has he tried contacts?"

"I tried them," Nick said, returning. "They were the size of paperweights—kept stretching out my eyelids."

"Sarah, I want you to meet Dr. Nick Polchak." Riley slid her arm behind Nick's back and looked intently into Sarah's eyes.

Sarah nodded slightly and turned to Nick. "It's really nice to meet you, Nick. Welcome to the McKay Coal Mine—duck your head as you enter."

Behind them a bedroom door opened and Gabriella appeared, lugging a black Samsonite carry-on in one hand and a small cosmetic bag in the other.

"What's going on?" Sarah said. "Are you two moving in?"

"We asked Gabriella to spend a few days with her family," Riley said.

"What? Why?"

Gabriella stepped past Sarah and opened the door. "Oh, Sarah—be careful."

"You too," Sarah replied. "Will somebody tell me what's going on here?"

Gabriella turned to Nick and Riley. "Should I go in to work tomorrow?"

"Go to work as you always do," Nick said. "Keep an ear out for anyone asking questions about Sarah's whereabouts. We'll check in with you—and *don't* come back here until we tell you to, understand?"

Gabriella nodded, gave Sarah a quick peck on the cheek, and pulled the door shut behind her.

Sarah turned to Nick and Riley. "Well, this is interesting. My sister and a tall, dark stranger mysteriously appear in my apartment late one night, and two minutes later my roommate moves out. What are you, Nick, an immigrations agent? I'm pretty sure Gabriella's got a green card."

Riley shook her head. "Sarah, there's so much to explain, and there isn't time. Do you trust me?"

"The last time you said that you set me up for a blind date with an anesthesiologist. I've been drowsy ever since."

"I want you to pack a bag. Pack enough for—" She looked at Nick.

"A few days. A week at most."

"A *week!* You know, this is a little sudden for a road trip. What's going on?"

"I can't explain it all now."

"So I'm supposed to just disappear for a week—from my job, from my friends, from the club—and just head with you two to parts unknown?"

"That's about the size of it," Nick said. "We can talk on the road."

"We can talk *now*," Sarah said. She strolled to the sofa, plopped down, and picked up a magazine from the coffee table. "I've got lots of time—I *live* here."

Riley charged over to the sofa, ripped the magazine from her hands, and threw it across the room. "You pack that bag," she said. "You pack it *now*. This is your big sister talking to you, and if you give me any more trouble, I swear I'll throw you over my shoulder and carry you out of here kicking and screaming—I've done it before, and you know I can do it again."

Sarah looked at her, then turned to Nick. "Are you sure you know what you're getting yourself into?"

"I'd do what she says," Nick said. "She's been very belligerent tonight."

Sarah gave her sister a bored look, shrugged, and headed for her bedroom.

"Five minutes," Riley called after her. "Don't make me come looking for you!"

"We'll take two cars," Nick said, "yours and Sarah's, if it's OK with her. Stop at an ATM and take what you can out of your checking account—no more credit cards, OK? I'll do the same, but I'll find an ATM in the opposite direction. If they check our bank activity, they'll know we're on the run—but they won't know where. Let's meet at the motel in thirty minutes. And build a fire under Sarah, will you?" Nick turned and headed for the door.

"Nick," she called after him.

He turned.

"You can't protect me."

"Thirty minutes," he said. "Don't make me come looking for you."

It was just after midnight when they checked into the King's Motel, a sixties-era relic complete with flat, gravel-covered roof and open hallways fenced in by black iron railings. Riley and Sarah checked in first; they took a room together on the second floor overlooking the street. Nick watched from the parking lot until they disappeared behind a peeling orange door; then he entered the small office himself and requested a room nearby. He paid in cash, and he registered under the name of William F. Burns. Five minutes later, he knocked softly on their door. Riley quietly slipped out and shut the door behind her.

"I put her to bed," she said. "I think she's a little overwhelmed."

Nick took her by the arm and led her down the hallway to a place where the elevator blocked them from view from the street. He reached up and twisted the incandescent bulb once, and the hallway instantly went dark.

"Your sister doesn't seem the type to be easily overwhelmed," Nick said.

"Sarah? She's as tough as an old razor strop."

"Sounds like someone I know."

Their shadows came together and touched once, then drifted apart again.

"This is a key to my room," Nick said. "I'm in 213, just a few doors down. If you need me, call. If the phone doesn't work for any reason, you come straight to my room—understand?"

She nodded. "Nick—what are we going to do next?"

"You're going to get some sleep. I'm going to do some thinking."

CHAPTER 35

Riley slipped the key into the lock and turned it gently; she felt the bolt give way. She pushed on the door, and it begrudgingly opened. The rubber weatherstrip dragging along the short-pile carpet made a sound like a stretching balloon.

She stepped quietly inside. It was just before six a.m., but every light in the room was on. In the center of the room, Nick straddled a wooden desk chair. His chin rested on his folded arms, which draped across the back of the chair. He sat utterly still; he stared directly ahead at an empty spot on the dingy wall, and his floating eyes were as still as two rafts on a glassy sea. Riley started forward in alarm, then stopped, recognizing telltale signs of life. Every day at the Coroner's Office she was reminded of the infinite difference between even a coma and death; Nick was lost in the depths of thought, but, thank God, he was still very much alive.

She approached him head-on, but there was no look of recognition or even awareness of her presence. She leaned down and looked into his face; at this distance his eyes were truly overwhelming, and for the very first time she saw them motionless. She felt a sense of gratitude, as though some rare or endangered species had allowed her to approach unchallenged. They were soft and dark, and Riley understood why few people could bear to look at them directly. But somehow she loved them; she loved the way they floated over her, calming her, like a groom with two soft brushes.

She reached out and stroked his chestnut hair. His eyes jumped suddenly like awakening birds and began to slowly take the room into focus. At last Nick straightened up and looked directly at her, but it was several seconds more before he spoke.

"I'm going to Leo's," he said. "You two stay here until I get back."

"Good morning to you too. Do you always sleep sitting up?"

Nick was still too lost in abstractions to engage in pleasantries. "I thought about it all night—what do we do next? We did the right thing first by grabbing Sarah and by sending Gabriella to her parents. But we can't stay on the defensive forever; the only way to eliminate the threat to us is to expose the ones who are threatening us."

"But how do we do that?"

"That's what I spent the night asking myself. Whoever we call next, whoever we choose to trust, we'd better be right about it—because making that contact will be like sending up a flare. Our problem is that we don't know who to trust. Santangelo is with the FBI; surely the entire Pittsburgh field office isn't in on it—at least, I hope not—but we don't know who would be safe to call. Your own office has been compromised—it may have been Lassiter's lone involvement, but then again he may have had help. It seems possible that at least two of your deputy coroners are in on it; they pick up the bodies at the death scene. And that raises the question of the police. They're at the death scene too—at least in cases like the drive-by shooting. Who can we trust within the police department? Who can we trust anywhere?"

"And the answer is . . ."

"The newspaper. We go to the *Pittsburgh Post-Gazette*."

Riley looked aghast. "Nick, that seems incredibly risky. First they're going to think we're nuts, and then they're going to start calling around to make inquiries. That will stir up everything."

"I hope so. Look, we've only got two things going for us: first, they don't know where to find us; and second, *we have physical evidence*. We have the shredded documents that prove that Mr.

Vandenborre picked up a spare kidney somewhere along the way. And we also have my entomological report and specimens, remember? That report could raise all kinds of awkward questions. The trick here is to reveal the physical evidence without exposing ourselves."

"How do we do that?"

"I'm going to swing by Leo's and grab the reconstructed documents. Then I'm going to drop them off at the *Post-Gazette* and head back here."

"Why can't Leo bring them here? Or why can't he take them to the newspaper himself?"

"Because I can't reach him. I've left messages, but I haven't heard back from him. This can't wait, Riley. They're searching for us right now, and they're looking for Sarah too. The sooner we get this out in the open, the safer we'll be—and the sooner I get this out of Leo's hands, the safer *he'll* be."

"I wish I could go with you," Riley said.

"You know better—Sarah needs you here. There's a very rich person somewhere waiting for one of her kidneys, and you need to make sure she doesn't do anything stupid. Don't dial out. If the phone rings, don't answer it. If it's me, I'll let it ring once, and then I'll call again. Got it?"

"Got it." She stroked his hair again. "Are you OK? You didn't sleep a wink."

"My species requires very little sleep."

Riley frowned. "If you're not careful, your species will be extinct."

Nick stopped half a block from Leo's apartment. He considered whether to park several blocks away and walk over, but he wanted to remove all the evidence at once, and it occurred to him that the sight of someone carrying an armload of trash bags several blocks would raise far more eyebrows than one quick trip to the street. He pulled his car into the same space he had occupied just the night before.

"Leo," he called out as he rounded the corner into the ever-open doorway. "Hey, Leo!" He headed directly for the bedroom. It was still early, and even tireless Leo might still be in bed. But the bedroom was empty, and the bed was unslept in—unless Leo was more fastidious than Nick remembered. He had hoped to find Leo here, to set his mind at ease and to brief him on their plans, but it didn't really matter. Right now all he needed was to collect the evidence and deliver it to the proper person at the *Pittsburgh Post-Gazette*.

He pushed open the bathroom door; it was empty. On a whim, he slid open the shower curtain and felt the inside; it was perfectly dry. It was possible that Leo made his bed *and* skipped his morning shower, Nick told himself. It was *possible*—but he moved to the kitchen with a crawling feeling on the back of his neck.

The kitchen table was completely bare; even the black-and-white trash bags surrounding it had been moved. But where had Leo taken them? Nick had asked him to *organize* the evidence, not to remove it. He assumed it would still be here on the kitchen table, where it had always been. Now he would have to search the whole apartment for it. Now he would have to—

He stopped.

Over the Formica counter, on the white ceramic kitchen floor, Nick saw the edge of a crimson pool.

He sat down hard on one of the kitchen chairs and stared at the wall below the counter that blocked his view of the kitchen beyond. He didn't need to look on the other side. He knew what was there—he could see it in every detail. He could see Leo's body stretched out facedown, just as it had first fallen, with a small slit below the rib cage or a gunshot wound through the occipital bone—or maybe even a crushed skull, depending on the savagery of his attacker. And somewhere on the floor there would be a wine bottle or a shattered cup of sugar, some small favor that Leo had been asked to fulfill that would cause him to pause momentarily in a vulnerable and accessible position. And in his mind he could hear the sound of the falling body, lifeless before it hit the floor without reflex or recoil, and the dull, flat sound of flesh slapping tile. Nick cringed and covered his ears with both hands.

He turned and looked across the room at the long computer workbench. The monitors were still in place, and the printers and scanners too—but the two computer towers had been removed, and their hard drives with them, along with all digital record of the reconstructed prescriptions. Nick ran his hand over the empty kitchen table. Leo didn't move the evidence—it had been removed by his attacker, and by now it was all completely destroyed.

Nick rose slowly to his feet and stumbled toward the kitchen. He had already seen it all in his mind—why did he have to look? But he knew he had to be a witness to the horror of his oldest friend's death—to do less would be cowardice. He owed it to Leo; somehow he knew that Leo would want him to look. "Drink it *all*, Nick," Leo would say. "If you leave any behind, you'll only regret it later." When he remembered the sound of Leo's voice, he felt alternating waves of rage and nausea. Why did he ever get Leo involved in this? How did he let things go this far? Leo was the most *alive* person he had ever met. He was all heart—he was *Nick's* heart. And now his heart was dead, and all he wanted to do was climb back up into his skull and lock the door forever.

He stepped into the kitchen and looked at the floor. He felt no additional shock, no fresh grief over the reality before him. Why should he? It was just as he knew it would be, down to the shattered bottle of claret and the deep green shards of glass lying in a stain of purplish red. He knelt down beside him; there was a trickle of red from the base of his skull. He leaned over the body and gently brushed back the wavy hair. Around the entry wound was the tattooing of gunpowder, indicating a close-range shot. There would be no exit wound; it was a small-caliber shell, intended to ricochet off the inside of his—Nick shut his eyes and pushed back the thought.

He began to stroke Leo's hair now. Teardrops gathered at the tips of his eyes and fell away into his glasses, pooling in the great lenses and washing all the terrible details from the image before him.

Nick sat back on the floor. It would have been quick and painless—he was sure of that, because pain produces noise, and noise is something no assassin can afford—especially from a victim who lives with open windows.

Open windows.

Nick looked up at the cream-colored walls. Above the sink he saw a tiny black speck, and two more above the counter. He struggled to his feet and hurried out into the living room; there were dozens more, dotting the walls above the computer workbench, surrounding the paintings like tiny visitors to an art gallery.

Mosquitoes.

He rushed to the door and down the hall, down the three flights of stairs to his waiting car. He leaned through the back window and pulled out his aerial sweep net. They would not stay long; they were female *Anopheles* or *Culex* mosquitoes, both late-night biters, who had engorged themselves on a meal of human blood. All night long they had rested, using the blood proteins to allow them to produce their eggs—but when the daytime temperatures rose again they would depart, searching for a source of standing water and a place to deposit their clutch.

Back in the apartment, Nick swung the net back and forth across the walls, allowing none of the tiny specks to escape. He was grateful that mosquitoes are slow fliers, reaching speeds of no more than a mile and a half per hour; Nick was used to netting far faster and more elusive carrion flies, and this was comparative child's play. The important thing was that he let none escape. He searched the walls carefully, waving his hand through the air to stir up any late risers, continuing until the walls were spotless and the tip of his net was flecked with gray-black specks.

He hurried back to the kitchen and began to open drawers, searching for a rubber band or clothes pin, something he could use to close off the tip of the net and trap its occupants until he could process them.

Suddenly he heard a quick knock on the doorframe and the sound of footsteps approaching from behind. Nick spun around.

"Hey, neighbor, I was wondering if you had any—"

The young man stood in the kitchen doorway. He looked at Nick, then down at the body lying in the crimson pool, then back at Nick again. There was a moment of horrified silence—then the man began to back away, his eyes still glued to Nick's.

"Wait," Nick said. "It's not how it looks."

The man held up one hand and continued to back across the living room; at the doorway, he turned and bolted down the hallway.

Nick took a last look at Leo, grabbed the aerial net, and ran for his car.

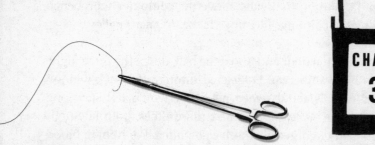

Nick rapped twice on the door, then stepped back from the peephole so he could be clearly seen. In his left hand he carried the aerial sweep net; his right arm encircled two plastic containers and two metal tins.

A moment later the door swung open. Riley smiled up at him, but Nick refused to meet her eyes. He brushed past her and charged into the motel room, heading directly for the small kitchenette.

"What happened?" Riley said.

Nick said nothing. He stepped to the counter and with a sweep of his arm sent a collection of small objects clattering onto the floor. He set down the net and peeled the tops off the two plastic containers.

"Nick—what's wrong?"

Sarah stepped out of the bathroom in a knee-length robe and a terry towel wrapped around her blond hair. "What's going on?"

Nick unscrewed the lid from the metal tin and poured the acrid liquid into one of the containers. In the bottom, an inch-thick layer of gypsum absorbed the fluid and kept it from spilling.

"This is ethyl acetate," he said without looking up. "Don't breathe it."

Riley stepped closer. "Nick, look at me."

"Somebody hasn't had his coffee yet," Sarah said, dabbing her ears with a towel.

Nick took the sacklike end of the sweep net and shook its occupants down into the extreme tip; then he draped it into the plastic container and pressed the lid on tight. Now he opened the other metal canister and poured the transparent fluid into the second container.

"I have to get them into ethanol as fast as possible," he said. "I've got to dry them out—moisture degrades the DNA."

Riley stepped up close to him now. She put her hand on Nick's arm and stared at him intently until he could no longer continue. He dropped his head and closed his eyes.

"Whatever it is, you have to tell me," she said gently.

Nick slowly turned his head and looked at her—and when his eyes met hers, she instantly knew.

Her knees buckled. Nick turned and caught her before she could fall. He pulled her in tight against him, and her body began to shake. She buried her face against Nick's chest and sobbed.

Sarah's eyes widened. "You guys are freaking me out. Will somebody tell me what's going on?"

But it was several minutes before anyone could speak.

"Leo's dead," Nick said to Sarah.

"Leo? The computer guy?"

"He was killed sometime last night."

Riley looked up at him. "How did it happen?"

"It doesn't matter."

"I want to know."

"The pathologist in you wants to know—but *you* don't. Just let it go, Riley. He's gone."

Sarah sunk down on one of the beds. "Last night? But you two were just there last night."

"If we had stayed any longer, they would have caught all three of us together."

Riley took a towel and wiped her eyes. "We thought they didn't know about Leo. How did they find out? How did they know where he lived?"

"I've underestimated them every step of he way," Nick said. "Not anymore." He turned back to the specimens again. He removed the net from the killing jar and shook its lifeless contents into a tiny black pile in the very tip of the bag. Then he placed the container of ethanol into the net and gently tipped the contents into the clear liquid. They floated to the bottom like tiny pieces of ash.

"What are you doing?" Riley asked.

"I'm going after Santangelo."

"What?"

"These are mosquitoes. I collected them from the walls in Leo's apartment—he always left his windows open, remember? These mosquitoes were there last night when the killer arrived—and I'm betting it was Santangelo. At least one of these mosquitoes drew blood from the killer, and that blood sample is still in its gut. I'm taking these specimens to Sanjay at Pitt; he'll do a DNA sequence on each of them. Now all I need is a sample of Santangelo's DNA, and if there's a match, we can prove that Santangelo was present at the murder scene."

"Now wait a minute," Sarah said. "You want to go *after* this guy? Aren't we supposed to be running away here? He just killed your friend *last night*."

"We have no choice—the physical evidence is gone. Santangelo took it all with him—the shredding, the computer hard drives, the trash bags—everything. Now what are we supposed to show the newspapers? What are we supposed to show anybody? If this mosquito evidence works out, we can shift to the offensive again."

"*If* it works out? How long will it take to find out?"

"A few days, tops . . . I think."

"You *think*?"

"Well, this has never actually been done before—at least, it's never been used in a court case. But it's been proven possible in a laboratory."

"And in the meantime we're supposed to stay here? Nick, we're still in Pittsburgh—surely they'll check the local motels. This guy knows more than you think he does—you said it yourself. He's just one step behind us. I think we need to put some distance between us."

"Sarah had an idea," Riley said. "I think it's a good one. We can go to our house in Mencken, remember? The place is deserted; no one would ever look for us there. There are no utilities, but there's a working pump in the backyard—and we can take food and supplies with us."

"It's perfect," Sarah said.

"I'm not going into hiding," Nick said. "I'm taking the fight to *them*. They started this—I'm going to finish it."

"I know I'm a newcomer here," Sarah said, "but it's my life, too, you know. I think we should get away from here."

"Then we split up."

"No!" Riley said. "Whatever we do, we do it *together*. There will be no splitting up!" She glared at both of them until their countenances softened.

Nick slumped down on the edge of the bed and lay backward. He rubbed his temples in long, slow circles, staring at the ceiling above. "Maybe you're right," he said. "Maybe we could—" He sat up suddenly. "We're going to Tarentum."

"Tarentum? But you just said—"

"Listen to me—Santangelo knows *everything*. He knew about the shredding, and he knew about Leo—and he knows about my entomological report and the blowfly specimens in my greenhouse in Tarentum. Santangelo has to destroy all the physical evidence; how long will it be before he heads to Tarentum?"

Riley looked at him in horror. "Oh, Nick—your mom."

Nick jumped up from the bed and began to gather the containers and canisters. Some clear fluid dripped down the edge of the specimen container; Nick wiped his hand on his trousers and turned to Sarah.

"Have you got something I can put this in? Something watertight?"

Sarah searched through her suitcase and found a Ziploc bag. She opened it, dumped out a hairbrush and a comb, and handed it to Nick. He sealed the leaking specimen container inside and set it with the others.

"You two get packed. I'm taking these specimens to Sanjay—I'll be back in a couple of hours. Then we're heading to Tarentum." He took out his cell phone and pushed an autodial number.

"Wait," Riley said. "Use the motel phone. They could be listening—"

Nick held up one hand. "Mama? Nick. Look, Riley and I are headed up there this afternoon. We need a place to get away for a couple of days. And I need a favor, OK? I need you to pack a bag and stay with a friend; we need the house to ourselves. What? No, it's not like that. No, really. Look, if it makes you feel any better, we're bringing a chaperone along with us, OK? What? I don't know, how about Mrs. Drewencki? Well, then, try Mrs. Teklinski. I don't know, Mama, you figure it out. You're the Queen of Poland, just tell them you're coming and they have to obey. Right. Now don't forget, I want you out of there by this afternoon. I'll call you when it's safe to come back. What? No, I said when it's *time* to come back—give your hearing aid a thump. I've got to go now. Thanks. Me too." He folded the phone and dropped it back in his pocket.

He turned to Sarah. "You're right, Sarah, we do need to put some distance between us—and we're going to need a day or two to hide out while these samples are being processed. We'll go to Tarentum, and then we'll head for Mencken—but after that, I go after Santangelo."

Nick gathered up the containers and turned for the door. Riley stepped in front of him.

"We go after Santangelo," she said.

CHAPTER
37

It was late afternoon before they arrived in Tarentum. Nick and Riley drove together, and Sarah followed in her own car close behind. They made the long drive up Route 28, with the Allegheny River winding beside them on their right like a long, green snake. At some points it came almost up to the roadway, then suddenly curved away and disappeared behind clusters of houses and trees and factories, only to reappear just as suddenly a few miles ahead. The rivers of Pittsburgh are the city's vascular system, and life surrounds the waterways like clusters of living cells around blood vessels. Opposite the river, narrow roads cut back through the steep, wooded hillsides, lined with gray-shingled houses that huddled close against the cold Pennsylvania winters.

They led Sarah to a small motel on the outskirts of town, where she checked in alone under an assumed name. Now it was dark, and Nick and Riley stood at a pay phone in the corner of a BP station across from the motel.

"No answer?"

"She must have packed up and left," Nick said. "Good girl."

"Now what?"

Nick thought for a minute. "I wish I could sneak in the greenhouse just long enough to grab those specimens."

"We can't chance that. What if Santangelo shows up and finds you? What if he's already there and waiting?"

Nick frowned.

"Why didn't you ask your mom to take them with her?"

"The greenhouse is filled with specimens. What was I supposed to tell her? 'Grab the *Phaenicia sericata* and the *Calliphora vicina*, but forget the *coeruleiviridis*.' My mom can't tell a palmetto bug from a pierogi."

Riley shivered. "That's the last time I eat her pierogies."

"Come on—we'll stick with our original plan."

They took a winding road to the very top of the hillside. They parked at the edge of the woods and made their way down on foot, approaching Nick's house from behind.

They emerged from the trees behind three sea green water tanks that sat like giant sentinels atop the Tarentum Plateau. The tanks were ancient, built before anyone could remember, holding a million gallons of water in reserve for the citizens of the town below. They were the tallest structures on the steep Tarentum hillside, boilerplated together from long, curving sheets of steel and welded together in rippling seams. From the rims, long brown lines of rust and corrosion dripped down the sides like icing on a cake.

"That one," Nick said, pointing to the tower on the right. "My house is on the other side."

Riley placed her left foot on the first rung of the metal ladder and looked up. Fifty feet above her, the curving rim of the water tank cut a dark slice from the evening sky. She climbed two rungs. Nick reached around her legs and grasped the sides of the ladder.

"Keep going," he said. "I'm right behind you."

Riley glanced down. She could already see the roof of Nick's house, the tiny backyard, and the shimmering glass of the greenhouse beyond. By the time they reached the top of the tank, they would have a perfect view of Nick's home—and of everything else in Tarentum as well. Riley checked her grip again; though she was no more than twenty feet off the ground, the hillside plummeting away to her left created the illusion of staggering height. She pulled herself tight against the ladder and looked at the rusting rivets that secured it to the side of the tank.

"Are you sure this is a good idea?"

"Trust me," Nick said, stepping up close behind her.

"The last time I trusted you I ended up in the Allegheny River."

"That's gratitude for you. Didn't I tell you I'd show you the town?"

They were only ten feet from the rim when Riley felt an overwhelming sense of exhaustion and a familiar dull ache in her lower back. She wrapped her arms around the ladder and shut her eyes.

"I have to rest," she said, panting. "It's the climbing—that's the hardest thing for me."

Nick climbed to the rung just below her and pressed his body tight against hers. "Take your time," he said softly. "Let me know when you're ready."

A few minutes later they pulled themselves up and over the curling rim and proceeded on hands and knees to the opposite side of the tank. Nick swung himself upright and casually draped his legs over the side of the tank; Riley approached the edge with considerably more caution.

Nick looked at her. "I thought you were queen of the bony pile."

"You can't fall off a bony pile," she said warily, but already she was feeling more accustomed to their lofty perch. She glanced back at the hillside rising up close behind them, which thankfully helped to diminish the sense of height. She sidled up beside Nick and took a seat, still focusing on the metal surface to help hold her fear in check. Now for the first time she raised her eyes and drew in a sharp breath.

The panorama before them was spectacular. Far below, the Allegheny River glistened blue white in the crystalline moonlight. Beyond the river, the dark bluffs of Lower Burrell and New Kensington ascended to heights equal to their own, the crest lined with glimmering dots of blue and gold. On their own side of the river, angular edges of boxcars, warehouses, and scrapyard conveyors cut sharp silhouettes against the white water. As the hillside rose to meet them, dots of light became individual streetlamps, and vague geometric shadows became houses and fences and yards. The streets around Nick's house were awash in orange light and visible in every detail, and the house and backyard lay at their feet. No one would be able to approach from any direction without their knowledge.

"I could get used to this," Riley said.

"I spent a lot of time here as a boy. In those days the tanks had no tops; I used to climb up here at night and walk the rim."

"Did your mom know?"

"Did you tell your dad you were climbing on the bony pile?"

She shook her head. "For some things, it's easier to ask forgiveness than permission."

"That's my life motto."

Neither one said anything for a few minutes. Reverential silence seemed to be the most appropriate response to the awesome vista before them.

"Do you think Sarah will be OK at that motel?"

"She'll be safe there—that's where *you* should be."

"Don't start," Riley said.

They heard the sound of an engine; a car approached from the left and pulled over to the curb just two blocks away. A man got out, locked the door, and entered the adjacent house.

"Mr. Jankowski," Nick said. "When his dog died a few years ago, I asked him if I could have the body. He's never looked at me the same way since."

Riley studied his face; the lenses of his glasses glowed like two white shields in the brilliant moonlight. From up here Nick could study the world's inhabitants like the insects in one of his terraria, but maintain a protective distance from all the pain and risk of personal contact. She wondered if anyone had ever shared this lofty vantage point with him before. She thought about Leo; she felt a hollow ache in her stomach, and tears flooded her eyes again as they had throughout the day.

"About Leo," she said. "Nick, I am so sorry—"

"Leo was not your fault."

"He was my *responsibility*. If it wasn't for me—"

"I asked him to help, not you. Leo was *my* responsibility."

Riley stroked his back. "Where did he live? Can you see his house from here?"

Nick pointed to a house several blocks closer to the river—then he pulled his hand away quickly, as if the contact had produced a painful spark. "It was Santangelo's fault," he said, "and I'm going to make sure he picks up the check."

"What about the rest of them? What about Lassiter and Zohar and Truett?"

"We only need one; he'll give us all the others."

Riley wiped the corners of her eyes and looked at the house below. "How do you know he'll come tonight?"

"That's what the phone call was for. I used my cell phone—they're bound to be listening in. And I left a forwarding address and phone number at the motel desk; I might as well have put up a billboard. Santangelo knows where we were headed, and he thinks we're planning to be here tonight. He won't pass up a chance to catch us here—and I don't think he'll come until night. He needs the cover of darkness to get in and out of here unseen."

For the next two hours they sat in silence, watching every passing car until it disappeared from sight and tracking every wandering pedestrian until a door closed securely behind him. About ten o'clock, a silver sedan approached from the direction of the river and pulled over about three blocks away. The engine stopped, the headlights blinked off, but no one emerged from the car for several minutes. Then the driver's door quietly opened; a single figure stepped out and glanced around. Nick and Riley both recognized Santangelo instantly.

Then the passenger door opened, and a young woman emerged with long auburn hair.

"Who is she?" Riley said.

Nick nodded slowly. "I was wondering about that. Unless I miss my guess, she's the lure."

"What lure?"

"Think about it: The murder of each of the 'donors' had to be carefully planned—a specific location, very precise timing. Now, how do you make sure your victim is in the right spot at the right time? What makes a man pull over to change a tire at night in the worst part of town? How do you get a man to hold still while someone sneaks up behind him and injects him with a syringe?

The answer is: you use a lure. I have a feeling we're looking at the last thing Leo ever saw."

Riley looked at her again, squinting hard. They were too far away for the features of their faces to be visible, but in the still of night sound traveled readily. As they approached, even their footsteps became audible; his were flat and dull-sounding, hers were sharper and higher in pitch. Santangelo cleared his throat once, and even that muffled sound drifted up to Riley's ears. They moved quickly toward the house, pausing in shadowy areas just long enough to search for prying eyes. With every step they came closer—closer to the street, closer to the house, closer to *them*. Riley felt terrified, but at the same time strangely exhilarated. It was like being an angel, floating passively in the sky above, looking down from the heavens on the sins of foolish men.

Suddenly, Santangelo looked directly at them.

CHAPTER
38

Can they see us?" she whispered to Nick.

"I doubt it. The moon is on the other side of the river." He lifted one hand slightly and waved. Riley grabbed his arm and jerked it back down.

Santangelo and the woman hesitated at the corner opposite the house. They stood for several minutes in the shadow of a tall hedge, watching the house and glancing up and down the street. When they finally moved, they moved quickly—not toward the front door, but around the house to the left and into the darkness of the backyard. They approached the back door silently and stopped, and Santangelo removed something from his coat pocket. While the woman stood watch, he bent over the doorknob and seemed to freeze like a statue.

Riley was almost directly above them now, looking down at the tops of their heads. Suddenly she began to feel faint. She felt herself being drawn irresistibly toward the edge of the water tower, and she imagined herself falling headlong and landing facedown on the grass just yards from the woman's feet. Riley propped herself up on wobbly arms, and there was the blank-faced woman staring at her; the woman turned to her companion, who slowly reached beneath his coat again and—

Riley's eyes began to droop shut—and then she felt two large hands grab her by the shoulders and pull back.

"Try breathing," Nick whispered. "You'll find it helps." He held her while she took several long, deep breaths. She looked at him and nodded.

Below them, the back door opened a crack. A streak of yellow light fell across the yard and disappeared into the trees. Santangelo stepped quietly inside and the woman followed. She pulled the door shut behind them.

"That's my cue," Nick said, rising to his feet.

Riley turned to him with a look of panicked protest. "Take me with you."

Nick shook his head. "What if we have to run? Sudden exertion is not your forte. I'll be OK; I should have plenty of time. And you'll be safe here—but stay back from the edge, will you? We can't catch these guys by falling on them." She watched him move quickly across the tower, turn, and back down the ladder.

Riley turned back to the edge of the tower; this time, she lay on her stomach and propped herself up slightly, with only her head protruding past the metal rim. She looked down to her left and saw Nick working his way around the side of the tank. She checked the back door of the house; it was still shut. Nick darted across the yard, around the side of the house, and momentarily disappeared from sight. A moment later he appeared again, standing under a streetlight on the front sidewalk, staring back at the house.

"Get out of the light!" Riley whispered. "They can see you!"

As if in response, Nick turned and hurried down a small alley between two houses.

Just then, the back door opened wide, and light flooded the backyard. Santangelo stepped out of the brightness and looked around; the woman was right behind him. Riley wriggled back from the edge until only her eyes were visible. Santangelo glanced to his left and spotted the greenhouse. He snapped his fingers and motioned to the woman; they turned together and headed directly for it, stopping briefly in the doorway before disappearing into the darkness inside.

Riley looked back at the streets and searched for Nick; he was nowhere to be found. Suddenly he emerged from a side alley less than half a block from Santangelo's car. He glanced both ways, then approached the passenger side. He tried the door, but it didn't open. He hurried around to the driver's side and tried again; still nothing.

From the corner of her eye, Riley glimpsed a flash of yellow light. She turned to the greenhouse and saw a light reflecting off three of the glass panes. She searched from side to side for the source: a flashlight, a passing car, a neighboring house. Suddenly she realized that the light was not reflecting off the glass—it was shining *through* it. The light appeared in a fourth pane now, then a fifth—and it grew brighter all the time.

Fire.

She looked back at Nick. He was on the passenger side again, but now he was facing away from the car. Thirty feet ahead of him was a house; shielding the house from the street was a tall hedge, and in front of the hedge was a short retaining wall. He seemed to be doing something with the retaining wall. He was holding on to it—no, he was *tugging* on it. He stumbled back away from the wall and looked down at something in his hand. He turned, raised his arm, and brought his hand down against the passenger-side window.

An instant later a sound like crunching gravel reached her ears, and right behind it came the shrill, piercing scream of a car alarm. Nick reached through the window, opened the door, and slid into the passenger seat.

Riley turned back to the greenhouse. She could hear the sound of the ceiling panes shattering from the heat and tinkling to the ground. Now the woman appeared in the doorway, silhouetted against the rising flames. She turned her head from side to side, searching for the source of the shrieking siren. She turned back to the greenhouse now and pointed urgently in the direction of the car. Santangelo bolted through the doorway and stopped, listening;

he took two halting steps forward, then took off running toward the street, with the woman not far behind.

Riley jumped to her own feet now, oblivious to the ominous edge and the fifty-foot plunge beyond. She searched frantically for Nick; he was out of the car again, standing on the sidewalk beside it, waving something in the air at her. She waved back with both arms, urging him away from there, desperately trying to warn him of the danger coming his way. She could see him clearly under the orange streetlamps—but could he see her? "I doubt it," Nick had said. "The moon is on the other side of the river."

Santangelo was on the street now, headed for the corner, and the woman was less than ten yards behind. In another few seconds they would round the corner, and Nick would be clearly visible less than two blocks away. Riley dropped her arms to her sides and staggered closer to the edge. Her utter helplessness almost overwhelmed her.

Moments from now Santangelo would round the corner and discover Nick standing by his car. Nick would turn and try to run, but Santangelo didn't need to overtake him. He only needed to get within firing distance, and then he would pull his gun and put an end to Nick's life, just as he had done to Leo—and all she could do was watch.

Riley took a deep breath, threw back her head, and screamed.

The sound rivaled the car alarm in intensity. On the street, Santangelo and the woman both skidded to a halt and turned to search for the source of the scream—but echoing off the hillside, it must have seemed to come from everywhere at once. Two blocks farther away, Nick heard the scream too. He started down the sidewalk toward the corner, then spun to his right and ducked into the tall hedge.

The thick brush rustled and shook, and an instant later Nick appeared on the other side. Riley held her breath, waiting for him to dart across the yard to safety behind the house—but to her dismay Nick remained where he was, kneeling in the darkness behind the hedge directly across from the car.

Nick! Get out of there!

Santangelo rounded the corner and raced down the sidewalk to the car. He threw open the driver's door, ducked inside, and silenced the wailing alarm. Riley could hear everything now—*everything*. The piercing siren had flayed her auditory nerves like sandpaper on the fingers of a safecracker, sensitizing her to even the tiniest sound. She heard the angry slam of the car door, the whispered curse from Santangelo's lips, and the grinding sound his soles made as he stepped through the bits of glass by the smashed-in passenger window. He pulled out a dangling piece of shattered safety glass and threw it aside; it landed like a beaded purse on a kitchen counter.

Hands on hips, Santangelo turned and surveyed the surrounding area: down the street toward the river, up the row of cars that lined the far sidewalk, over the shadows between the houses on the opposite side of the street. Now he turned to the hedge. He was looking almost directly at Nick now—there was no more than ten feet between them.

Half a block away, the woman with the long auburn hair had stopped running. She kicked off her shoes, picked them up, and continued at a walk. As she approached the car, Nick began to crane his neck up and down, trying for a better look.

Suddenly the porch light behind Nick went on, flooding the front yard with blinding luminescence. A storm door opened and an old man stepped out. "What's the problem out there?" he called to the street.

Nick jumped to his feet and spun around.

"Somebody broke into my car," Santangelo called back from the sidewalk. "Have you seen anybody around here?"

The old man looked at Nick. Nick gestured frantically for the old man not to answer.

"Nick, is that you? Nick Polchak? What are you doing out there?"

Without a word, Nick took off around the side of the house and disappeared into the shadows.

On the sidewalk, Santangelo began to dart from side to side, searching through the thick hedge for a glimpse of Nick—but he was staring directly into the blinding porch light. He turned away in anger and kicked the passenger door, leaving a noticeable dent.

The old man walked to the end of his porch and peered around the corner after Nick; then he slowly shook his head and turned his attention to the street again. "You want me to call the police?" he called over the hedge.

"No thanks," Santangelo said. "My insurance will cover it."

He hurried around the car and motioned for the woman to follow; she opened the passenger door, brushed off the seat, and climbed in. The engine raced, the car pulled away from the curb, and they headed back down the road toward the Allegheny River.

Riley sat down hard and rolled onto her back. She lay staring at the spinning stars above, trying to bring her breathing under control. The hollow water tower amplified her throbbing pulse like a massive bass drum.

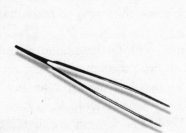

CHAPTER 39

"**W**here have you *been*?" Sarah said frantically. "You've been gone for hours!"

Riley slipped through the motel door, and Sarah quickly shut it behind her. "Pack your things," she said. "We're leaving."

"Right now? In the middle of the night?"

"It's an hour and a half to Mencken. We want to arrive before daylight."

"Doesn't this boyfriend of yours ever sleep?"

"We'll talk about it in *Mencken*. Right now we need to hurry."

"I've been worried sick about you! What happened out there? Where did you go?"

"We'll talk about it in Mencken." She tossed Sarah a pair of jeans and opened her suitcase on the bed.

They split up as before, with Nick and Riley driving one car and Sarah following behind—but this time they took an altogether different route. Route 28 was the single major artery in and out of Tarentum, and the one place Santangelo could lie in wait for them. Instead, they turned right across the Tarentum Bridge and into

Lower Burrell, heading for Mencken by a series of convoluted back roads that Santangelo could never follow. Even Pittsburgh natives cursed the bewildering tunnels, endless bridges, and cratered roads in the area; for the first time, they provided a measure of protection. Nick knew the back roads halfway to Mencken, and Riley and Sarah could lead them home.

"You're quiet," Nick said, glancing over at Riley.

"I'm tired. My species sleeps—most higher life forms do." She glared at him. "I'm also angry. What's wrong with you anyway?"

"We've only got an hour and a half. Can you be more specific?"

"Why did you stay behind that hedge? You scared me to death. I almost fell off the water tower!"

"That seems to be a recurring problem for you. Do you suffer from vertigo?"

"Santangelo was less than ten feet away from you. He could have reached through the hedge and grabbed you by the throat."

"He didn't know I was there. It's the last thing he would have expected. Sometimes the safest thing is the most unexpected."

Riley rolled her eyes. "You must be the safest person on earth."

"Besides, I was in darkness, and he was under a streetlamp. He couldn't see me."

"And when that old man turned the porch light on?"

"Mr. Davidek? I didn't count on him."

"But why didn't you just run in the first place? Why did you stay? What was the point?"

"I wanted to get a better look at the lure."

"What if Santangelo came after you? He would have killed you for sure."

"Out of doors? In front of Mr. Davidek? The one thing Santangelo fears most is exposure. That's why he wanted to catch us at home."

They cut through New Kensington and headed east on 56, then south on 66 toward the town of Greensburg. The narrow roads curved back and forth between the rounded hills, following the paths of ancient creek beds and valleys. Under the shadow of a hillside the road would lie in utter darkness, but just around the bend the asphalt would glisten in the bright moonlight.

"So what did she look like?" Riley asked.

"Who?"

"You know who."

"I never got a look at her. Mr. Davidek turned on the porch light before she got close enough to see. I only saw what you saw; she had long red hair." Nick glanced at her. "And great legs."

Riley stuck out her tongue at him.

"If you like that sort of thing," he added.

"Please, spare me. What did you take out of Santangelo's car?"

Nick held up a half-filled Aquafina water bottle.

"I get it," Riley nodded. "Saliva."

"If we run this through a centrifuge, we've got a sample of Santangelo's DNA. Now that we've lost the blowfly specimens, this is the only physical evidence we've got left."

"Sorry about your greenhouse. Won't the police figure out it was arson?"

"I doubt it. Santangelo knows his business—besides, I kept gallons of ethanol and ethyl acetate in there. The police will just think I left the cap off the wrong bottle. All it takes is a spark."

Riley glanced down at the water bottle. "How do you know it's Santangelo's? How do you know it's not hers?"

Nick held it up again. "No lipstick."

"Do assassins wear lipstick when they're on the job?"

"She's the lure," Nick said, "and lures need to be attractive."

They followed I-70 west almost to Washington, then headed south again on 79. They were well south of the city now. The area took on a much more rural look, and the names of the towns along the way reflected it: Lone Pine, Prosperity, Ruff Creek. At the town of Lippincott, Sarah flashed her lights at them and signaled for a left turn.

"Sarah's turning off," Nick said. "Should we go back?"

"She's just stopping for food. The last grocery store is in Lippincott. She'll meet us at the house; she knows the way."

"Mencken has no grocery store?"

"Mencken has no people."

Ten minutes later they came to a stop in front of two black-and-white barricades that completely blocked the road.

"It's not exactly the Welcome Wagon," Nick said.

Riley opened her door and stepped out. A moment later she appeared in front of the bright headlights; she lifted the end of each barricade and walked it slowly out of the way. Nick pulled ahead, and Riley slid back into the car. She winced as she stretched her back from side to side.

"I could have helped you with those," Nick said.

"I'm not helpless, you know."

"Never thought you were."

They drove slowly forward. Mencken was, in fact, a ghost town; it looked more like a movie set than a place of human habitation. The yards, untended for years, had reverted to coarse yellow buffalo grass. Tall brush grew in clumps right up to the roadside, and in places pushed its way up through cracks in the pavement.

"Stop here," Riley said.

Directly ahead of them, a jagged crack cut across the road, and wisps of smoke seeped out of it and vanished into the darkness.

"Problem?" Nick said.

"That wasn't here the last time I came. We've got a little ground subsidence problem here in Mencken. The coal vein runs right under the town. When they mined it out, they left huge columns of coal in place to help support the roof; but as the fire works its way through, it consumes those columns. Now there are huge areas that have no support at all, and they can collapse at any time."

"That's what you call a 'little problem'? Where are these areas?"

"There's no way to tell. Pull forward."

Nick drove slowly across the hissing crack. Riley watched through the rear windshield until the smoke appeared again behind them. She turned to Nick and smiled.

"That wasn't one of them."

Nick blinked at her and continued on.

They passed through the town itself now, with abandoned stores and offices lining the road like empty boxes. The structures themselves still looked solid, but badly in need of paint and repair. Most of the glass had been broken, courtesy of the Lippincott teenagers, and there were even charred patches where fires had apparently been set. The town ended just as abruptly as it began, and the storefronts gave way to a cluster of small single-family dwellings—all just as vacant as the town itself.

"Take a left here," Riley said. "It's just a little farther."

A quarter of a mile ahead, the road ended in front of a two-story white frame house. At first, it appeared to be on level ground, standing out like a beacon against the midnight sky. But as they drew closer, the blackness behind the house began to sparkle in the headlights. Nick leaned over the steering wheel and peered up, and far above he could see where the blackness ended and the true night sky began. It was the bony pile, and it was the size of a small mountain.

"No offense," Nick said, "but why have you kept this place?"

"What are we supposed to do with it? The town is condemned."

"Condemned? All of it?"

Riley nodded. "No one could afford the subsidence insurance, and no one wanted to live with the health risks. First the families left, then the store owners, then everybody just pulled out. There was a little money from the government, but not enough to go around. We're not the only coal-mine fire in Pennsylvania, you know."

To the left of the house was a large slatted shed. Nick pointed to it. "Is that empty?"

"Everything's empty. We can hide both cars in there. If we keep the drapes closed when we light the lamps, we'll be practically invisible."

"You've got drapes?"

"All the comforts of home."

They walked to the house together and stepped up onto the wooden porch. The boards under Nick's feet sagged ominously. He rocked from heel to toe and the boards produced a squeal like rusty hinges.

"A real fixer-upper," Riley said. "Priced to move."

She took a key ring from her purse.

"You keep it locked?" Nick said. "Is security really a problem around here?"

"It's still our home. We don't want it turning into a crack house."

They stepped through the doorway and into the darkness of a large open space; the hollow echo of their footsteps told them the room was empty. A pinpoint of white light appeared on Riley's key ring; she pointed the tiny flashlight quickly around the room and brought it to rest on a doorway on the opposite wall.

Through the doorway, on the right, was a closet door; it opened with a complaining groan and the pungent odor of mothballs. Riley handed Nick a Coleman lantern, matches, and a box of white candles. She took out two sleeping bags wrapped in plastic and a pair of ragged towels.

"You're well stocked," Nick said. "Come here often?"

"This is my water tower. I come out here from time to time to think things over."

"I've got a better view."

Riley headed for the wooden stairway. "You don't really climb up on that water tower to look at the river, do you? And I don't come here to stare at the bony pile. We both get away for the same reason, Nick—to look *back*."

They started up the narrow stairway—Riley first, then Nick. At the top of the stairs, the hallway led to three small bedrooms.

"Take your pick," Riley said. "They're all the same."

They entered the first room, facing the front of the house. On the right was a bare wooden dresser; on the left, a simple headboard and footboard with nothing but a metal bedframe in between. Riley stepped to the window, turned off her flashlight, and pulled open the dusty drapes. Moonlight colored the room with an even wash of greenish gray. She turned and looked at Nick, standing in the center of the room.

"You're a hard man to love," she said.

"So I've heard. Apparently I'm not a project for beginners."

"You almost died tonight."

He shrugged.

"I hope not." He walked across the room to her, brushed back the hair from her face, pulled her close, and kissed her. A moment later, she pulled away.

"You know," he said, "you're not easy to love either."

"Nick, I want to be fair with you."

"I don't want you to be fair; I want you to love me."

"The two go together."

"No they don't. When a woman say she wants to be fair, that's when everything starts to fall apart."

"Nick—we need to talk about the future."

"The future is an odd concept," he said. "It's a word we use for an imaginary collection of predictions, probabilities, and wild guesses.

The strange thing is, we let our fears about that imaginary world take all the enjoyment out of this one. Now does that seem *fair*?"

"Nick—there's something you don't know about me."

"What? After all the time I've known you?"

"Stop joking! I need to tell you something." She struggled for a way to begin.

The lenses in Nick's glasses flashed with a glaring light, then darkened again. He stepped past her to the window and looked out. He saw a car slowly turning off toward the open doors of the shed.

"It's Sarah," he said. "Let's grab something to eat; then we could all use a few hours sleep." He headed for the door.

"Nick," Riley said. "We need to have a talk."

"We'll have time for that," Nick called back.

"I hope so," she whispered.

CHAPTER 40

"Good morning," Sarah said, stretching as she entered the kitchen. Nick looked up from his coffee. "Good afternoon is more like it—it's after eleven."

She pointed to his cup. "Is there any more of that?"

"It tastes like rust," Nick said.

"You have to let the pump run for a while. It's a deep well, but iron from the mine gets into everything."

She stepped to the counter and reached into an open bag of bread. She took a spoon from a jar of strawberry preserves and absent-mindedly wiped it across the bread, then tested the side of the metal pot on the small camping stove. Nick watched her. She was a little taller than Riley, and her hair was an identical shade of blond. Her eyes were blue—both of them—and she had the same high cheekbones and fair complexion. She was quite beautiful—like her older sister—but minus a few of the lines and wrinkles awarded with a medical degree and residency. She was barefoot, and she wore a loose-fitting T-shirt over powder blue surgical scrubs. She pulled out a chair across from Nick and sat down.

"So you're the boyfriend," she said.

"Did Riley tell you that?"

"She didn't have to. How long have you two been an item?"

"That depends on who's doing the counting. I think I'm still trying to convince her."

"I think she's convinced." She stopped for a moment to sip her coffee. "What is it you do for a living, Nick?"

"I'm a forensic entomologist."

She looked at him blankly.

"I'm a bug man. I study the insects that inhabit human bodies when they die: blowflies, flesh flies, carrion beetles . . ."

Sarah shivered. "The things people do."

"Riley tells me you're a nurse. In what area?"

"OR, ER, ICU—I've done it all at one time or another. I'm in pediatrics right now. It's a lot more humane."

Nick looked around the room. It was long and narrow, with the cabinets and counters at one end and their table at the other. Behind them, a large window looked out on an ebony hillside. "So this is where the two of you grew up."

"Right here, in beautiful downtown Mencken."

He pointed over his shoulder. "And that's the volcano you used to climb on."

"Not me—you couldn't get me up on that thing. That was Riley's playground."

"With or without your dad's permission?"

Sarah smiled. "My sister has what you might call a stubborn streak—but I suppose you've noticed that by now."

"I've had a taste."

"Riley's like a weather vane. She has a way of always turning into the wind—she seems to follow the path of greatest resistance." She pointed out the window. "It's two hundred feet to the top of that thing, and the ground around here is fairly flat. When Riley climbed up there, she could see for miles. She could see out of Mencken; I think that's what she really wanted."

"And you?"

"Me? I didn't care. Our dad died when we were still teenagers.

Riley raised us both—she was both parent and sister. She made me go to college, and she made sure I got a good job. Then she went on to medical school and then a residency and now the coroner's office." She peered out the window again. "You know, I think she's still climbing."

"You love your sister, don't you?"

"Do you?"

Nick shifted in his chair. "That's . . . not an easy question."

"Sure it is. You just don't want to tell me yet. That's OK; I'm just a little overprotective."

"She seems to feel the same way about you."

"It's just the two of us, Nick. That's the way it's been for a long time. We look out for one another."

"I guess that makes me the third wheel."

"Wagons have four—one more and we've got a set. Have you got a brother?"

"Sorry."

Sarah snapped her fingers. "Just my luck."

"A woman like you can't be short of men."

"Ordinary men, sure—but the McKays settle for nothing but the best. Riley makes sure of it. You know, that says a lot about you."

"Do you ever get tired of your sister's influence?"

"Riley's more than my sister—she's my hero. Can you say that about anybody?"

"Not anymore."

"Well, it's a nice thing. A little overbearing at times, but nice."

Nick leaned closer across the table. "Can I ask you something about your sister?"

"Sure. I'm an expert."

"How is she? I mean, how is her health?"

Sarah paused. "How much do you know?"

"I know about her kidney disease. I've seen the edema in her ankles, and I know that she tires out easily—sudden exertion almost paralyzes her. What I want to know is, how serious is it?"

"What has Riley told you?"

Nick sat back in his chair. "You do look out for one another, don't you?"

She looked intently into his eyes. "Nick, I would do anything for Riley. Would you?"

"Would he what?" said a voice behind her. Riley tousled her sister's hair and headed straight for the coffee. "It's not decaf, is it?"

"It's the good stuff," Nick said. "Plus iron."

"Good. I'm fighting off anemia."

She poured herself a cup, turned, and leaned against the counter. "Were you two talking about me behind my back?"

"That's the best way," Sarah said.

"What did you tell him?"

"I told him about the guy who took you to the prom. I told him he got a little too forward, and you broke his hand."

She looked at Nick. "Did she really tell you that?"

"She did now."

"So you'd better be a gentleman," Sarah said.

Nick held up both hands. "There's not a mark on me." He pushed back from the table and began to collect his things. He walked over to the counter and gave Riley a peck on the forehead.

"Where are you going?"

"I'm late for work."

"What work? I thought we were hiding out here."

"I need to take the sample to Sanjay at Pitt. He'll run a DNA sequence on it, and in a day or two we'll know if we have a match."

At the table, Sarah set her bitter coffee down and slid the cup away from her. In the center of the table was a half-filled Aquafina water bottle.

"Well, be careful," Riley said. "Don't do anything unexpected."

"There is one 'unexpected' thing I plan to take care of," Nick said. "I just thought of it last night."

"What's that?"

Sarah twisted off the cap and lifted the bottle to her lips—

"Stop!" Nick shouted.

Sarah froze.

Nick gently took the bottle from her hand and replaced the cap. "That was close. You almost let the genie out of the bottle."

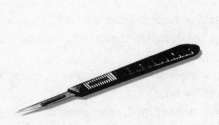

Julian Zohar held up the Money section of *USA Today* and searched the multicolored columns. Featured prominently on the second page was a story about the breathtaking progress in PharmaGen's research and development program and enthusiastic speculation about the much-anticipated date of their initial public offering. Zohar nodded and smiled.

He felt the table in front of him jostle slightly; he lowered the paper and looked across the table at an unexpected visitor.

"Do you know who I am?" Nick said, touching his glasses.

Zohar shook his head in astonishment. "You never cease to amaze me, Dr. Polchak. It's a pleasure to finally meet you." He extended his hand across the table. Nick ignored it.

"Your Web site photo is misleading," Nick said. "Photoshop does wonders."

"We all need a little touching up from time to time, don't we? So now we know how you recognized me; how did you know to find me here?"

"I followed you from your office. You don't strike me as the sort of man who packs his own lunch."

A waiter approached the table now. "Will you be joining us today, sir? Can I get you any—"

"Go away," Nick said without taking his eyes off Zohar.

"Perhaps just a glass of—"

"Now."

The waiter glanced at Zohar, who smiled and nodded reassuringly. He turned and waded back through the sea of bustling lunchtime tables.

"Dr. Polchak, I hope you're not planning to do anything embarrassing or physically violent—I abhor violence."

"Somehow I thought you would. That's why I figured it might be safe to drop in on you like this."

"I'm glad you did. We're overdue for a visit."

Nick glanced around the restaurant. "I don't suppose any of your henchmen are joining you here."

"*Henchmen?* I'm not a Mafioso, Dr. Polchak—I'm simply the proprietor of a small business enterprise."

"Have you joined the Chamber of Commerce yet?"

Zohar smiled. "As long as we're airing our suspicions, I don't suppose you're wearing a . . ." He gestured to Nick's shirt.

Nick unbuttoned his shirt partway and pulled it open. "No wires, no tape recorders—just me and you. What's the matter, Dr. Zohar, don't you trust me?"

"Forgive me. I sense that we're both a bit . . . *tentative.* But there can be no relationship without trust, now, can there? So why don't we both throw our cautions to the wind and dive right in?" Zohar cocked his head to one side and studied Nick. "Another man might come here today with a demand or an offer or a plea—but you, Dr. Polchak, you're not like other men, are you? I believe you came here with some *questions.*"

"How many people are involved in this 'business' of yours? How far does it go?"

Zohar grinned. "It involves every policeman, every federal agent, every person in any position of power or influence—that's what you need to believe right now. That's what keeps you from going to the authorities, isn't it?"

"Is this all about money? Is that it?"

"For some of our members, yes—it's all about money. Take our crime-scene investigators, for example. Do you know what a CSI makes in our city? Twenty thousand dollars a year. Can you believe that? The men and women who are responsible for collecting forensic evidence at a crime scene, the ones who may decide whether a killer is convicted or goes free."

"Welcome to capitalism," Nick said. "I thought you were a businessman."

"I despise a purely capitalistic system. It caters to the worst in all of us. It fulfills our every whim, but ignores our greatest needs. Think of it: an economic system where a man who can do nothing more than throw a little ball through a hoop is rewarded with millions, while someone like yourself—a college professor, a holder of a graduate degree—survives on a relative pittance."

"And you're planning to correct this system?"

"I'm planning to *use* it, simply by applying the law of supply and demand."

"What about the rest of your people—is it all about money for them too?"

"Motives are mysterious things, Dr. Polchak. Who can really say why a man does what he does? For Dr. Lassiter, yes, I suppose it's all about money. His cupidity never ceases to astound me. For others in our little group, it has more to do with excitement and danger—they simply enjoy living on the adrenaline edge. For Mr. Santangelo, I think it's largely about money—but then, Mr. Santangelo is by nature something of a predator. I suspect he would work for far less. As for the rest of us—well, there are *personal* motives involved."

"But it's not about money for you, is it?"

"Thank you for recognizing that—I was afraid you were about to insult me. No, Dr. Polchak, it's not about money for me. You might be interested to know that I do not benefit financially from our endeavors in any way."

"How noble of you."

"Not at all; I have nothing against making money. I simply have other motives."

"Such as?"

"Justice."

Nick slumped back against the booth. "Routine salvaging," he said. "That's what this is all about, isn't it?"

"Very good, Dr. Polchak. That's one of the things I admire about you—you have the most remarkable facility for making *connections*."

Nick leaned closer again. "As I understand it, routine salvaging has to do with dead people. These people you're stealing organs from—they're still alive. I find it slightly ironic that you call yourself an *ethicist*."

"Really? Why?"

"Has it ever occurred to you that what you're doing is . . . *wrong*?"

Zohar let out a sigh. "Let's talk about right and wrong, shall we? Suppose a man puts a gun to his head—a man with an otherwise healthy body. That one man's organs, tissues, and corneas could benefit more than *two hundred* people—and yet that man is allowed to take his life-saving tissues to the grave, simply out of selfishness or neglect. He's allowed to kill himself *and* someone else."

"That's his right."

"Two wrongs don't make a right, Dr. Polchak. Let me describe the scenario another way: A wealthy man lies dying; he calls his three closest friends to his bedside. He tells them, 'I'm going to take it with me.' He hands each of them an envelope containing a million dollars in cash. He says, 'At the graveside, as they're shoveling in the dirt, I want each of you to throw in his envelope.' At the funeral, each of them does as the man requested—he dutifully tosses his envelope in with the casket. Later, the three men meet to confer. The first one says, 'I have a confession to make: I kept fifty thousand dollars for myself.' The second says, 'I kept a hundred thousand.' The third man says, 'I'm surprised at both of you—I threw in a check for the full amount.' "

Nick said nothing.

"I'm disappointed. I thought you would have more of a sense of humor."

"I guess I'm not in the mood for jokes right now."

"It wasn't a joke, Dr. Polchak, it was a parable. The question behind the parable is: would *you* have thrown in the envelope? Because people do it every day—and I consider it a crime."

"More of a crime than what *you're* doing? Taking the lives of innocent people?"

"Innocent people? Look a little closer. The donor who lost his life in an apparent drive-by shooting—he was a family man, yes? A husband and a father. Did you also know that he was compulsively violent? That his loving wife refused to leave him, even though she had to undergo plastic surgery twice to repair the damage to her face? In time, he might have taken her life; instead, he saved one.

"And the donor who suffered the apparent heart attack, the one who was discovered lying facedown in a gutter—did you know he spent most of his adult life in a gutter? That's right, he was a hopeless alcoholic. His liver was almost certainly cirrhotic; fortunately, we're only in the kidney business—for now, that is."

"How do you know all this?"

"Do you know what I do for a living, Dr. Polchak? Do you know what I've done for the last forty years? I collect information about people—and I make connections, just as you do. And just like you, I'm very good at it."

"And that's how you justify all this? As some kind of social cleanup campaign?"

"Not at all. I'm simply saying that our selection process involves far more than financial considerations; there are ethical concerns as well. Yes, Dr. Polchak, *ethical* concerns. You may find it hard to believe, but I have an ethics board of my own, and we meet before every donor selection. I'm not a barbarian, you know. I simply draw a moral distinction between *worthwhile* lives and *useless* lives—between givers and takers. My goal is to save worthwhile lives—ideally, by taking the most worthless life I can find in trade. And with three hundred thousand people to draw from, I'm finding quite a few."

"How can you decide whose life is useless and whose is worthwhile? What gives you the right?"

"I have no *right,* as you call it; what I have is what Nietzsche called 'the will to power.' We live in a society that lacks the will to do what's best for its citizens—so I'm doing it *for* them. Try to see the larger picture here; try to understand what I'm after. This is about infinitely more than whether rich Mr. Vandenborre gets his kidney or not. Remember Prohibition? The Volstead Act declared the consumption of any alcoholic beverage to be illegal. If you think about it, it was a perfectly good law. Think of the reduction in alcohol-related crimes, automobile accidents—even domestic violence. The problem was with *demand;* the sheer demand for alcohol eventually led to the repeal of Prohibition through the Twenty-First Amendment.

"That's how it works, Dr. Polchak—demand creates law. I've shown a handful of the very wealthy that they can do more than wait around to die like dumb livestock; their demand can create a supply. I am, if you will, a kind of biological bootlegger. And as I extend this offer to more and more of the six thousand people who die on the waiting list each year, the victims of an antiquated ethical system, the demand will grow—and when it does, the laws will change. That's what I'm after, Dr. Polchak. I want to save six thousand lives a year—and if I have to do it at the expense of a handful of miscreants and reprobates, then so be it. You may call that unethical; I call it a greater good."

"I've got a parable for you," Nick said. "Three cowboys ride into town. The first cowboy ties his horse to the second horse, the second ties his horse to the third, and all three horses run off together. Why? Because none of the horses was tied to the hitching post."

Zohar shook his head. "You've been talking with Dr. Paulos, haven't you? I'm afraid he's infected you with a rather old-fashioned ethical system."

"I've always thought there was a difference between *old* and *old-fashioned*. Ian Paulos believes that all individuals have value—not because of their performance, but because they're made in the image of God. I find something very timely about that; it seems to keep the horses in check."

"Horses are born to run, Dr. Polchak."

"Horses need riders, or there's no telling where they'll run. How many times in history has someone looked past the individual to see some *greater good* that later turned out to be a disaster? Sorry, Dr. Zohar, I don't buy it."

"So you're adamantly opposed to what I'm doing? You think I'm misguided? Demented? Deceived?"

"I think you're a murderer—nothing more."

"Let's put this philosophical commitment of yours to the test, shall we? After all, 'virtue untested is not virtue at all.' "

"Don't tell me—you're going to offer me a position with your company."

"I wouldn't insult your intelligence. Tell me: how is Dr. McKay's health?"

Nick stiffened.

"I only ask, of course, because of the seriousness of her situation. You're aware, of course, that Riley McKay is dying."

Nick almost stood up. He caught himself and did his best to regain the appearance of ease. "That's a lie," he said.

"I can show you the transplant list for the University of Pittsburgh Medical Center if you like—a list she's been on for more than six years now."

Nick paused. *Leo.*

"Are you just learning this now? How very awkward. I have to say I'm a little surprised, since I understand that your relationship with Dr. McKay has become . . . personal."

Nick suddenly realized that he was slowly shaking his head. He stopped.

"End-stage renal disease is such a sad affair. The body begins to run down, the kidneys no longer able to purify the blood of all its pollutants. Like the rivers of Pittsburgh used to be—yes, that's a very good analogy. Choked with pollution, poisoned by toxins, life slowly ceases. What a tragedy that would be, considering what an outstanding human being Dr. McKay has become—but I don't have to tell you that, now, do I? I'm afraid she's in quite a predicament; she has a very rare compatibility problem that will make it virtually impossible for her to obtain her transplant in time—by conventional means."

"What are you asking me to do—trade someone else's life for Riley's?"

"I'm not asking you to do anything at all. All I'm saying is: Don't underrate your influence. Never underestimate the power of love. And let's not forget the influence that Riley McKay's death would have on *you*. Why, you've just barely come out of your cocoon, haven't you? Your new wings are barely dry. You've entrusted your heart to someone for the first time in—how long has it been, Dr. Polchak? And now she's going to be taken away from you, and who knows what you'll do then. You might very well crawl right back into that shell of yours and never come out again—and who could blame you?"

Nick stared at Zohar's face, but his eyes wouldn't focus. In his ears he heard an even, buzzing sound.

Zohar smiled. "That's another skill of mine—I know people. When you walk into a hospital waiting room; when you interrupt a family freshly grieving over the loss of a loved one; when you have less than an hour to find a way to say to them, 'I want your husband's liver and pancreas—someone is waiting for them across town'; then you learn to read every facial expression, you learn every nuance of posture and voice. And when I look at you, Dr. Polchak, do you know what I see? I see *fear*."

"Funny," Nick said, "that's what I was about to say to you."

"Me? And why should I be afraid?"

"I'd say you have plenty of reason. My friend Leo—the man you had murdered—he always left his windows open. When I found his body on the floor, I noticed mosquitoes all over his walls. I collected those mosquitoes, and I extracted the blood from their guts—blood from the man who killed my friend. When your boy Santangelo followed us to Tarentum the other night, I broke into his car and took his water bottle. I have a sample of his DNA, Dr. Zohar, and when I match it against the blood from those mosquitoes, I'll be able to prove that he was in the room the night my friend was murdered."

Zohar clapped his hands in delight. "Dr. Polchak, believe me, you have my most profound respect and admiration. But let's reexamine this little plan of yours. You say you'll be able to prove that Mr. Santangelo was in the room the night your friend was murdered—but why shouldn't he be? After all, you were interfering with an FBI investigation—he had contacted your little group before. And these mosquitoes of yours—can they tell you if Mr. Santangelo arrived *before* or *after* your friend expired?"

Nick said nothing.

"That seems a rather important point. And one other little item: have you considered that those mosquitoes may also contain samples of *other* DNA: your friend's, Dr. McKay's . . . even your own? Now what will the authorities make of that?"

Nick's thoughts raced, but they settled on nothing. His mind was a fog; Zohar's words ricocheted inside his skull like small-caliber bullets.

Zohar looked down at his plate again and picked up his knife and fork. "I wouldn't worry about Mr. Santangelo if I were you; I'd worry about Dr. McKay. Because she's going to die, Dr. Polchak, she is most certainly going to die—unless we do something about it."

Nick slowly rose from the table. To his surprise, his legs were unsteady. He looked down at Zohar. "One last thing: What about Sarah McKay? What's her social drawback? Why was she chosen as one of your donors?"

Zohar squinted at him. "Is it possible that you're not as clever as I thought?"

Nick stared at him blankly, his eyes darting like the fireflies on the Tarentum Plateau.

"Well, I could talk all day," Zohar said, "but as you can see, my lunch is growing cold. And besides—don't you have some mosquitoes to catch?"

Nick turned to the door and staggered out.

CHAPTER
42

Nick looked at his watch again. It was almost six o'clock now, ten minutes later than the last time he looked. He folded his arms and slumped despondently in the chrome-and-plastic chair. Across the hallway, a bulletin board was push-pinned full of departmental notices regarding fall registration, graduate teaching schedules, and a hundred other bits of minutiae relevant to graduate-student life. Nick had read all of them—several times.

He heard a sound; he jumped up from his chair. A student rounded the corner and padded quietly down the long corridor toward Nick, thoroughly absorbed in a fall course catalog.

"Have you seen Sanjay Patil?" Nick called out to him.

"Excuse me?"

"Dr. Sanjay Patil—he's a professor of molecular biology here."

"Sorry. I never had him."

"You don't have to take a class from him to know who he is. Have you seen him? I'm trying to locate him."

"Have you tried his office?"

Nick slumped down on the chair again and rocked back against the wall. "Try his *office*—now, why didn't I think of that? Look in the most obvious place first! And here I picked the most obscure place I could think of, just hoping he might wander by. Thank heaven you happened by—I might have been here all week."

The student avoided eye contact as he passed by.

Nick glanced at his watch. He bolted out of his chair again, sending it clattering across the linoleum floor. He turned to the door beside him and tried the knob; it was locked, just as it was the last six times he tried it. He cupped his hands and peered through the glass into the darkened room. The laboratory was a molecular biologist's toyland, complete with an ultracentrifuge, an electron microscope, a PhosphorImager, an X-ray diffractometer, and two state-of-the-art Applied Biosystems PRISM 377 DNA sequencers. The lab had everything a researcher could ever want—except for one critical, missing element: Dr. Sanjay Patil.

Nick began to pace the long corridor, his footsteps echoing behind him in the evening stillness. He thought again about Julian Zohar's words. Was it true? Was Riley really dying of her kidney disease? Would Leo purposely remove her name from UPMC's transplant waiting list, hiding the truth from him? He thought about Leo, and he knew instantly that he would. He would have done it to protect Riley—he would have done it to protect *him*. That was Leo—always trying to protect someone, but in his trusting and unsuspecting manner, unable to protect himself.

Riley. Is that what she tried to tell him last night? Is that what she meant when she said, "There's something you don't know about me"? Is that why she constantly pulled away from him, half-surrendering and half-resisting his advances? But why didn't she tell him long ago? Why didn't she trust him with this? Did she think he'd run away, refusing to get involved with a doomed woman? Or maybe she thought he would love her all the more— like a martyr—out of pity—as a service. Somewhere in his mind, a light began to dimly glow. He remembered something Leo used to say: "The heart has reasons that the mind knows nothing of." Zohar was right: Nick had a remarkable facility for making connections—but not connections like this.

Was it true what Zohar said—that Riley would never find a kidney through the official allocation system? "She is most certainly going to die," he said, "unless we do something about it." He felt a bead of cold sweat run down his back. He had been asked to make a deal with the devil himself—hadn't he? "I'm not asking you to do anything," Zohar said—but wasn't he? The devil never asks, Nick thought; *he just reaches into your mind and creates fear or panic or desperation, and before you know it, the deal is done.*

For the last four hours Nick had visited a very dark place within himself—a place he barely knew existed. Could he sit idly by and watch Riley die, her precious lifeblood slogging to a standstill like some toxic river? Nick had risked his own life a hundred times, but the life of someone else—the life of someone he *loved*—that was a different matter. Would he do nothing to save her? Wasn't her life worth more than that of some despicable wife-abuser or a hopeless gutter bum? Wasn't her life worth more than ... *anything*? "Let's test this philosophical commitment of yours," Zohar said. Nick shivered; the stench of sulfur was all over him.

And what if she did die? What then? Zohar's words flew in his face like a spray of acid. "She's going to be taken away from you, and who knows what you'll do then? You might very well crawl back into that shell of yours and never come out again." Did Zohar really know what was in Nick's heart? Had Nick become that obvious, that transparent? Or were his insights just an educated guess by a master manipulator, an off-the-cuff cold reading by the king of all con men? It didn't matter; either way, his words hit way too close to home.

Nick felt like an embarrassed child exposed in some shameful misdeed. He felt ravaged, he felt violated. He felt; that was the problem. For the first time in years he had opened his heart, and where had it got him? His work was sloppy, his thinking muddled. He had been a step behind Zohar from the very beginning—no, not a step, a *mile*. Now here he was to drop off Santangelo's DNA, the last of his physical evidence—and was it all for nothing? He tried to remember Zohar's words. Did Santangelo have a perfect excuse for being there that night? Could he claim that he visited Leo *before* the murder—could the blood from the mosquitoes prove nothing more? Worst of all, could Leo's death be blamed on Nick himself? He tried to focus his mind; he tried to sort out all the complexities of these options. But he was so tired, and he was in so much pain—more pain than he had felt in years. All he could do was push on and hope to somehow sort it all out along the way.

He heard footsteps from the opposite end of the hallway. He turned to see Sanjay Patil rounding the corner toward him. "Nick," he said simply.

"Where have you been?" Nick shouted. "I've looked everywhere for you—I've been waiting for hours!"

"Let me see." Sanjay handed his attaché case to Nick, who held it out for him like a tray. He flipped the brass latches, lifted the lid slightly, and peeked inside. "There it is—yes, I thought so—I have a *life*." He closed the lid and took the attaché back again. "You should get one yourself," he said. "I recommend it highly." He turned to the laboratory door and searched for his keys.

"Sanjay, this is a matter of life or death!"

"That is what your messages said—*all* of them—the ones you left at my office and on my pager and on my e-mail and with my research assistant and the *four* you left on my answering machine at home."

"Where have you been all day?"

"Have you ever heard of a *day off*? It is a fascinating new concept introduced to the Western world sometime in the last three millennia."

"I thought you'd come in *some* time today."

"Ah. You see, you misunderstand the concept of the *day off*. The idea is to *not* come in—to not work at all, all day long. A radical idea, is it not?" He pushed open the door and looked at Nick. "Do you know that you *filled* my answering machine with your messages? My wife called. She tried to leave me a message, a reminder to pick up my daughter from cello practice. But she could not, because of all *your* messages."

"So your daughter got an extra hour of cello practice."

"*Two* hours."

"Oh. Well, that's how you get to Carnegie Hall."

Sanjay squinted at him. "What is my daughter's name?"

"What?"

"My daughter—what is her name? What is my *wife's* name?"

"Mrs. Patil?"

"You see? That is the problem with you, Nick Polchak. Everything is *work* for you—everything is life or death. You will never respect the lives of other people until you get a life of your own."

"Sanjay, I'm *trying* to get a life of my own—but I'm about to lose it if you don't help me."

Sanjay studied his face. "Truly? Life or death?"

"Truly."

He stepped into the lab and flipped on the light switch. Bank after bank of fluorescents hummed on, flooding the room in blue white light. Nick picked up the water bottle from the floor beside his chair and followed.

"I have the results for you," Sanjay said. "We were able to identify four separate DNA sequences from the mosquitoes you captured."

"Great. Now I want you to do a sequence on this." He handed him the water bottle.

"What is this?"

"It should contain trace amounts of saliva. I want you to separate it in your centrifuge and then run it through one of your sequencers. I'm looking for a match with one of the four DNA samples from the mosquitoes."

Sanjay frowned. "But we already have a match."

"What are you talking about?"

"You brought me the mosquitoes preserved in alcohol, sealed in a plastic bag—yes? You said you were searching for a match."

"That's right—a match with *this*."

"I assumed you had given me all your samples. We already found your match."

Now Nick looked confused. "A match with what?"

Sanjay turned to the counter and picked up the Ziploc bag. He slipped on a pair of latex gloves, opened the bag, and carefully removed a single blond hair.

"With this," he said. "There were four of them in the bag with the specimen jar."

Nick turned for the door and ran.

CHAPTER 43

"You throw like a girl," Sarah said. "Watch me."

She sailed the walnut-sized rock toward the side of the building; it struck the corrugated siding with a metallic *clack* just inches from the single remaining windowpane. They stood in the road beside the Mencken Breaker, the multitiered structure once responsible for crushing large, sooty lumps of anthracite into smaller, cleaner nuggets. True to its name, at any given time half the windows in the Breaker were broken. Now, years after the mine had been abandoned and the building closed down, just a single piece of glass remained. Sarah reached down for another stone.

"Let it be," Riley said. "If it's lasted this long, maybe it deserves to live."

Daylight was almost gone now. The bony pile, hiding the sun behind its jagged crest, cast a premature gloom across the roadway. They started back toward home, past the old barracks where the single miners once lived, taking the same path their father had taken ten thousand times on his way home from the Mencken Mine. Riley stared at the gravel path, imagining that she was placing her feet in exactly the same ruts and furrows that her father once followed. Ruts and furrows—that's what a coal town was made out of—and once in them, it was almost impossible to escape.

"Remember summer mornings?" Sarah said. "If you slept with the windows open, you woke up with a ring of soot around your nose."

Riley nodded.

"And the water in the sink always had a layer of coal dust on it. Remember that?"

Riley said nothing. Sarah frowned.

"And the mountain lions—they used to sweep down from the hillsides and carry off the small children for dinner."

Riley nodded, then stopped abruptly. "What children?"

"Where *are* you? You haven't been paying attention all day."

"I've got a lot on my mind."

Sarah shook her head. "You always were a worrier."

"It's part of being a big sister. It comes with the territory."

"No, it's part of being a *mom*—that came with the territory too, didn't it? But you're not my mom, Riley—you never were."

Riley hooked her arm through Sarah's. "Can't a girl look out for her baby sister?"

"I'm not your baby sister anymore; I should be looking out for you now."

"For me? Why?"

"Well, let's see. Hmm. That's a tough one. Wait—I know. How about the fact that you're dying, and I'm not?"

Riley dropped her arm. "I'm not dying," she said.

"C'mon, Riley, get real. Have you heard anything from UPMC Presby?"

"You know I haven't. The odds are a million to one."

"So what are you going to do?"

"What can I do? It's called a *waiting* list, Sarah—there's a reason for that."

They walked in silence for the next few minutes.

"I like Nick," Sarah said.

"Really? What do you like about him?"

"He's intense. Especially those eyes of his—they're spooky."

"I like them. When he really looks at you . . ."

Sarah nodded. "I think Nick's the best one you've brought home in a long time. Do you love him?"

Riley looked mildly annoyed.

"What's the matter?" Sarah said. "Can't a girl look out for her big sister?"

"It's just that . . . it's kind of hard to say."

"Stop being a weasel. Do you love him or not?"

Riley glared at her, but her countenance slowly softened, and she finally nodded.

"Then say it. Say, 'I love Nick.' "

"Cut it out, Sarah."

"Go on—tell the truth and shame the devil."

"I don't have to say it."

"You don't mean it 'til you say it."

"I thought you weren't a baby anymore. You can be so *annoying.*"

"Chicken. Coward. Yellow belly."

"OK!" Riley said, turning to face her. "I love him! There, are you satisfied? I love Nick Polchak!" She stopped abruptly, stunned by the force of her own admission.

Sarah paused. "Does he love you?"

Riley rolled her eyes. "How am I supposed to know?"

"He hasn't told you yet?"

"Well, not in so many words."

"Not in *words*? How did he tell you, in smoke signals?"

Riley turned away and started down the road again. "I don't want to talk about this anymore."

"Well, *I* do," Sarah said, following right on her heels. "So you think he loves you?"

"I think he has a hard time saying it."

"Why?"

"I don't think love is his primary language."

"That's a crock. Men always say that."

"He didn't say that—that's just what *I* think. Nick comes from a pretty rough background."

"What is *this* place, Shangri-la?"

Riley stopped and looked at her. "Sarah, Nick has been hurt in the past."

"Oh, Riley, not another three-legged dog."

"No, it's not like that. He just needs . . . we *both* need to take it slow, that's all."

Sarah put her hands on her hips. "You haven't told him, have you? Nick doesn't know you're dying."

"He knows I'm sick—nothing more."

"He has a right to know, Riley."

"It's not that easy," she grumbled.

" 'Nick, I'm dying—I thought you should know.' Sounds easy enough to me."

"Easy for you, maybe—you're not the one who's dying. When was I supposed to say this, Sarah? 'Hello, Nick, I'm Riley. It's so nice to meet you; by the way, I'm dying, so don't get too close.' Or maybe after the first date: 'I had a nice time tonight, Nick. If you want to ask me out again, you'd better make it fast—I'm dying.' "

"Come on, Riley, you know what I mean."

"I didn't want his pity, OK? And to be honest, I didn't want to run him off either. For the first time in years I met a perfectly wonderful guy, someone who's just as weird and twisted as I am, and I wanted to know if we had a chance together—just as *people*. Is that so wrong?"

"Would you?" Sarah said. "Have a chance together, I mean?"

"I think we would," Riley said, "if only."

Sarah paused. "All the more reason to live."

"Do you think I *want* to die?"

"Everybody talks about the weather, but nobody does anything about it."

"What is it I'm supposed to do, Sarah? You tell me."

"OK, I will. How about moving to another transplant region—rich people do it all the time. Somewhere where you can be higher on the list, somewhere where there's more placement activity."

"More activity than Presby? You must be kidding—it's one of the top transplant centers in the country. Besides, Sarah, I can't just pack up and move—I've got a career to think about."

"Dead women don't have careers. How about moving overseas, have you ever thought of that? Someplace where the procurement laws are more flexible—somewhere where your odds might improve."

"You expect me to move *overseas*? Be serious."

"I *am* being serious. You said it yourself, your odds are one in a million here. Well, that's not good enough, Riley. You can't just sit around and wait to die."

Riley kicked stubbornly at the ground. "Well, it's my life."

"Sorry—it's not that simple. I love you, Riley, and so does Nick. That means a piece of your life belongs to me, and a piece belongs to him. You can't just take your ball and go home—you have a responsibility to both of us."

"I'm *sick* of responsibility."

"Well that's just too bad. Welcome to Mencken, Riley, welcome *home*. It's a world of responsibility—it always has been and it always will be. You have to *do* something to improve your chances. You've gone the conventional route—now you need to consider extreme measures."

"This all seems so simple to you, doesn't it?"

"You think it's hard to be the one who's dying? Try being the one who has to live—the one who has to stay behind. You're all I have in the whole world, Riley. Did you ever think of that? If you die, my whole world dies with you."

Riley looked into her sister's eyes; she saw the love, the devotion, the same furious intensity that used to fill her own eyes before her blood began to grow tainted and her spirit began to leech away. Now the last of her energy was leaving her—even her grief—and exhaustion weighed her down like a suit of armor. Her head throbbed, and her entire body felt like one dull ache. She threw her arms around her sister's neck—less out of affection than to support her own failing legs—and she began to gently weep.

"Oh, Sarah, what am I going to do?"

"You're going to live," Sarah said, "even if it kills us both."

They turned together toward the house, Sarah half-dragging, half-carrying her sister the last quarter mile. They struggled up the front steps together.

"When was your last dialysis?" Sarah said, pushing open the front door.

"Five days ago."

"That's too long. We need to—"

They stopped.

Standing in the center of the room, pointing a handgun directly at them, was Cruz Santangelo. He looked at Sarah.

"Hello, Angel," he said.

CHAPTER
44

Santangelo motioned them into the room.

"Ordinarily, I'd tell you to shut the door," he said. "But out here in the sticks I don't suppose it matters—does it, Angel?"

"Shut up, Cruz," Sarah said.

Riley looked from her sister to Santangelo and back again. She stared at Sarah wild-eyed, but Sarah refused to meet her gaze. Slowly, understanding began to break over her in pummeling waves.

"You're the one . . . the woman with the red hair. But then you must have . . . oh, Sarah, what have you done?" Riley sank down on the floor.

"Those were lousy directions," Santangelo said. "I thought I made a wrong turn somewhere. Do you know this place isn't even on the map anymore?"

Sarah lifted her sister to her feet and helped her to a chair—then she turned to Santangelo and held out her hand for the gun.

Santangelo shook his head. "Sorry—you *are* sisters, after all."

"You won't need the gun," Sarah said.

"I hope not—but then, that's up to you, isn't it?"

"We have a deal, remember?"

"Sure—the same deal we had in Tarentum." Santangelo looked at his watch. "You've got ten minutes."

Sarah helped Riley struggle to her feet again; they turned toward the back hallway.

"Whoa," Santangelo said. "Where do you think you're headed?"

"The kitchen," Sarah said. "Do you mind? This is personal—we'd like a little privacy."

Santangelo shrugged and took a seat on Riley's chair. "Make it fast. There's not much to do around here."

In the kitchen, Sarah deposited Riley in a chair and stood at the counter across from her. Riley looked up at her sister in unbelieving horror.

"Tell me it's all a mistake," Riley said. "Tell me he's confusing you with someone else."

"You're confusing me with someone else—with a baby sister who doesn't exist anymore. I've grown up a lot lately, Riley."

"Oh, Sarah—in God's name *why*?"

"To get you your kidneys, of course. Didn't you hear what I said back there? It's time to consider extreme measures."

"Like killing someone else to save my own life? Did you think I'd ever agree to something like that?"

"You were never supposed to *know*. When we found a match for you, all we had to do was make sure he had a donor card—we could have let his kidneys come up for transplant through the regular system. With your compatibility problem, you would have been number one on the match list. You would have gotten your kidneys, Riley, and you never would have known. That was the deal I made; that's why I agreed to work for them."

"And who would this 'donor' have been, Sarah? A mother?

Someone's husband? A woman my age with a sister just like you? Would you really trade my life for someone else's?"

"You don't understand. When they pick a donor, they consider more than medical factors. The man in the drive-by shooting—he was a wife-beater, did you know that? Do you know why he pulled over in that alley in Homewood? Not to change his tire, to change *mine*. I stood there by my car in a low-cut dress looking helpless—looking *available*—and he practically skidded to a stop. Do you think he would have stopped if I was old or ugly or overweight? Not a chance. That guy owed his wife a debt he could never repay, but there he was trying to hit on a younger woman. Are you asking me if I would trade that scumbag's life for yours? I'd trade *ten* of him for you."

"And what about your *clients*?" Riley said. "What do you know about them? Is Mr. Vandenborre some kind of angel? How does he treat *his* wife? Does he have an eye for younger women too—or is he even worse than that? You have no idea at all, do you?"

"I don't know—and I don't care. I know *you*, Riley. I love *you*. You've been my whole world since I was a little girl. What was I supposed to do, just stand by and watch you die?"

"So you find a match for me, and you help commit another murder; then I get my kidneys, and I marry Nick, and we all live happily ever after—is that the picture? Only we wouldn't all be happy, would we, Sarah? Because you couldn't live with yourself. You'd end up just like this town—burning underground, smoke seeping out through cracks, ready to collapse at any time. How many people have you helped murder?"

"No more than necessary."

"*Necessary*? Necessary for what—for me to live? For you to keep your happy family? Remember that verse from Sunday school: 'What does it profit a man to gain the whole world, and lose his own soul?' "

"First we save your life," Sarah said. "I'll worry about my soul later."

"I worry about *my* soul all the time—it comes with dying."

"You need to start thinking about the future."

"Dying is the future—it's everybody's future. So now what, Sarah? Why are we here in the kitchen? What is Santangelo expecting you to do? Are you supposed to try to change my mind about all of this? Are you supposed to *convince* me? Is that what these ten minutes are for?"

Sarah pulled out the chair across from Riley and slowly sat down. "It's a little more complicated than that. I didn't *ask* to work for these people, Riley—I never knew they existed. They asked *me*. Now, why do you suppose they did that? They liked the way I looked, sure. They also liked the fact that I've been a surgical nurse; but most of all, they knew I would have a motive. They knew about *you*, Riley. These people know everything—they're incredibly thorough."

"You could have said *no*."

"Could I? Remember about a week ago, that wealthy woman from Sewickley—the one who drowned? What was her name . . . Heybroek, wasn't that it?"

"I remember," Riley said. "I assisted on her autopsy."

"Funny, isn't it, a woman in a wheelchair falling into her own swimming pool? How careless of her. She didn't slip, Riley, she was pushed—but I don't suppose that showed up in the autopsy, now, did it? Do you want to know her real cause of death? She said *no* to Julian Zohar. He approached her about being a client, and she turned him down. But then she knew about the system, and Zohar couldn't have that—so she had to have an 'accident.' Do you understand what I'm saying? That's what happens when someone tells them *no*."

"You could have agreed at first—then you could have gone to the authorities later."

"I could have; I didn't *want* to. They knew me, Riley; they did their homework well. They offered me a chance to save your life—without you ever knowing about it—and I jumped at it. I *wanted* to say yes." Sarah reached across the table, took both her sister's hands, and looked intently into her eyes. "I wasn't talking about me, Riley. I was talking about you. *You* can't say no."

Riley jerked her hands away. "What are you telling me—that they're offering me my kidneys, and if I say no they'll kill me? Are you joking? Sarah, I'm dying anyway! What difference do a few months make?"

"It's not that simple. They're not just offering you your kidneys, Riley—they're offering you a *job*."

Riley's jaw dropped open.

"It's Lassiter," Sarah said. "He's an idiot. He's put the entire process at risk—he's the reason *you* caught on in the first place. They need a person at the coroner's office, Riley. They need someone to replace Lassiter."

"And what happens to Lassiter?"

Sarah shrugged. "Does he own a pool?"

"So that's the deal: I get my kidney, so I can no longer turn them in; then I spend the rest of my life working at the coroner's office, covering up strange little anomalies, passing off deliberate murders as accidental deaths. Are you out of your mind, Sarah? What in the world would ever motivate me to do such a thing?"

Sarah's eyes brimmed with tears. "Try this for starters: If you don't, they'll kill us *both*."

Riley stumbled out of her chair and reached for the counter to steady herself; Sarah was right behind her.

"When you and Nick started poking around—when you uncovered the system—they knew they had to deal with both of you. But with you they saw another option; they saw the chance to replace Lassiter. That's why they agreed to give me a chance to talk with you. That's why we came after you in Tarentum."

"You called him," Riley said. "You called Santangelo from the motel in Tarentum—and *you* were the one who wanted to come to Mencken!"

"They wanted us to get away. They wanted a quiet place where we could have some time together, where we would have a chance to talk."

"And if things didn't work out, they wanted a quiet place where they could *kill* us! And what about Nick, Sarah? What deal are they planning to offer him?"

Sarah said nothing.

"That's just great. Do you understand the choice you've given me? To live with you or to die with Nick. Well, I love Nick too, Sarah."

Sarah glanced nervously at her watch. "I tried to save your life," she said. "Now you have to save us both."

Riley turned on her. "Don't you put this on me! I was the only one dying here. Now you've killed us both—*and* Nick—and *Leo!*

Oh, Sarah, Leo! If only you'd *known* him. I'll *never* forgive you for that!"

"It would have worked," Sarah grumbled.

"Then what would have happened, Sarah? Did you really think they'd let you stop working for them? That they'd let you *retire*? What would have happened when you started to get a little older, or when you gained a few too many pounds—when the men would no longer pull over just to get a better look? You would have turned up in some swimming pool yourself."

"I didn't care," she said. "It was for a greater good."

Riley took her sister by the shoulders. "Listen to me. The greatest good is the good that's right in front of your nose. You cannot take an evil path to a good goal."

"All I did was love you."

"That's the problem, Sarah—all you did was love me. You've got to love something *more* than me, something greater, or even love gets twisted."

Sarah held out her watch. "Time's up. What are we going to tell Santangelo?"

Riley paced back and forth across the kitchen, her mind racing. "We have to buy some time," she said. "We'll tell him I agreed— that I bought the whole thing."

"These people are not idiots, Riley. Santangelo doesn't want this to work out—he despises loose ends; he'd rather kill us both and be done with it. If he detects the slightest hesitation on your part, if he picks up any hint of deception . . . all he wants to do is go back to Zohar and say, 'It didn't work. I took care of it.' Can you look Santangelo in the eye and convince him—unless you really mean it?"

Riley shook her head, trying to sort through the barrage of thoughts.

Sarah took her by the arm. "This can still work," she whispered. "You're right, we need to buy time—so take your kidneys, Riley, do that much—we can negotiate from there. Even about Nick—who knows what we might be able to work out?"

Riley twisted her arm free.

"Nick is coming back here," Sarah said. "If you say no, he'll be dead the minute he walks in the door. Do you really love him,

Riley? You're the only one who can save him—you're the only one who can save us all."

Riley lunged for the back door.

"Where are you going?"

"I'm going to save my soul," she said. "I'll worry about my life later."

"You can't run—not in your condition."

"It's a world of responsibility, Sarah—I can do anything I have to do."

"He'll follow you."

"Not where I'm going."

"Riley, he'll *follow* you—you don't know him."

She started out into the darkness.

"I won't be here if you make it back," Sarah called after her. "When he realizes you've run, I'm finished."

Riley didn't look back. She kept moving forward with all of her remaining strength, heading for the base of the bony pile. Now she was just a distant shadow, and Sarah called out to her sister for the last time.

"I love you, Riley."

Santangelo charged into the kitchen and saw Sarah alone, standing in the doorway, facing the empty darkness. "Where is she?" he demanded.

"She ran."

She heard his footsteps approach quickly. There was a moment of silence, and then she heard the click of a revolver hammer behind her head. She closed her eyes and waited . . .

She heard a second click, and then he pushed by her into the doorway. "I'm going after her," he said. "You wait here. If that Bug Man comes back, you do anything you have to do to hold him here until I get back, understand? No more screwups, Angel. Do this right, and I just might let you live."

He disappeared into the darkness.

Nick plowed through the barricades without stopping. They seemed to explode, sending splintered chunks of black-and-white wood clattering across the hood and over the roof. He kept the gas pedal to the floor, racing through town, the empty shanties whipping past like shuffling cards. As he rounded the last corner, his headlights played across a clump of brush just thirty yards from the house. Hidden behind the brush was a silver sedan with the passenger window open.

He's already here.

He killed his headlights and pulled in behind the sedan. If they were watching for him, it was already too late—in the perfect darkness of Mencken, approaching headlights would stand out like signal flares. He approached the house on foot; no sound of voices came from the house, no flicker of lantern light, no sign of life at all—maybe because there was no life. Nick tasted acid in the back of his throat.

He started to work his way around to the side of the house to try to get a look through a window—but just then, the front door opened and Sarah stepped out. A flashlight swept the ground in front of him.

"Nick! Is that you?"

"Where's Riley?" Nick called back.

"She isn't here! Come inside, we've got to talk!"

"Uh-uh," Nick said. "We'll talk out here."

Sarah ran wildly to meet him; Nick was startled by her apparent recklessness. He searched the surrounding brush, expecting to see an armed figure step out of the shadows at any moment—but Sarah arrived alone. She threw her arms around his neck and let out a sob. "I have to tell you something," she said.

Nick pried her arms from his neck and shoved her away. "I know who you are, Sarah. The mosquitoes that I took to Sanjay—the container was leaking, remember? I asked you for something to put it in. You handed me a plastic bag, but you took out a hairbrush and comb first. You left some of your hair in the bag, Sarah—your *real* hair, not that wig you wear on the job. Sanjay matched your DNA with the blood in the mosquitoes. It was *your* blood, Sarah—you were in the room the night Leo was killed. You're the lure, aren't you? You're the woman with the long red hair."

"That's what I was going to tell you."

"Save it," he said. "There are only two things I want to hear from you—where is Riley, and where is your partner Santangelo?"

"She's climbing up the bony pile—and Santangelo is right behind her! Come on, we've got to go after them!"

"You expect me to *follow* you? Where, Sarah? To some quiet spot where your partner is waiting for me?"

"Nick, this whole town is a 'quiet spot.' If I wanted to kill you, you never would have made it this far. You've got to trust me."

"*Trust* you? The way Leo trusted you?"

"Look, you can think whatever you want about me—but right now someone is trying to kill my sister."

"I know—*you* are."

"Don't be an idiot! Look, there isn't time to explain. Riley is about to *die*, Nick. Now maybe I'm lying to you—but if you love her half as much as I do, you won't be willing to take that chance."

Nick hesitated for only an instant. "Let's go."

"Do you have a gun?"

"Don't *you*?"

"Then how are we going to stop him?"

"I don't know," he said, "but we sure won't stop him standing here."

Nick took off running toward the bony pile, and Sarah was close behind.

Riley stumbled two hundred yards along the mountain's base before finding the first familiar landmark. As a six-year-old girl she had trampled down a sycamore sapling to point the way up—the safe way up. Now it was a full-grown tree, still bowing to the ground in memory of that day. She glanced back over her shoulder and started up the hillside.

The slope felt infinitely steeper than she remembered. Loose bits of coal and shale crumbled under her feet; she seemed to slide back half a step for every one she moved upward. She felt a surge of panic; she was trapped in a childhood nightmare, running as hard as she could to escape an approaching storm, but going nowhere. It was the wind—it wouldn't let her go. It kept tugging on her, holding her, pulling her back.

Even before she had reached the sycamore, her head was pounding and her back was throbbing with pain; now her exhaustion was almost overwhelming. Dull, aching pulses radiated from her failing kidneys like sonar waves, bouncing off the cap of her skull and down through her leaden limbs. She sank down on the hillside, panting, gathering the energy and summoning the will for the next upward advance.

"Ri-i-i-ley!"

She spun around in horror.

"Ri-i-i-ley!"

The voice sounded distant. He was still at the foot of the mountain, searching for the path she took upward—or was he? Did he only sound distant because he was calling in a quiet voice? Or was it all just a trick of the wind—was he right behind her in the darkness, just a few steps away? She held her breath—but her heart beat so loudly that she was sure the sound alone would give her away.

"I'm coming after you, Riley. I'm not far behind. You can't get away, not in your condition. Don't make me come up there after you—I'll be even angrier when I find you."

She looked down at herself. Thank God her clothing was dark, blending in against the ebony hillside—but her skin! She dug her fingers through the sooty coal, then rubbed her face and neck and arms until only her golden hair stood out in the moonlight—but she had no cap or hood to cover it. She looked up into the sky; ominous clouds passed intermittently across the face of the moon, momentarily blocking its light. Beneath the shadow of each cloud she vanished into the hillside—but when the moon slid out again, her hair lit up like a carbide lantern. She felt a drop of water on her face. She quickly rubbed the spot to cover it again.

She looked farther up the mountain, searching for the next marker: an ancient tangle of wheat-yellow brush that had somehow found a way to survive in the dusty soil. The hillside was dotted with such pockets of life: thorny brambles, twisted trees, and coarse tufts of buffalo grass enduring in meager deposits of soil and clay dumped along with other mine debris. Riley spotted the brush, about twenty yards up and as many yards to her left—and then it suddenly disappeared.

To her dismay, Riley saw that in the shadow of a covering cloud *everything* disappeared—every tree, every bush, every life-saving pointer and mark. The only time it was safe to navigate the smoldering hillside was when the moon shone bright—but that's when she herself was most visible. There was only one safe course of action: she would take her bearings in the moonlight, then move as fast as possible the instant darkness fell.

She scrambled for the scraggly brush, but not directly toward it; that was dangerous ground, she remembered—or was it? It had been almost two years since Riley sat on the back porch on a winter day, wrapped in a blanket, sipping coffee, and watching the falling snow map the contours of the underground fire. It had been far longer since she was on the bony pile, and from up close all the distances and proportions seemed to change. Was her memory reliable—and how much had the fire progressed in two years' time? She wasn't sure it was safe to move any farther—but she knew it would be fatal to remain where she was.

She headed straight up the mountain until she was even with the brush, then turned at a right angle and moved directly toward it. She ducked down behind the thick growth and listened.

"Ri-i-i-ley!"

He was on the hillside now. Riley traced her path back down the mountain; her sliding footsteps looked like craters in the undisturbed coal. And the *sound* she made—her feet, struggling through the crumbling slurry, seemed as loud as a car on a gravel driveway. What was the point in hiding? A blind man could have followed her.

"Ri-i-i-ley! Come on, Riley, my shoes are getting dirty. I only want to talk with you—didn't your sister tell you that? If I wanted to kill you, I could have shot you the minute you walked in the door."

Riley looked up the hillside again. Her next goal was a

dishwasher-sized lump of limestone thirty yards away. She looked back down the mountain, straining her eyes against the darkness— and she saw movement. In the moonlight, she could almost make out Santangelo's contour not far from her last stopping point. She turned to run—but then she stopped. She looked back at the path between her and Santangelo—not the path *she* had taken, not the *safe* path, but the one that he might take—if she called to him.

The idea seemed unthinkable—but what else could she do? She couldn't run from him forever; she could barely run at all. In another few minutes he would close the gap between them, and then—

"Here I am!" she called out from behind the brush. "Come on up and let's talk!"

There was a sharp crack. Riley heard a quick hiss and the sound of scattering rock behind her. Once again darkness fell, and she scrambled up the hill toward the lump of limestone. She heard a second crack—but this time she didn't hear the bullet hit. He was firing wildly, aiming at the sound of her footsteps.

She collapsed behind the boulder and waited. She could hear the *crunch-crunch-crunch* of his footsteps coming up the hill. They stopped; then they started again, moving away from her. Riley pounded her fist against the stone. In the darkness, he had followed the only thing he could see—her own footsteps, leading him safely across cooler ground.

She felt a raindrop on her arm, and then another one. She wiped furiously at the spots with coal dust, but then the drops began to come more quickly. Seconds later, it was a downpour. Washed by the cleansing rain, her fair skin began to reappear like a seashell in a receding tide.

She looked around her. The cloudburst was exposing her skin, but it was obscuring almost everything else—shapes, motion, even the raking sound of her footsteps. She had to take advantage of this blessing from above; she had to put distance between them—but which way? Up, of course—but there were no longer any markers visible, no signposts to guide her safely on her way. She closed her eyes and tried to assemble a mental map—but it came to her only in fragments and pieces. She sensed the cloudburst already beginning to lose intensity, and she knew she had to go, blind or not. She struggled to her feet and started climbing.

Twenty yards up the hill, then right; forward ten yards—no, a little more than that—then up again. Twenty yards, thirty yards—now left, leaving a wide berth for an especially dangerous section of ground. She stopped; this should be a safe spot. She sagged to her knees, exhausted—and felt a searing pain shoot up both legs. She leapt to her feet again.

Her pants were burned away at the knees, and the skin beneath was charred and blistered. She leaned down and extended her hand; a foot above the ground, the air was like an oven. Did she turn the wrong way? Did she travel too far—or not far enough? Or had the fire beneath her feet eaten away even more of the hillside, rendering her memory useless? She turned one way, and then the other . . . and then she stopped.

Riley stood paralyzed, utterly spent, her entire body throbbing with pain. She could see her heartbeat pulsing in her eyes. She tasted iron in the back of her mouth—was it the coal dust, or was it her own blood? She felt as though she were drifting away from the scene before her, becoming strangely distant, like a woman stepping back from a great picture window. It amazed her that she was somehow still standing. She wondered: don't you fall down when you die?

The rain stopped just as suddenly as it began, leaving her completely exposed on the open hillside. She looked at the sky; the last of the clouds slipped past the moon now, bathing the entire mountain in brilliant light. She looked up the slope; she was almost at the crest of the hill now, standing out in stark relief against the nighttime sky. She looked down at the abandoned buildings of Mencken, standing like little card houses in a darkened room. She saw the stores and the houses and the Breaker and even the old entrance to the mine itself. She saw her entire childhood all at once—and on the horizon, in the distance, she saw the lights of Pittsburgh.

She looked down at the base of the mountain. She imagined two tiny figures, scurrying from side to side, searching for the pathway up the hillside. She knew that they would never find it in time; Sarah didn't know about the sycamore. Sarah never climbed the bony pile as a child; Riley wouldn't let her. You have to look out for your baby sister; that's what big sisters do.

She lowered her eyes again. Just twenty-five yards below her, Cruz Santangelo searched for her in a patch of tall weeds.

"Not there," Riley called. "Not even close."

He turned. His own face was blackened with soot, just like hers, but at this distance Riley could see little white lines coursing down the sides of his face that freshets of sweat had washed clean. He stared up at her. She was so calm, so perfectly at peace. He whirled and pointed his gun at the darkness around him.

"There's nobody else—just me."

Santangelo turned back to her again. He widened his stance, squared his shoulders, and cupped the butt of the revolver in his left hand.

"Come on up," she said. "I'm not going anywhere. You could miss from there."

Santangelo raised the gun and took careful aim. "I bet I wouldn't."

"You're an expert—do it right. You owe me that much."

Santangelo slowly lowered the gun. "You know, you're a lot of trouble."

"I've always been that way. It's a specialty of mine."

He started forward, picking his way slowly across the shifting coal. Ten yards away from her, the ground stopped crumbling under his feet; it became hardened, encrusted, like the excess asphalt they dump on the side of a new road. The soles of his shoes began to make a peeling, sticking sound.

"You're sure you won't change your mind?" he said. "It seems a shame to lose a woman like you."

"It's a great offer—I just don't think I'd like working with a moron like you."

Santangelo smiled. "I have a specialty too. Want to see it?" He flipped open the cylinder of his revolver and slid in two brass cartridges.

Riley's body was like clay now, senseless, unfeeling—but somehow her mind was perfectly clear. Her thoughts seemed to her like the last high-pitched trill a television makes when it blinks off at night and the picture fades away. She raised her eyes and looked past Santangelo, over his shoulder, at a point halfway down the side of the mountain. She saw a solitary figure scrambling up the hillside toward them, oblivious to his own danger.

"I love Nick Polchak," she whispered.

Santangelo slowly raised the gun and pointed it at her head. "I'm going to enjoy this," he said.

She shook her head. "I bet you won't."

She tried to jump—her legs refused. She had no strength left, no power to move at all—so she simply told her legs to go ahead and die. An instant later they gratefully yielded, folding under her like strips of cloth, and she came down hard on the brittle mantle at Santangelo's feet.

Halfway up the mountain, Nick heard a howling scream. It was the voice of a man—or was it some kind of animal? It was impossible to tell; at that level of agony, all species seem to share a common voice.

He looked up the hillside near the crest—there, at the place where a moment ago two shadowy figures had stood, was a gaping, orange hole in the side of the mountain. The heat that belched from the jagged opening shook the air, and white-hot embers swirled above it and disappeared into the midnight sky. The glow from the inferno illuminated the hillside all around. Nick searched everywhere.

There was no one.

He sank to his knees and buried his face in his hands.

CHAPTER
46

Nick and Sarah sat across from each other on the wooden floor of the great room, leaning against opposite walls and staring at the empty space between them. They had spent most of the night pacing their own private prisons of grief and regret—but from time to time they talked. During those times Sarah poured out her heart, openly weeping, longing to explain her motives and actions. But if it was understanding she wanted, she didn't get it from Nick.

It was morning now. Their anguish, dulled by utter exhaustion, had begun to cool and crust over like the gaping hole on the crest of the bony pile. Nick lifted his eyes and looked at Sarah, curled in a fetal position against the wall.

"So there was no one else?"

"I already told you."

"Tell me again."

Sarah stiffly raised herself into a sitting position. "Julian Zohar— he's the organizer, he's the one who has access to the waiting lists. Tucker Truett provides genetic and medical information from western PA. Jack Kaplan—he's an ER surgeon at UPMC—he does the removals and transplants. Lassiter is the inside man at the coroner's office. There are two CSIs on the payroll too, but they don't know the whole system. That just leaves Santangelo."

"And *you*," Nick said. "Don't be so modest, Sarah. You were a valuable part of this team."

Sarah said nothing.

Nick leaned back against the wall and stared at the ceiling. It was a smaller operation than he ever imagined. Santangelo was the only contact at the FBI—and there were *none* in the Pittsburgh Police. He and Riley had no idea who they could turn to—they weren't sure that *anyone* was safe—but as it turned out, almost *everyone* was. Zohar was bluffing. He was just a little man who was adept at casting a very large shadow. Nick shook his head in disgust; he felt like vomiting.

Sarah looked at him. "What happens now?"

"Now? That's easy—I turn you over to the police, along with the DNA evidence that puts you in Leo's room the night he was murdered. Then you start squealing like a pig—you start naming names, you try to cut the best deal you can for yourself. Santangelo's already dead—you can blame most of it on him: a deranged federal agent, an ex–Hostage Rescue Team member who went over the edge—he *blackmailed* you, he threatened to *kill* you if you didn't help. That's good, Sarah. That just might play—except for one little problem: *me*. I'll be right there, telling them the rest of the story, making sure you get everything you deserve."

"I don't blame you for hating me," Sarah said.

Nick glared at her; his eyes were more than *intense;* they were like two great coal drills, piercing her black walls. "Last night—while you were sitting there—I thought about walking across the room and killing you myself. I *thought* about it, Sarah. I don't mean the idea just passed through my head—I mean I actually considered it."

"So why didn't you?"

"It's too quick," he said. *"Eight hundred degrees*—that's the temperature inside that mountain, did you know that? And it isn't fire exactly—it's more like a barbecue pit, that's what it is. I wonder: Is your body consumed immediately, or do you sort of *cook* first? How long can someone survive in that kind of heat—five seconds? Ten? Santangelo seemed to scream for an awfully long time—but pain is like that, isn't it? It seems to last—"

"Stop it!" Sarah buried her face in her hands and began to weep again.

"Might as well," Nick said. "You'll be thinking about it for the rest of your life anyway—and I hope it's a long life, Sarah, I really do. When the DA pushes for the death penalty, I plan to be there, pleading for leniency. Have pity on the poor girl, make it a life sentence instead—make it two—one for Riley and one for Leo. And I plan to visit you in prison, Sarah. I want to see you as the years go by. I want to watch you age *way* before your time; I want to see the way regret eats away at you—I guess that's what they mean when they give you *two* life sentences."

Sarah shuddered. "I can't do that, Nick. I can't."

"You'd be surprised what people can do—when they *have* to."

Sarah looked at him. "What about all the others—what about all the innocent people? Are you willing to destroy all of them too?"

"What innocent people?"

"Come on, Nick, think about it. Zohar is the chief executive officer of COPE—a legitimate organ procurement organization. They're the people who find organs for everybody else—the *honest* way. They're the ones who might have found Riley's kidneys for her, if only the odds had been better. COPE didn't go bad, Zohar did—he's like one of the execs at Enron. Are you planning to punish the whole organization because of what one man decided to do?"

"I guess it can't be helped."

"Can't it? COPE depends on public confidence, Nick. They need people to donate organs, they need people to trust them. They have to fight for every donation, because they're dealing with people's fears. If this whole thing comes out in the open, the loss of confidence will set their work back ten years—not just here, but everywhere. And you know who will be hurt the most? People like Riley; people on waiting lists, praying that other people won't lose faith."

"You picked a fine time to start thinking about all this," Nick said.

"I've been thinking about it all night. What about PharmaGen, Nick? It's a good company—if it survives. Personalized medicines, wonder drugs, new vaccines—I like that vision. But Truett took a shortcut; he needed cash. Truett made a mistake, not the whole company—but when this leaks out, the company is finished. What does that do to the future of personalized medicine? What does it do to other companies like PharmaGen, companies with their own population studies in other parts of the country?

"And what about the coroner's office? Lassiter deserves what he gets—but what about the rest of them? These are Riley's people, Nick—she was one of them. What will happen to their budget, their staffing, their fellowship program?"

"It's like a bomb," Nick said. "Innocent bystanders will get hurt." He leaned forward and looked into her eyes. "But whose fault is that?"

"It's *my* fault!" Sarah said. "I'm not blaming you for anything." She paused.

"I'm just asking you to let me do something about it. Nick, I have a favor to ask."

CHAPTER
47

My friends, I'd like to propose a toast."

Julian Zohar lifted his champagne flute; it sparkled gold and white against the nighttime sky. It was a perfect summer evening at the Point. Every dot of light from the Pittsburgh skyline stood out with crystalline clarity, perfectly reflected in the glassy water of the Allegheny River. The *PharmaGen* yacht lay floating at anchor directly in front of PNC Park. The Pirates were away on a three-day road trip, and the stadium lay black and cavernous before them. The hour was late, and there were no other boats in sight; they were alone on the river, minus the clinging barnacles that tended to collect around their splendid hull.

"To a new day," Zohar said, "and to ever more distant horizons."

They drank together.

"I love this boat," Kaplan said. "I've got to get one of these."

"Well, park it somewhere else," Truett said. "It won't look so good if we all pull up side by side in matching yachts. Besides—these are the hottest wheels in town. Go find your own strip to cruise." They both laughed.

"Where is Santangelo?" Lassiter asked. "What about the—you know—the problem? I want to hear the full report."

"Now, Nathan, calm yourself," Zohar said. "Angel is below deck right now, changing; she assures me that Mr. Santangelo will be joining us shortly. Her preliminary report informs me that everything went according to our expectations. I'm sure she will be more than happy to give us a complete account of her activities presently."

Just then the hatch swung open, and Sarah stepped up onto the deck. She was dressed in red, dressed as she had often been in Santangelo's company—except for the auburn wig. Tonight her blond hair drifted out behind her in the evening breeze.

All the men stared, but Kaplan was the only one to whistle. He held up one hand to block his view of her face. "*This* part I know," he said, "but I'm having a little trouble with the hair."

"Give it a chance," Sarah smiled, walking over to him. "You may learn to like it." She winked, then gave him a quick kiss on the lips.

"Whoa," Kaplan said. "Who lit *your* fire?"

"I do love red," Truett said, admiring her.

She turned to him and ran a finger down the buttons of his shirt. "I know—I wore it just for you." Now she slinked across the deck to where Zohar and Lassiter were standing. "Nathan." She nodded. "You're looking good tonight—as always." She turned to Zohar and offered her hand; he took it, kissed it, and smiled. She gave him a wink and reached for the ice chest. She lifted a champagne flute and drained it.

Now she turned, and every eye was on her.

"Do I have everyone's attention?" she smiled. "I do hope so— I'd hate to think I'm losing my touch. Dr. Zohar has asked me to make a report, and that's just what I'd like to do—only I'd like to expand it a bit. I get so tired of just *business* all the time, don't you? I think a moment like this calls for a few personal comments. I do hope you'll all listen. I promise not to bore you."

The men settled back against the railings and grinned.

"I want to thank you," she began, "each and every one of you. This last year has been—how can I describe it? An *education*. I have learned something from each of you, something of inestimable worth, and I want each of you to know what it is.

"Nathan, from you I've learned that no matter how much you have in life, you can always want more. I've learned that greed is really not about money or things at all—it's about *desire*. It's the wanting, not the having. You long for something, you think you'll die if you don't get it—but then when you do, you don't want it anymore. The *desire* is gone, and that's all you really wanted in the first place. The things themselves are insignificant, almost arbitrary—they're just hooks to hang our passions on, aren't they?"

Lassiter glanced uncomfortably at the other men.

"Nathan, you've taught me that it's worth sacrificing everything in pursuit of your desires: your friendships, your family, your reputation, your professionalism. I learned all that from you, Nathan, and I'm a different person because of it."

She held up her glass to him—and then she turned to Kaplan.

"And, Jack—what can I say? From you I've learned that it's possible to treat human beings as if they were inanimate objects— even in a caring profession! Your level of objectivity is astonishing, Jack—you really are above it all, aren't you? I've watched you cut into a man who's been dead for less than three minutes as though he were a med-school cadaver—that's really remarkable. That's what's allowed you to become what you are; that's what's permitted you to reach your incredible level of efficiency. You never let yourself get bogged down in the distractions of compassion or empathy or pity." She raised her glass again. "*Salud*, Jack. Because of you I know what I want, and I know how to get there—and nothing is going to stop me."

Now she looked at Truett.

"Tucker Truett—if ever there was a poster boy for success, it's you. You have so many remarkable gifts: intelligence, vision, business savvy, and let's not forget the package—women do love a nicely wrapped package, don't they? When you take all those gifts and pack them in tight together, it creates a kind of critical mass—an energy source, a *heat*." She held out one hand and wiggled her fingers. "I can feel it all the way over here. You don't lead people, you *compel* them. You're like . . . you're like this boat." She stepped into the cockpit, placing her hands on the wheel as if she were steering. "You're big and you're fast, and wherever you go you draw people into your wake."

She turned and looked at him. Truett smiled back and bowed slightly.

"What I've learned from you, Tucker, is that with the potential for success comes the *need* for success. You're like that big crystal ball in Times Square on New Year's Eve; everybody knows it will drop, everybody waits for it to drop—if it didn't, people would be so disappointed. That's you, Tucker. You're the crystal ball—so bright and so shiny and so ready to drop. You just *have* to make good, don't you? Because if you don't, there will be *shame*—and shame just doesn't fit in that perfect package of yours."

She raised her glass in tribute.

"To you, Tucker. From you I've learned that success is not an option."

Finally, she turned to Zohar. "And how could I forget you? Julian Zohar, our mentor, our founding father—from you I've learned so *many* things. Where do I even begin? I think most of all, I've learned from you that ethics is not about right and wrong or good and evil—it's just a way of talking. It's a way of getting *around* good and evil, really, a way of getting what you want. I've learned that almost anything can be justified in the name of some greater good—and the greater good itself never has to be justified at all. You're a kind of shaman, Julian; you give moral force to people. You give confidence, you give permission—to do right or wrong. But then, there's no such thing as *wrong*, is there?

"From you I've learned that you should always pursue the greatest good for the greatest number of people. And if someone is not a part of that 'greatest number,' well, he's just out of luck—because good can't slow down for individual people. You've given me the greatest gift of all, Julian: you've given me power—*moral* power—the kind that only comes once you abandon all sense of morality."

"Now, hold on," Kaplan said. "What about you, Angel? Let's not leave *you* out of this little roast of yours."

"You're right, Jack. That would be a terrible oversight—because I've learned more from myself than I have from any of you. I've learned that when you love something desperately—when you love something more than *anything* else—you'd better be careful what it is. I've learned that there's a kind of 'order of events' in the universe. If you put the right thing first, everything falls in line; if you get it wrong, everything falls apart."

She looked at each of them; no one was smiling now.

"Oh, please don't get the wrong idea. I'm not putting myself above any of you. In fact, that's the lesson I've learned most of all—I *belong* here. We really are a family, aren't we? We really belong together, and I have never felt more a part of this group than I do tonight."

The men began to relax.

"And now," Zohar said, "if we can get on with the—"

"Wait!" Sarah said. "I've forgotten someone—my very own partner, Cruz Santangelo. I have so much to thank him for. None of us appreciates him enough, you know—he's such a multitalented man. From him, I've learned how to kill—something every girl needs to know. I've learned how to do it quickly and quietly and with complete surprise; it's amazing what you can learn, spending a year in the company of a trained assassin.

"For example: I've learned that boats smaller than forty feet in length usually run on gasoline. Not this one; big yachts like this run on diesel fuel because it's less dangerous—because diesel fuel doesn't explode, it just burns. But big yachts like this, ones that carry Jet Skis or smaller boats on board, they often carry gasoline tanks—like this one does."

The men began to straighten. They looked at one another.

"The tanks are made of aluminum. They're nice and soft; you can punch right through them with an ice pick, and you can shove a little hose inside and let all the gasoline drain down into the bilge—right down into the engine room. Then all you have to do is remove one of the glow plugs, and leave it hanging in the air . . ."

Kaplan and Truett started toward her. Zohar stood frozen. Lassiter looked down at the river, contemplating the distance. But Sarah looked into the sky with a look of perfect peace.

"Forgive me, Riley."

She reached down to the console and turned the ignition key.

A hundred yards upriver, Nick Polchak sat in a small rowboat, watching the meeting on the PharmaGen yacht. He saw four men on the aft deck, leaning against the railings, transfixed. He saw a figure dressed in brilliant red standing in the cockpit, the object of everyone's attention. He watched her lift her face to the heavens . . . and then he saw a massive fireball erupt in the water, sending pieces of fiberglass and steel as far as the opposite bank. The blast shattered the stillness of the night, echoing off the buildings and the hills of Mount Washington beyond and sending a rippling shock wave in circles out across the river. A moment later, there was nothing left but a burning pool of diesel oil.

Nick sat motionless in the boat, his mind recording the event but his emotions untouched by it. The lenses of his glasses flashed from black to blinding white to orange and then back to black again.

As a writer of fiction, my job is to tell lies—but to use enough truth to make the story sound as though it just might happen. All of the characters in *Chop Shop* are fictional, though most of the settings are very real. There is a Pittsburgh, a Tarentum, and an Allegheny River. PharmaGen does not exist; the Fox Chapel Yacht Club does. The coal-mining town of Mencken does not exist; the Duquesne Incline does. In this kind of blending of fact and fiction, there's a chance that some very real person or group might inadvertently fall under the shadow of its fictional counterpart. This is potentially the case with two very fine organizations, and I wish to clarify any misconceptions here.

The Allegheny County Medical Examiner's Office—The Allegheny County Coroner's Office appears in my story. In the real world, the Allegheny County Medical Examiner's Office is one of the top forensic pathology facilities in the United States. The professionalism and skill of their staff are known and respected nationwide, and I wish to thank them for their forbearance and good humor toward my fictional tale. You can learn more about the real Allegheny County Medical Examiner's Office by visiting their informative Web site at www.alleghenycounty.us/me.

The Center for Organ Recovery and Education (CORE)—My story involves a fictional organ procurement organization based in Pittsburgh. In fact, there is an organ procurement organization based in Pittsburgh—the Center for Organ Recovery and Education. Since its inception twenty-five years ago, CORE has helped to provide more than 300,000 organs, tissues, and corneas for transplantation. They have saved innumerable lives and done immeasurable good, and I in no way wish to cast doubt or generate fear about legitimate organ donation. I have requested a little red heart to be placed on my driver's license, and I encourage my readers to do the same. You can learn more about organ donation and procurement by visiting CORE's Web site at www.core.org. Be sure to visit the link titled "Donation & Transplantation: Myths About Donation."